Two Irish National Tales

SELECTED NEW RIVERSIDE EDITIONS

Series Editor for the British Volumes
Alan Richardson

Oroonoko; or, The Royal Slave, Aphra Behn
Edited by Derek Hughes

The Mill on the Floss, George Eliot
Edited by Nancy Henry

Early Black British Writing, Olaudah Equiano, Mary Prince, and Others
Edited by Alan Richardson and Debbie Lee

Tess of the D'Urbervilles, Thomas Hardy
Edited by Linda M. Shires

Gulliver's Travels and Other Writings, Jonathan Swift
Edited by Clement Hawes

Two Gothic Novels: The Castle of Otranto, Horace Walpole, *and The Old English Baron,* Clara Reeve
Edited by Laura C. Mandell

The Picture of Dorian Gray, Oscar Wilde
Edited by Richard Kaye

Romantic Natural Histories, William Wordsworth, Charles Darwin, and Others
Edited by Ashton Nichols

For a complete listing of our American and British New Riverside Editions, visit our website at **http://college.hmco.com**

NEW RIVERSIDE EDITIONS
Series Editor for the British Volumes
Alan Richardson, Boston College

MARIA EDGEWORTH
Castle Rackrent
SYDNEY OWENSON (LADY MORGAN)
The Wild Irish Girl

Two Irish National Tales

Complete Texts with Introduction
Historical Contexts • Critical Essays

Edited by
James M. Smith
BOSTON COLLEGE

Introduction by Vera Kreilkamp
PINE MANOR COLLEGE

Houghton Mifflin Company
BOSTON • NEW YORK

Publisher: Patricia A. Coryell
Executive Editor: Suzanne Phelps Weir
Sponsoring Editor: Michael Gillespie
Development Manager: Sarah Helyar Smith
Associate Editor: Bruce Cantley
Editorial Assistant: Lisa Littlewood
Senior Project Editor: Tracy Patruno
Manufacturing Coordinator: Carrie Wagner
Marketing Manager: Cindy Graff Cohen
Marketing Assistant: Wendy Thayer

Cover image: Vine-Covered Castle Ruins, ©Tim Thompson/Corbis

Credits appear on page 447, which is a continuation of the copyright page.

Printed in the U.S.A.

Library of Congress Control Number: 2001133339
ISBN: 0-618-08487-8
1 2 3 4 5 6 7 8 9-MP-08 07 06 05 04

CONTENTS

ABOUT THIS SERIES
Alan Richardson

The Riverside imprint, stamped on a book's spine or printed on its title page, carries a special aura for anyone who loves and values books. As well it might: by the middle of the nineteenth century, Houghton Mifflin had already established the Riverside Edition as an important presence in American publishing. The Riverside series of British poets brought trustworthy editions of Milton and Wordsworth, Spenser and Pope, and (then) lesser-known writers like Herbert, Vaughan, and Keats to a growing nation of readers. There was both a Riverside Shakespeare and a Riverside Chaucer by the century's end, titles that would be revived and recreated as the authoritative editions of the late twentieth century. Riverside Editions of writers like Emerson, Hawthorne, Longfellow, and Thoreau helped establish the first canon of American literature. Early in the twentieth century, the Cambridge editions published by Houghton Mifflin at the Riverside Press made the complete works of dozens of British and American poets widely available in single-volume editions that can still be found in libraries and homes throughout the United States and beyond.

The Riverside Editions of the 1950s and 1960s brought attractive, affordable, and carefully edited versions of a range of British and American titles into the thriving new market for serious paperback literature. Prepared by leading scholars and critics of the time, the Riversides rapidly became known for their lively introductions, reliable texts, and lucid annotation. Though aimed primarily at the college market, the series was also created (as one editor put it) with the "general reader's private library" in mind. These were paperbacks to hold on to and read again, and many a "private" library was seeded with the colorful spines of Riverside Editions kept long after graduation.

Houghton Mifflin's New Riverside Editions now bring the combination of high editorial values and wide popular appeal long associated with the Riverside imprint into line with the changing needs and desires of twenty-first-century students and general readers. Inaugurated in 2000 with the first set of American titles under the general editorship of Paul Lauter, the New Riversides reflect both the changing canons of literature in English and the greater emphases on historical and cultural context that have helped a new generation of critics to extend and reenliven literary studies. The series not only is concerned with keeping the classic works of British and American literature alive, but also grows out of the excitement that a broader range of literary texts and cultural reference points has brought to the classroom. Works by formerly marginalized authors, including women writers and writers of color, will find a place in the series along with titles from the traditional canons that a succession of Riverside imprints helped establish beginning a century and a half ago. New Riverside titles will reflect the recent surge of interest in the connections among literary activity, historical change, and social and political issues, including slavery, abolition, and the construction of "race"; gender relations and the history of sexuality; the rise of the British Empire and of nationalisms on both sides of the Atlantic; and changing conceptions of nature and of human beings.

The New Riverside Editions respond to recent changes in literary studies not only in the range of titles but also in the design of individual volumes. Issues and debates crucial to a book's author and original audience find voice in selections from contemporary writings of many kinds as well as in early reactions and reviews. Some volumes will place contemporary writers into dialogue, as with the grouping of vampire stories by Bram Stoker, Sheridan Le Fanu, and John Polidori. Other volumes provide alternative ways of constructing literary tradition, juxtaposing Mary Shelley's *Frankenstein* with H. G. Wells's *Island of Dr. Moreau,* or Byron's *The Giaour,* an "Eastern Tale" in verse, with Frances Sheridan's *Nourjahad* and William Beckford's *Vathek,* its most important predecessors in Orientalist prose fiction. Chronologies, selections from major criticism, notes on textual history, and bibliographies will allow readers to go beyond the text and explore a given writer or issue in greater depth. Seasoned critics will find fresh new contexts and juxtapositions, and general readers will find intriguing new material to read alongside of familiar titles in an attractive format.

Houghton Mifflin's New Riverside Editions maintain the values of reliability and readability that have marked the Riverside name for well over a century. Each volume also provides something new—often unexpected—and each in a distinctive way. Freed from the predictable monotony and rigidity of a set template, editors can build their volumes around the special opportunities presented by a given title or set of related works. We hope that the resulting blend of innovative scholarship, creative format, and high production values will help the Riverside imprint continue to thrive well into the new century.

INTRODUCTION
Vera Kreilkamp

Nations as well as individuals gradually lose attachment to their identity, and the present generation is amused rather than offended by the ridicule that is thrown upon its ancestors. . . . When Ireland loses her identity by an union with Great Britain, she will look back with a smile of good-humoured complacency on the Sir Kits and Sir Condys of her former existence.

—*Castle Rackrent* 29

In this the dearest, most sacred, and most lasting of all human ties, let the names of Inismore and M____ be inseparably blended, and the distinctions of English and Irish, of protestant and catholic, for ever buried. And, while you look forward with hope to this family alliance being prophetically typical of a national unity of interests and affections between those who may be factiously severe, but who are naturally allied, lend your own individual efforts *towards the consummation of an event so devoutly to be wished by every liberal mind, by every benevolent heart.*

—*The Wild Irish Girl* 338[1]

Two historical events—the 1798 United Irishmen Rebellion and the 1800 Act of Union—loom over and shape *Castle Rackrent* and *The Wild Irish Girl*, the national tales first published together in this volume. In 1798, inspired by radical ideals disseminated by the recent American and French revolutions, descendants of Protestant settlers and members of a long-oppressed Catholic Irish population fought side by side against British colonial rule in Ireland. The

[1]Hereafter, references not otherwise identified are to this New Riverside Edition.

uprising occurred toward the end of the age of revolution, a period characterized by growing hostility to despotic aristocratic regimes and by a reactive counterrevolutionary suppression of republican sentiment throughout Europe. Ireland's long-standing political unreliability to Britain was made glaringly apparent in 1798, for the United Irishmen revolt was alarmingly (if inadequately) supported by French forces. Within two years of that brutally suppressed republican uprising, the Act of Union of Great Britain and Ireland annexed England's subversive neighboring island into the new political entity of the United Kingdom.

According to its supporters, a constitutional union was essential for the well-being of both islands, assuring England of security against further incursions by revolutionary France and bringing the benefits of economic modernization and an imperial partnership to a backward country. However, detractors like Henry Grattan, a leader of Ireland's independent parliament that had voted itself out of existence, condemned the new legislation as a mere absorption of one nation into another—a union in name only, which failed to bring a promised Catholic emancipation and retained London's economic and political control over a subordinate partner (Foster 283). The controversial act, passed only after the open bribery of Irish peers whose votes were needed to ensure its passage, ended Ireland's identity as a politically separate, if long colonized, kingdom.[2]

Maria Edgeworth's *Castle Rackrent, An Hibernian Tale. Taken from Facts, and from the Manners of the Irish Squires, before the Year 1782,* written for the most part in the turbulent decade of the 1790s, appeared anonymously in London in the same year as the Act of Union.[3] Sydney Owenson's *The Wild Irish Girl: A National Tale,* its subtitle flaunting a defiant assertion of Irish nationhood and announcing a new literary genre, was published in London only six years after the 1800 legislation. Together, the two works support not only Owenson's 1814 observation that fiction "forms the best history of nations" (Preface vii), but also the tendencies of recent interdisciplinary scholarship to undermine strict boundaries between imaginative literature and history (Dunne, "A Polemical Introduction"). Both tales should be read not only as key inaugural works of Irish fiction, but as cultural

---

[2]Irish nationalists came to see the Act of Union as the root cause of Ireland's troubles, and that legislation virtually defined Irish parliamentary politics for over a hundred years. After a long nineteenth century of growing insurgency, Union, in its 1800 form, survived until the partition of the island and the creation of the Irish Free State in the early 1920s.

[3]Marilyn Butler and Tim McLoughlin suggest that the first section of *Castle Rackrent* was written between 1794 and 1796, the second or Condy section between 1796 and 1798, and the Glossary added in 1799, when the book was already in press (Introductory Note, *Castle Rackrent* ix).

interventions in an ongoing discourse about the economic, political, and social "condition" of Ireland. That topic, having preoccupied English, settler, and native voices since the twelfth-century Norman conquest of the island, became increasingly heated in the decades surrounding Union. The contemporary literary buzz that surrounded both works suggests considerable English interest in the new member of the United Kingdom. King George III and Prime Minister William Pitt reportedly read *Castle Rackrent* with pleasure, and it was reprinted in Ireland and America and translated into French and German by 1802. Edgeworth went on to become an established novelist, well paid for her fiction, which was admiringly received in Britain, Europe, and America.

The reception of Owenson's national tale six years later was far more sensational, recently described as an early literary "media event" that plunged the author, her politics, and her fiction into the post-Union culture war (Connolly, "'*I accuse Miss Owenson*'"). By 1806, Robert Emmet's abortive 1803 rebellion and the continuing irritant of Britain's failure to grant Catholic Emancipation had revealed the incompleteness of the Act of Union—and the corresponding defensiveness of conservative voices. Within months of *The Wild Irish Girl*'s 1806 publication, the Irish Tory critic John Wilson Croker began a decades-long assault directed not only at what he termed Owenson's "bad novels and worse poetry," but also at her liberal Whig politics and her private character: "I accuse her of attempting to vitiate mankind—of attempting to undermine morality by sophistry, and the insidious mask of virtue, sensibility, and truth" (qtd. Connolly 98). Whereas Edgeworth's didactic novels about Irish landlords written after *Castle Rackrent* earned her praise as an advocate of enlightened agrarian reform within the structure of past colonial land settlements, Owenson's detractors identified her with a radical critique of Britain's Irish policies and with support of a suspiciously Jacobin ideology. Owenson's 1807 *Patriotic Sketches,* for example, cautions as to the effects of virulent contemporary religious bigotry against Catholics, of the vampiric rule of the Irish middleman, and of extortionate land policies—unheard of in England. Driving the Irish peasantry, she warned, "to the very barrier of penury and want should sometimes impel them beyond that of prudence and subordination" (*Patriotic Sketches* 384 in this volume). Taken up by liberal reform figures in Dublin and London at a time of growing anti-Catholic bigotry and political reaction, Owenson fused her fictional character Glorvina with her public identity as a literary celebrity, performing the role of the wild Irish girl for Dublin and London society hostesses. Soon after the novel's publication, Dublin jewelers were selling golden hair clasps modeled after the one affected by the Princess of Inismore, and drapers were displaying a "Glorvina mantle" (Stevenson 96–97). Significantly, in the year of her death the *Athenaeum* remembered Owenson as "less a woman of the pen than a patriot and a partizan. Her books were battles" (qtd. Ferris, "Writing on the Border" 87).

These two young women were to transform the anxieties of a revolutionary period and its aftermath into Ireland's first major works of fiction. Ironically, their achievement may explain the near invisibility of *Castle Rackrent* and *The Wild Irish Girl* in later histories of English fiction, the category into which, until recently, Irish novels were subsumed. Edgeworth's and Owenson's Irish works are distinguished not by the creation of a complex characterization so central to later canonical English novels, but by responses to the condition of Ireland. Both women wrote fiction not only to reflect, but also to change the course of a colonial society in the decades surrounding the Act of Union. After being frequently reprinted during their authors' lifetimes, *Castle Rackrent* and, to a far greater extent, *The Wild Irish Girl* largely disappeared from the literary landscape. Edgeworth's tale, one of her four fictional treatments of Ireland, survived in generic histories of the novel as a respected example of early regional fiction influencing Walter Scott. But although remaining in print, *Castle Rackrent* was little read or studied outside of Ireland. Until the second half of the twentieth century, Owenson's *The Wild Irish Girl,* more romance and propaganda than realistic novel in the English mode, was virtually forgotten, becoming accessible in an affordable classroom edition only in the 1990s. The present volume responds to a renewed interest in both texts emerging not only from feminist scholarship, but even more directly from a postcolonial criticism scrutinizing the interaction between imperialism and culture. *Castle Rackrent* and *The Wild Irish Girl* offer complex literary engagements with those political settlements and colonial conditions that created and, eventually, undermined the world's most powerful empire.

Viewing the promise or actuality of union from different perspectives, Maria Edgeworth and Sydney Owenson might well have objected to the appearance of their fiction side-by-side in this volume. Their remarks suggest reservations about each other's work, and both discouraged attempts to establish similarities between their careers. Edgeworth, who once privately objected to her literary rival's "disgusting affectation and *impropriety,*" testily maintained that all comparisons with her popular (and self-promoting) contemporary were "odious" (qtd. Butler, *Maria Edgeworth* 448). Owenson, although admitting the "useful, admirable, and most humorous" qualities of *Castle Rackrent,* more publicly (and thus diplomatically) declared that it "did not come under the same category" as her own fiction ("Prefatory Address" 255). Yet formal and historical relationships between these tales suggest ample reasons for juxtaposing them. For example, Edgeworth and Owenson's conflations of generic forms appear alien to the more seamless texts of much later British fiction. One critic's description of the "mongrel heterogeneity" of *The Wild Irish Girl* (Leerssen, *Remembrance* 55) applies, certainly, to both works, each of which combines multiple genres—such as fictional narrative, linguistic investigation, oral memory, antiquarian pedantry, and political speculation. As Claire Connolly observes of *Castle Rackrent,* the formal innovations of both works suggest how fiction registers "political conflict on the level of genre" ("'Completing the Union?'" 162). The two tales also influenced other Romantic-era novels, most notably Walter Scott's *Waverley* (1814), with its wildly popular depiction of an exotic Scottish history and landscape. Certainly the originality and unfamiliar generic forms of these hybrid literary productions, as well as their grounding in Irish colonial history, indicate various shared literary, biographical, and political contexts.

Together, Edgeworth and Owenson helped initiate a new literary form, the transborder national tale, emerging from geographic spaces peripheral to the metropolitan center of the British Empire (Trumpener 128–57; and Ferris, "Narrating Cultural Encounter" 408–21, in this volume). This hybrid genre of cultural encounter directs sentiment toward an often-maligned periphery, conducting readers into and through a strange Irish territory. It situates itself between political and literary borders—understood both geographically and generically—in order to explain and often to make claims for or about Ireland to an audience ignorant or misinformed about the country. With strong ties to travel writing about exotic places, and thus to later nineteenth-century empire fiction, the national tale represents Ireland as strikingly foreign to the domesticated world of its many English readers: comically disordered and in need of rational anglicized agrarian reform in *Castle Rackrent,* unjustly suppressed and romantically sublime in *The Wild Irish Girl.*[4]

Well versed in the growing literature of outsiders' accounts about Ireland, both writers reproduce, explicate, and on occasion undermine stereotypes about Irish national character that travelers such as de la Tocnaye or John Carr recorded (de la Tocnaye 357–59 and John Carr 368–73, both in this volume). Reading *Castle Rackrent* and *The Wild Irish Girl* in such contexts reveals their striking intertextuality, demonstrating how embedded they are in a range of contemporary and historical print sources. Edgeworth and Owenson read and to different degrees dramatized a view

[4]Owenson's publisher, Richard Phillips, encouraged her to consider contemporary travelogues, discussing those by John Carr and Daniel Augustus Beaufort; he reminded her that Ireland remained a strange world to metropolitan readers and regretted that she had chosen to write a novel rather than a book of travel letters (Connolly, Note on the Text, lix).

of Ireland's rural society that was informed, for example, by Arthur Young's late-eighteenth-century critique of the absentee Irish landlord and his dissipated and oppressive middleman (Young 343–56, in this volume). Thus we might surmise that Edgeworth's fictional rendition of Sir Kit's years in London emerges from what she learned about absentees from Young's *Tour of Ireland,* as well as from her familiarity with local absenteeism or her knowledge of family history. Similarly, Young's condemnation of the Irish middleman serves as a probable textual context for Owenson's depiction of the corrupt steward Clendinning.

In explicitly looking backwards in their tales, both Edgeworth and Owenson retrieve a version of Ireland's past, thus constructing theories of origin in the very period that Ireland seemed to have lost or to face losing its historical identity. Their motives for such retrieval, however, differ, for each tale invokes strikingly dissimilar visions of both pre- and post-Union Irish conditions. Despite Edgeworth and Owenson's shared liberal opposition to anti-Catholic bigotry and to the landlord's appalling record of estate management, encountering their tales side by side, the reader enters a cultural debate, a politically charged argument about the meaning of Ireland's past and its future. In the Preface to *Castle Rackrent,* which Edgeworth added to her text after completing the narrative of family decline, the "Editor" welcomes the imminent union with Great Britain. Often viewed as Maria and her father's attempt to contain the subversiveness of Thady Quirk's tale of big house collapse, the Preface argues that the Rackrents' reckless improvidence represents a safely distant past, just as the novel's full title reinforces a sense of the island's progress toward a new and more orderly governance. The editor's anglicized voice asserts that the origins of Ireland's disorder, embodied in the succeeding chronicle of four Rackrent generations, will be swept away by Union: "Nations as well as individuals gradually lose attachment to their identity, and the present generation is amused rather than offended by the ridicule that is thrown upon its ancestors" (29). However, subsequent versions of the national tale by Charles Maturin or John Banim, following the example of *The Wild Irish Girl,* counter any such easy effacement of a colonial history. Rather than offering a brisk elision of a well-dismissed past, Owenson provides compensatory assertions of the surviving cohesion of Gaelic culture. In her portrayal of the Prince of Inismore's banishment to a ruined castle on the Connamara coast, she reopens the scars of colonial settlements, retrieving the traditions of a suppressed native Irish history.

The persistent impulse of both texts to move beyond traditional novelistic narrative to the mode of explanation and, particularly in Owenson's case, to an explicit championing of Ireland, has perplexed readers more accustomed to the less hybrid forms of much subsequent English fiction.

Joep Leerssen, for example, suggests viewing Owenson's work as a tourist guide to Ireland, describing the country's sublime landscape and the pathos and charm of its impoverished peasantry (*Remembrance* 37). In their need to explain Ireland, Edgeworth and Owenson supplement their tales with multiple footnotes or glossaries; in a few cases these discursive digressions allude to personal experience, but more often to local lore or historical and antiquarian authorities about Ireland. Recent scholarship demonstrates how Maria Edgeworth brought her knowledge of family narrative, national history, and local popular culture to her Irish fiction (Butler, "Edgeworth's Ireland"). Even more centrally in *The Wild Irish Girl*—where in places the paratext overwhelms the narrative and where we find footnotes to footnotes—Sydney Owenson's discursive allusions to Irish antiquarianism recuperate national origins threatened by Union.[5]

During the second half of the eighteenth century, Irish scholars mobilized to document a precolonial history, demonstrating the ancient origins of an indigenous civilization and contesting colonial stereotypes of national barbarity. Owenson, unlike Edgeworth, includes these and even earlier, antiquarian responses to the accounts of Elizabethan chroniclers: hence her text directly engages and participates in major cultural controversies. *The Wild Irish Girl* reproduces the European-wide disagreements concerning the provenance of James Macpherson's *Ossian* poems (O'Halloran), as well as the debates surrounding Charles Vallancey's "Phoenican" thesis about the origins of the Irish language (Leerssen, *Mere Irish* 294–376). By offering a comprehensive annotation of Owenson's sources—for example, the scholarship of Joseph Cooper Walker, Charlotte Brooke, and Edward Bunting—this edition seeks to illustrate how her national tale invokes a dignified, ancient, but above all, civilized Irish culture.

Maria Edgeworth: Union as Solution?

Edgeworth's family and class background, unlike Owenson's, was firmly connected to a ruling-class Anglo-Irish colonial power structure. Moreover, her father, Richard Lovell Edgeworth, was largely educated in England, where he developed enduring relationships with liberal British reformers and scientists such as Erasmus Darwin, James Watt, and Josiah Wedgwood. After years of intermittent residence away from Ireland and the deaths of Maria's mother and first stepmother, he moved his third English wife and a growing family to his ancestral property in County Longford.

[5] A technique being revived in the late twentieth- and twenty-first-century fiction of, for example, David Foster Wallace and Dave Eggers.

There he vowed to devote his life to improving the country from which he drew his support. This 1782 resettlement, concurrent with the establishment of a newly independent Irish parliament, brought fifteen-year-old Maria to her permanent home in the midlands, the setting of her four novels about Ireland. At Edgeworthstown House, the self-effacing daughter devoted herself to educating her many siblings, serving as her father's estate assistant, and producing a body of writing that includes a treatise on education, two volumes of Richard Lovell Edgeworth's memoirs, at least nine major novels, and volumes of tales and stories. Until his death in 1817 she worked closely with her father, a famously energetic and opinionated eccentric to his Irish neighbors; he married four women, fathered twenty-two children, and occupied himself variously as an amateur inventor, scientist, estate manager, writer, educator of his children, and member of parliament. His intrusive role in Maria's writing life has earned the hostility of some readers, who celebrate *Castle Rackrent* as an inspired and uncharacteristically subversive work, with its central narrative produced with little paternal advice or interference.

The Edgeworth family, part of the "new English" settler community, had gained its Irish holdings in the seventeenth century with James I's redistribution of confiscated Catholic property to Protestants.[6] By the 1770s only 5 percent of the island's land remained in Catholic hands (Edwards 166). Nevertheless, as successive waves of anticolonial hostilities illustrate, Protestant settlers, even those like the Edgeworths who had on occasion intermarried with local Catholics, were never fully secure in a countryside surrounded by the native Irish descendants of dispossessed families. (With his speech advocating the Act of Union, the Earl of Clare notoriously depicted these "old inhabitants of the island, brooding over their discontents in sullen indignation" [qtd. Lecky 463].) In the 1641 rebellion, the English-born wife of Captain John Edgeworth, Maria's presumed model for Sir Patrick in *Castle Rackrent,* was driven naked with her infant into the fields, and, in family lore, rebels spared the big house on at least two occasions because it contained the portrait of a devoutly Catholic Edgeworth wife. More than a century later, during the 1798 uprising, the family was again forced to flee before an advancing rebel army, only to find that Richard Lovell Edgeworth's liberalism arose suspicions among his Loyalist neighbors that he was a French spy (see Edgeworth's letters from 1798, 361–65, in this volume).

To some extent, then, Maria Edgeworth's evasiveness about contemporary Ireland in *Castle Rackrent,* written during a decade of increasing

---

[6]The "new English" arrived in Ireland in Elizabeth I's reign or shortly after, in contrast to the "old English," the colonial population that emerged after the Norman conquest in the twelfth century.

political anxiety, was strategic. In County Longford, where almost all landlords were absentees with estates managed by illiberal Protestant agents, her father's early sympathies with the ideals of the French Revolution and his support of Catholic emancipation made him especially unpopular (Butler, *Maria Edgeworth* 115). *Castle Rackrent*'s full title conspicuously antedates the tale to the years before the family's 1782 resettlement in Ireland and before the optimistic period of a newly independent parliament in Dublin; thus Maria avoids any references to the local sectarian tensions preceding the rising that she witnessed as she worked on the text. When she briefly invokes the events of 1798 in her later novel *Ennui* (1809), she fearfully refers to the rebellion as an "epidemic infection" to be quelled when the influence of "men of property, and birth, and education, and character, once more prevailed" (*Castle Rackrent, Irish Bulls, Ennui* 245, 248).

Each of Edgeworth's post-*Rackrent* novels about Irish landlords—*Ennui* (1809), *The Absentee* (1812), and *Ormond* (1817)—reflects her father's plans for reforming his Irish estate, aspirations that were strikingly different not only from those of his contemporary gentry neighbors, but also from those of his ancestors. To the Edgeworths, father and daughter, these ancestral absentees, adventurers, and courtiers had viewed their Irish land solely as a means of support for their improvident lifestyles. Using her grandfather's 1768 chronicle of family exploits, *The Black Book of Edgeworthstown*, Maria loosely based the four generations of Rackrent landlords on family history, insisting that she was presenting "tales of other times" (29). Thus *Castle Rackrent* might be read as a narrative exorcism of past malfeasance that her father's land reform policies sought to bring about after 1782: the abolition of Sir Patrick's drunken extravagance, of Sir Murtagh's and his wife's greedy agrarian capitalism (disguised in the trappings of a defunct feudalism), of Kit's absenteeism, or Condy's improvidence.[7] Most transparently, the decaying and neglected Rackrent property invokes the landlord's failures—his greed, indolence, and irresponsibility that will be swept away with the advent of a modern, paternalistic (and anglicized) system of land tenure after Union.[8]

---

[7] By collecting his own rents, Richard Lovell Edgeworth rid his estate of oppressive land agents; similarly, he abolished long-standing burdens such as "duty-fowl" or "duty work" whereby the Murtaghs transformed older feudal custom into forms of agrarian capitalism (see Young 343–56, in this volume).

[8] Although a strong supporter of the benefits of Union, Richard Lovell Edgeworth, in a characteristically principled act, voted against the 1800 legislation because of opposition to it among his constituents and his disapproval of the government's attempts to buy votes (Butler, *Maria Edgeworth* 182).

Edgeworth's pervasive irony in *Castle Rackrent,* however, elicits a range of responses, signaling to some readers a typical Anglo-Irish condescension toward native Catholic Ireland. In a postcolonial interpretation of the tale reprinted in this volume, Mary Jean Corbett reads the ironic distance between the English editor and a seemingly unsophisticated and gullible Irish narrator as complicit with colonial strategies of control ("Another Tale To Tell" 391–407). Moreover, striking elisions and equivocations characterize Edgeworth's account of gentry history in this chronicle of decline—revealing not only her rejection of past misrule by all Irish landlords, but her anxious confrontations with the reality of an alarmingly colonial situation in the 1790s as she was writing the tale. *Castle Rackrent*'s editorial commentary, in the form of a preface, epilogue, footnotes, and long glossary notes explaining to English readers strange Irish customs and linguistic habits, significantly complicates a chronicle of ruling-class collapse related through the eyes of an ambivalently devoted servant. Added just before publication when the whole text was already in press, the Glossary, especially, implies irreconcilable differences between England and Ireland—linguistic, temperamental, and historic—thus belying the Preface's optimistic assurances that Ireland's disorderly past might be swept away from memory under Union. Edgeworth's depiction of the doomed Rackrent landlords as former O'Shaughlins—"related to the Kings of Ireland" (31)—signals her reluctance to assign full culpability for Ireland's contemporary discord to an Anglo-Irish colonial order. By bestowing a native Irish lineage on the Rackrents, Edgeworth tacitly encourages readers to assume that the family had converted to Protestantism in order to protect its property under the Penal Laws (see n. 10, 31). *Castle Rackrent,* thus, obliquely signals and deflects attention from the sectarian conflicts and colonial land policies that had long undermined Ireland and would continue to trouble the island throughout the long nineteenth century. Such stratagems, undertaken to assert Ireland's readiness for membership in a new union, betray Edgeworth's anxious depiction of a society that, despite her professed optimism, would be represented as a semicolonial outpost in much subsequent Irish fiction.

Two key figures in her tale, Thady Quirk and his son Jason, contribute to *Castle Rackrent*'s seemingly irresolvable ambiguities, again implying a far less optimistic reading of Ireland's future than the Preface asserts. Until recently, most readers viewed Thady as a transparently unreliable narrator, a loyal and simple retainer, whose devotion to his Rackrent masters unwittingly, and comically, reveals their flaws. Such readings took their cue from the author's 1834 explanation that Thady was modeled on John Langan, the Edgeworth family's steward, whose dialect and verbal habits she described herself as effortlessly mimicking.[9] A more skeptical, and by now more common, assessment emphasizes how Thady's craftily professed devotion to the Rackrents hastens their decline—and thus the rise of his ambitious son Jason, who connives to seize all of the family's property by the end of the tale (Newcomer; Dunne, *Maria Edgeworth and the Colonial Mind* 8–10). This darker view of a predatory Thady—and of the consequences of a colonial past—may well have been inflected by Edgeworth's familiarity with Elizabethan commentators like Edmund Spenser and John Davies and their preoccupation with native Irish deviousness.[10] In this reading, Thady is the consummate hypocrite, the servile colonized consciousness whose seeming loyalty to his foolhardy masters masks his deceit. His son Jason, a lawyer portrayed as an unscrupulous land-grabber, anticipates Anglo-Ireland's growing awareness of a threatening Catholic middle class. This social group was to bring down the Ascendancy big house, the symbol of British control of the Irish countryside. In 1834, after the granting of Catholic Emancipation in 1829 and the rise of Daniel O'Connell, Ireland's first great Catholic statesman/politician, Edgeworth announced that Ireland no longer provided fitting material for fiction. "It is impossible to draw Ireland as she now is in a book of fiction—realities are too strong, party passions too violent to bear to see, or care to look at their faces in the looking-glass. The people would only break the glass, and curse the fool who held the mirror up to nature—distorted nature, in a fever" (Letter to M. Pakenham Edgeworth 365–66, in this volume).

Sydney Owenson: Reimagining Union

Sydney Owenson's position within early nineteenth-century Irish society was shifting and marginal compared with the solidly Anglo-Irish gentry identity of Maria Edgeworth. Owenson's ancestry provided her with

---

[9] "The only character drawn from the life . . . is Thady himself, the teller of the story. He was an old steward (not very old, though at times I added to his age, to allow him time for the generations of the family). I heard him when I first came to Ireland, and his dialect struck me, and his character: and I became so acquainted with it, that I could think and speak in it without effort; so that when for mere amusement, without any idea of publishing, I began to write a family history as Thady would tell it, he seemed to stand beside me and dictate; and I wrote as fast as my pen could go, the characters all imaginary" (Letter to Mrs. Stark, 6 September, 1834. Edgeworth and Edgeworth, *A Memoir*, 3:152).

[10] See, for example, Edgeworth's note to Spenser's *View of the Present State of Ireland* on the Irish cloak. Thady's long coat is implicitly compared to the Irish mantle that Spenser describes as "a fit house for an outlaw, a meet bed for a rebel, and an apt cloak for a thief" (30). See Neill for a summary of recent readings of an opaque rather than transparent Thady.

remote connections to an Anglo-Irish power structure, but with stronger emotional alliances to Ireland's Gaelic past—an effective foundation for the central role she was to play in the post-Union culture wars. The mythology circulated about her birth—on a mailboat on the Irish Sea or in Dublin, probably in 1776 (the year of the American Revolution), but perhaps in 1783—itself invokes the turbulence she generated around her public persona. Her Catholic-born father, Robert Owenson (anglicized from MacOwen), who belonged to a dispossessed Connacht farming clan, married into an established Elizabethan settler family. Despite the anglicization of his name and his marriage to an evangelical English woman who reportedly hated Irish "potatoes and Papists" (Stevenson 7), throughout his life Robert claimed kin with Ireland's ancient tribes of Galway.

Owenson's daughter Sydney learned the Irish songs and dances she was later to perform in London and Dublin drawing rooms at his knee. Her attachment to her father, an improvident theater manager and itinerant actor performing stage-Irish roles throughout England and Ireland, was seemingly as formative an influence in her life as Maria Edgeworth's devotion to Richard Lovell Edgeworth. Just as Edgeworth's commitment to rational Enlightenment ideas emerged from parental tutelage, Owenson's engagement with Gaelic culture began with the oral lore she learned from her father. Educated in Dublin's French Huguenot school, she sought work as a governess and turned to writing as a promising source of income when Robert Owenson's stage career faltered. Even after marrying a respectable English doctor, whose powerful friends had arranged to have him knighted to encourage the match, she continued to regard herself as a professional writer, holding out for the highest advances she could negotiate in her new social and literary identity as Lady Morgan. Owenson's theatrical family background, liberal politics, and flamboyant self-promotion ensured that despite her literary success throughout the British Isles and Europe, in the view of ruling-class Dublin Ascendancy and London society her position was less respectable (and more controversial) than that of Edgeworth.[11]

Unlike *Castle Rackrent*, or Edgeworth's three subsequent Irish works written in a far more novelistic register, *The Wild Irish Girl* foregrounds rather than suppresses the brutal trauma of a colonial history. Owenson initiates an allegorical romance plot of reconciliation that would reappear, often in new political formulations, in subsequent national tales, and was to

[11]The controversy surrounding Owenson that began with the critical attacks on *The Wild Irish Girl* was to continue with her later publications. For example, her 1821 work of nonfiction, *Italy*, was banned by the Papacy and by Austria for its liberal political views. Owenson was, however, the first female recipient of a literary pension from the British government.

spread to Scotland, the new American Republic, and Latin America (Sommer). For an increasing number of nineteenth-century Irish novelists, the Act of Union, in its multiple failures to reconcile two countries, was itself the problem facing Ireland, not, as *Castle Rackrent*'s Preface had optimistically asserted, a solution to its conflicted history.[12] Central to Owenson's purpose, then, is the exposure of national disunion and the promotion of genuine reconciliation through a plot of travel, transformation, and love.

The protagonist of *The Wild Irish Girl* is a reluctant stranger journeying to the western edge of the British Isles. In this epistolary tale largely made up of his letters to an English friend, Horatio discovers not the savagery his British upbringing has led him to expect, but a richly cohesive culture and a people proudly surviving years of oppression. He learns that the cordoned-off Irish periphery that he initially dismisses as primitive offers a genuine civility he must acknowledge if the brutality of a past colonial history is to be appeased—and if union is to occur in more than name. A process of education, learning Ireland's language, literature, and antiquarian history, leads the visiting protagonist into visions of new identity. For the literary historian, of course, Horatio's changing responses to Ireland reflect what Seamus Deane describes as "the perceptible shift" at the turn of the nineteenth century from a pejorative identification of the idea of the primitive and barbaric to the new Romantic connotations of ancient cultures as embodying "the spontaneous and original" ("Irish National Character" 94).

After discovering that the Cromwellian founder of his family's Irish estate had murdered the ancestor of the dispossessed and impoverished Prince of Inismore, Horatio finds the old man now living in an ancestral ruin with his daughter—sworn in proud enmity toward the absentee owner of his former lands. Ina Ferris reads the nearly fatal meeting between the English landlord's son and the Irish prince's daughter Glorvina as an unsettling and confounding personal "ravishment" ("Narrating" 416). Horatio's first vision of Glorvina and the Prince disturbs his preconceptions and alters his very character. The setting of this encounter in the west of Ireland, the island's landscape most remote from the colonial pale, most Gaelic in identity, and most terrifyingly Gothic and sublime, initiates not just terror, but personal transformation. "I raised my eyes to the Castle of Inismore, and sighed, and almost wished I had been born the Lord of these beautiful ruins . . . the adored Chieftain of these affectionate and natural people" (146). The romance plot of sensibility grafted to a tale of colonial

[12]The literary historian Joep Leerssen observes that in the cultural record the Act of Union "came to stand for a wrong turn in Irish history. . . . From 1800 onward, we see a sudden increase in the tendency to view Irish history as unfinished business, as a set of outstanding grievances waiting to be addressed" (*Remembrance* 9).

encounter most transparently creates an allegory of personal and national union; Horatio's father, the Earl of M___, descendant of the Cromwellian invaders, pronounces that the new "family alliance" between Glorvina and his son will become "prophetically typical of a national unity of interests and affections" (338). Or as Robert Tracy suggests in another essay included in this volume, the two will rule her ancestral lands with a "double right: to his legal right she adds her own traditional right . . ." (428).

Owenson's imposition of the romance plot on an account of national struggle suggests the multiple and conflicted meanings of union operating in the generically hybrid national tale. For Mary Jean Corbett, the marriage between Horatio and Glorvina implies a continuing unequal union—and thus a perpetuation of the colonial representation of Ireland as female and, therefore, ripe for subjugation. In this reading, by possessing Glorvina, Horatio possesses and domesticates Ireland, bringing union not by the sword or through the imposition of law, but through the realm of feeling (Corbett, *Allegories of Union* 66–70). But competing interpretations might emphasize destabilizing and proto-feminist elements in Owenson's characterization of Glorvina as an enchanting harp-playing philosopher of Irish and western European culture. Moreover, the allegory of gender in *The Wild Irish Girl* is deeply rooted in tropes generated not solely by a long history of colonial representations of Ireland as female, but also by sources in early Gaelic culture. In allegorizing Glorvina as Ireland, Owenson deploys the cultural memory of the local tribal sovereignty goddess, whom the ancient king must marry to legitimize his kingship. Whereas Glorvina's skill on the harp places her in the world of the ancient bards, her bewildering combination of childlike traits and womanly authority, as well as her reading of the most advanced literature, confounds any easy objectification of the female Irish figure.

Once he arrives in the strange country that is Ireland, the male narrator suffers multiple disorientations, including those of gender and sexuality. Ferris's description of Horatio's confusing loss of gender authority before a group of Irish women who ridicule his ignorance of their language suggests a reversal of the customary male gaze. And if, suggests Ferris, in the course of the novel the much gazed-upon Glorvina becomes the erotic "locus of desire" for the visiting Englishman, she also exists as the "locus of guilt," who plunges him into feelings of his own inferiority and ignorance ("Narrating" 413–16). Like Edgeworth, whose chronicle of domestic as well as national disarray portrays reluctant and unruly Rackrent wives (holding on to their wealth and failing to perpetuate the family line), Owenson arguably subverts the very patriarchal form of matrimony she deploys.[13]

[13]Weekes 44–59. For another reading of the Rackrent wives, see Corbett, "Another" 402–07.

Not surprisingly, these two talented women, achieving literary fame and celebrity in a period of shifting expectations about women's roles and male authority, began to negotiate new versions of female identity in their fiction. As one reader observes of *The Wild Irish Girl*, "Love and marriage do not necessarily equate to reconciliation and submission" (Connolly, Introduction xxvi). The literary genre Edgeworth and Owenson initiated did not explicitly challenge the ideals of either political or matrimonial union. But by insistently connecting the political and private arenas, their fiction did begin to destabilize the traditional foundations of such arrangements in both public and domestic settings. Thus in the relationship between sexuality and nationality, Edgeworth and Owenson find complex ways to diagnose Ireland's wrongs and prescribe its future.

A NOTE ON THE TEXTS

The two novels reprinted in this New Riverside Edition present different textual and compositional histories. In an attempt to convey the texture of Edgeworth's and Owenson's tales as they appeared to their original readers, this volume for the most part reproduces the first-edition texts of each work.

The British Museum copy of the first edition of *Castle Rackrent,* published by Joseph Johnson (London, 1800), serves as this volume's base text. Johnson, the radical publisher of William Godwin and Mary Wollstonecraft and acquaintance of Maria Edgeworth's father, Richard Lovell Edgeworth, paid the young author the respectable sum of £100 for her "Hibernian Tale." Edgeworth would revise and correct the novel on at least seven occasions over the subsequent thirty-two years: two London editions in 1800 (there was also an Irish reprint), followed by editions in 1801, 1804, 1810, 1815, 1825 (as part of an early collected edition), and 1832 (as part of a fuller collected edition). The first American edition appeared in 1802, followed by an 1814 edition in Boston. The present New Riverside Edition deviates from the first edition in one important respect. When *Castle Rackrent* was already at press in 1799, Maria Edgeworth added a "Glossary" that the printer inserted after the "Preface." All subsequent editions repositioned the "Glossary" and "The Advertisement to the English Reader" to appear in the pages following Thady's narrative. Similarly, the 1815 edition incorporated the "Advertisement," initially printed on a separate page, into the "Glossary." The New Riverside Edition also places the "Glossary" at the end of the text; page references now accord with the present pagination.

The New Riverside choice of base text privileges the late eighteenth-century novel over the more polished product of some two generations later. This editorial choice captures the effect of idiosyncratic punctuation, the abundant use of what are now commonly called "feminine" dashes, and the deployment of parentheses within dialogue: "Jason! (says I) don't be trusting to him, Judy" (77). Typographical errors have been silently corrected and some spellings standardized. Similarly, certain variants and emendations, particularly changes to the early editions, are also silently adopted; for example, the variant surname "Stopgap" is replaced throughout by "Rackrent." Footnotes indicate which variants the editor regards as significant. Finally, while this edition retains the three footnotes deleted by Maria Edgeworth in later editions, it also incorporates a footnote and a glossary note added to the fifth edition (1810). In such cases, editorial notes [ED.] indicate changes.

The first edition of *The Wild Irish Girl*, published by Richard Phillips (London, 1806), serves as this volume's base text.[1] Imprisoned in 1792 for publishing Thomas Paine's *The Rights of Man*, Phillips paid Owenson the substantial sum of £300 for her "National Tale," but only after protracted negotiations in which she used discussions with Joseph Johnson to gain a financial advantage. Within two years of publication, Phillips produced three further British editions; Longman of London also published an edition in 1813. In 1846 Henry Colburn issued *The Wild Irish Girl* in his firm's "Standard Novels" series, on which occasion the author, now known as Lady Morgan, revised and edited the work for the first time and added a "Prefatory Address." Consistent with the stated objectives of this edition, neither the "Prefatory Address" nor the author's revisions are incorporated here. The novel was reprinted regularly throughout the nineteenth century, with American editions appearing in New York (1807, 1857, 1883), Philadelphia (1807, 1822), Boston (1808, 1832), Baltimore (1807), and Hartford (1850, 1855).

Owenson's extensive use of quotations and footnotes as part of the fabric of her text represents a formidable challenge to readers and editors of *The Wild Irish Girl.* The author quotes from an extensive array of sources: contemporary Irish antiquarian texts, works of English and foreign language literatures, as well as various forms of Greek and Roman myth and legend. Although earlier detractors accused Owenson of fabricating these footnotes and inventing her sources, the most recent edition of *The Wild Irish Girl* provides incontrovertible evidence of the author's serious scholarship. This New Riverside Edition, by providing a significant number of carefully selected citations, seeks to represent Owenson's intellectual achievement without burdening the reader with excessive commentary.

Despite their popularity when published, neither *Castle Rackrent* nor *The Wild Irish Girl* fared well in subsequent literary history. The former was primarily discussed in the context of the regional novel; the latter was largely ignored and remained out of print for much of the twentieth century. *Castle Rackrent* finally became available in an accurate and accessible

---

[1] The copy used belongs to Boston College's John J. Burns Library.

student edition in the 1960s; a comparable text of *The Wild Irish Girl* materialized only thirty years later. Moreover, unlike *Castle Rackrent,* Owenson's "National Tale" was generally ignored in critical and classroom discussions until the 1990s. Most significantly, the two novels, which were issued under the imprint of radical London publishers in a turbulent period of Irish history, now appear for the first time side by side in the New Riverside Edition.

Several previous editions of both novels, listed in the "Works Cited" section, inform this edition. In particular, I am indebted to Claire Connolly and Stephen Copley's scholarly textual edition of *The Wild Irish Girl* and Jane Demarais, Tim McLoughlin, and Marilyn Butler's scholarly textual edition of *Castle Rackrent.* Similarly, a number of reference works also listed in the "Works Cited," and online databases including *The Oxford English Dictionary, The Encyclopedia Britannica,* and *Literature Online,* silently inform the footnotes and editor's notes.

MARIA EDGEWORTH, SYDNEY OWENSON (LADY MORGAN), AND THEIR CULTURAL CONTEXT: A SELECT CHRONOLOGY

1768 Maria Edgeworth born on January 1, at Black Bourton, Oxfordshire, second child of Richard Lovell Edgeworth (1744–1817) and Anna Maria Elers.

1773 Maria's mother dies. Richard Lovell Edgeworth marries Honora Sneyd. Maria first visits Ireland.

1775–80 Edgeworth attends private school at Derby.

1776 Sydney Owenson born on Christmas Day (probably), first child of Irish actor Robert Owenson and Jane Hill. Arthur Young begins tour of Ireland (his account of it, *A Tour in Ireland*, published in 1780). Declaration of American Independence.

1777 Thomas Campbell publishes *Philosophical Survey of the South of Ireland.*

1780 Edgeworth attends private school at Upper Wimpole Street, London. Honora Sneyd dies. Richard Lovell Edgeworth marries her sister, Elizabeth.

1782 Maria settles at Edgeworthstown, her father's Irish estate in County Longford. Parliament in Dublin establishes independence. Poyning's Law amended. Catholic relief acts grant Catholics the right to purchase land and obtain an education.

1785 First meeting of Irish Academy (Royal Irish Academy by charter of January 28, 1786), later begins collections of Irish MSS with acquisition of "Book of Ballymote."

1786 Joseph Cooper Walker publishes *Historical Memoirs of the Irish Bards.*

1787 Maria Edgeworth begins *The Freeman Family;* resumed as *Patronage* in 1809. First bound volume of *Transactions of the Royal Irish Academy* appears.

1789 Jane Hill, Owenson's mother, dies. Charlotte Brooke publishes *Reliques of Irish Poetry.* French Revolution begins.

1789–92 Owenson and her sister Olivia attend Mme. Terson's Academy in Clontarf followed by Mrs. Anderson's finishing school in Earl Street, Dublin.

1790 Edmund Burke publishes *Reflections on the Revolution in France.* Edward Ledwich publishes *Antiquities of Ireland.*

1791 The Society of United Irishmen founded in Belfast, and later in Dublin.

1794 The Owenson family moves to Kilkenny, where Robert establishes a theatre. Statutes of Trinity College Dublin amended to allow Catholics to take degrees.

1795 Edgeworth publishes first book, *Letters for Literary Ladies.* Royal College of St. Patrick, a Catholic seminary, opens at Maynooth, Co. Kildare.

1796 Edgeworth publishes *The Parent's Assistant,* a collection of children's stories. French troops in Bantry Bay, Co. Cork, together with Theobald Wolfe Tone, prevented from invading Ireland due to bad weather.

1797 Elizabeth, Richard Lovell Edgeworth's third wife, dies. Edward Bunting publishes *A General Collection of the Ancient Irish Music.*

1798 Edgeworth publishes *Practical Education,* a textbook for children written with her father. Richard Lovell Edgeworth marries Frances Beaufort. United Irishmen rising in Wexford, Ulster, and, with the help of a French force landing in Killala Bay, Co. Mayo, in Connacht. French surrender at Ballinamuck, Co. Longford, near the Edgeworthtown estate. To avoid the rebels, Edgeworth family takes refuge in Longford. Wolfe Tone arrested and commits suicide in prison. Richard Lovell Edgeworth later elected to Irish parliament.

1800 Edgeworth anonymously publishes her first novel, *Castle Rackrent: An Hibernian Tale,* to overwhelming success. Owenson spends time with the Crofton family, her father's relations, in Sligo. Act of Union dissolves Irish parliament.

1801 Edgeworth publishes *Moral Tales for Young People,* a collection of stories for older children, and *Belinda,* her first novel of manners. Owenson publishes *Poems, Dedicated by Permission to the Countess of Moira.* She begins her career as a governess, first with the Featherstonehaugh family, Bracklin Castle, Co. Westmeath, and later with the Crawford family, Fort William, Co. Tipperary. Act of Union of Great Britain and Ireland takes effect.

1802 Edgeworth publishes *Essays on Irish Bulls,* written with her father's help. Travels on the Continent and meets a Swedish courtier, Abraham Edelcrantz. Peace of Amiens ends war between U.K. and France.

1803 Edgeworth back in England prior to resumption of Napoleonic wars. Owenson publishes her first novel, the sentimental *St Clair; or The Heiress of Desmond* (an earlier edition purportedly published in Dublin a year earlier, but no copy extant). Robert Emmet's rising in Dublin; rising fails and Emmet executed, September 20.

1804 Edgeworth publishes *Popular Tales,* a story collection written for the middle and lower classes. Napoleon becomes emperor of France.

1805 Edgeworth publishes *The Modern Griselda: A Tale.* Owenson publishes *Twelve Original Hibernian Melodies,* a collection of songs translated from Irish. William Parnell publishes *An enquiry into the causes of popular discontents in Ireland, by an Irish country gentleman.*

1806 Edgeworth publishes *Leonora,* a romantic epistolary novel. Owenson publishes *The Novice of Saint Dominick,* a historical romance, and *The Wild Irish Girl: A National Tale,* the latter resulting in celebrity status for the author.

1807 Owenson's only dramatic production, an opera entitled *The First Attempt, or Whim of a Moment,* performed at Dublin's Theatre Royal in which her father makes his final stage appearance. Also publishes *The Lay of an Irish Harp: or, Metrical Fragments*; and *Patriotic Sketches of Ireland, Written in Connaught.*

1808 Owenson acclaimed in London as the new force in writing about Ireland. First number of Thomas Moore's *Irish Melodies.*

1809 Edgeworth publishes *Tales of Fashionable Life*, i–iii, including *Ennui* and *Vivian*. Resumes work on *Patronage*. Owenson publishes *Woman, or, Ida of Athens*. Resides with the Abercorns at Baron's Court, Co. Tyrone, where she is introduced to Charles Morgan, the English physician to her patrons. Belfast Harp Society formed.

1810 Sir Thomas Lawrence paints Owenson's portrait while she is visiting London.

1811 Owenson publishes *The Missionary*, a novel set in India. Charles Morgan is knighted.

1812 Edgeworth publishes *Tales of Fashionable Life*, iv–vi, including *The Absentee*, an Irish novel. Owenson marries Sir Charles Morgan. Robert Owenson, Sydney's father, dies. The Morgans leave their residence with the Abercorns.

1813 Edgeworth visits London, meets Lord Byron and Humphry Davy. The Morgans move to 35 Kildare Street, Dublin.

1814 Edgeworth publishes *Patronage*, begun in 1787 and resumed in 1809. Edgeworth receives a copy of *Waverly*, and correspondence with Scott begins. Owenson publishes the very popular *O'Donnel—A National Tale*.

1815–16 Morgans travel to France after defeat of Napoleon in June.

1817 Edgeworth publishes *Harrington: A Tale* and *Ormond: A Tale*, two novellas. Richard Lovell Edgeworth writes "Preface," and part of *Ormond*, before dying on June 13. Owenson publishes the controversial *France*, a travel book advocating pro-revolutionary sentiments. Thomas Moore publishes *Lalla Rookh*.

1818 Owenson publishes *Florence Macarthy, an Irish Tale*. Irish Society for Promoting the Education of the Native Irish through the Medium of their own Language founded.

1819–20 Morgans again visit France, and Italy.

1820 Edgeworth publishes her father's memoirs, *Memoirs of Richard Lovell Edgeworth, Esq.; Begun by Himself and Concluded by his Daughter, Maria Edgeworth*. Visits Paris with her sisters, Fanny and Harriet. Rev. Charles Robert Maturin publishes *Melmoth the Wanderer*.

1821 Owenson publishes *Italy*, a travelogue, again advocating radical political ideas.

1822 With her husband, Owenson coauthors *The Mohawks: A Satirical Poem*.

1823 Edgeworth travels to Scotland, meets Scott for first time in Edinburgh, and later spends two weeks as his guest at Abbotsford. The Catholic Association founded at Dempsey's Tavern, Dublin. Daniel O'Connell leads campaign for Catholic Emancipation.

1824 Owenson publishes *The Life and Times of Salvator Rosa,* a biography of the Italian painter she much admired. O'Connell instigates the "catholic rent," a voluntary monetary contribution to aid the Catholic Association's campaign. Thomas Moore publishes *Memoirs of Captain Rock.*

1825 First collected edition of Edgeworth's works published, *Tales and Miscellaneous Pieces* (14 vols.). Scott visits Edgeworthstown. Owenson publishes *Absenteeism,* an essay on Ireland. Thomas Croften Croker publishes *The fairy legends and traditions of the south of Ireland.*

1827 Owenson publishes *The O'Briens and the O'Flahertys, a National Tale.* Sir Jonah Barrington publishes *Personal sketches of his own time.*

1828 Daniel O'Connell elected MP for Clare, first Irish Catholic to do so.

1829 Owenson publishes a collection of autobiographical sketches, *The Book of the Boudoir.* Also visits the Low Countries and France. Roman Catholic Relief Act, 1829, enables Catholics to enter Parliament, and hold military and civic offices—Catholic Emancipation. Gerald Griffin publishes *The Collegians.*

1830 Owenson publishes *France in 1829–30.* William Carleton publishes *Traits and stories of the Irish peasantry.*

1832 Second collected editions of Edgeworth's works published, *Tales and Novels* (18 monthly vols.), edited by the author. The Morgans visit England.

1833 Edgeworth visits Connemara. Owenson publishes *Dramatic Scenes from Real Life,* set in Ireland. First number of *Dublin University Magazine.* George Petrie reads paper, "An inquiry into the origin and uses of the round towers of Ireland," to Royal Irish Academy.

1834 Edgeworth publishes her last novel, and first since 1817, *Helen: A Tale.*

1835 Owenson publishes her last novel, *The Princess, or The Beguine.* Thomas Moore publishes *History of Ireland.*

1837 Owenson becomes the first woman to receive a literary pension from the British government, £300 a year. Morgans leave Dublin for Belgravia in London. Accession of Queen Victoria.

1838 Owenson publishes *Historic Sketches.* Irish Poor Law extends English system to Ireland. Trinity College Dublin establishes first chair of Irish (first appointment in 1840).

1840 Owenson publishes *Woman and her Master,* the first of a planned series on women's history.

1841 Owenson publishes *The Book Without a Name,* collected essays written with her husband. The Morgans visit Germany. Anthony Trollope arrives in Ireland as deputy post-office surveyor.

1843 Sir Charles Morgan dies.

1845–49 Great Irish Famine.

1848 Third collected editions of Edgeworth's works published, *Tales and Novels* (9 vols.).

1849 Maria Edgeworth dies on May 22.

1859 Sydney Owenson dies on April 16. Owenson's *Passages from my Autobiography* published.

1862 Publication of *Lady Morgan's Memoirs: Autobiography, Diaries, Correspondence.*

Part One

THE TALES

CASTLE RACKRENT,

R

AN

HIBERNIAN TALE.

TAKEN FROM FACTS,

AND FROM

THE MANNERS OF THE IRISH SQUIRES,

BEFORE THE YEAR 1782.[1]

Printed for J. JOHNSON, ST. PAUL'S CHURCH-YARD—1800.

By J. CROWDER, Warwick-ſquare.

Rackrent: an excessive or extortionate rent.

[1] 1782 is the year when Maria Edgeworth settled at her father's Irish estate in Edgeworthstown, and Ireland obtained an independent parliament in Dublin. The title page did not list the author's name until the third edition (1801).

Preface[2]

THE prevailing taste of the public for anecdote has been censured and ridiculed by critics, who aspire to the character of superior wisdom: but if we consider it in a proper point of view, this taste is an incontestible proof of the good sense and profoundly philosophic temper of the present times. Of the numbers who study, or at least who read history, how few derive any advantage from their labors! The heroes of history are so decked out by the fine fancy of the professed historian; they talk in such measured prose, and act from such sublime or such diabolical motives, that few have sufficient taste, wickedness or heroism, to sympathize in their fate. Besides, there is much uncertainty even in the best authenticated antient or modern histories; and that love of truth, which in some minds is innate and immutable, necessarily leads to a love of secret memoirs and private anecdotes. We cannot judge either of the feelings or of the characters of men with perfect accuracy from their actions or their appearance in public; it is from their careless conversations, their half finished sentences, that we may hope with the greatest probability of success to discover their real characters. The life of a great or of a little man written by himself, the familiar letters, the diary of any individual published by his friends, or by his enemies after his decease, are esteemed important literary curiosities. We are surely justified in this eager desire to collect the most minute facts relative to the domestic lives, not only of the great and good, but even of the worthless and insignificant, since it is only by a comparison of their actual happiness or misery in the privacy of domestic life, that we can form a just estimate of the real reward of virtue, or the real punishment of vice. That the great are not as happy as they seem, that the external circumstances of fortune and rank do not constitute felicity, is asserted by every moralist; the historian can seldom, consistently with his dignity, pause to illustrate this truth, it is therefore to the biographer we must have recourse. After we have beheld splendid characters playing their parts on the great theatre of the world, with all the

---

London: Johnson, 1800. (In addition to Edgeworth's footnotes, indicated in this edition by an asterisk (*), the glossary marker([g]) refers to Maria Edgeworth's original glossary, which is reprinted with minor changes in format on pages 81–95 immediately following the text. The footnotes provided by the volume editor of this New Riverside Edition (hereafter *TINT*) are indicated numerically or added parenthetically to Edgeworth's notes.)

[2]Presumed to have been written last, and possibly by Richard Lovell Edgeworth, Maria's father.

advantages of stage effect and decoration, we anxiously beg to be admitted behind the scenes, that we may take a nearer view of the actors and actresses.

Some may perhaps imagine, that the value of biography depends upon the judgment and taste of the biographer; but on the contrary it may be maintained, that the merits of a biographer are inversely as the extent of his intellectual powers and of his literary talents. A plain unvarnished tale is preferable to the most highly ornamented narrative.[3] Where we see that a man has the power, we may naturally suspect that he has the will to deceive us, and those who are used to literary manufacture know how much is often sacrificed to the rounding of a period or the pointing of an antithesis.

That the ignorant may have their prejudices as well as the learned cannot be disputed, but we see and despise vulgar errors; we never bow to the authority of him who has no great name to sanction his absurdities. The partiality which blinds a biographer to the defects of his hero, in proportion as it is gross ceases to be dangerous; but if it be concealed by the appearance of candor, which men of great abilities best know how to assume, it endangers our judgment sometimes, and sometimes our morals. If her Grace the Duchess of Newcastle, instead of penning her lord's elaborate eulogium, had undertaken to write the life of Savage, we should not have been in any danger of mistaking an idle, ungrateful libertine, for a man of genius and virtue.[4] The talents of a biographer are often fatal to his reader. For these reasons the public often judiciously countenance those, who without sagacity to discriminate character, without elegance of style to relieve the tediousness of narrative, without enlargement of mind to draw any conclusions from the facts they relate, simply pour forth anecdotes and retail conversations, with all the minute prolixity of a gossip in a country town.

The author of the following memoirs has upon these grounds fair claims to the public favor and attention: he was an illiterate old steward, whose partiality to *the family* in which he was bred and born must be obvious to the reader.[5] He tells the history of the Rackrent family in his vernacular idiom, and in the full confidence that Sir Patrick, Sir Murtagh, Sir Kit, and Sir Condy Rackrent's affairs, will be as interesting to all the world as they were to himself.[6] Those who were acquainted with the manners of

---

[3] William Shakespeare, *Othello*, I. iii. 90: "I will a round unvarnish'd tale deliver."

[4] Margaret Cavendish, Duchess of Newcastle (1624?–74) eulogized her husband in *The Life of William Cavendish* (1667). Samuel Johnson's *Life of Savage* (1744), reissued as one of his *Lives of the English Poets* (1779–81), similarly defends Richard Savage (d. 1743), poet, murderer, and alleged blackmailer. Both biographies notably skewed their subject.

[5] Based on John Langan, a steward to R. L. Edgeworth at Edgeworthstown.

[6] Spelled variously as "Kitt" and "Kit" throughout the first edition (1800), thereafter standardized as "Kit." After 1825, "Sir" was in lowercase throughout text.

a certain class of the gentry of Ireland some years ago, will want no evidence of the truth of honest Thady's narrative: to those who are totally unacquainted with Ireland, the following Memoirs will perhaps be scarcely intelligible, or probably they may appear perfectly incredible. For the information of the *ignorant* English reader a few notes have been subjoined by the editor, and he had it once in contemplation to translate the language of Thady into plain English; but Thady's idiom is incapable of translation, and besides, the authenticity of his story would have been more exposed to doubt if it were not told in his own characteristic manner. Several years ago he related to the editor the history of the Rackrent family, and it was with some difficulty that he was persuaded to have it committed to writing; however, his feelings for "*the honor of the family*," as he expressed himself, prevailed over his habitual laziness, and he at length completed the narrative which is now laid before the public.

The Editor hopes his readers will observe, that these are "tales of other times;" that the manners depicted in the following pages are not those of the present age: the race of the Rackrents has long since been extinct in Ireland, and the drunken Sir Patrick, the litigious Sir Murtagh, the fighting Sir Kit, and the slovenly Sir Condy, are characters which could no more be met with at present in Ireland, than Squire Western or Parson Trulliber in England. There is a time when individuals can bear to be rallied for their past follies and absurdities, after they have acquired new habits and a new consciousness. Nations as well as individuals gradually lose attachment to their identity, and the present generation is amused rather than offended by the ridicule that is thrown upon its ancestors.

Probably we shall soon have it in our power, in a hundred instances, to verify the truth of these observations.

When Ireland loses her identity by an union with Great Britain,[7] she will look back with a smile of good-humoured complacency on the Sir Kits and Sir Condys of her former existence.[8]

Squire Western: the boorish squire in Fielding's *Tom Jones* (1749).

Parson Trulliber: the mercenary country clergyman in Fielding's *Joseph Andrews* (1742).

[7]As early as 1799, when Edgeworth was completing *Castle Rackrent,* the Act of Union between Great Britain and Ireland seemed inevitable. R. L. Edgeworth was a member of the Dublin parliament and voted against the measure. Ultimately, George III signed the Act of Union on July 2, 1800, some six months after the novel's appearance.

[8]The 1832 edition added "1800" to the end of the Preface.

An Hibernian Tale

Castle Rackrent

Monday Morning.[g]

HAVING out of friendship for the family, upon whose estate, praised be Heaven! I and mine have lived rent free time out of mind, voluntarily undertaken to publish the Memoirs of the Rackrent Family, I think it my duty to say a few words, in the first place, concerning myself.—My real name is Thady Quirk, though in the family I have always been known by no other than "*honest Thady*"—afterwards, in the time of Sir Murtagh, deceased, I remember to hear them calling me "*old Thady,*" and now I'm come to "poor Thady"—for I wear a long great coat* winter and summer, which is very

*The cloak, or mantle, as described by Thady, is of high antiquity.—Spencer, in his "View of the State of Ireland," proves that it is not, as some have imagined, peculiarly derived from the Scythians, but that "most nations of the world anciently used the mantle; for the Jews used it, as you may read of Elias's mantle, &c.; the Chaldees also used it, as you may read in Diodorus; the Egyptians likewise used it, as you may read in Herodotus, and may be gathered by the description of Berenice, in the Greek Commentary upon Callimachus; the Greeks also used it anciently, as appeareth by Venus's mantle lined with stars, though afterwards they changed the form thereof into their cloaks, called Pallai, as some of the Irish also use: and the ancient Latins and Romans used it, as you may read in Virgil, who was a very great antiquary, that Evander, when Eneas came to him at his feast, did entertain and feast him, sitting on the ground, and lying on mantles; insomuch as he useth the very word mantile for a mantle,

'—— Humi mantilia sternunt.'

so that it seemeth that the mantle was a general habit to most nations, and not proper to the Scythians only."

Spencer knew the convenience of the said mantle, as housing, bedding, and cloathing.

"Iren. Because the commodity doth not countervail the discommodity; for the inconveniences which thereby do arise, are much more many; for it is a fit house for an outlaw, a meet bed for a rebel, and an apt cloak for a thief.—First, the outlaw being, for his many crimes and villanies, banished from the towns and houses of honest men, and wandering in waste places, far from danger of law, maketh his mantle his house, and under it covereth himself from the wrath of Heaven, from the offence of the earth, and from the sight of men. When it raineth, it is his penthouse; when it bloweth, it is his tent; when it freezeth, it is his tabernacle. In summer he can wear it loose; in winter he can wrap it close; at all times he can use it; never heavy, never cumbersome. Likewise for a rebel it is as serviceable; for in this war that he maketh (if at least it deserves the name of war), when he still flieth from his foe, and lurketh in the *thick woods, (this should be black bogs,)* and straight passages waiting for advantages; it is his bed, yea, and almost his household-stuff." [The quotation in Latin translates as, "They spread their cloaks on the ground," Edmund Spenser, *A View of the Present State of Ireland,* 56–57. Spenser (1552/3–99) was Lord Grey's secretary during the Irish campaign, finally settling a large estate at Kilcolman in Co. Cork. *A View* (written 1595–96, published 1633) argued for "root and branch" treatment of native Irish and Old English opposition to New English rule in Ireland. Ed.]

handy, as I never put my arms into the sleeves, (they are as good as new,) though, come Holantide next, I've had it these seven years; it holds on by a single button round my neck, cloak fashion—to look at me, you would hardly think "poor Thady" was the father of attorney Quirk; he is a high gentleman, and never minds what poor Thady says, and having better than 1500 a-year, landed estate, looks down upon honest Thady, but I wash my hands of his doings, and as I have lived so will I die, true and loyal to the family.[9]—The family of the Rackrents is, I am proud to say, one of the most ancient in the kingdom.—Every body knows this is not the old family name, which was O'Shaughlin, related to the Kings of Ireland—but that was before my time.—My grandfather was driver to the great Sir Patrick O'Shaughlin, and I heard him, when I was a boy, telling how the Castle Rackrent estate came to Sir Patrick—Sir Tallyhoo Rackrent was cousin-german to him, and had a fine estate of his own, only never a gate upon it, it being his maxim, that a car was the best gate.—Poor gentleman! he lost a fine hunter and his life, at last, by it, all in one day's hunt.—But I ought to bless that day, for the estate came straight into *the* family, upon one condition, which Sir Patrick O'Shaughlin at the time took sadly to heart, they say, but thought better of it afterwards, seeing how large a stake depended upon it, that he should, by Act of Parliament, take and bear the sirname and arms of Rackrent.[10]

Now it was that the world was to see what was *in* Sir Patrick.—On coming into the estate, he gave the finest entertainment ever was heard of in the country—not a man could stand after supper but Sir Patrick himself, who

---

Holantide: Halloween, October 31.

[9]A phrase with Jacobite connotations, referring probably to James Butler, second Duke of Ormonde (1665–1745), who served the last Stuart monarchs in Ireland.

[10]Sir Patrick's change of surname likely attends his conversion from Catholicism to the Established Anglican Church of Ireland, an action that would enable him legally to inherit a landed estate. Historically, "The Act to Prevent the Further Growth of Popery" (1704), one of the so-called Penal Laws, prohibited Catholics from buying land, inheriting land from Protestants, or taking leases longer than thirty-one years in duration. The statute also mandated that Catholic estates be divided equally among male heirs. Other measures barred Catholics from practicing law, from holding office in central or local government, and from membership of all grand juries and municipal corporations. Recent scholarship emphasizes that it was Ireland's remaining Catholic aristocracy (possessing roughly 14 percent of the land in 1703) who were chiefly targeted by these measures, but the general Catholic population also suffered. Catholic Relief Acts were passed in 1778, 1782, and 1792–93, and the passing of Catholic Emancipation in 1828 finally ended the "Penal Law" era.

could sit out the best man in Ireland, let alone the three kingdoms itself.[g]—He had his house, from one year's end to another, as full of company as ever it could hold, and fuller; for rather than be left out of the parties at Castle Rackrent, many gentlemen, and those men of the first consequence and landed estates in the country, such as the O'Neills of Ballynagrotty, and the Moneygawls of Mount Juliet's Town,[11] and O'Shannons of New Town Tullyhog, made it their choice, often and often, when there was no moon to be had for love nor money, in long winter nights, to sleep in the chicken house, which Sir Patrick had fitted up for the purpose of accommodating his friends and the public in general, who honoured him with their company unexpectedly at Castle Rackrent; and this went on, I can't tell you how long—the whole country rang with his praises—Long life to him!—I'm sure I love to look upon his picture, now opposite to me; though I never saw him, he must have been a portly gentleman—his neck something short, and remarkable for the largest pimple on his nose, which, by his particular desire, is still extant in his picture—said to be a striking likeness, though taken when young.—He is said also to be the inventor of raspberry whiskey, which is very likely, as nobody has ever appeared to dispute it with him, and as there still exists a broken punch-bowl at Castle Rackrent,[12] in the garret, with an inscription to that effect—a great curiosity.—A few days before his death he was very merry; it being his honour's birth-day, he called my great grandfather in, God bless him! to drink the company's health, and filled a bumper himself, but could not carry it to his head, on account of the great shake in his hand—on this he cast his joke, saying, "What would my poor father say to me if he was to pop out of the grave, and see me now?—I remember, when I was a little boy, the first bumper of claret he gave me after dinner, how he praised me for carrying it so steady to my mouth—Here's my thanks to him—a bumper toast"—Then he fell to singing the favourite song he learned from his father—for the last time, poor gentleman—he sung it that night as loud and as hearty as ever, with a chorus—

"He that goes to bed, and goes to bed sober,
Falls as the leaves do, falls as the leaves do, and dies in October—
But he that goes to bed, and goes to bed mellow,

---

[11] Castle-moneygawls (1800–25). Editor changed for conformity within text; see *Castle Rackrent* (hereafter *CR*) 50.

[12] Castle Stopgap (1800 first). Edgeworth contemplated using Stopgap as the family and estate name, a reference no doubt to Sir Tallyhoo's use of a car rather than a regular gate; see *CR* 31.

> Lives as he ought to do, lives as he ought to do, and dies an honest fellow."[13]

Sir Patrick died that night—just as the company rose to drink his health with three cheers, he fell down in a sort of a fit, and was carried off—they sat it out, and were surprised, on enquiry, in the morning, to find it was all over with poor Sir Patrick—Never did any gentleman live and die more beloved in the country by rich and poor—his funeral was such a one as was never known before or since in the county!—All the gentlemen in the three counties were at it—far and near, how they flocked—my great grandfather said, that to see all the women even in their red cloaks, you would have taken them for the army drawn out.—Then such a fine whillaluh![g] you might have heard it to the farthest end of the county, and happy the man who could get but a sight of the hearse!—But who'd have thought it, just as all was going on right, through his own town they were passing, when the body was seized for debt—a rescue was apprehended from the mob—but the heir who attended the funeral was against that, for fear of consequences, seeing that those villains who came to serve acted under the disguise of the law—So, to be sure, the law must take its course—and little gain had the creditors for their pains. First and foremost, they had the curses of the country; and Sir Murtagh Rackrent the new heir, in the next place, on account of this affront to the body, refused to pay a shilling of the debts, in which he was countenanced by all the best gentlemen of property, and others of his acquaintance, Sir Murtagh alledging in all companies, that he all along meant to pay his father's debts of honor; but the moment the law was taken of him, there was an end of honor to be sure. It was whispered, (but none but the enemies of the family believe it) that this was all a sham seizure to get quit of the debts, which he had bound himself to pay in honor.

It's a long time ago, there's no saying how it was, but this for certain, the new man did not take at all after the old gentleman—The cellars were never filled after his death—and no open house, or any thing as it used to be—the tenants even were sent away without their whiskey[g]—I was ashamed myself, and knew not what to say for the honor of the family—But I made the best of a bad case, and laid it all at my lady's door, for I did not like *her* any how, nor any body else—she was of the family of the Skinflints, and a widow—It was a strange match for Sir Murtagh; the people in the country thought he demeaned himself greatly[g]—but *I* said nothing—I knew how it was—Sir Murtagh was a great lawyer, and looked to the great Skinflint

[13]Watson dates this traditional song to the early seventeenth century, echoing lines in John Fletcher's play *Rollo: or the Bloody Brother* (1639) and in Thomas Fuller's *Gnomologa: Adages and Proverbs* (1732). See Watson 120, n. 16.

estate; there, however, he overshot himself; for though one of the co-heiresses, he was never the better for her, for she outlived him many's the long day—he could not foresee that, to be sure, when he married her. I must say for her, she made him the best of wives, being a very notable stirring woman, and looking close to every thing. But I always suspected she had Scotch blood in her veins, any thing else I could have looked over in her from a regard to the family. She was a strict observer for self and servants of Lent, and all Fast days, but not holidays. One of the maids having fainted three times the last day of Lent, to keep soul and body together we put a morsel of roast beef into her mouth, which came from Sir Murtagh's dinner, who never fasted, not he; but somehow or other it unfortunately reached my lady's ears, and the priest of the parish had a complaint made of it the next day, and the poor girl was forced as soon as she could walk to do penance for it, before she could get any peace or absolution in the house or out of it. However, my lady was very charitable in her own way. She had a charity school for poor children, where they were taught to read and write gratis, and where they were kept well to spinning gratis for my lady in return; for she had always heaps of duty yarn from the tenants, and got all her houshold linen out of the estate from first to last; for after the spinning, the weavers on the estate took it in hand for nothing, because of the looms my lady's interest could get from the Linen Board to distribute gratis. Then there was a bleach yard near us, and the tenant dare refuse my lady nothing, for fear of a law-suit Sir Murtagh kept hanging over him about the water course. With these ways of managing, 'tis surprising how cheap my lady got things done, and how proud she was of it. Her table the same way—kept for next to nothing—duty fowls, and duty turkies, and duty geese,[g] came as fast as we could eat 'em, for my lady kept a sharp look out, and knew to a tub of butter every thing the tenants had, all round. They knew her way, and what with fear of driving for rent and Sir Murtagh's law-suits, they were kept in such good order, they never thought of coming near Castle Rackrent without a present of something or other—nothing too much or too little for my lady—eggs—honey—butter—meal—fish —game, growse, and herrings, fresh or salt—all went for something. As for their young pigs, we had them, and the best bacon and hams they could make up, with all young chickens in spring; but they were a set of poor wretches, and we had nothing but misfortunes with them, always breaking and running away—This, Sir Murtagh and my lady said, was all their former landlord Sir Patrick's fault, who let 'em all get the half year's rent into arrear—there was something in that, to be sure—But Sir Murtagh was as much the contrary way—For let alone making English tenants[g] of them, every soul—he was

---

Linen Board: set up in 1711 to regulate the expanding Irish linen industry.

always driving and driving, and pounding and pounding, and canting[g] and canting, and replevying and replevying, and he made a good living of trespassing cattle—there was always some tenant's pig, or horse, or cow, or calf, or goose, trespassing, which was so great a gain to Sir Murtagh, that he did not like to hear me talk of repairing fences. Then his heriots and duty work[g] brought him in something—his turf was cut—his potatoes set and dug—his hay brought home, and in short all the work about his house done for nothing; for in all our leases there were strict clauses with heavy penalties, which Sir Murtagh knew well how to enforce—so many days duty work of man and horse, from every tenant, he was to have, and had, every year; and when a man vexed him, why the finest day he could pitch on, when the cratur was getting in his own harvest, or thatching his cabin, Sir Murtagh made it a principle to call upon him and his horse—so he taught 'em all, as he said, to know the law of landlord and tenant. As for law, I believe no man, dead or alive, ever loved it so well as Sir Murtagh. He had once sixteen suits pending at a time, and I never saw him so much himself—roads—lanes—bogs—wells—ponds—eel-wires—orchards—trees—tythes—vagrants—gravel-pits—sandpits—dung-hills and nuisances—every thing upon the face of the earth furnished him good matter for a suit. He used to boast that he had a law-suit for every letter in the alphabet. How I used to wonder to see Sir Murtagh in the midst of the papers in his office—why he could hardly turn about for them. I made bold to shrug my shoulders once in his presence, and thanked my stars I was not born a gentleman to so much toil and trouble—but Sir Murtagh took me up short with his old proverb, "learning is better than house or land."[14] Out of forty-nine suits which he had, he never lost one but seventeen;[g] the rest he gained with costs, double costs, treble costs sometimes—but even that did not pay. He was a very learned man in the law, and had the character of it; but how it was I can't tell, these suits that he carried cost him a power of money—in the end he sold some hundreds a year of the family estate—but he was a very learned man in the law, and I know nothing of the matter except having a great regard for the family. I could not help grieving when he sent me to post up notices of the sale of the fee simple of the lands and appurtenances of Timoleague.—"I know, honest Thady," says he to comfort me, "what I'm about better than you do; I'm only selling to get the ready money wanting, to carry on my suit with spirit with the Nugents of Carrickashaughlin."

---

replevying: the provisional restoration to the owner of goods invalidly appropriated, on his giving security to have the matter tried in court and to abide by the court's decision.

heriots: a feudal payment to the landlord on the death of a tenant, typically livestock.

fee simple: the right to possess land in perpetuity.

appurtenances: minor property, buildings, or rights that went with the land.

[14] See Garrick's Prologue to Goldsmith's *She Stoops to Conquer* (1773), 28.

He was very sanguine about that suit with the Nugents of Carrick-ashaughlin. He could have gained it, they say, for certain, had it pleased Heaven to have spared him to us, and it would have been at the least a plump two thousand a year in his way; but things were ordered otherwise, for the best to be sure. He dug up a fairy-mount*[g] against my advice, and had no luck afterwards. Though a learned man in the law, he was a little too incredulous in other matters. I warned him that I heard the very Banshee[†] that my grandfather heard, before I was born long, under Sir Patrick's window a few days before his death. But Sir Murtagh thought nothing of the Banshee, nor of his cough with a spitting of blood, brought on, I understand, by catching cold in attending the courts, and overstraining his chest with making himself heard in one of his favorite causes. He was a great speaker, with a powerful voice; but his last speech was not in the courts at all. He and my lady, though both of the same way of thinking in some things, and though she was as good a wife and great economist as you could see, and he the best of husbands, as to looking into his affairs, and making money for his family; yet I don't know how it was, they had a great deal of sparring and jarring between them.—My lady had her privy purse—and she had her weed ashes,[g] and her sealing money[g] upon the signing of all the leases, with something to buy gloves besides; and besides again often took money from the tenants, if offered properly, to speak for them to Sir Murtagh about abatements and renewals. Now the weed ashes and the glove money he allowed her clear perquisites; though once when he saw her in a new gown saved out of the weed ashes, he told her to my face, (for he could say a sharp thing) that she should not put on her weeds before her husband's death. But it grew more serious when they came to the renewal businesses. At last, in a dispute about an abatement, my lady would have the last word, and Sir Murtagh grew mad;[g] I was within hearing of the door, and now I wish I had made bold to step in. He spoke so loud, the whole kitchen was out on the stairs[g]—All on a sudden he stopped, and my lady

*These fairy-mounts are called ant-hills in England. They are held in high reverence by the common people in Ireland. A gentleman, who in laying out his lawn had occasion to level one of these hillocks, could not prevail upon any of his labourers to begin the ominous work. He was obliged to take a *loy* from one of their reluctant hands, and began the attack himself. The labourers agreed, that the vengeance of the fairies would fall upon the head of the presumptuous mortal, who first disturbed them in their retreat.

†The Banshee is a species of aristocratic fairy, who in the shape of a little hideous old woman has been known to appear, and heard to sing in a mournful supernatural voice under the windows of great houses, to warn the family that some of them are soon to die. In the last century every great family in Ireland had a Banshee, who attended regularly, but latterly their visits and songs have been discontinued.

***loy*:** a long, narrow asymmetric spade.

abatements: a legal term, bringing an end to an action or reducing a value.

too. Something has surely happened, thought I—and so it was, for Sir Murtagh in his passion broke a blood-vessel, and all the law in the land could do nothing in that case. My lady sent for five physicians, but Sir Murtagh died, and was buried. She had a fine jointure settled upon her, and took herself away to the great joy of the tenantry. I never said any thing, one way or the other, whilst she was part of the family, but got up to see her go at three o'clock in the morning—"It's a fine morning, honest Thady, says she; good bye to ye"—and into the carriage she stept, without a word more, good or bad, or even half-a-crown; but I made my bow, and stood to see her safe out of sight for the sake of the family.

Then we were all bustle in the house, which made me keep out of the way, for I walk slow and hate a bustle, but the house was all hurry-skurry, preparing for my new master.—Sir Murtagh, I forgot to notice, had no childer,* so the Rackrent estate went to his younger brother—a young dashing officer—who came amongst us before I knew for the life of me whereabouts I was, in a gig or some of them things, with another spark along with him, and led horses, and servants, and dogs, and scarce a place to put any Christian of them into; for my late lady had sent all the feather-beds off before her, and blankets, and household linen, down to the very knife cloths, on the cars to Dublin, which were all her own, lawfully paid for out of her own money—So the house was quite bare, and my young master, the moment ever he set foot in it out of his gig, thought all those things must come of themselves, I believe, for he never looked after any thing at all, but harum-scarum called for every thing as if we were conjurers, or he in a public-house. For my part, I could not bestir myself any how; I had been so much used to my late master and mistress, all was upside down with me, and the new servants in the servants' hall were quite out of my way; I had nobody to talk to, and if it had not been for my pipe and tobacco should, I verily believe, have broke my heart for poor Sir Murtagh.

But one morning my new master caught a glimpse of me as I was looking at his horse's heels, in hopes of a word from him—and is that old Thady! says he, as he got into his gig—I loved him from that day to this, his voice was so like the family—and he threw me a guinea out of his waistcoat pocket, as he drew up the reins with the other hand, his horse rearing too; I thought I never set my eyes on a finer figure of a man—quite another sort from Sir Murtagh, though withal *to me*, a family likeness—A fine life we should have led, had he stayed amongst us, God bless him!—he valued a guinea as little as any man—money to him was no more than dirt, and his gentleman and groom, and all belonging to him, the same—but the sporting season over, he grew tired of the place, and having got down a

* *Childer*—this is the manner in which many of Thady's rank, and others in Ireland, *formerly* pronounced the word *children*.

great architect for the house, and an improver for the grounds, and seen their plans and elevations, he fixed a day for settling with the tenants, but went off in a whirlwind to town, just as some of them came into the yard in the morning. A circular letter came next post from the new agent, with news that the master was sailed for England, and he must remit £500[15] to Bath for his use, before a fortnight was at an end—Bad news still for the poor tenants, no change still for the better with them—Sir Kit Rackrent, my young master, left all to the agent, and though he had the spirit of a Prince, and lived away to the honour of his country abroad, which I was proud to hear of, what were we the better for that at home? The agent was one of your middle men,* who grind the face of the poor, and can never bear a man with a hat upon his head—he ferretted the tenants out of their lives—not a week without a call for money—drafts upon drafts from Sir Kit—but I laid it all to the fault of the agent; for, says I, what can Sir Kit do with so much cash, and he a single man? but still it went.—Rents must be all paid up to the day, and afore—no allowance for improving tenants—no consideration for those who had built upon their farms—No sooner was a lease out, but the land was advertised to the highest bidder—all the old tenants turned out, when they spent their substance in the hope and trust of a renewal from the landlord.—All was now set at the highest penny to a parcel of poor wretches who meant to run away, and did so, after taking two crops out of the ground. Then fining down the year's rent[g] came into fashion—any thing for the ready penny, and with all this, and presents to the agent and the driver,[g] there was no such thing as standing it—I said nothing, for I had a regard for the family, but I walked about, thinking if his honour Sir Kit,

* *Middle men.*—There was a class of men termed middle men in Ireland, who took large farms on long leases from gentlemen of landed property, and set the land again in small portions to the poor, as under tenants, at exorbitant rents. The *head-landlord,* as he *was* called, seldom saw his *under tenants,* but if he could not get the *middle man* to pay him his rent punctually, he *went to the land, and drove the land for his rent,* that is to say, he sent his steward or bailiff, or driver, to the land, to seize the cattle, hay, corn, flax, oats, or potatoes, belonging to the under-tenants, and proceeded to sell these for his rent; it sometimes happened that these unfortunate tenants paid their rent twice over, once to the *middle man,* and once to the *head landlord.*

The characteristics of a middle man *were,* servility to his superiors, and tyranny towards his inferiors—The poor detested this race of beings. In speaking to them, however, they always used the most abject language, and the most humble tone and posture—"*Please your honour,—and please your honour's honour,*" they knew must be repeated as a charm at the beginning and end of every equivocating, exculpatory, or supplicatory sentence—and they were much more alert in doffing their caps to these new men, than to those of what they call *good old families.*—A witty carpenter once termed these middle men *journeymen-gentlemen.*

[15] 500l. (1832 and previous editions). Revised here for modern usage and for conformity throughout the text; e.g., see *CR* 39.

(long may he live to reign over us!) knew all this, it would go hard with him, but he'd see us righted—not that I had any thing for my own share to complain of, for the agent was always very civil to me, when he came down into the country, and took a great deal of notice of my son Jason.—Jason Quirk, though he be my son, I must say, was a good scholar from his birth, and a very 'cute lad—I thought to make him a priest,[g] but he did better for himself—Seeing how he was as good a clerk as any in the county, the agent gave him his rent accounts to copy, which he did first of all for the pleasure of obliging the gentleman, and would take nothing at all for his trouble, but was always proud to serve the family.—By and by, a good farm bounding us to the east fell into his honour's hands, and my son put in a proposal for it; why shouldn't he as well as another?—The proposals all went over to the master at the Bath, who knowing no more of the land than the child unborn, only having once been out a groussing on it before he went to England; and the value of lands, as the agent informed him, falling every year in Ireland, his honour wrote over in all haste a bit of a letter, saying he left it all to the agent, and that he must set it as well as he could to the best bidder, to be sure, and send him over £200 by return of post: with this the agent gave me a hint, and I spoke a good word for my son, and gave out in the country, that nobody need bid against us.—So his proposal was just the thing, and he a good tenant; and he got a promise of an abatement in the rent, after the first year, for advancing the half year's rent at signing the lease, which was wanting to compleat the agent's £200, by the return of the post, with all which my master wrote back he was well satisfied.—About this time we learned from the agent, as a great secret, how the money went so fast, and the reason of the thick coming of the master's drafts: he was a little too fond of play, and Bath, they say, was no place for a young man of his fortune, where there were so many of his own countrymen too haunting him up and down, day and night, who had nothing to lose—at last, at Christmas, the agent wrote over to stop the drafts, for he could raise no more money on bond or mortgage, or from the tenants, or any how, nor had he any more to lend himself, and desired at same time to decline the agency for the future, wishing Sir Kit his health and happiness, and the compliments of the season—for I saw the letter before ever it was sealed, when my son copied it.—When the answer came, there was a new turn in affairs, and the agent was turned out; and my son Jason, who had corresponded privately with his honor occasionally on business, was forthwith desired by his honor to take the accounts into his own hands, and look them over till further orders—It was a very spirited letter, to be sure: Sir Kit sent his service, and the compliments of the season, in return to the agent, and he would fight him with pleasure to-morrow, or any day, for sending him such a letter, if he was born a gentleman, which he was sorry (for both their sakes) to find (too late) he was not.—Then, in a private postscript, he condescended to tell us that all would be speedily settled to his satisfaction, and we should turn over a new leaf, for he was going to be married in a fortnight to the grandest heiress in England, and had only immediate occasion at present for £200, as he would not choose to touch his lady's fortune for travelling expences home to Castle Rackrent, where he intended to be, wind and weather permitting, early in the next month, and desired fires, and the house to be painted, and the new building to go on as fast as possible, for the reception of him and his lady before that time—with several words besides in the letter, which we could not make out, because, God bless him! he wrote in such a flurry—My heart warmed to my new lady when I read this; I was almost afraid it was too good news to be true—but the girls fell to scouring, and it was well they did, for we soon saw his marriage in the paper to a lady with I don't know how many tens of thousand pounds to her fortune—then I watched the post-office for his landing, and the news came to my son of his and the bride being in Dublin, and on the way home to Rackrent Gap—We had bonfires all over the country, expecting him down the next day, and we had his coming of age still to celebrate, which he had not time to do properly before he left the country; therefore a great ball was expected, and great doings upon his coming, as it were, fresh to take possession of his ancestors estate.—I never shall forget the day he came home—we had waited and waited all day long till eleven o'clock at night, and I was thinking of sending the boy to lock the gates, and giving them up for that night, when there came the carriages thundering up to the great hall door—I got the first sight of the bride; for when the carriage door opened, just as she had her foot on the steps, I held the flam[g] full in her face to light her, at which she shut her eyes, but I had a full view of the rest of her, and greatly shocked I was, for by that light she was little better than a blackamoor, and seemed crippled, but that was only sitting so long in the chariot—"You're kindly welcome to Castle Rackrent, my lady," says I, (recollecting who she was)—"Did your honor hear of the bonfires?" His honor spoke never a word, nor so much as handed her up the steps; he looked to me no more like himself than nothing at all; I know I took him for the skeleton of his honor—I was not sure what to say next to one or t'other, but seeing she was a stranger in a foreign country, I thought it but right to speak chearful to her, so I went back again to the bonfires—"My lady (says I, as she crossed the hall) there would have been fifty times as many, but for fear of the horses and frightening your ladyship—Jason and I forbid them, please your honor."—With that she looked at me a little bewildered— "Will I have a fire lighted in the state room to-night?" was the next question I put to her—but never a word she answered, so I concluded she could not speak a word of English, and was from foreign parts—The short and the long of it was, I couldn't tell what to make of her, so I left her to herself, and went straight down to the servants' hall to learn something for certain about her. Sir Kit's own man was tired, but the groom set him a talking at last, and we had it all out before ever I closed my eyes that night. The bride might well be a great fortune—she was a *Jewish* by all accounts, who are famous for their great riches. I had never seen any of that tribe or nation before, and could only gather that she spoke a strange kind of English of her own, that she could not abide pork or sausages, and went neither to church nor mass.—Mercy upon his honor's poor soul, thought I, what will become of him and his, and all of us, with his heretic Blackamore at the head of the Castle Rackrent estate. I never slept a wink all night for thinking of it, but before the servants I put my pipe in my mouth and kept my mind to myself; for I had a great regard for the family, and after this when strange gentlemen's servants came to the house, and would begin to talk about the bride, I took care to put the best foot foremost, and passed her for a Nabob, in the kitchen, which accounted for her dark complexion, and every thing.

The very morning after they came home, however, I saw how things were, plain enough, between Sir Kit and my lady, though they were walking together arm in arm after breakfast, looking at the new building and the improvements. "Old Thady, (said my master, just as he used to do) how do you do?"—"Very well, I thank your honor's honor," said I, but I saw he was not well pleased, and my heart was in my mouth as I walked along after him—"Is the large room damp, Thady?" said his honor—"Oh, damp, your honor! how should it but be as dry as a bone, (says I) after all the fires we have kept in it day and night—It's the barrack room your honor's talking on"—"And what is a barrack room,[g] pray, my dear"—were the first words I ever heard out of my lady's lips—"No matter, my dear," said he, and went on talking to me, ashamed like I should witness her ignorance.—To be sure to hear her talk, one might have taken her for an innocent,[g] for it was "what's this, Sir Kit? and what's that, Sir Kit?" all the way we went—To be sure, Sir Kit had enough to do to answer her—"And what do you call that, Sir Kit? (said she) that, that looks like a pile of black bricks, pray Sir Kit?" "My turf stack, my dear," said my master, and bit his lip—Where have you lived, my lady, all your life, not to know a turf stack when you see it, thought I, but I said nothing. Then, by-and-by, she takes out her glass and begins spying over the country—"And what's all that black swamp out yonder, Sir Kit?" says she—"My bog, my dear," says he, and went on whistling—"It's a very ugly prospect, my dear," says she—"You don't see it, my dear, (says he) for we've planted it out, when the trees grow up, in

---

Nabob: deputy governor of a province in India. Also refers to a wealthy person returning to England from the East.

summer time," says he—"Where are the trees, (said she) my dear," still looking through her glass—"You are blind, my dear, (says he) what are these under your eyes?"—"These shrubs?" said she—"Trees," said he—"May be they are what you call trees in Ireland, my dear, (says she) but they are not a yard high, are they?"—"They were planted out but last year, my lady" says I, to soften matters between them, for I saw she was going the way to make his honor mad with her—"they are very well grown for their age, and you'll not see the bog of Allyballycarricko'shaughlin at all at all through the skreen, when once the leaves come out—But, my lady, you must not quarrel with any part or parcel of Allyballycarricko'shaughlin, for you don't know how many hundred years that same bit of bog has been in the family, we would not part with the bog of Allyballycarricko'shaughlin upon no account at all; it cost the late Sir Murtagh two hundred good pounds to defend his title to it, and boundaries, against the O'Learys, who cut a road through it."—Now one would have thought this would have been hint enough for my lady, but she fell to laughing like one out of their right mind, and made me say the name of the bog over for her to get it by heart a dozen times—then she must ask me how to spell it, and what was the meaning of it in English—Sir Kit standing by whistling all the while—I verily believe she laid the corner stone of all her future misfortunes at that very instant—but I said no more, only looked at Sir Kit.

There were no balls, no dinners, no doings, the country was all disappointed—Sir Kit's gentleman said, in a whisper to me, it was all my lady's own fault, because she was so obstinate about the cross—"What cross? (says I) is it about her being a heretic?"—"Oh, no such matter, (says he) my master does not mind her heresies, but her diamond cross, it's worth I can't tell you how much, and she has thousands of English pounds concealed in diamonds about her, which she as good as promised to give up to my master before he married, but now she won't part with any of them, and she must take the consequences."

Her honey-moon, at least her Irish honeymoon, was scarcely well over, when his honour one morning said to me—"Thady, buy me a pig!"—and then the sausages were ordered, and here was the first open breaking out of my lady's troubles—my lady came down herself into the kitchen to speak to the cook about the sausages, and desired never to see them more at her table.—Now my master had ordered them, and my lady knew that—the cook took my lady's part, because she never came down into the kitchen, and was young and innocent in house-keeping, which raised her pity; besides, said she, at her own table, surely, my lady should order and disorder what she pleases—but the cook soon changed her note, for my master made it a principle to have the sausages, and swore at her for a Jew herself, till he drove her fairly out of the kitchen—then for fear of her place, and because he threatened that my lady should give her no discharge without the sausages, she gave up, and from that day forward always sausages or bacon, or pig meat, in some shape or other, went up to table; upon which my lady shut herself up in her own room, and my master said she might stay there, with an oath; and to make sure of her, he turned the key in the door, and kept it ever after in his pocket—We none of us ever saw or heard her speak for seven years after that*—he carried her dinner himself—then his honour had a great deal of company to dine with him, and balls in the house, and was as gay and gallant, and as much himself as before he was

*This part of the history of the Rackrent family can scarcely be thought credible; but in justice to honest Thady, it is hoped the reader will recollect the history of the celebrated Lady Cathcart's conjugal imprisonment.—The Editor was acquainted with Colonel M'Guire, Lady Cathcart's husband; he has lately seen and questioned the maid-servant who lived with Colonel M'Guire during the time of Lady Cathcart's imprisonment.—Her Ladyship was locked up in her own house for many years; during which period her husband was visited by the neighbouring gentry, and it was his regular custom at dinner to send his compliments to Lady Cathcart, informing her that the company had the honor to drink her ladyship's health, and begging to know whether there was any thing at table that she would like to eat? the answer was always—"Lady Cathcart's compliments, and she has every thing she wants"—An instance of honesty in a poor Irishwoman deserves to be recorded.—Lady Cathcart had some remarkably fine diamonds, which she had concealed from her husband, and which she was anxious to get out of the house, lest he should discover them: she had neither servant nor friend to whom she could entrust them; but she had observed a poor beggar-woman who used to come to the house—she spoke to her from the window of the room in which she was confined—the woman promised to do what she desired, and Lady Cathcart threw a parcel, containing the jewels, to her.—The poor woman carried them to the person to whom they were directed; and several years afterwards, when Lady Cathcart recovered her liberty, she received her diamonds safely.

At Colonel M'Guire's death, her ladyship was released.—The Editor, within this year, saw the gentleman who accompanied her to England after her husband's death.—When she first was told of his death, she imagined that the news was not true, and that it was told only with an intention of deceiving her.—At his death she had scarcely cloaths sufficient to cover her; she wore a red wig, looked scared, and her understanding seemed stupified; she said that she scarcely knew one human creature from another: her imprisonment lasted above twenty years.—These circumstances may appear strange to an English reader; but there is no danger in the present times, that any individual should exercise such tyranny as Colonel M'Guire's with impunity, the power being now all in the hands of government, and there being no possibility of obtaining from Parliament an act of indemnity for any cruelties. [Early readers of *Castle Rackrent* may have been familiar with the story of Elizabeth Malyn, Lady Cathcart (1692?–1789), from her obituary in *The Gentleman's Magazine,* lix (1789), 766–67. Malyn retained the name of her third husband, Baron Cathcart (d. 1740), when she married for a fourth time to the Irish fortune hunter, Colonel Hugh Maguire, in 1745. When she refused to surrender her property to him, he abducted her from England to his Irish estates, where she remained incarcerated until his death in 1764. See W. A. Maguire, "Castle Nugent and Castle Rackrent; fact and fiction in Maria Edgeworth." Ed.]

married—and at dinner he always drank my lady Rackrent's good health, and so did the company, and he sent out always a servant, with his compliments to my Lady Rackrent, and the company was drinking her ladyship's health, and begged to know if there was any thing at table he might send her; and the man came back, after the sham errand, with my lady Rackrent's compliments, and she was very much obliged to Sir Kit—she did not wish for any thing, but drank the company's health.—The country, to be sure, talked and wondered at my lady's being shut up, but nobody chose to interfere or ask any impertinent questions, for they knew my master was a man very apt to give a short answer himself, and likely to call a man out for it afterwards—he was a famous shot—had killed his man before he came of age, and nobody scarce dared look at him whilst at Bath.—Sir Kit's character was so well known in the country, that he lived in peace and quietness ever after, and was a great favorite with the ladies, especially when in process of time, in the fifth year of her confinement, my lady Rackrent fell ill, and took entirely to her bed, and he gave out that she was now skin and bone, and could not last through the winter.—In this he had two physicians' opinions to back him (for now he called in two physicians for her), and tried all his arts to get the diamond cross from her on her death bed, and to get her to make a will in his favour of her separate possessions—but she was there too tough for him—He used to swear at her behind her back, after kneeling to her to her face, and call her, in the presence of his gentleman, his stiff-necked Israelite, though before he married her, that same gentleman told me he used to call her (how he could bring it out I don't know!) "my pretty Jessica" [16]—To be sure, it must have been hard for her to guess what sort of a husband he reckoned to make her—when she was lying, to all expectation, on her death-bed, of a broken heart, I could not but pity her, though she was a Jewish; and considering too it was no fault of her's to be taken with my master so young as she was at the Bath, and so fine a gentleman as Sir Kit was when he courted her—and considering too, after all they had heard and seen of him as a husband, there were now no less than three ladies in our county talked of for his second wife, all at daggers drawing with each other, as his gentleman swore, at the balls, for Sir Kit for their partner—I could not but think them bewitched, but they all reasoned with themselves, that Sir Kit would make a good husband to any Christian, but a Jewish, I suppose, and especially as he was now a reformed rake; and it was not known how my lady's fortune was settled in her will, nor how the Castle Rackrent estate was all mortgaged, and bonds out against him, for he was never cured of his gaming tricks—but that was the only fault he had, God bless him!

---

[16] Shakespeare, *The Merchant of Venice* V. i. 21.

My lady had a sort of fit, and it was given out she was dead, by mistake; this brought things to a sad crisis for my poor master—one of the three ladies shewed his letters to her brother, and claimed his promises, whilst another did the same. I don't mention names—Sir Kit, in his defence, said he would meet any man who dared question his conduct, and as to the ladies, they must settle it amongst them who was to be his second, and his third, and his fourth, whilst his first was still alive, to his mortification and theirs. Upon this, as upon all former occasions, he had the voice of the country with him, on account of the great spirit and propriety he acted with.—He met and shot the first lady's brother—the next day he called out the second, who had a wooden leg, and their place of meeting by appointment being in a new ploughed field, the wooden leg man stuck fast in it.—Sir Kit seeing his situation, with great candour fired his pistol over his head, upon which the seconds interposed, and convinced the parties there had been a slight misunderstanding between them; thereupon they shook hands cordially, and went home to dinner together.—This gentleman, to shew the world how they stood together, and by the advice of the friends of both parties to re-establish his sister's injured reputation, went out with Sir Kit as his second, and carried his message next day to the last of his adversaries.—I never saw him in such fine spirits as that day he went out—sure enough he was within aims-ace of getting quit handsomely of all his enemies; but unluckily, after hitting the tooth-pick out of his adversary's finger and thumb, he received a ball in a vital part, and was brought home, in little better than an hour after the affair, speechless, on a hand-barrow, to my lady; we got the key out of his pocket the first thing we did, and my son Jason ran to unlock the barrack-room, where my lady had been shut up for seven years, to acquaint her with the fatal accident.—The surprize bereaved her of her senses at first, nor would she believe but we were putting some new trick upon her, to entrap her out of her jewels, for a great while, till Jason bethought himself of taking her to the window, and shewed her the men bringing Sir Kit up the avenue upon the hand-barrow, which had immediately the desired effect; for directly she burst into tears, and pulling her cross from her bosom, she kissed it with as great devotion as ever I witnessed, and lifting up her eyes to Heaven, uttered some ejaculation, which none present heard—but I take the sense of it to be, she returned thanks for this unexpected interposition in her favour, when she had least reason to expect it.—My master was greatly lamented—there was no life in him when we lifted him off the barrow, so he was laid out immediately, and *waked*

---

aims-ace: ambs-ace, a pair of aces, the lowest throw at dice.

waked: a ritual celebration around the body of a dead person prior to burial; see glossary note for "wake," *CR* 94.

the same night.—The country was all in an uproar about him, and not a soul but cried shame upon his murderer, who would have been hanged surely, if he could have been brought to his trial, whilst the gentlemen in the county were up about it, but he very prudently withdrew himself to the continent before the affair was made public.—As for the young lady who was the immediate cause of the fatal accident, however innocently, she could never shew her head after at the balls in the county or any place, and by the advice of her friends and physicians she was ordered soon after to Bath, where it was expected, if any where on this side of the grave, she would meet with the recovery of her health and lost peace of mind.—As a proof of his great popularity, I need only add, that there was a song made upon my master's untimely death in the newspapers, which was in every body's mouth, singing up and down through the country, even down to the mountains, only three days after his unhappy exit.—He was also greatly bemoaned at the Curragh,[g] where his cattle were well known, and all who had taken up his bets formerly were particularly inconsolable for his loss to society.—His stud sold at the cant[g] at the greatest price ever known in the country; his favourite horses were chiefly disposed of amongst his particular friends, who would give any price for them for his sake; but no ready money was required by the new heir, who wished not to displease any of the gentlemen of the neighbourhood just upon his coming to settle amongst them; so a long credit was given where requisite, and the cash has never been gathered in from that day to this.

But to return to my lady.—She got surprisingly well after my master's decease. No sooner was it known for certain that he was dead, than all the gentlemen within twenty miles of us came in a body as it were to set my lady at liberty, and to protest against her confinement, which they now for the first time understood was against her own consent. The ladies too were as attentive as possible, striving who should be foremost with their morning visits; and they that saw the diamonds spoke very handsomely of them, but thought it a pity they were not bestowed, if it had so pleased God, upon a lady who would have become them better. All these civilities wrought little with my lady, for she had taken an unaccountable prejudice against the country and every thing belonging to it, and was so partial to her native land, that after parting with the cook, which she did immediately upon my master's decease, I never knew her easy one instant, night or day, but when she was packing up to leave us. Had she meant to make any stay in Ireland, I stood a great chance of being a great favorite with her, for when she found I understood the weather-cock, she was always finding some pretence to be talking to me, and asking me which way the wind blew, and was it likely, did I think, to continue fair for England.—But when I saw she had made up her mind to spend the rest of her days upon her own income and jewels in England, I considered her quite as a foreigner, and not at all any longer as part of the family.—She gave no vails to the servants at Castle Rackrent at parting, notwithstanding the old proverb of "*as rich as a Jew,*" which, she being a Jewish, they built upon with reason—But from first to last she brought nothing but misfortunes amongst us; and if it had not been all along with her, his honor Sir Kit would have been now alive in all appearance.—Her diamond cross was, they say, at the bottom of it all; and it was a shame for her, being his wife, not to show more duty, and to have given it up when he condescended to ask so often for such a bit of a trifle in his distresses, especially when he all along made it no secret he married for money.—But we will not bestow another thought upon her—This much I thought it lay upon my conscience to say, in justice to my poor master's memory.

'Tis an ill wind that blows nobody no good—the same wind that took the Jew Lady Rackrent over to England brought over the new heir to Castle Rackrent.

Here let me pause for breath in my story, for though I had a great regard for every member of the family, yet without compare Sir Conolly, commonly called for short amongst his friends Sir Condy Rackrent, was ever my great favorite, and indeed the most universally beloved man I had ever seen or heard of, not excepting his great ancestor Sir Patrick, to whose memory he, amongst other instances of generosity, erected a handsome marble stone in the church of Castle Rackrent, setting forth in large letters his age, birth, parentage, and many other virtues, concluding with the compliment so justly due, that "Sir Patrick Rackrent lived and died a monument of old Irish hospitality."

---

vails: tips.

Continuation of the Memoirs of the Rackrent Family

History of Sir Conolly Rackrent[17]

SIR Condy Rackrent, by the grace of God, heir at law to the Castle Rackrent estate, was a remote branch of the family: born to little or no fortune of his own, he was bred to the bar, at which having many friends to push him, and no mean natural abilities of his own, he doubtless would in process of time, if he could have borne the drudgery of that study, have been rapidly made king's counsel at the least—But things were disposed of otherwise, and he never went the circuit but twice, and then made no figure for want of a fee, and being unable to speak in public. He received his education chiefly in the college of Dublin; but before he came to years of discretion, lived in the country in a small but slated house, within view of the end of the avenue. I remember him bare-footed and headed, running through the street of O'Shaughlin's town, and playing at pitch and toss, ball, marbles, and what not, with the boys of the town, amongst whom my son Jason was a great favorite with him. As for me, he was ever my white-headed boy*—often's the time when I would call in at his father's, where I was always made welcome, he would slip down to me in the kitchen, and love to sit on my knee whilst I told him stories of the family and the blood from which he was sprung, and how he might look forward, if the *then* present man should die without childer, to being at the head of the Castle Rackrent estate.—This was then spoke quite and clear at random to please the child, but it pleased Heaven to accomplish my prophecy afterwards, which gave him a great opinion of my judgment in business. He went to a little grammar school with many others, and my son amongst the rest, who was in his class, and not a little useful to him in his book learning, which he acknowledged with gratitude ever after. These rudiments of his education thus completed, he got a horseback, to which exercise he was ever addicted, and used to gallop over the country whilst yet but a slip of a boy, under the care of Sir Kit's

* *White-headed boy*—is used by the Irish as an expression of fondness.—It is upon a par with the English term *crony*.—We are at a loss for the derivation of this term. [Irish colloquialism. A favorite or one that can do no wrong. Edgeworth's footnote deleted after sixth edition (1815). ED.]

---

college of Dublin: Trinity College Dublin, founded in 1592 and not admitting Catholics until 1793.

[17]Although the exact dates for composition are widely debated, it is thought that Edgeworth completed the first section of the tale in 1794–95, with Sir Condy's tale following in 1796–98.

huntsman, who was very fond of him, and often lent him his gun and took him out a shooting under his own eye. By these means he became well acquainted and popular amongst the poor in the neighbourhood early, for there was not a cabin at which he had not stopped some morning or other along with the huntsman, to drink a glass of burnt whiskey out of an egg-shell, to do him good, and warm his heart, and drive the cold out of his stomach.—The old people always told him he was a great likeness of Sir Patrick, which made him first have an ambition to take after him, as far as his fortune should allow. He left us when of an age to enter the college, and there completed his education and nineteenth year; for as he was not born to an estate, his friends thought it incumbent on them to give him the best education which could be had for love or money, and a great deal of money consequently was spent upon him at college and Temple—He was very little altered for the worse, by what he saw there of the great world, for when he came down into the country to pay us a visit we thought him just the same man as ever, hand and glove with every one, and as far from high, though not without his own proper share of family pride, as any man ever you see. Latterly, seeing how Sir Kit and the *Jewish* lived together, and that there was no one between him and the Castle Rackrent estate, he neglected to apply to the law as much as was expected of him, and secretly many of the tenants, and others, advanced him cash upon his note of hand value received, promising bargains of leases and lawful interest should he ever come into the estate.—All this was kept a great secret, for fear the present man hearing of it should take it into his head to take it ill of poor Condy, and so should cut him off for ever by levying a fine, and suffering a recovery to dock the entail[g]—Sir Murtagh would have been the man for that, but Sir Kit was too much taken up philandering to consider the law in this case—or any other.—These practices I have mentioned account for the state of his affairs, I mean Sir Condy's, upon his coming into the Castle Rackrent estate.—He could not command a penny of his first year's income, which, and keeping no accounts, and the great sight of company he did, with many other causes too numerous to mention, was the origin of his distresses.—My son Jason, who was now established agent, and knew every thing, explained matters out of the face to Sir Conolly, and made him sensible of his embarrassed situation. With a great nominal rent-roll, it was almost all paid away in interest, which being for convenience suffered to run on, soon doubled the principal, and Sir Condy was obligated to pass new bonds for the interest, now grown principal, and so on. Whilst this was going on, my son requiring to be paid for his trouble, and many years service

---

Temple: Irish students frequently attended the Middle Temple at the Inns of Court in London.

in the family gratis, and Sir Condy not willing to take his affairs into his own hands, or to look them even in the face, he gave my son a bargain of some acres which fell out of lease at a reasonable rent; Jason set the land as soon as his lease was sealed to under-tenants, to make the rent, and got two hundred a year profit rent, which was little enough, considering his long agency. — He bought the land at twelve years purchase two years afterwards, when Sir Condy was pushed for money on an execution, and was at the same time allowed for his improvements thereon. There was a sort of hunting lodge upon the estate convenient to my son Jason's land, which he had his eye upon about this time; and he was a little jealous of Sir Condy, who talked of setting it to a stranger, who was just come into the country — Captain Moneygawl was the man; he was son and heir to the Moneygawls of Mount Juliet's town, who had a great estate in the next county to ours, and my master was loth to disoblige the young gentleman, whose heart was set upon the lodge; so he wrote him back that the lodge was at his service, and if he would honor him with his company at Castle Rackrent, they could ride over together some morning and look at it before signing the lease. — Accordingly the Captain came over to us, and he and Sir Condy grew the greatest friends ever you see, and were for ever out a shooting or a hunting together, and were very merry in the evenings, and Sir Condy was invited of course to Mount Juliet's town, and the family intimacy that had been in Sir Patrick's time was now recollected, and nothing would serve Sir Condy but he must be three times a week at the least with his new friends — which grieved me, who knew by the Captain's groom and gentleman how they talked of him at Mount Juliet's town, making him quite, as one may say, a laughing stock and a butt for the whole company: but they were soon cured of *that* by an accident that surprised 'em not a little, as it did me. — There was a bit of a scrawl found upon the waiting maid of old Mr. Moneygawl's youngest daughter Miss Isabella, that laid open the whole; and her father, they say, was like one out of his right mind, and swore it was the last thing he ever should have thought of when he invited my master to his house, that his daughter should think of such a match. — But their talk signified not a straw; for as Miss Isabella's maid reported, her young mistress was fallen over head and ears in love with Sir Condy, from the first time that ever her brother brought him into the house to dinner: the servant who waited that day behind my master's chair was the first who knew it, as he says; though it's hard to believe him, for he did not tell till a great while afterwards; but however, it's likely enough as the thing turned out that he was not far out of the way; for towards the middle of dinner, as he says, they were talking of stage plays, having a play-house, and being great play actors at Mount Juliet's town, and Miss Isabella turns short to my master and says — "Have you seen the play-bill, Sir Condy?" — "No, I have not," said he. — "Then more shame for you, (said the Captain her brother) not to know that my sister is to play Juliet tonight, who plays it better than any woman on or off the stage in all Ireland."—"I am very happy to hear it," said Sir Condy, and there the matter dropped for the present; but Sir Condy all this time, and a great while afterwards, was at a terrible nonplus, for he had no liking not he to stage plays, nor to Miss Isabella either; to his mind, as it came out over a bowl of whiskey punch at home, his little Judy M'Quirk, who was daughter to a sister's son of mine, was worth twenty of Miss Isabella—He had seen her often when he stopped at her father's cabin to drink whiskey out of the egg-shell, out of hunting, before he came to the estate, and as she gave out was under something like a promise of marriage to her—Any how I could not but pity my poor master, who was so bothered between them, and he an easy-hearted man that could not disoblige nobody, God bless him. To be sure it was not his place to behave ungenerous to Miss Isabella, who had disobliged all her relations for his sake, as he remarked; and then she was locked up in her chamber and forbid to think of him any more, which raised his spirit, because his family was, as he observed, as good as theirs at any rate, and the Rackrents a suitable match for the Moneygawls any day in the year; all which was true enough; but it grieved me to see that upon the strength of all this Sir Condy was growing more in the mind to carry off Miss Isabella to Scotland, in spite of her relations, as she desired.

"It's all over with our poor Judy!" said I, with a heavy sigh, making bold to speak to him one night when he was a little cheerful, and standing in the servant's hall all alone with me, as was often his custom—"Not at all (said he) I never was fonder of Judy than at this present speaking, and to prove it to you, (said he, and he took from my hand a halfpenny, change that I had just got along with my tobacco); and to prove it to you, Thady, says he, it's a toss up with me which I shall marry this minute, her or Mr. Moneygawl of Mount Juliet's Town's daughter—so it is"—"Oh, boo! boo!*(says I, making light of it, to see what he would go on to next)—your honor's joking, to be sure, there's no compare between our poor Judy and Miss Isabella, who has a great fortune, they say."—"I'm not a man to mind a fortune, nor never was, (said Sir Condy proudly,) whatever her friends may say; and to make short of it, (says he) I'm come to a determination upon the spot;" with that he swore such a terrible oath, as made me† cross myself—"and by this book, (said he, snatching up my ballad book, mistaking it for my prayer-book, which lay in the window)—and by this book, (said he) and by all the books that ever were shut and opened—it's come to

***Boo! Boo!* an exclamation equivalent to *Pshaw!* or *Nonsense.*

†*As made me cross myself*—The Roman Catholics. [Footnote deleted after fourth edition (1804). Ed.]

a toss up with me, and I'll stand or fall by the toss, and so, Thady, hand me over that* *pin* out of the ink-horn," and he makes a cross on the smooth side of the halfpenny—"Judy M'Quirk, (said he) her mark,"† God bless him! his hand was a little unsteadied by all the whiskey punch he had taken, but it was plain to see his heart was for poor Judy.—My heart was all as one as in my mouth, when I saw the halfpenny up in the air, but I said nothing at all, and when it came down, I was glad I had kept myself to myself, for to be sure now it was all over with poor Judy.—"Judy's out a luck," said I, striving to laugh—"I'm out a luck," said he, and I never saw a man look so cast down; he took up the halfpenny off the flag, and walked away quite sobered like by the shock.—Now though as easy a man you would think as any in the wide world, there was no such thing as making him unsay one of these sort of vows,‡ which he had learned to reverence when young, as I well remember teaching him to toss up for bog berries on my knee.—So I saw the affair was as good as settled between him and Miss Isabella, and I had no more to say but to wish her joy, which I did the week afterwards upon her return from Scotland with my poor master.

My new lady was young, as might be supposed of a lady that had been carried off by her own consent to Scotland,[18] but I could only see her at first through her veil, which, from bashfulness or fashion, she kept over her face—"And am I to walk through all this crowd of people, my dearest love," said she to Sir Condy, meaning us servants and tenants, who had gathered at the back gate—"My dear (said Sir Condy) there's nothing for it but to

**Pin* read *pen*—it formerly was vulgarly pronounced *pin* in Ireland.

†*Her mark*—It *was* the custom in Ireland for those who could not write, to make a cross to stand for their signature, as was formerly the practice of our English monarchs.—The Editor inserts the facsimile of an Irish *mark,* which may hereafter be valuable to a judicious antiquary—

Her
Judy X M'Quirk
Mark.

In bonds or notes, signed in this manner, a witness is requisite, as the name is frequently written by him or her.

‡ *Vows*—It has been maliciously and unjustly hinted, that the lower classes of the people in Ireland pay but little regard to oaths; yet it is certain that some oaths or vows have great power over their minds.—Sometimes they swear they will be revenged on some of their neighbours; this is an oath they never are known to break.—But what is infinitely more extraordinary and unaccountable, they sometimes make and keep a vow against whiskey; these vows are usually limited to a short time.—A woman who has a drunken husband is most fortunate if she can prevail upon him to go to the priest, and make a vow against whiskey for a year, or a month, or a week, or a day.

[18] Unlike English and Irish law at this time, Scottish law allowed persons under the age of twenty-one to marry without their parents' consent.

walk, or to let me carry you as far as the house, for you see the back road's too narrow for a carriage, and the great piers have tumbled down across the front approach, so there's no driving the right way by reason of the ruins"— "Plato, thou reasonest well!"[19] said she, or words to that effect, which I could no ways understand; and again, when her foot stumbled against a broken bit of a car wheel, she cried out—"Angels and ministers of grace, defend us!"[20]— Well, thought I, to be sure if she's no Jewish like the last, she is a mad woman for certain, which is as bad: it would have been as well for my poor master to have taken up with poor Judy, who is in her right mind any how.

She was dressed like a mad woman, moreover, more than like any one I ever saw afore or since, and I could not take my eyes off her, but still followed behind her, and her feathers on the top of her hat were broke going in at the low back door, and she pulled out her little bottle out of her pocket to smell to when she found herself in the kitchen, and said, "I shall faint with the heat of this odious, odious place"—"My dear, it's only three steps across the kitchen, and there's a fine air if your veil was up," said Sir Condy, and with that threw back her veil, so that I had then a full sight of her face; she had not at all the colour of one going to faint, but a fine complexion of her own, as I then took it to be, though her maid told me after it was all put on; but even complexion and all taken in, she was no way, in point of good looks, to compare to poor Judy; and with all she had a quality toss with her; but may be it was my over partiality to Judy, into whose place I may say she stept, that made me notice all this.—To do her justice, however, she was, when we came to know her better, very liberal in her house-keeping, nothing at all of the Skin-flint in her; she left every thing to the housekeeper, and her own maid, Mrs. Jane, who went with her to Scotland, gave her the best of characters for generosity; she seldom or ever wore a thing twice the same way, Mrs. Jane told us, and was always pulling her things to pieces, and giving them away, never being used in her father's house to think of expence in any thing—and she reckoned, to be sure, to go on the same way at Castle Rackrent; but when I came to enquire, I learned that her father was so mad with her for running off after his locking her up, and forbidding her to think any more of Sir Condy, that he would not give her a farthing; and it was lucky for her she had a few thousands of her own, which had been left to her by a good grandmother, and these were very convenient to begin with. My master and my lady set out in great stile; they had the finest coach and chariot, and horses and liveries, and cut the greatest dash in the county,

---

[19] Addison, *Cato: a tragedy* (1713), v. I. 1; Plato (c. 427–348 BC), founder of idealism in Greek philosophy.

[20] Shakespeare, *Hamlet,* I. iv. 39.

returning their wedding visits!—and it was immediately reported that her father had undertaken to pay all my master's debts, and of course all his tradesmen gave him a new credit, and every thing went on smack smooth, and I could not but admire my lady's spirit, and was proud to see Castle Rackrent again in all its glory.—My lady had a fine taste for building and furniture, and play-houses, and she turned every thing tops'y-turvy, and made the barrack-room into a theatre, as she called it, and she went on as if she had a mint of money at her elbow; and to be sure I thought she knew best, especially as Sir Condy said nothing to it one way or the other. All he asked, God bless him! was to live in peace and quietness, and have his bottle, or his whiskey punch at night to himself.—Now this was little enough, to be sure, for any gentleman, but my lady couldn't abide the smell of the whiskey punch.—"My dear, (says he) you liked it well enough before we were married, and why not now?"—"My dear, (said she) I never smelt it, or I assure you I should never have prevailed upon myself to marry you."—"My dear, I am sorry you did not smell it, but we can't help that now, (returned my master, without putting himself in a passion, or going out of his way, but just fair and easy helped himself to another glass, and drank it off to her good health). All this the butler told me, who was going backwards and forwards unnoticed with the jug, and hot water, and sugar, and all he thought wanting.—Upon my master's swallowing the last glass of whiskey punch, my lady burst into tears, calling him an ungrateful, base, barbarous wretch! and went off into a fit of hysterics, as I think Mrs. Jane called it, and my poor master was greatly frightened, this being the first thing of the kind he had seen; and he fell straight on his knees before her, and, like a good-hearted cratur as he was, ordered the whiskey punch out of the room, and bid 'em throw open all the windows, and cursed himself, and then my lady came to herself again, and when she saw him kneeling there, bid him get up, and not foreswear himself any more, for that she was sure he did not love her, nor never had: this we learnt from Mrs. Jane, who was the only person left present at all this—"My dear, (returns my master, thinking to be sure of Judy, as well he might) whoever told you so is an incendiary, and I'll have 'em turned out of the house this minute, if you'll only let me know which of them it was."—"Told me what?" says my lady, starting upright in her chair.—"Nothing, nothing at all, (said my master, seeing he had overshot himself, and that my lady spoke at random) but what you said just now that I did not love you, Bella, who told you that?"—"My own sense," said she, and she put her handkerchief to her face, and leant back upon Mrs. Jane, and fell to sobbing as if her heart would break.—"Why now Bella, this is very strange of you, (said my poor master) if nobody has told you nothing, what is it you are taking on for at this rate, and exposing yourself and me for this way?"—"Oh say no more, say no more, every word you say kills me, (cried my lady, and she ran on like one, as Mrs. Jane says, raving)—Oh Sir Condy, Sir Condy! I that had hoped to find in you—"[21] "Why now faith this is a little too much; do Bella, try to recollect yourself, my dear; am not I your husband, and of your own chusing, and is not that enough?"—"Oh too much! too much!" cried my lady, wringing her hands.—"Why, my dear, come to your right senses for the love of heaven—see is not the whiskey punch, jug and bowl and all, gone out of the room long ago? what is it in the wide world you have to complain of?"—But still my lady sobbed and sobbed, and called herself the most wretched of women; and among other out of the way provoking things, asked my master, was he fit for company for her, and he drinking all night.—This nettling him, which it was hard to do, he replied, that as to drinking all night, he was then as sober as she was herself, and that it was no matter how much a man drank, provided it did no ways affect or stagger him—that as to being fit company for her, he thought himself of a family to be fit company for any lord or lady in the land, but that he never prevented her from seeing and keeping what company she pleased, and that he had done his best to make Castle Rackrent pleasing to her since her marriage, having always had the house full of visitors, and if her own relations were not amongst them, he said, that was their own fault and their pride's fault, of which he was sorry to find her ladyship had so unbecoming a share—So concluding, he took his candle and walked off to his room, and my lady was in her tantarums for three days after, and would have been so much longer, no doubt, but some of her friends, young ladies and cousins and second cousins, came to Castle Rackrent, by my poor master's express invitation, to see her, and she was in a hurry to get up, as Mrs. Jane called it, a play for them, and so got well, and was as finely dressed and as happy to look at as ever, and all the young ladies who used to be in her room dressing of her said in Mrs. Jane's hearing, that my lady was the happiest bride ever they had seen, and that to be sure a love match was the only thing for happiness, where the parties could any way afford it.

As to affording it, God knows it was little they knew of the matter; my lady's few thousands could not last for ever, especially the way she went on with them, and letters from tradesfolk came every post thick and threefold, with bills as long as my arm of years and years standing; my son Jason had 'em all handed over to him, and the pressing letters were all unread by Sir Condy, who hated trouble and could never be brought to hear talk of business, but still put it off and put it off, saying—settle it any how, or bid 'em

[21] Based on Edgeworth's corrections to the Butler copy of the novel, Watson adds "my father, brother, husband, friend" (see Watson 123, n. 39). Not adopted in later editions.

call again to-morrow, or speak to me about it some other time.—Now it was hard to find the right time to speak, for in the mornings he was a-bed and in the evenings over his bottle, where no gentleman chuses to be disturbed.—Things in a twelvemonth or so came to such a pass, there was no making a shift to go on any longer, though we were all of us well enough used to live from hand to mouth at Castle Rackrent. One day, I remember, when there was a power of company, all sitting after dinner in the dusk, not to say dark in the drawing-room, my lady having rung five times for candles and none to go up, the housekeeper sent up the footman, who went to my mistress and whispered behind her chair how it was.—"My lady, (says he) there are no candles in the house."—"Bless me, (says she) then take a horse, and gallop off as fast as you can to Carrick O'Fungus and get some."—"And in the mean time tell them to step into the play-house, and try if there are not some bits left," added Sir Condy, who happened to be within hearing. The man was sent up again to my lady, to let her know there was no horse to go but one that wanted a shoe.—"Go to Sir Condy, then, I know nothing at all about the horses, (said my lady) why do you plague me with these things?"—How it was settled I really forget, but to the best of my remembrance, the boy was sent down to my son Jason's to borrow candles for the night. Another time in the winter, and on a desperate cold day, there was no turf in for the parlour and above stairs, and scarce enough for the cook in the kitchen, the little *gossoon** was sent off to the neighbours to see and beg or borrow some, but none could he bring back with him for love or money; so as needs must we were forced to trouble Sir Condy—"Well, and if there's no turf to be had in the town or country, why what signifies talking any more about it, can't ye go and cut down a tree?"—"Which tree, please your honor?" I made bold to say.—"Any tree at all that's good to burn, (said Sir Condy); send off smart, and get one down and the fires lighted before my lady gets up to breakfast, or the house will be too hot to hold us."—He was always very considerate in all things about my lady, and she wanted for nothing whilst he had it to give.—Well, when things were tight with them about this time, my son Jason put in a word again about the lodge, and made a genteel offer to lay down the purchase money to relieve Sir Condy's distresses.—Now Sir Condy had it from the best authority, that there were two writs come down to the Sheriff against his person, and the Sheriff, as ill luck would have it, was no friend of his, and talked how he must do his duty,

* *Gossoon*—a little boy—from the French word *Garçon.*—In most Irish families there *used* to be a bare-footed Gossoon, who was slave to the cook and the butler, and who in fact, without wages, did all the hard work of the house.—Gossoons were always employed as messengers.—The Editor has known a gossoon to go on foot, without shoes or stockings, fifty-one English miles between sun-rise and sun-set.

and how he would do it, if it was against the first man in the county, or even his own brother, let alone one who had voted against him at the last election, as Sir Condy had done.—So Sir Condy was fain to take the purchase money of the lodge from my son Jason to settle matters; and sure enough it was a good bargain for both parties, for my son bought the fee simple of a good house for him and his heirs for ever for little or nothing, and by selling of it for that same my master saved himself from a gaol. Every way it turned out fortunate for Sir Condy; for before the money was all gone there came a general election, and he being so well beloved in the county, and one of the oldest families, no one had a better right to stand candidate for the vacancy; and he was called upon by all his friends, and the whole county I may say, to declare himself against the old member, who had little thought of a contest. My master did not relish the thoughts of a troublesome canvas, and all the ill will he might bring upon himself by disturbing the peace of the county, besides the expence, which was no trifle; but all his friends called upon one another to subscribe, and formed themselves into a committee, and wrote all his circular letters for him, and engaged all his agents, and did all the business unknown to him, and he was well pleased that it should be so at last, and my lady herself was very sanguine about the election, and there was open house kept night and day at Castle Rackrent, and I thought I never saw my lady look so well in her life as she did at that time; there were grand dinners, and all the gentlemen drinking success to Sir Condy till they were carried off; and then dances and balls, and the ladies all finishing with a raking pot of tea[g] in the morning. Indeed it was well the company made it their choice to sit up all nights, for there were not half beds enough for the sights of people that were in it, though there were shake downs in the drawing-room always made up before sun-rise, for those that liked it. For my part, when I saw the doings that were going on, and the loads of claret that went down the throats of them that had no right to be asking for it, and the sights of meat that went up to table and never came down, besides what was carried off to one or t'other below stairs, I couldn't but pity my poor master who was to pay for all, but I said nothing for fear of gaining myself ill will. The day of election will come some time or other, says I to myself, and all will be over—and so it did, and a glorious day it was as any I ever had the happiness to see; huzza! huzza! Sir Condy Rackrent for ever, was the first thing I hears in the morning, and the same and nothing else all day, and not a soul sober only just when polling, enough to give their votes as became 'em, and to stand the brow-beating of the lawyers who came tight enough upon us; and many of our freeholders were knocked off, having never a freehold that they could safely swear to, and Sir Condy was not willing to have any man perjure himself for his sake, as was done on the other side, God knows, but no matter for that.—Some of our friends were dumb-founded, by the lawyers asking them—had they ever been upon the ground where their freeholds lay?—Now Sir Condy being tender of the consciences of them that had not been on the ground, and so could not swear to a freehold when cross-examined by them lawyers, sent out for a couple of cleaves-full of the sods of his farm of *Gulteeshinnagh*:* and as soon as the sods came into town he set each man upon his sod, and so then ever after, you know, they could fairly swear they had been upon the ground.†—We gained the day by this piece of honesty.[g] I thought I should have died in the streets for joy when I seed my poor master chaired, and he bare-headed and it raining as hard as it could pour; but all the crowds following him up and down, and he bowing and shaking hands with the whole town.—"Is that Sir Condy Rackrent in the chair?" says a stranger man in the crowd—"The same," says I—who else should it be? God bless him!"—"And I take it then you belong to him," says he.—"Not at all," (says I) "but I live under him, and have done so these two hundred years and upwards, me and mine."—"It's lucky for you, then," rejoins he, "that he is where he is, for was he any where else but in the chair this minute he'd be in a worse place, for I was sent down on purpose to put him up,‡ and here's my order for so doing in my pocket."—It was a writ that villain the wine merchant had marked against my poor master, for some hundreds of an old debt which it was a shame to be talking of at such a time as this.—"Put it in your pocket again, and think no more of it any ways for seven years to come, my honest friend, (says I), he's a member a Parliament now, praised be God, and such as you can't touch him; and if you'll take a fool's advice, I'd have you keep out of the way this day, or you'll run a good chance of getting your deserts amongst my master's friends, unless you chuse to drink his health like every body else."—"I've no objection to that in life," said he; so we went into one of the public houses kept open for my master, and we had a great deal of talk about this thing and that, and "how is it (says he) your master keeps on so well upon his legs; I heard say he was off Holantide twelve-month past."—"Never was

* At St Patrick's meeting, London, March, 1806, the Duke of Sussex said he had the honour of bearing an Irish title, and, with the permission of the company, he should tell them an anecdote of what he had experienced on his travels. When he was at Rome, he went to visit an Irish seminary, and when they heard who he was, and that he had an Irish title, some of them asked him, "Please your Royal Highness, since you are an Irish Peer, will you tell us if you ever trod upon Irish ground?" When he told them he had not, "O, then," said one of the order, "you shall soon do so." They then spread some earth, which had been brought from Ireland, on a marble slab, and made him stand upon it. [Footnote added to the fifth edition (1810). Ed.]

† This was actually done at an election in Ireland.

‡ *To put him up*—to put him in gaol.

better or heartier in his life," said I.—"It's not that I'm after speaking of, (said he) but there was a great report of his being ruined."—"No matter, (says I) the Sheriffs two years running were his particular friends, and the Sub-sheriffs were both of them gentlemen, and were properly spoken to; and so the writs lay snug with them, and they, as I understand by my son Jason the custom in them cases is, returned the writs as they came to them to those that sent 'em, much good may it do them, with word in Latin that no such person as Sir Condy Rackrent, Bart. was to be found in those parts."—"Oh, I understand all those ways better, no offence, than you," says he, laughing, and at the same time filling his glass to my master's good health, which convinced me he was a warm friend in his heart after all, though appearances were a little suspicious or so at first.—"To be sure, (says he, still cutting his joke) when a man's over head and shoulders in debt, he may live the faster for it and the better if he goes the right way about it—or else how is it so many live on so well, as we see every day, after they are ruined?"—"How is it, (says I, being a little merry at the time) how is it but just as you see the ducks in the chicken-yard just after their heads are cut off by the cook, running round and round faster than when alive."—At which conceit he fell a laughing, and remarked he had never had the happiness yet to see the chicken-yard at Castle Rackrent.—"It won't be long so, I hope, (says I) you'll be kindly welcome there, as every body is made by my master; there is not a freer spoken gentleman or a better beloved, high or low, in all Ireland."—And of what passed after this I'm not sensible, for we drank Sir Condy's good health and the downfall of his enemies till we could stand no longer ourselves—And little did I think at the time, or till long after, how I was harbouring my poor master's greatest of enemies myself. This fellow had the impudence, after coming to see the chicken-yard, to get me to introduce him to my son Jason—little more than the man that never was born did I guess at his meaning by this visit; he gets him a correct list fairly drawn out from my son Jason of all my master's debts, and goes straight round to the creditors and buys them all up, which he did easy enough, seeing the half of them never expected to see their money out of Sir Condy's hands. Then when this base-minded limb of the law, as I afterwards detected him in being, grew to be sole creditor over all, he takes him out a custodiam on all the denominations and sub-denominations, and every carton and half carton[g] upon the estate—and not content with that, must have an execution against the master's goods and down to the furniture, though little worth, of Castle Rackrent itself.—But this is a part of my story, I'm not come to yet, and it's

---

custodiam: under Irish law, a three-year grant of Crown lands made by the Exchequer to a lessee.

bad to be forestalling—ill news flies fast enough all the world over. To go back to the day of the election, which I never think of but with pleasure and tears of gratitude for those good times; after the election was quite and clean over, there comes shoals of people from all parts, claiming to have obliged my master with their votes, and putting him in mind of promises which he could never remember himself to have made—one was to have a freehold for each of his four sons—another was to have a renewal of a lease—another an abatement—one came to be paid ten guineas for a pair of silver buckles sold my master on the hustings, which turned out to be no better than copper gilt—another had a long bill for oats, the half of which never went into the granary to my certain knowledge, and the other half were not fit for the cattle to touch; but the bargain was made the week before the election, and the coach and saddle horses were got into order for the day, besides a vote fairly got by them oats—so no more reasoning on that head—but then there was no end to them that were telling Sir Condy he had engaged to make their sons exicisemen, or high constables, or the like; and as for them that had bills to give in for liquor, and beds, and straw, and ribands, and horses, and post-chaises for the gentlemen freeholders that came from all parts and other counties to vote for my master, and were not, to be sure, to be at any charges, there was no standing against all these; and worse than all the gentlemen of my master's committee, who managed all for him, and talked how they'd bring him in without costing him a penny, and subscribed by hundreds very genteelly, forgot to pay their subscriptions, and had laid out in agents and lawyers, fees and secret service money the Lord knows how much; and my master could never ask one of them for their subscription, you are sensible, nor for the price of a fine horse he had sold one of them, so it all was left at his door. He could never, God bless him again, I say, bring himself to ask a gentleman for money, despising such sort of conversation himself; but others, who were not gentlemen born, behaved very uncivil in pressing him at this very time, and all he could do to content 'em all was to take himself out of the way as fast as possible to Dublin, where my lady had taken a house fitting for him, as a Member of Parliament, to attend his duty in there all the winter.—I was very lonely when the whole family was gone, and all the things they had ordered to go and forgot sent after them by the stage. There was then a great silence in Castle Rackrent, and I went moping from room to room, hearing the doors clap for want of right locks, and the wind through the broken windows, that the glazier never would come to mend, and the rain coming through the roof and best ceilings all over the house for want of the slater, whose bill was not paid; besides our having no slates or shingles for that part of the old building which was shingled, and burnt when the chimney took fire, and had been open to the weather ever since. I took myself to the servants' hall in the evening to smoke my pipe as usual, but missed the bit of talk we used to have there sadly, and ever after was content to stay in the kitchen and boil my little potatoes,* and put up my bed there; and every post day I looked in the newspaper, but no news of my master in the house.—He never spoke good or bad—but, as the butler wrote down word to my son Jason, was very ill used by the government about a place that was promised him and never given, after his supporting them against his conscience very honorably, and being greatly abused for it, which hurt him greatly, he having the name of a great patriot in the country before. The house and living in Dublin too were not to be had for nothing, and my son Jason said Sir Condy must soon be looking out for a new agent, for I've done my part and can do no more—if my lady had the bank of Ireland to spend, it would go all in one winter, and Sir Condy would never gainsay her, though he does not care the rind of a lemon for her all the while.

Now I could not bear to hear Jason giving out after this manner against the family, and twenty people standing by in the street. Ever since he had lived at the Lodge of his own he looked down, howsomever, upon poor old Thady, and was grown quite a great gentleman, and had none of his relations near him—no wonder he was no kinder to poor Sir Condy than to his own kith or kin.†—In the spring it was the villain that got the list of the debts from him brought down the Custodiam, Sir Condy still attending his duty in Parliament; and I could scarcely believe my own old eyes, or the spectacles with which I read it, when I was shewn my son Jason's name joined in the Custodiam; but he told me it was only for form's sake, and to make things easier, than if all the land was under the power of a total stranger.—Well, I did not know what to think—it was hard to be talking ill of my own, and I could not but grieve for my poor master's fine estate, all torn by these vultures of the law; so I said nothing, but just looked on to see how it would all end.

It was not till the month of June that he and my lady came down to the country.—My master was pleased to take me aside with them to the brewhouse that same evening, to complain to me of my son and other matters, in which he said he was confident I had neither art nor part: he said a great deal more to me, to whom he had been fond to talk ever since he was my white-headed boy before he came to the estate, and all that he said about poor Judy I can never forget, but scorn to repeat.—He did not say an unkind

* *My little potatoes*—Thady does not mean by this expression that his potatoes were less than other people's, or less than the usual size—*little* is here used only as an *Italian* diminutive, expressive of fondness.

† *Kith and kin*—family or relations—*Kin* from *kind*—*Kith* from ——we know not what.

---

bank of Ireland: established in Dublin by royal charter in 1783 with a capital of £600,000.

word of my lady, but wondered, as well he might, her relations would do nothing for him or her, and they in all this great distress.—He did not take any thing long to heart, let it be as it would, and had no more malice or thought of the like in him than a child that can't speak; this night it was all out of his head before he went to his bed.—He took his jug of whiskey punch—My lady was grown quite easy about the whiskey punch by this time, and so I did suppose all was going on right betwixt them, till I learnt the truth through Mrs. Jane, who talked over their affairs to the housekeeper, and I within hearing. The night my master came home, thinking of nothing at all, but just making merry, he drank his bumper toast "to the deserts of that old curmudgeon my father-in-law, and all enemies at Mount Juliet's town."—Now my lady was no longer in the mind she formerly was, and did no ways relish hearing her own friends abused in her presence, she said.—"Then why don't they shew themselves your friends, (said my master,) and oblige me with the loan of the money I condescended, by your advice, my dear, to ask?—It's now three posts since I sent off my letter, desiring in the postscript a speedy answer by the return of the post, and no account at all from them yet."—"I expect they'll write to *me* next post," says my lady, and that was all that passed then; but it was easy from this to guess there was a coolness betwixt them, and with good cause.

The next morning being post day, I sent off the gossoon early to the post-office to see was there any letter likely to set matters to rights, and he brought back one with the proper post-mark upon it, sure enough, and I had no time to examine, or make any conjecture more about it, for into the servants' hall pops Mrs. Jane with a blue bandbox in her hand, quite entirely mad.—"Dear Ma'am, and what's the matter?" says I.—"Matter enough, (says she) don't you see my bandbox is wet through, and my best bonnet here spoiled, besides my lady's, and all by the rain coming in through that gallery window, that you might have got mended if you'd had any sense, Thady, all the time we were in town in the winter."—"Sure I could not get the glazier, Ma'am," says I.—"You might have stopped it up any how," says she.—"So I did, Ma'am, to the best of my ability, one of the panes with the old pillow-case, and the other with a piece of the old stage green curtain—sure I was as careful as possible all the time you were away, and not a drop of rain came in at that window of all the windows in the house, all winter, Ma'am, when under my care; and now the family's come home, and it's summer time, I never thought no more about it to be sure—but dear, it's a pity to think of your bonnet, Ma'am—but here's what will please you, Ma'am, a letter from Mount Juliet's town for my lady." With that she snatches it from me without a word more, and runs up the back stairs to my mistress; I follows with a slate to make up the window—this window was in the long passage, or gallery, as my lady gave out orders to have it called, in the gallery leading to my master's bed-chamber and her's, and when I went up with the slate, the door having no lock, and the bolt spoilt, was a-jar after Mrs. Jane, and as I was busy with the window, I heard all that was saying within.

"Well, what's in your letter, Bella, my dear? (says he) you're a long time spelling it over."—"Won't you shave this morning, Sir Condy," says she, and put the letter into her pocket.—"I shaved the day before yesterday, (says he) my dear,[22] and that's not what I'm thinking of now—but any thing to oblige you, and to have peace and quietness, my dear"—and presently I had the glimpse of him at the cracked glass over the chimney-piece, standing up shaving himself to please my lady.—But she took no notice, but went on reading her book, and Mrs. Jane doing her hair behind.—"What is it you're reading there, my dear?—phoo, I've cut myself with this razor; the man's a cheat that sold it me, but I have not paid him for it yet—What is it you're reading there? did you hear me asking you, my dear?" "The Sorrows of Werter,"[23] replies my lady, as well as I could hear.—"I think more of the sorrows of Sir Condy, (says my master, joking like).—What news from Mount Juliet's town?"—"No news, (says she) but the old story over again; my friends all reproaching me still for what I can't help now."—"Is it for marrying me, (said my master, still shaving) what signifies, as you say, talking of that when it can't be helped now."

With that she heaved a great sigh, that I heard plain enough in the passage.—"And did not you use me basely, Sir Condy, (says she) not to tell me you were ruined before I married you?"—"Tell you, my dear, (said he) did you ever ask me one word about it? and had not you friends enough of your own, that were telling you nothing else from morning to night, if you'd have listened to them slanders."—"No slanders, nor are my friends slanderers; and I can't bear to hear them treated with disrespect as I do, (says my lady, and took out her pocket handkerchief)—they are the best of friends, and if I had taken their advice—But my father was wrong to lock me up, I own; that was the only unkind thing I can charge him with; for if he had not locked me up, I should never have had a serious thought of running away as I did."—"Well, my dear, (said my master) don't cry and make yourself uneasy about it now, when it's all over, and you have the man of your own choice in spite of 'em all."—"I was too young, I know, to make a choice at the time you ran away with me, I'm sure," says my lady, and another sigh, which made my master, half shaved as he was, turn round upon her in surprise—"Why Bella, (says he) you can't deny what you know

---

[22] In the first edition (1800), "dear" was printed only as a catchword. Corrected in second edition (1800).

[23] Johann Wolfgang von Goethe, *Sorrows of Young Werther* (1774), translated into English by Richard Graves (1779), a popular sentimental classic.

as well as I do, that it was at your own particular desire, and that twice under your own hand and seal expressed, that I should carry you off as I did to Scotland, and marry you there."—"Well, say no more about it, Sir Condy, (said my lady, pettish like)—I was a child then, you know."—"And as far as I know, you're little better now, my dear Bella, to be talking in this manner to your husband's *face*; but I won't take it ill of you, for I know it's something in that letter you put into your pocket just now, that has set you against me all on a sudden, and imposed upon your understanding."—"It is not so very easy as you think it, Sir Condy, to impose upon *my* understanding," (said my lady)—"My dear, (says he) I have, and with reason, the best opinion of your understanding of any man now breathing, and you know I have never set my own in competition with it; till now, my dear Bella, (says he, taking her hand from her book as kind as could be,) till now—when I have the great advantage of being quite cool, and you not; so don't believe one word your friends say against your own Sir Condy, and lend me the letter out of your pocket, till I see what it is they can have to say."—"Take it then, (says she,) and as you are quite cool, I hope it is a proper time to request you'll allow me to comply with the wishes of all my own friends, and return to live with my father and family, during the remainder of my wretched existence, at Mount Juliet's Town."

At this my poor master fell back a few paces, like one that had been shot—"You're not serious, Bella, (says he) and could you find it in your heart to leave me this way in the very middle of my distresses, all alone?"—But recollecting himself after his first surprise, and a moment's time for reflection, he said, with a great deal of consideration for my lady—"Well, Bella, my dear, I believe you are right; for what could you do at Castle Rackrent, and an execution against the goods coming down, and the furniture to be canted, and an auction in the house all next week—so you have my full consent to go, since that is your desire, only you must not think of my accompanying you, which I could not in honour do upon the terms I always have been since our marriage with your friends; besides I have business to transact at home—so in the mean time, if we are to have any breakfast this morning, let us go down and have it for the last time in peace and comfort, Bella."

Then as I heard my master coming to the passage door, I finished fastening up my slate against the broken pane, and when he came out, I wiped down the window seat with my wig,* bade him a good morrow as kindly

* Wigs were formerly used instead of brooms in Ireland, for sweeping or dusting tables, stairs, &c. The Editor doubted the fact, till he saw a labourer of the old school sweep down a flight of stairs with his wig; he afterwards put it on his head again with the utmost composure, and said, "Oh please your honour, it's never a bit the worse."

It must be acknowledged that these men are not in any danger of catching cold by taking off their wigs occasionally, because they usually have fine crops of hair growing

as I could, seeing he was in trouble, though he strove and thought to hide it from me.—"This window is all racked and tattered, (says I,) and it's what I'm striving to mend." "It *is* all racked and tattered plain enough, (says he) and never mind mending it, honest old Thady, says he, it will do well enough for you and I, and that's all the company we shall have left in the house by-and-bye."—"I'm sorry to see your honour so low this morning, (says I,) but you'll be better after taking your breakfast."—"Step down to the servants' hall, (says he) and bring me up the pen and ink into the parlour, and get a sheet of paper from Mrs. Jane, for I have business that can't brook to be delayed, and come into the parlour with the pen and ink yourself, Thady, for I must have you to witness my signing a paper I have to execute in a hurry."—Well, while I was getting of the pen and ink-horn, and the sheet of paper, I ransacked my brains to think what could be the papers my poor master could have to execute in such a hurry, he that never thought of such a thing as doing business afore breakfast in the whole course of his life for any man living—but this was for my lady, as I afterwards found, and the more genteel of him after all her treatment.

I was just witnessing the paper that he had scrawled over, and was shaking the ink out of my pen upon the carpet, when my lady came in to breakfast, and she started as if it had been a ghost, as well she might, when she saw Sir Condy writing at this unseasonable hour.—"That will do very well, Thady," says he to me, and took the paper I had signed to, without knowing what upon the earth it might be, out of my hands, and walked, folding it up, to my lady—

"You are concerned in this, my lady Rackrent, (says he, putting it into her hands,) and I beg you'll keep this memorandum safe, and shew it to your friends the first thing you do when you get home, but put it in your pocket now, my dear, and let us eat our breakfast, in God's name."—"What is all this?" said my lady, opening the paper in great curiosity—"It's only a bit of a memorandum of what I think becomes me to do whenever I am able, (says my master); you know my situation, tied hand and foot at the present time being, but that can't last always, and when I'm dead and gone, the land will be to the good, Thady, you know; and take notice it's my intention your lady should have a clear five hundred a year jointure off the estate, afore any of my debts are paid."—"Oh, please your honour, says I, I can't expect to live to see that time, being now upwards of fourscore and ten years of age, and you a young man, and likely to continue so, by the help of God."—I was vexed to see my lady so insensible too, for all she said was—

under their wigs.—The wigs are often yellow, and the hair which appears from beneath them black; the wigs are usually too small, and are raised up by the hair beneath, or by the ears of the wearers.

"This is very genteel of you, Sir Condy—You need not wait any longer, Thady"—so I just picked up the pen and ink that had tumbled on the floor, and heard my master finish with saying—"You behaved very genteel to me, my dear, when you threw all the little you had in your own power, along with yourself, into my hands; and as I don't deny but what you may have had some things to complain of, (to be sure he was thinking then of Judy, or of the whiskey punch, one or t'other, or both); and as I don't deny but you may have had something to complain of, my dear, it is but fair you should have something in the form of compensation to look forward too agreeably in future; besides it's an act of justice to myself, that none of your friends, my dear, may ever have it to say against me I married for money, and not for love."—"That is the last thing I should ever have thought of saying of you, Sir Condy," said my lady, looking very gracious.—"Then, my dear, (said Sir Condy) we shall part as good friends as we met, so, all's right."

I was greatly rejoiced to hear this, and went out of the parlour to report it all to the kitchen.—The next morning my lady and Mrs. Jane set out for Mount Juliet's town in the jaunting car; many wondered at my lady's chusing to go away, considering all things, upon the jaunting car, as if it was only a party of pleasure; but they did not know till I told them, that the coach was all broke in the journey down, and no other vehicle but the car to be had; besides, my lady's friends were to send their coach to meet her at the cross roads—so it was all done very proper.

My poor master was in great trouble after my lady left us.—The execution came down, and every thing at Castle Rackrent was seized by the gripers, and my son Jason, to his shame be it spoken, amongst them—I wondered, for the life of me, how he could harden himself to do it, but then he had been studying the law, and had made himself attorney Quirk; so he brought down at once a heap of accounts upon my master's head—To Cash lent, and to ditto, and to ditto, and to ditto, and oats, and bills paid at the milliner's and linen-draper's, and many dresses for the fancy balls in Dublin for my lady, and all the bills to the workmen and tradesmen for the scenery of the theatre, and the chandler's and grocer's bills, and taylor's, besides butcher's and baker's, and worse than all, the old one of that base wine-merchant's, that wanted to arrest my poor master for the amount on the election day, for which amount Sir Condy afterwards passed his note of hand; bearing lawful interest from the date thereof; and the interest and compound interest was now mounted to a terrible deal on many other notes and bonds for money borrowed, and there was besides hush-money to the sub-sheriffs, and sheets upon sheets of old and new attornies' bills,

---

gripers: people who oppress others by extortionate or miserly means.

with heavy balances, *as per former account furnished,* brought forward with interest thereon; then there was a powerful deal due to the Crown for sixteen years arrear of quit-rent of the town lands of Carrickshaughlin, with drivers' fees, and a compliment to the receiver every year for letting the quit-rent run on, to oblige Sir Condy and Sir Kit afore him.—Then there was bills for spirits, and ribands at the election time, and the gentlemen of the Committee's accounts unsettled, and their subscription never gathered; and there were cows to be paid for, with the smith and farrier's bills to be set against the rent of the demesne, with calf and hay-money: then there was all the servants' wages, since I don't know when coming due to them, and sums advanced for them by my son Jason for clothes, and boots, and whips, and odd monies for sundries expended by them in journies to town and elsewhere, and pocket-money for the master continually, and messengers and postage before his being a parliament man—I can't myself tell you what besides; but this I know, that when the evening came on the which Sir Condy had appointed to settle all with my son Jason; and when he comes into the parlour, and sees the sight of bills and load of papers all gathered on the great dining table for him, he puts his hands before both his eyes, and cries out—"Merciful Jasus! what is it I see before me!"—Then I sets an arm chair at the table for him, and with a deal of difficulty he sits him down, and my son Jason hands him over the pen and ink to sign to this man's bill and t'other man's bill, all which he did without making the least objections; indeed, to give him his due, I never seen a man more fair, and honest, and easy in all his dealings, from first to last, as Sir Condy, or more willing to pay every man his own as far as he was able, which is as much as any one can do.—"Well, (says he, joking like with Jason) I wish we could settle it all with a stroke of my grey-goose-quill.—What signifies making me wade through all this ocean of papers here; can't you now, who understand drawing out an account, Debtor and Creditor, just sit down here at the corner of the table, and get it done out for me, that I may have a clear view of the balance, which is all I need be talking about, you know?"—"Very true, Sir Condy, nobody understands business better than yourself?" says Jason.—"So I've a right to do, being born and bred to the bar, (says Sir Condy)—Thady, do step out and see are they bringing in the things for the punch, for we've just done all we have to do for this evening."—I goes out accordingly, and when I came back, Jason was pointing to the balance, which was a terrible sight to my poor master.—"Pooh! pooh! pooh! (says he) here's so many noughts they dazzle my eyes, so they do, and put me in mind of all I suffered, larning of my numeration table, when I was a boy, at

---

quit-rent: a rent paid by a freeholder in lieu of services that might be legally required.

the day-school along with you, Jason—Units, tens, hundred, tens of hundreds.—Is the punch ready, Thady?" says he, seeing me—"Immediately, the boy has the jug in his hand; it's coming up stairs, please your honour, as fast as possible," says I, for I saw his honour was tired out of his life, but Jason, very short and cruel, cuts me off with—"Don't be talking of punch yet a while, it's no time for punch yet a bit—Units, tens, hundreds, goes he on, counting over the master's shoulder—units, tens, hundreds, thousands"—"A-a-agh! hold your hand, (cries my master,) where in this wide world am I to find hundreds, or units itself, let alone thousands."—"The balance has been running on too long, (says Jason, sticking to him as I could not have done at the time if you'd have given both the Indies and Cork to boot); the balance has been running on too long, and I'm distressed myself on your account, Sir Condy, for money, and the thing must be settled now on the spot, and the balance cleared off," says Jason. "I'll thank you, if you'll only shew me how," says Sir Condy.—"There's but one way, (says Jason) and that's ready enough; when there's no cash, what can a gentleman do but go to the land?"—"How can you go to the land, and it under custodiam to yourself already, (says Sir Condy) and another custodiam hanging over it? and no one at all can touch it, you know, but the custodees."—"Sure can't you sell, though at a loss?—sure you can sell, and I've a purchaser ready for you," says Jason.—"Have ye so? (said Sir Condy) that's a great point gained; but there's a thing now beyond all, that perhaps you don't know yet, barring Thady has let you into the secret."—"Sarrah bit of a sacret, or any thing at all of the kind has he learned from me these fifteen weeks come St. John's eve, (says I) for we have scarce been upon speaking terms of late—but what is it your honor means of a secret?"—"Why the secret of the little keepsake I gave my lady Rackrent the morning she left us, that she might not go back empty-handed to her friends."—"My lady Rackrent, I'm sure, has baubles and keepsakes enough, as those bills on the table will shew, (says Jason); but whatever it is, (says he, taking up his pen) we must add it to the balance, for to be sure it can't be paid for."—"No, nor can't till after my decease, (said Sir Condy) that's one good thing."—Then coloring up a good deal, he tells Jason of the memorandum of the five hundred a year jointure he had settled upon my lady; at which Jason was indeed mad, and said a great deal in very high words, that it was using a gentleman who had the management of his affairs, and was moreover his principal creditor, extremely ill, to do such a thing without consulting him, and against his knowledge and consent. To all which Sir Condy had nothing to reply, but that, upon his conscience, it was in a

---

Sarrah: literally, for sorrow.

hurry, and without a moment's thought on his part, and he was very sorry for it, but if it was to do over again he would do the same; and he appealed to me, and I was ready to give my evidence, if that would do, to the truth of all he said.

So Jason with much ado was brought to agree to a compromise. — "The purchaser that I have ready (says he) will be much displeased to be sure at the incumbrance on the land, but I must see and manage him — here's a deed ready drawn up — we have nothing to do but to put in the consideration money and our names to it. — And how much am I going to sell? — the lands of O'Shaughlin's-town, and the lands of Gruneaghoolaghan, and the lands of Crookaghnawaturgh, (says he, just reading to himself) — and — "Oh, murder, Jason! — sure you won't put this in — the castle, stable, and appurtenances of Castle Rackrent — Oh, murder! (says I, clapping my hands) this is too bad, Jason." — "Why so? (said Jason) when it's all, and a great deal more to the back of it, lawfully mine was I to push for it." "Look at him (says I, pointing to Sir Condy, who was just leaning back in his arm chair, with his arms falling beside him like one stupified) is it you, Jason, that can stand in his presence and recollect all he has been to us, and all we have been to him, and yet use him so at the last?" — "Who will he find to use him better, I ask you? (said Jason) — If he can get a better purchaser, I'm content; I only offer to purchase to make things easy and oblige him — though I don't see what compliment I am under, if you come to that; I have never had, asked, or charged more than sixpence in the pound receiver's fees, and where would he have got an agent for a penny less?" "Oh Jason! Jason! how will you stand to this in the face of the county, and all who know you, (says I); and what will people think and say, when they see you living here in Castle Rackrent, and the lawful owner turned out of the seat of his ancestors, without a cabin to put his head into, or so much as a potatoe to eat?" — Jason, whilst I was saying this and a great deal more, made me signs, and winks, and frowns; but I took no heed, for I was grieved and sick at heart for my poor master, and couldn't but speak.

"Here's the punch! (says Jason, for the door opened) — here's the punch!" — Hearing that, my master starts up in his chair and recollects himself, and Jason uncorks the whiskey — "Set down the jug here," says he, making room for it beside the papers opposite to Sir Condy, but still not stirring the deed that was to make over all. Well, I was in great hopes he had some touch of mercy about him, when I saw him making the punch, and my master took a glass; but Jason put it back as he was going to fill again, saying, "No, Sir Condy, it shan't be said of me, I got your signature to this deed when you were half-seas over; you know, your name and hand-writing in that condition would not, if brought before the courts, benefit me a straw, wherefore let us settle all before we go deeper into the punch-bowl."—"Settle all as you will, (said Sir Condy, clapping his hands to his ears) but let me hear no more, I'm bothered to death this night."—"You've only to sign," said Jason, putting the pen to him.—"Take all and be content," said my master—So he signed—and the man who brought in the punch witnessed it, for I was not able, but crying like a child; and besides Jason said, which I was glad of, that I was no fit witness, being so old and doating. It was so bad with me, I could not taste a drop of the punch itself, though my master himself, God bless him! in the midst of his trouble, poured out a glass for me and brought it up to my lips.—"Not a drop, I thank your honor's honor as much as if I took it though," and I just set down the glass as it was and went out; and when I got to the street door, the neighbour's childer who were playing at marbles there, seeing me in great trouble, left their play, and gathered about me to know what ailed me; and I told them all, for it was a great relief to me to speak to these poor childer, that seemed to have some natural feeling left in them: and when they were made sensible that Sir Condy was going to leave Castle Rackrent for good and all, they set up a whillalu that could be heard to the farthest end of the street; and one fine boy he was, that my master had given an apple to that morning, cried the loudest, but they all were the same sorry, for Sir Condy was greatly beloved amongst the childer* for letting them go a nutting in the demesne without saying a word to them, though my lady objected to them.—The people in the town who were the most of them standing at their doors, hearing the childer cry, would know the reason of it; and when the report was made known, the people one and all gathered in great anger against my son Jason, and terror at the notion of his coming to be landlord over them, and they cried, No Jason! No Jason!—Sir Condy! Sir Condy! Sir Condy Rackrent for ever! and the mob grew so great and so loud I was frightened, and made my way back to the house to warn my son to make his escape, or hide himself for fear of the consequences.—Jason would not believe me, till they came all round the house and to the windows with great shouts—then he grew quite pale, and asked Sir Condy what had he best do?—"I'll tell you what you'd best do, (said Sir Condy, who was laughing to see his fright) finish your glass first, then let's go to the window and shew ourselves, and I'll tell 'em, or you shall if you please, that I'm going to the Lodge for change of air for my health, and by my own desire, for the rest of my days."—"Do so," said Jason, who never meant it should have been so, but could not refuse him the Lodge at this unseasonable time. Accordingly Sir Condy threw up the sash and explained matters, and thanked all his friends, and bid 'em look in at the

*This is the invariable pronunciation of the lower Irish.[Footnote deleted after sixth edition (1815). Ed.]

punch bowl, and observe that Jason and he had been sitting over it very good friends; so the mob was content, and he sent 'em out some whiskey to drink his health, and that was the last time his honor's health was ever drunk at Castle Rackrent.

The very next day, being too proud, as he said to me, to stay an hour longer in a house that did not belong to him, he sets off to the Lodge, and I along with him not many hours after. And there was great bemoaning through all O'Shaughlin's town, which I stayed to witness, and gave my poor master a full account of when I got to the Lodge.—He was very low and in his bed when I got there, and complained of a great pain about his heart, but I guessed it was only trouble, and all the business, let alone vexation, he had gone through of late; and knowing the nature of him from a boy, I took my pipe, and while smoking it by the chimney, began telling him how he was beloved and regretted in the county, and it did him a deal of good to hear it.—"Your honor has a great many friends yet that you don't know of, rich and poor, in the county (says I); for as I was coming along the road I met two gentlemen in their own carriages, who asked after you, knowing me, and wanted to know where you was, and all about you, and even how old I was—think of that."—Then he wakened out of his doze, and began questioning me who the gentlemen were. And the next morning it came into my head to go, unknown to any body, with my master's compliments round to many of the gentlemen's houses where he and my lady used to visit, and people that I knew were his great friends, and would go to Cork to serve him any day in the year, and I made bold to try to borrow a trifle of cash from them.—They all treated me very civil for the most part, and asked a great many questions very kind about my lady and Sir Condy and all the family, and were greatly surprised to learn from me Castle Rackrent was sold, and my master at the Lodge for health; and they all pitied him greatly, and he had their good wishes if that would do, but money was a thing they unfortunately had not any of them at this time to spare. I had my journey for my pains, and I, not used to walking, nor supple as formerly, was greatly tired, but had the satisfaction of telling my master when I got to the Lodge all the civil things said by high and low.

"Thady, (says he) all you've been telling me brings a strange thought into my head; I've a notion I shall not be long for this world any how, and I've a great fancy to see my own funeral afore I die." I was greatly shocked at the first speaking to hear him speak so light about his funeral, and he to all appearance in good health, but recollecting myself, answered—"To be sure it would be a fine sight as one could see, I dared to say, and one I should be proud to witness, and I did not doubt his honor's would be as great a funeral as ever Sir Patrick O'Shaughlin's was, and such a one as that had never been known in the county afore or since." But I never thought he was in earnest about seeing his own funeral himself, till the next day he returns to it again.—"Thady, (says he) as far as the wake* goes, sure I might without any great trouble have the satisfaction of seeing a bit of my own funeral."—"Well, since your honor's honor's so bent upon it, (says I, not willing to cross him, and he in trouble) we must see what we can do."—So he fell into a sort of a sham disorder, which was easy done, as he kept his bed and no one to see him; and I got my shister, who was an old woman very handy about the sick, and very skilful, to come up to the Lodge to nurse him; and we gave out, she knowing no better, that he was just at his latter end, and it answered beyond any thing; and there was a great throng of people, men, women and childer, and there being only two rooms at the Lodge, except what was locked up full of Jason's furniture and things, the house was soon as full and fuller than it could hold, and the heat, and smoke, and noise wonderful great; and standing amongst them that were near the bed, but not thinking at all of the dead, I was started by the sound of my master's voice from under the great coats that had been thrown all at top, and I went close up, no one noticing.—"Thady, (says he) I've had enough of this, I'm smothering, and can't hear a word of all they're saying of the deceased."—"God bless you, and lie still quiet (says I) a bit longer, for my shister's afraid of ghosts, and would die on the spot with the fright, was she to see you come to life all on a sudden this way without the least preparation."—So he lays him still, though well nigh stifled, and I made all haste to tell the secret of the joke, whispering to one and t'other, and there was a great surprise, but not so great as we had laid out it would.—"And aren't we to have the pipes and tobacco, after coming so far to-night," said some; but they were all well enough pleased when his honor got up to drink with them, and sent for more spirits from a shebean-house,† where they very civilly let him have it upon credit—so the night passed off very merrily, but to my mind Sir Condy was rather upon the sad order in the midst of it all, not finding there had been such a great talk about himself after his death as he had always expected to hear.

The next morning when the house was cleared of them, and none but my shister and myself left in the kitchen with Sir Condy, one opens the door and walks in, and who should it be but Judy M'Quirk herself.—I forgot to notice that she had been married long since, whilst young Captain

* A wake[g] in England is a meeting avowedly for merriment—in Ireland, it is a nocturnal meeting avowedly for the purpose of watching and bewailing the dead; but in reality for gossipping and debauchery.

† *Shebean-house,* a hedge alehouse.—Shebean properly means weak small-bear, taplash.

---

taplash: washings of casks or glasses, stale leftovers from drinks, dregs.

Moneygawl lived at the Lodge, to the Captain's huntsman, who after a while listed and left her, and was killed in the wars. Poor Judy fell off greatly in her good looks after her being married a year or two, and being smoke-dried in the cabin and neglecting herself like, it was hard for Sir Condy himself to know her again till she spoke; but when she says, "It's Judy M'Quirk, please your honor, don't you remember her?"—"Oh, Judy, is it you? (says his honor)—yes, sure I remember you very well—but you're greatly altered, Judy."—"Sure it's time for me, (says she) and I think your honor since I *seen* you last, but that's a great while ago, is altered too."—"And with reason, Judy, (says Sir Condy, fetching a sort of a sigh)—but how's this, Judy, (he goes on) I take it a little amiss of you that you were not at my wake last night?" "Ah, don't be being jealous of that, (says she) I didn't hear a sentence of your honor's wake till it was all over, or it would have gone hard with me but I would have been at it sure—but I was forced to go ten miles up the country three days ago to a wedding of a relation of my own's, and didn't get home till after the wake was over; but (says she) it won't be so, I hope, the next time,* please your honor."—"That we shall see, Judy, (says his honor) and may be sooner than you think for, for I've been very unwell this while past, and don't reckon any way I'm long for this world." At this Judy takes up the corner of her apron, and puts it first to one eye and then to t'other, being to all appearance in great trouble; and my shister put in her word, and bid his honor have a good heart, for she was sure it was only the gout that Sir Patrick used to have flying about him, and that he ought to drink a glass or a bottle extraordinary to keep it out of his stomach, and he promised to take her advice, and sent out for more spirits immediately; and Judy made a sign to me, and I went over to the door to her, and she said—"I wonder to see Sir Condy so low!—Has he heard the news?" "What news?" says I.—"Didn't ye hear it, then? (says she) my lady Rackrent that was is kilt[g] and lying for dead, and I don't doubt but it's all over with her by this time."—"Mercy on us all, (says I) how was it?"—"The jaunting car, it was that that ran away with her, (says Judy).—I was coming home that same time from Biddy M'Guggin's marriage, and a great crowd of people too upon the road coming from the fair of Crookaghnawatur, and I sees a jaunting car standing in the middle of the road, and with the two wheels off and all tattered.—What's this? says I."—"Didn't ye hear of it? (says they that were looking on) it's my lady Rackrent's car that was running away from her husband, and the horse took fright at a carrion that lay across the road, and so ran away with the jaunting car, and my lady Rackrent and her

* At the coronation of one of our monarchs, the king complained of the confusion which happened in the procession—The great officer who presided told his majesty, "That it should not be so next time."

maid screaming, and the horse ran with them against a car that was coming from the fair, with the boy asleep on it, and the lady's petticoat hanging out of the jaunting car caught, and she was dragged I can't tell you how far upon the road, and it all broken up with the stones just going to be pounded, and one of the road makers with his sledge hammer in his hand stops the horse at the last; but my lady Rackrent was all kilt* and smashed, and they lifted her into a cabin hard by, and the maid was found after, where she had been thrown, in the gripe of the ditch, her cap and bonnet all full of bog water—and they say my lady can't live any way. Thady, pray now is it true what I'm told for sartain that Sir Condy has made over all to your son Jason?"—"All," says I.—"All entirely," says she again.—"All entirely," says I.—"Then (says she) that's a great shame, but don't be telling Jason what I say."—"And what is it you say? (cries Sir Condy, leaning over betwixt us, which made Judy start greatly)—I know the time when Judy M'Quirk would never have stayed so long talking at the door, and I in the house." "Oh, (says Judy) for shame, Sir Condy, times are altered since then, and it's my lady Rackrent you ought to be thinking of."—"And why should I be thinking of her, that's not thinking of me now?" says Sir Condy.—"No matter for that, (says Judy, very properly) it's time you should be thinking of her if ever you mean to do it at all, for don't you know she's lying for death?"—"My lady Rackrent! (says Sir Condy in a surprise) why it's but two days since we parted, as you very well know, Thady, in her full health and spirits, and she and her maid along with her going to Mount Juliet's town on her jaunting car."—"She'll never ride no more on her jaunting car, (said Judy) for it has been the death of her sure enough."—"And is she dead then?" says his honor.—"As good as dead, I hear, (says Judy) but there's Thady here has just learnt the whole truth of the story as I had it, and it is fitter he or any body else should be telling it you than I, Sir Condy—I must be going home to the childer."—But he stops her, but rather from civility in him, as I could see very plainly, than any thing else, for Judy was, as his honor remarked, at her first coming in, greatly changed, and little likely, as far as I could see—though she did not seem to be clear of it herself—little likely to be my lady Rackrent now, should there be a second toss-up to be made.—But I told him the whole story out of the face, just as Judy had told it to me, and he sent off a messenger with his compliments to Mount

* *Kilt and smashed*—Our author is not here guilty of an anticlimax.—The mere English reader, from a similarity of sound between the words *kilt* and *killed*, might be induced to suppose that their meanings are similar, yet they are not by any means in Ireland synonymous terms. Thus you may hear a man exclaim—"I'm kilt and murdered!"—but he frequently means only that he has received a black eye, or a slight contusion.—*I'm kilt all over*—means that he is in a worse state than being simply *kilt*—Thus—*I'm kilt with the cold*—is nothing to—*I'm kilt all over with the rheumatism.*

Juliet's town that evening to learn the truth of the report, and Judy bid the boy that was going call in at Tim M'Enerney's shop in O'Shaughlin's town and buy her a new shawl.—"Do so, (says Sir Condy) and tell Tim to take no money from you, for I must pay him for the shawl myself."—At this my shister throws me over a look, and I says nothing, but turned the tobacco in my mouth, whilst Judy began making a many words about it, and saying how she could not be beholden for shawls to[24] any gentleman. I left her there to consult with my shister, did she think there was any thing in it, and my shister thought I was blind to be asking her the question, and I thought my shister must see more into it than I did, and recollecting all past times and every thing, I changed my mind, and came over to her way of thinking, and we settled it that Judy was very like to be my lady Rackrent after all, if a vacancy should have happened.

The next day, before his honor was up, somebody comes with a double knock at the door, and I was greatly surprised to see it was my son Jason.—"Jason, is it you? (says I) what brings you to the Lodge? (says I) is it my lady Rackrent? we know that already since yesterday." "May be so, (says he) but I must see Sir Condy about it."—"You can't see him yet, (says I) sure he is not awake." "What then, (says he) can't he be wakened? and I standing at the door."—"I'll not be disturbing his honor for you, Jason (says I); many's the hour you've waited in your time, and been proud to do it, till his honor was at leisure to speak to you.—His honor," says I, raising my voice—at which his honor wakens of his own accord, and calls to me from the room to know who it was I was speaking to. Jason made no more ceremony, but follows me into the room.—"How are you, Sir Condy, (says he) I'm happy to see you looking so well; I came up to know how you did to-day, and to see did you want for any thing at the Lodge."—"Nothing at all, Mr. Jason, I thank you, (says he, for his honor had his own share of pride, and did not chuse, after all that had passed, to be beholden, I suppose, to my son)—but pray take a chair and be seated, Mr. Jason."—Jason sat him down upon the chest, for chair there was none, and after he had sat there some time, and a silence on all sides—"What news is there stirring in the country, Mr. Jason M'Quirk?" says Sir Condy, very easy, yet high like.—"None that's news to you, Sir Condy, I hear (says Jason) I am sorry to hear of my lady Rackrent's accident."—"I am much obliged to you, and so is her ladyship, I'm sure," answered Sir Condy, still stiff; and there was another sort of a silence, which seemed to lie the heaviest on my son Jason.

"Sir Condy, (says he at last, seeing Sir Condy disposing himself to go to sleep again) Sir Condy, I dare say you recollect mentioning to me the little

---

[24] "shawls by any" until seventh edition (1825), but corrected in "ERATTUM" at end of first edition (1800).

memorandum you gave to lady Rackrent about the £500 a year jointure."—"Very true, (said Sir Condy) it is all in my recollection."—"But if my lady Rackrent dies there's an end of all jointure," says Jason. "Of course," says Sir Condy.—"But it's not a matter of certainty that my lady Rackrent won't recover," says Jason.—"Very true, Sir," says my master.—"It's a fair speculation then, for you to consider what the chance of the jointure on those lands when out of custodiam will be to you."—"Just five hundred a year, I take it, without any speculation at all," said Sir Condy.—"That's supposing the life dropt and the custodiam off, you know, begging your pardon, Sir Condy, who understand business, that is a wrong calculation."—"Very likely so, (said Sir Condy) but Mr. Jason, if you have any thing to say to me this morning about it, I'd be obliged to you to say it, for I had an indifferent night's rest last night, and wouldn't be sorry to sleep a little this morning."—"I have only three words to say, and those more of consequence to you, Sir Condy, than me. You are a little cool, I observe, but I hope you will not be offended at what I have brought here in my pocket,"—and he pulls out two long rolls, and showers down golden guineas upon the bed. "What's this? (said Sir Condy) it's long since"—but his pride stops him—"All these are your lawful property this minute, Sir Condy, if you please," said Jason.—"Not for nothing, I'm sure, (said Sir Condy, and laughs a little)—nothing for nothing, or I'm under a mistake with you, Jason."—"Oh, Sir Condy, we'll not be indulging ourselves in any unpleasant retrospects, (says Jason) it's my present intention to behave, as I'm sure you will, like a gentleman in this affair.—Here's two hundred guineas, and a third I mean to add, if you should think proper to make over to me all your right and title to those lands that you know of."—"I'll consider of it," said my master; and a great deal more, that I was tired listening to, was said by Jason, and all that, and the sight of the ready cash upon the bed worked with his honor; and the short and the long of it was, Sir Condy gathered up the golden guineas and tied them up in a handkerchief, and signed some paper Jason brought with him as usual, and there was an end of the business; Jason took himself away, and my master turned himself round and fell asleep again.

I soon found what had put Jason in such a hurry to conclude this business. The little gossoon we had sent off the day before with my master's compliments to Mount Juliet's town, and to know how my lady did after her accident, was stopped early this morning, coming back with his answer through O'Shaughlin's town, at Castle Rackrent by my son Jason, and questioned of all he knew of my lady from the servant at Mount Juliet's town; and the gossoon told him my lady Rackrent was not expected to live over night, so Jason thought it high time to be moving to the Lodge, to make his bargain with my master about the jointure afore it should be too late, and afore the little gossoon should reach us with the news. My master was greatly vexed, that is, I may say, as much as ever I seen him, when he found how he had been taken in; but it was some comfort to have the ready cash for immediate consumption in the house any way.

And when Judy came up that evening, and brought the childer to see his honor, he unties the handkerchief, and God bless him! whether it was little or much he had, 'twas all the same with him, he gives 'em all round guineas a-piece.—"Hold up your head, (says my shister to Judy, as Sir Condy was busy filling out a glass of punch for her eldest boy)—Hold up your head, Judy, for who knows but we may live to see you yet at the head of the Castle Rackrent estate."—"May be so, (says she) but not the way you are thinking of."—I did not rightly understand which way Judy was looking when she makes this speech, till a while after.—"Why Thady, you were telling me yesterday that Sir Condy had sold all entirely to Jason, and where then does all them guineas in the handkerchief come from?" "They are the purchase money of my lady's jointure," says I.—Judy looks a little bit puzzled at this.—"A penny for your thoughts, Judy, (says my shister)—hark, sure Sir Condy is drinking her health."—He was at the table in *the room*,* drinking with the exciseman and the gauger, who came up to see his honor, and we were standing over the fire in the kitchen.—"I don't much care is he drinking my health or not (says Judy), and it is not Sir Condy I'm thinking of, with all your jokes, whatever he is of me." "Sure you wouldn't refuse to be my lady Rackrent, Judy, if you had the offer?" says I.—"But if I could do better?" says she. "How better?" says I and my shister both at once.—"How better! (says she) why what signifies it to be my lady Rackrent and no Castle? sure what good is the car and no horse to draw it?"—"And where will ye get the horse, Judy," says I.—"Never you mind that, (says she)—may be it is your own son Jason might find that."—"Jason! (says I) don't be trusting to him, Judy. Sir Condy, as I have good reason to know, spoke well of you, when Jason spoke very indifferently of you, Judy."—"No matter (says Judy), it's often men speak the contrary just to what they think of us."—"And you the same way of them, no doubt, (answers I).—Nay don't be denying it, Judy, for I think the better of ye for it, and shouldn't be proud to call ye the daughter of a shister's son of mine, if I was to hear ye talk ungrateful, and any way disrespectful of his honor."—"What disrespect, (says she) to say I'd rather, if it was my luck, be the wife of another man?" "You'll have no luck, mind my words, Judy," says I; and all I remembered about my poor master's goodness in tossing up for her afore he married at all came

* *The room*—the principal room in the house.

---

gauger: a person who measures the quantity of liquor in a cask; especially an exciseman.

across me, and I had a choaking in my throat that hindered me to say more.—"Better luck, any how, Thady, (says she) than to be like some folk, following the fortunes of them that have none left." "Oh King of Glory! (says I) hear the pride and ungratitude of her, and he giving his last guineas but a minute ago to her childer, and she with the fine shawl on her he made her a present of but yesterday!"—"Oh troth, Judy, you're wrong now," says my shister, looking at the shawl.—"And was not he wrong yesterday then, (says she) to be telling me I was greatly altered, to affront me."—"But Judy, (says I) what is it brings you here then at all in the mind you are in—is it to make Jason think the better of you?"—"I'll tell you no more of my secrets, Thady, (says she) nor would have told you this much, had I taken you for such an unnatural fader as I find you are, not to wish your own son pre-farred to another."—"Oh troth, *you* are wrong, now, Thady," says my shis-ter.—Well, I was never so put to it in my life between these womens, and my son and my master, and all I felt and thought just now, I could not upon my conscience tell which was the wrong from the right.—So I said not a word more, but was only glad his honor had not the luck to hear all Judy had been saying of him, for I reckoned it would have gone nigh to break his heart; not that I was of opinion he cared for her as much as she and my shis-ter fancied, but the ungratitude of the whole from Judy might not plase him, and he could never stand the notion of not being well spoken of or beloved like behind his back. Fortunately for all parties concerned, he was so much elevated at this time, there was no danger of his understanding any thing, even if it had reached his ears. There was a great horn at the Lodge, ever since my master and Captain Moneygawl was in together, that used to belong originally to the celebrated Sir Patrick, his ancestor, and his honor was fond often of telling the story that he larned from me when a child, how Sir Patrick drank the full of this horn without stopping, and this was what no other man afore or since could without drawing breath.—Now Sir Condy challenged the gauger, who seemed to think little of the horn, to swallow the contents, and it filled to the brim, with punch; and the gauger said it was what he could not do for nothing, but he'd hold Sir Condy a hundred guineas he'd do it.—"Done, (says my master) I'll lay you a hun-dred golden guineas to a tester* you don't."—"Done," says the gauger, and done and done's enough between two gentlemen. The gauger was cast, and my master won the bet, and thought he'd won a hundred guineas, but by

* *Tester*—Sixpence—from the French word tête, a head. A piece of silver stamped with a head, which in old French was called, "un testion," and which was about the value of an old English sixpence.—Tester is used in Shakspeare. [A silver coin, usually of debased metal. Shakespeare, *2 Henry IV*, III. ii. 269 and *Merry Wives of Windsor*, I. iii. 83. Ed.]

the wording it was adjudged to be only a tester that was his due, by the exciseman. It was all one to him, he was as well pleased, and I was glad to see him in such spirits again.

The gauger, bad luck to him! was the man that next proposed to my master to try himself could he take at a draught the contents of the great horn.—"Sir Patrick's horn! (said his honor) hand it to me—I'll hold you your own bet over again I'll swallow it."—"Done, (says the gauger) I'll lay ye any thing at all you do no such thing."—"A hundred guineas to sixpence I do, (says he) bring me the handkerchief."—I was loth, knowing he meant the handkerchief with the gold in it, to bring it out in such company, and his honor not very well able to reckon it. "Bring me the handkerchief then, Thady," says he, and stamps with his foot; so with that I pulls it out of my great coat pocket, where I had put it for safety.—Oh, how it grieved me to see the guineas counting upon the table, and they the last my master had. Says Sir Condy to me—"Your hand is steadier than mine tonight, Old Thady, and that's a wonder; fill you the horn for me."—And so wishing his honor success, I did—but I filled it, little thinking of what would befall him.—He swallows it down, and drops like one shot.—We lifts him up, and he was speechless and quite black in the face. We put him to bed, and in a short time he wakened raving with a fever on his brain. He was shocking either to see or hear.—"Judy! Judy! have ye no touch of feeling? won't you stay to help us nurse him?" says I to her, and she putting on her shawl to go out of the house.—"I'm frightened to see him, (says she) and wouldn't, nor couldn't stay in it—and what use?—he can't last till the morning." With that she ran off.—There was none but my shister and myself left near him of all the many friends he had. The fever came and went, and came and went, and lasted five days, and the sixth he was sensible for a few minutes, and said to me, knowing me very well—"I'm in burning pain all within side of me, Thady,"—I could not speak, but my shister asked him, would he have this thing or t'other to do him good?—"No, (says he) nothing will do me good no more"—and he gave a terrible screech with the torture he was in—then again a minute's ease—"brought to this by drink (says he)—where are all the friends?—where's Judy?—Gone, hey?—Aye, Sir Condy has been a fool all his days"—said he, and there was the last word he spoke, and died. He had but a very poor funeral, after all.

If you want to know any more, I'm not very well able to tell you; but my lady Rackrent did not die as was expected of her, but was only disfigured in the face ever after by the fall and bruises she got; and she and Jason, immediately after my poor master's death, set about going to law about that jointure; the memorandum not being on stamped paper, some say it is worth nothing, others again it may do; others say, Jason won't have the lands at any rate—many wishes it so—for my part, I'm tired wishing for any thing in this world, after all I've seen in it—but I'll say nothing; it would be a folly to be getting myself ill will in my old age. Jason did not marry, nor think of marrying Judy, as I prophesied, and I am not sorry for it—who is?—As for all I have here set down from memory and hearsay of the family, there's nothing but truth in it from beginning to end, that you may depend upon, for where's the use of telling lies about the things which every body knows as well as I do?

The Editor could have readily made the catastrophe of Sir Condy's history more dramatic and more pathetic, if he thought it allowable to varnish the plain round tale of faithful Thady. He lays it before the English reader as a specimen of manners and characters, which are perhaps unknown in England. Indeed the domestic habits of no nation in Europe were less known to the English than those of their sister country, till within these few years.

Mr. Young's picture of Ireland, in his tour through that country, was the first faithful portrait of its inhabitants.[25] All the features in the foregoing sketch were taken from the life, and they are characteristic of that mixture of quickness, simplicity, cunning, carelessness, dissipation, disinterestedness, shrewdness and blunder, which in different forms, and with various success, has been brought upon the stage or delineated in novels.

It is a problem of difficult solution to determine, whether an Union[26] will hasten or retard the melioration of this country. The few gentlemen of education who now reside in this country will resort to England: they are few, but they are in nothing inferior to men of the same rank in Great Britain. The best that can happen will be the introduction of British manufacturers in their places.

Did the Warwickshire militia, who were chiefly artisans, teach the Irish to drink beer, or did they learn from the Irish to drink whiskey?[27]

---

[25] Arthur Young (1741–1820), English agronomist, travel writer, and author of *A Tour in Ireland* (1780). See *TINT* 343–56.

[26] See *CR* 29, n. 7.

[27] The Sixth Regiment of Foot of the Warwickshire Militia was part of the military force (estimated at 80,000) diverted to Ireland in the 1790s from the war with France. In the aftermath of the 1798 rebellion the regiment was based at Moate and Athlone, within twenty-five miles of Edgeworthstown, perhaps explaining local knowledge that the forces drank.

GLOSSARY[28]

SOME friends who have seen Thady's history since it has been printed have suggested to the Editor, that many of the terms and idiomatic phrases with which it abounds could not be intelligible to the English reader without farther explanation. The Editor has therefore furnished the following Glossary.

Page 30 *Monday morning.*—Thady begins his Memoirs of the Rackrent Family by dating *Monday morning,* because no great undertaking can be auspiciously commenced in Ireland on any morning but *Monday morning.*—"Oh, please God we live till Monday morning, we'll set the slater to mend the roof of the house—On Monday morning we'll fall to and cut the turf—On Monday morning we'll see and begin mowing—On Monday morning, please your honor, we'll begin and dig the potatoes," &c.

All the intermediate days between the making of such speeches and the ensuing Monday are wasted, and when Monday morning comes it is ten to one that the business is deferred to *the next* Monday morning. The Editor knew a gentleman who, to counteract this prejudice, made his workmen and laborers begin all new pieces of work upon a Saturday.

Page 32 *Let alone the three kingdoms itself.*—*Let alone,* in this sentence, means *put out of consideration.* This phrase *let alone,* which is now used as the imperative of a verb, may in time become a conjunction, and may exercise the ingenuity of some future etymologist. The celebrated Horne Tooke has proved most satisfactorily, that the conjunction *but* comes from the imperative of the Anglo-Saxon verb (*beoutan*) *to be out;* also that *if*

[28]The addition of a glossary was unusual but not without precedent for eighteenth-century novels. See, for example, Robert Burns's Kilmarnock edition of *Poems, Chiefly in the Scottish Dialect* (1786). Scott, in some of the Waverley novels, was to follow Edgeworth's example of providing a glossary, and Edgeworth provided one for Mary Leadbeater's *Cottage Dialogues among the Irish Poor* (1811).

comes from *gif*, the imperative of the Anglo-Saxon verb which signifies *to give*, &c. &c. [John Horne Tooke, *The Diversions of Purley* (London, 1786), 185. Tooke gives "beon-utan," not "beoutan." Ed.]

Page 33 *Whillaluh.*—Ullaloo, Gol, or lamentation over the dead—

"*Magnoque ululante tumultu.*"

—*Virgil.*

"*Ululatibus omne*
Implevere nemus."
— *Ovid.*

[Virgil, *Aeneid*, xi. 662. As they return from battle, the women exult "in a great ululating tumult"; Ovid, *Metamorphoses*, iii. 179–80. On seeing a man the naked nymphs "filled the whole wood with shrieks." Ed.]

A full account of the Irish Gol or Ullaloo, and of the Caoinan or Irish funeral song, with its first semichorus, second semichorus, full chorus of sighs and groans, together with the Irish words and music, may be found in the fourth volume of the Transactions of the Royal Irish Academy. For the advantage of *lazy* readers, who would rather read a page than walk a yard, and from compassion, not to say sympathy with their infirmity, the Editor transcribes the following passages. [The following passage is excerpted from William Beauford, "Caoinam: or some account of the ancient Irish lamentations," *Transactions of the Royal Irish Academy*, 4 (1790), 41–54. Ed.]

"The Irish have been always remarkable for their funeral lamentations, and this peculiarity has been noticed by almost every traveller who visited them. And it seems derived from their Celtic ancestors, the primaeval inhabitants of this isle." * * * *

"It has been affirmed of the Irish, that to cry was more natural to them than to any other nation, and at length the Irish cry became proverbial." * * * *

"Cambrensis in the twelfth century says, the Irish then musically expressed their griefs; that is, they applied the musical art, in which they excelled all others, to the orderly celebration of funeral obsequies, by dividing the mourners into two bodies, each alternately singing their part, and the whole at times joining in full chorus." * * * * * * [Giraldus Cambrensis (1146?– 1220?), an Anglo-Norman prelate who visited Ireland as secretary to Prince John in 1184 and wrote two books about the country: *Expugnatio Hibernica* (1189), or *The Conquest of Ireland*, and *Topographia Hibernica* (1188), or *The Topography and History of Ireland*. For the passage cited, see his *Topographia*, pt. III, ch. 12. Ed.]

"The body of the deceased, dressed in grave clothes and ornamented with flowers, was placed on a bier or some elevated spot. The relations and keepers *(singing mourners)* ranged themselves in two divisions, one at the head and the other at the feet of the corpse. The bards and croteries had before prepared the funeral Caoinan. The chief bard of the head chorus began by singing the first stanza in a low, doleful tone, which was softly accompanied by the harp: at the conclusion the foot semichorus began the lamentation, or Ullaloo, from the final note of the preceding stanza, in which they were answered by the head semichorus; then both united in one general chorus. The chorus of the first stanza being ended, the chief bard of the foot semichorus began the second Gol or lamentation, in which he was answered by that of the head and then as before both united in the general full chorus. Thus alternately were the song and chorusses performed during the night. The genealogy, rank, possessions, the virtues and vices of the dead were rehearsed, and a number of interrogations were addressed to the deceased: as, Why did he die? If married, whether his wife was faithful to him, his sons dutiful, or good hunters or warriors? If a woman, whether her daughters were fair or chaste? If a young man, whether he had been crossed in love? or if the blue-eyed maids of Erin treated him with scorn?"

We are told that formerly the feet (the metrical feet) of the Caoinan were much attended to, but on the decline of the Irish bards these feet were gradually neglected, the Caoinan fell into a sort of slip-shod metre amongst women. Each province had different Caoinans, or at least different imitations of the original. There was the Munster cry, the Ulster cry, &c. It became an extempore performance, and every set of keepers varied the melody according to their own fancy.

It is curious to observe how customs and ceremonies degenerate. The present Irish cry or howl cannot boast of such melody, nor is the funeral procession conducted with much dignity. The crowd of people who assemble at these funerals sometimes amounts to a thousand, often to four or five hundred. They gather as the bearers of the hearse proceed on their way, and when they pass through any village, or when they come near any houses, they begin to cry—Oh! Oh! Oh! Oh! Oh! Agh! Agh! raising their notes from the first *Oh!* to the last *Agh!* in a kind of mournful howl. This gives notice to the inhabitants of the village that *a funeral is passing,* and immediately they flock out to follow it. In the province of Munster it is a common thing for the women to follow a funeral, to join in the universal cry with all their might and main for some time, and then to turn and ask—"Arrah! who is it that's dead?—who is it we're crying for?"—Even the poorest people have their own burying-places, that is, spots of ground in the church-yards, where they say that their ancestors have been buried ever since the wars of Ireland: and if these burial-places are ten miles from the place where a man dies, his friends and neighbours take care to carry his corpse thither. Always one priest, often five or six priests attend these funerals; each priest repeats a mass, for which he is paid sometimes a shilling, sometimes half a crown, sometimes half a guinea, or a guinea, according to their circumstances, or as they say, according to the *ability* of the deceased. After the burial of any very poor man who has left a widow or children, the priest makes what is called *a collection* for the widow; he goes round to every person present, and each contributes sixpence or a shilling, or what they please. The reader will find in the note upon the word *Wake* more particulars respecting the conclusion of the Irish funerals.

Certain old women, who cry particularly loud and well, are in great request, and, as a man said to the Editor, "Every one would wish and be proud to have such at his funeral, or at that of his friends." The lower Irish are wonderfully eager to attend the funerals of their friends and relations, and they make their relationships branch out to a great extent. The proof that a poor man has been well beloved during his life, is his having a crowded funeral. To attend a neighbour's funeral is a cheap proof of humanity, but it does not, as some imagine, cost nothing. The time spent in attending funerals may be safely valued at half a million to the Irish nation: the Editor thinks that double that sum would not be too high an estimate. The habits of profligacy and drunkenness which are acquired at *wakes* are here put out of the question. When a labourer, a carpenter, or a smith is not at his work, which frequently happens, ask where he is gone, and ten to one the answer is—"Oh faith, please your honor, he couldn't do a stroke to-day, for he's gone to *the* funeral."

Even beggars, when they grow old, go about begging *for their own funerals;* that is, begging for money to buy a coffin, candles, pipes and tobacco.—For the use of the candles, pipes and tobacco, see *Wake.*

Those who value customs in proportion to their antiquity, and nations in proportion to their adherence to antient customs, will doubtless admire the Irish *Ullaloo,* and the Irish nation, for persevering in this usage from time immemorial. The Editor, however, has observed some alarming symptoms, which seem to prognosticate the declining taste for the Ullaloo in Ireland. In a comic theatrical entertainment represented not long since on the Dublin stage, a chorus of old women was introduced, who set up the Irish howl round the relics of a physician, who is supposed to have fallen under the wooden sword of Harlequin. After the old women have continued their Ullaloo for a decent time, with all the necessary accompaniments of wringing their hands, wiping or rubbing their eyes with the corners of their gowns or aprons, &c. one of the mourners suddenly suspends her lamentable cries, and turning to her neighbour, asks—"Arrah now, honey, who is it we're crying for?"

Page 33 *The tenants were sent away without their whiskey.*—It is usual with some landlords to give their inferior tenants a glass of whiskey when they pay their rents. Thady calls it *their* whiskey; not that the whiskey is actually the property of the tenants, but that it becomes their *right,* after it has been often given to them. In this general mode of reasoning respecting *rights,* the lower Irish are not singular, but they are peculiarly quick and tenacious in claiming these rights.—"Last year your honor gave me some straw for the roof of my house, and I *expect* your honor will be after doing the same this year."—In this manner gifts are frequently turned into tributes. The high and low are not always dissimilar in their habits. It is said that the Sublime Ottoman Porte is very apt to claim gifts as tributes: thus it is dangerous to send the Grand Seignor a fine horse on his birth-day one year, lest on his next birth-day he should expect a similar present, and should proceed to demonstrate the reasonableness of his expectations.

Page 33 *He demeaned himself greatly*—Means, he lowered, or disgraced himself much.

Page 34 *Duty fowls—and duty turkies—and duty geese.*—In many leases in Ireland, tenants were *formerly* bound to supply an inordinate quantity of poultry to their landlords. The Editor knew of thirty turkies being reserved in one lease of a small farm. [Edgeworth corrected this to "sixty" turkeys in the margin of the Butler copy. Not adopted in later editions (see Watson 126, n. 65). Ed.]

Page 34 *English tenants.*—An English tenant does not mean a tenant who is an Englishman, but a tenant who pays his rent the day that it is due. It is a common prejudice in Ireland, amongst the poorer classes of people, to believe that all tenants in England pay their rents on the very day when they become due. An Irishman, when he goes to take a farm, if he wants to prove to his landlord that he is a substantial man, offers to become an *English tenant.* If a tenant disobliges his landlord by voting against him, or against his opinion, at an election, the tenant is immediately informed by the agent that he must become *an English tenant.* This threat does not imply that he is to change his language or his country, but that he must pay all the arrear of rent which he owes, and that he must thence-forward pay his rent on the day when it becomes due.

Page 35 *Canting*—Does not mean talking or writing hypocritical nonsense, but selling substantially by auction.

Sublime Ottoman Porte: the Ottoman court at Constatinople.

Page 35 *Duty work.*—It was formerly common in Ireland to insert clauses in leases, binding tenants to furnish their landlords with laborers and horses for several days in the year. Much petty tyranny and oppression have resulted from this feudal custom. Whenever a poor man disobliged his landlord, the agent sent to him for his duty work, and Thady does not exaggerate when he says, that the tenants were often called from their own work to do that of their landlord. Thus the very means of earning their rent were taken from them: whilst they were getting home their landlord's harvest, their own was often ruined, and yet their rents were expected to be paid as punctually as if their time had been at their own disposal. This appears the height of absurd injustice.

In Esthonia, amongst the poor Sclavonian race of peasant slaves, they pay tributes to their lords, not under the name of duty work, duty geese, duty turkies, &c. but under the name of *righteousnesses.* The following ballad is a curious specimen of Esthonian poetry:

> "This is the cause that the country is ruined,
> And the straw of the thatch is eaten away,
> The gentry are come to live in the land—
> Chimneys between the village,
> And the proprietor upon the white floor!
> The sheep brings forth a lamb with a white forehead;
> This is paid to the lord for a *righteousness sheep.*
> The sow farrows pigs,
> They go to the spit of the lord.
> The hen lays eggs,
> They go into the lord's frying-pan.
> The cow drops a male calf,
> That goes into the lord's herd as a bull.
> The mare foals a horse foal,
> That must be for my lord's nag.
> The boor's wife has sons,
> They must go to look after my lord's poultry." [Unidentified. Ed.]

Page 35 *Out of forty-nine suits which he had, he never lost one—but seventeen.*—Thady's language in this instance is a specimen of a mode of rhetoric common in Ireland. An astonishing assertion is made in the beginning of a sentence, which ceases to be in the least surprizing when you hear the qualifying explanation that follows. Thus a man who is in the last stage of staggering drunkenness will, if he can articulate, swear to you—"Upon his conscience now (and may he never stir from the spot alive if he is telling a lie) upon his conscience he has not tasted a drop of any thing, good or bad, since morning at-all-at-all—but half a pint of whiskey, please your honor."

Page 36 *Fairy Mounts—Barrows.*—It is said that these high mounts were of great service to the natives of Ireland, when Ireland was invaded by the Danes. Watch was always kept on them, and upon the approach of an enemy a fire was lighted to give notice to the next watch, and thus the intelligence was quickly communicated through the country. *Some years ago,* the common people believed that these Barrows were inhabited by fairies, or as they call them, by the *good people.*—"Oh troth, to the best of my belief, and to the best of my judgment and opinion, (said an elderly man to the Editor) it was only the old people that had nothing to do, and got together and were telling stories about them fairies, but to the best of my judgment there's nothing in it.—Only this I heard myself not very many years back, from a decent kind of a man, a grazier, that as he was coming just *fair and easy (quietly)* from the fair, with some cattle and sheep that he had not sold, just at the church of ___, at an angle of the road like, he was met by a good looking man, who asked him where he was going? And he answered, 'Oh, far enough, I must be going all night.'—'No, that you mustn't nor won't (says the man), you'll sleep with me the night, and you'll want for nothing, nor your cattle nor sheep neither, nor your *beast (horse);* so come along with me.'—With that the grazier *lit* (alighted) from his horse, and it was dark night; but presently he finds himself, he does not know in the wide world how, in a fine house, and plenty of every thing to eat and drink—nothing at all wanting that he could wish for or think of—And he does not *mind (recollect,* or *know)* how at last he falls asleep; and in the morning he finds himself lying, not in ever a bed or a house at all, but just in the angle of the road where first he met the strange man: there he finds himself lying on his back on the grass, and all his sheep feeding as quiet as ever all round about him, and his horse the same way, and the bridle of the beast over his wrist. And I asked him what he thought of it, and from first to last he could think of nothing but for certain sure it must have been the fairies that entertained him so well. For there was no house to see any where nigh hand, or any building, or barn, or place at all, but only the church and the *mote, (barrow).* There's another odd thing enough that they tell about this same church, that if any person's corpse, that had not a right to be buried in that church-yard, went to be burying there in it, no not all the men, women, or childer in all Ireland could get the corpse any way into the church-yard; but as they would be trying to go into the church-yard, their feet would seem to be going backwards instead of forwards; aye, continually backwards the whole funeral would seem to go; and they would never set foot with the corpse in the church-yard. Now they say, that it is the fairies do all this; but it is my opinion it is all idle talk, and people are after being wiser now."

The country people in Ireland certainly *had* great admiration mixed with reverence, if not dread of fairies. They believed, that beneath these fairy mounts were spacious subterraneous palaces inhabited by *the good people,* who must not on any account be disturbed. When the wind raises a little eddy of dust upon the road, the poor people believe that it is raised by the fairies, that it is a sign that they are journeying from one of the fairies' mounts to another, and they say to the fairies, or to the dust as it passes—"God speed ye, gentlemen, God speed ye." This averts any evil that *the good people* might be inclined to do them. There are innumerable stories told of the friendly and unfriendly feats of these busy fairies; some of these tales are ludicrous, and some romantic enough for poetry. It is a pity that poets should lose such convenient, though diminutive machinery.—By the by, Parnell, who shewed himself so deeply "skilled in faerie lore," was an Irishman; and though he has presented his faeries to the world in the ancient English dress of "Britain's Isle, and Arthur's days," it is probable that his first acquaintance with them began in his native country. [Thomas Parnell (1679–1718), poet; born in Dublin and educated at Trinity College. Moved to London in 1712 and became part of the Scriblers circle, making friends of Swift and Pope. Ed.]

Some remote origin for the most superstitious or romantic popular illusions or vulgar errors may often be discovered. In Ireland, the old churches and church-yards have been usually fixed upon as the scenes of wonders. Now the antiquarians tell us, that near the ancient churches in that kingdom caves of various constructions have from time to time been discovered, which were formerly used as granaries or magazines by the ancient inhabitants, and as places to which they retreated in time of danger. There is (p. 84 of the R. I. A. Transactions for 1789) a particular account of a number of these artificial caves at the West end of the church of Killossy, in the county of Kildare. Under a rising ground, in a dry sandy soil these subterraneous dwellings were found: they have pediment roofs, and they communicate with each other by small apertures. In the Brehon laws these are mentioned, and there are fines inflicted by those laws upon persons who steal from the subterraneous granaries. All these things shew, that there was a real foundation for the stories which were told of the appearance of lights and of the sounds of voices near these places. The persons who had property concealed there very willingly countenanced every wonderful relation, that tended to make these places objects of sacred awe or superstitious terror. [William Beauford, "A Memoir respecting the Antiquities of the Church of Killossy, in the County Kildare . . ." *Transactions of the Royal Irish Academy,* 3 (1790), 84. Ed.]

Page 36 *Weed-ashes.*—By antient usage in Ireland, all the weeds on a farm belonged to the farmer's wife, or to the wife of the squire who holds the ground in his own hands. The great demand for alkaline salts in bleaching rendered these ashes no inconsiderable perquisite.

Page 36 *Sealing-money.*—Formerly it was the custom in Ireland for tenants to give the squire's lady from two to fifty guineas as a perquisite upon the sealing of their leases. The Editor not very long since knew of a baronet's lady accepting fifty guineas as sealing money, upon closing a bargain for a considerable farm.

Page 36 *Sir Murtagh grew mad.*—Sir Murtagh grew angry.

Page 36 *The whole kitchen was out on the stairs.*—Means that all the inhabitants of the kitchen came out of the kitchen and stood upon the stairs. These, and similar expressions, shew how much the Irish are disposed to metaphor and amplification.

Page 38 *Fining down the yearly rent.*—When an Irish gentleman, like Sir Kit Rackrent, has lived beyond his income, and finds himself distressed for ready money, tenants obligingly offer to take his land at a rent far below the value, and to pay him a small sum of money in hand, which they call fining down the yearly rent. The temptation of this ready cash often blinds the landlord to his future interest. [Correction in Butler copy has "distressed for want of ready money." Not adopted in later editions (see Watson 126, n. 66). Ed.]

Page 38 *Driver.*—A man who is employed to drive tenants for rent; that is, to drive the cattle belonging to tenants to pound. The office of driver is by no means a sinecure.

Page 39 *I thought to make him a priest.*—It was customary amongst those of Thady's rank, in Ireland, whenever they could get a little money, to send their sons abroad to St. Omer's, or to Spain, to be educated as priests. Now they are educated at Maynooth. The Editor has lately known a young lad, who began by being a post-boy, afterwards turn into a carpenter; then quit his plane and work-bench to study his *Humanities*, as he said, at the college of Maynooth: but after he had gone through his course of Humanities, he determined to be a soldier instead of a priest. [Under the Penal Laws (see *CR* 31, n. 10), Catholic seminaries were banned and Catholics were excluded from attending Trinity College. Consequently, Irish seminarians traveled to the Continent, and St. Omer's near Calais was the closest seminary to Ireland. After political reform in 1793, St. Patrick's College, Maynooth, Co. Kildare opened in 1795 as the national seminary. Ed.]

Page 40 *Flam.*—Short for flambeau.

Page 41 *Barrack room.*—Formerly it was customary, in gentlemen's houses in Ireland, to fit up one large bedchamber with a number of beds for the reception of occasional visitors. These rooms were called Barrack rooms.

Page 41 *An innocent*—in Ireland, means a simpleton, an idiot.

Page 46 *The Curragh*—is the Newmarket of Ireland. [An Irish word for racecourse. Set about thirty miles west of Dublin in Co. Kildare, the Curragh remains a major horseracing venue today. Ed.]

Page 46 *The Cant.*—The auction.

Page 49 *And so should cut him off for ever, by levying a fine, and suffering a recovery to dock the entail.*—The English reader may perhaps be surprised at the extent of Thady's legal knowledge, and at the fluency with which he pours forth law terms; but almost every poor man in Ireland, be he farmer, weaver, shopkeeper, or steward, is, beside his other occupations, occasionally a lawyer. The nature of processes, ejectments, custodiams, injunctions, replevins, &c. is perfectly known to them, and the terms as familiar to them as to any attorney. They all love law. It is a kind of lottery, in which every man, staking his own wit or cunning against his neighbour's property, feels that he has little to lose and much to gain.

"I'll have the law of you, so I will!"—is the saying of an Englishman who expects justice. "I'll have you before his honor"—is the threat of an Irishman who hopes for partiality. Miserable is the life of a justice of the peace in Ireland the day after a fair, especially if he resides near a small town. The multitude of the *kilt* (*kilt* does not mean *killed,* but hurt) and wounded who come before his honor with black eyes or bloody heads is astonishing, but more astonishing is the number of those, who, though they are scarcely able by daily labour to procure daily food, will nevertheless, without the least reluctance, waste six or seven hours of the day lounging in the yard or hall of a justice of the peace, waiting to make some complaint about—nothing. It is impossible to convince them that *time is money.* They do not set any value upon their own time, and they think that others estimate theirs at less than nothing. Hence they make no scruple of telling a justice of the peace a story of an hour long about a *tester* (sixpence): and if he grows impatient, they attribute it to some secret prejudice which he entertains against them.

Their method is to get a story completely by heart, and to tell it, as they call it, *out of the face,* that is, from the beginning to the end, without interruption.

"Well, my good friend, I have seen you lounging about these three hours in the yard; what is your business?"

"Please your honor, it is what I want to speak one word to your honor."

"Speak then, but be quick—What is the matter?"

"The matter, please your honor, is nothing at-all-at-all, only just about the grazing of a horse, please your honor, that this man here sold me at the fair of Gurtishannon last Shrove fair, which lay down three times with myself, please your honor, and *kilt* me; not to be telling your honor of how, no later back than yesterday night, he lay down in the house there within and all the childer standing round, and it was God's mercy he did not fall a'-top of them, or into the fire to burn himself. So please your honor, to-day I took him back to this man, which owned him, and after a great deal to do I got the mare again I *swopped (exchanged)* him for; but he won't pay the grazing of the horse for the time I had him, though he promised to pay the grazing in case the horse didn't answer; and he never did a day's work, good or bad, please your honor, all the time he was with me, and I had the doctor to him five times, any how. And so, please your honor, it is what I expect your honor will stand my friend, for I'd sooner come to your honor for justice than to any other in all Ireland. And so I brought him here before your honor, and expect your honor will make him pay me the grazing, or tell me, can I process him for it at the next assizes, please your honor?"

The defendant now, turning a quid of tobacco with his tongue into some secret cavern in his mouth, begins his defence with—

"Please your honor, under favor, and saving your honor's presence, there's not a word of truth in all this man has been saying from beginning to end, upon my conscience, and I wouldn't for the value of the horse itself, grazing and all, be after telling your honor a lie. For please your honor, I have a dependance upon your honor that you'll do me justice, and not be listening to him or the like of him. Please your honor, it's what he has brought me before your honor, because he had a spite against me about some oats I sold your honor, which he was jealous of, and a shawl his wife got at my shister's shop there without, and never paid for; so I offered to set the shawl against the grazing, and give him a receipt in full of all demands, but he wouldn't out of spite, please your honor; so he brought me before your honor, expecting your honor was mad with me for cutting down the tree in the horse park, which was none of my doing, please your honor—ill luck to them that went and belied me to your honor behind my back!—So if your honor is pleasing, I'll tell you the whole truth about the horse that he swopped against my mare, out of the face.—Last Shrove fair I met this man, Jemmy Duffy, please your honor, just at the corner of the road where the bridge is broken down that your honor is to have the presentment for this year—long life to you for it!—And he was at that time coming from the fair of Gurtishannon, and I the same way. "How are you, Jemmy?" says I.—"Very well, I thank ye kindly, Bryan," says he; "shall we turn back to

Paddy Salmon's, and take a naggin of whiskey to our better acquaintance?"—"I don't care if I did, Jemmy," says I; "only it is what I can't take the whiskey, because I'm under an oath against it for a month." Ever since, please your honor, the day your honor met me on the road, and observed to me I could hardly stand I had taken so much—though upon my conscience your honor wronged me greatly that same time—ill luck to them that belied me behind my back to your honor!—Well, please your honor, as I was telling you, as he was taking the whiskey, and we talking of one thing or t'other, he makes me an offer to swop his mare that he couldn't sell at the fair of Gurtishannon, because nobody would be troubled with the beast, please your honor, against my horse, and to oblige him I took the mare—sorrow take her! and him along with her!—She kicked me a new car, that was worth three pounds ten, to tatters the first time ever I put her into it, and I expect your honor will make him pay me the price of the car, any how, before I pay the grazing, which I've no right to pay at-all-at-all, only to oblige him.—But I leave it all to your honor—and the whole grazing he ought to be charging for the beast is but two and eight pence half-penny, any how, please your honor. So I'll abide by what your honor says, good or bad. I'll leave it all to your honor."

I'll leave *it* all to your honor—literally means, I'll leave all the trouble to your honor.

The Editor knew a justice of the peace in Ireland, who had such a dread of *having it all left to his honor,* that he frequently gave the complainants the sum about which they were disputing to make peace between them, and to get rid of the trouble of hearing their stories *out of the face.* But he was soon cured of this method of buying off disputes, by the increasing multitude of those who, out of pure regard to his honor, came "to get justice from him, because they would sooner come before him than before any man in all Ireland."

Page 57 *A raking pot of tea.*—We should observe, this custom has long since been banished from the higher orders of Irish gentry. The mysteries of a raking pot of tea, like those of the Bona Dea, are supposed to be sacred to females, but now and then it has happened that some of the male species, who were either more audacious or more highly favored than the rest of their sex, have been admitted by stealth to these orgies. The time when the festive ceremony begins varies according to circumstances, but it is never earlier than twelve o'clock at night; the joys of a raking pot of tea depending on its being made in secret, and at an unseasonable hour. After a ball, when the more discreet part of the company has departed to rest, a few

---

Bona Dea: the Roman goddess of chastity whose temple was the preserve of women.

chosen female spirits, who have footed it till they can foot it no longer, and till the sleepy notes expire under the slurring hand of the musician, retire to a bed-chamber, call the favorite maid, who alone is admitted, bid her *put down the kettle,* lock the door, and amidst as much giggling and scrambling as possible, they get round a tea-table, on which all manner of things are huddled together. Then begin mutual railleries and mutual confidences amongst the young ladies, and the faint scream and the loud laugh is heard, and the romping for letters and pocket-books begins, and gentlemen are called by their surnames, or by the general name of fellows—pleasant fellows! charming fellows! odious fellows! abominable fellows!—and then all prudish decorums are forgotten, and then we might be convinced how much the satyrical poet was mistaken when he said,

> "There is no woman where there's no reserve." [Edward Young, *Love of Fame* (1725–8), Satire VI. 1. 45. ED.]

The merit of the original idea of a raking pot of tea evidently belongs to the washerwoman and the laundry-maid. But why should not we have *Low life above stairs,* as well as *High life below stairs?* [David Garrick, *High Life below Stairs* (1759), a popular comedy during the 1790s. Variously attributed to James Townley. ED.]

Page 58 *We gained the day by this piece of honesty.*—In a dispute which occurred some years ago in Ireland, between Mr. E. and Mr. M., about the boundaries of a farm, an old tenant of Mr. M.'s cut a *sod* from Mr. M.'s land, and inserted it in a spot prepared for its reception in Mr. E.'s land; so nicely was it inserted, that no eye could detect the junction of the grass. The old man, who was to give his evidence as to the property, stood upon the inserted sod when the *viewers* came, and swore that the ground he *then stood upon* belonged to his landlord, Mr. M.

The Editor had flattered himself that the ingenuous contrivance which Thady records, and the similar subterfuge of this old Irishman, in the dispute concerning boundaries, were instances of *'cuteness* unparalleled in all but Irish story: an English friend, however, has just mortified the Editor's national vanity by an account of the following custom, which prevails in part of Shropshire. It is discreditable for women to appear abroad after the birth of their children till they have been *churched.* To avoid this reproach, and at the same time to enjoy the pleasure of gadding, whenever a woman goes abroad before she has been to church, she takes a tile from the roof of her house, and puts it upon her head: wearing this panoply all the time she pays her visits, her conscience is perfectly at ease; for she can afterwards safely declare to the clergyman, that she "has never been from under her own roof till she came to be churched." [Added to the fifth edition (1810). ED.]

Page 59 *Carton, or half Carton.*—Thady means cartron or half cartron. "According to the old record in the black book of Dublin, a *cantred* is said to contain 30 *villatas terras,* which are also called *quarters* of land (quarterons, *cartrons*); every one of which quarters must contain so much ground as will pasture 400 cows and 17 plough-lands. A knight's fee was composed of 8 hydes, which amount to 160 acres, and that is generally deemed about a *plough-land.*"

The Editor was favored by a learned friend with the above Extract, from a MS. of Lord Totness's in the Lambeth library. [Sir George Carew (1555–1629), provincial president of Munster 1600–03, serving Elizabeth I. His archive of Irish papers was deposited at Lambeth Palace in London. Ed.]

Page 72 *Wake.*—A wake, in England, means a festival held upon the anniversary of the Saint of the parish. At these wakes rustic games, rustic conviviality, and rustic courtship, are pursued with all the ardour and all the appetite, which accompany such pleasures as occur but seldom.—In Ireland a wake is a midnight meeting, held professedly for the indulgence of holy sorrow, but usually it is converted into orgies of unholy joy. When an Irish man or woman of the lower order dies, the straw which composed his bed, whether it has been contained in a bag to form a mattress, or simply spread upon the earthen floor, is immediately taken out of the house, and burned before the cabin door, the family at the same time setting up the death howl. The ears and eyes of the neighbours being thus alarmed, they flock to the house of the deceased, and by their vociferous sympathy excite and at the same time sooth the sorrows of the family.

It is curious to observe how good and bad are mingled in human institutions. In countries which were thinly inhabited, this custom prevented private attempts against the lives of individuals, and formed a kind of Coroner's inquest upon the body which had recently expired, and burning the straw upon which the sick man lay became a simple preservative against infection. At night the dead body is waked, that is to say, all the friends and neighbours of the deceased collect in a barn or stable, where the corpse is laid upon some boards, or an unhinged door supported upon stools, the face exposed, the rest of the body covered with a white sheet. Round the body are stuck in brass candlesticks, which have been borrowed perhaps at five miles distance, as many candles as the poor person can beg or borrow, observing always to have an odd number. Pipes and tobacco are first distributed, and then according to the *ability* of the deceased, cakes and ale, and sometimes whiskey, are *dealt* to the company.

"Deal on, deal on, my merry men all,
Deal on your cakes and your wine,

For whatever is dealt at her funeral to-day
Shall be dealt to-morrow at mine." [Traditional song. ED.]

After a fit of universal sorrow, and the comfort of a universal dram, the scandal of the neighbourhood, as in higher circles, occupies the company. The young lads and lasses romp with one another, and when the fathers and mothers are at last overcome with sleep and whiskey, *(vino & somno)* the youth become more enterprizing and are frequently successful. It is said that more matches are made at wakes than at weddings. [Glossary-note written by R. L. Edgeworth. See unpublished letter from Maria Edgeworth to Charlotte Sneyd (?September 1806), "Written by my father & which does not read quite well from a lady's pen" (Edgeworth Papers, National Library of Ireland, MS 10-166f. 539). ED.]

Page 73 *Kilt.*—This word frequently occurs in the preceding pages, where it means not *killed,* but much *hurt.* In Ireland, not only cowards, but the brave "die many times before their death." *There killing is no murder.* [Shakespeare, *Julius Caesar,* II. ii. 32. ED.]

THE

WILD IRISH GIRL;

A NATIONAL TALE.

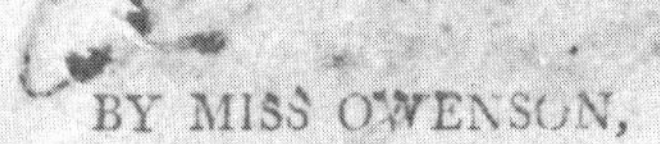

BY MISS OWENSON,

AUTHOR OF ST. CLAIR, THE NOVICE OF ST. DOMINICK, *&c. &c. &c.*

IN THREE VOLUMES.

VOL. I.

"Questa gente benche mostra selvagea
E pur gli monte la contrada accierba
Nondimeno l'e dolcie ad cui l'assagia."

This race of men, tho' savage they may seem,
The country, too, with many a mountain rough,
Yet are they sweet to him who tries and tastes them."

Fazio Delli Uberti's Travels through Ireland
in the 14th Century.[1]

LONDON:

PRINTED FOR RICHARD PHILLIPS,
6, BRIDGE STREET, BLACKFRIARS.

1806.

[1] 14th century author, Frazio Delli Uberti (c. 1305–67), *Il Dittamondo (The Book of the World)*, IV, xxvi, ll. 37–39. For source of translation, see Earl of Charlemont, "The Antiquity of the Woollen Manufacture in Ireland, Proved from a Passage of an Antient Florentine Poet," *Transactions of the Royal Irish Academy*, I (1787): 17–24.

The Wild Irish Girl

Introductory Letters

THE EARL OF M____ TO THE HON. HORATIO M____, KING'S BENCH

Castle M___, Leicestershire,
Feb. —, 17—

IF there are certain circumstances under which a fond father can address an imprisoned son, without suffering the bitterest heart-rendings of paternal agony, such are not those under which I now address you. To sustain the loss of the most precious of all human rights, and forfeit our liberty at the shrine of virtue, in defence of our country abroad, or of our public integrity and principles at home, brings to the heart of the sufferer's dearest sympathising friend a soothing solace, almost concomitant to the poignancy of its afflictions, and leaves the decision difficult, whether in the scale of human feelings, triumphant pride or affectionate regret preponderate.

"I would not," said the old Earl of Ormond, "give up my dead son for twenty living ones."[2] Oh! how I envy such a father the possession, and even the *loss* of such a child: with what eagerness my heart rushes back to that period when *I* too triumphed in my son,—when I beheld him glowing in all the unadulterated virtues of the happiest nature, flushed with the proud consciousness of superior genius, refined by a taste intuitively elegant, and warmed by an enthusiasm constitutionally ardent; his character indeed tinctured with the bright colouring of romantic eccentricity, but marked by the indelible traces of innate rectitude, and ennobled by the purest principles of native generosity, the proudest sense of inviolable honour, I beheld him rush eagerly on life, enamoured of its seeming good, incredulous of its latent evils, till fatally fascinated by the magic spell of the former, he fell an early victim to the successful lures of the latter. The growing influence of his passions kept pace with the expansion of his mind, and the moral powers of the *man* of *genius*, gave way to the overwhelming propensities of the *man* of

---

London: Phillips, 1806. (In addition to Owenson's footnotes, indicated in this edition by an asterisk (*), the footnotes provided by the volume editor of this New Riverside Edition are indicated numerically or added parenthetically to Owenson's notes.)

King's Bench: Court of common law at Westminster, and later a division of the High Court. Criminals sentenced therein housed at its dedicated prison.

[2]Quoted in David Hume, *The History of Great Britain, from the Accession of James I to the Revolution of 1688,* 8 vols. (London, 1770), v. 8, 173.

pleasure. Yet in the midst of these exotic vices (for as such even yet I would consider them), he continued at once the object of my parental partiality and anxious solicitude; I admired while I condemned, I pitied while I reproved. * * * * * * *

The rights of primogeniture, and the mild and prudent cast of your brother's character, left me no cares either for his worldly interest or moral welfare: born to titled affluence, his destination in life was ascertained previous to his entrance on its chequered scene; and equally free from passions to mislead, or talents to stimulate, he promised to his father that series of temperate satisfaction which, if unillumined by those coruscations *your* superior and promising genius flashed on the parental heart, could not prepare for its sanguine feelings that mortal disappointment with which *you* have destroyed all its hopes. On the recent death of my father I found myself possessed of a very large but encumbered property: it was requisite I should make the same establishment for my eldest son, that my father had made for me; while I was conscious that my youngest was in some degree to stand indebted to his own exertions, for independence as well as elevation in life.

You may recollect that during your first college vacation, we conversed on the subject of that liberal profession I had chosen for you, and you agreed with me, that it was congenial to your powers, and not inimical to your taste; while the part I was anxious you should take in the legislation of your country, seemed at once to rouse and gratify your ambition; but the pure flame of laudable emulation was soon extinguished in the destructive atmosphere of pleasure, and while *I* beheld you, in the visionary hopes of my parental ambition, invested with the crimson robe of legal dignity, or shining brightly conspicuous in the splendid galaxy of senatorial luminaries, *you* were idly presiding as the high priest of libertinism at the nocturnal orgies of vitiated dissipation, or indolently lingering out your life in elegant but unprofitable pursuits.

It were as vain as impossible to trace you through every degree of error on the scale of folly and imprudence, and such a repetition would be more heart-wounding to me than painful to you, were it even made under the most extenuating bias of parental fondness.

I have only to add, that though already greatly distressed by the liquidation of your debts, at a time when I am singularly circumstanced with respect to pecuniary resources, I will make a struggle to free you from the chains of this your present *Iron*-hearted creditor, though the retrenchment of my *own* expences, and my temporary retreat to the solitude of my Irish estate, must be the result; provided that by this sacrifice I purchase your acquiescence to my wishes respecting the destiny of your future life, and an unreserved abjuration of the follies which have governed your past.

Your &c. &c.

M____.

TO THE EARL OF M____.

My Lord,

SUFFER me, in the fulness of my heart, and in the language of one prodigal and penitent as myself, to say, "I have sinned against Heaven and thee, and am no longer worthy to be called thy son."[3] Abandon me then, I beseech you, as such; deliver me up to the destiny that involves me, to the complicated tissue of errors and follies I have so industriously woven with my own hands; for though I am equal to sustain the judgment my own vices have drawn down on me, I cannot support the cruel mercy with which your goodness endeavours to avert its weight.

Among the numerous catalogue of my faults, a sordid selfishness finds no place. Yet I should deservedly incur its imputation, were I to accept of freedom on such terms as you are so generous to offer. No, my Lord, continue to adorn that high and polished circle in which you are so eminently calculated to move; nor think so lowly of one who, with all his faults, is *your son,* as to believe him ready to purchase *his* liberty at the expence of *your* banishment from your native country.

I am, &c. &c.

H. M.

King's Bench.

TO THE HON. HORATIO M____.

AN act to which the exaggeration of *your* feelings gives the epithet of banishment, I shall consider as a voluntary sequestration from scenes of which I am weary, to scenes which, though thrice visited, still preserve the poignant charms of novelty and interest. Your hasty and undigested answer to my letter (written in the prompt emotion of the moment, ere the probable consequence of a romantic rejection to an offer not unreflectingly made, could be duly weighed or coolly examined), convinces me experience has contributed little to the modification of your feelings, or the prudent regulation of your conduct. It is this promptitude of feeling, this

---

[3] The parable of the prodigal son, Luke 15:18–19.

contempt of prudence, that formed the predisposing cause of your errors and your follies. Dazzled by the brilliant glare of the splendid virtues, you saw not, you would not see, that prudence was among the first of moral excellencies; the director, the regulator, the standard of them all;—that it is in fact the corrective of virtue herself; for even *virtue,* like the *sun,* has her *solstice,* beyond which she ought not to move.

If you would retribute what you seem to lament, and unite restitution to penitence, leave this country for a short time, and abandon with the haunts of your former blameable pursuits, those associates who were at once the cause and punishment of your errors. I myself will become your partner in exile, for it is to my estate in Ireland I *banish* you for the summer. You have already got through the "first rough brakes" of your profession: as you can now serve the last term of this season, I see no cause why *Coke upon Lyttelton* cannot be as well studied amidst the wild seclusion of Connaught scenery, and on the solitary shores of the "steep Atlantic," as in the busy bustling precincts of the Temple.[4]

I have only to add, that I shall expect your undivided attention will be given up to your professional studies; that you will for a short interval resign the fascinating pursuits of polite literature and belles lettres, from which even the syren spell of pleasure could not tear you, and which snatched from vice many of those hours I believed devoted to more serious studies. I know you will find it no less difficult to resign the elegant theories of your favourite *Lavater,*[5] for the dry facts of law reports, than to exchange your duodecimo editions of the amatory poets for heavy tomes of cold legal disquisitions; but happiness is to be purchased, and labour is the price; fame and independence are the result of talent united to great exertion, and the elegant enjoyments of literary leisure are never so keenly relished as when tasted under the shade of that flourishing laurel which our own efforts have reared to mature perfection. Farewell! my agent has orders respecting the arrangement of your affairs. You must excuse the procrastination of our interview till we meet in Ireland, which I fear will not be so immediate as my wishes would incline. I shall write to my banker in Dublin to replenish your purse

---

Temple: An Inner and a Middle Temple made up the Inns of Court in London.

[4]Sir Edward Coke (1522–1634), jurist who defended common law in the face of Stuart claims of privilege; Sir Thomas Littelton (1422–81), jurist and author of first vernacular works on English law; "Connaught" is the western-most province of Ireland; for "steep Atlantic," see John Milton, *Cosmus, A Maske Presented at Ludlow Castle* (1634), i. 97.

[5]Johann Kaspar Lavater (1741–1801), Swiss philosopher, author of *Physiognomische Fragmente* (1775–78).

on your arrival in Ireland, and to my Connaught steward, to prepare for your reception at M___ house. Write to me by return.

Once more, farewell!

M___.

TO THE EARL OF M___.

My Lord,

HE who agonized on the bed of Procrostus reposed on a couch of down, compared to the sufferings of him who, in the heart he has stabbed, beholds the pulse of generous affection still beating with an invariable throb for the being who has inflicted the wound.

I shall offer you no thanks, my Lord, for the generosity of your conduct, nor any extenuation for the errors of mine.

The gratitude the one has given birth to—the remorse which the other has awakened, bid equal defiance to expression. I have only (fearfully) to hope, that you will not deny my almost forfeited claim to the title of your son.

H. M.

TO J. D. ESQ. M. P.

Holyhead.

WE are told in the splendid Apocrypha of ancient Irish fable, that when one of the learned was missing on the Continent of Europe, it was proverbially said,

"*Amandatus est ad disciplinum in Hibernia.*"[6]

But I cannot recollect that in its fabulous or veracious history, Ireland was ever the mart of voluntary exile to the man of pleasure; so that when you and the rest of my precious associates miss the track of my footsteps in the oft-trod path of dissipation, you will never think of tracing its pressure to the wildest of the Irish shores, and exclaim, "*Amandatus est ad,*" *&c. &c. &c.*

However, I am so far advanced in the land of *Druidism,* on my way to the "Island of Saints,"[7] while you, in the emporium of the world, are drinking

---

Procrostus: Robber in Greek legend who stretched his victims so they fit his bed.

[6]Latin: "He was sent to Ireland for instruction." Quoted in Sylvester O'Halloran, *Introduction to the Study of the History and Antiquities of Ireland* (London, 1772), x.

[7]Referring to Ireland in this manner suggests the post–Counter-Reformation effort to substantiate precolonial Irish civilization. *Druidism* refers to the religious and philosophical system of priests and teachers among the ancient Celtic peoples of Ireland and Britain.

from the cup of conjugal love a temporary oblivion to your past sins and wickedness, and revelling in the first golden dreams of matrimonial illusion.

I suppose an account of my high crimes and misdemeanours, banishment, &c. &c. have already reached your ears; but while my brethren in transportation are offering up their wishes and their hopes on the shore, to the unpropitious god of winds, indulge me in the garrulity of egotism, and suffer me to correct the overcharged picture of that arch caricature *report*, by giving you a correct *ebauche* of the recent circumstances of my useless life.

When I gave you convoy as far as Dover on your way to France, I returned to London, to

——"Surfeit on the same
surfeit and yawn my joys——"[8]

And was again soon plunged in that dreadful vacillation of mind from which your society and conversation had so lately redeemed me.

Vibrating between an innate propensity to *right*, and an habitual adherence to *wrong;* sick of pursuits I was too indolent to relinquish, and linked to vice, yet still enamoured of virtue; weary of the useless, joyless inanity of my existence, yet without energy, without power to regenerate my worthless being; daily losing ground in the minds of the inestimable few who were still interested for my welfare; nor compensating for the loss, by the gratification of any one feeling in my own heart, and held up as an object of fashionable popularity for sustaining that character, which of all others I most despised; my taste impoverished by a vicious indulgence, my senses palled by repletion, my heart chill and unawakened, every appetite depraved and pampered into satiety, I fled from myself, as the object of my own utter contempt and detestation, and found a transient pleasurable inebriety in the well-practised blandishments of Lady C___.

You who alone know me, who alone have *openly* condemned, and *secretly* esteemed me, you who have wisely culled the blossom of pleasure, while I have sucked its poison, know that I am rather a *mechant par air,* than from any irresistible propensity to indiscriminate libertinism. In fact, the *original sin* of my nature militates against the hackneyed modes of hackneyed licentiousness; for I am too profound a voluptuary to feel any exquisite gratification from such gross pursuits as the "*swinish multitude*"[9]

---

ebauche: French: a sketch; a rough-hewn sculpture, a first draft.

mechant par air: French: malicious or spiteful person.

[8] Edward Young, *Night Thoughts on Life, Death, and Immortality* (1742–44), Night III, ll. 334–35.

[9] Edmund Burke, *Reflections on the Revolution in France* (Hardmondsworth: Penguin, 1986), 173.

of fashion ennoble with that name so little understood, *pleasure.* Misled in my earliest youth by "passion's meteor ray,"[10] even then, my heart called (but called in vain), for a thousand delicious refinements to give poignancy to the mere transient impulse of sense.

Oh! my dear friend, if in that sunny season of existence when the ardours of youth nourish in our bosom a thousand indescribable emotions of tenderness and love, it had been *my* fortunate destiny to have met with a being, who—but this is an idle regret, perhaps an idle supposition;—the moment of ardent susceptibility is over, when woman becomes the sole spell which lures us to good or ill, and when her omnipotence, according to the bias of her own nature, and the organization of those feelings on which it operates, determines in a certain degree our destiny through life—leads the mind through the medium of the heart to the noblest pursuits, or seduces it through the medium of the passions to the basest career.

That I became the dupe of Lady C___, and her artful predecessor, arose from the want of that "something still unpossessed," to fill my life's dreadful void. I sensibly felt the want of an object to interest my feelings, and laboured under that dreadful interregnum of the heart, reason and ambition; which leaves the craving passions open to every invader. Lady C___ perceived the situation of my mind, and—but spare me the detail of a connexion which even in memory, produces a *nausea* of every sense and feeling. Suffice it to say, that equally the victim of the husband's villany as the wife's artifice, I stifled on its birth a threatened prosecution,[11] by giving my bond for a sum I was unable to liquidate: it was given as for a gambling debt, but my father, who had long suspected, and endeavoured to break this fatal connexion, guessed at the truth, and suffered me to become a guest (*mal voluntaire*) in the King's Bench. This unusual severity on his part, lessened not on mine the sense of his indulgence to my former boundless extravagance, and I determined to remain a prisoner for life, rather than owe my liberty to a new imposition on his tenderness, by such solicitings as have hitherto been invariably crowned with success, though answered with reprehension.

I had been already six weeks a prisoner, deserted by those gay moths that had fluttered round the beam of my transient prosperity; delivered up to all the maddening meditation of remorse, when I received a letter from my father (then with my brother in Leicestershire), couched in his usual

---

mal voluntaire: French: against my will.

[10] Conventional poetic phrase; see Robert Burns, *The Vision,* l. 105, or William Falconer, *The Demagogue,* l. 430, among others.

[11] A reference to the common law provision recognizing a husband's legal right to recover damages from an adulterer.

terms of reprehension, and intervals of tenderness; ascertaining every error with judicial exactitude, and associating every fault with some ideal excellence of parental creation, alternately the father and the judge; and as you once said, when I accused him of partiality to his eldest born, "talking *best* of Edward, but *most* of me."

In a word, he has behaved like an Angel! So well, that by Heavens! I can scarcely bear to think of it. A spurious half-bred generosity—a little tincture of illiberality on his side, would have been Balm of Gilead to my wounded conscience; but with unqualified goodness he has paid all my debts, supplied my purse beyond my wants, and only asks in return, that I will retire for a few months to Ireland, and this I believe merely to wean me from the presence of an object which he falsely believes still hangs about my heart with no moderate influence.

And yet I wish his mercy had flowed in any other channel, even though more confined and less liberal.

Had he banished me to the savage desolations of Siberia, my exile would have had some character; had he even transported me to a South-Sea Island, or thrown me into an Esquimaux hut, my new species of being would have been touched with some interest; for in fact, the present relaxed state of my intellectual system requires some strong transition of place, circumstance, and manners, to wind it up to its native tone, to rouse it to energy, or awaken it to exertion.

But sent to a country against which I have a decided prejudice—which I suppose semi-barbarous, semi-civilized; has lost the strong and hardy features of savage life, without acquiring those graces which distinguish polished society—I shall neither participate in the poignant pleasure of awakened curiosity and acquired information, nor taste the least of those enjoyments which courted my acceptances in my native land. Enjoyments did I say! And were they indeed enjoyments? How readily the mind adopts the phraseology of habit, when the sentiment it once clothed no longer exists. Would that my past pursuits wore even in *recollection*, the aspect of enjoyments. But even my memory has lost its character of energy, and the past, like the present, appears one unvaried scene of chill and vapid existence. No sweet point of reflection seizes on the recollective powers. No actual joy woos my heart's participation, and no prospect of future felicity glows on the distant vista of life, or awakens the quick throb of hope and expectation; all is cold, sullen, and dreary.

Laval seems to entertain no less prejudice against this country than his master, he has therefore begged leave of absence until my father comes

---

Balm of Gilead: a soothing resin from the aromatic leaves of the mastic tree.

over. Pray have the goodness to send me by him a box of Italian crayons, and a good thermometer; for I must have something to relieve the *tedium vitae* of my exiled days; and in my articles of stipulation with my father, chemistry and belles lettres are *specially* prohibited. It was a useless prohibition, for Heaven knows chemistry would have been the last study I should have flown to in my present state of mind. For how can he look minutely into the intimate structure of things, and resolve them into their simple and elementary substance, whose own disordered mind is incapable of analyzing the passions by which it is agitated, of ascertaining the reciprocal relation of its incoherent ideas, or combining them in different proportions (from those in which they were united by chance), in order to join a new and useful compound for the benefit of future life? As for belles lettres! so blunted are all those powers once so

> "Active and strong, and feelingly alive
> To each fine impulse,"[12]

that not *one "pensée couleur de rose"* lingers on the surface of my faded imagination, and I should turn with as much apathy from the sentimental sorcery of *Rousseau,* as from the voluminous verbosity of an high German doctor; yawn over the "the Pleasures of Memory," and run the risk of falling fast asleep with the brilliant *Madame de Sevigne* in my hand.[13] So send me a FAHRENHEIT, that I may bend the few coldly mechanical powers left me, to ascertain the temperature of my wild western *territories,* and expect my letters from thence to be only filled with the summary results of meteoric instruments, and synoptical views of common phenomena.

Adieu,

H. M.

---

tedium vitae: Latin: tediousness of life.

pensée couleur de rose: French: rose-colored thought.

[12] Mark Akenside, *The Pleasures of Imagination* (1744), Book III, ll. 516–17.

[13] John-Jacques Rousseau (1712–78), philosopher and novelist. Owenson refers frequently to his work *Julie, ou La Nouvelle Héloïse* (1761) and thus the phrase "sentimental sorcery"; "high German Doctor" likely refers to Johann Wolfgang von Goethe (1749–1832), the accomplished German poet and writer; Samuel Rogers's (1763–1855) *Pleasures of Memory* (1792) was in its fifteenth edition by 1806; Maria de Rabutin-Chantal (1626–96), Madame de Sévigné, author of letters recording life in Paris under Louis XIV, published posthumously in 1725.

The Wild Irish Girl

Letter I

TO J. D. ESQ. M. P.

Dublin, March—, 17—.

I REMEMBER, when I was a boy, meeting somewhere with the quaintly written travels of *Moryson* through Ireland, and being particularly struck with his assertion, that so late as the days of Elizabeth, an Irish chieftain and his family were frequently seen seated round their domestic fire in a state of perfect nudity.[14] This singular anecdote (so illustrative of the barbarity of the Irish at a period when civilization had made such a wonderful progress even in its sister countries), fastened so strongly on my boyish imagination, that whenever the *Irish* were mentioned in my presence, an *Esquimaux* group circling round the fire which was to dress a dinner, or broil an enemy, was the image which presented itself to my mind; and in this trivial source, I believe, originated that early formed opinion of Irish ferocity, which has since been nurtured into a *confirmed prejudice.* So true it is, that almost all the erroneous principles which influence our maturer being, are to be traced to some fatal association of ideas received and formed in early life. But whatever may be the *cause,* I feel the strongest objection to becoming a resident in the remote part of a country which is still shaken by the convulsions of an anarchical spirit; where for a series of ages the olive of peace has not been suffered to shoot forth *one* sweet blossom of national concord, which the sword of civil dissention has not cropt almost in the germ; and the natural character of whose factious sons, as we are still taught to believe, is turbulent, faithless, intemperate, and cruel; formerly destitute of arts, letters, or civilization, and still but slowly submitting to their salutary and ennobling influence.

To confess the truth, I had so far suffered prejudice to get the start of unbiassed liberality, that I had almost assigned to these rude people scenes appropriately barbarous; and never was more pleasantly astonished, than when the morning's dawn gave to my view one of the most splendid spectacles in the scene of picturesque creation I had ever beheld, or indeed ever conceived; the bay of Dublin.

---

[14]Fynes Moryson (1566–1630), one in a series of English chroniclers who visited Ireland during the Elizabethan era. His works, *An History of Ireland, From the Year 1599, to 1603 . . .* (1735) and his travelogue *An Itinerary* (1617), like Spenser's *A View of the Present State of Ireland* (1598/1633) and John Davies's *A Discovery of the True Causes Why Ireland Was Never Entirely Subdued . . .* (1612), portray the native Irish and Old English populations as barbarous and uncivilized.

A foreigner on board the packet, compared the view to that which the bay of Naples affords: I cannot judge of the justness of the comparison, though I am told one very general and common-place; but if the scenic beauties of the Irish bay are exceeded by those of the Neapolitan, my fancy falls short in a just conception of its charms. The springing up of a contrary wind kept us for a considerable time beating about this enchanting coast: the weather suddenly changed, the rain poured in torrents, a storm arose, and the beautiful prospect which had fascinated our gaze, vanished in mists of impenetrable obscurity.

As we had the mail on board, a boat was sent out to receive it, the oars of which were plied by six men, whose statures, limbs, and features, declared them the lingering progeny of the once formidable race of Irish giants. Bare-headed, they "bided the pelting of the pitiless storm,"[15] with no other barrier to its fury, than what tattered check trowsers, and shirts open at the neck, and tucked above the elbows afforded; and which, thus disposed, betrayed the sinewy contexture of forms, which might have individually afforded a model to sculpture, for the colossal statue of an Hercules, under all the different aspects of strength and exertion.*

A few of the passengers proposing to venture in the boat, I listlessly followed, and found myself seated by one of these sea monsters, who in an accent and voice that made me startle, addressed me in English at least as pure and correct as a Thames boatman would use; and with so much courtesy, cheerfulness, and respect, that I was at a loss how to reconcile such civilization of manner to such ferocity of appearance; while his companions, as they stemmed the mountainous waves, or plied their heavy oars, displayed such a vein of low humour and quaint drollery, and in a language so curiously expressive and original, that no longer able to suppress my surprize, I betrayed it to a gentleman who sat near me, and by whom I was assured that this species of colloquial wit was peculiar to the lower classes of the Irish, who borrowed much of their curious phraseology from the peculiar idiom of their own tongue, and the cheeriness of manner from the native exility of their temperament; "and as for their courteousness," he continued, "you will find them on a further intercourse, civil even to *adulation,* as long as you treat them with apparent kindness, but an opposite conduct will prove their manner proportionably uncivilized."

"It is very excusable," said I, "they are of a class in society to which the modification of the feelings are unknown, and to be sensibly alive to *kindness or to unkindness,* is, in my opinion, a noble trait in the national character of an unsophisticated people."

* This little marine sketch is by no means a fancy picture; it was actually copied from the life, in the summer of 1805.

---

[15] Shakespeare, *King Lear,* III. iv. 29.

While we spoke, we landed, and for the something like pleasurable emotion, which the first on my list of Irish acquaintance produced in my mind, I distributed among these "sons of the waves" more silver than I believe they expected. Had I bestowed a principality on an Englishman of the same rank, he would have been less lavish of the *eloquence* of gratitude on his benefactor, though he might equally have felt the *sentiment.*—So much for my voyage *across the Channel!*

This city is to London like a small temple of the Ionic order, whose proportions are delicate, whose character is elegance, compared to a vast palace whose Corinthian pillars at once denote strength and magnificence.

The wonderous extent of London excites our amazement; the compact uniformity of Dublin our admiration. But as dispersion is less within the *coup-d'oeil* of observance, than aggregation, the small, but harmonious features of Dublin seize at once on the eye, while the scattered but splendid traits of London, excite a less immediate and more progressive admiration, which is often lost in the intervals that occur between those objects which are calculated to excite it.

In London, the miserable shop of a gin seller, and the magnificent palace of a Duke, alternately create disgust, or awaken approbation.

In Dublin the buildings are not arranged upon such democratic principles. The plebeian hut offers no foil to the patrician edifice, while their splendid and beautiful public structures are so closely connected, as with *some* degree of policy to strike *at once* upon the eye in the happiest combination.*

In other respects this city appears to me to be the miniature copy of our imperial original, though minutely imitative in show and glare. Something less observant of life's prime luxuries, order and cleanliness, there is a certain class of wretches who haunt the streets of Dublin, so emblematic of vice, poverty, idleness, and filth, that disgust and pity frequently succeed in the minds of the stranger to sentiments of pleasure, surprize, and admiration. For the origin of this evil, I must refer you to the supreme police of the city; but whatever may be the cause, the effects (to an Englishman especially) are dreadful and disgusting beyond all expression.[16]

* Although in one point of view, there may be a policy in this close association of splendid objects, yet it is a circumstance of general and just condemnation to all strangers who are not confined to a *partial* survey of the city.

---

coup-d'oeil: French: a glance.

[16]The Dublin Metropolitan Police were introduced in 1786 representing the first city in the British Isles to have a uniformed, armed, and government-controlled police force. Dublin underwent a major physical transformation during the eighteenth century (e.g., the building of Parliament House, Four Courts, College Green, Dublin Castle).

Although my father has a large connexion here, yet he only gave me a letter to his banker, who has forced me to make his house my home for the few days I shall remain in Dublin, and whose cordiality and kindness sanctions all that has ever been circulated of Irish hospitality.

In the present state of my feelings, however, a party on the banks of the *Ohio*, with a tribe of Indian hunters, would be more consonant to my inclinations than the refined pleasures of the most polished circles in the world. Yet these warm-hearted people, who find in the name of stranger, an irresistible lure to every kind attention, will force me to be happy in despite of myself, and overwhelm me with invitations, some of which it is impossible to resist. My prejudices have received some mortal strokes, when I perceived that the natives of this barbarous country have got goal for goal with us, in every elegant refinement of life and manners; the only difference I can perceive between a London and a Dublin *rout* is, that here, even amongst the first class, there is a warmth and cordiality of address, which, though perhaps not more sincere than the cold formality of British ceremony, is certainly more fascinating.*

It is not, however, in Dublin I shall expect to find the tone of national character and manner; in the first circles of all great cities (as in courts), the native features of national character are softened into general uniformity, and the genuine feelings of nature are suppressed or exchanged for a political compliance with the reigning modes and customs, which hold their tenure from the sanction and example of the seat of government. Before I close this, I must make one observation, which I think will speak more than volumes for the refinement of these people.

During my short residence here, I have been forced, in the true spirit of Irish dissipation, into three parties of a night; and I have upon these occasions observed, that the most courted objects of popular attention, were those whose talents alone endowed them with distinction. Besides amateurs, I have met with many professional persons, whom I knew in London as public characters, and who are here incorporated in the first and most brilliant circles, appearing to feel no other inequality, than what their own superiority of genius confers.

I leave Dublin to-morrow for M___ house. It is situated in the county of___, on the north-west coast of Connaught, which I am told is the classic ground of Ireland.[17] The native Irish, pursued by religious and political

* "Every unprejudiced traveller who visits them (the Irish), will be as much pleased with their cheerfulness as obliged by their hospitality; and will find them a brave, polite, and liberal people." —*Philosophical Survey through Ireland by* Mr. YOUNG. [Arthur Young, *A Tour in Ireland*, vol. 2, 156. See *TINT* 343–56. ED.]

[17] The native Irish were driven from their lands and transplanted to Connacht during the Cromwellian wars.

bigotry, made it the asylum of their sufferings, and were separated by a provincial barrier from an intercourse with the rest of Ireland, until after the Restoration; so I shall have a fair opportunity of beholding the Irish character in all its *primeval* ferocity.

Direct your next to Bally___, which I find is the nearest post town to my *Kamscatkan palace;* where, with no other society than that of Blackstone and Co. I shall lead such a life of animal existence, as PRIOR gives to his Contented Couple—

> "They ate and drank, and slept—what then?
> Why, slept and drank, and ate again."—[18]

Adieu,

H. M.

Letter II

TO J. D. ESQ. M. P.

M___ House.

IN the various modes of penance invented by the various *penance mongers* of pious austerity, did you ever hear the travelling in an *Irish post-chaise* enumerated as a punishment, which by far exceeds horse-hair shirts and voluntary flagellation? My first day's journey from Dublin being as wet a one as this moist climate and capricious season ever produced, my berlin answered all the purposes of a *shower bath,* while the ventilating principles on which the windows were constructed, gave me all the benefit to be derived from the *breathy* influence of the four cardinal points.

Unable any longer to sit tamely enduring the "*penalty of Adam, the season's change,*"[19] or to sustain any longer the "hair-breadth 'scapes," which the most dismantled of vehicles afforded me, together with delays and stoppages of every species to be found in the catalogue of procrastination

---

post-chaise: a traveling carriage, hired from stage to stage.

berlin: an old-fashioned four-wheeled covered carriage.

[18] Reference to the remote Kamchatka Peninsula in far eastern Russia; Sir William Blackstone (1723–80), English jurist and author of *Commentaries on the Laws of England,* 4 vols. (1765–69). The work became the basis of university legal education in England and North America; the quoted lines likely refer to Matthew Prior's (1664–1721) "An Epitaph" (1718), ll. 9–10.

[19] Shakespeare, *As You Like It,* II. i. 5–6.

and mischance, I took my seat in a mail coach which I met at my third stage, and which was going to a town within twenty miles of Bally___. These twenty miles, by far the most agreeable of my journey, I performed as we once (in days of boyish errantry) accomplished a tour of Wales—on foot.

I had previously sent my baggage, and was happily unincumbered with a servant, for the fastidious delicacy of Monsieur Laval would never have been adequate to the fatigues of a pedestrian tour through a country wild and mountainous as his own native *Savoy.* But to me every difficulty was an effort of some good *genius* chacing the daemon of lethargy from the usurpations of my mind's empire. Every obstacle that called for exertion was a temporary revival of latent energy; and every unforced effort worth an age of indolent indulgence.

To him who derives gratification from the embellished labours of art, rather than the simple but sublime operations of nature, *Irish* scenery will afford little interest; but the bold features of its varying landscape, the stupendous attitude of its "cloud-capt"[20] mountains, the impervious gloom of its deep embosomed glens, the savage desolation of its uncultivated heaths, and boundless bogs, with those rich veins of a picturesque champagne, thrown at intervals into gay expansion by the hand of nature, awaken in the mind of the poetic or pictoral traveller, all the pleasures of tasteful enjoyment, all the sublime emotions of a rapt imagination. And if the glowing fancy of Claude Loraine would have dwelt enraptured on the paradisial charms of English landscape, the superior genius of Salvator Rosa would have reposed its eagle wing amidst those scenes of mysterious sublimity, with which the wildly magnificent landscape of Ireland abounds.[21] But the liberality of nature appears to me to be here but frugally assisted by the donations of art. Here *agriculture* appears in the least felicitous of her aspects. The rich treasures of Ceres seldom wave their golden heads over the earth's fertile bosom; the verdant drapery of young plantation rarely skreens out the coarser features of a rigid soil, the cheerless aspect of a gloomy bog; while the unvaried surface of the perpetual pasturage which satisfies the eye of the interested grazier, disappoints the glance of the tasteful spectator.

Within twenty miles of Bally___ I was literally dropt by the stage at the foot of a mountain, to which your native *Wrekin* is but an hillock. The

---

Savoy: kingdom in Italy.

Ceres: Roman goddess of grain and protector of agriculture.

Wrekin: a district in Shropshire between the towns of Telford and Shrewsbury.

[20] Shakespeare, *The Tempest,* IV. i. 152.

[21] Contemporary discussions of picturesque landscape painting invariably turned to evaluations of the French painter Claude Lorraine (1600–82) and Italian Salvator Rosa (1615–73). Owenson published her *Life and Times of Salvator Rosa* in 1824.

dawn was just risen, and flung its grey and reserved tints on a scene of which the mountainous region of Capel Cerig will give you the most adequate idea.

Mountain rising over mountain, swelled like an amphitheatre to those clouds which, faintly tinged with the sun's prelusive beams, and rising from the earthly summits where they had reposed, incorporated with the kindling aether of a purer atmosphere.

All was silent and solitary—a tranquillity tinged with terror, a sort of "delightful horror,"[22] breathed on every side.—I was alone, and felt like the presiding genius of desolation!

As I had previously learned my route, after a few minute's contemplation of the scene before me, I pursued my solitary ramble along a steep and trackless path, which wound gradually down towards a great lake, an almost miniature sea, that lay embosomed amidst those stupendous heights whose rugged forms, now bare, desolate, and barren, now clothed with yellow furze, and creeping underwood, or crowned with misnic forests, appeared towering above my head in endless variety. The progress of the sun convinced me that *mine* must have been slow, as it was perpetually interrupted by pauses of curiosity and admiration, and by long and many lapses of thoughtful reverie; and fearing that I had lost my way (as I had not yet caught a view of the village, in which, seven miles distant from the spot where I had left the stage, I was assured I should find an excellent breakfast), I ascended that part of the mountain where, on one of its vivid points, a something like a human habitation hung suspended, and where I hoped to obtain a *carte du pays:* the exterior of this *hut,* or *cabin,* as it is called, like the few I had seen which were not built of mud, resembled in one instance the magic palace of Chaucer, and was erected with loose stones,

> "Which, cunningly, were without mortar laid,"[23]

thinly thatched with straw; an aperture in the roof served rather to *admit* the air than *emit* the smoke, a circumstance to which the wretched inhabitants of those wretched hovels seem so perfectly naturalized, that they live in a constant state of fumigation; and a fracture in the side wall (meant I suppose as a substitute for a casement) was stuffed with straw, while the door, off its hinges, was laid across the threshold, as a barrier to a little crying boy, who

---

Capel Cerig: located near Snowdonia National Park, in North Wales.

carte du pays: French: map of the country.

[22] Edmund Burke, *A Philosophical Enquiry into the Origin of Our Ideas of the Sublime and Beautiful,* pt. 2, "Infinity."

[23] Quotation not from Chaucer. Rather Edmund Spenser, *The Faerie Queene* (1590–96), I. iv. 4.

sitting within, bemoaned his captivity in a tone of voice not quite so mellifluous as that which Mons. de Sanctyon ascribes to the crying children of a certain district in Persia, but perfectly in unison with the vocal exertions of the companion of his imprisonment, a large sow. I approached—removed the barrier: the boy and the animal escaped together, and I found myself alone in the centre of this miserable asylum of human wretchedness—the residence of an *Irish peasant.* To those who have only contemplated this useful order of society in England, "where every rood of ground maintains its man,"[24] and where the peasant liberally enjoys the *comforts* as well as the necessaries of life, the wretched picture which the interior of an *Irish* cabin presents, would be at once an object of compassion and disgust.*

Almost suffocated, and not surprised that it was deserted *pro tempo,* I hastened away, and was attracted towards a ruinous barn by a full chorus of females—where a group of young females were seated round an old hag

*Sometimes excavated from a hill, sometimes erected with loose stones, but most generally built of mud; the *cabin* is divided into two apartments, the one littered with straw and coarse rugs, and sometimes (but very rarely) furnished with the luxury of *a chaff bed,* serves as a dormitory not only to the family of both sexes, but in general to any animal they are so fortunate as to possess; the other chamber answers for every purpose of domesticity, though almost destitute of every domestic implement, except the iron pot in which the potatoes are boiled, and the stool on which they are flung. From these wretched hovels (which often appear amidst scenes that might furnish the richest models to poetic imitation) it is common to behold a group of children rush forth at the sound of a horse's foot or carriage wheel (regardless of the season's rigours), in a perfect state of nudity, or covered with the drapery of wretchedness, which gives to their appearance a still stronger character of poverty; yet even in these miserable huts you will seldom find the spirit of urbanity absent—the genius of hospitality *never.* I remember meeting with an instance of both, that made a deep impression on my heart: in the autumn of 1804, in the course of a morning's ramble with a charming Englishwoman, in the county of Sligo, I stopped to rest myself in a cabin, while she proceeded to pay a visit to the respectable family of the O'H______s, of Nymph's Field: when I entered I found it occupied by an old woman and her three granddaughters; two of the young ones were engaged in scutching flax, the other in some domestic employment. I was instantly hailed with the most cordial welcome: the hearth was cleared, the old woman's seat forced on me, eggs and potatoes roasted, and an apology for the deficiency of bread politely made, while the manners of my hostages betrayed a courtesy that almost amounted to adulation. They had all laid by their work on my entrance, and when I requested I might not interrupt their avocations, one of them replied, "I hope we know better—we can work any day, but we cannot any day have such a lady as you under our roof." Surely this was not the manners of a cabin, but a court.

---

a chaff bed: a bed or mattress stuffed with straw.

pro tempo: Latin: temporarily.

scutching: the process of beating flax with sticks in preparation for making fabric.

[24] Oliver Goldsmith, *The Deserted Village* (1770), ll. 58.

who formed the centre of the circle; they were all busily employed at their *wheels*, which I observed went merrily round in exact time with their song, and so intently were they engaged by both, that my proximity was unperceived. At last the song ceased—the wheel stood still—every eye was fixed on the old *primum mobile* of the circle, who, after a short pause, began a *solo* that gave much satisfaction to her young auditors, and taking up the strain, they again turned their wheels round in unison.—The whole was sung in Irish, and as soon as I was observed, suddenly ceased; the girls looked down and tittered—and the old woman addressed me *sans ceremonie*, and in a language I now heard for the first time.*

Supposing that some one among the number must understand English, I explained with all possible politeness the cause of my intrusion on this little harmonic society. The old woman looked up in my face and shook her head; *I* thought contemptuously—while the young ones, stifling their smiles, exchanged looks of compassion, doubtlessly at my ignorance of their language.

"So many languages a man knows," said Charles V, "so many times is he a man,"[25] and its certain *I* never felt myself less invested with the dignity of one, than while I stood twirling my stick, and "biding the encounter of

*These *conventions* of female industry, so frequent in many parts of Ireland, especially in the west and north, are called *Ouris*, and are thus ingeniously traced to their origin by General Vallancey:—Speaking of the Scythian religion, he observes, that the ceremonies pertaining to their worship were comprehended in the word "*Haman*," or "*Mann*." From this *Mann* many of our mountains receive their names. "Take an old Irish fable still in every one's mouth, of *Shliabhna Mann Mountain;* they say it was first inhabited by foreigners, who came from very distant countries; that they were of both sexes, and taught the Irish the art of *Oshíris*, or *Ouris;* that is, the management of flax or hemp, &c. &c. The word *Ouris*, now means a meeting of women or girls at one house or barn, to card a quantity of flax, and sometimes there are a hundred together. Wherever there is an *Ouris* the *Mann* comes invisibly and assists."—*Collectanea de Rebus Hibernica*, vol. iv. Preface, p. 8. [Charles Vallancey, ed., *Collecteana de Rebus Hibernicis*, 6 vols. (Dublin, 1770–1804), vol. 4, viii. Vallancey (1721–1812) was a military engineer and an important antiquarian in the late eighteenth-century movement to rediscover Ireland's past. Founded antiquarian journal *Collecteana de Rebus Hibernicis* (1770–1804) and published the influential *Grammar of the Hiberno-Celtic or Irish Language* (1773). Proposed a Phoenician source for Irish, associating it with the language of the Carthaginians and the Persians. See *Wild Irish Girl* (hereafter *WIG*) 255, n. 138. On the Irish Antiquarian Movement, in general, see O'Halloran's "Irish Re-Creations of the Gaelic Past" and Leerssen's *Mere Irish and Fíor-Ghael*, 294–376. Ed.]

---

primum mobile: Latin: prime mover.

sans ceremonie: French: without ceremony.

[25] A reference to William Robertson's *The History of the Reign of the Emperor Charles V*, 4 vols. (London, 1774).

the eyes," and smiles of these "spinners in the sun."[26] Here, you will say, was prejudice opposed to prejudice with a vengeance; but I comforted myself with the idea that the natives of Greenland, the most gross and savage of mortals, compliment a stranger by saying, "he is as well bred as a Greenlander."[27]

While thus situated, a sturdy looking young fellow, with that boldness of figure and openness of countenance so peculiar to the young Irish peasants, and with his hose and brogues suspended from a stick over his shoulder, approached, and hailed the party in Irish: the girls instantly pointed his attention towards me; he courteously accosted me in English, and having learnt the nature of my dilemma, offered to be my guide—"it will not take me above a mile out of my way, and if it did *two,* it would make no *odds,*" said he. I accepted his offer, and we proceeded together over the summit of the mountain.

In the course of our conversation (which was very fluently supported on his side), I learnt, that few strangers ever passing through this remote part of the province, and even very many of the gentry here speaking Irish, it was a rare thing to meet with any one wholly unacquainted with the language, which accounted for the surprise, and I believe contempt, my ignorance had excited.

When I inquired into the nature of those choral strains I had heard, he replied—"O! as to that, it is according to the old woman's fancy;" and in fact I learnt that Ireland, like Italy, has its *improvisatorés,* and that those who are gifted with the impromptu talent are highly estimated by their rustic compatriots;* and by what he added, I discovered that their inspirations are either drawn from the circumstances of the moment, from some striking

*In the romantic story of the beautiful *Deirdre,* as related in Keating's History of Ireland (page 176), it is mentioned, that Conor, King of Ulster, gave his ward a governess celebrated for her poetic talents, named *Leabharchan,* "as she could deliver *extempore* verses on any subject, and was consequently much respected by the nobility."—This was A. M. 3940. [Geoffrey Keating, *The General History of Ireland,* trans. Dermod O'Conner (2nd ed.; Dublin, 1723), 176. Keating [Seatrún Céitínn] (c. 1580–c. 1644), an Old English Catholic writer who wrote in Irish (*Foras Feasa ar Éireann*), set out to challenge Elizabethan representations of Ireland. Later commentators considered his work a foundational text. See *WIG* 107, n. 14. Ed.]

---

improvisatorés: French: improvisers.

[26] Unidentified.

[27] Goldsmith, *Natural History of Animals* (1776), vol. ii, 217: "It is common with them [Greenlanders], when they see a quiet stranger, to say that he is almost as well bred as a Greenlander."

excellence or palpable defect in some of the company present, or from some humorous incident or local event generally known.

As soon as we arrived at the little *auberge* of the little village, I ordered my courteous guide his breakfast, and having done all due honour to my own, we parted.

My route from the village to Bally___ lay partly through a desolate bog, whose burning surface, heated by a vertical sun, gave me no inadequate idea of *Arabia Deserta;* and the pangs of an acute head-ach, brought on by exercise more violent than my still delicate constitution was equal to support, determined me to defer my journey until the meridian ardors were abated; and taking your Horace from my pocket, I wandered into a shady path, "impervious to the noon-tide ray." Throwing my "listless length" at the foot of a spreading beech, I had already got to that sweet ode to Lydia, which Scaliger in his enthusiasm,[28] declares he would rather have written than to have possessed the monarchy of Naples, when somebody accosted me in Irish, and then with a "God save you, Sir!" I raised my eyes, and beheld a poor peasant driving, or rather soliciting, a sorry lame cow to proceed.

"May be," said he, taking off his hat, "your Honour would be after telling me what's the hour?" "Later than I supposed, my good friend," replied I; rising, "it is past two." He bowed low, and stroking the face of his companion, added, "well, the day is yet young, but you and I have a long journey before us, my poor Driminduath."[29]

"And how far are you going, friend?"

"Please your Honour, two miles beyond Bally___."

"It is my road exactly, and you, Driminduath, and I, may perform the journey together." The poor fellow seemed touched and surprized by my condescension, and profoundly bowed his sense of it, while the curious *triumviri* set off on their pedestrian tour together.

I now cast an eye over the person of my *compagnon de voyage.* It was a tall, thin, athletic figure, "bony and gaunt,"[30] with an expressive countenance,

---

auberge: French: inn.

triumviri: Latin: commissions, boards, ruling bodies comprising three members.

compagnon de voyage: French: traveling companion.

[28] Quintus Horatius Flaccus (65 BC–8 BC), Roman lyric poet and satirist; see his *Odes,* I. viii; Edward Moore, *Solomon, A Serenata* (1745), pt. II, l. 26: "impervious to the noon-tide ray"; Thomas Gray, *Elegy Written in a Country Church-Yard* (1751), ll. 104: "His listless length at noontide would he stretch"; Julius Caesar Scaliger (1484–1558), classical scholar and author of *Poetice* (1561).

[29] Likely a reference to "Droimfhionn Donn Dilis," a traditional song with Jacobite resonances. Literal translation from the Irish is "the black white-backed cow."

[30] James Thomson, *The Seasons* (1726–30), "Winter," 1. 394.

marked features, a livid complexion, and a quantity of coarse black hair hanging about the face; the drapery was perfectly appropriate to the wearer—an under garment composed of "*shreds* and *patches*,"[31] was partially covered with an old great coat of coarse frize, fastened on the breast with a large wooden skewer, the sleeves hanging down on either side unoccupied,* and a pair of yarn hose which scarcely reached *mid-leg*, left the ancle and foot naked.†

Driminduath seemed to share in the obvious poverty of her master—she was almost an anatomy, and scarcely able to crawl. "Poor beast!" said he, observing I looked at her, "Poor beast! little she dreamed of coming back the road she went, and little able she is to go it, poor soul; not that I am *overly* sorry I could not get nobody to take her off my hands at all at all; though to be sure 'tis better loose one's cow nor one's wife, any day in the year."

"And had you no alternative?" I asked.

"Anan!" exclaimed he, staring.

"Were you obliged to part with one or the other?" Sorrow is garrulous, and in the natural selfishness of its suffering, seeks to lessen the weight of its woe by participation. In a few minutes I was master of Murtoch O'Shaughnassey's story:‡ he was the husband of a sick wife; the father of six children, and a labourer, or *cotter*, who worked daily throughout the year for the hut that sheltered the heads, and the little potatoe rick which was the sole subsistence, of his family. He had taken a few acres of ground, he said, from his employer's steward, to set grass potatoes in, by which he hoped to make something handsome; that to enable himself to pay for them, he had gone to work in Leinster during the last harvest, "where, please your Honour," he added, "a poor man gets more for his labour than in Connaught;§ but here it was my luck (and bad luck it was), to get

* This manner of wearing the coat, so general among the peasantry, is deemed by the natives of the county of Galway a remnant of the Spanish modes.

† They are called "*triathians*."—Thus in a curious dissertation on an ancient marble statue, of a bag-piper, by Signor Canonico Orazio Maccari, of Cortona, he notices, "*Nudi* sono i piedi ma due rozze calighe pastorali cuoprone *le gambe*." [Italian: The feet are bare, but two rough sandals cover the legs. Ed.]

‡ Neither the rencontre with, nor the character or story of Murtoch, partakes in the least degree of fiction.

§ This is a very general practice, and though attended frequently with fatal consequences, still pursued; for by over labour, over heatings, fatigue and colds (caught by

---

frize: a type of coarse woolen cloth associated with Ireland.

cotter: Farm laborer in pre-famine Ireland who, in return for a cottage, a small plot of land, and turf-cutting rights, paid rent by working a predetermined number of days for his landlord.

[31] Shakespeare, *Hamlet*, III. iv. 103.

the shaking fever upon me, so that I returned sick and sore to my poor people, without a cross to bless myself with, and then there was an end of my fine grass potatoes, for devil receive the sort they'd let me dig till I paid for the ground; and what was worse, the steward was going to turn us out of our cabin, because I had not worked out the rent with him as usual, and not a potatoe had I for the children, besides finding my wife and two boys in a fever: the boys got well, but my poor wife has been decaying away ever since; so I was fain to sell my poor Driminduath here, which was left me by my gossip, in order to pay my rent and get some nourishment for my poor woman, who I believe was just weak at heart for the want of it; and so, as I was after telling your Honour, I left home yesterday for a *fair* twenty-five good miles off, but my poor Driminduath has got such bad usage of late, and was in such bad plight, that nobody would bid nothing for her, and so we are both returning home as we went, with full hearts and empty stomachs."

This was uttered with an air of despondency that touched my very soul, and I involuntarily presented him some sea biscuit I had in my pocket. He thanked me, and carelessly added, "that it was the first morsel he had tasted for twenty-four hours;* not," said he, "but I can fast with any one, and well

lying in numbers together on the earth, and only covered with a blanket), these poor adventurers return home to their expecting families with fevers lurking in their veins, or suffering under violent ague fits, which they call shaking fevers.

It is well known that within these thirty years the Connaught peasant laboured for *three-pence* a day and two meals of potatoes and milk, and four-pence when he maintained himself; while in Leinster the harvest hire rose from eight-pence to a shilling. Riding out one day near the village of Castletown Delvin, in Westmeath, in company with the younger branches of the respectable family of the F___ns, of that country, we observed two young men lying at a little distance from each other in a dry ditch, with some lighted turf burning near them; they both seemed on the verge of eternity, and we learned from a peasant who was passing, that they were Connaught men who had come to Leinster to work; that they had been disappointed, and owing to want and fatigue, had been first seized with agues and then with fevers of so fatal a nature, that no one would suffer them to remain in their cabins; owing to the benevolent exertions of my young friends we, however, found an asylum for these unfortunates, and had the happiness of seeing them return comparatively well and happy to their native province.

*The temperance of an Irish peasant in this respect is almost incredible; many of them are satisfied with one meal a day—none of them exceed two—breakfast and supper; which invariably consists of potatoes, sometimes with, sometimes without milk. One of the rules observed by the *Finian band*, or ancient militia of Ireland, was to eat but once in the twenty-four hours.—See *Keating's History of Ireland*. [Keating, *The History of Ireland*, 270. Ed.]

---

gossip: godparent.

it is for me I can." He continued brushing an intrusive tear from his eye; and the next moment whistling a lively air, he advanced to his cow, talked to her in Irish, in a soothing tone, and presenting her such wild flowers and blades of grass as the scanty vegetation of the bog afforded, turned round to me with a smile of self satisfaction and said, "One can better suffer themselves a thousand times over than see one's poor dumb beast want: it is next, please your Honour, to seeing one's child in want—God help him who has witnessed both!"

"And art thou then (I mentally exclaimed) that intemperate, cruel, idle savage, an Irish peasant? with an heart thus tenderly alive to the finest feelings of humanity; patiently labouring with daily exertion for what can scarce afford thee a bare subsistence; sustaining the unsatisfied wants of nature without a murmur; nurtured in the hope (the *disappointed hope*) of procuring nourishment for *her* dearer to thee than thyself, tender of thy animal as thy child, and suffering the consciousness of *their* wants to absorb all consideration of thy own; and yet resignation smooths the furrow which affliction has traced upon thy brow, and the national exility of thy character cheers and supports the natural susceptibility of thy heart." In fact, he was at that moment humming an Irish song by my side.

I need not tell you that the first village we arrived at I furnished him with means of procuring a comfortable dinner for himself and Driminduath, and advice and medicine from the village apothecary for his wife. Poor fellow! his surprise and gratitude was expressed in the true hyperbola of Irish emotion.

Meantime I walked on to examine the ruins of an abbey, where in about half an hour I was joined by Murtoch and his patient companion, whom he assured me he had regaled with some hay, as he had himself with a glass of whiskey.—What a breakfast for a famishing man!

"It is a dreadful habit, Murtoch," said I.

"It is so, please your Honour," replied he, "but then it is meat, drink, and clothes to us, for we forget we have but little of one and less of the other, when we get *the drop* within us;* Och, long life to them that

* "J'ai souvent entendu reprocher la paresse et l'ivrogné au paysan. Mais lorsque on est reduit a mourir de faim, n'est-ce pas preferâble de ne rien faire, puisque le travail le plus assidus ne sauroit-en empecher; dans cette situation n'est il pas fort simple de boire quand on le peut une goutte de fleuve de Lethe pour oublier sa misere."—*La Tocknay.* [Chevalier de la Tocnaye, *Promenade d'un Françaïse dans l'Irelande,* 2 vols. (Dublin, 1797), 147. John Stevenson's translation, *A Frenchman's Walk through Ireland 1796–97* reads: "Often I have heard the peasant reproached for his idleness and drunkenness, but when one is reduced to danger of dying from hunger, is it not a better thing to do nothing, since the most assiduous work will hinder the evil from arriving? In such a situation also, is it not natural to drink when one can, a drop from the waters of Lethe, in order to forget one's misery?" 127–28. See *TINT* 357–59. Ed.]

lightened the tax on the whiskey,[32] for by my safe conscience, if they had left it on another year we should have forgotten how to drink it."

I shall make no comment on Murtoch's unconscious philippic against the legislature, but surely a government has but little right to complain of those popular disorders to which in a certain degree it may be deemed accessary, by removing the strongest barrier that confines within moral bounds the turbulent passions of the lower orders of society.

To my astonishment, I found that Murtoch had only purchased for his sick wife a little wine and a small piece of bacon:* both, he assured me, were universal and sovereign remedies, and better than any thing the *physicianers* could prescribe, to keep the disorder *from the heart*.† The spirits of Murtoch were now quite afloat, and during the rest of our journey the vehemence, pliancy, and ardour of the Irish character strongly betrayed itself in the manners of this poor unmodified Irishman; while the natural facetiousness of a temperament "complexionally pleasant,"[33] was frequently succeeded by such heart-rending accounts of poverty and distress, as shed involuntary tears on those cheeks which but a moment before were distended by the exertions of a boisterous laugh.

Nothing could be more wildly sweet than the whistle or song of the ploughman or labourer as we passed along; it was of so singular a nature, that I frequently paused to catch it; it is a species of voluntary recitative, and so melancholy, that every plaintive note breathes on the heart of the auditor a tale of hopeless despondency or incurable woe. By heavens! I could have wept as I listened, and found a luxury in tears.‡

The evening was closing in fast, and we were within a mile of Bally____, when to a day singularly fine, succeeded one of the most violent storms of

* It is common to see them come to gentlemen's houses with a little vial bottle to beg a table spoonful of wine (for a sick relative), which they esteem the elixir of life.

† To be able to keep any disorder from the heart, is supposed (by the lower orders of the Irish) to be the secret of longevity.

‡ Mr. Walker, in his Historical Memoir of the Irish Bards, has given a specimen of the Irish plough-tune; and adds, "While the Irish ploughman drives his team, and the female peasant milks her cow, they warble a succession of wild notes which bid defiance to the rules of composition, yet are inexpressibly sweet."—Page 132. [Joseph Cooper Walker, *Historical Memoirs of the Irish Bards* (Dublin, 1786). Walker (1761–1810), an important antiquarian, greatly influenced Owenson's novel. His *Historical Memoirs* affirms the dignity of Irish culture in its examination of music, painting, and dress. Ed.]

---

philippic: a bitter attack, invective, or denunciation.

[32] As part of an ongoing campaign to persuade the Irish peasant to drink beer rather than whiskey, the Irish parliament abolished the tax on beer in 1795. Also, see *CR* 80.

[33] Robert Blair, *The Grave* (1753), ll. 115–16.

rain and wind I had ever witnessed. Murtoch, who seemed only to regard it on my account, insisted on throwing his great coat over me, and pointed to a cabin at a little distance, where, he said, "if my Honour would demean myself so far, I could get good shelter for the night."

"Are you sure of that, Murtoch?" said I.

Murtoch shook his head, and looking full in my face, said something in Irish; which at my request he translated—the words were—"Happy are *they* whose roof shelters the head of the traveller."

"And is it indeed a source of happiness to you, Murtoch?"

Murtoch endeavoured to convince me it *was*, even upon a *selfish* principle: "For (said he) it is thought right lucky to have a stranger sleep beneath one's roof."

If superstition was ever thus on the side of benevolence, even reason herself would hesitate to depose her.—We had now reached the door of the cabin, which Murtoch opened without ceremony, saying as he entered—"May God and the Virgin Mary pour a blessing on this house"!* The family, who were all circled round a fine turf fire that blazed on the earthen hearth, replied, "Come in, and a thousand welcomes"—for Murtoch served interpreter, and translated as they were spoken these warm effusions of Irish cordiality. The master of the house, a venerable old man, perceiving me, made a low bow, and added, "You are welcome, and ten thousand welcomes, *gentleman*."†

So you see I hold my letter patent of nobility in my countenance, for I had not yet divested myself of Murtoch's costume—while in the act, the best stool was wiped for me, the best seat at the fire forced on me, and on being admitted into the social circle, I found its central point was a round oaken stool heaped with smoking potatoes thrown promiscuously over it.

To partake of this national diet I was strongly and courteously solicited, while as an incentive to an appetite that needed none, the old dame pro-

* A *salutation* and a *benediction* are synonymous, among the lower orders of the Irish.

† "*Failte augus cead ro ag duine uasal.*" The term *gentleman,* however, is a very inadequate version of the Irish UASAL, which is an epithet of superiority that indicates more than mere gentility of birth can bestow, although that requisite is also included. In a curious dialogue between Ossian and St. Patrick, in an old Irish poem, in which the former relates the combat between Oscar and Illan, St. Patrick solicits him to the detail, addressing him as, "*Ossian uasal, a mhic Fionne.*" "*Ossian the Noble*—the son of Fingal." [Ossian refers to Oisín, son of Fionn mac Cumhaill, mythical heroes of the "Fionn Cycle." These stories featured Irish society in the third century AD, but according to the tradition, a number of the *fianna* survived into the Christian era. The dialogues between Oisín and St. Patrick bridge these two civilizations and often result in heated debate. For the "old Irish poem," see Charlotte Brooke's *Reliques of Irish Poetry* (Dublin, 1789), 73n. ED.]

duced what she called a *madder* of sweet milk, in contradistinction to the sour milk of which the rest partook; while the cow which supplied the luxury* slumbered most amicably with a large pig at no great distance from where I sat; and Murtoch glancing an eye at *both,* and then looking at me, seemed to say, "You see into what snug quarters we have got." While I (as I sat with my damp clothes smoking by the turf fire, my madder of milk in one hand, and hot potatoe in the other), assured him by a responsive glance, that I was fully sensible of the comforts of our situation.

As soon as supper was finished the old man said grace, the family piously blessed themselves, and the stool being removed, the hearth swept, and the fire replenished from the bog, Murtoch threw himself on his back along a bench,† and unasked began a song, the wild and plaintive melody of which went at once to the soul.

When he had concluded, I was told it was the lamentation of the poor Irish for the loss of their *glibbs,* or long tresses, of which they were deprived by the arbitrary will of Henry VIII.—The song (composed in his reign), is called the *Cualin,*‡ which I am told is literally, the fair ringlet.

When the English had drawn a pale round their conquests in this country, such of the inhabitants as were compelled to drag on their existence beyond the barrier, could no longer afford to cover their heads with metal, and were necessitated to rely on the resistance of their matted locks. At length this necessity became "the fashion of their choice." [34]

The partiality of the ancient Irish to long hair is still to be traced in their descendants of both sexes, the women in particular; for I observed that the

* To supply the want of this (by them) highly esteemed luxury, they cut an onion into a bowl of water, into which they dip their potatoes.—This they call a *scadan caoch,* or blind herring.

† This curious vocal position is of very ancient origin in Connaught, though now by no means prevalent. Formerly the songster not only lay on his back, but had a weight pressed on his chest. The author's father recollects to have seen a man in the county of Mayo, of the name of O'Melvill, who sung for him in this position some years back.

‡ The Cualin is one of the most popular and beautiful Irish airs extant.

---

madder: a square wooden drinking vessel.

pale: the area around Dublin (typically including the medieval counties of Dublin, Meath, Louth, and Kildare) under English control and fortified against incursions from Gaelic Ireland.

[34] Sir Edward Poynings, lord deputy of Ireland 1494–95, introduced a series of laws in 1494 ("Poynings's Laws"), the goal of which was to reinforce English control within the pale. Henry VIII continued these practices during his reign, and restricted aspects of Irish dress including the "glib," or the wearing of long hair that could cover the face.

young *ones* only wore their "native ornament of *hair*,"[35] which sometimes flows over their shoulders, sometimes is fastened up in tresses, with a pin or bodkin. A fashion more in unison with grace and nature, though less in point with formal neatness, than the round-eared caps and large hats of our rustic fair in England.

Almost every word of Murtoch's lamentation was accompanied by the sighs and mournful lamentations of his auditors, who seemed to sympathize as tenderly in the sufferings of their progenitors, as though they had themselves been victims to the tyranny which had caused them. The arch-policy of the "ruthless king," who destroyed at once the records of a nation's woes, by extirpating "the tuneful race,"[36] whose art would have perpetuated them to posterity, never appeared to me in greater force than at that moment.

In the midst, however, of the melancholy which involved the mourning auditors of Murtoch, a piper entered, and seating himself by the fire, *sans façon,* drew his pipes from under his coat, and struck up an Irish lilt of such inspiring animation, as might have served St. Basil of Limoges, the merry patron of dancing, for a jubilate.

In a moment, in the true pliability of Irish temperament, the whole pensive group cheered up, flung away their stools, and as if bit to merry madness by a tarantula, set to dancing jigs with all their hearts, and all their *strength* into the bargain. Murtoch appeared not less skilled in the dance than song; and every one (according to the just description of Goldsmith, who was a native of this province), seemed

"To seek renown,
By holding out to tire each other down."[37]

Although much amused by this novel style of devotion at the shrine of Terpsichore, yet as the night was now calm, and an unclouded moon dispersed the gloom of twilight obscurity, I arose to pursue my journey. Murtoch would accompany me, though our hospitable friends did their utmost to prevail on both to remain for the night.

---

sans façon: French: without ceremony.

jubilate: a call to rejoice.

Terpsichore: the muse of dancing.

[35] John Dryden, "Meleager and Atalanta" (1700), ll. 69.

[36] Thomas Gray, "The Bard: a Pindaric Ode" (1757), I. l. i: "Ruin seize thee, ruthless king"; many examples of "the tuneful race" in eighteenth-century poetry; see Henry Needler's "To the Earl of Roscommon" (1724), l. i, and Alexander Pope's *The Iliad of Homer,* Book II, l. 722.

[37] Goldsmith, *The Deserted Village,* ll. 25–26.

When I insisted on my host receiving a trifle, I observed poverty struggling with pride, and gratitude superior to both: he at last reluctantly consented to be prevailed on, by my assurance of forgetting to call on them again when I passed that way, if I were now denied. I was followed for several paces by the whole family, who parted *with,* as they *received* me, with blessings;—for their courtesy upon all occasions, seems interwoven with their religion, and not to be pious in their forms of etiquette, is not to be polite.

Benevolent and generous beings! whose hard labour

"Just gives what life requires, but gives no more;"[38]

yet who, with the ever ready smile of heart-felt welcome, are willing to share that hard-earned little with the weary traveller whom chance conducts to your threshold, or the solitary wanderer whom necessity throws upon your bounty. How did my heart smite me, while I received the cordial rites of hospitality from your hands, for the prejudices I had hitherto nurtured against your characters. But your smiling welcome, and parting benediction, retributed my error—in the feeling of remorse they awakened.

It was late when I reached Bally___, a large, ugly, irregular town, near the sea coast; but fortunately meeting with a chaise, I threw myself into it, gave Murtoch my address, (who was all amazement at discovering I was son to the Lord of the Manor), and arrived without further adventure at this antique *chateau,* more gratified by the result of my little pedestrian tour, than if (at least in the present state of my feelings), I had performed it Sesostris-like, in a triumphal chariot drawn by kings; for "so weary, stale, flat, and unprofitable,"[39] appear to me the tasteless pleasures of the world I have left, that every sense, every feeling, is in a state of revolt against its sickening joys, and their concommitant sufferings.

Adieu! I am sending this off by a courier extraordinary, to the next post-town, in the hope of receiving one from you by the same hand.

H. M.

Letter III

TO J. D. ESQ. M. P.

I PERCEIVE my father emulates the policy of the British Legislature, and delegates English ministers to govern his Irish domains. Who, do you

---

Sesostris: Sesostris I–III were kings of Egypt in the Egyptian twelfth dynasty, c. 1908–1818 BC.

[38] Goldsmith, *The Deserted Village,* l. 60.

[39] Shakespeare, *Hamlet,* I. ii. 132.

think, is his *fac-totum* here? The rascally son of his cunning Leicestershire steward who unites all his father's artifice to a proportionable share of roguery of his own. I have had some reason to know the fellow; but his servility of manner, and apparent rigid discharge of his duties, has imposed on my father; who, with all his superior mind, is to be imposed on, by those who know how to find the clue to his point of fallibility: his noble soul can never stoop to dive into the minute vices of a rascal of this description.

Mr. Clendinning was absent from M___ house when I arrived, but attended me the next morning at breakfast, with that fawning civility of manner I abhor, and which, contrasted with the manly courteousness of my late companion, never appeared more grossly obvious. He endeavoured to amuse me with a detail of the ferocity, cruelty, and uncivilized state of those among whom (as he hinted), I was banished for my sins. He had now, he said, been near five years among them, and had never met an individual of the lower order who did not deserve an halter at least: for his part, he kept a tight hand over them, and he was justified in so doing, or his Lord would be the sufferer; for few of them would pay their rents till their cattle were driven, or some such measure was taken with them. And as for the labourers and workmen, a slave-driver was the only man fit to deal with them: they were all rebellious, idle, cruel, and treacherous; and for his part, he never expected to leave the country with his life.

It is not possible a better defence for the imputed turbulence of the Irish peasantry could be made, than that which lurked in the unprovoked accusations of this narrow-minded sordid steward, who, it is evident, wished to forestall the complaints of those on whom he had exercised the native tyranny of his disposition (even according to his own account), by every species of harassing oppression within the compass of his ability. For if power is a dangerous gift even in the regulated mind of elevated rank, what does it become in the delegated authority of ignorance, meanness and illiberality?*

* "A horde of tyrants exist in Ireland, in a class of men that are unknown in England, in the multitude of *agents of absentees*, small proprietors, who are the pure Irish squires, middle men who take large farms, and squeeze out a forced kind of profit by letting them in small parcels; lastly, the little farmers themselves, who exercise the same insolence they receive from their superiors, on those unfortunate beings who are placed at the extremity of the scale of degradation—the Irish Peasantry!"—*An Enquiry into the Causes of Popular Discontents in Ireland, &c. &c.* [William Parnell, *An Inquiry into the Causes of Popular Discontents in Ireland. By an Irish Country Gentleman*, 2nd ed. (London, 1805), 30. Also see Edgeworth's note on "*Middle-men*," *CR* 38, and Young's "On the Tenantry of Ireland," *TINT* 344–52. Ed.]

---

fac-totum: a servant who has the entire management of his master's affairs.

My father, however, by frequent visitations to his Irish estates (within these few years at least), must afford to his suffering tenantry an opportunity of redress; for who that ever approached him with a *tear* of suffering, left his presence with a tear of gratitude! But many, very many of the English nobility who hold immense tracts of land in this country, and draw from hence in part the suppliance of their luxuries, have never visited their estates, since conquest first put them in the possession of their ancestors. Ours, you know, fell to us in the Cromwellian wars,[40] but since the time of General M___, who earned them by the sword, my father, his lineal descendant, is the first of the family who ever visited them. And certainly a wish to conciliate the affections of his tenantry, could alone induce him to spend so much of his time here as he has done; for the situation of this place is bleak and solitary, and the old mansion, like the old manor houses of England, has neither the architectural character of an antique structure, nor the accommodation of a modern one.

"*Ayant l'air delabri, sans l'air antique.*"

On inquiring for the key of the library, Mr. Clendinning informed me his Lord always took it with him, but that a box of books had come from England a few days before my arrival.

As I suspected, they were all law books—well, be it so; there are few sufferings more acute than those which forbid complaint, because they are self-created.

Four days have elapsed since I began this letter, and I have been prevented from continuing it merely for want of something to say.

I cannot now sit down, as I once did, and give you a history of my ideas or sensation, in the deficiency of fact or incident; for I have survived my sensations, and my ideas are dry and exhausted.

I cannot now trace my joys to their source, or my sorrows to their spring, for I am destitute of their present, and insensible to their former existence. The energy of youthful feeling is subdued, and the vivacity of warm emotion worn out by its own violence. I have lived too fast in a moral as well as a physical sense, and the principles of my intellectual, as well as my natural constitution are, I fear, fast hastening to decay. I live the tomb of my expiring mind, and preserve only the consciousness of my wretched

---

"Ayant l'air . . .": French: "Dilapidated without being ancient."

[40]Oliver Cromwell (1600–58) campaigned in Ireland between August 15, 1649, and May 26, 1650. His forces sacked Drogheda (September 11, 1649) and Wexford (October 11, 1649), resulting in massacres of the native Irish population. After the military campaign, Cromwell rewarded many of his supporters with lands appropriated from Catholic landowners.

state, without the power, and almost without the wish to be otherwise than what I am. And yet, God knows I am nothing less than contented.

Would you hear my journal? I rise late to my solitary breakfast, because it is solitary; then to study, or rather to yawn over *Giles* versus *Haystack*, until (to check the creeping effects of lethargy), I rise from my reading desk, and lounge to a window, which commands a boundless view of a boundless bog; then "with what appetite I may,"[41] sit down to a joyless dinner. Sometimes, when seduced by the blandishments of an evening singularly beautiful, I quit my *den*, and *prowl* down to the sea-shore, where, throwing myself at the foot of some cliff that "battles o'er the deep,"[42] I fix my vacant eye on the stealing waves that

"Idly swell against the rocky coast,
And break—as break those glittering shadows,
Human joys."[43]

Then wet with the ocean spray and evening dew, return to bed, merely to avoid the intrusive civilities of Mr. Clendinning. "Thus wear the hours away."

I had heard that the neighbourhood about M___ house was good: I can answer for its being populous. Although I took every precaution to prevent my arrival being known, yet the natives have come down on me in hordes, and this in all the form of *haut ton,* as the innumerable cards of the clans of Os and Macs evince. I have, however, neither been visible to the visitants, nor accepted their invitations; for "man delights me not, nor woman either."[44] Nor woman either! Oh! uncertainty of all human propensities! Yet so it is, that every letter that composes the word *woman!* seems cabilistical, and rouses every principle of aversion and disgust within me; while I often ask myself with Tasso,

"Se pur ve nelle amor alcun diletto."[45]

It is certain, that the diminutive body of our worthy steward, is the abode of the transmigrated soul of some *West Indian* planter. I have been engaged these two days in listening to, and retributing those injuries his

---

haut ton: French: high style.

cabilistical: possessing a hidden meaning.

[41] Samuel Bishop, "Dinner" (1796), ll. 35.

[42] Shakespeare, *Hamlet,* II. ii. 310.

[43] Young, *Night Thoughts* (1742–45), Night V, ll. 1040–42.

[44] Shakespeare, *Hamlet,* II. ii. 309–10.

[45] Torquato Tasso, *Aminta* (1573), I. i. 9–10.

tyranny has inflicted, in spite of his rage, eloquence, and threats, none of which have been spared. The victims of his oppression haunt me in walks, fearful lest their complaints should come to the knowledge of this puissant *major domo.*

"But why," said I to one of the sufferers, after a detail of seized geese, pounded cows, extra-labour, cruelty extorted, ejectments, &c. &c. given in all the tedious circumlocution of Irish oratory,—"why not complain to my father when he comes among you?"

"Becaise, please your Honour, my Lord stays but a few days at a time here together, nor that same neither: besides, we be loath to trouble his Lordship, for feard it would be after coming to measter Clendinnin's ears, which would be the ruination of us all; and then when my Lord is at the Lodge, which he mostly is, he is always out amongst the quality, so he is."

"What Lodge?" said I.

"Why, please your Honour, where my Lord mostly takes up when he comes here, the place that belonged to measter Clendinnin, who called it the *Lodge,* becaise the good old Irish name that was upon it happened not to hit his fancy."

In the evening I asked Clendinning if my father did not sometimes reside at the Lodge? He seemed surprised at my information, and said, that was the name he had given to a ruinous old place which, with a few acres of indifferent land, he had purchased out of his hard labour, and which his Lord having taken an unaccountable liking to, rented from him, and was actually the tenant of his own steward.

O! what arms of recrimination I should be furnished with against my rigidly moral father, should I discover this remote *Cassino* (for remote I understand it is), to be the *harem* of some wild Irish *Sultana;* for I strongly suspect "that metal more attractive"[46] than the cause he assigns, induces him to pay an annual visit to a country to which, till within these few years, he nurtured the strongest prejudices. You know there are but 19 years between him and my brother; and his feelings are so unblunted by vicious pursuits, his life has been guided by such epicurean principles of enjoyment, that he still retains much of the first warm flush of juvenile existence, and has only sacrificed to time, its follies and its ignorance. I swear, at this moment he is a younger man than either of his sons; the one chilled by the coldness of an icy temperament into premature old age, and the other!!!

* * * * * * * * * *

major domo: Italian and Spanish: head servant of a wealthy household.

Cassino: Italian: little house by the sea.

[46] Shakespeare, *Hamlet,* III. ii. 110.

Murtoch has been to see me. I have procured him a little farm, and am answerable for the rent. I sent his wife some rich wine; she is recovering very fast. Murtoch is all gratitude for the wine, but I perceive his faith still lies in the *bacon!*

Letter IV

TO J. D. ESQ. M. P.

I CAN support this wretched state of non-existence, this *articula mortis,* no longer. I cannot read—I cannot think—nothing touches, nothing interests me; neither is it permitted me to indulge my sufferings in solitude. These hospitable people still weary me with their attentions, though they must consider me as a sullen misanthropist, for I persist in my invisibility. I can escape them no longer but by flight—professional study is out of the question, for a time at least. I mean, therefore, to "take the wings of"[47] some fine morning and seek a change of being in a change of place; for a perpetual state of evagation alone, keeps up the flow and ebb of existence in my languid frame. My father's last letter informs me he is obliged by business to postpone his journey for a month; this leaves me so much the longer master of myself. By the time we meet, my mind may have regained its native tone. *Laval* too, writes for a longer leave of absence, which I most willingly grant. It is a weight removed off my shoulders; I would be savagely free.

I thank you for your welcome letters, and will do what I can to satisfy your antiquarian taste; and I would take your advice, and study the Irish language, were my powers of comprehension equal to the least of the philological excellencies of *Tom Thumb,* or *Goody Two Shoes,*—but alas!

"Se perchetto a me Stesso quale acquisto,
Faro mai che me piaccia." *[48]

Villa di Marino, Atlantic Ocean.

Having told Mr. Clendinning that I should spend a few days in wandering about the country, I mounted my horse. So I determined to roam free

* Torquatto Tasso.

---

articula mortis: Latin: moment or state of death.

[47] Psalm 139:9: "If I take the wings of the morning, and dwell in the uttermost parts of the sea."

[48] Torquato Tasso, *Aminta* (1573), I. ii. 22–25: "what conquest can I make who can appease me?"

and unrestrained by the presence of a servant, to Mr. Clendinning's utter amazement, I ordered a few changes of linen, my drawing-book and pocket escritoire, to be put in a small valise, which, with all due humility, I had strapped on the back of my steed, whom, by the bye, I expect will be as celebrated as the *Rozinante* of Don Quixote, or the *Beltenebros L'Amadis de Gaul;*[49] and thus accoutred, set off on my peregrination, the most listless knight that ever entered on the lists of errantry.

You will smile, when I tell you my first point of attraction was the *Lodge;* to which (though with some difficulty) I found my way; for it lies in a most wild and unfrequented direction, but so infinitely superior in situation to M___ house, that I no longer wonder at my father's preference. Every feature that constitutes either the beauty or sublime of landscape, is here finely combined. Groves druidically venerable—mountains of Alpine elevation—expansive lakes, and the boldest and most romantic sea coast I ever beheld, alternately diversify and enrich its scenery; while a number of young and flourishing plantations evince the exertion of a taste in my father, he certainly has not betrayed in the disposition of his hereditary domains. I found this *Tusculum* inhabited only by a decent old man and his superannuated wife. Without informing them who I was, I made a feigned wish to make the place a pretext for visiting it. The old man smiled at the idea, and shook his head, presuming that I must be indeed a stranger in the country, as my accent denoted, for that this spot belonged to a great *English Lord,* whom he verily believed would not resign it for his own fine place some miles off; but when, with some jesuitical artifice, I endeavoured to trace the cause of this attachment, he said it was his Lordship's fancy, and that there was no accounting for people's fancies.

"That is all very true," said I; "but is it the house only that seized on your Lord's fancy?"

"Nay, for the matter of that," said he, "the lands are far more finer; the house, though large, being no great things." I begged in this instance to judge for myself, and a few shillings procured me not only free egress, but the confidence of the ancient *Cicerone.*

This fancied *harem,* however, I found not only divested of its expected fair inhabitant, but wholly destitute of furniture, except what filled a

---

escritoire: a writing-desk, a bureau or secretary.

Tusculum: a favorite resort of the wealthy, fifteen miles southeast of Rome, where Cicero had a villa.

Cicerone: a guide who shows the antiquities of a place to strangers.

[49]The hero in Miguel de Cervantes's *Don Quixote* (1605–15) named his worn-down horse Rozinante. *Amadis De Gaula,* possibly Portuguese, a series of chivalrous prose romances dating from 1508.

bed-room occupied by my father, and an apartment which was *locked.* The old man with some tardiness produced the key, and I found this mysterious chamber was only a study; but closer inspection discovered, that almost all the books related to the language, history, and antiquities of Ireland.

So you see, in fact, my father's *Sultana* is no other than the *Irish Muse;* and never was son so tempted to become the rival of his father, since the days of Antiochus and Stratonice.[50] For, at a moment when my taste, like my senses, is flat and palled, nothing can operate so strongly as an incentive, as novelty. I strongly suspect that my father was aware of this, and that he had despoiled the temple, to prevent me becoming a worshipper at the same shrine. For the old man said he had received a letter from his Lord, ordering away all the furniture (except that of his own bed-room and study) to the manor house; the study and bed room however, will suffice me, and here I shall certainly pitch my head-quarters until my father's arrival.

I have already had some occasions to remark, that the warm susceptible character of the Irish is open to the least indication of courtesy and kindness.

My *politesse* to this old man, opened every sluice of confidence in his breast, and, as we walked down the avenue together, having thrown the bridle over my horse's neck, and offered him my arm, for he was lame, I inquired how this beautiful farm fell into the hands of Lord M___; still concealing from him that it was his son who demanded the question.

"Why, your Honour," said he, "the farm, though beautiful, is small; however, it made the best part of what remained of the patrimony of the Prince, when—"

"What Prince?" interrupted I, amazed.

"Why, the Prince of Inismore, to be sure, jewel, whose great forefathers once owned the half of the barony, from the Red Bog to the sea coast. Och! it is a long story, but I have heard my grandfather tell it a thousand times, how a great Prince of Inismore, in the wars of Queen Elizabeth,[51] here had a castle and a great tract of land on the *borders,* of which he was deprived, as the story runs, becaise he would neither cut his *glibbs,* shave his upper lip, nor shorten his shirt;* and so he was driven with the rest of us beyond

* From the earliest settlement of the English in this country, an inquisitorial persecution had been carried on against the national costume. In the reign of Henry V, there was an act passed against even the English colonists wearing a whisker on the upper lip, like the

[50] Antiochus the Great (242–187 BC), one of the Seleucid kings of the Hellenistic Syrian Empire. Married his stepmother, Stratonice, with consent of his father, Seleucus I Nicator.

[51] Elizabeth, Queen of England (1533–1603), maintained Henry VIII's policy of subduing native Irish rebellion. Lord Mountjoy finally defeated Irish forces, led by Hugh O'Neill, at the battle of Kinsale in December 1601.

the *pale.* The family, however, after a while, flourished greater nor ever. Och, and its themselves that might, for they were true Milesians[52] bred and born, every mother's soul of them. O! not a drop of *Strongbonean*[53] flowed in their Irish veins agrah! Well, as I was after telling your Honour, the family flourished, and beat all before them, for they had an army of *galloglasses* at their back,* until the Cromwellian wars broke out, and those same cold-hearted Presbyterians battered the fine *old ancient* castle of Inismore, and left it in the condition it now stands; and what was worse nor that, the poor old Prince was put to death in the arms of his fine young son, who tried to save him, and that by one of Cromwell's English Generals, who received the town-lands of Inismore, which lie near Bally___, as his reward. Now this English General who murdered the Prince, was no other than the ancestor of my Lord, to whom these estates descended from father to son. Aye, you may well start, Sir, it was a woeful piece of business; for of all their fine estates, nothing was left to the Princes of Inismore, but the ruins of their old castle, and the rocks that surround it; except this tight little bit of an estate here, on which the father of the present Prince built this house; becaise his Lady, with whom he got a handsome fortune, and who was descended from the Kings of Connaught, took a dislike to the castle; the story going that it was haunted by the murdered Prince; and what with building this house, and living like an Irish Prince, as he was every inch of him, and spending £3000 a-year out of £300, when he died (and the sun never shone upon such a funeral; the whiskey ran about like *ditch water,* and the country was stocked with pipes and tobacco for many a long year after. For the present Prince his son, would not be a bit behind with his father in any thing, and so signs on him, for he is not worth one guinea this blessed day, Christ save him);—well, as I was saying, when he died, he left things in a sad way, which his son has not the man to mind, for he was the spirit of a King, and lives in as much state as one to this day."

Irish; and in 1616, the Lord Deputy, in his instructions to the Lord President and Council, directed, that such as appeared in Irish robes or mantles, should be punished by fine and imprisonment.

*The second order of military in Ireland. [Gallowglasses were armored foot soldiers, and were considered valuable for their ability to sustain a cavalry charge. Ed.]

---

[52] Derived from *Milesius,* whose sons according to the *Leabhar Gabhála (Book of Invasions)* led the Goidelic conquest of Ireland. Since the sixteenth century, writers suggested that Milesius and his Phoenician followers settled in Ireland.

[53] Refers to Richard fitz Gilbert, alias Richard de Clare (d. 1176). After military victories at Waterford and Dublin, Strongbow recognized King Henry II as overlord of all his Irish acquisitions. Thus began the Anglo-Norman conquest of Ireland.

"But where, where does he live?" interrupted I, with breathless impatience.

"Why," continued this living Chronicle, in the true spirit of Irish replication, "he did live there in that Lodge, as they call it now, and in that room where my Lord keeps his books, was our young Princess born; her father never had but her, and loves her better than his own heart's blood, as well he may, the blessing of the Virgin Mary and the Twelve Apostles light on her sweet head. Well, the Prince would never let it come near him, that things were not going on well, and continued to take at great rents, farms that brought him in little; for being a Prince and a Milesian, it did not become him to look after such matters, and every thing was left to stewards and the like, until things coming to the worst, a rich English gentleman, as it was said, came over here, and offered the Prince, through his steward, a good round sum of money on this place, which the Prince, being harassed by his *spalpeen* creditors, and wanting a little ready money more than any other earthly thing, consented to receive the gentleman; sending him word he should have his own time; but scarcely was the mortgage a year old, when this same Englishman, (Oh, my curse lie about him, Christ pardon me), foreclosed it, and the fine old Prince not having as much as a shed to shelter his grey hairs under, was forced to fit up part of the old ruined castle, and open those rooms which it had been said were haunted. Discharging many of his old servants, he was accompanied to the castle by the family steward, the *fosterers*, the *nurse*,* the harper, and Father John, the chaplain.

"Och, it was a piteous sight the day he left this: he was leaning on the Lady Glorvina's arm, as he walked out to the chaise. "James Tyral," says he to me in Irish, for I caught his eye; "James Tyral," but he could say no more, for the old tenants kept crying about him, and he put his mantle to his eyes and hurried into the chaise; the Lady Glorvina kissing her hand to us all, and crying bitterly till she was out of sight. But then, Sir, what would you have of it: the Prince shortly after found out that this same Mr. *Mortgagee*,

*The custom of retaining the nurse who reared the children, has ever been, and is still in force among the most respectable families in Ireland, as it is still in modern, and was formerly in ancient *Greece*, and they are probably both derived from the same origin. We read, that when Rebecca left her father's house to marry Isaac at Beersheba, the nurse was sent to accompany her. But in Ireland, not only the nurse herself, but her husband and children, are objects of peculiar regard and attention, and are called *fosterers;* the claims of these fosterers frequently descend from generation to generation, and the tie which unites them is indissoluble. Sometimes, however, it is cemented by a less disinterested sentiment than affection; and the claims of the fosterers become an hereditary tax on the bounty of the fostered. [Genesis 24:59. Ed.]

---

spalpeen: Irish: a common workman or laborer, also implying small-minded.

was no other than a spalpeen steward of Lord M___'s. It was thought he would have at first run mad, when he found that almost the last acre of his hereditary lands was in the possession of the servant of his hereditary enemy; for so deadly is the hatred he bears my Lord, that upon my conscience, I believe the young Prince who held the bleeding body of his murdered father in his arms, felt not greater for the murdered, than our Prince does for the murderer's descendant.

"Now, my Lord is just such a man as God never made better, and wishing with all the veins in his heart to serve the old Prince, and do away all difference between them, what does he do jewel? but writes him a mighty pretty letter, offering this house and part of the land as a present. O! divil a word a lie I'm after telling you; but what would you have of it, but this offer sets the Prince madder than all; for you know that this was an insult on his honour, which warmed every drop of Milesian blood in his body, for he would rather starve to death all his life, than have it thought he would be obligated to any body at all at all for wherewithal to support him; so with that the Prince writes him a letter: it was brought by the old steward, who knew every line of the contents of it, though divil a line in it but two, and that same was but one and half, as one may say, and this it was, as the old steward told me:

'The son of the son of the son's son of Bryan Prince of Inismore, can receive no favour from the descendant of his ancestor's murderer.'

"Now it was plain enough to be seen, that my Lord took this to heart, as well he might faith; however, he considered that it came from a misfortunate Prince, he let it drop, and so this was all ever passed between them; however, he was angry enough with his steward, but measter Clendinnin put his *comehither* on him, and convinced him that the biggest rogue alive was an honest man."

"And the Prince!" I interrupted eagerly.

"Och, jewel, the Prince lives away in the old Irish fashion, only he has not a Christian soul now at all at all, most of the old Milesian gentry having quit the country; besides, the Prince being in a bad state of health, and having nearly lost the use of his limbs, and his heart being heavy, and his purse light; for all that he keeps up the old Irish customs and dress, letting nobody eat at the same table but his daughter,* not even his Lady, when she was alive."

* M'Dermot, Prince of Coolavin, never suffered his wife to sit at table with him; although his daughter-in-law was permitted to that honour, as she was descended from the royal family of the *O'Conor*.

When the Earl of K___, Mr. O'H___, member for Sligo, and Mr. S___, a gentleman of fortune, waited on the Prince, be received them in the following manner: —"K___

"And do you think the son of Lord M___ would have no chance of obtaining an audience from the Prince?"

"What, the young gentleman that they say is come to M___ house? why about as much chance as his father, but by my conscience that's a bad one."

"And your young Princess, is she as implacable as her father?"

"Why faith! I cannot well tell you what the Lady Glorvina is, for she is like nothing upon the face of God's creation but herself. I do not know how it comes to pass, that every mother's soul of us love her better nor the Prince; aye, by my conscience, and fear her too; for well may they fear her, on the score of her great learning, being brought up by Father John, the chaplain, and spouting Latin faster nor the priest of the parish: and we may well love her, for she is a saint upon earth, and a great *physicianer* to boot; curing all the sick and maimed for twenty miles round. Then she is so proud, that divil a one soul of the quality will she visit in the whole barony, though she will sit in a smoky cabin for hours together, to talk to the poor: besides all this, she will sit for hours at her Latin and Greek, after the family are gone to bed, and yet you will see her up with the dawn, running like a doe about the rocks; her fine yellow hair streaming in the wind, for all the world like a mermaid. Och! my blessing light on her every day she sees the light, for she is the jewel of a child."

"A child! say you?"

"Why, to be sure I think her one; for many a time I carried her in these arms, and taught her to bless herself in Irish; but she is no child either, for as one of our old Irish songs says, 'Upon her cheek we see love's letter sealed with a damask rose.'* But if your Honour has any curiosity you may judge for yourself; for matins and vespers are celebrated every day in the year, in the old chapel belonging to the castle, and the whole family attend."

"And are strangers also permitted?"

"Faith and its themselves that are; but few indeed trouble them, though none are denied. I used to get mass myself sometimes, but it is now too far to walk for me."

you are welcome; O'H___, you may sit down; but for you," (turning to Mr. S___, who was unfortunately of English extraction), "I know nothing of you." The compliment paid to Mr. O'H___, arose from his mother being the descendant of Milesian ancestry.

*This is a line in a song of one Dignum, who composed in his native language, but could neither read or write, nor spoke any language but his own.

"I have seen," said the celebrated Edmund Burke (who in his boyish days had known him), "some of his effusions translated into English, but was assured by judges, that they fell far short of the originals; yet they contained some graces 'snatched beyond the reach of art.'"—Vide *Life of Burke.* [See Charles Henry Wilson, ed., *The Beauties of the Late Right Honourable Edmund Burke,* 2 vols. (London, 1798), vol. 1, 115. Ed.]

This was sufficient, I waited to hear no more, but repaid my communicative companion for his information, and rode off, having inquired the road to Inismore from the first man I met.

It would be vain, it would be impossible, to describe the emotion which the simple tale of this old man awakened. The descendant of a murderer! The very scoundrel steward of my father revelling in the property of a man, who shelters his aged head beneath the ruins of those walls where his ancestors bled under the uplifted sword of mine.

Why this, you will say, is the romance of a novel-read school boy. Are we not all, the little and the great, descended from assassins; was not the first born man a fratricide? and still, on the field of unappeased contention, does not "man the murderer, meet the murderer, man?"

Yes, yes, 'tis all true; humanity acknowledges it and shudders. But still I wish *my* family had never possessed an acre of ground in this country, or possessed it on other terms. I always knew the estate fell into our family in the civil wars of Cromwell, and in the world's language, was the well-earned meed of my progenitors' valour; but I seemed to hear it now for the first time.

I am glad, however, that this old Irish chieftain is such a ferocious savage; that the pity his fate awakens, is qualified by aversion for his implacable, irascible disposition. I am glad his daughter is *red headed,* a pedant, and a romp; that she spouts Latin like the priest of the parish, and cures sore fingers; that she avoids genteel society, where her ideal rank would procure her no respect, and her unpolished ignorance, by force of contrast, make her feel her real inferiority; that she gossips among the poor peasants, over whom she can reign liege Lady; and, that she has been brought up by a Jesuitical priest, who has doubtlessly rendered her as bigotted and illiberal as himself. All this soothes my conscientious throes of feeling and compassion; for Oh! if this savage chief was generous and benevolent, as he is independent and spirited; if this daughter was amiable and intelligent, as she must be simple and unvitiated! But I dare not pursue the supposition. It is better as it is.

You would certainly never guess that the *Villa di Marino,* from whence I date the continuation of my letter, was simply a *fisherman's hut* on the sea coast, half way between the Lodge and Castle of Inismore, that is, seven miles distant from each. Determined on attending vespers at Inismore, I was puzzling my brain to think where or how I should pass the night, when this hut caught my eye, and I rode up to it to inquire if there was any inn in the neighbourhood, where a *Chevalier Errant* could shelter his adventurous

---

Chevalier Errant: French: a wandering knight, e.g., *Don Quixote.*

head for a night; but I was informed the nearest inn was fifteen miles distant, so I bespoke a little fresh straw, and a clean blanket, which hung airing on some fishing tackle outside the door of this *marine hotel,* in preference to riding so far for a bed, at so late an hour as that in which the vespers would be concluded.

This, mine host of the Atlantic promised me, pointing to a little board suspended over the door, on which was written

"*Good Dry Lodging.*"

My landlord, however, convinced me his hotel afforded something better than good dry lodging; for entreating I would alight, till a shower passed over which was beginning to fall, I entered the hut, and found his wife, a sturdy lad their eldest son, and two naked little ones, seated at their dinner, and enjoying such a feast, as Apicius, who sailed to Africa from Rome to eat good oysters, would gladly have voyaged from Rome to Ireland, to have partaken of; for they were absolutely dining on an immense turbot (whose fellow-sufferers were floundering in a boat that lay anchored near the door). A most cordial invitation on their part, and a most willing compliance on mine, was the ceremony of a moment; and never did an English alderman on turtle day, or Roman Emperor on lampreys and peacocks' livers, make a more delicious repast, than the chance guest of these good people, on their boiled turbot and roasted potatoes, which was quaffed down with the pure phalernian of a neighbouring spring.

Having learnt that the son was going with the compeers of the demolished turbot to Bally___, I took out my little escritoire to write you an account of the first adventure of my chivalrous tour; while one of spring's most grateful sunny showers, is pattering on the leaves of the only tree that shades this simple dwelling, and my *Rosinante* is nibbling a scanty dinner from the patches of vegetation that sprinkle the surrounding cliffs. Adieu! the vesper hour arrives. In all "my orisons thy sins shall be remembered." [54] The spirit of adventure wholly possesses me, and on the dusky horizon of life, some little glimmering of light begins to dawn.

Encore adieu,

H. M.

Apicius: Quintus Gavius Apicus, Roman gourmet and author of cookbook.
turtle day: turtle soup, an exclusive dish reserved for special occasions.
lampreys: a fish resembling an eel in shape and having no scales.
turbot: a large flat fish and much esteemed as food.
phalernian: a celebrated Roman wine.
[54] Shakespeare, *Hamlet,* III. i. 88–89.

Letter V

TO J. D. ESQ. M. P.

Castle of Inismore, Barony of___.

AYE, 'tis even so—point your glass, and rub your eyes, 'tis all one; here I am, and here I am likely to remain for some time. But whether a prisoner of war, or taken up on a suspicion of espionage, or to be offered as an appeasing sacrifice to the *manes* of the old Prince of Inismore, you must for a while suspend your patience to learn.

According to the *carte du pays* laid out for me by the fisherman, I left the shore and crossed the summit of a mountain that "battled o'er the deep,"[55] and which after an hour's ascension, I found sloped almost perpendicularly down to a bold and rocky coast, its base terminating in a peninsula, that advanced for near half a mile into the ocean. Towards the extreme western point of this peninsula, which was wildly romantic beyond all description, arose a vast and grotesque pile of rocks, which at once formed the scite and fortifications of the noblest mass of ruins on which my eye ever rested. Grand even in desolation, and magnificent in decay—it was the Castle of Inismore. The setting sun shone brightly on its mouldering turrets, and the waves which bathed its rocky basis, reflected on their swelling bosoms the dark outlines of its awful ruins.*

As I descended the mountain's brow, I observed that the little isthmus which joined the peninsula to the mainland, had been cut away, and a curious danger-threatening bridge was rudely thrown across the intervening gulf, flung from the rocks on one side to an angle of the mountain on the other, leaving a yawning chasm of some fathoms deep beneath the foot of the wary passenger. This must have been a very perilous pass in days of civil warfare; and in the intrepidity of my daring ancestor, I almost forgot his crime. Amidst the interstices of the rocks which skirted the shores of this interesting peninsula, patches of the richest vegetation were to be seen, and the trees, which sprung wildly among its venerable ruins, were bursting into all the vernal luxuriancy of spring. In the course of my descent, several cabins of a better description than I had yet seen, appeared scattered beneath the shelter of the mountain's innumerable projections; while in the air and dress of their inhabitants (which the sound of my horse's feet

*Those who have visited the Castle of Dunluce, near the Giants' Causeway, may, perhaps, have some of its striking features in this rude draught of the Castle of Inismore.

---

manes: departed ancestors; also custom or manners.

[55] See *WIG* 128, n. 42.

brought to their respective doors), I evidently perceived a something original and primitive, I had never noticed before in this class of persons here.

They appeared to me, I know not why, to be in their holiday garb, and their dress, though grotesque and coarse, was cleanly and characteristic. I observed that round the heads of the elderly dames were folded several wreaths of white or coloured linen,* that others had handkerchiefs† lightly folded round their brows, and curiously fastened under the chin; while the young wore their hair fastened up with wooden bodkins. They were all enveloped in large shapeless mantles[56] of blue frize, and most of them had a rosary hanging on their arm, from whence I inferred they were on the point of attending vespers at the chapel of Inismore. I alighted at the door of a cabin a few paces distant from the Alpine bridge, and entreated a shed for my horse, while I performed my devotions. The man to whom I addressed myself, seemed the only one of several who surrounded me, that understood English, and appeared much edified by my pious intention, saying, "that God would prosper my Honour's journey, and that I was welcome to a shed for my horse, and a night's lodging for myself into the bargain." He then offered to be my guide, and as we crossed the draw-bridge, he told me I was out of luck by not coming earlier, for that high mass had been celebrated that morning for the repose of the soul of a Prince of Inismore, who had been murdered on this very day of the month. "And when this day comes round," he added, "we all attend dressed in our best; for my part, I never wear my poor old grandfather's *berrad* but on the like occasion," taking off a curious cap of a conical form, which he twirled round his hand, and regarded with much satisfaction.‡

* "The women's ancient head-dress so perfectly resembles that of the Egyptian Isis, that it cannot be doubted but that the modes of Egypt were preserved among the Irish."—*Walker on the Ancient Irish Dress,* page 62.

The Author's father, who lived in the early part of his life in a remote skirt of the Province of Connaught, remembers to have seen the heads of the female peasantry encircled with folds of linen in form of a turban. [Joseph Cooper Walker, *An Historical Essay on the Dress of the Ancient and Modern Irish* (Dublin, 1788), 62n. See *WIG* 121, Ed.'s n. Ed.]

† These handkerchiefs they call *Binnogues:* it is a remnant of a very ancient mode.

‡ A few years back, Hugh Dugan, a peasant of the County of Kilkenny, who affected the ancient Irish dress, seldom appeared without his *berrad.* [See Walker, *An Historical Essay,* 8. Ed.]

---

berrad: the barrad, or Irish conical cap.

[56] The mantle was long considered a symbol of Irish opposition to English rule, and they were banned in 1537. See Edgeworth's long note on the mantle where she quotes from Spenser's *A View, CR* 30–31.

By heavens! as I breathed this region of superstition, so strongly was I infected, that my usual scepticism was scarcely proof against my inclination to mount my horse and gallop off, as I shudderingly pronounced,

"I am then entering the Castle of Inismore, on the anniversary of that day on which my ancestors took the life of its venerable Prince!"

You see, my good friend, how much we are the creatures of situation and circumstance, and with what pliant servility the mind resigns itself to the impressions of the senses, or the illusions of the imagination.

We had now reached the ruined cloisters of the chapel; I paused to examine their curious but delapidated architecture when my guide, hurrying me on said, "if I did not quicken my pace, I should miss getting a good view of the Prince," who was just entering by a door opposite to that we had passed through. Behold me then mingling among a group of peasantry, and, like them, straining my eyes to that magnet which fascinated every glance.

And sure, Fancy, in her boldest flight, never gave to the fairy vision of poetic dreams, a combination of images more poetically fine, more strikingly picturesque, or more impressively touching. Nearly one half of the chapel of Inismore has fallen into decay, and the ocean breeze, as it rushed through the fractured roof, wafted the torn banners of the family which hung along its dismantled walls. The red beams of the sinking sun shone on the glittering tabernacle which stood on the altar, and touched with their golden light the sacerdotal vestments of the two officiating priests, who ascended its broken steps at the moment that the Prince and his family entered.

The first of this most singular and interesting group, was the venerable Father John, the chaplain. Religious enthusiasm never gave to the fancied form of the first of the Patriarchs, a countenance of more holy expression, or divine resignation; a figure more touching by its dignified simplicity, or an air more beneficently mild—more meekly good. He was dressed in his pontificals, and with his eyes bent to earth, his hands spread upon his breast, be joined his coadjutors.

What a contrast to this saintly being now struck my view; a form almost gigantic in stature, yet gently thrown forward by evident infirmity; limbs of Herculean mould, and a countenance rather furrowed by the inroads of vehement passions, than the deep trace of years. Eyes still emanating the ferocity of an unsubdued spirit, yet tempered by a strong trait of benevolence; which, like a glory, irradiated a broad expansive brow, a mouth on which even yet the spirit of convivial enjoyment seemed to hover, though

---

glory: a ring of light.

shaded by two large whiskers on the upper lip,* which still preserved their ebon hue; while time or grief had bleached the scattered hairs, which hung their snows upon the manly temple. The drapery which covered this striking figure was singularly appropriate, and, as I have since been told, strictly conformable to the ancient costume of the Irish nobles.†

The only part of the under garment visible, was the ancient Irish *truis*, which closely adhering to the limbs from the waist to the ancle, includes the pantaloon and hose, and terminates in a kind of buskin, not dissimilar to the Roman *perones.* A triangular mantle of bright *scarlet* cloth, embroidered and fringed round the edges, fell from his shoulders to the ground, and was fastened at the breast with a large circular golden broach,‡ of a workmanship most curiously beautiful; round his neck hung a golden collar, which seemed to denote the wearer of some order of knighthood, probably hereditary in his family; a dagger, called a *skiene* (for my guide explained every article of the dress to me), was sheathed in his girdle, and was discerned by the sunbeam that played on its brilliant haft. And as he entered the chapel, he removed from his venerable head a cap, or berrad, of the same form as that I had noticed with my guide, but made of velvet, richly embroidered.

The chieftain moved with dignity—yet with difficulty—and his colossal, but infirm frame, seemed to claim support from a form so almost

*"I have been confidently assured, that the grandfather of the present Rt. Hon. John O'Neil, (great grandfather to the present Lord O'Neil), the elegant and accomplished owner of Shanes' Castle, wore his beard after the *prohibited* Irish mode."—*Walker*, p. 62. [Walker, *An Historical Essay*, 40. Ed.]

†The Irish mantle, with the fringed or shagged borders sewed down the edges of it, was not always made of frize and such coarse materials, which was the dress of the lower sort of people, but, according to the rank and quality of the wearer, was sometimes made of the finest cloth, bordered with silken fringe of scarlet, and various colours—*Ware*, vol. ii. p. 75. [James Ware, *De Hibernia et Antiquitatibus Eius Disquisitiones* (London, 1654), trans. as *The Whole Works of Sir James Ware Concerning Ireland*, 3 vols. (London, 1739–45), vol. 2, 175. Ware (1594–1666) published the first printed version of Edmund Spenser's *A View of the Present State of Ireland* (1633). Ed.]

‡Several of these useful ornaments (in Irish, *dealg fallain*), some gold, some silver, have been found in various parts of the kingdom, and are to be seen in the cabinets of our national *virtuosi.* Joseph Cooper Walker, Esq. to whose genius, learning, and exertions, Ireland stands so deeply indebted, speaking of a broach he had seen in the possession of R. Ousley, Esq. says—"Neither my pen or pencil can give an adequate idea of the elegant gold filligree work with which it is composed." ["Virtuosi" refers to "a student or collector of antiquities, a connoisseur." Walker, *An Historical Essay*, vi. Ed.]

---

truis: close-fitting trousers.

impalpably delicate, that as it floated on the gaze, it seemed like the incarnation of some pure etherial spirit, which a sigh too roughly breathed would dissolve into its kindred air; yet to this sylphid elegance of spheral beauty was united all that symmetrical *contour* which constitutes the luxury of human loveliness. This scarcely "mortal mixture of earth's mould,"[57] was vested in a robe of vestal white, which was enfolded beneath the bosom with a narrow girdle embossed with precious stones.

From the shoulder fell a mantle of scarlet silk, fastened at the neck with a silver bodkin, while the fine turned head was enveloped in a veil of point lace, bound round the brow with a band, or diadem, ornamented with the same description of jewels as encircled her arms.*

Such was the *figure* of the Princess of Inismore!—But Oh! not once was the face turned round towards that side where I stood. And when I shifted my position, the envious veil intercepted the ardent glance which eagerly sought the fancied charms it concealed: for was it possible to doubt the face would not "keep the promise which the form had made."

The group that followed was grotesque beyond all powers of description. The ancient bard, whose long white beard

"Descending, swept his aged breast,"[58]

the incongruous costume—half modern, half antique—of the bare-footed domestics; the ostensible air of the steward, who closed the procession—and above all, the dignified importance of the *nurse,* who took the lead in it immediately after her young lady: her air, form, countenance, and dress, were indeed so singularly fantastic and *outrê,* that the genius of masquerade might have adopted her figure as the finest model of grotesque caricature.

Conceive for a moment a form whose longitude bore no degree of proportion to her latitude; dressed in a short jacket of brown cloth, with loose

*This was, with little variation, the general costume of the female *noblesse* of Ireland from a very early period. In the 15th century the veil was very prevalent, and was termed fillag, or scarf; the Irish ladies, like those of ancient and modern Greece, seldom appearing unveiled. As the veil made no part of the Celtic costume, its origin was probably merely oriental.

The great love of ornaments betrayed by the Irish ladies of other times, "the beauties of the heroes of old," are thus described by a quaint and ancient author:—"Their necks are hung with chains and carkanets—their arms wreathed with many bracelets." [Walker, *An Historical Essay,* 73 and 64. Ed.]

---

outrê: breaking with convention or propriety.

[57] Milton, *Comus,* l. 244.

[58] Goldsmith, *The Deserted Village,* l. 152.

sleeves from the elbow to the wrist, made of red camblet, striped with green, and turned up with a broad cuff—a petticoat of scarlet frize, covered by an apron of green serge, longitudinally striped with scarlet tape, and sufficiently short to betray an ancle that sanctioned all the libels ever uttered against the ancles of the Irish fair—true national brogues set off her blue worsted stockings and her yellow hair, dragged over an high roll, was covered on the summit with a little coiff, over which was flung a scarlet handkerchief, which fastened in a large bow under her rubicund chin.*

As this singular and interesting group advanced up the centre aisle of the chapel, reverence and affection were evidently blended in the looks of the multitude, which hung upon their steps; and though the Prince and his daughter seemed to lose in the meekness of true religion all sense of temporal inequality, and promiscuously mingled with the congregation, yet *that* distinction they humbly avoided, was reverentially forced on them by the affectionate crowd, which drew back on either side as they advanced—until the chieftain and his child stood alone, in the centre of the ruined choir—the winds of Heaven playing freely amidst their garments—the sun's setting beam enriching their beautiful figures with its orient tints, while he, like Milton's ruined angel,

> "Above the rest,
> In shape and feature proudly eminent,
> Stood like a tower;"[59]

and she, like the personified spirit of Mercy, hovered round him, or supported more by her tenderness than her strength, him from whom she could no longer claim support.

Those grey-headed domestics too—those faithful though but nominal vassals, who offered that voluntary reverence with their looks, which his repaid with fatherly affection, while the anguish of a suffering heart hung on his pensive smile, sustained by the firmness of that indignant pride which lowered on his ample brow!

What a picture!

As soon as the first flush of interest, curiosity, and amazement, had subsided, my attention was carried towards the altar; and then I thought, as I

*Such was the dress of Mary Morgan, a poor peasant, in the neighbourhood of Drogheda, in 1786.—"In the close of the last century Mrs. Power, of Waterford, vulgarly called the *Queen of Credan,* appeared constantly in this dress, with the exception of ornaments being gold, silver and fine Brussels lace."—See *Walker's Essay on Ancient Irish Dress,* p. 73. [Walker, *An Historical Essay,* 73. Ed.]

[59]Milton, *Paradise Lost* (1674), Book I, ll. 589–91.

watched the impressive avocation of Father John, that had I been the Prince, I would have been the *Caiphas* too.

What a religion is this! How finely does it harmonize with the weakness of our nature; how seducingly it speaks to the senses; how forcibly it works on the passions; how strongly it seizes on the imagination; how interesting its forms; how graceful its ceremonies; how awful its rites.—What a captivating, what a *picturesque* faith! Who would not become its proselyte, were it not for the stern opposition of reason—the cold suggestions of philosophy!

The last strain of the vesper hymn died on the air as the sun's last beam faded on the casements of the chapel; and the Prince and his daughter, to avoid the intrusion of the crowd, withdrew through a private door, which communicated by a ruinous arcade with the castle.

I was the first to leave the chapel, and followed them at a distance as they moved slowly along. Their fine figures sometimes concealed behind a pillar, and again emerging from the transient shade, flushed with the deep suffusion of the crimsoned firmament.

Once they paused, as if to admire the beautiful effect of the retreating light, as it faded on the ocean's swelling bosom; and once the Princess raised her hand and pointed to the evening star, which rose brilliantly on the deep cerulean blue of a cloudless atmosphere, and shed its fairy beam on the mossy summit of a mouldering turret.

Such were the sublime objects which seemed to engage their attention, and added their *sensible* inspiration to the fervour of those more abstracted devotions in which they were so recently engaged. At last they reached the portals of the castle, and I lost sight of them. Yet still spell-bound, I stood transfixed to the spot from whence I had caught a last view of their receding figures.

While I felt like the victim of superstitious terror when the spectre of its distempered fancy vanishes from its strained and eager gaze, all I had lately seen revolved in my mind like some pictured story of romantic fiction. I cast round my eyes; all still seemed the vision of awakened imagination—Surrounded by a scenery grand even to the boldest majesty of nature, and wild even to desolation—the day's dying splendours awfully involving in the gloomy haze of deepening twilight—the grey mists of stealing night gathering on the still faintly illumined surface of the ocean, which awfully spreading to infinitude, seemed to the limited gaze of human vision to incorporate with the heaven whose last glow it reflected—the rocks, which on every side rose to Alpine elevation, exhibiting, amidst the soft obscurity,

---

Caiphas: the high priest during the trial of Jesus, see Matthew 26:57.

forms savagely bold or grotesquely wild; and those finely interesting ruins which spread grandly desolate in the rear, and added a moral interest to the emotions excited by this view of nature in her most awful, most touching aspect.

Thus suddenly withdrawn from the world's busiest haunts, its hackneyed modes, its vicious pursuits, and unimportant avocations—dropt as it were amidst scenes of mysterious sublimity—alone—on the wildest shores of the greatest ocean of the universe; immersed amidst the decaying monuments of past ages; still viewing in recollection such forms, such manners, such habits (as I had lately beheld), which to the worldly mind may be well supposed to belong to a race long passed beyond the barrier of existence with "the years beyond the flood,"[60] I felt like the being of some other sphere newly alighted on a distant orb. While the novel train of thought which stole on my mind seemed to seize its tone from the awful tranquillity by which I was surrounded, and I remained leaning on the fragment of a rock, as the waves dashed idly against its base, until their dark heads were silvered by the rising moon, and while my eyes dwelt on her silent progress, the castle clock struck nine. Thus warned, I arose to depart, yet not without reluctance. My soul, for the first time, had here held commune with herself; the "lying vanities"[61] of life no longer intoxicating my senses, appeared to me for the first time in their genuine aspect, and my heart still fondly loitered over those scenes of solemn interest, where some of its best feelings had been called into existence.

Slowly departing, I raised my eyes to the Castle of Inismore, and sighed, and almost wished I had been born the Lord of these beautiful ruins, the Prince of this isolated little territory, the adored Chieftain of these affectionate and natural people. At that moment a strain of music stole by me, as if the breeze of midnight stillness had expired in a manner on the Eolian lyre. Emotion, undefinable emotion, thrilled on every nerve. I listened. I trembled. A breathless silence gave me every note. Was it the illusion of my now all awakened fancy, or the professional exertions of the bard of Inismore? Oh, no! for the voice it symphonized; the low wild tremulous voice, which sweetly sighed its soul of melody o'er the harp's responsive chords, was the voice of *a woman!*

Directed by the witching strain, I approached an angle of the building from whence it seemed to proceed; and perceiving a light which streamed through an open casement, I climbed, with some difficulty, the ruins of a parapet wall, which encircled this wing of the castle, and which rose so

---

[60] Young, *Night Thoughts*, Night, l. 60.

[61] James Thomson, *The Seasons*, "Winter," l. 209.

immediately under the casement as to give me, when I stood on it, a perfect view of the interior of that apartment to which it belonged.

Two tapers which burned on a marble slab, at the remotest extremity of this vast and gloomy chamber, shed their dim blue light on the saintly countenance of Father John; who, with a large folio open before him, seemed wholly wrapt in studious meditation; while the Prince, reclined on an immense gothic couch, with his robe thrown over the arm that supported his head, betrayed by the expression of his countenance, those emotions which agitated his soul, while he listened to those strains which spoke once to the heart of the father, the patriot, and the man—breathed from the chords of his country's emblem—breathed in the pathos of his country's music—breathed from the lips of his apparently inspired daughter! The "white rising of her hands upon the harp;"[62] the half-drawn veil, that imperfectly discovered the countenance of a seraph; the moon-light that played round her fine form, and partially touched her drapery with its silver beam—her attitude! her air! But how cold—how inanimate—how imperfect this description! Oh! could I but seize the touching features—could I but realize the vivid tints of this enchanting picture, as they then glowed on my fancy! By heavens! you would think the mimic copy fabulous; the "celestial visitant"[63] of an over-heated imagination. Yet as if the independent witchery of the lovely minstrel was not in itself all, all-sufficient, at the back of her chair stood the grotesque figure of her antiquated nurse. O! the precious contrast. And yet it heightened, it finished the picture.

While thus entranced in breathless observation, endeavouring to support my precarious tenement, and to prolong this rich feast of the senses and the soul, the loose stones on which I tottered gave way under my feet, and impulsively clinging to the wood-work of the casement, it mouldered in my grasp. I fell—but before I reached the earth I was bereft of sense. With its return I found myself in a large apartment, stretched on a bed, and supported in the arms of the Prince of Inismore! His hand was pressed to my bleeding temple; while the priest applied a styptic to the wound it had received; and the nurse was engaged in binding up my arm, which had been dreadfully bruised and fractured a little above the wrist. Some domestics, with an air of mingled concern and curiosity, surrounded my couch; and at her father's side stood the Lady Glorvina, her looks pale and disordered—her trembling hands busily employed in preparing bandages, for which my skilful doctress impatiently called.

---

[62] James Macpherson, *Temora* (1763), Book VII, 210.

[63] Frequent description in eighteenth-century letters, e.g., Francis Sheridan, *The History of Nourjahad* (1767), 15.

While my mind almost doubted the evidence of my senses, and a physical conviction alone *painfully* proved to me the reality of all I beheld, my wandering, wondering eyes met those of the Prince of Inismore! A volume of pity and benevolence was registered in their glance; nor were mine, I suppose, inexpressive of my feelings, for he thus replied to them:—

"Be of good cheer, young stranger; you are in no danger; be composed; be confident; conceive yourself in the midst of friends; for you are surrounded by those who would wish to be considered as such."

I attempted to speak, but my voice faultered; my tongue was nerveless; my mouth dry and parched. A trembling hand presented a cordial to my lip. I quaffed the philtre, and fixed my eyes on the face of my ministering angel.—That angel was Glorvina!—I closed them, and sunk on the bosom of her father.

"Oh, he faints again!" cried a sweet and plaintive voice.

"On the contrary," replied the priest, "the weariness of acute pain something subsided, is lulling him into a soft repose; for see, the colour reanimates his cheek, and his pulse quickens."

"It indeed beats most wildly;" returned the sweet physician—for the pulse which responded to her finger's thrilling pressure, moved with no languid throb.

"Let us retire," added the priest, "all danger is now, thank heaven, over; and repose and quiet the most salutary requisites for our patient."

At these words he arose from my bed-side; and the Prince gently withdrawing his supporting arms, laid my head upon the pillow. In a moment all was death-like stillness, and stealing a glance from under my half-closed eyes, I found myself alone with my skilful doctress, the nurse; who, shading the taper's light from the bed, had taken her distaff and seated herself on a little stool at some distance.

This was a golden respite to feelings wound up to that vehement excess which forbade all expression, which left my tongue powerless, while my heart overflowed with emotion the most powerful.

Good God! I, the son of Lord M___, the hereditary object of hereditary detestation, beneath the roof of my implacable enemy! Supported in his arms; relieved from anguish by his charitable attention; honored by the solicitude of his lovely daughter; overwhelmed by the charitable exertions of his whole family; and reduced to that bodily infirmity that would of necessity oblige me to continue for some time the object of their beneficent attentions.

What a series of emotions did this conviction awaken in my heart! Emotions of a character, an energy, long unknown to my apathized feelings; while gratitude to those who had drawn them into existence, combined with the interest, the curiosity, the admiration, they had awakened, tended to confirm my irresistible desire of perpetuating the immunities I enjoyed, as the guest and patient of the Prince and his daughter. And while the touch of this Wild Irish Girl's hand thrilled on every sense—while her voice of tenderest pity murmured on my ear, and I secretly triumphed over the prejudices of her father, I would not have exchanged my broken arm and wounded temple for the strongest limb and soundest head in the kingdom; but the same chance which threw me in the supporting arms of the irasible Prince, might betray to him in the person of his patient, the son of his hereditary enemy: it was at least probable he would make some inquiries relative to the object of his benevolence, and the singular cause which rendered him such; it was therefore a necessary policy in me to be provided against this scrutiny.

Already deep in adventure, a thousand seducing reasons were suggested by my newly awakened heart, to go on with the romance, and to secure for my future residence in the castle, that interest, which, if known to be the son of Lord M___, I must eventually have forfeited, for the cold aversion of irreclaimable prejudice. The imposition was at least innocent, and might tend to future and mutual advantage; and after the ideal assumption of a thousand fictitious characters, I at last fixed on that of an itinerant artist, as consonant to my most cultivated talent, and to the testimony of those witnesses which I had fortunately brought with me, namely, my drawing book, pencils, &c. &c.—self-nominated *Henry Mortimer,* to answer the initials on my linen, the only proofs against me, for I had not even a letter with me.

I was now armed at all points for inspection; and as the Prince lived in a perfect state of isolation, and I was unknown in the country, I entertained no apprehensions of discovery during the time I should remain at the castle; and full of hope, strong in confidence, but wearied by incessant cogitation, and something exhausted by pain, I fell into that profound slumber I did before but feign.

The mid-day beam shone brightly through the faded tints of my bed curtains before I awakened the following morning, after a night of such fairy charms as only float round the couch of

> "Fancy trained in bliss."

The nurse, and the two other domestics, relieved the watch at my bed-side during the night; and when I drew back the curtain, the former complimented me on my somniferous powers, and in the usual mode of inquiry, but in a very unusual accent and dialect, addressed me with much kindness and good-natured solicitude. While I was endeavouring to express my gratitude for her attentions, and what seemed most acceptable to her, my high opinion of her skill, the Father Director entered.

To the benevolent mind, distress or misfortune is ever a sufficient claim on all the privileges of intimacy; and, when Father John seated himself by my bed-side, affectionately took my hand, lamented my accident, and assured me of my improved looks, it was with an air so kindly familiar, so tenderly intimate, that it was impossible to suspect the sound of his voice was yet a stranger to my ear.

Prepared and collected, as soon as I had expressed my sense of his and the Prince's benevolence, I briefly related my feigned story; and in a few minutes I was a young Englishman, by birth a gentleman, by inevitable misfortunes reduced to a dependence on my talents for a livelihood, and by profession an artist. I added, that I came to Ireland to take views, and seize some of the finest features of its landscapes; that having heard much of the wildly picturesque charms of the north-west coasts, I had penetrated thus far into this remote corner of the province of Connaught; that the uncommon beauty of the views surrounding the castle, and the awful magnificence of its ruins, had arrested my wanderings, and determined me to spend some days in its vicinity: that having attended divine service the preceding evening in the chapel, I continued to wander along the romantic shores of Inismore, and in the adventuring spirit of my art, had climbed part of the mouldering ruins of the castle, to catch a fine effect of light and shade, produced by the partially-veiled beams of the moon, and had then met with the accident which now threw me on the benevolence of the Prince of Inismore; an unknown in a strange country, with a fractured limb, a wounded head, and an heart oppressed with the sense of gratitude under which it laboured.

"That you were a stranger and a traveller, who had been led by curiosity or devotion to visit the chapel of Inismore," said the priest, "we were already apprised of, by the peasant who brought to the castle last night the horse and valise left at his cabin, and who feared, from the length of your absence, some accident had befallen you. What you have yourself been kind enough to detail, is precisely what will prove your best letter of recommendation to the Prince. Trust me, young gentleman, that your standing in need of his attention, is the best claim you could make on it; and your admiration of his native scenes, of that ancient edifice, the monument of that decayed ancestral splendour still dear to his pride; and your having so severely suffered through an anxiety by which he must be flattered, will induce him to consider himself as even *bound* to administer every attention that can meliorate the unpleasantness of your present situation."

What an idea did this give me of the character of him whose heart I once believed divested of all the tender feelings of humanity. Every thing that mine could dictate on the subject, I endeavoured to express, and borne away by the vehemence of my feelings, did it in a manner that more than once fastened the eyes of Father John on my face, with that look of surprise and admiration which, to a delicate mind, is more gratifying than the most finished verbal eulogium.

Stimulated by this silent approbation, I insensibly stole the conversation from myself to a more general theme; one thought was the link to another—the chain of discussion gradually extended, and before the nurse brought up my late breakfast, we had ranged through the whole circle of *sciences*. I found that this intelligent and amiable being, had trifled a good deal in his young days with chemistry, which he still spoke like a lover who, in mature life fondly dwells on the charms of that object who first awakened the youthful raptures of his heart. He is even still an enthusiast in botany, and as free from monastic pedantry as he is rich in the treasures of classical literature, and the elegancies of belles lettres. His feelings even yet preserve something of the ardour of youth, and in his mild character, evidently appears blended, a philosophical knowledge of human nature, with the most perfect worldly inexperience, and the manly intelligence of an highly-gifted mind, with the sentiments of a recluse, and the simplicity of a child. His still ardent mind seemed to dilate to the correspondence of a kindred intellect, and two hours bed-side chit chat, with all the unrestrained freedom such a situation sanctions, produced a more perfect intimacy, than an age would probably have effected under different circumstances.

After having examined and dressed the wounded temple, which he declared to be a mere scratch, and congratulated me on the apparent convalescence of my looks, he withdrew, politely excusing the length of his visit, by pleading the charms of my conversation as the cause of his detention. There is, indeed, an evident vein of French suavity flowing through his manners, that convinced me he had spent some years of his life in that region of the graces. I have since learned that he was partly educated in France; so that, to my astonishment, I have discovered the manners of a gentleman, the conversation of a scholar, and sentiments of a philanthropist, united in the character of an Irish priest.[64]

While my heart throbbed with the natural satisfaction arising from the consciousness of having awakened an interest in those whom it was my ambition to interest, my female Esculapius came and seated herself by me; and while she talked of fevers, inflammations, and the Lord knows what, insisted on my not speaking another word for the rest of the day. Though by no means appearing to labour under the same Pythagorean[65] restraint

---

Esculapius: Asclepius, Greco-Roman god of medicine, son of Apollo.

[64]On the Penal Laws and their implications for Catholic clerics in eighteenth-century Ireland, see *CR* 31, n. 10, and *CR* 89, Ed.'s n.

[65]School founded by Pythagoras (c. 580–c. 500 BC), the Greek philosopher and mathematician, whose followers were guided by strict rules and ascetic conduct.

she had imposed on me; and after having extolled her own surgical powers, her celebrity as the best bone-setter in the barony, and communicated the long list of patients her skill had saved, her tongue at last rested on the only theme I was inclined to hear.

"Arrah! now jewel," she continued, "there is our Lady Glorvina now, who with all her skill, and knowing every leaf that grows, why she could no more set your arm than she could break it. Och! it was herself that turned white, when she saw the blood upon your face, for she was the first to hear you fall, and hasten down to have you picked up; at first, faith, we thought you were a robber; but it was all one to her; into the castle you must be brought, and when she saw the blood spout from your temple—Holy Virgin! she looked for all the world as if she was kilt dead herself."

"And is she," said I, in the selfishness of my heart, "is she always thus humanely interested for the unfortunate?"

"Och! it is she that is tender-hearted for man or beast," replied my companion. "I shall never forget till the day of my death, *nor then* either, faith, the day that Kitty Mulrooney's cow was bogged: you must know, honey, that a bogged cow * * * * * * * *
* * * * * * * * * * *

Unfortunately, however, the episode of Kitty Mulrooney's cow was cut short, for the Prince now entered, leaning on the arm of the priest.

Dull indeed must be every feeling, and blunted every recollective faculty, when the look, the air, the smile, with which this venerable and benevolent Chieftain, approaching my bed, and kindly taking me by the hand, addressed me in the singular idiom of his expressive language.

"Young man," said he, "the stranger's best gift is upon you, for the eye that sees you for the first time, wishes it may not be the last; and the ear that drinks your words, grows thirsty as it quaffs them. So says our good Father John here; for you have made him your friend ere you are his acquaintance; and as the *friend of my friend*, my heart opens to you—you are welcome to my house, as long as it is pleasant to you; when it ceases to be so, we will part with you with regret, and speed your journey with our wishes and our prayers."

Could my heart have lent its eloquence to my lip—but that was impossible; very imperfect indeed was the justice I did to my feelings; but as my peroration was an eulogium on these romantic scenes and interesting ruins, the contemplation of which I had nearly purchased with my life, the Prince seemed as much pleased as if my gratitude had poured forth with *Ciceronian* eloquence, and he replied,

---

***Ciceronian* eloquence:** Marcus Tullius Cicero (106–43 BC), Roman statesman, lawyer, scholar, and writer. Remembered in modern times as the greatest Roman orator.

"When your health will permit, you can pursue here uninterrupted your charming art. Once, the domains of Inismore could have supplied the painter's pencil with scenes of smiling felicity, and the song of the band—with many a theme of joy and triumph; but the harp can now only mourn over the fallen greatness of its sons; and the pencil has nothing left to delineate, but the ruins which shelter the grey head of the last of their descendants."

These words were pronounced with an emotion that shook the debilitated frame of the Prince, and the tear which dimmed the spirit of his eye, formed an associate in that of his auditor. He gazed on me for a moment with a look that seemed to say, "you feel for me then—yet you are an Englishman;" and taking the arm of Father John, he walked towards a window which commanded a view of the ocean, whose troubled bosom beat wildly against the castle cliffs.

"The day is sad," said he, "and makes the soul gloomy: we will summons O'Gallagher to the hall, and drive away sorrow with music."

Then turning to me, he added, with a faint smile, "the tones of an Irish harp have still the power to breathe a spirit over the drooping soul of an Irishman; but if its strains disturb your repose, command its silence: the pleasure of the host always rests in that of his guest."

With these words, and leaning on the arm of his chaplain, he retired; while the nurse, looking affectionately after him, raised her hands, and exclaimed,

"Och! there you go, and may the blessing of the Holy Virgin go with you, for it's yourself that's the jewel of a Prince!"

The impression made on me by this brief but interesting interview, is not to be expressed. You should see the figure, the countenance, the dress of the Prince; the appropriate scenery of the old Gothic chamber, the characteristic appearance of the priest and the nurse, to understand the combined and forcible effect the whole produced.

Yet, though experiencing a pleasurable emotion, strong as it was novel there was still one little wakeful wish throbbing vaguely at my heart.

Was it possible that my chilled, my sated misanthropic feelings, still sent forth one sigh of wishful solicitude for woman's dangerous presence! No, the sentiment the daughter of the Prince inspired, only made a *part* in that general feeling of curiosity, which every thing in this new region of wonders continued to nourish into existence. What had I to expect from the unpolished manners, the confined ideas of this Wild Irish Girl? Deprived of all those touching allurements which society only gives; reared in wilds and solitudes, with no other associates than her nurse, her confessor, and her father; endowed indeed by nature with some personal gifts, set off by the advantage of a singular and characteristic dress, for which she is indebted to whim and natural prejudice, rather than native taste:—I, who had fled in disgust even from those to whose natural attraction the bewitching blandishments of education, the brilliant polish of fashion, and the dazzling splendour of *real* rank, contributed their potent spells.

And yet, the roses of Florida,[66] though the fairest in the universe, and springing from the richest soil, emit no fragrance; while the mountain violet, rearing its timid form from a steril bed, flings on the morning breeze the most delicious perfume.

While given up to such reflections as these—while the sound of the Irish harp arose from the hall below, and the nurse muttered her prayers in Irish over her beads by my side, I fell into a gentle slumber, in which I dreamed that the Princess of Inismore approached my bed, drew aside the curtains, and raising her veil, discovered a face I had hitherto rather guessed at, than seen. Imagine my horror—it was the face, the head, of a *Gorgon!*

Awakened by the sudden and terrific motion it excited, though still almost motionless, as if from the effects of a night-mare (which in fact, from the position I lay in, had oppressed me in the form of the Princess), I cast my eyes through a fracture in the old damask drapery of my bed, and beheld—not the horrid spectre of my recent dream, but the form of a cherub hovering near my pillow—it was the Lady Glorvina herself! Oh! how I trembled lest the fair image should only be the vision of my slumber: I scarcely dared to breathe, lest it should dissolve.

She was seated on the nurse's little stool. Her elbow resting on her knee, her cheek reclined upon her hand; for once the wish of Romeo appeared no hyperbola.[67]

Some snow-drops lay scattered in her lap, on which her downcast eyes shed their beams; as though she moralized over the modest blossoms, which, in fate and delicacy, resembled herself. Changing her pensive attitude, she collected them into a bunch, and sighed, and waved her head as she gazed on them. The dew that trembled on their leaves seemed to have flowed from a richer source than the exhalation of the morning's vapour—for the flowers were faded—but the drops that gem'd them were fresh.

At that moment the possession of a little kingdom would have been less desirable to me, than the knowledge of that association of ideas and feelings which the contemplation of these honoured flowers awakened. At last, with a tender smile, she raised them to her lip, and sighed, and placed them in her bosom; then softly drew aside my curtain. I feigned the stillness of

---

Gorgon: in Greek mythology, one of three female personages, with snakes for hair, whose look turned the beholder into stone.

[66] See Wilson, ed., *Beauties of Edmund Burke,* vol. 1, 10.

[67] Shakespeare, *Romeo and Juliet,* II. i. 23–25: "See how she leans her cheek upon her hand! / O that I were a glove upon that hand, / That I might touch that cheek!"

death—yet the curtain remained unclosed—many minutes elapsed—I ventured to unseal my eyes, and met the soul dissolving glance of my sweet attendant spirit, who seemed to gaze intently on her charge. Emotion on my part the most delicious, on hers the most modestly confused, for a moment prevented all presence of mind; the beautiful arm still supported the curtain—my ardent gaze was still rivetted on a face alternately suffused with the electric flashes of red and white. At last the curtain fell, the priest entered, and the vision, the sweetest, brightest, vision of my life, dissolved!

Glorvina sprung towards her tutor, and told him aloud, that the nurse had entreated her to take her place, while she descended to dinner.

"And no place can become thee better, my child," said the priest, "than that which fixes thee by the couch of suffering and sickness."

"However," said Glorvina, smiling, "I will gratify you by resigning for the present in your favour;" and away she flew, speaking in Irish to the nurse, who passed her at the door.

The benevolent confessor then approached, and seated himself beside my bed, with that premeditated air of chit-chat sociality, that it went to my soul to disappoint him. But the thing was impossible. To have tamely conversed in mortal language on mortal subjects, after having held "high communion" with an ethereal spirit; when a sigh, a tear, a glance, were the delicious vehicles of our souls' secret intercourse—to stoop from this "coloquy sublime!"[68] I could as soon have delivered a logical essay on identity and diversity, or any other subject equally interesting to the heart and imagination.

I therefore closed my eyes, and breathed most sonorously; the good priest drew the curtain and retired on tip-toe, and the nurse once more took her distaff, and for her sins was silent.

These good people must certainly think me a second Epimenides, for I have done nothing but sleep, or feign to sleep, since I have been thrown amongst them.

Letter VI

TO J. D. ESQ. M. P.

I HAVE already passed four days beneath this hospitable roof. On the third, a slight fever with which I had been threatened passed off, my head was disencumbered, and on the fourth I was able to leave my bed, and to

---

Epimenides: Legendary figure (sixth century BC), reputed to have awakened from a boyhood sleep after fifty-seven years.

[68] Milton, *Paradise Lost,* Book VIII, l. 455.

scribble thus far of my journal. Yet these kind solicitous beings will not suffer me to leave my room, and still the nurse at intervals gives me the pleasure of her society, and hums old *cronans,* or amuses me with what she calls a little *shanaos,** as she plies her distaff; while the priest frequently indulges me with his interesting and intelligent conversation. The good man is a great logician, and fond of displaying his metaphysical prowess, where he feels that he is understood, and we diurnally go over *infinity, space,* and *duration,* with innate, simple, and complex ideas, until our own are exhausted in the discussion; and then we generally relax with Ovid, or trifle with Horace and Tibullus, for nothing can be less austerely pious than this cheerful and gentle being: nothing can be more innocent than his life; nothing more liberal than his sentiments.

The Prince, too, has thrice honoured me with a visit. Although he possesses nothing of the erudition which distinguishes his all-intelligent chaplain, yet there is a peculiar charm, a spell in his conversation, that is irresistibly fascinating; and chiefly arising, I believe, from the curious felicity of his expressions, the originality of the ideas they clothe, the strength and energy of his delivery, and the enthusiasm and simplicity of his manners.

He seems not so much to speak the English language, as literally to translate the Irish; and he borrows so much and so happily, from the peculiar idiom of his vernacular tongue, that though his conversation were deficient in matter, it would still possess a singular interest from its manner. But it is far otherwise; there is indeed in the uncultivated mind of this man, much of the *vivida vis anima* of native genius, which neither time or misfortune has wholly damped, and which frequently flings the brightest

* *Shanaos* pronounced, but properly spelt *Sheanachus,* is a term in very general use in Ireland, and is applied to a kind of genealogical chit-chat, or talking over family antiquity, family anecdotes, descent, alliances, &c. &c. to which the lower, as well as the higher order of Irish in the provincial parts are much addicted. I have myself conversed with several old ladies in Connaught and Munster, who were living chronicles of transactions in their families of the most distant date and complicated nature. *Senachy,* was the name of the antiquary retained in every noble family to preserve its exploits, &c. &c. [Shanaos or "sean-nós," a term used to denote the native Irish song tradition, when songs were passed on from one singer to another. "Senachy" refers to the Irish "seanchaí," the bearer of "old lore." Ed.]

---

cronans: cronán, Irish: a tune hummed in a low key.

Ovid: Publius Ovidius Naso (43 BC–AD 17), Roman poet noted especially for his *Ars Amatoria* and *Metamorphoses.*

Horace: see *WIG* 117, n. 28.

Tibullus: Albius Tibullus (c. 55–c. 19 BC), Roman elegiac poet.

vivida vis anima: Latin: the lively force of the mind.

corruscations of thought over the generally pensive tone that pervades his conversation. The extent of his knowledge on subjects of national interest is indeed wonderful; his memory is rich in oral tradition, and most happily faithful to the history and antiquities of his country, which, notwithstanding peevish complaints of its degeneracy, he still loves with idolatrous fondness. On these subjects he is always borne away, but upon no subject whatever does he speak with coolness or moderation; he is always in extremes, and the vehemence of his gestures and looks ever corresponds to the energy of his expressions or sentiments. Yet he possesses an infinite deal of that *suaviter in modo,* so prevailing and insinuating, even among the lower classes of this country; and his natural, or, I should rather say, his national politeness, frequently induces him to make the art in which he supposes me to excel, the topic of our conversation. While he speaks in rapture of the many fine views this country affords to the genius of the painter, he dwells with melancholy pleasure on the innumerable ruined palaces and abbeys which lie scattered amidst the richest scenes of this romantic province: he generally thus concludes with a melancholy apostrophe:

"But the splendid dwelling of princely grandeur, the awful asylum of monastic piety, are just mouldering into oblivion with the memory of those they once sheltered. The sons of little men triumph over those whose arm was strong in war, and whose voice breathed no impotent command; and the descendant of the mighty chieftain has nothing left to distinguish him from the son of the peasant, but the decaying ruins of his ancestors' castle; while the blasts of a few storms, and the pressure of a few years, shall even of them leave scarce a wreck to tell the traveller the mournful tale of fallen greatness."

When I shewed him a sketch I had made of the Castle of Inismore, on the evening I had first seen it from the mountain's summit, he seemed much gratified, and warmly commended its fidelity, shaking his head as he contemplated it, and impressively exclaiming,

"Many a morning's sun has seen me climb that mountain in my boyish days, to contemplate these ruins, accompanied by an old follower of the family, who possessed many strange stories of the feats of my ancestors, with which I was then greatly delighted. And then I dreamed of my arm wielding the spear in war, and my hall resounding to the song of the bard, and the mirth of the feast; but it was only a dream!"

As the injury sustained by my left arm (which is in a state of rapid convalescence) is no impediment to the exertions of my right, we have already

---

suaviter in modo: Latin: gentle in manner.

talked over the various views I am to take; and he enters into every little plan with that enthusiasm, which childhood betrays in the pursuit of some novel object, and seems wonderfully gratified in the idea of thus perpetuating the fast decaying features of this "time honoured" edifice.[69]

The priest assures me, I am distinguished in a particular manner by the partiality and condescension of the Prince.

"As a man of genius," said he this morning, "you have awakened a stronger interest in his breast, than if you had presented him with letters patent of your nobility, except, indeed, you had derived them from *Milesius* himself.

"An enthusiastic love of talents is one of the distinguishing features of the true ancient Irish character; and, independent of your general acquirements, your professional abilities coinciding with his ruling passion, secures you a larger portion of his esteem and regard than he generally lavishes upon any stranger, and almost incredible, considering you are an Englishman. But national prejudice ceases to operate when individual worth calls for approbation; and an Irishman seldom asks or considers the country of him whose sufferings appeal to his humanity, whose genius makes a claim on his applause."

But, my good friend, while I am thus ingratiating myself with the father, the daughter (either self-wrapt in proud reserve, or determined to do away that temerity she may have falsely supposed her condescension and pity awakened) has not appeared even at the door of my chamber, with a charitable inquiry for my health, since our last silent, but eloquent, interview; and I have lived for these three days on the recollection of those precious moments which gave her to my view, as I last beheld her, like the angel of pity hovering round the pillow of mortal suffering.

Ah! you will say, this is not the language of an apathist, of one "whom man delighteth not, nor *woman* either."[70] But let not your vivid imagination thus hurry over at once the scale of my feelings from one extreme to the other, forgetting the many intermediate degrees that lie between the deadly chill of the coldest, and the burning ardor of the most vehement of all human sentiments.

If I am less an apathist, which I am willing to confess, trust me, I am not a whit more the lover.—Lover!—Preposterous!—I am merely interested for this girl on a philosophical principle. I long to study the purely national, natural character of an Irishwoman: in fine, I long to behold any woman in such lights and shades of mind, temper, and disposition, as Nature has

---

[69] Shakespeare, *Richard II*, I. i. 1.

[70] See *WIG* 128, n. 44.

originally formed her in. Hitherto I have only met servile copies, sketched by the finger of art, and finished off by the polished touch of fashion.

I fear, however, that this girl is already spoiled by the species of education she has received. The priest has more than once spoke of her erudition! *Erudition!* the pedantry of a school-boy of the third class, I suppose. How much must a woman lose, and how little can she gain, by that commutation which gives her our acquirements for her own graces! For my part, you know I have always kept clear of the *bas-bleus;* and would prefer one playful charm of a *Ninon,* to all the classic lore of a *Dacier.*

But you will say, I could scarcely come off worse with the pedants than I did with the dunces; and you will say right. And, to confess the truth, I believe I should have been easily led to desert the standard of the pretty *fools,* had female pedantry ever stole on my heart under such a form as the little *soi-disant* Princess of Inismore. 'Tis, indeed, impossible to look *less* like one who spouts Latin with the priest of the parish, than this same Glorvina. There is something beautifully wild about her air and look, that is indescribable; and, without a very perfect regularity of feature, she possesses that effulgency of countenance, that bright *lumine purpureo,* which poetry assigns to the dazzling emanations of divine beauty. In short, there are a thousand little fugitive graces playing around her, which are not beauty, but the cause of it; and were I to personify the word *spell,* she should sit for the picture. . . . . A thousand times she swims before my sight, as I last beheld her; her locks of living gold parting on her brow of snow, yet seeming to separate with reluctance, as they were lightly shaken off with that motion of the head, at once so infantine and graceful; a motion twice put into play, as her recumbent attitude poured the luxuriancy of her tresses over her face and neck, for she was unveiled, and a small gold bodkin was unequal to support the redundancy of that beautiful hair, which I more than once apostrophized in the words of Petrarch:

> "Onde totse amor l'oro e di qual vena
> Per far due treccie biondê," &c.[71]

---

bas-bleus: French: blue stockings, or intellectual women.

Ninon: Anne De Lenclos, "Ninon" (1620–1705), celebrated French courtesan.

Dacier: Anne Dacier (1654–1720), classical commentator, translator, and editor; highly regarded translations of the *Iliad* (1717) and the *Odyssey* (1716).

soi-distant: French: so-called.

lumine purpureo: Latin: purple or crimson glow.

[71] Francesco Petrarca, *Canzoniere,* sonnet 20, ll. 1–2: "From what vein did love exhume the gold to make these two fair braids?"

I understand a servant is dispatched once a week to the next post-town, with and for letters; and this intelligence absolutely amazed me; for I am astonished that these beings, who

"Look not like the inhabitants of the earth,
And yet are on it,"[72]

should hold any intercourse with the world.

This is post-day, and this packet is at last destined to be finished and dispatched. On looking it over, the titles of prince and princess so often occur, that I could almost fancy myself at the court of some foreign potentate, basking in the warm sunshine of regal favour, instead of being the chance guest of a poor Irish gentleman, who lives on the produce of a few rented farms, and, infected with a species of pleasant mania, believes himself as much a prince as the heir apparent of boundless empire and exhaustless treasures.

Adieu! Direct as usual: for though I certainly mean to accept the invitation of the Prince, yet I intend, in a few days, to return home, to obviate suspicion, and to have my books and wardrobe removed to the Lodge, which now possesses a stronger magnet of attraction than when I first fixed on it as my head-quarters.

Letter VII

TO J. D. ESQ. M. P.

THIS is the sixth day of my convalescence, and the first of my descent from my western tower; for I find it is literally in a tower, or turret, which terminates a wing of these ruins, I have been lodged. These good people, however, would have persuaded me into the possession of a slow fever, and confined me to my room another day, had not the harp of Glorvina, with "supernatural solicitings,"[73] spoken more irresistibly to my heart than all their eloquence.

I had just made my *toilette,* for the first time since my arrival at the castle; and with a black ribbon of the nurse's across my forehead, and silk handkerchief of the priest's supporting my arm, with my own "customary suit of solemn black,"[74] tintless cheek, languid eye, and pensive air, I looked indeed as though "melancholy had marked me for her own;"[75] or an excellent personification of "pining atrophy"[76] in its last stage of decline.

---

[72] Shakespeare, *Macbeth,* I. iii. 41–42.

[73] Shakespeare, *Macbeth,* I. iii. 130–31.

[74] Shakespeare, *Hamlet,* I. ii. 78.

[75] Gray, *Elegy Written in a Country Church-Yard,* Epitaph, l. 120.

[76] John Philips, *Cyder* (1727), Book II, l. 473.

While I contemplated my *memento mori* of a figure in the glass, I heard a harp tuning in an underneath apartment. The Prince, I knew, had not yet left his bed, for his infirmities seldom permit him to rise early; the priest had rode out; and the venerable figure of the old harper at that moment gave a fine effect to a ruined arch under which he was passing, led by a boy, just opposite my window. "It is Glorvina then," said I, "and alone!" and down I sallied; but not with half the intrepidity that Sir Bertram followed the mysterious blue flame along the coridors of the enchanted castle.[77]

A thousand times since my arrival in this *trans-mundane region,* I have had reason to feel how much we are the creatures of situation; how insensibly our minds and our feelings take their tone from the influence of existing circumstances. You have seen me frequently the very prototype of *nonchalance,* in the midst of a circle of birth-day beauties, that might have put the fabled charms of the *Mount Ida triumviri* to the blush of inferiority. Yet here I am, groping my way down the dismantled stone stairs of a ruined castle in the wilds of Connaught, with my heart fluttering like the pulse of green eighteen in the presence of its first love, merely because on the point of appearing before a simple rusticated girl, whose father calls himself a *prince,* with a *potatoe ridge* for his *dominions!* O! with what indifference I should have met her in the drawing-room, or at the Opera!—there she would have been merely a woman!—here, she is the fairy vision of my heated fancy.

Well, having finished the same circuitous journey that a squirrel diurnally performs in his cage, I found myself landed in a dark stone passage, which was terminated by the identical chamber of fatal memory already mentioned, and the vista of a huge folding door, partly thrown back, beheld the form of Glorvina! She was alone, and bending over her harp; one arm was gracefully thrown over the instrument, which she was tuning; with the other she was lightly modulating on its chords.

Too timid to proceed, yet unwilling to retreat, I was still hovering near the door, when, turning round, she observed me, and I advanced. She blushed to the eyes, and returned my profound bow with a slight inclination of the head, as if I were unworthy a more marked obeisance.

Nothing in the theory of sentiment could be more diametrically opposite, than the bashful indication of that crimson blush, and the haughty

---

memento mori: Italian: a reminder of death.

trans-mundane region: that is or lies beyond the world.

Mount Ida triumviri: Hera, Athena, and Aphrodite each tried to bribe Paris after Zeus charged him with deciding who was the most beautiful goddess.

[77]John and Laetitia Aikin, "Of the Pleasure derived from Objects of Terror; with Sir Bertrand, a Fragment," *Miscellaneous Pieces, In Prose* (1773), 119–37.

spirit of that graceful bow. What a logical analysis would it have afforded to Father John, on innate and acquired ideas! Her blush was the effusion of nature; her bow the result of inculcation—the one spoke the native woman; the other the *ideal* princess.

I endeavoured to apologize for my intrusion; and she, in a manner that amazed me, congratulated me on my recovery; then drawing her harp towards her, she seated herself on the great Gothic couch, with a motion of the hand, and a look, that seemed to say, "there is room for you too." I bowed my acceptance of the silent welcome invitation.

Behold me then seated *téte-à-téte* with this Irish Princess!—my right arm thrown over her harp, and her eyes rivetted on my left.

"Do you still feel any pain from it?" said she so naturally, as though we had actually been discussing the accident it had sustained.

Would you believe it! I never thought of making her an answer; but fastened my eyes on her face. For a moment she raised her glance to mine, and we both coloured, as if she read there—I know not what!

"I beg your pardon," said I, recovering from the spell of this magic glance—"you made some observation, Madam?"

"Not that I recollect," she replied, with a slight confusion of manner, and running her finger carelessly over the chords of the harp, till it came in contact with my own, which hung over it. The touch circulated like electricity through every vein. I impulsively arose, and walked to the window from whence I had first heard the tones of that instrument which had been the innocent accessary to my present unaccountable emotion. As if I were measuring the altitude of my fall, I hung half my body out of the window, thinking, Heaven knows, of nothing less than *that* fall, of nothing more than its fair cause, until abruptly drawing in my dizzy head, I perceived her's (such a cherub head you never beheld!) leaning against her harp, and her eye directed towards me. I know not why, yet I felt at once confused and gratified by this observation.

"My fall," said I, glad of something to say, to relieve my school-boy bashfulness, "was greater than I suspected."

"It was dreadful!" she replied shuddering. "What could have led you to so perilous a situation?"

"That," I returned, "which has led to more certain destruction, senses more strongly fortified than mine—the voice of a syren!"

I then briefly related to her the rise, decline, and fall, of my physical empire; obliged, however, to qualify the gallantry of my *debut* by the subsequent plainness of my narration, for the delicate reserve of her air made me tremble, lest I had gone too far.

By Heavens! I cannot divest myself of a feeling of inferiority in her presence, as though I were actually that poor, wandering, unconnected being I have feigned myself.

My compliment was received with a smile and a blush; and to the eulogium which rounded my detail on the benevolence and hospitality of the family of Inismore, she replied, that "had the accident been of less material consequence to myself, the family of Inismore must have rejoiced at any event which enriched its social circle with so desirable an acquisition."

The *matter* of this little *politesse* was nothing; but the *manner*, the air, with which it was delivered! Where can she have acquired this elegance of manner!—reared amidst rocks, and woods, and mountains! deprived of all those graceful advantages which society confers—a manner too that is at perpetual variance with her looks, which are so *naif*—I had almost said so wildly simple—that while she speaks in the language of a court, she looks like the artless inhabitant of a cottage:—a smile, and a blush, rushing to her cheek, and her lip, as the impulse of fancy or feeling directs, even when smiles and blushes are irrelevant to the etiquette of the moment.

This elegance of manner, then, must be the pure result of elegance of soul; and if there is a charm in woman, I have hitherto vainly sought, and prized beyond all I have discovered, it is this refined, celestial, native elegance of soul, which effusing its spell through every thought, word, and motion, of its enviable possessor, resembles the peculiar property of gold, which subtilely insinuates itself through the most minute and various particles, without losing any thing of its own intrinsic nature by the amalgamation.

In answer to the flattering observation which had elicited this digression, I replied:

That far from regretting the consequences, I was enamoured of an accident that had procured me such happiness as I now enjoyed (even with the risk of life itself); and that I believed there were few who, like me, would not prefer peril to security, were the former always the purchase of such felicity as the latter, at least on me, had never bestowed.

Whether this reply savoured too much of the world's common-place gallantry, or that she thought there was more of the head than the heart in it, I know not; but, by my soul, in spite of a certain haughty motion of the head not unfrequent with her, I thought she looked wonderfully inclined to laugh in my face, though she primed up her pretty mouth, and fancied she looked like a nun, when her lip pouted with the smiling archness of an Hebe.

In short, I never felt more in all its luxury the comfort of looking like a fool; and to do away the not very agreeable sensation which the conviction of being laughed at awakens, as a *pis-aller*, I began to examine the harp, and expressed the surprise I felt at its singular construction.

Hebe: daughter of Zeus and Hera, goddess of youth in Greek mythology.

pis-aller: French: last resort or stopgap.

"Are you fond of music?" she asked with *naiveté.*

"Sufficiently so," said I, "to risk my life for it."

She smiled, and cast a look at the window, as much as to say, "I understand you."

As I now was engaged in examining her harp, I observed that it resembled less any instrument of that kind I had seen, than the drawings of the Davidic lyre in Montfaucon.[78]

"Then," said she with animation, "this is another collateral proof of the antiquity of its origin, which I never before heard adduced, and which sanctions that universally received tradition among us, by which we learn, that we are indebted to the first Milesian colony that settled here, for this charming instrument, although some modern historians suppose that we obtained it from Scandinavia." *

"And is this, Madam?" said I, "the original ancient Irish harp?"

* The supposition is advanced by Dr. Ledwich; but neither among the "Sons of Song," or by those of the interior part of the island, who are guided in their faith by "tradition's volubly transmitting tongue," could I ever find *one* to agree in the supposition. "That the harp was the common musical instrument of the Anglo-Saxons, might be inferred from the very word itself, which is not derived from the British, or any other Celtic language, but of genuine Gothic original, and current among every branch of that people, viz. Angl-Sax. þearpe, þearpa. Iceland. þaurpa. Dan. and Bel. þarpa. Ger. Harpffa. Gal. Harpe. Span. Harpa. Ital. Arpa, &c. &c."—Vide *Essay on Ancient Minstrels in England, by Dr. Percy. Reliques of Ancient English Poetry.*

It is reserved then for the national *Lyre* of *Erin* only, to claim a title independent of a Gothic origin. For *clarseach,* is the only Irish epithet for the harp,* a name more in unison with the cithera of the Greeks, and even the *chinor* of the Hebrew, than the Anglo-Saxon harp. "I cannot but think the *clarseach,* or Irish harp, one of the most ancient instruments we have among us, and had perhaps its origin in remote periods of antiquity."—*Essay on the Construction, &c. &c. of the Irish Harp, by Dr. Beauford.* [Edward Ledwich (1738–1823), author of *Antiquities of Ireland* (1790), opposed Charles Vallencey's "Phoenician" theory of Irish origins (*Collecteana,* ix, 1781). He expressed his views on the origins of Irish music in a letter to Joseph Walker; see Edward Ledwich, "A Letter to Joseph C. Walker M.R.I.A. on the Style of the Ancient Irish Music," Appendix to Walker, *Historical Memoirs,* 8; Thomas Percy, "Essay on the Ancient Minstrels in England," Appendix 1, *Reliques of Ancient English Poetry,* 3 vols. (1765), vol. 1, 390; William Beauford, "An Essay on the Construction and Capability of the Irish Harp in its Present and Pristine State," Appendix to Walker, *Historical Memoirs,* 115. On Arthur O'Neill, the blind harper, see Donal O'Sullivan, *Life, Times and Music of an Irish Harper* (London, 1858). Ed.]

*A few months back the Author having played the Spanish guitar in the hearing of some Connaught peasants, they called it a *clarseach beg,* or little harp.

[78] Bernard de Montfauçon (1655–1741), *Antiquity Explained and Represented in Diagrams,* 5 vols. (London, 1721–25), vol. 3, 218ff.

"Not exactly, for I have strung it with gut instead of wire, merely for the gratification of my own ear;* but it is, however, precisely the same form as that preserved in the Irish university, which belonged to one of the most celebrated of our heroes, Brian Boru; for the warrior and the bard often united in the character of our kings, and they sung the triumphs of those departed chiefs whose feats they emulated.

"You see," she added, with a smile, while my eager glance pursued the kindling animation of her countenance as she spoke,—"you see, that in all which concerns my national music, I speak with national enthusiasm; and much indeed do we stand indebted to the most charming of all the sciences

* As the modern Irish harp is described in a letter I have just received from a very eminent modern Irish bard, Mr. O'Neil, I beg leave to quote the passage which relates to it.

"My harp has thirty-six strings" (the harp of *Brian Boiromh* had but 28 strings), "of four kinds of wire, increasing in strength from treble to bass; your method of tuning yours (by octaves and fifths) is perfectly correct; but a change of keys or half tones, can only be effected by the tuning hammer. As to my mode of travelling, the privation of sight has long obliged me to require a servant who carries the harp for me. I remember in this neighbourhood, fifteen ladies proficients on the Irish harp, two in particular excelled, a Mrs. Bailly, and a Mrs. Hermar; but all are now dead; so is Rose Moony (a professional bardess), who was likewise celebrated. Fanning I knew, and thought well of his performance."

Fanning was an eminent professional harper, and, like O'Neil, and some others of the Bardic order, rode about the country attended by a servant who carried his harp. It was thus, in ancient times, the "light of song" was effused over Europe. "The Minstrel," says Dr. Percy, "had sometimes his servant to carry his harp, and even to sing his music." Thus in the old romantic legend of "King Estmere," we find the younger Prince proposing to accompany his brother in the disguise of a minstrel, and carry his harp.

And you shall be a harper's brother,
Out of the north countrye,
And I'll be your boy so fine of sighte,
And bear your harp by your knee.
And thus they renesht them to ryde
On two good Renish steedes,
And when they came to King Adland's hall
Of red gold shone their weedes.

Vide *Percy's Reliques,* page 62.

Dr. Percy justly observes, that in this ballad, the character of the old minstrels (those successors to the bards) is placed in a very respectable light; for that "here we see one of them represented mounted on a *fine horse,* accompanied with an attendant to bear his harp, &c. &c." And I believe in Ireland only, is the minstrel of remote antiquity justly represented in the itinerant bard of modern days. [See Percy, *Reliques,* vol. 1, 85–98. Ed.]

Brian Boru: Brian Boru (941–1014), High King of Ireland. Defeated the Vikings at the Battle of Clontarf near Dublin on April 23, 1014.

for the eminence it has obtained us; for in *music only,* do *you* English allow us poor Irish any superiority; and therefore your King, who made the *harp* the armorial bearing of Ireland, perpetuated our former musical celebrity beyond the power of time or prejudice to destroy it."[79]

Not for the world would I have annihilated the triumph which this fancied superiority seemed to give to this patriotic little being, by telling her, that we thought as little of the music of her country, as of every thing else that related to it; and that all we knew of the style of its melodies, reached us through the false medium of comic airs, sung by some popular actor, who, in coincidence with his author, caricatures those national traits he attempts to delineate.

I therefore simply told her, that though I doubted not the former musical celebrity of her country, yet that I perceived the *Bardic* order in Wales seemed to have survived the tuneful race of *Erin;* for that though every little Cambrian village had its harper, I had not yet met one of the profession in Ireland.

She waved her head with a melancholy air, and replied—"The rapid decline of the Sons of Song, once the pride of our country, is indeed very evident; and the tones of that tender and expressive instrument which gave birth to those which now survive them in happier countries, no longer vibrates in our own; for of course you are not ignorant that the importation of Irish bards and Irish instruments into Wales,* by *Griffith ap Conan,* formed an epocha in Welsh music, and awakened there a genius of style in composition, which still breathes a kindred spirit to that from whence it derived its being, and that even the invention of Scottish music is given to Ireland."†

"Indeed," said I, "I must plead ignorance to this singular fact, and almost to every other connected with this *now* to me, most interesting country."

"Then suffer me," said she, with a most insinuating smile, "to indulge another national little triumph over you, by informing you, that we learn

*Cardoc (of Lhancarvan), without any of that illiberal partiality so common with national writers, assures that the Irish devised all the instruments, tunes, and measures, in use among the Welsh. *Cambrensis* is even more copious in its praise, when he peremptorily declares that the Irish, above any other nation, is incomparably skilled in symphonal music.—See *Walker's Hist. Mem. of the Irish Bards.* [See Walker, *Historical Memoirs,* Appendix, 19. Ed.]

†See Doctor Campbell, Phil. Surv. Letter 44; and Walker's Hist. of Irish Bards, page 131–32. [Thomas Campbell (1733–95) took issue with antiquarians Vallancey and O'Conor; see *A Philosophical Survey of the South of Ireland, in a series of letters to K. Watkinson* (1777), 454. Ed.]

[79] Glorvina's views here echo those of Edward Ledwich; see Walker, *Historical Memoirs,* Appendix, 11.

from musical record, that the first piece of music ever seen in *score*, in Great Britain, is an air sung time immemorial in this country on the opening of summer—an air which, though animated in its measure, yet still, like all the Irish melodies, breathes the very soul of melancholy." *

"And do your melodies then, Madam, breathe the soul of melancholy?" said I.

"Our national music," she returned, "like our national character, admits of no medium in sentiment: it either sinks our spirit to despondency, by its heart-breaking pathos, or elevates it to wildness by its exhilarating animation.

"For my own part, I confess myself the victim of its magic—an Irish planxty cheers me into maddening vivacity; an Irish lamentation depresses me into a sadness of melancholy emotion, to which the energy of despair might be deemed comparative felicity."

Imagine how I felt while she spoke—but you cannot conceive the feelings, unless you beheld and heard the object who inspired them—unless you watched the kindling lumination of her countenance, and the varying hue of that mutable complexion, which seemed to ebb and flow to the impulse of every sentiment she expressed; while her round and sighing voice modulated in unison with each expression it harmonized.

After a moment's pause, she continued:

"This susceptibility to the influence of my country's music, discovered itself in a period of existence, when no associating sentiment of the heart could have called it into being; for I have often wept in convulsive emotion at an air, before the sad story it accompanied was understood: but now—now—that feeling is matured, and understanding awakened. Oh! you cannot judge—cannot feel—for you have no national music; and your country is the happiest under heaven!"

Her voice faultered as she spoke—her fingers seemed impulsively to thrill on the chords of the harp—her eyes, her tear-swollen beautiful eyes, were thrown up to heaven, and her voice, "low and mournful as the song of the tomb,"[80] sighed over the chords of her national lyre, as she faintly murmured Campbell's beautiful poem to the ancient Irish air of *Erin go Brach!*

Oh! is there on earth a being so cold, so icy, so insensible, as to have made a comment, even an *encomiastic* one, when this song of the soul

*Called in Irish, "*Ta an Samradth teacht,*" or, "*We brought Summer along with us.*" [See Edward Bunting, *A General Collection of the Ancient Irish Music* (London, 1796). Ed.]

---

planxty: a harp tune, usually associated with Turlough O'Carolan.

Erin go Brach: Irish: Ireland for ever. A slogan of the United Irishmen organization.

[80] Macpherson, *Dar-Thula: A Poem* (1805), 402.

ceased to breathe! God knows how little I was inclined or empowered to make the faintest eulogium, or disturb the sacred silence which succeeded to her music's dying murmur. On the contrary, I sat silent and motionless, with my head unconsciously leaning on my broken arm, and my handkerchief to my eyes: when at last I withdrew it, I found her hurried glance fixed on me with a smile of such expression! Oh! I could weep my heart's most vital drop for such another glance—such another smile!—they seemed to say, but who dares to translate the language of the soul, which the eye only can express?

In (I believe) equal emotion, we both arose at the same moment, and walked to the window. Beyond the mass of ruins which spread in desolate confusion below, the ocean, calm and unruffled, expanded its awful bosom almost to infinitude; while a body of dark sullen clouds, tinged with the partial beam of a meridian sun, floated above the summits of those savage cliffs which skirt this bold and rocky coast; and the tall spectral figure of Father John, leaning on a broken pediment, appeared like the embodied spirit of philosophy moralizing amidst the ruins of empires, on the instability of all human greatness.

What a sublime assemblage of images!

"How consonant," thought I, gazing at Glorvina, "to the sublimated tone of our present feelings." Glorvina waved her head in accedence to the idea, as though my lips had given it birth.

How think you I felt, on this sweet involuntary acknowledgment of a mutual intelligence?

Be that as it may, my eyes, too faithful I fear to my feelings, covered the face on which they were passionately rivetted, with blushes.

At that moment Glorvina was summoned to dinner by a servant, for she only is permitted to dine with the Prince, as being of royal descent. The vision dissolved—she was again the proud Milesian Princess, and I, the poor wandering *artist*—the eleemosynary guest of her hospitable mansion.

The priest and I dined *téte-à-téte;* and, for the first time, he had all the conversation to himself; and got deep in Locke and Malbranche, in solving quidities, and starting hypotheses, to which I assented with great gravity, and thought only of Glorvina.

---

encomiastic: a formal or high-flown expression of praise.

eleemosynary: charitable.

Locke: John Locke (1632–1704), English philosopher, author of *An Essay Concerning Human Understanding* (1690), and initiator of the Enlightenment in England.

Malbranche: Nicholas Malebranche (1638–1715), French Roman Catholic priest, theologian, and Cartesian philosopher.

I again beheld her gracefully drooping over her harp—I again caught the melody of her song, and the sentiment it conveyed to the soul; and I entered fully into the idea of the Greek painter, who drew *Love,* not with a bow and arrow, but a lyre.

I could not avoid mentioning with admiration her great musical powers.

"Yes," said he, "she inherits them from her mother, who obtained the appellation of *Glorvina,* from the sweetness of her voice, by which name our little friend was baptized at her mother's request." *

Adieu! Glorvina has been confined in her father's room during the whole of the evening—to this circumstance you are indebted for this long letter.

Adieu!

H. M.

Letter VIII

TO J. D. ESQ. M. P.

THE invitation I received from the hospitable Lord of these ruins, was so unequivocal, so cordial, that it would have been folly, not delicacy, to think of turning out of his house the moment my health was re-established. But then, I scarcely felt it warranted that length of residence here, which, for a thousand reasons, I am now anxious to make.

To prolong my visit till the arrival of my father in this country was my object; and how to effect the desired purpose, the theme of cogitation during the whole of the restless night which succeeded my interview with Glorvina; and to confess the truth, I believe this interview was not the least potent spell which fascinated me to Inismore.

Wearied by my restlessness, rather than refreshed by my transient slumbers, I arose with the dawn, and carrying my *port-feuille* and pencils with me, descended from my tower, and continued to wander for some time among the wild and romantic scenes which surround these interesting ruins, while

"La sainte recueilment le paisible innocence
Sembler de ces lieus habiter le silence;"

* To derive an appellation from some eminent quality or talent, is still very common in the interior parts of Ireland. The Author's grandmother was known in the neighbourhood where she resided (in the County of Mayo), by the appellative of *Clarseach na Vallagh,* or, the *Village Harp;* for the superiority of her musical abilities. *Glor-bhin* (pronounced *vin*), is literally "sweet voice."

Love: Eros, in Greek religion, god of love.

port-feuille: French: portfolio.

"La sainte . . . le silence": French: "Holy reflection, and peaceful innocence seems to live in the silence of these places."

until, almost wearied in the contemplation of the varying sublimities which the changes of the morning's seasons shed over the ocean's boundless expanse, from the first grey vapour that arose from its swelling wave, to that splendid refulgence with which the risen sun crimsoned its bosom, I turned away my dazzled eye, and fixed it on the ruins of Inismore. Never did it appear in an aspect so picturesquely felicitous: it was a golden period for the poet's fancy or the painter's art; and in a moment of propitious genius, I made one of the most interesting sketches my pencil ever produced. I had just finished my successful *ebauche,* when Father John, returning from matins, observed, and instantly joined me. When he had looked over, and commended the result of my morning's avocation, he gave my port-folio to a servant who passed us, and taking my arm, we walked down together to the sea shore.

"This happy specimen of your talent," said he, as we proceeded, "will be very grateful to the Prince. In him, who has no others left, it is a very innocent pride, to wish to perpetuate the fading honours of his family—for as such the good Prince considers these *ruins.* But, my young friend, there is another and a surer path to the Prince's heart, to which I should be most happy to lead you."

He paused for a moment, and then added:

"You will, I hope, pardon the liberty I am going to take; but as I boast the merit of having first made your merit known to your worthy host, I hold myself in some degree (smiling, and pressing my hand) accountable for your confirming the partiality I have awakened in your favour.

"The daughter of the Prince, and my pupil, of whom you can have yet formed no opinion, is a creature of such rare endowments, that it should seem Nature, as if foreseeing her isolated destiny, had opposed her own liberality to the chariness of fortune; and lavished on her such intuitive talents, that she almost sets the necessity of education at defiance. To all that is most excellent in the circle of human intellect, or human science, her versatile genius is constantly directed; and it is my real opinion, that nothing more is requisite to perfect her in any liberal or elegant pursuit, but that method or system which even the strongest native talent, unassisted, can seldom attain (without a long series of practical experience), and which is unhappily denied her; while her doating father incessantly mourns over that poverty, which withholds from him the power of cultivating those shining abilities that would equally enrich the solitude of their possessor, or render her an ornament to that society she may yet be destined to grace. Yet the occasional visits of a strolling dancing-master, and a few musical

---

ebauche: French: rough draft or outline.

lessons received in her early childhood from the family bard, are all the advantages these native talents have received.

"But who that ever beheld her motions in the dance, or listened to the exquisite sensibility of her song, but would exclaim—'here is a creature for whom Art can do nothing—Nature has done all!'

"To these elegant acquirements, she unites a decided talent for drawing, arising from powers naturally imitative, and a taste, early imbibed (from the contemplation of her native scenes), for all that is most sublime and beautiful in Nature. But this, of all her talents, has been the least assisted, and yet is the most prized by her father, who, I believe, laments his inability to detain you here as her preceptor; or rather, to make it worth your while to forego your professional pursuits, for such a period as would be necessary to invest her with such rudiments in the art, as would form a basis for her future improvement. In a word, can you, consistently with your present plans, make the Castle of Inismore your head-quarters for two or three months, from whence you can take frequent excursions amidst the neighbouring scenery, which will afford to your pencil subjects rich and various as almost any other part of the country?"

Now, in the course of my life, I have had more than one occasion to remark certain desirable events, brought about by means diametrically opposite to the supposition of all human probability;—but that this worthy man should (as if infected with the intriguing spirit of a French Abbé reared in the purlieus of the *Louvre*)—should thus forward my views, and effect the realization of my wishes, excited so strong an emotion of pleasurable surprise, that I with difficulty repressed my smiles, or concealed my triumph.

After, however, a short pause, I replied with great gravity, that I always conceived with Pliny, that the dignity we possess by the good offices of a friend, is a kind of sacred trust, wherein we have his judgment as well as our own character to maintain, and therefore to be guarded with peculiar attention; that consequently, on his account, I was as anxious as on my own, to confirm the good opinion conceived in my favour through the medium of his partiality; and with very great sincerity I assured him, that I knew of no one event so coincident to my present views of happiness, as the power of making the Prince some return for his benevolent attentions, and of becoming his (the priest's) coadjutor in the tuition of his highly-gifted pupil.

"Add then, my dear Sir," said I, "to all the obligations you have forced on me, by presenting my respectful compliments to the Prince, with the

---

Pliny: Gaius Plinius Caecilius Secundus (Pliny the Younger, c. AD 61–112). Roman author and administrator, noted for his collection of private letters.

offer of my little services, and an earnest request that he will condescend to accept of them: and if you think it will add to the delicacy of the offer, let him suppose that it voluntarily comes from a heart deeply impressed with a sense of his kindness."

"That is precisely what I was going to propose," returned this excellent and unsuspecting being. "I would even wish him to think you conceive the obligation all on your own side; for the pride of fallen greatness is of all others the most sensitive."

"And God knows so I do," said I, fervently;—then carelessly added, "do you think your pupil has a decided talent for the art?"

"It may be partiality," he replied; "but I think she has a decided talent for every elegant acquirement. If I recollect right, somebody has defined *genius* to be 'the various powers of a strong mind directed to one point:'[81] making it the *result* of combined force, not the vital source whence all intellectual powers flow; in which light, the genius of Glorvina has ever appeared to me as a beam from heaven, an emanation of divine intelligence, whose nutritive warmth cherishes into existence that richness and variety of talent which wants only a little care to rear it to perfection.

"When I first offered to become the preceptor to this charming child, her father, I believe, never formed an idea that my tuition would have extended beyond a little reading and writing; but I soon found that my interesting pupil possessed a genius that bore all before it—that almost anticipated instruction by force of its intuitive powers, and prized each task assigned it, only in proportion to the difficulty by which it was to be accomplished.

"Her young ambitious mind even emulated rivalry with mine, and that study in which she beheld me engaged, seldom failed to become the object of her desires and her assiduity. Availing myself, therefore, of this innate spirit of emulation—this boundless thirst of knowledge, I left her mind free in the election of its studies, while I only threw within its power of acquisition, that which could tend to render her a rational, and consequently a benevolent being; for I have always conceived an informed, intelligent, and enlightened mind, to be the best security for a good heart; although the many who mistake talent for intellect, and unfortunately too often find the former united to vice, are led to suppose that the heart loses in goodness what the mind acquires in strength, as if (as a certain paradoxical writer has asserted), there was something in the natural mechanism of the human frame necessary to constitute a fine genius, that is not altogether favourable to the heart.

---

[81] Samuel Johnson, "Life of Cowley," *Lives of the English Poets* (1779–81).

"But here comes the unconscious theme of our conversation."

And at that moment Glorvina appeared, springing lightly forward, like Gresset's beautiful personification of Health:

"As Hebe swift, as Venus fair,
Youthful, lovely, light as air."[82]

As soon as she perceived me she stopt abruptly, blushed, and returning my salutation, advanced to the priest, and twining her arm familiarly in his, said with an air of playful tenderness,

"O! I have brought you something you will be glad to see—here is the spring's first violet, which the unusual chillness of the season has suffered to steal into existence: this morning as I gathered herbs at the foot of the mountain, I inhaled its odour ere I discovered its purple head, as solitary and unassociated it drooped beneath the heavy foliage of a neighbouring plant.

"It is but just you should have the first violet, as my father has already had the first snow-drop. Receive, then, my offering," she added with a smile; and while she fondly placed it in his breast, with an air of exquisite *naiveté*, to my astonishment she repeated from B. Tasso, those lines so consonant to the tender simplicity of the act in which she was engaged:

"Poiche d'altro honorate
Non posso, prendi lieta
Queste negre viole
Dall umor rugiadose."

The priest gazed at her with looks of parental affection, and said,
"Your offering, my dear, is indeed the

"Incense of the heart;"[83]

and more precious to the receiver, than the richest donation that ever decked the shrine of Loretto. How fragrant it is!" he added, presenting it to me.

I took it in silence, but raised it no higher than my lip—the eye of Glorvina met mine, as my kiss breathed upon her flower: Good God! what an undefinable, what a delicious emotion thrilled through my heart at that

---

"Poiche d'altro . . . rugiadose": Italian: "Since I cannot honour thee in any other way, take these black pansies damp with dew."

Loretto: shrine of the house of the Blessed Virgin Mary near Ancona in Italy, supposedly transported there by angels in 1291.

[82] Likely a translation from the work of Jean-Baptiste Gresset (1709–77), the French poet and dramatist, author of the irreverently comic narrative poem *Ver-Vert* (1734).

[83] Numerous examples in eighteenth-century writing, e.g., Nathaniel Cotton, *The Fireside*, l. 65, and Thomas Godfrey, *The Prince of Parthia*, II. vii. 30.

moment! and the next—yet I know not how it was, or whether the motion was made by her, or by me, or by the priest—but somehow, Glorvina had got between us, and while I gazed at her beautiful flower, I personified the blossom, and addressed to her the happiest lines that form "*La Guirlande de Julie,*" while, as I repeated

> "Mais si sur votre front je peux briller un jour,
> La plus humble des fleurs sera la plus superbe;"

I reposed it for a moment on her brow in passing it over to the priest.

"Oh!" said she, with an arch smile, "I perceive you too will expect a tributary flower for these charming lines; and the summer's first rose"—she paused abruptly; but her eloquent eye continued, "should be thine, but that thou may'st be far from hence when the summer's first rose appears." I thought too—but it might be only the fancy of my wishes, that a sigh floated on the lip, when recollection checked the effusion of the heart.

"The *rose,*" (said the priest with simplicity, and more engaged with the classicality of the idea, than the inference to be drawn from it), "the rose is the flower of Love."

I stole a look at Glorvina, whose cheek now emulated the tint of the theme of our conversation; and plucking a thistle that sprung from a broken pediment, she blew away its down with her balmy breath, merely to hide her confusion.

Surely she is the most sensient of all created beings!

"I remember," continued the priest, "being severely censured by a rigid old priest, at my college in St. Omers, who found me reading the Idylium of Ausonius, in which he so beautifully celebrates the rose, when the good father believed me deep in St. Augustus."

"The rose," said I, "has always been the poet's darling theme. The impassioned Lyre of Sappho has breathed upon its leaves. Anacreon has wooed it in the happiest effusions of his genius; and poesy seems to have exhausted her powers in celebrating the charms of the most beautiful and transient of flowers.

"Among its modern panegyrists, few have been more happily successful than Monsieur de Bernard, in that charming little ode beginning—

"Mais si sur . . . la plus superbe": French: "But if I can shine on your brow one day, the humblest flower will be the proudest."

St. Omers: See *CR* 89, Ed.'s n.

Ausonius: Decimus Magnus Ausonius (c. 310–c. 395), Latin poet and rhetorician.

St. Augustus: presumably St. Augustine of Hippo (354–430), influential theologian.

Sappho: Sappho (c. 610–c. 580 BC), female love poet of Lesbos.

Anacreon: Anacreon (c. 582–c. 485 BC), Greek lyric poet.

'Tendre fruits des pleurs d'aurore,
Objets des baisers du zephyrs,
Reine de l'empire de Flore,
Hâte toi d'epanouir.'

"O! I beseech you go on," exclaimed Glorvina; and at her request, I finished the poem.

"Beautiful, beautiful!" said she, with enthusiasm. "O! there is a certain delicacy of genius in elegant trifles of this description, which I think the French possess almost exclusively: it is a language formed almost by its very construction *d'eterniser la bagatelle,* and to clothe the fairy effusions of fancy in the most appropriate drapery.

"I thank you for this beautiful ode; the rose was always my idol flower; in all its different stages of existence, it speaks a language my heart understands; from its young bud's first crimson glow, to the last sickly blush of its faded bosom. It is the flower of sentiment in all its sweet transitions; it breathes a moral, and seems to preserve an undecaying soul in that fragrant essence which still survives the bloom and symmetry of the fragile form which every beam too ardent, every gale too chill, injures and destroys."

"And is there," said I, "no parallel in the moral world for this lovely offspring of the natural?"—

Glorvina raised her humid eyes to mine, and I read the parallel there.

"I vow," said the priest with affected pettishness, "I am half tempted to fling away my violet, since this *idol* flower has been decreed to Mr. Mortimer; and to revenge myself, I will shew him your ode on the rose."

At these words, he took out his pocket-book, laughing at his gratified vengeance, while Glorvina coaxed, blushed, and threatened; until snatching the book out of his hand, as he was endeavouring to put it into mine, away she flew like lightning, laughing heartily at her triumph, in all the elixity and playfulness of a youthful spirit.

"What a *Hebe!*" said I, as she kissed her hand to us in her airy flight.

"Yes," said he, "she at least illustrates the possibility of a woman uniting in her character, the extremes of intelligence and simplicity: you see, with all her information and talent, she is a mere child."

When we reached the castle, we found her waiting for us at the breakfast table, flushed with her race—all animation, all spirits! her reserve seemed gradually to vanish, and nothing could be more interesting, yet

---

'Tendre fruits . . . d'epanouir': "Tender fruits of the tears of daybreak / Objects of kisses of the winds / Queen of the empire of the Flowers / Hasten to blossom."

d'eterniser la bagatelle: French: to eternalize trifles.

more *enjoueé,* than her manner and conversation. While the fertility of her imagination supplied incessant topic of conversation, always new, always original, I could not help reverting in idea to those languid *tête-à-têtes,* even in the hey-day of our intercourse, when Lady C___ and I have sat yawning at each other, or biting our fingers, merely for want of something to say, in those intervals of passion, which every connexion even of the tenderest nature, must sustain—she in the native dearth of her mind, and I, in the habitual apathy of mine.

But here is a creature who talks of a violet or a rose with the artless air of infancy, and yet fascinates you in the simple discussion, as though the whole force of intellect was roused to support it.

By Heaven! if I know my own heart, I would not love this being for a thousand worlds; at least as I have hitherto loved. As it is, I feel a certain commerce of the soul—a mutual intelligence of mind and feeling with her, which a look, a sigh, a word is sufficient to betray—a sacred communion of spirit, which raises me in the scale of existence almost above mortality; and though we had been known to each other by looks only, still would this amalgamation of soul (if I may use the expression), have existed.

What a nausea of every sense does the turbulent agitation of gross common-place passion bring with it. But the sentiment which this seraph awakens, "brings with it no satiety." There is something so pure, so refreshing about her, that in the present state of my heart, feelings, and constitution, she produces the same effect on me as does the health-giving breeze of returning spring to the drooping spirit of slow convalescence!

After breakfast she left us, and I was permitted to kiss his Highness's hand, on my instalment in my new and enviable office. He did not speak much on the subject, but with his usual energy. However, I understood I was not to waste my time, as he termed it, for nothing.

When I endeavoured to argue the point (as if the whole business was not a *farce*), the Prince would not hear me; so behold me to all intents and purposes an hireling tutor. Faith, to confess the truth, I know not whether to be pleased or angry with this wild romance: this too, in a man whose whole life has been a laugh at romancers of every description.

What, if my father learns the extent of my folly, in the first era too of my probation! Oh! what a spirit of *bizarté* ever drives me from the central point of common sense, and common prudence! With what tyranny does impulse rule my wayward fate? and how imperiously my heart still takes the lead of my head! yet if I could ever consider the "meteor ray"[84] that has

---

enjoueé: French: playful, sprightly.

[84] See *WIG* 103, n. 10.

hitherto misled my wanderings, as a "light from heaven,"[85] it is now, when virtue leads me to the shrine of innocent pleasure; and the mind becomes the better for the wanderings of the heart.

"But what," you will say with your usual foreseeing prudence—"what is the aim, the object of your present romantic pursuit?"

Faith, none; save the simple enjoyment of present felicity, after an age of cold, morbid apathy; and a self-resignation to an agreeable illusion, after having recently sustained the actual burthen of real sufferings (sufferings the more acute, as they were self-created), succeeded by that dearth of feeling and sensation which, in permitting my heart to lie *fallow* for an interval, only rendered it the more genial to those exotic seeds of happiness which the vagrant gale of chance has flung on its surface. But whether they will take deep root, or only wear "the perfume and suppliance of a moment,"[86] is an unthought of "circumstance still hanging in the stars;"[87] to whose decision I commit it.

Would you know my plans of meditated operation, they run thus:—In a few days I shall avail myself of my professional vocation, and fly home, merely to obviate suspicion in Mr. Clendinning, receive and answer letters, and get my books and wardrobe sent to the Lodge, previous to my own removal there, which I shall effect under the plausible plea of the dissipated neighbourhood of M___ house being equally inimical to the present state of my constitution and my studious pursuits; and in fact, I must either associate with, or offend these hospitable Milesians—an alternative by no means consonant to my inclinations.

From Inismore to the Lodge, I can make constant sallies, and be in the way to receive my father, whose arrival I think I may still date at some weeks' distance; besides, should it be necessary, I think I should find no difficulty in bribing the old steward of the Lodge to my interest. His evident aversion to Clendinning, and attachment to the Prince, renders him ripe for any scheme by which the latter could be served, or the former outwitted; and I hope in the end to effect both: for, to unite this old Chieftain in bonds of amity with my father, and to punish the rascality of the worthy Mr. Clendinning, is a double "consummation devoutly to be wished."[88] In short, when the heart is interested in a project, the stratagems of the imagination to forward it are inexhaustible.

---

[85] Burns, *The Vision* (1786), l. 108.

[86] Shakespeare, *Hamlet,* I. iii. 9.

[87] Shakespeare, *Romeo and Juliet,* I. iv. 107.

[88] Shakespeare, *Hamlet,* III. i. 62–63.

It should seem that the name of M. is interdicted at Inismore: I have more than once endeavoured (though remotely) to make the residence of our family in this country a topic of conversation; but every one seemed to shrink from the subject, as though some fatality was connected with its discussion. To avoid speaking ill of those of whom we have but little reason to speak well, is the temperance of aversion, and seldom found but in great minds.

I must mention to you another instance of liberality in the sentiments of these isolated beings:—I have only once attended the celebration of divine service here since my arrival; but my absence seemed not to be observed, or my attendance noticed; and though, as an Englishman, I may be naturally supposed to be of the most popular faith, yet for all they know to the contrary, I may be Jew, Mussulman or Infidel; for, before me at least, religion is a topic never discussed.

Adieu!

H. M.

END OF VOL. I

The Wild Irish Girl

[Volume II]

Letter IX

TO J. D. ESQ. M. P.

I HAVE already given two lessons to my pupil, in an art in which, with all due deference to the judgment of her quondam tutor, she was never destined to excel.

Not, however, that she is deficient in talent—very far from it; but it is too progressive, too tame a pursuit for the vivacity of her genius. It is not sufficiently connected with those lively and vehement emotions of the soul she is so calculated to feel and to awaken. She was created for a musician—there she is borne away by the magic of the art in which she excels, and the natural enthusiasm of her impassioned character: she can sigh, she can weep, she can smile, over her harp. The sensibility of her soul trembles in her song, and the expression of her rapt countenance harmonizes with her voice. But at her drawing-desk, her features lose their animated character—the smile of rapture ceases to play, and the glance of inspiration to beam. And with the transient extinction of those feelings from which each touching charm is derived, fades that all-pervading interest, that energy of admiration which she usually excites.

Notwithstanding, however, the pencil is never out of her hand; her harp lies silent, and her drawing-book is scarcely ever closed. Yet she limits my attendance to the first hour after breakfast, and then I generally lose sight of her the whole day, until we all meet *en-famille* in the evening. Her improvement is rapid—her father delighted, and she quite fascinated by the novelty of her avocation; the priest congratulates me, and I alone am dissatisfied.

But, from the natural impatience and volatility of her character (both very obvious), this, thank heaven! will soon be over. Besides, even in the hour of tuition, from which I promised myself so much, I do not enjoy her society—the priest always devotes that time to reading out to her; and this too at her own request:—not that I think her innocent and unsuspicious nature cherishes the least reserve at her being left *téte-à-téte* with her less venerable preceptor; but that her ever active mind requires incessant exercise; and in fact, while I am hanging over her in uncontrouled emotion,

---

quondam: at one time.

en-famille: French: as a family.

she is drawing as if her livelihood depended on the exertions of her pencil, or commenting on the subject of the priest's perusal, with as much ease as judgment; while she minds me no more than if I was a well-organized piece of mechanism, by whose motions her pencil was to be guided.

What if, with all her mind, all her genius, this creature had no heart! And what were it to me, though she had? * * * * * * * * * * * * * * * * * *

The Prince fancies his domestic government to be purely patriarchal, and that he is at once the "Law and the Prophet" to his family; never suspecting that he is all the time governed by a girl of nineteen, whose soul, notwithstanding the playful softness of her manner, contains a latent ambition, which sometimes breathing in the grandeur of her sentiments, and sometimes sparkling in the haughtiness of her eye, seems to say, "I was born for empire!"

It is evident that the tone of her mind is naturally stronger than her father's, though to a common observer, *he* would appear a man of nervous and masculine understanding; but the difference between them is this—his energies are the energies of the passions—hers of the mind!

Like most other Princes, *mine* is governed much by *favouritism;* and it is evident I already rank high on the list of partiality.

I perceive, however, that much of his predilection in my favour, arises from the coincidence of my present curiosity and taste with his favourite pursuits and national prejudices. Newly awakened (perhaps by mere force of novelty) to a lively interest for every thing that concerns a country I once thought so little worthy of consideration; in short, convinced by the analogy of existing habits, with recorded customs, of the truth of those circumstances so generally ranked in the apocryphal tales of the history of this vilified country; I have determined to resort to the witness of time, the light of truth, and the corroboration of living testimony, in the study of a country which I am beginning to think, would afford to the mind of philosophy a rich subject of analysis, and to the powers of poetic fancy a splendid series of romantic detail.

"Sir William Temple," says Dr. Johnson,[89] "complains that Ireland is less known than any other country, as to its ancient state, because the natives have little leisure, and less encouragement for inquiry; and that a stranger, not knowing its language, has no ability."

Law and the Prophet: Matthew 7:12.

[89]Sir William Temple (1628–99), English statesman and author of *The Advancement of Trade in Ireland* (1673). Samuel Johnson (1709–84), English author and lexicographer. See letter from Samuel Johnson to Charles O'Conor, April 9, 1757, included in *James Boswell's Life of Johnson: an edition of the original manuscript,* vol. 1, 230. Charles O'Conor, the Elder (1710–91), unlike many of his contemporary antiquarians, knew Irish and had direct access to manuscripts and sources.

This impediment, however, shall not stand in the way of *one* stranger, who is willing to offer up his national prejudices at the Altar of Truth, and expiate the crime of an unfounded but habitual antipathy, by an impartial examination, and an unbiassed inquiry. In short, I have actually began to study the Irish language; and though I recollect to have read the opinion of Temple, "that the Celtic dialect used by the native Irish is the purest and most original language that yet remains;"[90] yet I never suspected that a language spoken *par routine,* and chiefly by the lower classes of society, could be acquired upon *principle,* until the other day, when I observed in the Prince's truly national library some philological works, which were shewn me by Father John, who has offered to be my preceptor in this wreck of ancient dialect, and who assures me he will render me master of it in a short time—provided I study *con amore.*

"And I will assist you," said Glorvina.

"We will *all* assist him," said the Prince.

"Then I shall study *con amore!* indeed," returned I.

Behold me then, buried amidst the monuments of past ages!—deep in the study of the language, history, and antiquities of this ancient nation—talking of the invasion of Henry II as a recent circumstance—of the Phoenician migration hither from Spain, as though my grandfather had been delegated by Firbalgs to receive the Milesians on their landing—and of those transactions passed through

"The dark posterns of time long elapsed,"[91]

as though their existence was but freshly registered in the annals of recollection.

In short, infected by my antiquarian conversation with the Prince, and having fallen in with some of those monkish histories which, on the strength of Druidical tradition, trace a series of wise and learned Irish monarchs before the Flood, I am beginning to have as much faith in antediluvian records as Dr. Parsons[92] himself, who accuses *Adam* of authorship, or Thomas Banguis, who almost gives *fac-similies* of the hand-writing of Noah's progenitors.

---

par routine: French: as a matter of course.

con amore: Italian: with love.

Henry II: King of England (1154–89). Landed in Waterford in October 1171 and established an English colonial presence in Ireland. Also see *WIG* 133, n. 53.

[90] See *The Works of Sir William Temple,* 4 vols. (1770), vol. 3, 82.

[91] Young, *Night Thoughts,* Night I, l. 224.

[92] Lawrence Parsons, *Observations on the Bequest of Henry Flood, Esq. To Trinity College Dublin, with a Defence of the Ancient History of Ireland* (Dublin, 1795). Parsons claimed Ireland was known to the Phoenicians two generations before Moses.

Seriously, however, I enter on my new studies with avidity, and read from the morning's first dawn till the usual hour of breakfast, which is become to me as much the banquet of the heart, as the Roman supper was to the Augustan wits "the feast of reason and the flow of soul,"[93] for it is the only meal at which Glorvina presides.

Two hours each day does the kind priest devote to my philological pursuits, while Glorvina, who is frequently present on these occasions, makes me repeat some short poem or song after her, that I may catch the pronunciation (which is almost unattainable), then translates them into English, which I word for word write down. Here then is a specimen of Irish poetry, which is almost always the effusion of some blind itinerant bard, or some rustic minstrel, into whose breast the genius of his country has breathed inspiration, as he patiently drove the plough, or laboriously worked in the bog.*

"*CATHBEIN NOLAN.*

I.

"My love, when she floats on the mountain's brow, is like the dewy cloud of the summer's loveliest evening. Her forehead is as a pearl; her spiral locks are of gold; and I grieve that I cannot banish her from my memory.

II.

"When she enters the forest like the bounding doe, dispersing the dew with her airy steps, her mantle on her arm, the axe in hand, to cut the branches of flame; I know not which is the most noble—the King of the Saxons,† or Cathbein Nolan."[94]

* Miss Brooks, in her elegant version of the works of some of the Irish Bards, says, "'Tis scarcely possible that any language can be more adapted to lyric poetry than the Irish; so great is the smoothness and harmony of its numbers: it is also possessed of a refined delicacy, a descriptive power, and an exquisite tender simplicity of expression: two or three little artless words, or perhaps a single epithet, will sometimes convey such an image of sentiment or suffering, to the mind, that one lays down the book to look at the picture." [See Charlotte Brooke, *Reliques of Irish Poetry* (1789), 229–30. Brooke (c. 1740–93), translator and anthologist. Her *Reliques* offered some of the first translations of Irish songs into English, publishing both original and translation side by side. Ed.]

† The King of England is still called by the common Irish, *Riagh Sasseanach.*

---

[93] Alexander Pope, *Imitations of Horace: Satires,* II, Satire I, l. 130.

[94] The song's title should read "Cathlein Nolan." All instances changed in the 1846 edition.

This little song is of so ancient a date, that Glorvina assures me, neither the name of the composer (for the melody is exquisitely beautiful) nor the poet, have escaped the oblivion of time. But if we may judge of the rank of the poet by that of his mistress, it must have been of a very humble degree; for it is evident that the fair Cathbein, whose form is compared, in splendour, to that of the Saxon Monarch, is represented as cutting wood for the fire.

The following songs, however, are by the most celebrated of all the modern Irish bards, Turloch Carolan,* and the airs to which he has composed them, possess the *arioso* elegance of Italian music, united to the heart-felt pathos of Irish melody.

I.

"I must sing of the youthful plant of gentlest mien—Fanny, the beautiful and warm-soul'd—the maid of the amber-twisted ringlets; the air-lifted and light-footed virgin—the elegant pearl and heart's treasure of Erin; then waste not the fleeting hour—let us enjoy it in drinking to the health of Fanny, the daughter of David.

II.

"It is the maid of the magic lock I sing, the fair swan of the shore—for whose love a multitude expires: Fanny, the beautiful, whose tresses are like the evening sun-beam; whose voice is like the black-bird's morning song: O, may I never leave the world until dancing *in the air*

* He was born in the village of Nobber, county Westmeath, in 1670, and died in 1739. He never regretted the loss of sight, but used gayly to say, "my eyes are only transplanted into my ears." Of his poetry, the reader may form some judgment from these examples: of his music, it has been said by O'Connor, the celebrated historian (who knew him intimately), "so happy, so elevated was he in some of his compositions, that he excited the wonder, and obtained the approbation, of a great master who never saw him, I mean Geminiani." And his execution on the harp was rapid and impressive—far beyond that of all the professional competitors of the age in which he lived. The charms of women, the pleasures of conviviality, and the power of poesy and music, were at once his theme and inspiration; and his life was an illustration of his theory: for until its last ardour was chilled by death, he loved, drank, and sung. He was the welcome guest of every house, from the peasant to the prince; but, in the true wandering spirit of his profes-sion, he never stayed to exhaust that welcome. He lived and died poor. While in the fervor of composition, he was constantly heard to pass sentence on his own effusions, as they arose from his harp, or breathed on his lips; blaming and praising with equal vehemence, the unsuccessful effort and felicitous attempt. [For Charles O'Conor's description of Carolan, see "Life of Turlough O'Carolan," Appendix to Walker, *Historical Memoirs*, 97. Francesco Geminiani (1687–1762), Italian composer, resided in Dublin after 1759. Ed.]

---

arioso: musical direction for a composition indicating melodious, songlike cantabile.

(this expression in the Irish is beyond the power of translation) at her wedding, I shall send away the hours in drinking to Fanny, the daughter of David."*

"*GRACY NUGENT.*

I.

"I delight to talk of thee! blossom of fairness! Gracy, the most frolic of the young and lovely—who from the fairest of the province bore away the palm of excellence—happy is he who is near her, for morning nor evening grief, nor fatigue, cannot come near him: her mien is like the mildness of a beautiful dawn; and her tresses flow in twisted folds—she is the daughter of the branches.—Her neck has the whiteness of alabaster—the softness of the cygnet's bosom is hers; and the glow of the summer's sun-beam is on her countenance. Oh! blessed is he who shall obtain thee, fair daughter of the blossoms—maid of the spiry locks!

II.

"Sweet is the word of her lip, and sparkling the beam of her blue rolling eye; and close round her neck cling the golden tresses of her head; and her teeth are arranged in beautiful order.—I say to the maid of youthful mildness, thy voice is sweeter than the song of birds; every grace, every charm play round thee; and though my soul delights to sing thy praise, yet I must quit the theme—to drink with a sincere heart to thy health, Gracy of the soft waving ringlets."†

* She was daughter to David Power, Esq. of the county of Galway, and mother to the late Lord Cloncarty. The epithet bestowed on her, of *swan of the shore,* arose from her father's mansion being situated on the edge of *Lough Leah, or the grey lake,* of which many curious legends are told. When Carolan, alone, and in the act of composing the music and words of the above song, hung over his harp, wrapt in the golden visions of his art, the theme of his effusions suddenly entered the room where he sat, and, by the noise which the rustling of her silks made, disturbed the poetic reveries of the bard, who, enraged at the interruption, which probably put to flight some happy inspiration of genius, flung at the unknown intruder a large sapling stick which he always carried with him. Miss Power, however, fortunately escaped the frenzied intention of the passionate minstrel, which, had it been realized, would have turned his panegyric strains to elegies of woe. This anecdote the Author had from her father, who had the honour of hearing it from the lips of the lady herself, and who, though at that period in an advanced era of life, retained strong traces of that exquisite beauty for which she was so justly celebrated in the strains of her native bard.

† She was the daughter of John Nugent, Esq. of Castle Nugent, Culambre, at whose hospitable mansion the bard was frequently entertained. In the summer of 1797, the Author conversed with an old peasant in Westmeath, who had frequently listened to the tones of Carolan's harp in his boyish days. [For the melody of "Gracey Nugent," see Bunting, *A General Collection.* Maria Edgeworth used the name in *The Absentee* (1812). Ed.]

Does not this poetical effusion awakened by the charms of the fair Gracy, recall to your memory the description of Helen by Theocritus, in his beautiful epithalamium on her marriage?—

"She is like the rising of the golden morning, when the night departeth, and when the winter is over and gone—she resembleth the cypress in the garden, the horse in the chariot of Thessaly."

While the invocation to the enjoyment of convivial pleasure which breathes over the termination of every verse, glows with the festive spirit of the Tean bard.

When I remarked the coincidence of style which existed between the early Greek writers and the bards of Erin, Glorvina replied, with a smile,

"In drawing this analogy, you think, perhaps, to flatter my national vanity; but the truth is, we trace the spirit of Milesian poetry to a higher source than the spring of Grecian genius; for many figures in Irish song are of oriental origin; and the bards who ennobled the train of our Milesian founders, and who awakened the soul of song here, seem, in common with the Greek poets, 'to have kindled their poetic fires at those unextinguished lamps which burn within the tomb of oriental genius.' Let me, however, assure you, that no adequate version of an Irish poem can be given; for the peculiar construction of the Irish language, the felicity of its epithets, and force of its expressions, bid defiance to all translation."

"But while your days and nights are thus devoted to Milesian literature," you will say, "what becomes of Blackstone and Coke?"

Faith, e'en what may for me—the mind, the mind, like the heart, is not to be forced in its pursuits; and, I believe, in an intellectual as in a physical sense, there are certain antipathies which reason may condemn, but cannot vanquish. Coke is to me a dose of ipecacuhana, and my present studies, like those poignant incentives which stimulate the appetite without causing repletion. It is in vain to force me to a profession, against which my taste, my habits, my very nature, revolts; and if my father persists in his determination, why, as a *dernier resort.* I must turn *historiographer* to the Prince of Inismore.

*　　*　　*　　*　　*　　*

Theocritus: Theocritus (c. 300–260 BC), Greek writer of pastoral poetry. See his *Idylls,* VIII, stanza 4.

epithalamium: a nuptial song or poem in praise of the bride and bridegroom.

Thessaly: region in northern Greece. In Greek legend, Admentus' suit of Alcestis, daughter of Pelias, King in Thessaly, required him to harness a lion and a boar to a chariot.

Tean bard: variant form of "Teian" and frequent eighteenth- and nineteenth-century poetic synonym for Anacreon. See *WIG* 174.

ipecacuhana: [*sic*] "ipecacuanha." A purgative, emetic, agent to induce vomiting.

Like the spirit of Milton, I feel myself, in this new world, "vital in every part:"

"All heart I live, all head, all eye, all ear,
All intellect, all sense."[95]

Letter X

TO J. D. ESQ. M. P.

THE more I know of this singular girl, the more the happy *discordia concors* of her character awakens my curiosity and surprise. I never beheld such an union of intelligence and simplicity, infantine playfulness and profound reflexion, as her character exhibits. Sometimes when I think I am trifling with a child, I find I am conversing with a philosopher; and sometimes in the midst of the most serious and interesting conversation, some impulse of the moment seizes on her imagination, and a vein of frolic humour and playful sarcasm is indulged at the expence of my most sagacious arguments or philosophic gravity. Her reserve (unknown to herself) is gradually giving way to the most bewitching familiarity.

When the priest is engaged, I am suffered to tread with her the "pathless grass,"[96] climb the mountain's steep, or ramble along the sea-beat coast, sometimes followed by her nurse, and sometimes by a favourite little dog only.

Of nothing which concerns her country is she ignorant; and when a more interesting, a more soul-felt conversation, cannot be obtained, I love to draw her into a little national chit-chat.

Yesterday, as we were walking along the base of that mountain from which I first beheld her dear residence (and sure I may say with Petrarch, "Benedetto sia il fiorno e'l Mese e'lanno"),[97] several groups of peasants (mostly females) passed us, with their usual courteous salutations, and apparently dressed in their holiday garbs.

"Poor souls!" said Glorvina—"this is a day of jubilee to them, for a great annual fair is held in the neighbourhood."

---

dernier resort: French: last resort.

discordia concors: Latin: harmonious discord.

[95] Milton, *Paradise Lost,* Book VI, ll. 350–51.

[96] Thomas Parnell, *The Hermit* (1722), l. 29.

[97] Italian: Petrarch, *Canzoniere,* sonnet 61, 1: "Blessed be the day and the month and the year."

"But from whence," said I, "do they draw the brightness of those tints which adorn their coarse garments; those gowns and ribbons, that rival the gay colouring of that heath hedge; those bright blue and scarlet mantles? Are they, too, vestiges of ancient modes and ancient taste?"

"Certainly they are," she replied, "and the colours which the Irish were celebrated for wearing and dying a thousand years back, are now most prevalent. In short, the ancient Irish, like the Israelites, were so attached to this many-coloured *costume,* that it became the mark by which the different classes of the people were distinguished. Kings were limited to seven colours in their royal robes; and six were allowed the bards. What an idea does this give of the reverence paid to superior talent in other times by our forefathers! But that bright yellow you now behold so universally worn, has been in all ages their favourite hue. Spenser thinks this custom came from the East; and Lord Bacon accounts for the propensity of the Irish to it, by supposing it contributes to longevity."[98]

"But where," said I, "do these poor people procure so expensive an article as saffron, to gratify their prevailing taste?" *

"I have heard Father John say," she returned, "that saffron, as an article of importation, could never have been at any time cheap enough for general use. And I believe formerly, as *now,* they communicated this bright yellow tinge with indigenous plants, with which this country abounds.

"See," she added, springing lightly forward, and culling a plant which grew from the mountain's side—"see this little blossom, which they call here, 'yellow lady's bed-straw,' and which you, as a botanist, will better recognize as the *Galicens borum;* it communicates a beautiful yellow; as does the *Lichen juniperinus,* or 'cypress moss,' which you brought me yesterday; and I think the *resida Luteola,* or 'yellow weed,' surpasses them all.†

* "A Portuguese physician attempts to account for their use of this yellow dye, by alledging that it was worn as a vermifuge. He should first demonstrate that all the people were infected with worms."—*Dr. Patterson's Observations on the Climate of Ireland.* [Patterson, *Observations* . . . , 85n. Ed.]

† Purple, blue, and green dyes, were introduced by *Tighwmas* the Great, in the year of the world 2815. The Irish also possessed the art of dyeing a fine scarlet; so early as the day of St. Bennia, a disciple of St. Patrick, scarlet clothes and robes highly embroidered, are mentioned in the book of *Glandelogh.* [Patterson, *Observations* . . . , 88 and 92. Ed.]

Spenser: see *CR* 30–31, Ed.'s n.

Lord Bacon: Francis Bacon (1561–1626), Lord Chancellor of England (1618–21), philosopher, and essayist.

vermifuge: an agent capable of destroying or expelling parasitic worms.

[98] Near direct quotation from William Patterson, *Observations on the Climate of Ireland* (Dublin, 1804), 84–85, who borrowed it from Walker, *An Historical Essay* (1788).

"In short, the botanical treasures of our country, though I dare say little known, are inexhaustible.

"Nay," she continued, observing, I believe, the admiration that sparkled in my eyes, "give me no credit, I beseech you, for this local information, for there is not a peasant girl in the neighbourhood, but will tell you more on the subject."

While she was thus dispensing knowledge with the most unaffected simplicity of look and manner, a group of boys advanced towards us, with a car laden with stones, and fastened to the back of an unfortunate dog, which they were endeavouring to train to this new species of canine avocation, by such unmerciful treatment as must have procured the wretched animal a speedy release from all his sufferings.

Glorvina no sooner perceived this, than she flew to the dog, and while the boys looked all amaze, effected his liberation, and by her caresses endeavoured to soothe him into forgetfulness of his late sufferings; then turning to the ringleader, she said:

"Dermot, I have so often heard you praised for your humanity to animals, that I can scarcely believe it possible that you have been accessary to the sufferings of this useful and affectionate animal; he is just as serviceable to society in his way, as you are in your's, and you are just as well able to drag a loaded cart as he is to draw that little car. Come now, I am not so heavy as the load you have destined him to bear, and you are much stronger than your dog, and now you shall draw me home to the castle; and then give me your opinion on the subject."

In one moment his companions, laughing vociferously at the idea, had the stones flung out of the little vehicle, and fastened its harness on the broad shoulders of the half-pouting, half-smiling Dermot; and the next moment this little agile sylph was seated in the car.

Away went Dermot, dragged on by the rest of the boys, while Glorvina, delighted as a child, with her new mode of conveyance, laughed with all her heart, and kissed her hand to me as she flew along; while I, trembling for her safety, endeavoured to keep pace with her triumphal chariot, till her wearied, breathless Phaeton, unable to run any further with his lovely, laughing burthen, begged a respite.

"How!" said she, "weary of this amusement, and yet you have not at every step been cruelly lashed, like your poor dog."

The panting Dermot hung his head, and said in Irish, "the like should not happen again."

Phaeton: In Greek mythology, Phaethon drove Helios's sun chariot but failed to control it. Zeus intervened to prevent Phaethon setting the world on fire. In modern usage, refers to various light four-wheeled horse-drawn vehicles.

"It is enough," said Glorvina, in the same language—"we are all liable to commit a fault, but let us never forget it is in our power to correct it. And now go to the castle, where you shall have a good dinner, in return for the good and pleasant exercise you have procured me."

The boys were as happy as kings. Dermot was unyoked, and the poor dog, wagging his tail in token of his felicity, accompanied the gratified group to the castle.

When Glorvina had translated to me the subject of her short dialogue with Dermot, she added, laughing,

"Oh! how I should like to be dragged about this way for two or three hours every day: never do I enter into any little folly of this kind, that I do not sigh for those sweet hours of my childhood when I could play the fool with impunity."

"Play the fool!" said I—"and do you call this playing the fool?—this dispensation of humanity, this culture of benevolence in the youthful mind, these lessons of truth and goodness, so sweetly, simply given."

"Nay," she returned, "you always seem inclined to flatter me into approbation of myself! but the truth is, I was glad to seize on the opportunity of lecturing that urchin Dermot, who, though I praised his humanity, is the very beadle to all the unfortunate animals in the neighbourhood. But I have often had occasion to remark, that by giving a virtue to those neglected children, which they do not possess, I have awakened their emulation to attain it."

"To say that you are an angel," said I, "is to say a very common-place thing, which every man says to the woman he either does, or affects to admire; and yet"—

"Nay,"—interrupted she, laying her hand on my arm, and looking up full in my face with that arch glance I have so often caught revelling in her eloquent eye—"I am not emulous of a place in the angelic choir; canonization is more consonant to my *papistical* ambition; then let me be your saint—your tutelar saint, and"—

"And let me," interrupted I, impassionately—"let me, like the members of the Greek church, adore my saint, not by prostration, but by a kiss;"—and, for the first time in my life, I pressed my lips to the beautiful hand which still rested on my arm, and from which I first drew a glove that has not since left my bosom, nor been redemanded by its charming owner.

This little freedom (which, to another, would have appeared nothing), was received with a degree of blushing confusion, that assured me it was the first of the kind ever offered; even the fair hand blushed its sense of my

---

tutelar saint: a patron saint.

boldness, and enhanced the pleasure of the theft by the difficulty it promised of again obtaining a similar favour.

By Heaven there is an infection in the sensitive delicacy of this creature, which even my hardened confidence cannot resist!

No *prieux Chevalier,* on being permitted to kiss the tip of his liege lady's finger, after a seven years' siege, could feel more pleasantly embarrassed than I did, as we walked on in silence, until we were happily relieved by the presence of the old garrulous nurse, who came out in search of her young lady—for, like the princesses in the Greek tragedies, *my* Princess seldom appears without the attendance of this faithful representative of fond maternity.

For the rest of the walk she talked mostly to the nurse in Irish, and at the castle-gate we parted—she to attend a patient, and I to retire to my own apartment, to ruminate on my morning's ramble with this fascinating *lusus naturae.*

Adieu!

H. M.

Letter XI

TO J. D. ESQ. M. P.

THE drawing which I made of the castle is finished—the Prince is charmed with it, and Glorvina insisted on copying it. This was as I expected—as I wished; and I took care to finish it so minutely, that her patience (of which she has no great store), should soon be exhausted in the imitation, and I should have something more of her attention than she generally affords me at the drawing-desk.

Yesterday, in the absence of the priest, I read to her as she drew. After a thousand little symptoms of impatience and weariness—"here," said she, yawning—"here is a straight line I can make nothing of—do you know, Mr. Mortimer, I never could draw a perpendicular line in my life. See now my pencil *will* go into a curve or an angle; so you must guide my hand, or I shall draw it all zig-zag."

(I "guide her hand to draw a straight line!")

"Nay then," said I, with the ostentatious gravity of a pedagogue master, "I may as well do the drawing myself."

"Well then," said she playfully, "*do* it yourself."

---

prieux Chevalier: French: gallant knight.

lusus naturae: Latin: sport of nature.

Away she flew to her harp; while I, half lamenting, half triumphing, in my forbearance, took her pencil and her seat. I perceived, however, that she had not even drawn a single line of the picture, and yet her paper was not a mere *carte-blanche*—for close to the margin was written in a fairy hand, '*Henry Mortimer,* April 2d, 10 o'clock,'—the very day and hour of my entrance into the castle; and in several places, the half-defaced features of a face evidently a copy my own, were still visible.

If any thing could have rendered this little circumstance more deliciously gratifying to my heart, it was, that I had been just reading to her the anecdote of "the *Maid of Corinth.*"

I raised my eyes from the paper to her with a look that must have spoken my feelings; but she, unconscious of my observation, began a favourite air of her favourite Carolan's, and supposed me to be busy at the *perpendicular line.*

Wrapt in her charming avocation, she seemed borne away by the magic of her own numbers, and thus inspired and inspiring as she appeared, faithful, as the picture it formed was interesting, I took her likeness. Conceive for a moment a form full of character, and full of grace, bending over an instrument singularly picturesque—a profusion of auburn hair fastened up to the top of the finest formed head I ever beheld, with a golden bodkin—an armlet of curious workmanship glittering above a finely turned elbow, and the loose sleeves of a flowing robe drawn up unusually high, to prevent this drapery from sweeping the chords of the instrument. The expression of the divinely touching countenance breathed all the fervour of genius under the influence of inspiration, and the contours of the face, from the peculiar uplifted position of the head, were precisely such, as lends to painting the happiest line of feature, and shade of colouring. Before I had near finished the lovely picture, her song ceased; and turning towards me, who sat opposite her, she blushed to observe how intensely my eyes were fixed on *her.*

"I am admiring," said I, carelessly, "the singular elegance of your costume: it is indeed to me a never-failing source of wonder and admiration."

"I am not sorry," she replied, "to avail myself of my father's prejudices in favour of our ancient national costume, which, with the exception of the drapery being made of modern materials (on the antique model), is absolutely drawn from the wardrobes of my great grandames. This armlet, I have heard my father say, is near four hundred years old, and many of the ornaments and jewels you have seen me wear, are of a date no less ancient."

Maid of Corinth: credited with the invention of clay modeling, and the concept of mimesis.

"But how," said I, while she continued to tune her harp, and I to ply the pencil, "how comes it that in so remote a period, we find the riches of Peru and Golconda contributing their splendour to the magnificence of Irish dress?"

"O!" she replied, smiling, "we too had our Peru and Golconda in the bosom of our country—for it was once thought rich not only in gold and silver mines, but abounded in pearls,* amethysts, and other precious stones: even a few years back, Father John saw some fine pearl taken out of the river Ban;† and Mr. O'Halloran, the celebrated Irish historian, declares that within his memory, amethysts of immense value were found in Ireland.‡[99]

"I remember reading in the life of St. Bridget, that the King of Leinster presented to her father, a sword set with precious stones, which the pious saint, more charitable than honest, devoutly stole, and sold for the benefit of the poor; but it should seem that the sources of our national treasures are now shut up, like the gold mines of La Valais, for the public weal, I suppose; for we now hear not of amethysts found, pearls discovered, or gold mines worked; and it is to the caskets of my female ancestors that I stand indebted that my dress or hair is not fastened or adorned like those of my humbler countrywomen, with a wooden bodkin."

"That, indeed," said I, "is a species of ornament I have observed very prevalent with your fair *paysannes*; and of whatever materials it is made,

* "It should seem," says Mr. Walker, in his ingenious and elegant essay on Ancient Irish Dress—"that Ireland teemed with gold and silver, for as well as in the laws recited, we find an act ordained 35th Henry VIII that merchant strangers should pay 40 pence custom for every pound of silver they carried out of Ireland; and Lord Strafford, in one of his letters from Dublin, to his royal master, says, 'with this I land you an ingot of silver of 300 oz.'" [See Walker, *An Historical Essay,* 23n. Ed.]

† Pearls abounded, and still are found in this country; and were in such repute in the 11th century, that a present of them was sent to the famous Bishop Anselm, by a Bishop of Limerick. [Anselm, Archbishop of Canterbury from 1093 to his death in 1109, canonized in 1163. See O'Halloran, *History and Antiquities of Ireland,* 116. Ed.]

‡ The Author is indebted to—Knox, Esq. barister at law, Dublin, for the sight of some beautiful amethysts, which belonged to his female ancestors, and which many of the lapidaries of London, after a diligent search, found it impossible to match.

Golconda: historic city in the Andhra Pradesh state, southwest India, famous for its diamonds.

St. Bridget: Also Brigid, Brigit, or Bride (d. c. 525), founder of convent at Kildare, second only to St. Patrick among Irish saints, and a figure of Celtic mythology.

wooden bodkin: an ornamental hairpin or brooch. See Walker, *An Historical Essay,* 14.

paysannes: French: countrywomen.

[99] See Walker, *An Historical Essay,* 21–22n.

when employed in such an happy service as I *now* behold it, has an air of simple useful elegance, which in my opinion constitutes the great art of female dress."

"It is at least," replied she, "the most ancient ornament we know here—for we are told that the celebrated palace of Emania,* erected previous to the Christian era, was sketched by the famous Irish Empress Macha, with her bodkin.

"I remember a passage from a curious and ancient romance in the Irish language, that fastened wonderfully upon my imagination when I read it to my father in my childhood, and which gives to the bodkin a very early origin:—it ran thus, and is called the '*Interview between Fionn M'Cumhal and Cannan.*'

'Cannan, when he said this, was seated at table; on his right hand was seated his wife, and upon his left his beautiful daughter, so exceedingly fair, that the snow driven by the winter storms surpassed not her in fairness, and her cheeks wore the blood of a young calf; her hair hung in curling ringlets, and her teeth were like pearl—a spacious veil hung from her lovely head down her delicate form, and the veil was fastened by a golden bodkin.'

"The bodkin, you know, is also an ancient Greek ornament, and mentioned by Vulcan, as among the trinkets he was obliged to forge."†

By the time she had finished this curious quotation in favour of the antiquity of her dress, her harp was tuned, and she began another exquisite old Irish air, called the "Dream of the Young Man,"[100] which she accompanied rather by a plaintive *murmur,* than with her voice's full melodious powers. It is thus this creature winds round the heart, while she enlightens the mind, and entrances the senses.

*The resident palace of the Kings of Ulster of which Colgan speaks as "*redolens spelndorem.*" [John Colgan (c. 1592–1658), Franciscan friar and hagiographer who studied at St. Anthony's College in Louvain. Helped produce a Counter-Reformation ecclesiastical history of Ireland. His publications *Acta Sanctorum Hiberniae* (1645) and *Trias Thaumaturga* (1647) reflect access to manuscripts at Louvain that are no longer extant. Ed.]

†See Iliad, 13, 17. [See Pope's translations of the *Iliad* (1715–20), Book XVIII, ll. 431–78. Ed.]

Empress Macha: In Ulster Cycle, one of three war goddesses and great earth mother, used her bodkin to draw the design for the palace at Eamania.

[100]For the melody of "Dream of the Young Man," see Bunting, *A General Collection* (1796).

I had finished the sketch in the meantime, and just beneath the figure, and above her flattering inscription of my name, I wrote with my pencil,

"'Twas thus Apelles bask'd in beauty's blaze,
Nor felt the danger of the stedfast gaze;"[101]

while she, a few minutes after, with that restlessness that seemed to govern all her actions to-day, arose, put her harp aside, and approached me with

"Well, Mr. Mortimer, you are very indulgent to my insufferable indolence—let me see what you have done for me;" and looking over my shoulder, she beheld not the ruins of her castle, but a striking likeness of her blooming self; and bending her head close to the paper, read the lines, and that name honoured by the inscription of her own fair hand.

For the world I would not have looked her full in the face; but from beneath my downcast eye I stole a transient glance: the colour did not rush to her cheek (as it usually does under the influence of any powerful emotion), but rather deserted its beautiful standard, and she stood with her eyes rivetted on the picture, as though she dreaded by their removal she should encounter those of the artist.

After about three minutes endurance of this mutual confusion, (could you believe me such a blockhead!)—the priest, to our great relief, entered the room.

Glorvina ran and shook hands with him, as though she had not seen him for an age, and flew out of the room; while I, effacing the quotation, but not the honoured inscription, asked Father John's opinion of my effort at portrait painting. He acknowledged it was a most striking resemblance, and added,

"Now you will indeed give a *coup de grace* to the partiality of the Prince in your favour, and you will rank so much the higher in his estimation, in proportion as his daughter is dearer to him than his *ruins.*

Thus encouraged, I devoted the rest of the day to copying out this sketch; and I have finished the picture in that light tinting, so effective in these kind of characteristic drawings. That beautifully pensive expression which touches the countenance of Glorvina, when breathing her native strains, I have most happily caught; and her costume, attitude, and harp, form as happy a combination of traits, as a single portrait perhaps ever presented.

When it was shewn to the Prince, he gazed on it in silence, till tears obscured his glance; then laying it down, he embraced me, but said nothing. Had he detailed the merits and demerits of the picture in all the technical

coup de grace: French: a finishing stroke.

[101] Anna Seward, "Monody on Major André" (1781), ll. 75–76.

farrago of *cognoscenti* phrase, his comments would not have been half so eloquent as this simple action, and the silence which accompanied it.

Adieu!

H. M.

Letter XII

TO J. D. ESQ. M. P.

HERE is a *bonne bouche* for your antiquarian taste, and *Ossianic*[102] palate! Almost every evening after vespers, we all assemble in a spacious hall,* which had been shut up for near a century, and first opened by the present prince when he was driven for shelter to his paternal ruins.

This *Vengolf,* this *Valk-halla,* where the very spirit of Woden seems to preside, runs the full length of the castle as it now stands (for the center of the building only, has escaped the dilapidations of time), and its beautifully arched roof is enriched with numerous devices, which mark the spirit of that day in which it was erected. This very curious roof is supported by two rows of pillars of that elegant spiral lightness which characterizes the Gothic order in a certain stage of its progress. The floor is a finely tesselated pavement; and the ample but ungrated hearths which terminate it at either extremity, blaze every evening with the cheering contributions of a neighbouring bog. The windows, which are high, narrow, and arched, command on one side a noble view of the ocean, on the other they are closed up.

When I inquired of Father John the cause of this singular exclusion of a very beautiful land view, he replied, "that from those windows were to be

* "Amidst the ruins of Buan Ratha, near Limerick, is a princely hall and spacious chambers; the fine stucco in many of which is yet visible, though uninhabitable for near a century." — *O'Halloran's Introduction to the Study of the Hist. and Antiq. of Ireland,* p. 8.

There are very few, if any, of those venerable mansion houses, such as in England bear the stamp of that style of architecture so prevalent about two hundred years back, to be found in Ireland. But in town, every village, every considerable tract of land, the spacious ruins of princely residence or religious edifices, the palace, the castle, or the abbey, are to be seen. [O'Halloran, *History and Antiquities of Ireland,* 84. Ed.]

---

cognoscenti: Italian: connoisseur.

bonne bouche: French: tidbit.

Vengolf: In Scandinavian mythology, fallen warriors join Woden (see below) in Vengolf, the hall of slain warriors.

Woden: Woden, one of the principal gods in Scandinavian mythology.

tesselated: mosaic pattern.

[102] For Ossian, see *WIG* 122, Ed.'s n. and *WIG* 200, n. 104.

seen the greater part of that rich tract of land which once formed the territory of the Princes of Inismore;* and since," said he, "the possessions of the present Prince are limited to a few hereditary acres, and a few rented farms, he cannot bear to look on the domains of his ancestors, nor ever goes beyond the confines of this little peninsula."

This very curious apartment is still called the banquetting-hall—where

> "Stately the feast and high the cheer,
> Girt with many a valiant Peer,"[103]

was once celebrated in all the boundless extravagance and convivial spirit of ancient Irish hospitality. But it now serves as an armory, a museum, a cabinet of national antiquities, and national curiosities. In short, it is the receptacle of all those precious relics, which the Prince has been able to rescue from the wreck of his family splendour.

Here, when he is seated by a blazing hearth in an immense arm-chair, made, as he assured me, of the famous wood of *Shilelah,* his daughter by his side, his harper behind him, and his *domestic altar* not destitute of that national libation which is no disparagement to princely taste, since it has received the sanction of imperial approbation;† his gratified eye wandering over the scattered insignia of the former prowess of his family; his gratified heart expanding to the reception of life's sweetest ties—domestic joys and social endearments;—he forgets the derangement of his circumstances—he forgets that he is the ruined possessor of a visionary title; he feels only that he is a man—and an Irishman! While the transient happiness that lights up the vehement feelings of his benevolent breast, effuses its warmth o'er all who come within its sphere.

Nothing can be more delightful than the evenings passed in this *vengolf*—this hall of Woden; where my sweet Glorvina hovers round us, like one of the beautiful *valkyries* of the Gothic paradise, who bestow on the

*I understand that it is only a few years back, since the present respectable representative of the M'Dermot family opened these windows, which the Prince of Coolavin closed up, upon a principle similar to that by which the Prince of Inismore was actuated. [MacDermott of Coolavin is named by Owenson in the "Prefatory Address" to the 1846 edition as a model for the Prince of Inishmore. Ed.]

†Peter the Great of Russia, was remarkably fond of whiskey, and used to say, "Of all wine, Irish wine is the best." [Peter the Great, ruled Russia 1682–1725. Ed.]

Shilelah: Shillelagh, a barony and village in Co. Wicklow. Known for its woods.

valkyries: in Scandinavian mythology, the group of maidens who chose the slain worthy of a place in the Vengolf.

[103] Thomas Warton, *Ode XIII. The Grave of King Arthur* (1777), ll. 1–2.

spirit of the departed warrior that heaven he eagerly rushes on death to obtain. Sometimes she accompanies the old bard on her harp, or with her voice; and frequently as she sits at her wheel (for she is often engaged in this simple and primitive avocation), endeavours to lure her father to speak on those subjects most interesting to him or to me; or, joining the general conversation, by the playfulness of her humour, or the original whimsicality of her sallies, materially contributes to the "*molle atque facetum*" of the moment.

On the evening of the day of the picture scene, the absence of Glorvina (for she was attending a sick servant) threw a gloom over our little circle. The Prince, for the first time, dismissed the harper, and, taking me by the arm, walked up and down the hall in silence, while the priest yawned over a book.

I have already told you, that this curious hall is the *emporium* of the antiquities of Inismore, which are arranged along its walls, and suspended from its pillars.—As much to draw the Prince from the gloomy reverie into which he seemed plunged, as to satisfy my own curiosity and yours, I requested his Highness to explain some characters on a collar which hung from a pillar, and appeared to be plated with gold.

Having explained the motto, he told me that this collar had belonged to an order of knighthood hereditary in his family—of an institution more ancient than any in England, by some centuries.

"How!" said I, "was chivalry so early known in Ireland? and rather, did it ever exist here?"

"Did it!" said the Prince, impatiently, "I believe, young gentleman, the origin of knighthood may be traced in Ireland upon surer ground than in any other country whatever.* Long before the birth of Christ, we had an hereditary order of knighthood in Ulster, called the Knights of the *Red Branch.* They possessed, near the royal palace of Ulster, a seat, called the

* Mr. O'Halloran, with a great deal of spirit and ingenuity, endeavours to prove, that the German knighthood (the earliest we read of in chivalry) was of Irish origin: with what success, we leave it to the impartial reader to judge. It is, however, certain, that the German *Ritter,* or knight, bears a very close analogy to the Irish *riddaire.* In 1395, Richard II in his tour through Ireland, offered to knight the four provincial Kings who came to receive him in Dublin. But they excused themselves, as having received that honour from their parents at seven years old—that being the age in which the Kings of Ireland knighted their eldest sons.—See *Froissart.* [O'Halloran, *History and Antiquities of Ireland,* 43–44; Jean Froissart (c. 1333–c. 1400), French medieval poet whose *Chroniques* (1388–1410) narrate fourteenth-century chivalric and courtly ideals. Ed.]

---

molle atque facetum: Latin: tenderness and wit.

Academy of the Red Branch; and an adjoining hospital, expressively termed *the House of the Sorrowful Soldier.*

"There was also an order of chivalry hereditary in the royal families of Munster, named the *Sons of Deagha,* from a celebrated hero of that name, probably their founder. The Connaught Knights were called the *Guardians of Jorus,* and those of Leinster, *the Clan of Boisgna.* So famous, indeed, were the knights of Ireland, for the elegance, strength, and beauty of their forms, that they were distinguished, by way of pre-eminence, by the name of *the Heroes of the Western Isles.*

"Our annals teem with instances of this romantic bravery and scrupulous honour. My memory, though much impaired, is still faithful to some anecdotes of both. During a war between the Connaught and Munster Monarchs, in 192, both parties met in the plains of Lena, in this province; and it was proposed to Goll M'Morni, chief of the Connaught Knights, to attack the Munster army at midnight, which would have secured him victory. He nobly and indignantly replied: 'On the day the arms of a knight were put into my hands, I swore never to attack my enemy at night, by surprize, or under *any kind of disadvantage;* nor shall that vow now be broken.'

"Besides those orders of knighthood which I have already named, there are several others* still hereditary in noble families, and the honourable titles of which are still preserved: such as the *White Knights of Kerry,* and the *Knights of Glynn:* that hereditary in my family was the *Knights of the Valley;* and this collar,† an ornament never dispensed with, was found about fifty years back in a neighbouring bog, and worn by my father till his death.

"This gorget," he continued, taking down one which hung on the wall, and apparently gratified by the obvious pleasure evinced in the countenance of his auditor,—"This gorget was found some years after in the same bog."‡

"And this helmet?" said I—

* The respectable families of the Fitzgeralds still bear the title of their ancestors, and are never named but as the Knights of Kerry, and of Glynn.

† One of these collars was in the possession of Mr. O'Halloran. [The Prince is quoting from O'Halloran, 46. Ed.]

‡ In the Bog of Cullen, in the county of Tipperary, some golden gorgets were discovered, as were also some corselets of pure gold in the lands of Clonties, county of Kerry.—See *Smith's History of Kerry.* [Charles Smith, *The Ancient and Present State of the County of Kerry* (London, 1756), 186–87; and Campbell, *A Philosophical Survey,* 469–78. Ed.]

---

gorget: Old French: a piece of armor for the throat, a collar.

"It is called in Irish," he replied, "*salet,* and belonged, with this coat of mail, to my ancestor who was murdered in this castle."

I coloured at this observation, as though I had been myself the murderer.

"As you refer, Sir," said the priest, who had flung by his book and joined us, "to the ancient Irish for the origin of knighthood,* you will perhaps send us to the Irish *Mala,* for the derivation of the word mail."

"Undoubtedly," said the national Prince, "I should; but pray, Mr. Mortimer, observe this shield. It is of great antiquity. You perceive it is made of wicker, as were the Irish shields in general; although I have also heard they were formed of silver, and one was found near Slimore, in the county of Cork, plated with gold, which sold for seventy guineas."

"But here," said I, "is a sword of curious workmanship, the hilt of which seems of gold."

"It is in fact so," said the priest—"Golden hilted swords have been in great abundance through Ireland; and it is a circumstance singularly curious, that a sword found in the Bog of Cullen should be of the exact construction and form of those found upon the plains of Canae. You may suppose that the advocates for our Milesian origin gladly seize on this circumstance, as affording new arms against the sceptics to the antiquity of our nation.

"Here too is a very curious hauberjeon, once perhaps impregnable! And this curious battle-axe," said I—

"Was originally called," returned the Prince, "*Tuath Catha,* or axe of war, and was put into the hands of our Galloglasses, or second rank of military."

"But how much more elegant," I continued, "the form of this beautiful spear; it is of course of a more modern date."

*At a time when the footstep of an English invader had not been impressed upon the Irish coast, the celebrity of the Irish Knights was sung by the British minstrels. Thus in the old romantic tale of Sir Cauline:

> In Ireland, *ferr* over the sea,
> There dwelleth a bonnye kinge,
> And with him a yong and comlye knight,
> Men call him Syr Cauline.

Sir Cauline's antagonist, the Eldridge knight, is described as being "*a foul paynim,*" which places the events the romantic tale delineates, in the earliest era of Christianity in Ireland. [For ballad, "Sir Cauline" (or Cawline), see Percy, *Reliques,* vol. 1, 61, stanza 1. "a foul paynim" means "a profane pagan." Ed.]

---

hauberjeon: haubergeon, French: a sleeveless coat or jacket of mail or scale armor.

"On the contrary," said the Prince, "this is the exact form of the cranuil or lance, with which Oscar is described to have struck Art to the earth."

"Oscar!" I repeated, almost starting—but added—"O, true Mr. Macpherson[104] tells us the Irish have some wild improbable tales of Fingal's heroes among them, on which they found some claim to their being natives of this country."

"Some claims!" repeated the Prince, and by one of those motions which speak more than volumes, he let go my arm, and took his usual station by the fire-side, repeating *some claims!*

While I was thinking how I should repair my involuntary fault, the good-natured priest said with a smile,

"You know, my dear Sir, that by one half of his English readers, Ossian is supposed to be a Scottish bard of ancient days; by the other he is esteemed the legitimate offspring of Macpherson's own muse. But here," he added, turning to me, "We are certain of his Irish origin, from the testimony of tradition, from proofs of historic fact, and above all, from the internal evidences of the poems themselves, even as they are given us by Mr. Macpherson.

"We who are from our infancy taught to recite them,* who bear the appellations of their heroes to this day, and who reside amidst those very scenes of which the poems, even according to their *ingenious,* but not always *ingenuous* translator, are descriptive—*we* know, believe, and assert them to be translated from the fragments of the Irish bards, or seanachies, whose surviving works were almost equally diffused through the Highlands as through this country. Mr. Macpherson combined them in such

*The Irish, like the Greeks, are passionately fond of traditional fictions, fables and romances. Nothing can be more relevant to this asserted analogy, than a passage translated from the works of Monsieur de Guys. Speaking of fables and romances, he says, "The modern Greeks are excessively attached to them, and much delighted with those received from the Arabians, and other eastern nations; they are particularly pleased with the marvellous, and have, like the Greeks, their Milesian fables."—*Lettres sur la Grece.* [Pierre Guys, *Sentimental Journey Through Greece in a Series of Letters,* 3 vols. (Dublin, 1773), vol. 2, 91–92. Ed.]

Fingal: Scottish King, central to most of Macpherson's poems, and a distortion of Fionn MacCumail.

[104]James Macpherson (1736–96), Scottish poet, works include *Fragments of Ancient Poetry Collected in the Highlands of Scotland* (1760), *Fingal* (1761), *Temora* (1763), and *The Works of Ossian* (1765), all of which he claimed were translations from Gaelic poetry originally composed by Ossian. The ensuing controversy regarding their authenticity waged throughout the British Isles and much of Europe, and was particularly divisive between the literati in Scotland and Ireland. Also, see *WIG* 122, Ed.'s n and *WIG* 195, n. 102.

forms as his judgment (too classically correct in this instance) most approved; retaining the old names and events, and altering the dates of his originals as well as their matter and form, in order to give them an higher antiquity than they really possess; suppressing many proofs which they contain of their Irish origin, and studiously avoiding all mention of St. Patrick, whose name frequently occurs in the original poems; only occasionally alluding to him under the character of a *Culdee;* conscious that any mention of the *Saint* would introduce a suspicion that these poems were not the true compositions of Ossian, but of those *Fileas* who, in an after day, committed to verse the traditional details of one equally renowned in song and arms."*

Here, you will allow, was a blow furiously aimed at all my opinions respecting these poems, so long the objects of my enthusiastic admiration: you may well suppose I was for a moment quite stunned. However, when I had a little recovered, I went over the arguments used by Macpherson, Blair,[105] &c. &c. &c. to prove that Ossian was an Highland bard, whose works were handed down to us by *oral* tradition, through a lapse of fifteen hundred years.

"And yet," said the priest, having patiently heard me out—"Mr. Macpherson confesses that the ancient language and traditional history of the Scottish nation became confined to the natives of the Highlands, who falling, from several concurring circumstances, into the last degree of ignorance and barbarism, left the Scots so destitute of historic facts, that they were reduced to the necessity of sending John Fordun[106] to Ireland for their history, from whence he took the entire first part of his book. For Ireland, owing to its being colonized from Phoenicia,[107] and conse-

* *Samuir,* daughter of Fingal, having married Cormac Cas, their son (says Keating) *Modh Corb,* retained as his friend and confident his uncle, Ossian, contrary to the orders of Cairbre Liffeachair, the then monarch, against whom the Irish militia had taken up arms. Ossian was consequently among the number of rebellious chiefs. [See Keating, *The General History of Ireland,* 286. Ed.]

Culdee: a member of an ancient Scottish-Irish religious order.

Fileas: a "file," or a poet in Gaelic society.

[105] Hugh Blair (1718–1800), Scottish clergyman and professor of rhetoric at Edinburgh University. His *Critical Dissertation on the Poems of Ossian* (1763) steadfastly defended the authenticity of Macpherson's Ossianic poems.

[106] Fordun (d. c. 1384) attempted a continuous history of Scotland in *Chronica Gentis Scotorum* (c. 1385). Walter Bower completed the project after his death. Fordun made extensive use of Irish source material. See O'Halloran, *History and Antiquities of Ireland,* v.

[107] See Parsons, *Observations on the Bequest of Henry Flood,* 167–68. Ireland's Phoenician origins is a thesis generally associated with Vallancey; see *WIG* 115, Ed. n.

quent early introduction of letters there, was at that period esteemed the most enlightened country in Europe: and indeed Mr. Macpherson himself avers, that the Irish, for ages antecedent to the Conquest, possessed a competent share of that kind of learning which prevailed in Europe; and from their superiority over the Scots, found no difficulty in imposing on the ignorant Highland seanachies, and established that historic system which afterwards, for want of any other, was universally received.

"Now, my dear friend, if historic fact and tradition did not attest the poems of Ossian to be Irish, probability would establish it. For if the Scotch were obliged to Ireland, according to Mr. Macpherson's own account, not only for their history, but their tradition, so remote a one as Ossian must have come from the Irish; for Scotland, as Dr. Johnson asserts, when he called on Mr. Macpherson to shew his originals, had not an Erse manuscript two hundred years old. And Sir George M'Kenzie,[108] though himself a Scotchman, declares, "that he had in his possession, an Irish manuscript written by Cairbre Liffeachair,* monarch of Ireland, who flourished before St. Patrick's mission."

"But," said I, "even granting these beautiful poems to be effusions of Irish genius, it is strange that the feats of your own heroes could not supply your bards with subjects for their epic verse."

"Strange indeed it would have been," said the priest, and therefore they have chosen the most renowned chiefs in their annals of national heroism, as their Achilleses, their Hectors, and Agamemnons."

"How!" exclaimed I, "is not Fingal a Caledonian chief? Is he not expressly called King of Morven?"

"Allowing he were, in the originals, which he is not," returned the priest, "give me leave to ask you where Morven lies?"

"Why, I suppose of course in Scotland," said I, a little unprepared for the question.

"Mr. Macpherson supposes so too," replied he, smiling, "though he certainly is at no little pains to discover where in Scotland. The fact is, however, that the epithet of *Riagh Mór Fhionne*, which Mr. Macpherson translates King of Morven, is literally King or Chief of the Fhians, or Fians, a

* Mr. O'Halloran, in his introduction to the study of Irish History, &c. quotes some lines from a poem still extant, composed by Torna Ligis, chief poet to Nial the Great, who flourished in the fourth century. [See O'Halloran, *History and Antiquities of Ireland*, 177. Ed.]

Erse: the dialect of Irish spoken in the Scottish Highlands.

Achilleses, . . . Hectors, . . . Agamemnons: Greek heroes of the Trojan wars.

[108] Sir George Mackenzie (1636–91) wrote *A Defence of the Antiquity of the Royal Line of Scotland* (1685), where he claimed "Hibernia" often referred to "Scotland."

body of men of whom Mr. Macpherson makes no mention, and which, indeed, either in the annals of Scottish history or Scottish poetry, would be vainly sought. Take then their history, as extracted from the book of Howth into the Transactions of the Royal Irish Academy in 1786.*

"In Ireland there were soldiers called *Fynne Erin,* appointed to keep the sea coast, fearing foreign invasion, or foreign princes to enter the realm; the names of these soldiers were, Fin M'Cuil, Coloilon, Keilt, Oscar, M'Ossyn, Dermot, O'Doyne, Collemagh, Morna, and divers others. These soldiers waxed bold, as shall appear hereafter, and so strong, that they did contrary to the orders and institutions of the kings of Ireland, their chiefs and governors, and became very strong, and stout, and at length would do things without licence of the King of Ireland, &c. &c." It is added, that one of these heroes was alive till the coming of St. Patrick, who recited the actions of his compeers to the Saint. This hero was Ossian, or, as we pronounce it, *Ossyn;* whose dialogues with the Christian missionary is in the mouth of every peasant, and several of them preserved in old Irish manuscripts. Now the Fingal of Mr. Macpherson (for it is thus he translates *Fin M'Cuil,* sometimes pronounced and spelled Fionne M'Cumhal, or *Fionn* the son of Cumhal) and his followers, appear like the earth-born myrmidons of Deucalion, for they certainly have no human origin; bear no connexion with the history of their country; are neither to be found in the

* *Fionn,* the son of Cumhal (from whom, says Keating, the established militia of the kingdom were called *Fion Erinne*), was first married to Graine, daughter to Cormac, King of Ireland, and afterwards to her sister, and descended in a sixth degree from Nuagadh Neacht, King of Leinster. The history, laws, requisites, &c. &c. of the Fion-na-Erin, are to be found in Keating's History of Ireland, page 269.

Cormac, at the head of the Fion, and attended by Fingal, sailed to that part of Scotland opposite Ireland, where he planted a colony as an establishment for Carbry Riada, his cousin-german. This colony was often protected from the power of the Romans by the Fion, under the command of Fingal, occasionally stationed in the circumjacent country. "Hence," says Mr. Walker, "the claim of the Scots to Fin." In process of time this colony gave monarchs to Scotland, and their posterity at this day reign over the British empire. Fingal fell in an engagement at Rathbree, on the banks of the Boyne, A.D. 294; from whence the name of Rathbree was changed into that of Killeen, or Cill-Fhin, the tomb of Fin. [Matthew Young, "Ancient Gaelic Poems, Respecting the Race of the Fions, Collected in the Highlands of Scotland in the Year 1784," *Transactions of the Royal Irish Academy,* I (1787), 43–119, 118–19; Keating, *General History of Ireland,* 269; and Walker, *Historical Memoirs,* 37–38. Ed.]

Deucalion: In Greek mythology, Deucalion was the son of Prometheus and husband of Pyrrha. Having escaped the flood created by Zeus, who was resolved to destroy humanity, Deucalion and his wife threw stones over their shoulders and created sons and daughters.

poetic legend or historic record* of Scotland, and are even furnished with appellations which the Caledonians neither previously possessed nor have since adopted. They are therefore abruptly introduced to our knowledge, as living in a barbarous age, yet endowed with every perfection that renders them the most refined, heroic, and virtuous of men. So that while we grant to the interesting poet and his heroes our boundless admiration, we cannot help considering them as solecisms in the theory of human nature.

"But with *us*, Fingal and his chiefs are beings of real existence, their names, professions, rank, characters, and feats, attested by historic fact as well as by poetic eulogium. Fingal is indeed romantically brave; benevolent and generous; but he is turbulent, restless, and ambitious: he is a man as well as a hero; and both his virtues and his vices bear the stamp of the age and country in which he lived. His name and feats, as well as those of his chief officers, bear an intimate connexion with our national history.

"Fionne, or Finnius, was the grandsire of Milesius; and it is not only a name to be met with through every period of our history, but there are few old families even at this day in Ireland, who have not the appellative of Finnius in some one or other of its branches; and a large tract of the province of Leinster is called *Fingal*: a title in possession of one of our most noble and ancient families.

*I know but of one instance that contradicts the assertion of Father John, and that I borrow from the allegorical *Palace of Honour* of Gawin Douglas, Bishop of Dunkeld, who places Gaul, son of Morni and Fingal, among the distinguished characters in the annals of legendary romance; yet even *he* mentions them not as the heroes of Scottish celebrity, but as the almost fabled demigods of Ireland.

> "And now the wran cam out of Ailsay,
> And Piers Plowman, that made his workmen few,
> Great Gow MacMorne and Fyn M'Cowl, and how
> They suld be goddis in Ireland, as they say."

It is remarkable, that the genius of the Ossianic style still prevails over the wild effusions of the modern and unlettered bards of Ireland; while even the remotest lay of Scottish minstrelsy respires nothing of that soul which breathes in "the voice of Cona;" and the metrical flippancy which betrays its existence, seems neither to rival, or cope with that touching sublimity of measure through whose impressive medium the genius of Ossian effuses its inspiration, and which, had it been known to the early bards of Scotland, had probably been imitated and adopted. In Ireland, it has ever been and is still the measure in which the Sons of Song breathe "their wood-notes wild." [For "And now the wran . . . ," see Gavin Douglas, *The Palice of Honour*, Book III, 1713–16; for "their wood-notes wild," see John Milton, *L'Allegro*, l. 134. Ed.]

---

solecisms: improprieties or irregularities in speech or diction.

"Nay, if you please, you shall hear our old nurse run through the whole genealogy of Macpherson's hero, which is frequently given as a theme to exercise the memory of the peasant children."*

"Nay," said I, nearly overpowered, "Macpherson assures us the Highlanders also repeat many of Ossian's poems in the original Erse: nay, that even in the Isle of Sky, they still shew a stone which bears the form and name of Cuchullin's dog."†

"This is the most flagrant error of all," exclaimed the Prince, abruptly breaking his sullen silence—"for he has synchronized heroes who flourished in two distant periods; both Cuchullin and Conal Cearneath are historical characters with us; they were Knights of the *Red Branch,* and flourished about the birth of Christ. Whereas Fingal, with whom he has united them, did not flourish till near three centuries after. It is indeed Macpherson's pleasure to inform us, that by the Isle of Mist is meant the Isle of Sky, and on that circumstance alone to rest his claim on *Cuchullin*'s being a Caledonian; although, through the whole poems of Fingal and Temora, he is not once mentioned as such: it is by the translator's notes only we are informed of it."

"It is certain," said the priest—"that in the first mention made of *Cuchullin* in the poem of Fingal, he is simply denominated 'the Son of Semo,' 'the Ruler of High Temora,' 'Mossy Tura's Chief.'‡ So called, says

*They run it over thus: "Oscar Mac Ossyn, Mac Fionn, Mac Cuil, Mac Cormic, Mac Arte, Mac Fiervin, &c. &c. That is, Oscar the son of Ossian, the son of Fionn, &c. &c.

†There is an old tradition current in Connaught, of which *Bran,* the favourite dog of Ossian, is the hero. In a war between the King of Lochlin and the Fians, a battle continued to be fought on equal terms for so long a period, that it was at last mutually agreed that it should be decided in a combat between Ossian's *Bran* and the famous *Cu dubh,* or dark greyhound, of the Danish Monarch. This greyhound had already performed incredible feats, and was never to be conquered until his name was found out. The warrior dogs fought in a space between the two armies, and with such fury, says the legend, in a language absolutely untranslatable, that they tore up the stony bosom of the earth, until they rendered it perfectly soft, and again trampled on it with such force, that they made it of a rocky substance. The *Cu dubh* had nearly gained the victory, when the *bald-headed Conal,* turning his face to the east, and *biting his thumb* a ceremony difficult to induce him to perform, and which always endowed him with the gift of divination, made a sudden exclamation of encouragement to *Bran,* the first word of which found the name of the greyhound, who lost at once his prowess and the victory. The chief Order of Denmark was instituted in memory of the fidelity of a dog, "though it is injuriously called the Order of the Elephant," says Pope. [See Macpherson, *Fingal,* 54 and *Temora,* Book VI, 274 and Book VIII, 288. Ed.]

‡The groves of Tura, or Tuar, are often noticed in Irish song. *Emunh Acnuic,* or Ned of the Hill, has mentioned it in one of his happiest and most popular poems. It was supposed to be in the county of Armagh, province of Ulster. [See Owenson, *Twelve Original Hibernian Melodies* (Dublin, 1805) for song "Eamon an Chnoic," or "Ned of the Hill." Ed.]

Macpherson, from his castle on the coast of Ulster, where he dwelt before he took the management of the affairs of Ireland into his hands; though the singular cause which could induce the lord of the Isle of Sky to reside in Ireland previous to his political engagements in the Irish state, he does not mention.

"In the same manner we are told, that his three nephews came from Streamy Etha, one of whom married an Irish lady; but there is no mention made of the real name of the place of their nativity, although the translator assures us, in another note, that they also were Caledonians. But in fact, it is from the internal evidences of the poems themselves, not from the notes of Mr. Macpherson, nor indeed altogether from his beautiful but unfaithful translation, that we are to decide on the nation to which these poems belong. In Fingal, the first and most perfect of the collection, that hero is first mentioned by Cuchullin as Fingal, *King of Desarts*—in the original—*Inis na bfhiodhuide,* or *Woody Island;* without any allusion whatever to his being a Caledonian. And afterwards he is called King of Selma, by Swaran, a name, with little variation, given to several castles in Ireland. Darthulla's castle is named Selma; and another, whose owner I do not remember, is termed Selemath. *Slimora,* to whose fir the spear of Foldath is compared, is a mountain in the province of Munster, and throughout the whole even of Mr. Macpherson's translation, the characters, names, allusions, incidents, and scenery are all Irish. And in fact, our *Irish spurious ballads,* as Mr. Macpherson calls them, are the very originals out of which he has spun the materials for his version of Ossian.*

"Dr. Johnson,[109] who strenuously opposed the idea of *Ossian* being the work of a Scotch bard of the third century, asserts that the 'Erse never was

* "Some of the remaining footsteps of these old warriors are known by their first names at this time (says Keating), as for instance, *Suidhe Finn,* or the Palace of Fin, at *Sliabh na Mann,* &c. &c. &c." There is a mountain in Donegal still called *Alt Ossoin,* surrounded by all that wild sublimity of scenery so exquisitely delineated through the elegant medium of Mr. Macpherson's translation of Ossian; and in its environs many Ossianic tales are still extant.

In an extract given by Camden from an account of the manners of the native Irish in the sixteenth century—"they think (says the author) the souls of the deceased are in communion with the famous men of those places, of whom they retain many stories and sonnets—as of the giants Fin, Mac Huyle, Osker, Mac Osshin, &c. &c. and they say, through illusion, they often see them." [Keating, *General History of Ireland,* 267–68. William Camden (1551–1623), English antiquarian and author of *Britannia* (1586), the first comprehensive topographical survey of England. Ed.]

[109] See Samuel Johnson, *A Journey to the Western Islands of Scotland* (1775), 114–15.

a written language, and that there is not in the world a written Erse manuscript an hundred years old.' He adds, 'The Welsh and Irish are cultivated tongues, and two hundred years back insulted their English neighbours for the instability of their orthography. Even the ancient Irish *letter* was unknown in the Highlands in 1690, for an Irish version of the Bible being given there by Mr. Kirk, was printed in the Roman character.'[110]

"When Dr. Young,* led by tasteful enterprize; visited the Highlands (on an Ossianic research) in 1784, he collected a number of Gaelic poems respecting the race of the Fiens, so renowned in the annals of Irish heroism,† and found, that the orthography was less pure than that among us; for he says, 'the Erse being only a written language within these few years, no means were yet afforded of forming a decided orthographic standard.' But he augurs, from the improvement which had lately taken place, that we soon may expect to see the Erse restored to the original purity which it possesses in the *mother* country. And these very poems, whence Mr. Macpherson has chiefly constructed his Ossian, bear such strong internal proof of their Irish origin, as to contain in themselves the best arguments that can be adduced against the Scottish claimants on the poems of the bard. But in their translation,‡ many passages are perverted, in order to deprive Ireland of being the residence of Fingal's heroes."

* Dr. Young, late Bishop of Clonfert, who united in his character the extremes of human perfection—the most unblemished virtue to the most exalted genius. [Dr. Matthew Young (1750–1800), Anglican Bishop of Clonfert, philosopher who supported Catholic education. Ed.]

† See Transactions of the Royal Irish Academy, 1786. [See Young, "Ancient Gaelic Poems," 50–51. Ed.]

‡ "From the remotest antiquity we have seen the military order distinguished in Ireland, codes of military laws and discipline established, and their dress, and rank in the state, ascertained. The learned Keating, and others, tell us, that these *militia* were called *Fine,* from *Fion Mac Cumhal;* but it is certainly a great error; the word *Fine* strictly implying a *military corps.* Many places in the island retain, to this day, the names of some of the leaders of this famous body of men, and whole volumes of poetical fictions have been grafted upon their exploits. The manuscript which I have, after giving a particular account of *Finn's* descent, his inheritance, his acquisitions from the King of Leinster, and his great military command, immediately adds—'but the reader must not expect to meet here with such stories of him and his heroes *as the vulgar Irish have.*'" —*Dr. Warner.* [See Ferdinando Warner, *The History of Ireland; from the Earliest Authentic Accounts to the Year 1171,* 2 vols. (Dublin, 1763), vol. 1, 278. Ed.]

[110] Robert Kirke's *An Bíobla Naomhtha* (1690), an Irish-language edition of the Bible, was published in London for use in Scotland, representing the first time Roman type face was used for Irish. See Young, "Ancient Gaelic Poems," 50.

"I remember," said the Prince, "when you read to me a description of a sea-fight between Fingal and Swaran, in Macpherson's translation, that I repeated to you, in Irish, the very poem whence it was taken, and which is still very current here, under the title of *Laoid Mhanuis M'hoir.*"

"True," returned the priest, "a copy of which is deposited in the University of Dublin, with another Irish MS. entitled, '*Oran eadas Ailte agus do Maronnan,*' whence the Battle of Lora is taken."

The Prince then, desiring Father John to give him down a bundle of old manuscripts which lay on a shelf in the hall, dedicated to national tracts, after some trouble, produced a copy of a poem, called "The Conversation of Ossian and St. Patrick," the original of which, Father John assured me, was deposited in the library of the Irish University.[111]

It is to this poem that Mr. Macpherson alludes, when he speaks of the dispute reported to have taken place between Ossian and a Culdee.

At my request, he translated this curious controversial tract.* The dispute was managed on both sides with a great deal of polemic ardour. St. Patrick, with apostolic zeal, shuts the gates of Mercy on all whose faith differs from his own, and, with an unsaintly vehemence, extends the exclusion, in a pointed manner, to the ancestors of Ossian, who, he declares, are suffering in the *limbo* of tortured spirits.

The bard tenderly replies, "It is hard to believe thy tale, O man of the white book! that Fian, *or one so generous,* should be in captivity with God or man."

When, however, the Saint persists in the assurance, that not even the generosity of the departed hero could save him from the house of torture, the failing spirit of "the King of Harps" suddenly sends forth a lingering flash of its wonted fire; and he indignantly declares, "that if the Clan of Boisgna were still in being, they would liberate their beloved general from this threatened hell."

The Saint, however, growing warm in the argument, expatiates on the great difficulty of *any* soul entering the court of God: to which the infidel bard beautifully replies:—"Then he is not like *Fionn M'Cuil,* our chief of

*Notwithstanding the sceptical obstinacy that Ossian here displays, there is a current tradition of his having been present at a baptismal ceremony performed by the Saint, who accidentally struck the sharp point of his crozier through the bard's foot, who, supposing it part of the ceremony, remained transfixed to the earth without a murmur.

---

[111] Trinity College Dublin (see *CR* 48), a center of renewed antiquarian interest and Irish manuscript collection. Henry Flood's bequest to the college in the 1790s resulted in a major controversy; see *WIG* 181, n. 92.

the Fians; for every man upon the face of the earth might enter *his* court, without asking his permission."

Thus, as you perceive, fairly routed, I however artfully proposed terms of capitulation, as though my defeat was yet dubious.

"Were I a Scotchman," said I, "I should be furnished with more effectual arms against you; but as an Englishman, I claim an armed neutrality, which I shall endeavour to preserve between the two nations. At the same time that I feel the highest satisfaction in witnessing the just pretensions of that country (which now ranks in my estimation next to my own) to a work which would do honour to *any* country so fortunate as to claim its author as her son."

The Prince, who seemed highly gratified by this avowal, shook me heartily by the hand, apparently flattered by his triumph; and at that moment Glorvina entered.

"O, my dear!" said the Prince, "you are just come in time to witness an amnesty between Mr. Mortimer and me."

"I should much rather witness the amnesty than the breach," returned she, smiling.

"We have been battling about the country of Ossian," said the priest "with as much vehemence as the claimants on the birth-place of Homer."[112]

"O! I know of old," cried Glorvina, "that you and my father are natural allies on that point of contention; and I must confess, it was ungenerous in both, to oppose your united strength against Mr. Mortimer's single force."

"What, then," said the Prince, good humouredly, "I suppose you would have deserted your national standard, and have joined Mr. Mortimer, merely from motives of compassion."

"Not so, my dear Sir," said Glorvina, faintly blushing, "but I should have endeavoured to have compromised between you. To you I would have accorded that Ossian was an Irishman, of which I am as well convinced as of any other self-evident truth whatever, and to Mr. Mortimer I would have acknowledged the superior merits of Mr. Macpherson's poems, as compositions, over those wild effusions of our Irish bards whence he compiled them.

"Long before I could read, I learned on the bosom of my nurse, and in my father's arms, to recite the songs of our national bards, and almost since I could read, the Ossian of Macpherson has been the object of my enthusiastic admiration.

---

[112] For competitive claims regarding Homer's birthplace, see Thomas Blackwell, *An Enquiry into the Life and Writings of Homer* (1735), 5–12. Blackwell was both tutor to and an important influence on Macpherson.

"In the original Irish poems, if my fancy is sometimes dazzled by the brilliant flashes of native genius, if my heart is touched by strokes of nature, or my soul elevated by sublimity of sentiment, yet my interest is often destroyed, and my admiration often checked, by relations so wildly improbable, by details so ridiculously grotesque, that though these stand forth as the most undeniable proofs of their authenticity and the remoteness of the day in which they were composed, yet I reluctantly suffer my mind to be convinced at the expence of my feeling and my taste. But in the soul-stealing strains of "the Voice of Cona,"[113] as breathed through the refined medium of Macpherson's genius, no incongruity of style, character, or manner, disturbs the profound interest they awaken. For my own part, when my heart is coldly void, when my spirits are sunk and drooping, I fly to my English Ossian, and then my sufferings are soothed, and every desponding spirit softens into a sweet melancholy, more delicious than joy itself; while I experience in its perusal a similar sensation as when, in the stillness of an autumnal evening, I expose my harp to the influence of the passing breeze, which faintly breathing on the chords, seems to call forth its own requiem as it expires."

"Oh, Macpherson!" I exclaimed, "be thy spirit appeased, for thou hast received that apotheosis thy talents have nearly deserved, in the eulogium of beauty and genius, and from the lip of an Irishwoman."

This involuntary and impassioned exclamation extorted from the Prince a smile of gratified parental pride, and overwhelmed Glorvina with confusion. She could, I believe, have spared it before her father, and received it with a bow and a blush. Shortly after she left the room.

Adieu! I thought to have returned to M___ house, but I know not how it is—

"Mais un invincible contraint
Malgrè moi fixe ici mes pas,
Et tu sais que pour aller à Corinth,
Le desir seul ne suffit pas."

Adieu!

H. M.

Mais un . . . suffit pas: French: "But an invincible constraint holds me here despite myself, and you know that desire alone is not enough to go to Corinth."

[113]Cona is Fingal's homeport in Scotland. See Macpherson's "The Songs of Selma," *The Poems of Ossian* (1805), 468.

Letter XIII

TO J. D. ESQ. M. F.

THE conduct of this girl is inexplicable. Since the unfortunate picture scene three days back, she has excused herself twice from the drawing-desk; and to-day appeared at it with the priest by her side. Her playful familiarity is vanished, and a chill reserve, uncongenial to the native ardour of her manner, has succeeded. Surely she cannot be so vain, so weak, as to mistake my attentions to her as a young and lovely woman; my admiration of her talents, and my surprize at the originality of her character, for a serious passion. And supposing me to be a wanderer and an hireling, affect to reprove my temerity by haughtiness and disdain.

Would you credit it! By Heavens, I am sometimes weak enough to be on the very point of telling her who and what I am, when she plays off her little airs of Milesian pride and female superciliousness. You perceive, therefore, by the conduct of this little Irish recluse, that on the subject of love and vanity, woman is every where, and in all situations, the same. For what coquet reared in the purlieus of St. James, could be more *a portée* to those effects which denote the passion, or more apt to suspect she had awakened it into existence, than this inexperienced, unsophisticated being? who I suppose never spoke to ten men in her life, save the superannuated inhabitants of her paternal ruins. Perhaps, however, she only means to check the growing familiarity of my manner, and to teach me the disparity of rank which exists between us; for, with all her native strength of mind, the influence of invariable example and frequent precept has been too strong for her, and she has unconsciously imbibed many of her father's prejudices respecting antiquity of descent and nobility of birth. She will frequently say, "O! such a one is a true Milesian!"—or, "he is a descendant of the *English* Irish;"—or, "they are new people—we hear nothing of them till the wars of Cromwell," and so on. Yet at other times, when reason lords it over prejudice, she will laugh at that weakness in others, she sometimes betrays in herself.

The other day, as we stood chatting at a window together, pointing to an elderly man who passed by, she said, "there goes a poor Connaught gentleman, who would rather starve than work—he is a *follower* of the family, and has been just entertaining my father with an account of our ancient splendour. We have too many instances of this species of *mania* among us.

---

purlieus of St. James: fashionable area in London surrounding St. James's Palace.

a portée: French: inclined.

***English* Irish:** Old English, the settler/colonial community that emerged in Ireland after the Anglo-Norman invasion, and distinct from the New English, or Elizabethan settlers, in the sixteenth and seventeenth centuries.

"The celebrated Bishop of Cloyne[114] relates an anecdote of a kitchen-maid, who refused to carry out cinders, because she was of Milesian descent. And Father John tells a story of a young gentleman in Limerick, who being received under the patronage of a nobleman going out as Governor-General of India, sacrificed his interest to his *national pride;* for having accompanied his Lordship on board the vessel which was to convey them to the East, and finding himself placed at the foot of the dining-table, he instantly arose, and went on shore, declaring that "as a *true Milesian,* he would not submit to any indignity, to purchase the riches of the East India Company." *

"All this," continued Glorvina, "is ridiculous, nay it is worse, for it is highly dangerous and fatal to the community at large. It is the source of innumerable disorders, by promoting idleness, and consequently vice. It frequently checks the industry of the poor, and limits the exertions of the rich, and perhaps is not among the least of those sources whence our national miseries flow. At the same time I must own, I have a very high idea of the virtues which exalted birth does or ought to bring with it. Marmontel elegantly observes, 'nobility of birth is a letter of credit given us on our country, upon the security of our ancestors, in the conviction that at a proper period of life we shall acquit ourselves with honour to those who stand engaged for us.'"

Observe, that this passage was quoted in the first person, and not, as in the original, in the second, and with an air of dignity that elevated her pretty little head some inches.

"Since," she continued, "we are all the beings of education, and that its most material branch, example, lies vested in our parents, it is natural to suppose that those superior talents or virtues which in early stages of society are the purchase of worldly elevation, become hereditary, and that the noble principles of our ancestors should descend to us with their titles and estates."

"Ah," said I, smiling, "these are the ideas of an Irish Princess, reared in the palace of her ancestors on the shores of the Atlantic Ocean."

* Not long since, the Author met a person in the capacity of a writing-master in a gentleman's family, who assured her that he was a *Prince* by lineal descent, and that the name of his Principality was *Sliabh-Ban.* This Principality of *Sliabh-Ban,* however, is simply a small and rugged mountain, whose rigid soil bids defiance to culture.

East India Company: By the late eighteenth century, popular opinion associated wealth and fortune with those involved in the East India Company.

Marmontel: Jean-François Marmontel (1723–99), French writer and critic, remembered for his moral tales, *Contes Moraux* (1761).

[114] George Berkeley (1685–1753), philosopher, scientist, and Anglican bishop. For the anecdote, see Warner, *The History of Ireland,* vol. 1, 257.

"They may be," she returned, "the ideas of an inexperienced recluse, but I think they are not less the result of rational supposition, strengthened by the evidence of internal feeling; for though I possessed not that innate dignity of mind which instinctively spurned at the low suggestion of vicious dictates, yet the consciousness of the virtues of those from whom I am descended, would prevent me from sullying by an unworthy action of mine, the unpolluted name I had the honour to bear."

She then repeated several anecdotes of the heroism, rectitude, and virtue of her ancestors of both sexes, adding, "this was once the business of our Bards, Fileas, and Seanachies; but we are now obliged to have recourse to our own memories, in order to support our own dignity.

"But do not suppose I am so weak as to be dazzled by a *sound*, or to consider mere title in any other light than as a golden toy judiciously worn to secure the respect of the vulgar, who are incapable of appreciating that 'which passeth show,'*[115] which, as my father says, is sometimes given to him who saves, and sometimes bestowed on him who betrays, his country. O! no; for I would rather possess *one* beam of that genius which elevates *your* mind above all worldly distinction, and those principles of integrity which breathe in your sentiments and ennoble your soul, than"—

Thus hurried away by the usual impetuosity of her feelings, she abruptly stopped, fearful, perhaps, that she had gone too far. And then, after a moment added—"but who will dare to bring the souls of nobility in competition with the short-lived elevation which man bestows on man!"

This was the first direct compliment she ever paid me; and I received it with a silent bow, a throbbing heart, and a colouring cheek.

Is she not an extraordinary creature! I meant to have given you an unfavourable opinion of her prejudices; and in transcribing my documents of accusation, I have actually confirmed myself in a better opinion of her heart and understanding than I ever before indulged in. For to think well of *her*, is a positive indulgence to my philanthropy, after having thought so ill of all her sex.

But her virtues and her genius have nothing to do with the ice which crystallizes round her heart; and which renders her as coldly indifferent to the talents and virtues with which her fancy has invested me, as though they were in possession of an hermit of four score. Yet God knows,

* "He feels no ennobling principles in his own heart, who wishes to level all the artificial institutes which have been adopted for giving body to opinion, and permanence to future esteem."—*Burke*. [Burke, *Reflections on the Revolution in France*, 245. Ed.]

Bards, Fileas, and Seanachies: Versifier, poet, and storyteller/historiographer.

[115] Shakespeare, *Hamlet*, I. ii. 85.

nothing less than cold does her character appear. That mutability of complexion which seems to flow perpetually to the influence of her evident feelings and vivid imagination, that ethereal warmth which animates her manners; the force and energy of her expressions, the enthusiasm of her disposition, the uncontroulable smile, the involuntary tear, the spontaneous sigh!—Are these indications of an icy heart? And yet, shut up as we are together, thus closely associated, the sympathy of our tastes, our pursuits! But the fact is, I begin to fear that I have imported into the shades of Inismore some of my London presumption; and that after all, I know as little of this charming *sport of Nature,* as when I first beheld her—possibly my perceptions have become as sophisticated as the objects to whom they have hitherto been directed; and want refinement and subtilty to enter into all the delicate *minutiae* of her superior and original character, which is at once both *natural* and *national.*

Adieu!

H. M.

Letter XIV

TO J. D. ESQ. M. P.

TO day I was present at an interview granted by the Prince to two contending parties, who came to *ask law of him,* as they term it. This, I am told, the Irish peasantry are ready to do upon every slight difference; so that they are the most litigious, or have the nicest sense of *right* and *justice,* of any people in the world.

Although the language held by this little judicial meeting was Irish, it was by no means necessary it should be understood, to comprehend, in some degree, the subject of discussion; for the gestures and countenances both of the judge and the clients, were expressive beyond all conception; and I plainly understood, that almost every other word on both sides was accompanied by a species of *local oath,* sworn on the first object that presented itself to their hands, and strongly marked the vehemence of the national character.

When I took notice of this to Father John, he replied,

"It is certain, that the habit of confirming every assertion with an oath, is as prevalent among the Irish as it *was* among the ancient, and *is* among the modern, Greeks. And it is remarkable, that even at this day, in both countries, the nature and form of their adjurations and oaths are perfectly

---

sport of Nature: See *WIG* 190.

similar: a Greek will still swear by his parents, or his children; an Irishman frequently swears 'by my father, who is no more!' 'by my mother in the grave!' Virgil makes his pious Aeneas swear by his head. The Irish constantly swear, 'by my hand,'—'by this hand,'—or, 'by the hand of my gossip!'* There is one who has just sworn by *the Cross;* another, by the blessed stick he holds in his hand. In short, no intercourse passes between them where confidence is required, in which oaths are not called in to confirm the transaction."

I am this moment returned from my *Vengolf,* after having declared the necessity of my absence for some time, leaving the term, however, indefinite; so that in this instance, I can be governed by my inclination and convenience, without any violation of promise. The good old Prince looked as much amazed at my determination, as though he expected I were never to depart; and I really believe, in the old-fashioned hospitality of his Irish heart, he would be better satisfied I never should. He said many kind and cordial things in his own curious way; and concluded by pressing my speedy return, and declaring that my presence had created a little jubilee among them.

The priest was absent; and Glorvina, who sat at her little wheel by her father's side, snapped her thread, and drooped her head close to her work, until I casually observed, that I had already passed above three weeks at the castle—then she shook back the golden tresses from her brow, and raised her eyes to mine with a look that seemed to say, "can that be possible!" Not even by a glance did I reply to the flattering question; but I felt it not the less.

When we arose to retire to our respective apartments, and I mentioned that I should be off at dawn, the Prince shook me cordially by the hand, and bid me farewell with an almost paternal kindness.

Glorvina, on whose arm he was leaning, did not follow his example—she simply wished me "a pleasant journey."

*The mention of this oath recalls to my mind an anecdote of the bard Carolan, as related by Mr. Walker, in his inimitable Memoir of the Irish Bards. "He (Carolan) went once on a pilgrimage to *St. Patrick's Purgatory,* a cave in an island in Lough Dergh (county of Donegal), of which more wonders are told than even of the Cave of Triphonius. On his return to shore, he found several pilgrims waiting the arrival of the boat which had conveyed him to the object of his devotion. In assisting some of those devout travellers to get on board, he chanced to take a lady's hand, and instantly exclaimed, '*dar lamh mo Chairdais Criost (i.e.* by the hand of my gossip) this is the hand of Bridget Cruise.' His sense of feeling did not deceive him—it *was* the hand of her whom he once adored." ["Life of Turlough O'Carolan," Appendix to Walker, *Historical Memoirs,* 69. Ed.]

"But where," said the Prince, "do you sojourn to?"

"To the town of Bally___," said I, "which has been hitherto my head-quarters, and where I have left my clothes, books, and drawing utensils. I have also some friends in the neighbourhood, procured me by letters of introduction with which I was furnished in England."

You know that a great part of this neighbourhood is now my father's property, and once belonged to the ancestors of the Prince. He changed colour as I spoke, and hurried on in silence.

Adieu! the castle clock strikes twelve! What creatures we are! when the tinkling of a bit of metal can affect our spirits. Mine, however (though why, I know not), were prepared for the reception of sombre images. This night may be, in all human probability, the last I shall sleep in the castle of Inismore; and what then—it were perhaps as well I had never entered it. A generous mind can never reconcile itself to the practices of deception; yet to prejudices so inveterate, I had nothing but deception to oppose. And yet, when in some happy moment of parental favour, when all my past sins are forgotten, and my present state of regeneration only remembered—I shall find courage to disclose my romantic adventure to my father, and through the medium of that strong partiality the son has awakened in the heart of the Prince, unite in bonds of friendship these two worthy men, but *unknown* enemies—then I shall triumph in my impositions, and, for the first time, adopt the maxim, that good consequences may be effected by means not strictly conformable to the rigid laws of truth.

I have just been at my window, and never beheld so gloomy a night—not a star twinkles through the massy clouds that are driven impetuously along by the sudden gusts of a rising storm—not a ray of light partially dissipates the profound obscurity, save what falls on a fragment of an opposite tower, and seems to issue from the window of a closet which joins the apartment of Glorvina. She has not yet then retired to rest, and yet 'tis unusual for her to sit up so late. For I have often watched that little casement—its position exactly corresponds with the angle of the castle where I am lodged.

If I should have any share in the vigils of Glorvina!!!

I know not whether to be most gratified or hurt at the manner in which she took leave of me. Was it indifference, or resentment, that marked her manner? She certainly was surprised, and her surprise was not of the most pleasing nature—for where was the magic smile, the sensient blush, that ever ushers in and betray every emotion of her ardent soul? Sweet being! whatever may be the sentiments which the departure of the supposed unfortunate wanderer awakens in thy bosom, may that bosom still continue the hallowed asylum of the dove of peace! May the pure heart it enshrines still throb to the best impulses of the happiest nature, and beat with the soft palpitation of innocent pleasure and guileless transport, veiled from the rude intercourse of that world to which thy elevated and sublime nature is so eminently superior: long amidst the shade of the venerable ruins of thy forefathers mayest thou bloom and flourish in undisturbed felicity! the ministering angel of thy poor compatriots, who look up to thee for example and support—thy country's muse, and the bright model of the genuine character of her daughters, when unvitiated by erroneous education, and by those fatal prejudices which lead them to seek in foreign refinement for those talents, those graces, those virtues, which are no where to be found more flourishing, more attractive, than in their native land.

H. M.

Letter XV

TO J. D. ESQ. M. P.

M___ House

IT certainly requires less nicety of perception to distinguish differences in kind than differences in degree; but though my present, like my past situation, is solitudinous in the extreme, it demands no very great discernment to discover, that my late life was a life of solitude—my present, of desolation.

In the castle of Inismore I was estranged from the world: here I am estranged from myself. Yet so much more sequestered did that sweet interesting spot appear to me, that I felt, on arriving at this vast and solitary place (after having passed by a few gentlemen's seats, and caught a distant view of the little town of Bally___), as though I were returning to the world—but felt as if that world had no longer any attraction for me.

What a dream was the last three weeks of my life! But it was a dream from which I wished not to be awakened. It seemed to me as if I had lived in an age of primeval simplicity and primeval virtue. My senses at rest, my passions soothed to philosophic repose, my prejudices vanquished, all the powers of my mind gently breathed into motion, yet calm and unagitated—all the faculties of my taste called into exertion, yet unsated even by boundless gratification. My fancy restored to its pristine warmth, my heart to its native sensibility. The past given to oblivion, the future unanticipated, and the present enjoyed, with the full consciousness of its pleasurable existence. Wearied, exhausted, satiated by a boundless indulgence of hackneyed pleasures, hackneyed occupations, hackneyed pursuits, at a moment when I was sinking beneath the lethargic influence of apathy, or hovering on the brink of despair, a new light broke upon my clouded mind, and discovered to my inquiring heart, something yet worth living for. What that mystic something is, I can scarcely yet define myself; but a magic spell now irresistibly binds me to that life which but lately,

> "Like a foul and ugly witch, did limp
> So tediously away."[116]

The reserved tints of a grey dawn had not yet received the illuminating beams of the east, when I departed from the castle of Inismore. None of the family were risen, but the hind who prepared my *rosinante*, and the nurse, who made my breakfast.

I rode twice round that wing of the castle where Glorvina sleeps: the curtain of her bed-room casement was closely drawn; but as I passed by it the second time, I thought I perceived a shadowy form at the window of the adjoining casement. As I approached it seemed to retreat; the whole, however, might have only been the vision of my wishes—my *wishes!!!* But this girl piques me into something of interest for her.

About three miles from the castle, on the summit of a wild and desolate heath, I met the good Father Director of Inismore. He appeared quite amazed at the rencontre. He expressed great regret at my absence from the castle, insisting that he should accompany me a mile or two of my journey, though he was only then returning after having passed the night in ministering temporal as well as spiritual comfort to an unfortunate family at some miles distance.

"These poor people," said he, "were tenants on the skirts of Lord M.'s estate, who, though by all accounts a most excellent and benevolent man, employs a steward of a very opposite character. This unworthy delegate having considerably raised the rent on a little farm held by these unfortunate people, they soon became deeply in arrears, were ejected, and obliged to take shelter in an almost roofless hut, where the inclemency of the season, and the hardships they endured, brought on disorders by which the mother and two children are now nearly reduced to the point of death;* and yesterday, in their last extremity, they sent for me."

While I commiserated the sufferings of these unfortunates (and cursed the villain Clendinning in my heart), I could not avoid adverting to the humanity of this benevolent priest.

* The lower orders of Irish are very subject to dreadful fevers, which are generally the result of colds caught by the exposed state of their damp and roofless hovels.

---

hind who prepared my *rosinante*: farm servant who prepared my horse.

rencontre: French: chance encounter.

[116] Shakespeare, *Henry V*, IV, Prologue. 21–22.

"These offices of true charity, which you so frequently perform," said I, "are purely the result of your benevolence, rather than a mere observance of your duty."

"It is true," he replied, "I have no parish; but the incumbent of that in which these poor people reside is so old and infirm, as to be totally incapacitated from performing such duties of his calling as require the least exertion. The duty of one who professes himself the minister of religion, whose essence is charity, should not be confined within the narrow limitation of prescribed rules; and I should consider myself as unworthy of the sacred habit I wear, should my exertions be confined to the suggestions of my interest and my duty only."

"The faith of the lower order of Catholics here in their priest," he continued, "is astonishing: even his presence they conceive an antidote to every evil. When he appears at the door of their huts, and blends his cordial salutation with a blessing, the spirit of consolation seems to hover at its threshold—pain is alleviated, sorrow soothed, and hope, rising from the bosom of strengthening faith, triumphs over the ruins of despair. To the wicked he prescribes penitence and confession, and the sinner is forgiven; to the wretched he asserts, that suffering here, is the purchase of felicity hereafter, and he is resigned; and to the sick he gives a consecrated charm, and by the force of faith and imagination he is made well. Guess then the influence which this order of men hold over the aggregate of the people; for while the Irish peasant, degraded, neglected, and despised,* vainly seeks one beam of conciliation in the eye of overbearing superiority; condescension, familiarity and kindness win his gratitude to him whose spiritual elevation is in his mind above all temporal rank."

"You shed," said I, "a patriarchal interest over the character of priesthood among you here; which gives that order to my view in a very different aspect from that in which I have hitherto considered it. To what an excellent purpose might this boundless influence be turned!"

"If," interrupted he, "priests *were not men*—men too, generally speaking, without education (which is in fact character, principle, every thing), except such as tends rather to narrow than enlarge the mind—men in a certain degree shut out from society, except of the lower class; and men who, from their very mode of existence (which forces them to depend on the eleemosynary contributions of their flock), must eventually in many

* "The common people of Ireland have no rank in society—they *may* be treated with contempt, and consequently are with inhumanity."—"*An Inquiry into the Causes,*" &c. &c. [Parnell, *Popular Discontents in Ireland,* 31. Ed.]

instances imbibe a degradation of spirit which is certainly not the parent of the liberal virtues."

"Good God!" said I, surprised, "and this from one of their own order!"

"These are sentiments I should never have hazarded," returned the priest, "could I not have opposed to those natural conclusions, drawn from well known facts, innumerable instances of benevolence, piety, and learning, among the order. While to the whole body let it be allowed as *priests,* whatever may be their failings as *men,* that the activity of their lives,* the punctilious discharge of their duty, and their ever ready attention to their flock, under every moral and even under every physical suffering, renders them deserving of that reverence and affection which, above the ministers of any other religion, they receive from those over whom they are placed."

"And which," said I, "if opposed to the languid performance of periodical duties, neglect of the moral functions of their calling, and the habitual indolence of the ministers of other sects, they may certainly be deemed zealots in the cause of the faith they profess, and the charity they inculcate!"

While I spoke, a young lad, almost in a state of nudity, approached us, yet in the crown of his leafless hat were stuck a few pens, and over his shoulder hung a leathern satchel full of books.

"This is an apposite rencontre," said the priest—"behold the first stage of *one* class of Catholic priesthood among us; a class however no longer very prevalent."

The boy approached, and, to my amazement, addressed us in Latin, begging with all the vehement eloquence of an Irish mendicant, for some money to buy ink and paper. We gave him a trifle, and the priest desired him to go on to the castle, where he would get his breakfast, and that on his return he would give him some books into the bargain.

The boy, who had solicited in Latin, expressed his gratitude in Irish; and we trotted on.

"Such," said Father John, "formerly was the frequent origin of our Roman Catholic priests. This is a character unknown to you in England, and is called here, '*a poor scholar.*' If a boy is too indolent to work, and his parents too poor to support him, or, which is more frequently the case, if he

* "A Roman Catholic clergyman is the minister of a very *ritual* religion; and by his profession, subject to many restraints; his life is full of strict observances, and his duties are of a laborious nature towards himself, and of the highest possible trust towards others."—*Letter on the Penal Laws against the Irish Catholics, by the Right Honourable Edmund Burke.* [Edmund Burke, "A Letter to a Peer of Ireland on the Penal Laws Against Irish Catholics" (1782), rpt. *Field Day Anthology of Irish Writing,* vol. 1, 819. Ed.]

discovers some natural talents, or, as they call it *takes to his learning,* and that they have not the means to forward his improvement, he then becomes by profession a *poor scholar,* and continues to receive both his mental and bodily food at the expence of the community at large.

"With a leathern satchel on his back, containing his portable library, he sometimes travels not only through his own province, but frequently over the greater part of the kingdom.* No door is shut against the poor scholar, who, it is supposed, at a future day may be invested with the apostolic key of Heaven. The priest or school-master of every parish through which he passes, receives him for a few days into his bare-footed seminary, and teaches him bad Latin and worse English; while the most opulent of his school-fellows eagerly seize on the young peripatetic philosopher, and provide him with maintenance and lodging; and if he is a boy of talent or *humour* (a gift always prized by the naturally laughter-loving Milesians), they will struggle for the pleasure of his society.

"Having thus had the seeds of dependence sown *irradically* in his mind, and finished his peripatetic studies, he returns to his native home, and with an empty satchel on his back, goes about raising contributions on the pious charity of his poor compatriots: each contributes some necessary article of dress, and assists to fill a little purse, until completely equipped; and for the first time in his life, covered from head to foot, the divine in embryo sets out for some sea-port, where he embarks for the colleges of Douay or St. Omers; and having begged himself, *in forma pauperis,* through all the necessary rules and discipline of the seminary, he returns to his own

*It has been justly said, that "Nature is invariable in her operations; and that the principles of a polished people will influence even their latest posterity." And the ancient state of letters in Ireland, may be traced in the love of learning and talent even still existing among the inferior class of the Irish to this day. On this point it is observed by Mr. Smith, in his *History of Kerry,* "that it is well known that classical reading extends itself even to a fault, among the lower and poorer kind of people in this country (Munster), many of whom have greater knowledge in this way than some of the better sort in other places." He elsewhere observes, that Greek is taught in the mountainous parts of the province. And Mr. O'Halloran asserts, that classical reading has most adherents in those retired parts of the kingdom where strangers had least access, and that as good classical scholars were found in most parts of Connaught, as in any part of Europe. ["Preface" to Guys, *Sentimental Journey Through Greece,* vol. 1, iv; Smith, *The Ancient and Present State of the County of Kerry,* 67, 418; Sylvester O'Halloran, *A General History of Ireland from the Earliest Accounts to the Close of the Twelfth Century,* 2 vols. (London, 1778), vol. 2, 118–19. Ed.]

Douay: Like St. Omers, Douay in Belgium was a Jesuit seminary attended by Irish seminarians during the Penal Laws era. See *CR* 89, Ed.'s n.

country, and becomes the minister of salvation to those whose generous contributions enabled him to assume the sacred profession.*

"Such is the man by whom the minds, opinions, and even actions of the people are often influenced; and if man is but the creature of education and habit, I leave you to draw the inference. But this is but *one* class of priesthood, and its description rather applicable to twenty or thirty years back than to the present day. The other two may be divided into the sons of tradesmen and farmers, and the younger sons of Catholic gentry.

"Of the latter order am I; and the interest of my friends on my return from the Continent procured me what was deemed the best parish in the diocese. But the good and the evil attendant on every situation in life, is rather to be estimated by the feelings and sensibility of the objects whom they affect, than by their own intrinsic nature. It was in vain I endeavoured to accommodate my mind to the mode of life into which I had been forced by my friends. It was in vain I endeavoured to assimilate my spirit to that species of exertion necessary to be made for my livelihood.

"To owe my subsistence to the precarious generosity of those wretches, whose every gift to me must be the result of a sensible deprivation to themselves; to be obliged to extort (even from the altar where I presided as the minister of the Most High) the trivial contributions for my support, in a language which, however appropriate to the understandings of my auditors, sunk me in my own esteem to the last degree of self-degradation; or to receive from the religious affection of my flock such voluntary benefactions as, under all the pressure of scarcity and want, their rigid economy to themselves enabled them to make to the pastor whom they revered.† In a word, after three years miserable dependence on those for whose poverty and wretchedness my heart bled, I threw up my situation, and became chaplain to the Prince of Inismore, on a stipend sufficient for my little wants, and have lived with him for thirty years, on such terms as you have witnessed for these three weeks back.

"While my heart-felt compassion, my tenderest sympathy, is given to those of my brethren who are by birth and education divested of that low

* The French Revolution, and the foundation of the Catholic college at Maynooth, in Leinster, has put a stop to these pious emigrations. [Maynooth was founded in 1795. See *CR* 89, Ed.'s n. Ed.]

† "Are these men supposed to have no sense of justice, that, in addition to the burthen of supporting their own establishment exclusively, they should be called on to pay ours; that, where they pay sixpence to their own priest, they should pay a pound to our clergyman; that, while they can scarce afford their own horse, they should place ours in his carriage; and that when they cannot build a mass-house to cover their multitudes, they should be forced to contribute to build sumptuous churches for half a dozen Protestants to pray under a shed!"—*Inquiry into the Causes of Popular Discontents, &c. &c.* page 27. [Parnell, *Popular Discontents in Ireland*, 27. Ed.]

scale of thought, and obtuseness of feeling, which distinguish those of the order, who, reared from the lowest origin upon principles the most servilising, are callous to the innumerable humiliations of their dependent state—"

Here an old man mounted on a mule, rode up to the priest, and with tears in his eyes informed him that he was just going to the castle to humbly entreat his Reverence would visit a poor child of his, who had been looked on with "*an evil eye*" a few days back,* and who had ever since been pining away.

"It was our misfortune," said he, "never to have tied a gospel about her neck, as we did round the other children's, or this heavy sorrow would never have befallen us. But we know if your Reverence would only be pleased to say a prayer over her, all would go well enough!"

The priest gave me a significant look, and shaking me cordially by the hand, and pressing my speedy return to Inismore, rode off with the suppliant.

Thus, in his duty, "prompt at every call," after having passed the night in acts of religious benevolence, his humanity willingly obeyed the voice of superstitious prejudice which endowed him with the fancied power of alleviating fancied evils.

"As I rode along reflecting on the wondrous influence of superstition, and the nature of its effects, I could not help dwelling on the strong analogy which in so many instances appears between the vulgar errors of this country and that of the ancient as well as modern Greeks.

St. Crysostom† relating the bigotry of his own times, particularly mentions the superstitious horror which the Greeks entertained against "*the evil eye.*" And an elegant modern traveller assures us, that even in the present day they "combine cloves of garlic, talismans, and other charms, which they hang about the neck of their infants, with the same intention of keeping away *the evil eye.*"

Adieu!

H. M.

* It is supposed among the lower order of Irish, as among the Greeks, that some people are born with *an evil eye,* which injures every object on which it falls, and they will frequently go many miles out of their direct road, rather than pass by the house of one who has *an evil eye.* To frustrate its effects, the priest hangs a consecrated charm around the necks of their children, called *a gospel;* and the fears of the parents are quieted by their faith.

† "Some write on the hand the names of several rivers; while others make use of ashes, tallow, and salt, for the like purpose—all this being to divert the *evil eye.*" [St. John Chrysostom (AD 347–407), archbishop of Constantinople. Guys extracts the work of St. John Chrysostom in his *Sentimental Journey through Greece,* and is the source for the novel's repeated reference to "the evil eye," vol. 1., 179. ED.]

Letter XVI

TO J. D. ESQ. M. P.

I WISH you were to have seen the look with which the worthy Mr. Clendinning met me, as I rode up the avenue to M___ House.

To put an end at once to his impertinent surmises, curiosity, and suspicion, which I evidently saw lurking in his keen eye, I made a display of my fractured arm, which I still wore in a sling; and naturally enough accounted for my absence, by alleging that a fall from my horse, and a fractured limb, had obliged me to accept the humane attentions of a gentleman, near whose house the accident had happened, and whose guest and patient I had since been. Mr. Clendinning affected the tone of regret and condolence, with some appropriate suppositions of what his Lord would feel when he learnt the unfortunate circumstance.

"In a word, Mr. Clendinning," said I, "I do not choose my father's feelings should be called in question on a matter which is now of no ill consequence; and as there is not the least occasion to render him unhappy to no purpose, I must insist that you neither write or mention the circumstance to him on any account."

Mr. Clendinning bowed obedience, and I contrived to ratify his promise by certain inuendoes; for as he is well aware many of his villanies have reached my ear, he hates and fears me with all his soul.

My first inquiry was for letters. I found two from my father, and one, only one, from you.

My father writes in his usual style. His first is merely an epistle admonitory; full of prudent axioms, and fatherly solicitudes. The second informs me, that his journey to Ireland is deferred for a month or six weeks, on account of my brother's marriage with the heiress of the richest banker in the city. It is written in his best style, and a brilliant flow of spirit pervades every line. In the plenitude of his joy, all *my* sins are forgiven: he even talks of terminating my exile sooner than I had any reason to expect: and he playfully adds, "of changing my banishment into slavery"—"knowing, from experience, that provided my shackles are woven by the rosy fingers of beauty, I can wear them patiently and pleasurably enough. In short," he adds, "I have a connexion in my eye for you, not less brilliant in point of fortune than that your brother has made; and which will enable you to forswear your Coke, and burn your Blackstone."

In fact, the spirit of matrimonial establishment seems to have taken such complete possession of my good speculating *dad,* that it would by no means surprise me though he were on the point of sacrificing at the Hymeneal altar himself. You know he has more than once, in a frolic, passed for my elder brother; and certainly has more sensibility than should belong to *forty-five.* Nor should I at all wonder if some insinuating coquette should one day or other *sentimentalize* him into a Platonic passion, which would terminate *in the old way.* I have, however, indulged in a little triumph at his expence; and have answered him in a strain of apathetic content—that habit and reason have perfectly reconciled me to my present mode of life, which leaves me without a wish to change it.

Now for your letter. With respect to the advice you demand, I have only to repeat the opinion already advanced, that * * * * * * * * * * * * * *

But with respect to that you give me—

> "Go bid physicians preach our veins to health,
> And with an argument new set a pulse."[117]

And as for your prediction—of this be certain, that I am too hackneyed in *les affaires du coeur,* ever to fall in love beyond all redemption with any woman in existence. And even this little Irish girl, with all her witcheries, is to me a subject of philosophical analysis, rather than amatory discussion.

You ask me if I am not disgusted with her brogue? If she had one, I doubt not but I should; but the accent to which we English apply that term, is here generally confined to the lower orders of society; and I certainly believe, that purer and more grammatical English is spoken generally through Ireland, than in any part of England whatever; for here you are never shocked by the barbarous and unintelligible dialect peculiar to each shire in England. As to Glorvina, an aptitude to learn languages is, you know, peculiar to her country; but in her it is a decided and striking talent: even her Italian is, "*la langua Toscana, nel' bocca Romana;*" and her English, grammatically correct, and elegantly pure, is spoken with an accent that could never denote her country. But it is certain that in *that* accent there is a species of languor very distinct from the brevity of ours. Yet (to me at least) it only renders the lovely speaker more interesting. A simple question from her lip seems rather tenderly to solicit, than abruptly to demand. Her

---

Hymeneal altar: the marriage altar.

les affaires du coeur: French: the affairs of the heart.

la langua Toscana, nel' bocca Romana: Italian: the language of Tuscany, in a Roman mouth.

[117] Perhaps an inaccurate reference to Samuel Wesley's "Reflections Upon these two Verses of Mr. Oldham . . ." (1743), ll. 47–48: "Go! bid Physicians heal our Pain,/Without enquiring the Disease."

every request is a soft supplication; and when she stoops to entreaty, there is in her voice and manner such an energy of supplication, that while she places *your* power to grant in the most ostensible light to yourself, you are insensibly vanquished by that soft persuasion whose melting meekness bestows your fancied exaltation. Her sweet-toned mellifluous voice, is always sighed forth rather below than above its natural pitch, and her mellowed softened mode of articulation is but imperfectly expressed by the *susaro susingando,* or *coaxy murmurs,* of Italian persuasion.

To Father John, who is the first and most general linguist I ever met, she stands highly indebted; but to Nature, and her own ambition to excell, still more.

I am now but six hours in this solitary and deserted mansion, where I feel as though I reigned the very king of desolation. Let me hear from you by return.

Adieu!

H. M.

Letter XVII

TO J. D. ESQ. M. P.

I FORGOT to mention to you in my last, that to my utter joy and surprise, our *premier* here has been recalled. On the day of my return, he received a letter from his Lord, desiring his immediate attendance in London, with all the rents he could collect; for I suppose the necessary expenditures requisite for my brother's matrimonial establishment, will draw pretty largely on our family treasury.

This change of things in our domestic politics has changed all my plans of operation. This arch spy being removed, obviates the necessity of my retreat to the Lodge. My establishment here consists only of two females, who scarcely speak a word of English; an old gardener, who possesses not one *entire sense;* and a groom, who, having nothing to do, I shall discharge: so that if I should find it my pleasure to return, and remain any time at the castle of Inismore, I shall have no one here to watch my actions, or report them to my father.

There is something Boeotian in this air. I can neither read, write, or think. Does not Locke assert, that the soul sometimes dozes? I frequently think I

Boeotian: Boeotia, a district of ancient Greece proverbial for the stupidity of its inhabitants.

have been bit by a torpedo, or that I partake in some degree of the nature of the seven sleepers, and suffer a transient suspension of existence. What if this Glorvina has an *evil eye,* and has overlooked me? The witch haunts me, not only in my dreams, but when *I fancy myself,* at least, awake. A thousand times I think I hear the tones of her voice and harp. Does she feel my absence at the accustomed hour of tuition, the fire-side circle in the *Vengolf,* the twilight conversation, the noon-tide ramble?—Has my presence become a want to her? Am I missed, and missed with regret? It is scarcely vanity to say, *I am—I must be.* In a life of so much sameness, the most trivial incident, the most inconsequent character, obtains an interest in a certain degree.

One day I caught her weeping over a pet robin, which died on her bosom. She smiled, and endeavoured to hide her tears. "This is very silly, I know," said she, "but one must feel even the loss of *a bird,* that has been the *companion of one's solitude!*"

To day I flung by my book, in downright deficiency of comprehension to understand a word in it, though it was a simple case in the Reports of ____; and so in the most *nonchalante* mood possible, I mounted my *rosinante,* and throwing the bridle over her neck, said, "please thyself:" and it was her pious pleasure to tread on consecrated ground: in short, after a ride of half an hour, I found myself within a few paces of the parish mass-house, and recollected that it was the Sabbath day; so that you see my mare reproved me, though in an oblique manner, with little less gravity than the ass of Balaam did his obstinate rider.

The mass-house was of the same order of architecture as the generality of Irish cabins; with no other visible mark to ascertain its sacred designation than a stone cross, roughly hewn, over its entrance. I will not say that it was merely a sentiment of piety which induced me to enter it; but it certainly required, at first, an effort of energy to obtain admittance, as for several yards round this simple tabernacle, a crowd of *devotees* were prostrated on the earth, praying over their beads with as much fervour as though they were offering up their orisons in the golden-roofed temple of Solyman.

When I had fastened my horse's bridle to a branch of an hawthorn, I endeavoured to make my way through the pious crowd, who all arose the moment I appeared—for the *last mass,* I learnt, was over; and those who had

---

torpedo: a fish with the ability to emit electrical discharges.

ass of Balaam: See Numbers 22: 22–31. Balaam, a non-Israelite prophet, whose ass communicated with him on articles of faith.

temple of Solyman: See I Kings 6. Solomon, son of David, King of the Hebrews, had an opulent temple.

prayed *par hazard,* without hearing a word the priest said within, departed. While I pressed my way into the body of the chapel, it was so crowded that with great difficulty I found means to fix myself by a large triangular stone vessel filled with holy water, where I fortunately remained (during the sermon) unnoticed.

This sermon was delivered by a little old mendicant, in the Irish language. Beside him stood the parish priest in pontificalibus, and with as much self-invested dignity as the *dalai lama* of Little Thibet[118] could assume before his votarists. When the shrivelled little mendicant had harangued them some time on the subject of Christian charity, for so his countenance and action indicated, a general *secula seculorum* concluded his discourse; and while he meekly retreated a few paces, the priest mounted the steps of the little altar, and after preparing his lungs, he delivered an oration, to which it would be impossible to do any justice. It was partly in Irish, partly in English; and intended to inculcate the necessity of contributing to the relief of the mendicant preacher, if they hoped to have the benefit of his prayers; addressing each of his flock by their name and profession, and exposing their faults and extolling their virtues, according to the nature of their contributions. While the friar, who stood with his face to the wall, was with all human diligence piously turning his beads to two accounts—with one half he was making intercession for the souls of his good subscribers, and with the other diligently keeping count of the sum total of their benefactions. As soon as I had sent in mine, almost stifled with heat, I effected my escape.

In contrasting this parish priest with the chaplain of Inismore, I could not help exclaiming with Epaminondas—"It is the *man* who must give dignity to the situation—not the situation to the man."

Adieu!

H. M.

---

par hazard: French: by guesswork.

pontificalibus: Latin: official or ceremonial attire.

secula seculorum: Latin: now and for always.

Epaminondas: Greek statesman and military tactician, who led Thebes and Boeotia in their defeat of Sparta (371 BC).

[118] For a contemporary view of Tibet, see "An Account of a Journey to Tibet, made by Poorungeer, a Goseyn," in William Jones, *Dissertations and Miscellaneous Pieces, Relating to the History and Antiquities, the Arts, Sciences and Literature of Asia* (Dublin, 1793), 352–66.

Letter XVIII.

TO J. D. ESQ. M. P.

"LA solitude est certainement une belle chose, mais il-y-a plaisir d'avoir quelqu'une qui en sache repondre, a qui on puis dire, la solitude est une belle chose."

So says Monsieur de Balsac, and so repeats my heart a thousand times a day. In short, I am devoured by *ennui*, by apathy, by discontent! What should I do here? Nothing. I have spent but four days here, and all the symptoms of my old disease begin to re-appear; in short, like other impatient invalids, I believed my cure was effected when my disease was only on the decline. I must again fly to sip from the fountain of intellectual health at Inismore, and receive the vivifying drops from the hand of the presiding priestess, or stay here, and fall into an incurable atrophy of the heart and mind!

Having packed up a part of my wardrobe, and a few books, I sent them by a young rustic to the little *Villa di Marino*, and in about an hour after I followed myself. The old fisherman and his dame seemed absolutely rejoiced to see me, and having my valise laid in their cabin, and dismissed my attendant, I requested they would permit their son to carry my luggage as far as the next *cabaret*, where I expected a man and horse to meet me. They cheerfully complied, and I proceeded with my *compagnon de voyage* to a hut which lies half way between the fisherman's and the castle. This hut they call a *Sheebeen House*, and is something inferior to a certain description of a Spanish inn. Although a little board informs the weary traveller he is only to expect "good dry lodgings," yet the landlord contrives to let you know in an *entre nous* manner, that he keeps some real *Inishone* (or spirits, smuggled from a tract of country so called) for his particular friends. So having dismissed my second courier, and paid for the whiskey I did not taste, and the potatoes I did not eat, I sent my host forward, mounted on a sorry mule, with my travelling equipage, to the cabin at the foot of the draw-bridge; and by these precautions obviated all possibility of discovery.

"La solitude . . . belle chose": French: "Solitude is certainly a beautiful thing, but there is pleasure in having someone to whom one can say, solitude is a beautiful thing."

Balsac: Jean-Louis Guez de Balzac (1597–1654), French writer and critic, and major influence on the development of classical French prose.

cabaret: French: tavern.

entre nous: French: between us.

As I now proceeded on my route, every progressive step awakened some new emotion; while my heart was agitated by those unspeakable little flutterings which are alternately excited and governed by the ardour of hope, or the timidity of fear. "And shall I, or shall I not be welcome?" was the problem which engaged my thoughts during the rest of my little journey.

As I descended the mountain at whose base the peninsula of Inismore reposes, I perceived a form at some distance, whose drapery ("*nebulam lineam*") seemed light as the breeze on which it floated. It is impossible to mistake the figure of Glorvina, when its graces are called forth by motion. I instantly alighted, and flew to meet her. She too sprang eagerly forward. We were almost within a few paces of each other, when she suddenly turned back, and flew down the hill with the bounding step of a fawn. This would have mortified another—I was charmed. And the bashful consciousness which repelled her advances, was almost as grateful to my heart as the warm impulse which had nearly hurried her into my arms. How freshly does she still wear the first gloss of nature!

In a few minutes, however, I perceived her return, leaning on the arm of the Father Director. You cannot conceive what a festival of the feelings my few days absence had purchased for me. Oh! he knows nothing of the doctrine of enjoyment, who does not purchase his pleasures at the expence of temporary restraint. The good priest, who still retains something of the etiquette of his foreign education, embraced me *à la Française.* Glorvina, however, who *malhereusement,* was not reared in France, only offered me her *hand,* which I had not the courage to raise to my unworthy lip, although the cordial *cead mille a falta* of her country revelled in her shining eyes, and her effulgent countenance was lit up with an unusual blaze of animation.

When we reached the castle the Prince sent for me to his room, and told me, as he pressed my hand, that "his heart warmed at my sight." In short, my return seems to have produced a carnival in the whole family.

You who know, that notwithstanding my late vitiated life, the simple pleasures of the heart were always dead to mine, may guess how highly gratifying to my feelings is this interest which, independent of all adventitious circumstances of rank and fortune, I have awakened in the bosoms of these cordial, ingenuous beings.

The late insufferable reserve of Glorvina has given way to the most bewitching (I had almost said *tender*) softness of manner.

---

nebulam lineam: Latin: flaxen cloud or mist.

à la Française: French: in the French way.

malhereusement: French: unfortunately.

cead mille a falta: céad míle fáilte, Irish: a hundred thousand welcomes; a conventional greeting.

As I descended from paying my visit to the Prince, I found her and the priest in the hall.

"We are waiting for you," said she—"there is no resisting the fineness of this evening."

And as we left the door, she pointed towards the west, and added—

"See—

'The weary sun hath made a golden set,
And by yon ruddy brightness of the clouds,
Gives tokens of a goodly day to-morrow.'[119]

"O! *a-propos,* Mr. Mortimer, you are returned in most excellent time—for to-morrow is the *first of May.*"

"And is the arrival of a guest," said I, "on the *eve* of that day, a favourable omen?"

"The arrival of such a guest," said she, "must be at least ominous of happiness. But the first of May is our great national festival; and you who love to trace modern customs to ancient origins, will perhaps feel some curiosity and interest to behold some of the rites of our heathen superstitions still lingering among our present ceremonies."

"What then," said I, "have you, like the Greeks, the festivals of the spring among you?"

"It is certain," said the priest, "that the ancient Irish sacrificed on the *first of May* to *Beal,* or the *Sun;* and that day, even at this period, is called *Beal.*"

"By this idolatry to the God of Light and Song," said I, "one would almost suppose that Apollo was the tutelar deity of your Island."

"Why," returned he, "Hecataeus tells us that the Hyperborean Island was dedicated to Apollo, and that most of its inhabitants were either priests or bards, and I suppose you are not ignorant that we claim the honour of being those happy Hyperboreans, which were believed by many to be a fabulous nation.

"And if the peculiar favour of the God of Poetry and Song may be esteemed a sufficient proof, it is certain that our claims are not weak. For surely no nation under Heaven was ever more enthusiastically attached to poetry and music than the Irish. Formerly every family had its poet or bard, called Filea and Crotarie; and indeed the very language itself seems most felicitously adapted to be the vehicle of poetic images; for its energy,

---

Beal: Bealtaine, Irish: May. O'Halloran, *History and Antiquities of Ireland,* 34–35.

Hecataeus: Hecataeus of Mietus (fl. c. 500 BC), early Greek chronicler and geographer.

Hyperborean Island: in Greek mythology, lay to the north and usually described in utopian terms.

[119] Shakespeare, *Richard III,* V. iii. 19–21.

strength, expression, and luxuriancy, never leave the bard at a loss for apposite terms to realize 'the thick coming fancies' [120] of his genius." *

"But," said Glorvina, "the first of May was not the only festival held sacred by the Irish to their tutelar deity: on the 24th of June they sacrificed to the Sun, to propitiate his influence in bringing the fruit to perfection; and to this day those lingering remains of heathen rites are performed with something of their ancient forms. '*Midsummer's Night,*' as it is called, is with us a night of universal lumination—the whole country blazes: from the summit of every mountain, every hill, ascends the flame of the bonfire, while the unconscious perpetuators of the heathen ceremony dance round the fire in circles, or, holding torches to it made of straw, run with the burning brands wildly through the country with all the gay frenzy of so many Bacchantes. But though I adore our inspiring *Beal* with all my soul, I worship our popular deity *Samhuin* with all my heart—he is the god of the heart's close-knitting socialities, for the domesticating month of November is sacred to him."

"And on its eve," said the priest, "the great fire of *Samhuin* was illuminated, all the culinary fires in the kingdom being first extinguished, as it was deemed sacrilege to awaken the winter's social flame, except by a spark snatched from this sacred fire,† and so deep rooted are the customs of our forefathers among us, that the present Irish have no other name for the month of November than *Samhuin.*

"Over our mythological accounts of this *winter god,* an almost impenetrable obscurity seems to hover; but if *Samhuin* is derived from *Samhfhuin,* as it is generally supposed, the term literally means the gathering or closing of summer; and in fact, on the eve of the first of November we make our offerings round the domestic altar (the fireside), of such fruits as the lingering seasons afford, besides playing a number of curious gambols, and

* Mr. O'Halloran informs us, that in a work entitled "*Uiraceacht na Neaigios,*" or Poetic Tales, above an hundred different species of Irish verse is exhibited. O'Molloy, in his Irish and Latin Grammar, has also given rules and specimens of our modes of versification, which may be seen in Dr. Lhuid's *Achaeologia.* [O'Halloran, *History and Antiquities of Ireland,* 75. Edward Llwyd, author of the philological study *Archaeologia Brittanica* (1701) that argued for connections between Welsh and Irish. Ed.]

† To this day, the inferior Irish look upon bonfires as sacred; they say their prayers walking round them; the young dream upon their ashes, and the old steal away the fire, to light up their domestic hearths with it.

Bacchantes: women who celebrated at the feast of Bacchus, the Roman god of wine.

Samhuin: in Celtic mythology, a time when the normal order is suspended, allowing free passage between the natural and supernatural worlds; celebrated on November 1.

[120] Shakespeare, *Macbeth,* V. iii. 38.

performing many superstitious ceremonies, in which our young folk find great pleasure, and put great faith."

"For my part," said Glorvina, "I love all those old ceremonies which force us to be periodically happy, and look forward with no little impatience to the gay-hearted pleasures which to-morrow will bring in its train."

The little post-boy has this moment tapped at my door for my letter, for he tells me he sets off before dawn, that he may be back in time for the sport. It is now past eleven o'clock, but I could not resist giving you this little scrap of Irish mythology, before I wished you good night.

H. M.

Letter XIX

TO J. D. ESQ. M. P.

ALL the life-giving spirit of spring, mellowed by the genial glow of summer, shed its choicest treasures on the smiling hours which yesterday ushered in the most delightful of all the seasons.

I arose earlier than usual; the elixity of my mind would not suffer me to rest, and the scented air, as it breathed its odours through my open casement, seduced me abroad. I walked as though I scarcely touched the earth, and my spirit seemed to ascend like the lark which soared over my head to hail the splendour of the dewy dawn. There is a fairy vale in the little territories of Inismore, which is almost a miniature *Tempé,* and which is indeed the only spot on the peninsula where the luxuriant charms of the most bounteous nature are evidently improved by taste and cultivation. In a word, it is a spot sacred to the wanderings of Glorvina. It was there our theological discourse was held on the evening of my return, and thither my steps were now with an irresistible impulse directed.

I had scarcely entered this Eden, when the form of the Eve to whose picturesque fancy it owes so many charms, presented itself. She was standing at a little distance *en profile*—with one hand she supported a part of her drapery filled with wild flowers gathered ere the sun had kissed off the tears which night had shed upon their bosoms: with the other she seemed carefully to remove some branches that entwined themselves through the sprays of a little hawthorn hedge richly embossed with the first-born blossoms of May.

Tempé: a beautiful valley in Thessaly in northern Greece.

As I stole towards her, I exclaimed, as Adam did when he first saw Eve—

> "——Behold her,
> Such as I saw her in my dream adorned,
> With all that earth or heaven could bestow."[121]

She started and turned round, and in her surprise let fall her flowers, yet she smiled, and seemed confused—but pleasure, pure animated life-breathing pleasure, was the predominant expression of her countenance. The Deity of Health was never personified in more glowing colours—her eye's rich blue, her cheek's crimson blush, her lip's dewy freshness, the wanton wildness of her golden tresses, the delicious languor that mellowed the fire of her beamy glance—I gazed, and worshiped! but neither apologized for my intrusion, nor had the politeness to collect her scattered flowers.

"If Nature," said I, "had always such a priestess to preside at her altar, who would worship at the shrine of Art?"

"I am her votarist only," she replied, smiling, and, pointing to a wild rose which had just begun to unfold its blushing breast amidst the snowy blossoms of the hedge—added, "see how beautiful! how orient its hue appears through the pure crystal of the morning dew-drop! It is nearly three weeks since I discovered it in the germ, since when I have screened it from the noon-day ardors, and the evening's frost, and now it is just bursting into perfection to reward my cares."

At these words, she plucked it from the stem. Its crimson head drooped with the weight of the gems that spangled it. Glorvina did not shake them off, but imbibed the liquid fragrance with her lip; then held the flower to me!

"Am I to pledge you?" said I.

She smiled, and I quaffed off the fairy nectar, which still trembled on the leaves her lip had consecrated.

"We have now," said I, "*both* drank from the same cup; and if the delicious draught which Nature has prepared for us, circulates with mutual effect through our veins—If"—I paused, and cast down my eyes. The hand which still sustained the rose, and was still clasped in mine, seemed to tremble with an emotion scarcely inferior to that which thrilled through my whole frame.

After a minute's pause—"Take the rose," said Glorvina, endeavouring to extricate the precious hand which presented it—"Take it; it is the first of the season! My father has had his snow-drop—the confessor his violet—and it is but just you should have your *rose*."

---

votarist: devoted to some particular pursuit or person.

[121] Milton, *Paradise Lost*, Book VIII, ll. 481–83.

At that moment the classical remark of the priest rushed, I believe, with mutual influence, to both our hearts. I, at least, was borne away by the rapturous feelings of the moment, and knelt to receive the offering of my lovely votarist.

I kissed the sweet and simple tribute with pious ardor; but with a devotion more fervid, kissed the hand that presented it. I would not have exchanged that moment for the most pleasurable hours of the most pleasurable era of my existence. The blushing radiance that glowed on the cheek, sent its warm suffusion even to the hand I had violated with my unhallowed lip; while the sparkling fluid of her eyes, turned on mine in almost dying softness, beamed on the latent powers of my once-chilled heart, and awakened there a thousand delicious transports, a thousand infant wishes and chaste desires, of which I lately thought its worn-out feelings were no longer susceptible.

As I arose, I plucked off a small branch of that myrtle which here grows wild, and which, like my rose, was dripping in dew, and putting it into the hand I still held, said,

"This offering is indeed less beautiful, less fragrant, than that which you have made; but remember, it is also less *fragile*—for the sentiment of which it is an emblem, carries with it an eternity of duration."

Glorvina took it in silence, and placed it in her bosom; and in silence we walked together towards the castle; while our eyes, now timidly turned on each other, now suddenly averted (Oh, the insidious danger of the abruptly downcast eye!), met no object but what breathed of love, whose soul seemed

"——Sent abroad,
Warm thro' the vital air, and on the heart
Harmonious seiz'd."[122]

The morning breeze flushed with ethereal fervour; the luxury of landscape through which we wandered, the sublimity of those stupendous cliffs which seemed to shelter two hearts from the world, to which their profound feelings were unknown, while

"——Every copse
Deep tangled, but irregular, and bush,
Bending with dewy moisture o'er the heads
Of the coy quiresters that lodg'd within,
Were prodigal of harmony;"[123]

---

[122] Thomson, *The Seasons,* "Spring," ll. 579–81.

[123] Thomson, *The Seasons,* "Spring," ll. 591–95.

and crowned imagination's wildest wish, and realized the fancy's warmest vision.

"Oh! my sweet friend!" I exclaimed, "since now I feel myself entitled thus to call you—well indeed might your nation have held this day sacred; and while the heart which now throbs with an emotion to which it has hitherto been a stranger, beats with the pulse of life, on the return of this day will it make its offering to that glorious orb, to whose genial nutritive beams this precious rose owes its existence."

As I spoke, Father John suddenly appeared. Vexed as I was at his unseasonable intrusion, yet in such perfect harmony was my spirit with the whole creation, that in the true hyperbola of Irish cordiality, I wished him a thousand happy returns of this season!

"Spoken like a true-born Irishman!" said the priest, laughing, and shaking me heartily by the hand—"While with something of the phlegm of an Englishman, I wish you only as many returns of it as shall bring health and felicity in their train."

Then looking at the myrtle which reposed on the bosom of Glorvina, and the rose which I so proudly wore, he added—"So, I perceive you have both been sacrificing to *Beal;* and, like the priests and priestesses of this country in former times, are adorned with the flowers of the season. For you must know, Mr. Mortimer, *we* had our Druidesses as well as our Druids; and both, like the ministers of Grecian mythology, were crowned with flowers at the time of sacrifice."

At this apposite remark of the good priest's, I stole a glance at *my* lovely priestess. Hero, at the altar of the deity she rivalled, never looked more attractive in the eyes of the enamoured Leander.[124]

We had now come within a few steps of the portals of the castle, and I observed that since I had passed that way, the path and entrance were strewed with green flags, rushes, and wild crocusses;* while the heavy framework of the door was hung with garlands, and bunches of flowers tastefully displayed.

"This, Madam," said I to Glorvina, "is doubtless the result of your happy taste."

* "Seeing the doors of the Greeks on the first of May, profusely ornamented with flowers, would certainly recall to your mind the many descriptions of that custom which you have met with in the Greek and Latin poets."—*Letters on Greece, by Monsieur De Guys,* vol. i. p. 153. [Guys, *Sentimental Journey Through Greece,* vol. 1, 153. Ed.]

---

[124] Two lovers celebrated in Greek legend. Leander swam the Hellespont at night to visit Hero, a priestess of Aphrodite, guided by a light from her tower. He drowned on a night when the light was extinguished by a storm, and, seeing his body, Hero drowned herself.

"By no means," she replied—"this is a custom prevalent among the peasantry time immemorial."

"And most probably was brought hither," said the priest, "from Greece by our Phoenician progenitors; for we learn from Athenaeus, that the young Greeks hung garlands on the doors of their favourite mistresses on the first of May. Nor indeed does the Roman *floralia* differ in any respect from ours."

"Those, however, which you now admire," said Glorvina, smiling, "are no offerings of rustic gallantry; for every hut in the country, on this morning, will bear the same fanciful decorations. The wild crocus, and indeed every flower of that rich tint, is peculiarly sacred to this day."

And, in fact, when, in the course of the day, I rambled out alone, and looked into the several cabins, I perceived not only their floors covered with flags and rushes, but a "May-bush," as they call it, or small tree, planted before all the doors, covered with every flower the season affords.

I saw nothing of Glorvina until evening, except for a moment, when I perceived her lost over a book (as I passed her closet window), which, by the Morocco binding, I knew to be the Letters of the impassioned Heloise. Since her society was denied me, I was best satisfied to resign her to Rousseau. *A-propos!* it was among the books I brought hither; and they were all precisely such books as Glorvina had *not*, yet *should* read, that she may know herself, and the latent sensibility of her soul. They have, of course, all been presented to her, and consist of "*La Nouvelle Heloise,*" de Rousseau—the unrivalled "*Lettres sur la Mythologie,*" de Moustier—the "*Paul et Virginie*" of St. Pierre—the *Werter* of Göethe—the *Dolbreuse* of Lousel, and the *Attila* of Chateaubriand.[125] Let our English novels carry away the prize of morality from the romantic fictions of every other country; but you will find they rarely seize on the imagination through the medium of the heart; and as for their heroines, I confess that though they are the most perfect of beings, they are also the most stupid. Surely virtue would not be the less attractive for being united to genius and the graces.

But to return to the never-to-be-forgotten *first of May!* Early in the evening the Prince, his daughter, the priest, the bard, the old nurse, and indeed all the household of Inismore, adjourned to the vale, which being the only

---

Athenaeus: Greek grammarian and author of *Deipnosophistai (The Gastronomers).*

[125]Works of sentimental fiction influenced by Rousseau: Jean-Jacques Rousseau, *Julie, ou La Nouvelle Héloïse* (1761); Charles-Albert de Moustier, *Lettres à Émilie sur la mythologie* (1786–99); Jacques-Henri Bernardin de Saint-Pierre, *Paul et Virginie* (1788); Goethe's *The Sorrows of Young Werther* (1774); Joseph-Marie Loaisel-Tréogate, *Dolbreuse; ou, L'Homme du siécle, ramené à la verité par le sentiment et par la raison* (1783); and François René, vicomte de Chateaubriand, *Atala* (1801).

level ground on the peninsula, is always appropriated to the sports of the rustic neighbours. It was impossible I should enter this vale without emotion; and when I beheld it crowded with the vulgar throng, I felt as it were profanation for the

> "Sole of unblest feet!"[126]

to tread that ground sacred to the most refined emotions of the heart.

Glorvina, who walked on before the priest and me, supporting her father, as we entered the vale stole a glance at me; and a moment after, as I opened the little wicker through which we passed, I murmured in her ear—*La val di Rosa!*

We found this charming spot crowded with peasantry of both sexes, and all ages.* Since morning they had planted a May-bush in the centre, which was hung with flowers, and round the seats appropriated to the Prince and his family, the flag, crocus, and primrose, were profusely scattered. Two blind fiddlers, and an excellent piper,† were seated under the shelter of the very hedge which had been the nursery of my precious rose; while the old bard, with true druidical dignity, sat under the shade of a venerable oak, near his master.

*In the summer of 1802 the Author was present at a rural festival at the seat of an highly respected friend in Tipperary, from which this scene is partly copied.

†Although the bagpipe is not an instrument indigenous to Ireland, it holds an high antiquity in the country. It was the music of the Kearns, in the reign of Edward the Third.* It is still the favourite accompaniment of those mirthful exertions with which laborious poverty crowns the temporary cessation of its weekly toil, and the cares and solicitudes of the Irish peasant ever dissipate to the spell which breathes in the humorous drones of the Irish pipes. To Scotland we are indebted for this ancient instrument, who received it from the Romans; but to the native musical genius of Ireland are we indebted for its present form and improved state. "That at present in use in Ireland," says Dr. Burney, in a letter to J. C. Walker, Esq. "is an improved bagpipe, on which I have heard some of the natives play very well in two parts, without the drone, which, I believe, is never attempted in Scotland. The tone of the lower notes resembles that of an hautboy and clarinet, and the high notes, that of a German flute; and the whole scale of one I heard lately was very well in tune, which has never been the case of any Scottish bagpipe that I have yet heard." [Letter from Burney quoted in Walker, *Historical Memoirs,* 78–80n. Ed.]

> *See Smith's Hist. of Cork, p. 43. [Charles Smith describes the kerns as, "among the Irish, light arm'd foot . . . their common names were Kerns, from the Irish Keathern, which signifies a company of soldiers. . . . Their musick was the bagpipe, as Aulius Gellius informs us, was also that of the Lacedemonians" (Charles Smith, *The Ancient and Present State of the County and City of Cork,* 2 vols. (Dublin, 1774), vol. 2, 43n). Ed.]

[126] Milton, *Paradise Lost,* Book I, ll. 237–38.

The sports began with a wrestling-match;* and in the gymnastic exertions of the youthful combatants there was something, I thought, of Spartan energy and hardihood.

But, as "breaking of ribs is no sport for ladies,"[127] Glorvina turned from the spectacle in disgust; which I wished might have been prolonged, as it procured me (who leaned over her seat) her undivided attention; but it was too soon concluded, though without any disagreeable consequences, for neither of the combatants were hurt, though one was laid prostrate. The victorious wrestler was elected King of the May; and, with "all his blushing honours thick about him,"[128] came timidly forward, and laid his rural crown at the feet of Glorvina. Yet he evidently seemed intoxicated with his happiness, and though he scarcely touched the hand of his blushing charming queen, yet I perceived a thousand saucy triumphs basking in his fine black eyes, as he led her out to dance. The fellow was handsome too. I know not why, but I could have knocked him down with all my heart.

"Every village has its Caesar," said the priest, "and this is ours. He has been elected King of the May for these five years successively. He is second son to our old steward, and a very worthy, as well as very fine young fellow."

"I do not doubt his worth," returned I peevishly, "but it certainly cannot exceed the condescension of his young mistress."

"There is nothing singular in it, however," said the priest. "Among us, over such meetings as these, inequality of rank holds no *obvious* jurisdiction, though in fact it is not the less regarded; and the condescension of the master or mistress on these occasions, lessens nothing of the respect of the servant upon every other; but rather secures it, through the medium of gratitude and affection."

The piper had now struck up one of those lilts, whose mirth-inspiring influence it is almost impossible to resist.† The Irish jig, above every other

* The young Irish peasantry particularly prize themselves on this species of exertion: they have almost reduced it to a science, by dividing it into two distinct species—the one, called *sparniaght,* engages the arms only; the other, *carriaght,* engages the whole body.

† Besides the Irish jig, tradition has rescued from that oblivion which time has hung over the ancient Irish dance, the *rinceadh-fada,* which answers to the festal dance of the Greeks; and the *rinceadh,* or war dance, "which seems," says Mr. Walker, "to have been of the nature of the armed dance, which is so ancient, and with which the Grecian youth amused themselves during the siege of Troy."

Previous to the adoption of the French style in dancing, Mr. O'Halloran asserts, that both our private and public balls always concluded with the *rinceadh-fada.* On the arrival of James the Second at Kinsale, his adherents received the unfortunate Prince on the shore with this dance, with whose taste and execution he was infinitely delighted;

---

[127] Shakespeare, *As You Like It,* I. ii. 138–39.

[128] Shakespeare, *Henry VIII,* III. ii. 354.

dance, leaves most to the genius of the dancer; and Glorvina, above all the women I have ever seen, seems most formed by Nature to excell in the art. Her little form, pliant as that of an Egyptian *alma,* floats before the eye in all the swimming languor of the most graceful motion, or all the gay exility of soul-inspired animation. She even displays an exquisite degree of comic humour in some of the movements of her national dance; and her eyes, countenance, and air, express the wildest exhilaration of pleasure, and glow with all the spirit of health, mirth, and exercise.

I was so struck with the grace and elegance of her movements, the delicacy of her form, and the play of her drapery gently agitated by the air, that I involuntarily gave to my admiration an audible existence.

"Yes," said the priest, who overheard me, "she performs her national dance with great grace and spirit. But the Irish are all dancers; and, like the Greeks, we have no idea of any festival here which does not conclude with a dance;* old and young, rich and poor, all join here in the sprightly dance."

Glorvina, unwearied, still continued to dance with unabated spirit, and even seemed governed by the general principle which actuates all the Irish dancers—of not giving way to any competitor in the exertion; for she actually outdanced her partner, who had been jigging with all his *strength,* while she had only been dancing with all her *soul;* and when he retreated, she dropped a simple curtsey (according to the laws of jig-dancing here) to another young rustic, whose seven-leagued brogues finally prevailed, and Glorvina at last gave way, while he made a scrape to a rosy-cheeked, barefooted damsel, who out-jigg'd him and his two successors; and thus the chain went on.

Glorvina, as she came panting and glowing towards me, exclaimed, "I have done my duty for the evening;" and threw herself on a seat, breathless and smiling.

"Nay," said I, "more than your duty; for you even performed a work of supererogation." And I cast a pointed look at the young rustic who had been the object of her election.

and even still, in the county of Limerick, and many other parts of Ireland, the *rinceadh-fada* is danced on the eve of May. [See Walker, *Historical Memoirs,* 150–55, reflecting communication with Sylvester O'Halloran and Charles O'Connor. Ed.]

* "The passion of the Greeks for dancing is common to both sexes, who neglect every other consideration, when they have an opportunity of indulging that passion." [Guys, *Sentimental Journey Through Greece,* vol. 1, 201. Ed.]

---

alma: dancing girl.

supererogation: performance of more than duty or circumstance requires.

"O!" she replied eagerly—"it is the custom here, and I should be sorry, for the indulgence of an overstrained delicacy, to violate any of those established rules to which, however trifling, they are devotedly attached. Besides, you perceive," she added, smiling, "this condescension on the part of the females who are thus 'won unsought,'[129] does not render the men more presumptuous. You see what a distance the youth of both sexes preserve—a distance which always exists in these kind of public meetings."

And in fact, the lads and lasses were ranged opposite to each other, with no other intercourse that what the communion of the eyes afforded, or the transient intimacy of the jig bestowed.*

"And will not you dance a jig?" asked Glorvina.

"I seldom dance," said I—"Ill health has for some time back coincided with my inclination, which seldom led me to try my skill at the *Poetry of Motion.*"

"*Poetry of Motion!*" repeated Glorvina—"What a beautiful idea!"

"It is so," said I, "and if it had been my own, it must have owed its existence to you; for your dancing is certainly the true poetry of motion, and *Epic* poetry too."

"I love dancing with all my heart," she replied: "when I dance I have not a care on earth—every thing swims gayly before me; and I feel as if swiftly borne away in a vortex of pleasurable sensation."

"Dancing," said I, "is the talent of your sex—that pure grace which must result from a symmetrical form, and that elixity of temperament which is the effect of woman's delicate organization, creates you dancers. And while I beheld your performance this evening, I no longer wondered that the gravity of Socrates could not resist the spell which lurked in the graceful motions of Aspasia, but followed her in the mazes of the dance."

She bowed, and said, "I flattered too agreeably, not to be listened to with *pleasure,* if not with *faith.*"

In short, I have had a thousand occasions to observe, that while she receives a decided compliment with the ease of almost *bon ton nonchalance,* a look, a broken sentence, a word, has the power of overwhelming her with

*This custom, so prevalent in some parts of Ireland, is of a very ancient origin. We read in Keating's History of Ireland, that in the remotest periods, when the Irish brought their children to the fair of Tailtean, in order to dispose of them in marriage, the strictest order was observed: the men and women having distinct places assigned them, at a certain distance from each other.—See *Keating,* page 216. [Keating, *General History of Ireland,* 216. Ed.]

Aspasia: mistress of the Athenian statesman Pericles.

bon ton nonchalance: French: a fine nonchalant manner.

[129] Shakespeare, *Twelfth Night,* III. i. 156.

confusion, or awakening all the soul of emotion in her bosom. All this I can understand.

As the dew of the evening now began to fall, the invalid Prince and his lovely daughter arose to retire. And those who had been rendered so happy by their condescension, beheld their retreat with regret, and followed them with blessings. Whiskey, milk, and oaten bread, were now distributed in abundance by the old nurse and the steward; and the dancing was recommenced with new ardor.

The priest and I remained behind, conversing with the old and jesting with the young—he in Irish and I in English, with such as understood it. The girls received my little gallantries with considerable archness, and even with some point of repartee; while the priest rallied them in their own way, for he seems as playful as a child among them, though evidently worshipped as a saint. And the moon rose resplendently over the vale, before it was restored to its wonted solitary silence.

Glorvina has made the plea of a head-ach these two mornings back, for playing the truant at her drawing-desk; but the fact is, her days and nights are devoted to the sentimental sorcery of Rousseau; and the effects of her studies are visible in her eyes. When we meet, their glance sinks beneath the ardor of mine, in soft confusion: her manner is no longer childishly playful, or carelessly indifferent, and sometimes a sigh, scarce breathed, is discovered by the blush which glows on her cheek for the inadvertency of her lip. Does she then begin to feel she has an heart? Does "*Le besoin de l'ame tendre,*" already throb with vague emotion in her bosom? Her abstracted air, her delicious melancholy, her unusual softness, betray the nature of the feelings by which she is overwhelmed—they are new to herself; and sometimes I fancy, when she turns her melting eyes on me, it is to solicit their meaning. O! if I dared become the interpreter between her and her heart—if I dared indulge myself in the hope, the belief, that——And what then? 'Tis all folly, 'tis madness, 'tis worse! But who ever yet rejected the blessing for which his soul thirsted?—And in the scale of human felicities, if there is one in which all others are summed up—above all others supremely elevated—It is the consciousness of having awakened the first sentiment of the sweetest, the sublimest of all human passions, in the bosom of youth, genius, and sensibility.

Adieu!

H. M.

Le besoin de l'ame tendre: French: "The need of a tender soul."

Letter XX

TO J. D. ESQ. M. P.

I HAD just finished my last by the beams of a gloriously setting sun, when I was startled by a pebble being thrown in at my window. I looked out, and perceived Father John in the act of flinging up another, which the hand of Glorvina (who was leaning on his arm) presented.

"If you are not engaged in writing to your mistress," said he, "come down and join us in a ramble."

"And though I were," I replied, "I could not resist your challenge." And down I flew—Glorvina laughing, sent me back for my hat, and we proceeded on our walk.

"This is an evening," said I, looking at Glorvina, "worthy of the morning of the first of May, and we have seized it in that happy moment so exquisitely described by Collins:

—'While now the bright hair'd sun
Sits in yon western tent, whose cloudy skirts,
With brede ethereal wove
O'erhang his wavy bed.'"[130]

"O! that beautiful Ode!" exclaimed Glorvina, with all her wildest enthusiasm—"never can I read—never hear it repeated, but with emotion. The perusal of Ossian's 'Song of other Times,' the breezy respiration of my harp at twilight, the last pale rose that outlives its season, and bears on its faded breast the frozen tears of the wintry dawn, and Collins's Ode to Evening, awaken in my heart and fancy the same train of indescribable feeling, of exquisite yet unspeakable sensation. Alas! the solitary pleasure of feeling thus alone the utter impossibility of conveying to the bosom of another those ecstatic emotions by which our own is sublimed."

While my very soul followed this brilliant comet to her perihelium of sentiment and imagination, I fixed my eyes on her "mind-illumin'd face,"[131] and said,

"And is expression then necessary for the conveyance of such profound, such exquisite feeling? May not a similarity of refined organization exist between souls, and produce that mutual intelligence which sets the

---

"Song of Other times": term used repeatedly in Macpherson's poems.

perihelium: perihelion, the point in the orbit of a planet, comet, or other heavenly body at which it is nearest to the sun.

[130] William Collins, "Ode to Evening" (1746), ll. 5–8.

[131] Thomas Dermody, *The Histionade: Or, Theatric Tribunal* (1802), Part I, ll. 87–88.

necessity of cold verbal expression at defiance? May not the sympathy of a kindred sensibility in the bosom of another, meet and enjoy those delicious feelings by which yours is warmed, and, sinking beneath the inadequacy of language to give them birth, feel like you in silent and sacred emotion?"

"Perhaps," said the priest, with his usual simplicity, "this sacred sympathy between two refined, elevated, and sensible souls, in the sublime and beautiful of the moral and natural world, approaches nearest to the rapturous and pure emotions which uncreated spirits may be supposed to feel in their heavenly communion, than any other human sentiment with which we are acquainted."

For all the looks of blandishment which ever flung their spell from beauty's eye, I would not have exchanged the glance which Glorvina at that moment cast on me. While the priest, who seemed to have been following up the train of thought awakened by our preceding observations, abruptly added, after a silence of some minutes—

"There is a species of metaphorical taste, if I may be allowed the expression, whose admiration for certain objects is not deducible from the established rules of beauty, order, or even truth; which *should* be the basis of our approbation; yet which ever brings with it a sensation of more lively pleasure; as for instance, a chromatic passion in music, will awaken a thrill of delight which a simple chord could never effect."

"Nor would the most self-evident truth," said I, "awaken so vivid a sensation, as when we find some sentiment of the soul illustrated by some law or principle in science. To an axiom we grant our assent, but we lavish our most enthusiastic approbation when Rousseau tells us that, 'Les ames humaines veulent être accomplies pour valoir toute leurs prix, et la force unie des ames *comme celles des larmes d'un aimant artificiel,* est incomparablement plus grands que la somme de leurs force particulier.'"

As this quotation was meant *all* for Glorvina, I looked earnestly at her as I repeated it. A crimson torrent rushed to her cheek, and convinced me that she felt the full force of a sentiment so applicable to us both.

"And why," said I, addressing her in a low voice, "was Rousseau excluded from the sacred coalition with Ossian, Collins, your twilight harp, and winter rose?"

Glorvina made no reply; but turned full on me her "eyes of dewy light."[132] Mine almost sunk beneath the melting ardor of their soul-beaming glance.

"Les ames . . . force particulier": French: "Human souls want to be completed, and the united force of arms, like those of the tears of an artificial lover, is incomparably greater than the sum of their individual force."

[132] William Collins, "Ode to Pity" (1747), ll. 11–12.

Oh! child of Nature! child of genius and of passion! why was I withheld from throwing myself at thy feet; from offering thee the homage of that soul thou hast awakened; from covering thy hands with my kisses, and bathing them with tears of such delicious emotion, as thou only hast power to inspire?

While we thus "*buvames à longs traits le philtre de l'amour,*" Father John gradually restored us to common-place existence, by a common-place conversation on the fineness of the weather, promising aspect of the season, &c. until the moon, as it rose sublimely above the summit of the mountain, called forth the melting tones of my Glorvina's syren voice.

Casting up her eyes to that Heaven whence they seem to have caught their emanation, she said, "I do not wonder that unenlightened nations should worship the moon. Our ideas are so intimately connected with our senses, so ductilely transferrable from cause to effect, that the abstract thought may readily subside in the sensible image which awakens it. When, in the awful stillness of a calm night, I fix my eyes on that mild and beautiful orb, the *created* has become the awakening medium of that adoration I offered to the *Creator.*"

"Yes," said the priest, "I remember, that even in your childhood, you used to fix your eyes on the moon, and gaze and wonder. I believe it would have been no difficult matter to have plunged you back in the heathenism of your ancestors, and to have made it one of the gods of your idolatry."

"And was the chaste Luna in the *album sanctorum* of your Druidical mythology?" said I.

"Undoubtedly," said the priest, "we read in the life of our celebrated saint, St. Columba, that on the altar-piece of a Druidical temple, the sun, moon, and stars, were curiously depicted; and the form of the ancient Irish oath of allegiance, was to swear by the sun, moon, and stars, and other deities, celestial as well as terrestrial."

"How," said I, "did your mythology touch so closely on that of the Greeks? had you also your Pans and your Daphnes, as well as your Dians and Apollos?"

"Here is a curious anecdote that evinces it," returned the priest—"It is many years since I read it in a black-letter memoir of St. Patrick.[133]

"buvames . . . l'amour:" French: "drank the philter of love in long draughts."

album sanctorum: Latin: sacred volume.

St. Columba: St. Columba, or Colum Cile (c. 521–97), established monasteries in Ireland and later at Iona, Scotland.

[133] St. Patrick's extant prose writings include *Epistola ad Milites Corotici (Letter to the Soldiers of Coroticus)* and *Confessio.* Although often attributed to him popularly, the *Lorica* or *Breastplate of St. Patrick* is believed to be of later provenance.

The Saint, says the biographer, attended by three bishops, and some less dignified of his brethren, being in this very province, arose early one morning, and with his pious associates placed himself near a fountain or well, and began to chaunt a hymn. In the neighbourhood of this honoured fountain, stood the palace of *Cruachan,* where the two daughters of the Emperor Laogaire were educating in retirement; and as the saints sung by no means *sotto voce,** their pious strains caught the attention of the royal fair ones, who were enjoying an early ramble, and who immediately sought the sanctified choristers. Full of that curiosity so natural to the youthful recluses, they were by no means sparing of interrogations to the Saint, and among other questions, demanded 'and who is your God? where dwells he, in heaven or on earth, or beneath the earth, or in the mountain or the valley; or the sea or the stream?'—And indeed even to this day, we have Irish for a river god, which we call *Divona.* You perceive, therefore, that our ancient religion was by no means an unpoetical one."

While he spoke, we observed a figure emerging from a coppice, towards a small well, which issued from beneath the roots of a blasted oak. The priest motioned us to stop, and be silent—the figure (which was that of an ancient female wrapt in a long cloak), approached, and having drank of the well out of a little cup, she went three times round it on her knees, praying with great fervency over her beads; then rising after this painful ceremony, she tore a small part of her under garb, and hung it on the branch of the tree which shaded the well.

"This ceremony, I perceive," said the priest, "surprises you; but you have now witnessed the remains of one of our most ancient superstitions.— The ancient Irish, like the Greeks, were religiously attached to the consecrated fountain, the *Vel expiatoria;* and our early missionaries discovering the fondness of the natives for these sanctified springs, artfully averted the course of their superstitious faith, and dedicated them to Christian saints."

*A musical voice was an indispensable quality in an Irish Saint, and *lungs of leather* no trivial requisite towards obtaining canonization. St. Columbkill, we are told, sung so loud, that, according to an old Irish poem, called *Amhra Choilluim chille,* or the Vision of *Columbkill,*

"His hallow'd voice beyond a mile was heard." [For the quotation, see Adamnan's *Vita Columbae (Life of Columba):* "his voice did not seem louder than that of others; [. . .] persons more than a mile away heard it so distinctly [. . .] for his voice sounded the same whether far or near," <ftp://ftp.ucc.ie/pub/celt/texts/T201040.txt>. Ed.]

---

sotto voce: musical term. Latin: softly.

Divona: Irish river god. See O'Halloran, *History and Antiquities,* 32.

"There is really," said I, "something truly classic in this spot; and here is this little shrine of Christian superstition hung with the same votive gifts as Pausanius tells us obscured the statue of Hygeia in Secyonia."

"This is nothing extraordinary here," said the priest—"these consecrated wells are to be found in every part of the kingdom. But of all our *Aquae Sanctificatae,* Lough Derg is the most celebrated.[134] It is the *Loretto* of Ireland, and votarists from every part of the kingdom resort to it. So great, indeed, is the still-existing veneration among the lower orders for these holy wells, that those who live at too great a distance to make a pilgrimage to one, are content to purchase a species of amulet made of a sliver of the tree which shades the well (and imbued in its waters), which they wear round their necks. These curious amulets are sold at fairs, by a species of sturdy beggar called a *Bacagh,* who stands with a long pole, with a box fixed at the top of it, for the reception of alms; while he alternately extols the miraculous property of the amulet, and details his own miseries; thus at once endeavouring to interest the faith and charity of the always benevolent, always credulous multitude."

"Strange," said I, "that religion in all ages, and in all countries, should depend so much on the impositions of one half of mankind, and the credulity and indolence of the other. Thus the Egyptians (to whom even Greece herself stood indebted for the principles of those arts and sciences by which she became the most illustrious country in the world), resigned themselves so entirely to the impositions of their priests, as to believe that the safety and happiness of life itself depended on the motions of an ox, or the tameness of a crocodile.

"Stop, stop," interrupted Father John, smiling—"you forget, that though you wear the *San-Benito,* or robe of heresy yourself, you are in the company of those who—"

"Exactly think on *certain points,*" interrupted I, "even as my heretical self."

This observation led to a little controversial dialogue, which, as it would stand a very poor chance of being read by you, will stand none at all of being transcribed by me.

Pausanius: Greek traveler, geographer, and author of *Periegesis Hellados (Description of Greece).*

Hygeia: In Greek mythology, Hygeia is the goddess of health. See Guys, vol. 1, 170.

San-Benito: during the Spanish Inquisition, a penitential garment worn by a confessed and penitent heretic.

[134]Lough Derg, a religious site of pilgrimage associated with St. Patrick's forty-day fast on a lake-island in southeast Co. Donegal. Also see description in "The Life of Turlough O'Carolan," Appendix to Walker, *Historical Memoirs,* 69. For "Loretto," see *WIG* 173.

When we returned home we found the Prince impatiently watching for us at his window, fearful lest the dews of heaven should have fallen too heavily on the head of his heart's idol, who finished her walk in silence—either I believe not much pleased with the turn given to the conversation by the priest, or not sufficiently interested to participate in it.

I know not how it is, but since the morning of the first of May, I feel as though my soul had entered into a sacred covenant with hers—as though our very beings were indissolubly interwoven with each other. And yet the freedom which once existed in our intercourse is fled. I approach her trembling; and she repels the most distant advances with such dignified softness, such chastely modest reserve, that the restraint I sometimes labour under in her presence, is almost concomitant to the bliss it bestows.

This morning, when she came to her drawing-desk, she held a volume of *De Moustier* in her hand—"I have brought this," said she, "for our *bon Pere Directeur* to read out to us."

"He has commissioned me," said I, "to make his excuses—he is gone to visit a sick man on the other side of the mountain."

At this intelligence she blushed to the eyes; but suddenly recovering herself, she put the book into my hands, and said with a smile, "then you must officiate for him."

As soon as she was seated at the drawing desk I opened the book, and by chance at the beautiful description of the *Boudoir*:

"J'aime une boudoir etroite qu'un demi jour eclaire,
La mon coeur est chez lui, le premier demi jour
Fuit par la volupte, menagé pour l'amour,
La discrete amitiè, veut aussi du mystere.
Quand de nos bons amis dans un lieu limité,
Le cercle peu nombreux pres de nous le rassemble
Le sentiment, la paix, la franche liberté
Preside en commun," &c. &c.

I wish you could see this creature, when any thing is said or read that comes home to her heart, or strikes in immediate unison with the exquisite tone of her feelings. Never sure was there a finer commentary, than her looks and gestures pass on any work of interest which engages her attention. Before I had finished the perusal of this charming little fragment, the

"J'aime une . . . Preside en commun," &c. &c: French: "I love a small boudoir lit by twilight: there my heart is at home, the first twilight fled by voluptuousness, cared for by love and discrete friendship. When the limited circle of our good friends assemble around us sentiment, peace, and open-hearted freedom reign in common."

pencil had dropped from her fingers; and often she waved her beautiful head and smiled, and breathed a faint exclamation of delight; and when I laid down the book, she said, while she leaned her face on her clasped hands—

"And I too have a boudoir!—but even a *boudoir* may become a dreary solitude, except"—she paused; and I added, from the poem I had just read, except that within its social little limits

'La confidence ingenû rapproche deux amis.'"

Her eyes, half raised to mine, suddenly cast down, beamed a tender acquiescence to the sentiment.

"But," said I, "if the being worthy of sharing the bliss such an intercourse in such a place must confer, is yet to be found, is its hallowed circle inviolable to the intrusive footstep of an inferior, though perhaps not less ardent votarist?"

"Since you have been here," said she, "I have scarcely ever visited this once favourite retreat myself."

"Am I to take that as a compliment or otherwise?" said I.

"Just as it is meant," said she—"as a fact;" and she added, with an inadvertent simplicity into which the ardor of her temper often betrays her—"I never can devote myself partially to any thing—I am either all enthusiasm or all indifference."

Not for the world would I have made her *feel* the full force of this avowal; but requested permission to visit this now deserted boudoir.

"Certainly," she replied—"it is a little closet in that ruined tower, which terminates the corridor in which your apartment lies."

"Then I am privileged?" said I.

"Undoubtedly," she returned; and the Prince, who had risen unusually early, entered the room at that moment, and joined us at the drawing-desk.

The absence of the good priest left me to a solitary dinner. Glorvina (as is usual with her) spent the first part of the evening in her father's room; and thus denied her society, I endeavoured to supply its want—its soul-felt want, by a visit to her boudoir.

There is a certain tone of feeling when fancy is in its acmé, when sentiment holds the senses in subordination, and the visionary joys which float in the imagination shed a livelier bliss on the soul than the best pleasures cold reality ever conferred. Then, even the presence of a beloved object is not more precious to the heart than the spot consecrated to her memory;

"La confidence . . . amis": French: "Candid intimacy draws two friends together."
acmé: the highest point of perfection.

where we fancy the very air is impregnated with her respiration; every object is hallowed by her recent touch, and that all around breathes of her.

In such a mood of mind, I ascended to Glorvina's boudoir; and I really believe, that had she accompanied me, I should have felt less than when alone and unseen I stole to the asylum of her pensive thoughts. It lay as she had described; and almost as I passed its threshold, I was sensibly struck by the incongruity of its appearance—it seemed to me as though it had been partly furnished in the beginning of one century, and finished in the conclusion of another. The walls were rudely wainscotted with oak, black with age; yet the floor was covered with a Turkey carpet, rich, new, and beautiful—better adapted to cover a Parisian dressing-room than the closet of a ruined tower. The casements were high and narrow, but partly veiled with a rich drapery of scarlet silk: a few old chairs, heavy and cumbrous, were interspersed with stools of an antique form; one of which lay folded up on the ground, so as to be portable in a travelling trunk. On a pondrous Gothic table (which seemed a fixture coeval with the building), was placed a silver *escritoire*, of curious and elegant workmanship, and two small, but beautiful antique vases (filled with flowers) of Etrurian elegance. Two little book-shelves, elegantly designed, but most clumsily executed (probably by some hedge carpenter), were filled with the best French, English, and Italian poets; and, to my utter astonishment, not only some new publications scarce six months old, but two London newspapers of no distant date, lay scattered on the table, with some MS. music, and unfinished drawings.

Having gratified my curiosity, by examining the singular incongruities of this paradoxical boudoir, I leaned for some time against one of the windows, endeavouring to make out some defaced lines cut on its panes with a diamond, when Glorvina herself entered the room.

As I stood concealed by the silken drapery, she did not perceive me. A basket of flowers hung on her arm, from which she replenished the vases, having first flung away their faded treasures. As she stood thus engaged, and cheering her sweet employment with a murmured song, I stole softly behind her, and my breath disturbing the ringlets which had escaped from the bondage of her bodkin, and seemed to cling to her neck for protection, she turned quickly round, and with a start, a blush, and a smile, said, "Ah! *so soon* here!"

"You perceive," said I, "your immunity was not lost on me! I have, have been here this half hour!"

"Indeed!" she replied, and casting round a quick inquiring glance, hastily collected the scattered papers, and threw them into a drawer;

Etrurian: ancient culture in central Italy, predating and influencing Rome.

adding, "I intended to have made some arrangements in this deserted little place, that you might see it in its best garb; but had scarcely began the necessary reform this morning, when I was suddenly called to my father, and could not till this moment find leisure to return hither."

While she spoke I gazed earnestly at her. It struck me there was a something of mystery over this apartment; yet wherefore should mystery dwell where all breathes the ingenuous simplicity of the golden age. Glorvina moved towards the casement, threw open the sash, and laid her fresh gathered flowers on the seat. Their perfume scented the room; and a new fallen shower still glittered on the honeysuckle which she was endeavouring to entice through the window, round which it crept.

The sun was setting with rather a mild than a dazzling splendour, and the landscape was richly impurpled with his departing beams, which, as they darted through the scarlet drapery of the curtain, shed warmly over the countenance and figure of Glorvina, "*Love's proper hue.*"

We both remained silent, until her eye accidentally meeting mine, a more "celestial rosy red"[135] invested her cheek. She seated herself in the window, and I drew a chair, and sat near her. All within was the softest gloom—all without the most solemn stillness. The grey vapours of twilight were already stealing amidst the illumined clouds that floated in the atmosphere—the sun's golden beams no longer scattered round their rich suffusion; and the glow of retreating day was fading even from the horizon where its parting glories faintly lingered.

"It is a sweet hour," said Glorvina, softly sighing.

"It is a *boudoirizing* hour," said I.

"It is a golden one for a poetic heart," she added.

"Or an enamoured one," I returned.

"It is the hour in which the soul best knows herself; when every low-thoughted care is excluded, and the pensive pleasures take possession of the dissolving heart."

'Ces douces lumieres
Ces sombre clairtés
Sont les *jours* de la volupté.'

And what was the *voluptas* of Epicurus, but those refined and elegant enjoyments which must derive their spirit from virtue and from health;

"Ces douces . . . la volupté": French: "These soft lights, these somber illuminations are the days of voluptuousness."

Epicurus: Greek philosopher, author of an ethical philosophy of simple pleasure, friendship, and retirement.

[135] Milton, *Paradise Lost,* Book VIII, l. 619: "Celestial rosie red, Loves proper hue."

from a vivid fancy, susceptible feelings, and a cultivated mind; and which are never so fully tasted as in this sweet season of the day? then the influence of sentiment is buoyant over passion; the soul, alive to the sublimest impression, expands in the region of pure and elevated meditation: the passions, slumbering in the soft repose of Nature, leave the heart free to the reception of the purest, warmest, tenderest sentiments—when all is delicious melancholy, or pensive softness—when every vulgar wish is hushed, and a rapture, an indefinable rapture, thrills with sweet vibration on every nerve."

"It is thus *I* have felt," said the all-impassioned Glorvina, clasping her hands, and fixing her humid eyes on mine—"thus, in the dearth of all *kindred* feeling, have *I* felt. But never, Oh! till *now—never!*"—and she abruptly paused, and dropped her head on the back of my chair, over which my hand rested, and felt the soft pressure of her glowing cheek, while her balmy sigh breathed its odour on my lip.

Oh! had not her celestial confidence, her angelic purity, sublimed every thought, restrained every wish—at that moment—that too fortunate—too dangerous moment!!!—Yet even as it was, in the delicious agony of my soul, I secretly exclaimed, with the legislator of Lesbos—"*It is too difficult to be always virtuous!*"[136] while I half audibly breathed on the ear of Glorvina—

"Nor I, O first of all created beings! never, never till I beheld thee, did I know the pure rapture which the intercourse of a kindred soul awakens—of that sacred communion with a superior intelligence, which, while it raises me in my own estimation, tempts me to emulate that excellence I adore."

Glorvina raised her head—her melting eyes met mine, and her cheek rivalled the snow of that hand which was pressed with passionate ardor to my lips. Then her eyes were bashfully withdrawn—she again drooped her head—not on the chair, but on my shoulder. What followed, angels might have attested—but the eloquence of bliss is silence.

Suffice it to say, that I am now certain of at least being understood; and that in awakening her comprehension, I have roused my own. In a word, I *now* feel I love!!—for the first time I feel it. For the first time my heart is alive to the most profound, the most delicate, the most ardent, and most refined of all human passions. I am now conscious that I have hitherto mistaken the senses for the heart, and the blandishments of a vitiated imagination for the pleasures of the soul. In short, I now feel myself in that state of beatitude, when the fruition of all the heart's purest wishes leaves me nothing to desire, and the innocence of those wishes nothing to fear. You

---

[136] Assertion of Pittacus (c. 650–c. 570 BC), Dictator of Mytilene, one of the Seven Wise Men of ancient Greece.

know but little of the sentiment which now pervades my whole being, and blends with every atom of my frame, if you suppose I have formerly told Glorvina I loved her, or that I appear even to suspect that I am (rapturous thought!) beloved in return. On the contrary, the same mysterious delicacy, the same delicious reserve still exist. It is a sigh, a glance, a broken sentence, an imperceptible motion (imperceptible to all eyes but our own), that betrays us to each other. Once I used to fall at the feet of the "*Cynthia of the moment,*"[137] avow my passion, and swear eternal truth. Now I make no genuflexion, offer no vows, and swear no oaths; and yet feel more than ever—More!—dare I then place in the scale of comparison what I now feel with what I ever felt before? The thought is sacrilege!

This Child of Nature appears to me each succeeding day, in a *phasis* more bewitchingly attractive than the last. She now feels her power over me (with woman's *intuition,* where the heart is in question!); and this consciousness gives to her manners a certain roguish tyranny, that renders her the most charming tantalizing being in the world. In a thousand little instances she contrives to teaze me; most, when most she delights me! and takes no pains to conceal my simple folly from others, while she triumphs in it herself. In short, she is the last woman in the world who would incur the risk of satiating him who was blest in her love; for the variability of her manner, always governed by her ardent, though volatilized, feelings, keeps suspense on the eternal *qui vive!* and the sweet assurance given by the eyes one moment, is destroyed in the next by some arch sally of the lip.

To day I met her walking with the nurse. The old woman, very properly, made a motion to retire as I approached. Glorvina would not suffer this, and twined her arm round that of her foster-mother. I was half inclined to turn on my heel, when a servant came running to the nurse for the keys. It was impossible to burst them from her side, and away she hobbled after the bare-footed *laquais.* I looked reproachfully at Glorvina, but her eyes were fixed on an arbutus tree rich in blossom.

"I wish I had that high branch," said she, "to put in my vase." In a moment I was climbing up the tree like a great school-boy, while she, standing beneath, received the blossoms in her extended drapery; and I was on the point of descending, when a branch, lovelier than all I had culled,

---

phasis: Greek: aspect.

qui vive: French: alertness.

laquais: French: lackey.

[137] Alexander Pope, *An Epistle to a Lady: Of the Character of Women* (1743), l. 20.

attracted my eye: this I intended to present in *propria persona,* that I might get a kiss of the hand in return. With my own hands sufficiently engaged in effecting my descent, I held my Hesperian branch in my teeth, and had nearly reached the ground, when Glorvina playfully approached her lovely mouth to snatch the prize from mine. We were just in contact—I suddenly let fall the branch—and—Father John appeared walking towards us; while Glorvina, who, it seems, had perceived him before she had placed herself in the way of danger, now ran towards him, covered with blushes and malignant little smiles. In short, she makes me feel in a thousand trivial instances, the truth of Epictetus's maxim, that to *bear* and *forbear,* are the powers that constitute a wise man: to *forbear* alone, would, in my opinion, be a sufficient test.

Adieu!

H. M.

Letter XXI.

TO J. D. ESQ. M. P.

I CANNOT promise you any more Irish history. I fear my *Hiberniana* is closed, and a volume of more dangerous, more delightful tendency, draws towards its betwitching subject every truant thought. To him who is deep in the *Philosophia Amatoria,* every other science is cold and vapid.

The oral legend of the Prince and the historic lore of the priest, all go for nothing! I shake my head, look very wise, and appear to listen, while my eyes are rivetted on Glorvina—who, not unconscious of the ardent gaze, sweeps with a feathery touch the chords of her harp, or plies her fairy wheel with double vigilance. Meantime, however, I am making a rapid progress in the Irish language, and well I may; for besides that I now listen to the language of Ossian with the same respect a Hindoo would to the Shanscrit of the Bramins, the Prince, the priest, and even Glorvina, contribute their exertions to my progress. The other evening, as we circled round the evening fire in the great hall, the Prince would put my improvements to the test, and taking down a grammar, he insisted on my conjugating a verb. The verb he chose was "*to love.*"—"Glorvina," said he, seeing me hesitate, "go through the verb."

---

propria persona: Latin: in person.

Epictetus: Greek philosopher (AD 55–140), associated with the Stoics.

Hiberniana: Latin: volume of knowledge about Ireland.

Philosophia Amatoria: Latin: philosophy of love.

Glorvina had it at her fingers' ends; and in her eyes swam a thousand delicious comments on the text she was expounding.

The Prince, who is as unsuspicious as an infant, would have us repeat it together, that I might catch the pronunciation from her lip!

"*I love,*" faintly articulated Glorvina.

"*I love,*" I more faintly repeated.

This was not enough—the Prince would have us repeat the plural twice over; and again and again we murmured together—"*we love!*"

Heavens and earth! had you at that moment seen the preceptress and the *pupil!* The attention of the simple Prince was rivetted on Vallancy's grammar:[138] he grew peevish at what he called our stupidity, and said we knew nothing of the verb to love, while in fact we were running through all its moods and tenses with our eyes and looks.

Good God! to how many delicious sensations is the soul alive, for which there is no possible mode of expression.

Adieu!—The little post-boy is at my elbow. I observe he goes more frequently to post than usual; and one morning I perceived Glorvina eagerly watching his return, from the summit of a rock. Whence can this solicitude arise? Her father may have some correspondence on business—she can have none.

Letter XXII

TO J. D. ESQ. M. P.

THIS creature is deep in the metaphysics of love. She is perpetually awakening ardor by restraint, and stealing enjoyment from privation. She still persists in bringing the priest with her to the drawing-desk; but it is evident she does not the less enjoy that casual absence which leaves us sometimes alone; and I am now become such an epicure in sentiment, that I scarcely regret the restraint the presence of the priest imposes; since it gives a keener zest to the transient minutes of felicity his absence bestows—even though they are enjoyed in silent confusion. For nothing can be more seducing than her looks, nothing can be more dignified than her manners. If, when we are alone, I even offer to take her hand, she grows pale, and shrinks from my touch.—Yet I regret not that careless confidence which once prompted the innocent request that I would guide her hand to draw a perpendicular line.

---

[138] Vallancey's *Grammar of the Hiberno-Celtic or Irish Language* (1773) characterized Irish as capable of complex articulation and abstract subtlety. See *WIG* 115, Ed.'s n.

"Solitude (says the Spectator) with the person beloved, even to a woman's mind, has a pleasure beyond all the pomp and splendor in the world."[139]

O! how my heart subscribes to a sentiment I have so often laughed at, when my ideas of pleasure were very different from what they are at present. I cannot persuade myself that three weeks have elapsed since my return hither; and still less am I willing to believe that it is necessary I should return to M___ House. In short, the rocks which embosom the peninsula of Inismore bound all my hopes, all my wishes; and my desires, like the *radii* of a *circle,* all point towards one and the same centre. This creature grows on me with boundless influence: her originality, her genius, her sensibility, her youth and person! In short, their united charms in this profound solitude thus closely associated, is a species of witchcraft. * *
* * * * *

* * * * * *

It was indispensably necessary I should return to M___ House, as my father's visit to Ireland is drawing near; and it was requisite I should receive and answer his letters. At last, therefore, I summoned up resolution to plead my former excuses to the Prince for my absence; who insisted on my immediate return—which I promised should be in a day or two; while the eyes of Glorvina echoed her father's commands, and mine looked implicit obedience. With what different emotions I now left Inismore, to those which accompanied my last departure! My feelings were then unknown to myself—now I am perfectly aware of their nature.

I found M___ House, as usual, cold, comfortless, and desolate—with a few wretched looking peasants working languidly about the grounds. In short, every thing breathed the deserted mansion of an *absentee.*

The evening of my arrival I answered my father's letters—one from our pleasant but libertine friend D___n—read over yours three times—went to bed—dreamed of Glorvina—and set off for Inismore the next morning. I rode so hard, that I reached the castle about that hour which we usually devoted to the exertions of the pencil. I flew at once to that vast and gloomy room which her presence alone cheers and illumines. Her drawing-desk lay open; she seemed but just to have risen from the chair placed before it; and her work-basket hung on its back. Even this well known little work-basket is to me an object of interest. I kissed the muslin it contained; and in raising it, perceived a small book splendidly bound and gilt. I took it up, and read on its cover, marked in letters of gold—"*Breviare du Sentiment.*"

Impelled by the curiosity which this title excited, I opened it—and

---

Breviare du Sentiment: A breviary, in the Roman Catholic Church, is a book containing psalms, prayers, and hymns. In this case, indicating a diary.

[139] *Spectator,* No. 149 (Tuesday, 21 August, 1711).

found between its first two leaves several faded snow-drops *stained with blood.* Under them was written, in Glorvina's hand,

> "Prone to the earth we bowed our pallid flowers —
> And caught the drops divine, the purple dyes
> Tinging the lustre of our native hues."*

A little lower in the page was traced—"Culled from the spot where he fell—April the 1st, 17—."

Oh! how quickly my bounding heart told me who was that *he,* whose vital drops had stained these *treasured* blossoms, thus, "tinging the lustre of their native hues"—While the sweetest association of ideas convinced me that these were the identical flowers which Glorvina had hallowed with a tear, as she watched by the couch of him with whose blood they were polluted.

While I pressed this sweet testimony of a pure and lively tenderness to my lips, she entered. At sight of *me,* pleasurable surprise invested every feature; and the most innocent joy lit up her countenance, as she sprang forward and offered me her hand. While I carried it eagerly to my lips, I pointed to the snow-drops. Glorvina, with the hand which was disengaged, covered her blushing face, and would have fled. But the look which preceded this natural motion discovered the wounded feelings of a tender but proud heart. I felt the indelicacy of my conduct, and still clasping her struggling hand, exclaimed—

"Forgive, forgive, the vain triumph of a being intoxicated by your pity—transported by your condescension."

"*Triumph!*" repeated Glorvina, in an accent tenderly reproachful, yet accompanied by a look proudly indignant—"*Triumph!*"

How I cursed the coxcomical expression in my heart, while I fell at her feet, and kissing the hem of her robe, without daring to touch the hand I had relinquished, said,

"Does this look like triumph, Glorvina?"

Glorvina turned towards me a face in which all the witcheries of her sex were blended—playful fondness, affected anger, animated tenderness, and soul-dissolving languishment. Oh! she should not have looked thus, or I should have been more or less than man.

With a glance of undeniable supplication, she released herself from that glowing fold, which could have pressed her for ever to an heart where she must for ever reign unrivalled. I saw she wished I should think her very angry, and another pardon was to be solicited, for the transient indulgence

* From the Italian of Lorenzo de Medicis. [Lorenzo de Medici, *Canzoniere,* sonnet 136, ll. 9–11. Ed.]

---

coxcomical: like a fool, a conceited person, a fop.

of that passionate impulse her own seducing looks had called into existence. The pardon, after some little pouting playfulness, *was* granted, and I was suffered to lead her to that Gothic sofa where our first *téte-à-téte* had taken place; and partly by artifice, partly by entreaty, I drew from her the little history of the treasured snow-drops, and read in her eloquent eyes, more than her bashful lips will ever dare to express.

Thus, like the *assymtotes* of an hyperbola, without absolutely rushing into contact, we are, by a sweet impulsion, gradually approximating closer and closer towards each other.

Ah! my dear friend, this is the golden age of love; and I sometimes think, with the refined Weiland, that the passion begins with the first sigh, and ends, in a certain degree, with the first kiss—mine, therefore, is now in its climacteric.

The impetuosity with which I rush on every subject that touches her, often frustrates the intention with which I sit down to address you. I left this letter behind me unfinished, for the purpose of filling it up on my return, with answers to those I expected to receive from you. The arguments which your friendly foresight and prudent solicitude have furnished you, are precisely such as the understanding cannot refute, nor the heart subscribe to.

You say my *wife* she *cannot* be—and my mistress!—perish the thought! What! I repay the generosity of the father by the destruction of the child! I steal this angelic being from the peaceful security of her native shades, with all her ardent tender feelings thick about her: I

> "Crop this fair rose, and rifle all its sweetness!"[140]

No; you do me but common justice when you say, that though you have sometimes known me *affect* the character of a libertine, yet never, even for a moment, have you known me forfeit that of a man of honour. I would not be understood to speak in the mere common-place worldly acceptation of the word, but literally, according to the text of all moral and divine laws.

"Then what," you ask me, "is the aim, the object, in pursuing this *ignus fatuus* of the heart and fancy?"

---

assymtotes: a line that approaches nearer and nearer to a given curve, but does not meet it within a finite distance.

hyperbola: a plane curve consisting of two separate, equal and similar, infinite branches.

Weiland: Christoph Martin Wieland (1733–1813), German sentimental writer and forerunner of Romanticism in his work.

climacteric: a critical stage in human life.

ignus fatuus: Latin: false fire.

[140] Robert Colvill, "To the Memory of Mrs. Kilnock of Gilmerton," ll. 60–61.

In a word, then, virtue is my object—felicity my aim; or, rather, I am lured towards the former through the medium of the latter. And whether the tye which binds me at once to moral and physical good, is of a fragile texture and transient existence, or whether it will become "close twisted with the fibres of the heart, and breaking, break it," time only can determine—to time, therefore, I commit my fate; but while thus led by the hand of virtue, I inebriate at the living spring of bliss,

> "Wild reeling thro' a wilderness of joy,"[141]

can you wonder that I fling off the goading chain of prudence, and in daring to be *free,* at once be virtuous and be happy?

My father's letter is brief, but pithy. My brother is married, and has sold his name and *title* for a hundred thousand pounds; and *his* brother has a chance of selling his happiness for ever for something about the same sum. And who, think you, is to be the purchaser? Why our old sporting friend D___. In my last grousing visit at his seat, you may remember the pretty *pert* little girl, his only daughter, who, he assured us, was that day *unkennelled* for the first time, in honour of our success, and who rushed upon us from the nursery in all the bloom of fifteen, and all the boldness of a hoyden; whose society was the housekeeper and the chamber-maid, and whose ideas of pleasure extended no further than blind-man's buff in the servants' hall, and a game of hot cockles with the butler and footman in the pantry. I had the good fortune to touch her heart at cross-purposes, and completely vanquished her affections by a romping match in the morning; and so it seems the fair *susceptible* has pined in thought ever since, but not "let concealment prey on her damask cheek,"[142] for she *told* her love to an old maiden aunt, who told it to another confidential friend, until the whole neighbourhood was full of the tale of the *victim of constancy* and the *cruel deceiver.*

The father, as is usual in such cases, was the last to hear it; and believing me to be an excellent shot, and a keen sportsman, all he requires in a son-in-law, except a good family, he proposed the match to my father, who gladly embraces the offer, and fills his letter with blooms, blushes, and unsophisticated charms; congratulates me on my conquest, and talks either of recalling me shortly to England, or bringing the fair *fifteen* and old *Nimrod* to Ireland on a visit with him. But the former he will not easily effect, and the latter I know business will prevent for some weeks, as he writes that he

---

Nimrod: a mighty hunter, see Genesis 10:8–12.

[141] Young, *Night Thoughts,* Night III, l. 21.

[142] Shakespeare, *Twelfth Night,* II. iv. 111–12.

is still up to his ears in parchment deeds, leases, settlements, and jointures. Mean time,

> "Song, beauty, youth, love, virtue, joy, this group
> Of bright ideas, flowers of Paradise as yet unforfeit,"[143]

crown my golden hours of bliss; and whatever may be my future destiny, I will at least rescue one beam of unalloyed felicity from its impending clouds—for, oh! my good friend, there is a prophetic something which incessantly whispers me, that in clouds and storms will the evening of my existence expire.

Adieu!

H. M.

Letter XXIII

TO J. D. ESQ. M. P.

IT is certain, that you men of the world are nothing less than men of *pleasure:*—would you taste it in all its essence, come to Inismore. Ah! no, pollute not with your presence the sacred *palladium* of all the primeval virtues; attempt not to participate in those pure joys of the soul it would be death to me to divide even with you. Here Plato might enjoy, and Epicurus revel: here we are taught to feel according to the doctrine of the latter, that the happiness of mankind consists in *pleasure,* not such as arises from the gratification of the senses, or the pursuits of vice—but from the enjoyments of the mind, the pleasures of the imagination, the affections of the heart, and the sweets of virtue. And here we learn, according to the precepts of the former, that the summit of human felicity may be attained, by removing from the material, and approaching nearer to the intellectual world; by curbing and governing the passions, which are so much oftener inflamed by imaginary than real objects; and by borrowing from temperance, that zest which can alone render pleasure forever poignant, and forever new. Ah! you will say, like other lovers, you now see the moral as well as the natural world through a prism; but would this unity of pleasure and virtue be found in the wilds of Inismore, if Glorvina was no longer there?

I honestly confess to you, I do not think it would, for where yet was pleasure ever found where woman was not? and when does the heart so warmly receive the pure impressions of virtue, as when its essence is imbibed from woman's lip?

---

palladium: a safeguard, a protecting institution.

Plato: See *CR* 53, n. 19.

Epicurus: See *WIG* 251.

[143] Young, *Night Thoughts,* Night III, ll. 94–96.

My life passes away here in a species of delectability to which I can give no name; and while, through the veil of delicate reserve which the pure suggestions of the purest nature have flung over the manners of my sweet Glorvina, a thousand little tendernesses unconsciously appear. Her amiable preceptor clings to me with a parent's fondness; and her father's increasing partiality for his hereditary enemy, is visible in a thousand instances; while neither of these excellent, but inexperienced men, suspect the secret intelligence which exists between the younger tutor and his lovely pupil. As yet, indeed, it has assumed no determinate character. With me it is a delightful dream, from which I dread to be awakened, yet feel that it is but a dream; while she, bewildered, amazed, at those vague emotions which throb impetuously in her unpractised heart, resigns herself unconsciously to the sweetest of all deliriums, and makes no effort to dissolve the vision!

If, in the refined epicurism of my heart, I carelessly speak of my departure for England in the decline of summer, Glorvina changes colour; the sainted countenance of Father John loses its wonted smile of placidity; and the Prince replies by some peevish observation on the solitude of their lives, and the want of attraction at Inismore to detain a man of the world in its domestic circle.

But he will say, "it was not always thus—this hall once echoed to the sound of mirth and the strain of gaiety; for the day was, when none went sad of heart from the castle of Inismore!"

I much fear that the circumstances of this worthy man are greatly deranged, though it is evident his pride would be deeply wounded if it was even suspected. Father John, indeed, hinted to me, that the Prince was a great agricultural speculator some few years back; "and even still," said he, "likes to hold more land in his hands than he is able to manage."

I have observed too, that the hall is frequently crowded with importunate people, whom the priest seems endeavouring to pacify in Irish; and twice, as I passed the Prince's room last week, an ill-looking fellow appeared at the door, whom Glorvina was shewing out. Her eyes were moist with tears; and at sight of me she deeply coloured, and hastily withdrew. It is impossible to describe my feelings at that moment!

Notwithstanding, however, the Prince affects an air of grandeur, and opulence—he keeps a kind of open table in his servants' hall, where a crowd of labourers, dependents, and mendicants, are daily entertained;*

*The kitchen, or servants' hall, of an Irish country gentleman, is open to all whom distress may lead to its door. Professed and indolent mendicants take advantage of this indiscriminating hospitality, enter without ceremony, seat themselves by the fire, and seldom (indeed never) depart with their demands unsatisfied, by the misapplied benevolence of an old Irish custom, which in many instances would be—"more honoured in the breach than the observance." [Shakespeare, *Hamlet,* I. iv. 16. Ed.]

and it is evident his pride would receive a mortal stab, if he supposed that his guest, and that guest an Englishman, suspected the impoverished state of his circumstances.

Although not a man of very superior understanding, yet he evidently possesses that innate grandeur of soul, which haughtily struggles with distress, and which will neither yield to, nor make terms with misfortune; and when, in the dignity of that pride which scorns the revelation of its woes, I behold him collecting all the forces of his mind, and asserting a right to a better fate, I feel my own character energize in the contemplation of his, and am almost tempted to envy him those trials which call forth the latent powers of human fortitude and human greatness.

H. M.

END OF VOL. II

The Wild Irish Girl

[Volume III]

Letter XXIV

TO J. D. ESQ. M. P.

> "Tout s'evanouit sous les cieux,
> Chaque instant varie à nos yeux
> Le tableau mouvant de la vie."

ALAS! that even this solitude, where all seems

> "The world forgetting, by the world forgot."[144]

should be subject to that mutability of fate which governs the busiest haunts of man. Is it possible, that among these dear ruins, where all the "life of life" has been restored to me, the worst of human pangs should assail my full all-confiding heart. And yet I am jealous only on surmise; but who was ever jealous on conviction; for where is the heart so weak, so mean, as to cherish the passion when betrayed by the object. I have already mentioned to you the incongruities which so forcibly struck me in Glorvina's *boudoir.* Since the evening, the happy evening in which I first visited it, I have often stolen thither when I knew her elsewhere engaged, but always found it locked till this morning, when I perceived the door standing open. It seemed as though its mistress had but just left it, for a chair was placed near the window, which was open, and her book and work-basket lay on the seat. I mechanically took up the book, it was my own *Eloisa,* and was marked with a slip of paper in that page where the character of Wolmar is described;[145] I read through the passage, I was throwing it by when some writing on the *paper mark* caught my eye; supposing it to be Glorvina's, I endeavoured to decypher the lines, and read as follows: "Professions, my lovely friend, are for the world. But I would at least have you believe, that *my* friendship, like gold, though not *sonorous,* is indestructible." This was all I could make out—and this I read a hundred times—the hand writing was a man's—but it was not the priest's—it could not be her father's. And

---

"Tout s'evanouit . . . de la vie": French: "Everything under the heavens vanishes/Every instant the moving tableau of life varies in front of our eyes."

144 Alexander Pope, *Eloisa to Abelard* (1717), l. 208.

145 In Rousseau's *Julie, ou la Nouvelle Héloïse* (1761), portraying a relationship between Julie and her tutor, she ultimately marries another man, Baron Wolmar.

yet, I thought the hand was not entirely unknown to me, though it appeared disguised. I was still engaged in gazing on the *sibyl leaf* when I heard *Glorvina* approach. I never was mistaken in her little feet's light bound; for she seldom walks, and hastily replacing the book, I appeared deeply engaged in looking over a fine *Atlas* that lay open on the table. She seemed surprised at my appearance, so much so, that I felt the necessity of apologizing for my intrusion. "But," said I, "an immunity granted by you is too precious to be neglected," and if I have not oftener availed myself of my valued privileges, I assure you the fault was not mine."

Without noticing my innuendo she only bowed her head, and asked me with a smile, "what favourite spot on the globe I was tracing with such earnestness when her entrance had interrupted my geographic pursuits."

I placed my finger on that point of the north-west shores of Ireland, where we then stood, and said in the language of *St. Preux*, "The world in my imagination is divided into two regions—that where *she is*—and that where she is not."[146]

With an air of bewitching insinuation she placed her hand on my shoulder, and with a faint blush and a little smile shook her head, and looked up in my face, with a glance half incredulous—half tender. I kissed the hand by whose pressure I was thus honoured, and said, "professions, my lovely friend, are for the world, but I would at least have you believe that my friendship, like gold, though not sonorous, is indestructible."

This is I said, in the irascibility of my jealous heart, for, though too warm for another, oh! how cold for me! Glorvina started as I spoke, I thought changed colour! while at intervals she repeated, "strange!—nor is this the only coincidence!" "Coincidence!" I eagerly repeated, but she affected not to hear me, and appeared busily engaged in selecting for herself a bouquet from the flowers which filled one of those *vases* I before noticed to you. "And is that beautiful vase," said I, "another family antiquity? it looks as though it stole its elegant form from an Etruscan model: is this too an effort of ancient Irish taste?" "No," said she, I thought confusedly, "I believe it came from Italy."

"Has it been long in the possession of the family?" said I, with persevering impertinence. "It was a present from a friend of my father's," she replied, colouring, "to me!" The bell at that moment rang for breakfast, away she flew, apparently pleased to be released from my importunities.

"A friend of her father's!" and who can this friend be, whose delicacy of judgment so nicely adapts the gifts to the taste of her on whom they are lavished. For undoubtedly the same hand that made the offering of the vases,

[146] St. Preux is the tutor and hero of Rousseau's *Julie.* For Owenson's line, see William Kenrick's translation of the novel (1803), vol. 3, 38.

presented also those other portable elegancies which are so strongly contrasted by the rude original furniture of the *boudoir*. The tasteful *doneur* and the author of that letter whose torn fragment betrayed the sentiment of no common mind, are certainly one and the same person. Yet who visits the castle? scarcely any one; the pride, and circumstances of the *Prince* equally forbid it. Sometimes, though rarely, an old Milesian cousin, or poor relation will drop in, but those of them that I have seen, are more common-place people. I have indeed heard the Prince speak of a cousin in the Spanish service, and a nephew in the Irish brigades,[147] now in Germany. But the cousin is an old man, and the nephew he has not seen since he was a child. Yet after all, these presents may have come from one of these relatives; if so, as Glorvina has no recollection of either, how I should curse that jealous temper which has purchased for me some moments of torturing doubts. I remember you used often to say, that any woman could *pique* me into love, by affecting indifference, and that the native jealousy of my disposition, would always render me the slave of any woman who knew how to play upon my dominant passion. The fact is, when my heart erects an idol for its secret homage, it is madness to think that another should even bow at the shrine, much less that his offerings should be propitiuosly received.

But it is the silence of Glorvina on the subject of this generous friend, that distracts me; if after all—oh! it is impossible—it is sacrilege against heaven to doubt her—she practised in deception! she, whose every look, every motion, betrays a soul that is all truth, innocence, and virtue! I have endeavoured to sound the priest on the subject, and affected to admire the vases; repeating the same questions with which I had teased Glorvina. But he too carelessly replied, "they were given her by a friend of her father's."

Letter XXV

TO J. D. ESQ. M. P.

JUST as I had finished my last, the Prince sent for me to his room; I found him alone, and sitting up in his bed! he only complained of the effects of years and sickness, but it was evident some recent cause of uneasiness preyed on his mind. He made me sit by his bed-side, and said, that my good-nature upon every occasion, induced him to prefer a request, he was induced to hope would not meet with a denial. I begged he would change

---

doneur: French: giver.

[147] Refers to the Irish regiments in continental armies, originally in France, who went into exile after being dispossessed during the seventeenth-century land settlements. Often referred to popularly as the "Wild Geese."

that request to a command, and rely in every instance on my readiness to serve him. He thanked and told me in a few words, that the priest was going on a very particular, but not very pleasing business for him (the Prince) to the *north;* that the journey was long, and would be both solitary and tedious to his good old friend, whose health I might have observed was delicate and precarious, except I had the goodness to cheat the weariness of the journey by giving the priest my company. "I would not make the request" he added, "but that I think your compliance will be productive of pleasure and information to yourself; in a journey of an hundred miles, many new sources of observation to your inquiring mind will appear. Besides, you who seem to feel so lively an interest in all which concerns this country, will be glad to have an opportunity of viewing the Irish character in a new aspect; or rather of beholding the Scotch character engrafted upon ours. "But," said the Prince, with his usual nationality, "that *exotic* branch is not very distinguishable from the old stock."

I need not tell you that I complied with this request with *seeming* readiness, but with real reluctance.

In the evening, as we circled round the fire in the great hall, I proposed to *Father John* to accompany him on his journey the following day. The poor man was overjoyed at the offer, while Glorvina betrayed neither surprise nor regret at my intention, but looked first at her father, and then at me, with kindness and gratitude.

Were my heart more at ease, were my confidence in the affections of Glorvina something stronger, I should greatly relish this little tour, but as it is, when I found every thing arranged for my departure, without the concurrence of my own wishes, I could not check my pettishness, and for want of some other mode of venting it, I endeavoured to ridicule a work on the subject of *ancient Irish* history which the priest was reading aloud, while Glorvina worked, and I was trifling with my pencil.

"What," said I, after having interrupted him in many different passages, which I thought favoured of natural Hyperbole, "what can be more forced than that very supposition of your partial author, that *Albion,* the most ancient name of Britain, was given it as though it were another, or *second Ireland,* because Banba was one of the ancient names of your country?"

"It may appear to you a FORCED etymology," said the priest, "yet it has the sanction of *Camden,* who first risked the supposition. But it is the fate

---

Scotch character: As a result of the plantations in the seventeenth century, Ulster was largely settled by Scottish Presbyterians.

Banba: an ancient name for Ireland.

Camden: William Camden (1551–1623), English antiquarian and author of *Britannia* (1586).

of our unhappy country to receive as little credit in the present day, for its former celebrity, as for its great antiquity,* although the former is attested by *Bede,* and many other early British writers, and the latter is authenticated by the testimony of the most ancient Greek authors. For *Jervis*[148] is mentioned in the *Argonautica* of *Orpheus,* long before the name of England is any where to be found in Grecian literature. And surely it had scarcely been first mentioned, had it not been first known."

"Then you really suppose," said I, smiling incredulously, "we are indebted to you for the name of our country." "I know," said the priest, returning my smile, "the fallacies in general of all etymologists, but the only part of your island, anciently called by any name that bore the least affinity to *Albion,* was *Scotland,* then called *Albin,* a word of *Irish* etymology, *Albin* signifying mountainous, from Alb, a mountain.

"But, my dear friend," I replied, "admitting the great antiquity of your country, allowing it to be early inhabited by a lettered and civilized people, and that it was the *Nido paterno* of western literature when the rest of Europe was involved in darkness; how is it that so few monuments of your ancient learning and genius remain? Where are your manuscripts, your records, your annals, stamped with the seal of antiquity, to be found."

"Manuscripts, annals, and records, are not the treasures of a colonized or a conquered country," said the priest; "it is always the policy of the conqueror, (or the invader) to destroy those mementi of ancient national

*It has been the fashion to throw an odium on the modern Irish, by undermining the basis of their ancient history, and vilifying their ancient national character. If an historian professes to have acquired his information from the records of the country, whose history he writes, his accounts are generally admitted as authentic, as the commentaries of *Garcilorsso de Vega* are considered as the chief pillars of Peruvian history, though avowed by their author to have been compiled from the old national ballads of the country; yet the old writers of Ireland, (the psalter of Cashel in particular) though they refer to those ancient records of *their* country, authenticated by existing manners and existing habits, are plunged into the oblivion of contemptuous neglect, or read, only to be discredited. [Garcilaso de la Vega (1539–1616), sixteenth-century Spanish chronicler, especially on the history of South America. Born the illegitimate son of a Spanish conquistador and an Inca princess, he absorbed both the traditions of the Incas and the stories told by his father's Spanish associates. Author of *Royal Commentaries on the Incas and General History of Peru* (1609). Ed.]

Bede: "The Venerable" Bede (c. 673–735), Anglo-Saxon theologian and historian. His *Ecclesiastical History of the English People* (731) praised the Irish clergy's role in converting the English to Christianity.

Nido paterno: Latin: the paternal nest.

[148]In the 1846 edition, Owenson corrected "Jervis" as "Iernis," an ancient name for Ireland. Fr. John's comments directly echo Parsons, *Observations on the Bequest of Henry Flood,* 82–83.

splendour which keep alive the spirit of the conquered or the invaded;* the dispersion at various periods,† of many of the most illustrious Irish families into foreign countries, has assisted the depredations of time and policy, in the plunder of her literary treasures; many of them are now mouldering in public and private libraries on the Continent, whither their possessors conveyed them from the destruction which civil war carries with it, and many of them (even so far back as the Elizabeth day) were conveyed to Denmark. The Danish monarch applied to the English court for some learned man to translate them, and one *Donald O'Daly,* a person eminently qualified for the task, was actually engaged to perform it, until the illiberality of the English court prevented the intention, on the poor plea of its prejudicing the English interest. I know myself that many of our finest and most valuable MSS. are in libraries in France, and have heard that not a few of them enrich the Vatican at Rome."‡

"But," said I, "are not many of those MSS. supposed to be Monkish impositions?" "Yes," replied the Priest, "by those who *never saw them,* and if

* Sir George Carew, in the reign of Elizabeth, was accused of bribing the family historian of the M'CARTHIES, to convey to him some curious *MSS.* "But what," says the author of the '*Analect,*' "CAREW did in *one* province (Munster) *Henry Sidney,* and his predecessors, did all over the kingdom, being charged to collect all the MSS. they could, that they might effectually destroy every vestige of antiquity and letters throughout the kingdom. And St. Patrick, in his apostolic zeal, committed to the flames several hundred druidical volumes." [Sir George Carew (1555–1629), President of Munster (1600–03) and antiquarian noted for his service in Ireland during Elizabeth I's reign. See his *Pacata Hibernia: Ireland Appeased and Reduced* (1633). Henry Sidney (1641–1704), Earl of Romney, served as secretary of state and then as lord lieutenant of Ireland (1692–93). ED.]

† Fourteen thousand Irish took advantage of the articles of Limerick, and bade adieu to their native country for ever. [The Treaty of Limerick (3 Oct. 1691) provided a peace between the Irish Jacobite and Williamite forces. Jacobite soldiers, under the leadership of Patrick Sarsfield, were offered free passage to France, where they helped constitute the Irish Brigade. See *WIG* 265, n.147. ED.]

‡ In a conversation which passed in Cork, between the author's father, and the celebrated Dr. O'Leary, the latter said he had once intended to have written a history of Ireland. And added, "but in truth I found after various researches, that I could not give such a history as I would wish should come from my pen, without visiting the Continent; more particularly *Rome,* where alone the best documents for the history of Ireland are to be had. But it is now too late in the day for me to think of such a journey, or such exertions as the task would require." "Mr. O'Hallaran informs me," (Says Mr. Walker, *Mem. of Irish Bards, p.* 141.) "that he lately got in a collection from Rome, several poems of the most eminent bards of the two last centuries." [See O'Halloran, *History and Antiquities of Ireland,* 95–96; Rev. Arthur O'Leary (1729–1802), Capuchin friar and controversialist, educated in France, author of *An Essay on Toleration* (1780); Walker's *Historical Memoirs,* 141n. ED.]

they did were too ignorant of the Irish language to judge of their authenticity by the internal evidences they contain."

"And if they were the works of Monks," said the priest, "Ireland was always allowed to possess at that era, the most devout and learned ecclesiastics in Europe, from which circumstance it received its title of *Island of Saints.* By them indeed many histories of the ancient Irish were composed in the early ages of christianity, but it was certainly from pagan records and traditions, they received their information; besides, I do not think any arguments can be advanced more favourable to the truth of their histories, than that the fiction of those histories simply consists in ascribing natural phenomena to super-natural agency."

"But," returned I, "granting that your island was the *Athens* of a certain age, how is the barbarity of the present day to be reconciled with the civilization of the enlightened past?"

"When you talk of our *barbarity,*" said the Priest, "you do not speak as you *feel,* but as you *hear,*" I blushed at this mild reproof, and said, "what I *now* feel for this country, it would not be easy to express, but I have always been taught to look upon the *inferior* Irish as beings forming an humbler link than humanity in the chain of nature." "Yes," said the priest, "in your country it is usual to attach to that class of society in ours, a ferocious disposition amounting to barbarity; but this, with other calumnies, of national indolence, and obstinate ignorance, of want of principle, and want of faith, is unfounded and illiberal;"* 'cruelty' says Lord Sheffield, 'is not

*To endeavour to efface from the Irish character the odium of cruelty, by which the venom of prejudiced aversion has polluted its surface, would be to retrace a series of complicated events from the first period of British invasion to a recent day. And by the *exposition* of CAUSES accomplish the extenuation of EFFECTS. To such a task neither the limits of this little work, nor the abilities of its author are competent; much indeed has been already said, and finely said, on the subject by those whose powers were adequate to the task, and who were induced by the mere principle of national affection, to the noble effort of national defence. But the champions were *Irish men,* and the *motive* of the patriotic exertion became its sole reward.

Had the *Historiographer* of MONTEZUMA or ATALIBA defended the *resistance* of his country-men, or recorded the woes from whence it sprung, though his QUIPAS was

---

Montezuma: Montezuma II (1466–1520), ninth Aztec emperor of Mexico, famous for his confrontation with the Spanish conquistador Hernán Cortés.

Ataliba: Atahuallpa (c. 1502–1533), thirteenth and last emperor of the Inca, captured, held for ransom, and executed by Francisco Pizarro.

Quipas: quipu, also spelled quipo, an Incan accounting apparatus consisting of ropes and various knots, created and maintained as historical records.

in the nature of these people, more than of other men, for they have many customs among them which discover uncommon gentleness, kindness,

bathed in their blood, or embued with their tears, he would have unavailingly recorded them; for the victorious *Spaniard* was insensible to the woes he had created, and called the resistance it gave birth to CRUELTY. But when *nature* is wounded through all her dearest ties, she must *turn* on the hand that stabs, and endeavour to wrest the poniard from the *grasp* that aims at the life-pulse of *her* heart. And this she will do in obedience to that immutable law, which blends the instinct of self-preservation with every atom of human existence. And for this in *less felicitous* times, when *oppression and sedition* succeeded alternately to each other, was the name, *Irishman,* blended with the horrid epithet of cruel. But when the sword of the *oppressor* was *sheathed,* the spirit of the *oppressed* reposed, and the opprobrium it had drawn down on him was no longer remembered, until the unhappy events of a late anarchical period, revived the faded characters in which that opprobrium had been traced. The events alluded to were the *atrocities* which chiefly occurred in the county of Wexford, and its adjoining, and confederate district. Wexford is an English colony planted by Henry the second, where scarcely any feature of the original Irish character, or any trace of the Irish language is to be found. While in the *Barony* of *Forth,* not only the customs, manners, habits, and *costume,* of the ancient British settlers still prevail, but the ancient Celtic language has been preserved with infinitely less corruption than in any part of *Britain,* where it has been interwoven with the Saxon, Danish, and French languages. In fact here may be found a remnant of an ancient *British Colony,* more pure and unmixed, than in any other part of the world. And here were committed those barbarities, which have recently attached the epithet of cruel to the name of *Irishman!* Strongly as the ancient British character may be found extant in the natives of *Wexford and its environs,* equally pure will the primitive character of the Irish be met with in the provinces of *Connaught and Munster;* yet if the footstep of resistance was sometimes impressed on that soil, which had been the asylum of *ancient* Irish independence, its *track* was bloodless; if the energy of a *once* oppressed, but ever *unsubdued* spirit, sometimes burst beyond the boundary of prudent restraint and politic submission, mercy still hung upon its perilous enterprise, and the irritated vehemence of that soul which dared to *oppose,* was tempered by the generous feelings of that heart which disdained to oppress!

"In the parliament held by king James, after the abdication, the Irish solemnly complained, that the injustice and misrepresentation of their governors had forced them to those unwilling acts of violence by which the Irish gentry had attempted to maintain their security and honour, in the numerous conflicts which took place before and subsequent to that period; the national character of Ireland never deserved the disgraceful epithets of sanguinary: had we affixed it to the transactions of the civil war, we should only conclude that, roused by a series of wrongs too great for human patience, a desperate and desponding people had submitted, in a wild paroxysm of rage, to the fierce impulse of nature on their untutored minds, and sacrificed to their feelings those men whom they regarded as the authors or the instruments of their misfortunes; even on this hypothesis, which the concurring testimony of history and probability compel us to reject, we might palliate, though we could not justify, the frenzy. [For the record of Wex-

and affection; they are so far from possessing natural indolence, that they are constitutionally of an active nature, and capable of the greatest exertions; and of as good dispositions as any nation in the same state of improvement; their generosity, hospitality, and bravery, are proverbial; intelligence and zeal in whatever they undertake will never be wanting: *but it has been the fashion to judge of them by their outcasts.*'"[149]

"It is strange," said the prince, "that the earliest British writers should be as diffuse in the praise, as the moderns are in calumniating our unhappy country. Once we were every where, and by all, justly famed for our patriotism, ardor of affection, love of letters, skill in arms and arts, and refinement of manners; but no sooner did there arise a connexion between us and a sister country, than the reputed virtues and well-earned glory of the Irish sunk at once into oblivion: as if" continued this enthusiastic *Milesian*, rising from his seat with all his native vehemence—"as if the moral world was subject to those convulsions which shake the *natural* to its centre, burying by a single shock the monumental splendors of countless ages. Thus it should seem, that when the bosom of national freedom was rent asunder, the national virtues which derived their nutriment from its source sunk into the abyss; while on the barren surface which covers the wreck of Irish greatness, the hand of prejudice and illiberality has sown the seeds of calumny and defamation, to choak up those healthful plants, indigenous to the soil, which still raise their oft-crushed heads, struggling for existence, and which, like the palm-tree, rise in proportion to those efforts made to suppress them."

To repeat the words of the prince is to deprive them of half their effect: his great eloquence lies in his air, his gestures, and the forcible expression of his dark rolling eye. He sat down exhausted with the impetuous vehemence with which he had spoken.

"If we are to believe Doctor Warner, however," said the priest, "the modern Irish are a degenerated race, comparatively speaking; for he asserts that, even in the days of Elizabeth, 'the old natives had degenerated, and

ford, see O'Halloran, *A General History of Ireland*, 34; for the 1641 and 1798 rebellions, both referenced in this long note, see Leerssen, *Mere Irish and Fíor-Ghael*, 332 and Kevin Whelan, *Tree of Liberty*, 133–76. Ed.]

---

[149] John Baker Holroyd, Lord Sheffield, *Observations on the Manufactures, Trade, and Present State of Ireland* (Dublin, 1785), Part I, 4. The final comment on cruelty is unidentified.

that the *wars of several centuries* had reduced them to a state far inferior to that in which they were found in the days of Henry the Second.'[150] But still, like the modern Greeks, we perceive among them strong traces of a free, a great, a polished, and an enlightened people."

Wearied by a conversation in which my heart now took little interest, I made the *palinode* of my *prejudices*, and concluded by saying, "I perceive that on *this* ground I am always destined to be vanquished, yet always to win by the loss, and gain by the defeat; and therefore I ought not in common policy to cease to *oppose*, until nothing further can be obtained by opposition."

The prince, who was getting a little testy at my "*heresy* and *schism*," seemed quite appeased by this avowal; and the priest, who was gratified by a compliment I had previously paid to his talents, shook me heartily by the hand, and said, I was the most generous opponent he had ever met with. Then taking up his book, was suffered to proceed in its perusal uninterrupted. During the whole of the evening, Glorvina maintained an uninterrupted silence; she appeared lost in thought, and unmindful of our conversation, while her eyes, sometimes turned on me, but oftener on her father, seemed humid with a tear, as she contemplated his lately much altered appearance. Yet when the debility of the man was for a moment lost in the energy of the patriot, I perceived the mind of the daughter kindling at the sacred fire which illumined the father's; and through the tear of natural affection sparkled the bright beam of national enthusiasm.

I suspect that the embassy of the good priest is not of the most pleasant nature. To-night, as he left me at the door of my room, he said, that we had a long journey before us; for that the house of the nobleman to whom we were going lay in a remote part of the province of Ulster; that he was a Scotchman, and only occasionally visited this country (where he had an immense property) to receive his rents. "The prince (said he) holds a large but unprofitable farm from this highland chief, the lease of which he is anxious to throw up: that surly-looking fellow who dined with us the other day is his steward; and if the master is as inexorable as the servant, we shall undertake this journey to very little purpose."

Adieu—I endeavour to write and think on every subject but that nearest my heart, yet *there* Glorvina and her mysterious friend still awaken the throb of jealous doubt and anxious solicitude. I shall drop this for you in the post-office of the first post-town I pass through; and probably

---

palinode: a retraction.

[150] See Warner, *The History of Ireland*, vol. 1, 41.

endeavour to forget myself, and my anxiety to return hither, at your expence, by writing to you in the course of my journey.

Adieu,

H. M.

Letter XXVI

TO J. D. ESQ. M.P.

CAN you recollect who was that rational moderate youth who exclaimed in the frenzy of passion, "O Gods! annihilate both *time* and *space*, and make two lovers happy." [151]

For my part, I should indeed wish the hours annihilated till I again behold Glorvina; but for the space which divides us, it was requisite I should be fifty miles from her to be more entirely with her; to appreciate the full value of her society; and to learn the nature of those wants my heart must ever feel when separated from her. The priest and I arose this morning with the sun. Our lovely hostess was ready at the breakfast-table to receive us. I was so selfish as to observe without regret the air of languor that invested her whole form, and the heaviness that weighed down her eye-lids, as though the influence of sleep had not renovated the lustre of those downcast eyes they veiled. Ah! if I dared believe that these wakeful hours were given to me. But I fear at that moment her heart was more occupied by her father than her lover: for I have observed, in a thousand instances, the interest she takes in his affairs; and indeed the priest hinted to me, that her good sense has frequently retrieved those circumstances the imprudent speculations of her father have as constantly deranged.

During breakfast she spoke but little, and once I caught her eyes turned full on me, with a glance in which tenderness, regret, and even something of despondency was mingled. Glorvina despond! So young, so lovely, so virtuous, and so highly gifted! Oh! at that moment had I been master of worlds! But, dependent myself on another's will, I could only sympathize in the sufferings while I adored the sufferer.

When we arose to depart, Glorvina said, "If you will lead your horses I will walk to the draw-bridge with you."

Delighted at the proposal, we ordered our horses to follow us; and with an arm of Glorvina drawn through either of ours, we left the

---

[151] Christopher Smart (1722–71), *The Hilliad: An Epic Poem*, Book I, l. 17n.

castle.—"This," said I, pressing the hand which rested on mine, "is commencing a journey under favourable auspices."

"God send it may be so!" said Glorvina fervently.

"Amen!" said the priest.

"Amen!" I repeated; and looking at Glorvina, read all the daughter in her eyes.

"We shall sleep to-night," said the priest, endeavouring to dissipate the gloom which hung over us by indifferent chit-chat; "we shall sleep to-night at the hospitable mansion of a true-born *Milesian,* to whom I have the honour to be distantly allied; and where you will find the old *Brehon* law, which forbids that a sept should suddenly break up lest the traveller should be disappointed of the expected feast, was no fabrication of national partiality."

"What, then," said I, "we shall not enjoy ourselves in all the comfortable unrestrained freedom of *an inn*?"

"We poor Irish," said the priest, "find the unrestrained freedom of an inn not only in the house of every friend, but of every acquaintance however distant; and indeed if you are at all known, you may travel from one end of a province to another without entering a house of public entertainment;* the host always considering himself the debtor of the guest, as though the institution of the *Beataghs*† were still in being. And besides a cordial welcome from my hospitable kinsman, I promise you an introduction to his three handsome daughters. So fortify your heart, for I warn you it will run some risk before you return."

* "Not only have I been received with the greatest kindness, but I have been provided with every thing which could promote the execution of my plan. In taking the circuit of Ireland I have been employed eight or nine months; during which time I have been every where received with an hospitality which is nothing surprising in Ireland: that in such a length of time I have been but six times at an inn will give a better idea of this hospitality than could be done by the most laboured praise." *M. de Latocknay.* [de la Tocnaye, *A Frenchman's Walk Through Ireland,* v–vi. See *WIG* 120, Ed.'s n and *TINT* 357–59. Ed.]

† In the excellent system of the ancient Milesian government, the people were divided into classes;—the *Literati* holding the next rank to royalty itself, and the *Beataghs* the fourth; so that as in China the state was so well regulated, that every one knew his place from the prince to the peasant. "These Beataghs," says M. O'Halleran, "were keepers of open houses for strangers or poor distressed natives; and as honorable stipends were settled on the Literati, so were particular tracts of land on the Beataghs to support, with proper munificence, their station; and there are lands and villages in many places to this day which declare by their names their original appointment." [O'Halloran, *History and Antiquities of Ireland,* 44–45. Ed.]

Brehon law: system of law operating in Ireland before English settlement.

sept: a branch of a family or a clan.

"Oh!" said Glorvina archly, "I dare say that, like St. Paul, he will 'count it all joy to fall into divers temptations.'"[152]

"Or rather," returned I, "I shall court them, like the saints of old, merely to prove my powers of resistance; for I bear a charmed spell about me; and *now* 'none of *woman born* can harm *Macbeth*.'"[153]

"And of what nature is your spell?" said Glorvina smiling, while the priest remained a little behind us talking to a peasant. "Has father John given you a gospel? or have you got an amulet, thrice passed through the *thrice blessed* girdle of St. Bridget, our great Irish charm?" *

"My charm," returned I, "in some degree certainly partakes of your religious and national superstitions; for since it was presented me by YOUR hand, I could almost believe that its very *essence* has been changed by a touch!" And I drew from my breast the withered remains of my once blooming rose. At that moment the priest joined us; and though Glorvina was silent, I felt the pressure of her arm more heavily on mine, and saw her pass the draw-bridge without a recollection on her part that it was to have been the boundary of her walk. We had not, however, proceeded many paces, when the most wildly mournful sounds I ever heard rose on the air and slowly died away.

"Hark!" said Glorvina, "some one is going to '*that bourne from whence no traveller returns*.'"[154] As she spoke an hundred voices seemed to ascend to the skies; and, as they subsided, a fainter strain lingered on the air, as though this truly savage choral symphony was reduced to a recitativo, chanted by female voices. All that I had heard of the *Irish howl,* or funeral song, now rushed to my recollection; and turning at that moment the angle of the mountain of Inismore, I perceived a procession advancing towards a little cemetery, which lay by a narrow path-way to the left of the road.

The body, in a plain deal coffin, covered with a white shirt, was carried by four men, immediately preceded by several old women, covered in their mantles, and who sung at intervals in a wild and rapid tone.† Before them walked a number of young persons of both sexes, each couple holding by a

* On St. Bridget's day it is usual for the young people to make a long girdle or rope of straw, which they carry about to the neighbouring houses, and through which all persons who have faith in the charm pass nine times, uttering at each time a certain form of prayer in Irish, which they thus conclude: "If I enter this thrice-blessed girdle, well may I come out of it nine times better." [St. Bridget's day is celebrated on 1 February. ED.]

† Speaking of the ancient Irish funeral, Mr. Walker observes: — "Women, whose voices recommended them, were taken from the lower classes of life, and instructed in music,

---

[152] James 1:2: "My brethren, count it all joy when ye fall into divers temptations."

[153] Shakespeare, *Macbeth,* IV. i. 80–81.

[154] Shakespeare, *Hamlet,* III. i. 78–79.

white handkerchief, and strewing flowers along the path. An elderly woman, with eyes overflown with tears, disheveled hair, and distracted mien, followed the body, uttering many passionate exclamations in Irish; and the procession was filled up by upwards of three hundred people; the recitative of the female choristers relieved at intervals by the combined howlings of the whole body. In one of the pauses of this dreadful death-chorus, I expressed to Glorvina my surprize at the multitude which attended the funeral of a peasant, while we stood on a bank as they passed us.

"The lower order of Irish," she returned, "entertain a kind of posthumous pride respecting their funerals; and from sentiments that I have heard them express, I really believe there are many among them who would prefer living neglected to the idea of dying unmourned, or unattended, by a host to their last home." To my astonishment she then descended the bank, and, accompanied by the priest, mingled with the crowd.

"This will surprise you," said Glorvina; "but it is wise to comply with those prejudices which we cannot vanquish. And by those poor people it is not only reckoned a mark of great disrespect not to follow a funeral (met by chance) a few paces, but almost a species of impiety." "And mankind, you know," added the priest, "are always more punctilious with respect to ceremonials than fundamentals. However *you should* see an Irish Roman Catholic funeral; to a protestant and a stranger it must be a spectacle of some interest.

"With respect to the attendant ceremonies on death," he continued, "I know of no country which the Irish at present resemble but the modern Greeks. In both countries when the deceased dies unmarried, the young attendants are chiefly dressed in white, carrying garlands, and strewing flowers as they proceed to the grave. Those old women who sing before the body are professional *improvisatori;* they are called *Caoiners* or *Keeners,* from the *Caoine* or death song, and are *hired* to celebrate the virtues of the deceased. Thus we find St. Chrysostom censuring the Greeks of his day, for the purchased lamentations and hireling mourners that attended their funerals. And so far back with us as in the days of druidical influence, we find it was part of the profession of the bards to perform the funeral ceremonies, to

and the *cur sios,* or elegiac measure, that they might assist in heightening the melancholy which that ceremony was calculated to inspire. This custom prevailed among the Hebrews, from whom it is not improbable we had it immediately."

Dr. Campbell is of opinion that the word *Ululate* or *hullalor,* the choral burden of the Caoine, and the Greek word of the same import, have a strong affinity to each other. *Phil. Surv. of South of Ireland, Letter* 2, 3. [Walker, *Historical Memoirs,* 19–20; and Campbell, *A Philosophical Survey,* 208. Ed.]

St. Chrysostom: See *WIG* 223, Ed.'s n.

sing to their harps the virtues of the dead, and to call on the living to emulate their deeds.* This you may remember is a custom frequently alluded to in the poems of Ossian.† Pray observe that frantic woman who tears her hair and beats her bosom:—It is the mother of the deceased. She is following her only child to an early grave; and did you understand the nature of her lamentations you would compare them to the complaints of the mother of Euriales in the Eneid:—[155] the same passionate expressions of sorrow, and the same wild extravagance of grief. They even still most religiously preserve here that custom never lost among the Greeks, of washing the body before interment, and strewing it with flowers."

"And have you also," said I, "the funeral feast, which among the Greeks composed so material a part of the funeral ceremonies?"

"A *wake,* as it is called among us," he replied, "is at once the season of lamentation and sorrow, and of feasting and amusement. The immediate relatives of the deceased sit near the body, devoted to all the luxury of woe,

*The *Caoine,* or funeral song, was composed by the *Filea* of the departed, set to music by one of his oirfidegh, and sung over the grave by the racasaide, or rhapsodist, who accompanied his "song of the tomb" with the mourning murmur of his harp, while the inferior order of minstrels at intervals mingled their deep-toned chorus with the strain of grief, and the sighs of lamenting relatives breathed in unison to the tuneful sorrow. Thus was "the stones of his fame" raised over the remains of the Irish chief with a ceremony resembling that with which the death of the Trojan hero was lamented:

> "A melancholy choir attend around,
> With plaintive sighs and music's solemn sound."

But the singular ceremonies of the Irish funeral, which are even still in a certain degree extant, may be traced to a remoter antiquity than Grecian origin; for the pathetic lamentations of David for the friend of his soul, and the *conclamatio* breathed over the Phoenician Dido, has no faint coincidence to the *Caoine* or funeral song of the Irish. [Alexander Pope, *The Iliad of Homer,* Book XXIV, l. 900. Also see Campbell, *A Philosophical Survey,* 209. In Greek legend, Dido was the Queen of Carthage. Virgil attributed Dido's self-immolation to the grief suffered after Jupiter forced her to leave Aeneas. See Virgil, *Aeneid,* Book IV, ll. 663–705. Ed.]

†Thus over the tomb of Cucullin vibrated the song of the bard:—"Blest be thy soul, son of Semo! thou wert mighty in battle, thy strength was like the strength of the stream, thy speed like the speed of the eagle's wing, thy path in the battle was terrible, the steps of death were behind thy sword; blest be thy soul, son of Semo! Car-borne chief of Dunscaith. The mighty were dispersed at Temora—there is none in Cormac's hall. The king mourns in his youth, for he does not behold thy coming; the sound of thy shield is ceased, his foes are gathering round. Soft be thy rest in thy cave, chief of Erin's wars." [See Macpherson, *The Death of Cuchulain,* 139. Ed.]

[155] In Virgil's *Aeneid,* Ilium, mother of Euralyus and Nisus, learns that her sons are dead and their heads displayed on the spears of their enemies. In her lament, such is her grief that she, too, seeks death. See Book IX, ll. 473–503.

which revives into the most piercing lamentations at the entrance of every stranger, while the friends, acquaintances, and guests give themselves up to a variety of amusements; feats of dexterity, and even some exquisite pantomimes are performed; though in the midst of all their games should any one pronounce an *Ave Maria,* the merry groupe are in a moment on their knees; and the devotional impulse being gratified, they recommence their sports with new vigour. The *wake,* however, is of short duration; for here, as in Greece, it is thought an injustice to the dead to keep them long above ground; so that interment follows death with all possible expedition."

We had now reached the burial ground; near which the funeral was met by the parish priest, and the procession went three times round the cemetery, preceded by the priest, who repeated the *De profundis,* as did all the congregation.[156]

"This ceremony," said Father John, "is performed by us instead of the funeral service, which is denied to the Roman Catholies. For *we* are not permitted, like the protestant ministers, to perform the last solemn office for our departed fellow creatures."

While he spoke we entered the church yard, and I expressed my surprise to Glorvina, who seemed wrapt in solemn meditation, at the singular appearance of this rustic little cemetery, where instead of the monumental marble,

> "The storied urn, or animated bust,"[157]

an osier, twisted into the form of a cross, wreathed with faded foliage, garlands made of the pliant sally, twined with flowers; alone distinguished the "narrow house," where

> "The rude forefathers of the hamlet slept."[158]

Without answering, she led me gently forward towards a garland which seemed newly planted. We paused. A young woman who had attended the funeral, and withdrawn from the crowd, approached the garland at the same moment, and taking some fresh gathered flowers from her apron, strewed them over the new made grave, then kneeling beside it wept, and prayed. "It is the tomb of her lover," said I.—"*Of her Father!*" said Glorvina,

---

[156] de la Tocnaye refers to "the De profundis which the priests in Catholic countries chant while following the dead to the grave, a ceremony of which the people in Ireland are deprived, but of which, perhaps, they have an unconscious recollection," 90. See *WIG* 120, Ed.'s n and *TINT* 357–59.

[157] Gray, *Elegy Written in a Country Church-Yard,* ll. 41–42.

[158] Gray, *Elegy Written in a Country Church-Yard,* ll. 15–16.

in a voice whose affecting tone sunk to my heart, while her eyes, raised to heaven, were suffused with tears. The filial mourner now arose and departed, and we approached the simple shrine of her sorrowing devotion. Glorvina took from it a sprig of rosemary—its leaves were humid! "It is not *all* dew," said Glorvina with a sad smile, while her own tears fell on it, and she presented it to me.

"Then you think me worthy of sharing in these divine feelings," I exclaimed as I kissed off the sacred drops; while I was now confirmed in the belief that the tenderness, the sufferings, and declining health of her father rendered him at that moment the sole object of her solicitude and affection. And with him only could I, without madness, share the tender, sensible, angelic heart of this sweet interesting being.

Observing her emotion increase, as she stood near the spot sacred to filial grief, I endeavoured to draw away her attention by remarking, that almost every tomb had now a votarist. "It is a strong instance," said Glorvina, "of the sensibility of the Irish, that they repair at intervals to the tombs of their deceased friends to drop a tender tear, or heave a heart-breathed sigh, to the memory of those so lamented in death, so dear to them in life. For my own part, in the stillness of a fine evening, I often wander towards this solemn spot, where the flowers newly thrown on the tombs, and weeping with the tears of departed day, always speak to my heart a tale of woe it feels and understands. While, as the breeze of evening mourns softly round me, I involuntarily exclaim, 'And when *I* shall follow the crowd that presses forward to eternity, what affectionate hand will scatter flowers over *my* solitary tomb; for haply ere that period arrive, *my* trembling hand shall have placed the cypress on the tomb of him who alone loved me living, and would lament me dead.' "

"*Alone!*" I repeated, and pressing her hand to my heart, inarticulately added, "Oh! Glorvina, did the pulses which now throb against each other throb in unison, you would understand, that even *love* is a cold inadequate term for the sentiments you have inspired in a soul, which would claim a closer kindred to yours than even parental affinity can assert; if (though but by a glance) yours would deign to acknowledge the sacred union."

We were standing in a remote part of the cemetery, under the shade of a drooping cypress—we were alone—we were unobserved. The hand of Glorvina was pressed to my heart, her head almost touched my shoulders, her lips almost effused their balmy sighs on mine. A glance was all I required—a glance was all I received.

In the succeeding moments I know not what passed; for an interval all was delirium. Glorvina was the first to recover presence of mind; she released her hand, which was still pressed to my heart, and covered with blushes advanced to Father John. I followed, and found her with her arm entwined in his, while those eyes from whose glance my soul had lately quaffed the essence of life's richest bliss, were now studiously turned from me in love's own downcast bashfulness.

The good Father Director now took my arm: and we were leaving this (to me), interesting spot, when the filial mourner who had first drawn us from his side, approached the priest, and taking out a few shillings from the corner of her handkerchief, offered them to him, and spoke a few words in Irish; the priest returned her an answer and her money at the same time: she curtseyed low, and departed in silent and tearful emotion. At the same moment another female advanced towards us, and put a piece of silver and a little fresh earth into the hand of Father John; he blessed the earth and returned the little offering with it. The woman knelt and wept, and kissed his garment; then addressing him in Irish, pointed to a poor old man, who, apparently overcome with weakness, was reposing on the grass. Father John followed the woman, and advanced to the old man, while I, turning towards Glorvina, demanded an explanation of this extraordinary scene.

"The first of those poor creatures," said she, "was offering the fruits of many an hour's labour to have a mass said for the soul of her departed father, which she firmly believes will shorten his sufferings in purgatory: the last is another instance of weeping humanity stealing from the rites of superstition a solace for its woes. She brought that earth to the priest, that he might bless it ere it was flung into the coffin of a dear friend, who, she says, died this morning; for they believe that this consecrated earth is a substitute for those religious rites which are denied them on this awful occasion. And though these tender cares of mourning affection may originate in error, who would not pardon the illusion, that soothes the sufferings of a breaking heart? Alas! I could almost envy these ignorant prejudices, which lead their possessors to believe, that by restraining their own enjoyments in this world, they can alleviate the sufferings, or purchase the felicity of the other for the objects of their tenderness and regret. Oh! that I could thus believe!"

"Then you do not," said I, looking earnestly at her, "you do not receive all the doctrines of your church as infallible?"

Glorvina approached something closer towards me, and in a few words convinced me that on the subject of religion, as upon every other, her strong mind discovered itself to be an emanation of that divine intelligence, which her pure soul worships 'in spirit and in truth,'

"The bright effluence of bright essence uncreate."[159]

When she observed my surprise and delight, she added, "believe me, my dear friend, the age in which religious error held her empire undisputed, is

[159] Milton, *Paradise Lost,* Book III, l. 6.

gone by. The human mind, however slow, however opposed its progress, is still, by a divine and invariable law, propelled towards truth, and must finally attain that goal which reason has erected in every breast. Of the many who are the inheritors of *our* persuasion, *all* are not devoted to its errors, or influenced by its superstitions. If its professors are coalesced, it is in the sympathy of their destinies, not in the dogmas of their belief. If they are allied, it is by the tye of temporal interest, not by the bond of speculative opinion; they are united as *men,* not as sectaries; and once incorporated in the great mass of general society, their feelings will become diffusive as their interests; their affections, like their privileges, will be in common; the limited throb with which their hearts now beat towards each other, under the influence of a kindred fate, will then be animated to the nobler pulsation of universal philanthropy; and, as the acknowledged members of the first of all human communities, they will forget they had ever been the *individual* adherents of an alienated body."

The priest now returned to us, and was followed by the multitude, who crowded round this venerable and adored pastor: some to obtain his benediction for themselves, others his prayers for their friends, and all his advice or notice; while Glorvina, whom they had not at first perceived, stood like an idol in the midst of them, receiving that adoration which the admiring gaze of some, and the adulatory exclamations of others, offered to her virtues and her charms. While those personally known to her, she addressed with her usual winning sweetness in their native language, I am sure that there was not an individual among this crowd of ardent and affectionate people that would not risk their lives "to avenge a look that threatened her with danger."[160]

Our horses now coming up to the gate of the cemetery, we insisted on walking back as far as the draw bridge with Glorvina. When we reached it, the priest saluted her cheek with paternal freedom, and gave her his blessing. While I was put off with an offer of the hand; but when, for the first time, I felt its soft clasp return the pressure of mine, I no longer envied the priest his cold salute; for oh! cold is every enjoyment which is unreciprocated. Reverberated bliss alone can touch the heart.

When we had parted with Glorvina, and caught a last view of her receding figure, we mounted our horses and proceeded a considerable way in silence. The morning though fine was gloomy; and though the sun was scarcely an hour high, we were met by innumerable groupes of peasantry of both sexes, laden with their implements of husbandry, and already

---

sectaries: zealous in the cause of a sect.

[160] See Burke, *Reflections on the Revolution in France,* 170.

beginning the labours of the day. I expressed my surprise at observing almost as many women as men working in the fields and bogs. "Yes," said the priest, "toil is here shared in common between the sexes, the women as well as the men cut the turf, sow the potatoes, and even assist to cultivate the land; both rise with the sun to their daily labour; but his repose brings not theirs; for after having worked all day for a very trivial remuneration (as nothing here is rated at a lower price than human labour), they endeavour to snatch a beam from retreating twilight; by which they labour in that little spot of ground, which is probably the sole support of a numerous family."

"And yet," said I, "idleness is the chief vice laid to the account of your peasantry."

"It is certain," returned he, "that there is not, generally speaking, that active spirit of industry among the inferior orders here, which distinguishes the same rank in England. But neither have they the same encouragement to awaken their exertions. 'The laziness of the Irish,' says Sir William Petty, 'seems rather to proceed from want of employment, and encouragement to work, than the constitution of their bodies.'[161] And an intelligent and liberal countryman of yours, Mr. Young, the celebrated traveller, is persuaded that, circumstances considered, the Irish do not in reality deserve the character of indolence; and relates a very extraordinary proof of their great industry and exertion in their method of procuring lime for manure; which the mountaineers bring on the backs of their little horses many miles distance, to the foot of the steepest acclivities; and from thence to the summit on their own shoulders, while they pay a considerable rent for liberty to cultivate a barren, waste, and rigid soil.[162] In short, there is not in the creation a more laborious animal than an Irish peasant, with less stimulus to exertion, or less reward to crown his toil.* He is indeed in many instances the creature of the soil, and works independent of that hope, which is the best stimulus to every human effort, the hope of reward. And yet it is not rare to find among these oft misguided beings, some who really believe themselves the hereditary proprietors of the soil they cultivate."

* "Si le pauvre voyait clairement que la travail pouvoit ameliorer sa situation, il abandonneroit bientot cette apathie, cette indifference qui au fait n'est que l'habitude du desespoir."

M. de la Tocknay.

[de la Tocnaye, "If the poor man could really feel that work would ameliorate his situation, he would quickly abandon that apathy and indifference which are born of despair," 128. See *WIG* 120, Ed.'s n and *TINT* 357–59. Ed.]

[161] Sir William Petty (1623–87), English political economist and cartographer. Completed the Down Survey (1654–59), and his Irish works describe the land, people, and natural resources of the country. See *The Political Anatomy of Ireland* (1691), 98–99.

[162] Young, *Tour in Ireland*, vol. 2, 43. See *CR* 80, n. 25 and *TINT* 343–56.

"But surely," said I, "the most ignorant among them must be well aware that all could not have been proprietors?"

"The fact is," said the priest, "the followers of many a great family having anciently adopted the name of their chiefs, that name has descended to their progeny, who now associate to the name an erroneous claim on the confiscated property of those to whom their progenitors were but vassals or dependants.* And this false but strong rooted opinion, co-operating with their naturally active and impetuous characters, renders them alive to every enterprize, and open to the impositions of the artful or ambitious. But a brave, though misguided, people is not to be dragooned out of a train of ancient prejudices, nurtured by fancied interest and real ambition, and confirmed by ignorance, which those who deride, have made no effort to dispel. It is not by physical force, but moral influence, the illusion is to be dissolved. The darkness of ignorance must be dissipated before the light of truth can be admitted, and though an Irishman may be argued out of an error, it has been long proved he will never be forced. His understanding may be convinced, but his spirit will never be subdued. He may culminate to the meridian of loyalty† or truth by the influence of kindness, or the convictions of reason, but he will never be forced towards the one, nor oppressed into the other, by the lash of power, or the "insolence of office."[163]

"This has been strongly evinced by the attachment of the Irish to the House of Stuart, by whom they have always been so cruelly, so ungratefully treated. For what the coercive measures of 400 years could not effect, the accession of *one* prince to the throne accomplished. Until that period, the

*Although ignorance and interest may cherish this erroneous opinion, its existence is only to be traced among some of the lower orders of Irish, but its influence seldom extends to a superior rank, among many of whom are to be found the *real* descendants of those whose estates were forfeited shortly after the English invasion, and during the reigns of James the First, Oliver Cromwell and William the Third, *particularly. They* consider that "The property has now been so long vested in the hands of the present proprietors that the interests of justice and utility would be more offended by dispossessing them than they could be advanced by reinstating the original owners." And that a "term of prescription is always paramount to the rights of lineal descent."

†Speaking of the people of Ireland, Lord Minto thus expresses himself. "In these (the Irish) we have witnessed exertions of courage, activity, perseverance, and spirit, as well as *fidelity* and *honour* in fulfilling the engagements of their connexion with us, and the protection and defence of their own country, which challenges the thanks of Great Britain, and the approbation of the world." [Minto, Gilbert Elliot-Murray, first Earl of Melgund (1751–1814), friend of Edmund Burke, spoke during the debate regarding the Act of Union (1800). Ed.]

House of Stuart: Royal house ruling Scotland from 1371 to 1603, and ruling Scotland and England from 1603 to 1714, except during the establishment of the Commonwealth (1649–60).

[163] Shakespeare, *Hamlet,* III. i. 72.

unconquered Irish, harassing and harassed, struggled for that liberty which they at intervals obtained, but never were permitted to enjoy. Yet the moment a Prince of the Royal line of Milesius placed the British diadem on his brow, the sword of resistance was sheathed, and those principles which force could not vanquish yielded to the mild empire of national and hereditary affection: the Irish of *English* origin from natural tenderness, and those of the *true old stock,* from the firm conviction that they were *then* governed by a *Prince* of their own blood. Nor is it now unknown to them that in the veins of his present Majesty, and his ancestors, from James the First, flows the Royal blood of the *three* kingdoms united."

"I am delighted to find," said I, "the lower ranks of a country, to which I am now so endeared, thus rescued from the obloquy thrown on them by prejudiced illiberality; and from what you have said, and indeed from what I have myself observed, I am convinced that were endeavours* for their improvement more strictly promoted, and their respective duties obviously made clear, their true interests fully represented by reason and common sense, and their unhappy situations ameliorated by justice and humanity, they would be a people as happy, contented, and prosperous, in a political sense, as in a natural and a national one. They are brave, hospitable, liberal, and ingenious."

We now continued to proceed through a country, rich in all the boundless extravagance of picturesque beauty, where Nature's sublimest features every where present themselves, carelessly disposed in wild magnificence; unimproved, and, indeed, almost unimproveable by art. The far-stretched ocean, mountains of alpine magnitude, heaths of boundless desolation, vales of romantic loveliness, navigable rivers, and extensive lakes, alternately succeeding to each other, while the ruins of an ancient castle, or the mouldering remains of a desolated abbey, gave a moral interest to the pleasure derived from the contemplation of Nature in her happiest and most varied aspect.

"Is it not extraordinary," said I, as we loitered over the ruins of an abbey, "that though your country was so long before the introduction of

*"Connomara (says Mr. de la Tocknay in his Travels through Ireland,) a district in the county of Galway, sixty miles long, and forty broad, is less known than the islands in the Pacific Ocean; and, consequently, the people remain much in their natural uncultivated state. But it is an error to suppose, that even in this sequestered spot the peasants are either ignorant or stupid. On the contrary, I never saw any class of men better disposed to serve their country; and though their huts are miserable, and their general situation comparatively wretched, they are humane and would be industrious, if they found that labour and industry produced advantage or amelioration." [de la Tocnaye, 156. See *WIG* 120, Ed.'s n and *TINT* 357–59. Ed.]

---

diadem: crown.

christianity inhabited by a learned and ingenious people, yet that among your gothic ruins, no traces of a more ancient and splendid architecture are to be discovered. From the ideas I have formed of the primeval grandeur of Ireland, I should almost expect to see a Balbec or Palmyra rising amidst these stupendous mountains, and picturesque scenes."

"My dear Sir," he replied, "a country may be civilized, enlightened, and even learned and ingenious, without attaining to any considerable perfection in those arts, which give to posterity *sensible* memorials of its passed splendour. The ancient Irish, like the modern, had more *soul,* more genius, than worldly prudence, or cautious calculating forethought. The feats of the hero engrossed them more than the exertions of the mechanist; works of imagination seduced them from pursuing works of utility. With an enthusiasm, bordering on a species of *mania,* were they devoted to poetry and music; and to '*Wake the soul of song*' was to them an object of more interesting importance, than to raise that edifice which would betray to posterity their ancient grandeur; besides, at that period to which you allude, the Irish were in that era of society, when the iron age was yet distant, and the artist confined his skill to the elegant workmanship of gold, and brass, which is ascertained by the number of warlike implements and beautiful ornaments of dress of those metals, exquisitely worked, which are still frequently found in the bogs of Ireland."

"If, however," said I, "there are no remnants of a Laurentinum, or Tusculum, to be discovered, I perceive that at every ten or twelve miles, in the fattest of the land, the ruins of an abbey and its granaries are discernible."

"Why," returned the priest laughing, "you would not have the good father abbots advise the dying but generous sinner to leave the *worst* of his lands to God! that would be sacrilege—but besides the voluntary donation of *estates* from rich penitents, the regular monks of Ireland had *landed properties* attached to their convents. Sometimes they possessed immense tracts of a country, from which the officiating clergy seldom or ever derived any benefit; and I believe that many, if not *most,* of the bishops' leases now existing are the confiscated revenues of these ruined abbeys."

"So," said I, "after all it is only a transfer of property from one opulent ecclesiastic to another;* and the great difference between the luxurious abbot of other times, and the rich church dignitary of the present, lies in a few

* For instance, the abbey of Raphoe was founded by St. Columbkill, who was succeeded in it by St. Eanon. The first Bishop of Raphoe having converted the abbey into a cathedral see. It is now a protestant bishoprick.

Balbec or Palmyra: ancient cities renowned for their splendor.

Laurentinum: an ancient city in Italy named after a sacred laurel tree.

Tusculum: See *WIG* 131.

speculative theories which, whether they are or are not consonant to reason and common sense, have certainly no connexion with *true* religion or *true* morality. While the bishopricks now, like the abbeys of old, are estimated rather by the profit gained to the temporal, than the harvest reaped to the heavenly Lord. However I suppose they borrow a sanction from the perversion of scriptural authority, and quote the Jewish law, not intended for the benefit of *individuals* to the detriment of a whole body, but which extended to the whole tribe of Levi, and doubtlessly strengthen it by a sentiment of St. Paul: 'If we sow unto you spiritual things is it not just we reap your carnal, &c.' It is, however, lucky for your country that your abbots are not as numerous in the present day as formerly."

"Numerous, indeed, as you perceive," said the priest, "by these ruins; for we are told in the Life of St. Rumoloi, that there were a greater number of monks and superb monasteries in Ireland than in any other part of Europe. St. Columbkill, and his contemporaries, alone erected in this kingdom upwards of 200 abbeys, if their biographers are to be credited; and the luxury of their governors kept pace with their power and number.

"In the abbey of Enis a sanctuary was provided for the cowls of the friars and the veils of the nuns, which were costly and beautifully wrought. We read that, knights excepted, the prelates only were allowed to have gold bridles and harnesses; and that among the rich presents bestowed by Bishop Snell, in 1146, on a cathedral, were gloves, pontificals, sandals, and silken robes, interwoven with golden spots, and adorned with precious stones.

"There is a monument of monkish luxury still remaining among the interesting ruins of Sligo Abbey. This noble edifice stands in the midst of a rich and beautiful scenery, on the banks of a river, near which is a spot still shewn, where (as the tradition runs) a box or weir was placed in which the fish casually entered, and which contained a spring that communicated, by a cord, with a bell hung in the refectory. The weight of the fish pressed down the spring; the cord vibrated; the bell rung; and the unfortunate captive thus taken suffered martyrdom, by being placed on the fire alive."

"And was served up," said I, "I suppose on a fast day, to the *abstemious* monks, who would, however, have looked upon a morsel of flesh meat thrown in this way as a lure to eternal perdition."

Already weary of a conversation in which my heart took little interest, I now suffered it to die away; and while father John began a parley with a traveller who socially joined us, I gave up my whole soul to love and to Glorvina.

'If we sow . . . carnal, &c.': See 1 Corinthians 9:11.

St. Columbkill: See *WIG* 245.

In the course of the evening we arrived at the house of our destined host. Although it was late the family had not yet gone to dinner, as the servant who took our horses informed us that his master had but that moment returned from a fair. We had scarcely reached the hall, when, the report of our arrival having preceded our appearance, the whole family rushed out to receive us. What a group!—the father looking like the very *Genius of Hospitality,* the mother like the personified spirit of a cordial welcome, three laughing *Hebe* daughters, two fine young fellows supporting an aged grandsire (a very *Silenus* in appearance), and a pretty demure little governess with a smile and a hand ready as the others.

The priest, according to the good old Irish fashion, saluted the cheeks of the ladies, and had his hands nearly shaken off by the men; while I was received with all the cordiality that could be lavished on a friend, and all the politeness that could be paid to a stranger. A welcome shone in every eye; ten thousand welcomes echoed from every lip; and the arrival of the unexpected guests seemed a festival of the social feelings to the whole warm-hearted family. If this is a true specimen of the first rites of hospitality among the *independent country gentlemen of Ireland,** it is to me the most captivating of all possible ceremonies.

When the first interchange of courtesies had passed on both sides, we were conducted to the refreshing comforts of a dressing-room; but the domestics were not suffered to interfere, all were in fact our servants.

The plenteous dinner was composed of every luxury the season afforded; though only supplied by the demesne of our host and the neighbouring sea-coast, and though served up in a style of perfect elegance, was yet so abundant, so *over plenteous,* that compared to the compact neatness and simple sufficiency of English fare in the same rank of life, it might have been thought to have been "more than hospitably good."[164] But to my surprize, and indeed not much to my satisfaction, during dinner the door was left open for the benefit of receiving the combined efforts of a very indifferent fiddler and a tolerable piper, who, however, seemed to hold the life and spirits of the family in their keeping. The ladies left us early after the cloth was removed; and though besides the family there were three strange gentlemen, and that the table was covered with excellent wines, yet conversation circulated with much greater freedom than the bottle; every

*To those who have witnessed (as I so often have) the celebration of these endearing rites, this picture will appear but a very cold and languid sketch.

Genius: here referring to the guiding or controlling spirit.

Silenus: in Greek mythology, the foster father of Bacchus, and leader of the satyrs.

[164]Thomas Parnell, "The Hermit" (1719), ll. 55–56.

one did as he pleased, and the ease of the guest seemed the pleasure of the host.* For my part, I arose in less than an hour after the retreat of the ladies, and followed them to the drawing-room. I found them all employed; one at the piano, another at her work, a third reading; mamma at her knitting, and the pretty little duenna copying out music.

They received me as an old acquaintance, and complimented me on my temperance in so soon retiring from the gentlemen, for which I assured them they had all the credit. It is certain, that the frank and open ingenuousness of an Irishwoman's manners forms a strong contrast to that placid but distant reserve which characterizes the address of my own charming countrywomen. For my part, since I have known Glorvina, I shall never again endure that perpetuity of air, look, and address, which those who mistake formality for good-breeding are so apt to assume. Manners, like the graduated scale of the thermometer, should betray, by degrees, the expansion or contraction of the feelings, as they are warmed by emotion or chilled by indifference. They should *breathe* the soul in order to *win* it.

Nothing could be more animated yet more modest than the manners of these charming girls; nor should I require any stronger proof of that pure and exquisite chastity of character which, from the earliest period, has distinguished the women of this country, than that ingenuous candour and enchanting frankness which accompanies their every look and word.

> "The soul as sure to be admired as seen,
> Boldly steps forth, nor keeps a thought within."

But although the Miss O'D___s are very charming girls, although their mother seems a very rational and amiable being, and although their governess appears to be a young woman of distinguished education and considerable talent; yet I in vain sought in their conversation for that soul-seizing charm which with a magic undefinable influence breathes round the syren *princess of Inismore.* O! it was requisite I should mingle, converse, with other women to justly appreciate all I possess in the society of Glorvina; for surely she is *more,* or every other woman is *less,* than mortal!

* "Drunkenness ought no longer to be a reproach to them; for any table I was at in Ireland I saw a perfect freedom reign, every person drank as little as they pleased, nor have I ever been asked to drink a single glass more than I had an inclination for. I may go farther, and assert, that hard drinking is very rare among people of fortune; yet it is certain that they sit much longer at table than in England." *Young's Tour through Ireland, &c.* [Young, *Tour in Ireland,* vol. 2, 152. See *TINT* 343–56. Ed.]

---

duenna: a chaperone.

Before the men joined us in the drawing-room, I was quite *boudoirized* with these unaffected and pleasing girls. One wound her working-silk off my hands, another would try my skill at battledore, and the youngest, a charming little being of thirteen, told me the history of a pet dove that was dying in her lap; while all intreated I would talk to them of the princess of Inismore.

"For my part," said the youngest girl, "I always think of her as of the Sleeping Beauty in the Wood, or some other princess in a fairy tale."

"We know nothing of her, however," said Mrs. O'D___, "but by report; we live at too great a distance to keep up any connexion with the Inismore family; besides that it is generally understood to be Mr. O'Melville's wish to live in retirement."

This is the first time I ever heard my soi-disant prince mentioned without his title; but I am sure I should never endure to hear my Glorvina called Miss O'Melville. For to me too does she appear more like the Roganda of a fairy tale than "any mortal mixture of earth's mould." [165]

The gentlemen now joined us, and as soon as tea was over the piper struck up in the hall, and in a moment every one was on their feet. My long journey was received as a sufficient plea for my being a spectator only; but the priest refused the immunity, and led out the lady mother; the rest followed, and the idol amusement of the gay-hearted Irish received its usual homage. But though the women danced with considerable grace and spirit, they did not, like Glorvina,

"Send the soul upon a jig to heaven." [166]

The dance was succeeded by a good supper; the supper by a cheerful song, and every one seemed unwilling to be the first to break up a social compact over which the spirit of harmony presided.

As the priest and I retired to our rooms, "You have now," said he, "had a specimen of the mode of living of the Irish gentry of a certain rank in this country: the day is devoted to agricultural business, the evening to temperate festivity and innocent amusement; but neither the avocations of the morning nor the engagements of the evening suspend the rites of hospitality."

Thus far I wrote before I retired that night to rest, and the next morning at an early hour we took our leave of these courteous and hospitable Milesians; having faithfully promised on the preceding night to repeat our visit on our return from the north.

---

battledore: a game played with a small racket involving two players striking a shuttlecock back and forth.

[165] George Colman (1732–94), *Comus: A Masque*, I. ii. 100–01.

[166] Alexander Pope, *Epistle IV*, "To Richard *Earl* of Burlington," l. 141–42.

We are now at a sorry little inn, within a mile or two of the nobleman's seat to whom the priest is come, and on whom he waits to-morrow, having just learned that his lordship passed by here to-day on his way to a gentleman's house in the neighbourhood, where he dines. The little post-boy at this moment rides up to the door; I shall drop this in his bag, and begin a new journal on a fresh sheet.

Adieu,

H. M.

Letter XXVII

TO J. D. ESQ. M. P.

THE priest is gone on his embassy. The rain which batters against the casement of my little hotel prevents my enjoying a ramble. I have nothing to read, and I must write or yawn myself to death.

Yesterday, as we passed the imaginary line which divides the province of Connaught from that of Ulster, the priest said, "As we now advance northward, we shall gradually lose sight of the genuine Irish character, and those ancient manners, modes, customs, and language with which it is inseparably connected. Not long after the chiefs of Ireland had declared James the First universal monarch of their country, a sham plot was pretended, consonant to the usual ingratitude of the House of Stuart, by which six entire counties of the north became forfeited, which James with a liberal hand bestowed on his favourites;* so that this part of Ireland may in some respects be considered as a Scottish colony; and in fact, Scotch dialect, Scotch

* "The pretext of rebellion was devised as a specious prelude to predetermined confiscations, and the inhabitants of six counties, whose aversion to the yoke of England the shew of lenity might have disarmed, were compelled to encounter misery in desarts, and, what is perhaps still more mortifying to human pride, to behold the patrimony of their ancestors, which force had wrested from their hands, bestowed the prey of a more favoured people. The substantial view of providing for his indigent countrymen might have gratified the national partiality of James; the favourite passion of the English was gratified by the triumph of protestantism, and the downfal of its antagonists: men who professed to correct a system of peace did not hesitate to pursue their purpose through a scene of iniquity which humanity shudders to relate; and by an action more criminal, because more deliberate, than the massacre of St. Bartholomew, two thirds of an extensive province were offered up in one great hecatomb, on the altar of false policy and theological prejudice. Here let us survey with wonder the mysterious operations of divine wisdom, which, from a measure base in its means, and atrocious in its execution, has derived a source of fame, freedom, and industry to Ireland." — *Vide A Review of some interesting periods of Irish History.* [On August 24/25, 1572, French Huguenots (Protestants)

manners, Scotch modes, and the Scotch character almost universally prevail. Here the ardor of the Irish constitution seems abated, if not chilled. Here the *cead-mile falta* of Irish cordiality seldom lends its welcome home to the stranger's heart. The bright beams which illumine the gay images of Milesian fancy are extinguished; the convivial pleasures, dear to the Milesian heart, scared at the prudential maxims of calculating interest, take flight to the warmer regions of the south; and the endearing socialities of the soul, lost and neglected amidst the cold concerns of the counting-house and the *bleach green*, droop and expire in the deficiency of that nutritive warmth on which their tender existence depends. So much for the shades of the picture, which however possesses its lights, and those of no dim lustre. The north of Ireland may be justly esteemed the palladium of Irish industry and Irish trade, where the staple commodity of the kingdom is reared and manufactured; and while the rest of Ireland is devoted to that species of agriculture, which, in lessening the necessity of human labour, deprives man of subsistence; while the wretched native of the Southern provinces (where little labour is required, and consequently little hire given) either famishes in the midst of an helpless family, or begs his way to England, and offers those services *there* in harvest time, which his own country rejects. Here, both the labourer and his hire rise in the scale of political consideration: here more hands are called for than can be procured; and the peasant, stimulated to exertions by the rewards it reaps for him, enjoys the fruits of his industry, and acquires a relish for the comforts and conveniencies of life. Industry, and this taste for comparative luxury, mutually re-act; and the former, while it bestows the *means*, enables them to gratify the suggestions of the latter; while their wants, nurtured by enjoyment, afford fresh allurement to continued exertion. In short, a mind not too deeply fascinated by the florid virtues, the warm overflowings of generous and ardent qualities, will find in the Northerns of this island much to admire and more to esteem; but on the heart they make little claims, and from its affections they receive but little tribute."*

"Then in the name of all that is warm and cordial," said I, "let us hasten back to the province of Connaught."

were massacred in Paris. Many Huguenots settled in Ireland, and Owenson attended a Huguenot school in Dublin; see [Theobald McKenna], *A Review of Some Interesting Periods of Irish History* (London, 1786), 15–16. Ed.]

*Belfast cannot be deemed the *metropolis* of Ulster, but may almost be said to be the *Athens* of Ireland. It is at least the CYNOSURE of the province in which it stands; and those beams of genius which are there concentrated send to the extremest point of the hemisphere in which they shine, no faint ray of lumination.

"That you may be sure we shall (returned father John): for I know none of these sons of trade; and until we once more find ourselves within the pale of Milesian hospitality, we must set up at a sorry inn, near a tract of the sea coast, called the Magilligans, and where one *solitary fane* is raised to the once tutelar deity of Ireland; in plain English, where one of the last of the race of *Irish bards* shelters his white head beneath the fractured roof of a wretched hut." Although the evening sun was setting on the western wave when we reached the auberge, yet, while our fried eggs and bacon were preparing, I proposed to the priest that we should visit the old bard before we put up our horses. Father John readily consented, and we enquired his address.

"What the *mon wi the twa heads*?" said our host. I confessed my ignorance of this hydra epithet, which I learnt was derived from an immense wen on the back of his head.

"O!" continued our host, "A wull be telling you weel to gang tull the auld Kearn, and one of our wains wull shew the road. Ye need nae fear trusting yoursels to our wee Willy, for he os an uncommon canie chiel." Such was the dialect of this Hibernian Scot, who assured me he had never been twenty miles from his "aine wee hame."

We however dispensed with the guidance of *wee Wully,* and easily found our way to the hut of the man "*wi the twa heads.*" It stood on the right hand by the road side. We entered it without ceremony, and as it is usual for strangers to visit this last of the "Sons of Song," his family betrayed no signs of surprize at our appearance. His ancient dame announced us to her husband. When we entered, he was in bed; and when he arose to receive us (for he was dressed, and appeared only to have lain down from debility), we perceived that his harp had been the companion of his repose, and was actually laid under the bed-clothes with him. We found the venerable bard cheerful *

* The following account of the Bard of the Magilligans was taken from his own lips, July 3d, 1805, by the Rev. Mr. Sampson, of Magilligan, and forwarded to the author (through the medium of Dr. Patterson, of Derry) previous to her visit to that part of the North, which took place a few weeks after. [The Reverend Sampson, member of the Royal Irish Academy and author of *Statistical Survey of the County of Londonderry* (1802). Dr. Patterson, also a member of the Royal Irish Academy, author of *Observations on the Climate of Ireland.* See *WIG* 187, n. 98. Ed.]

Umbrae, July 3d, 1805,
Magilligan.

"I MADE the survey of the man with two heads, according to your desire; but not till yesterday on account of various *impossibilities.* Here is my report—

---

hydra: the many-headed snake in Greek mythology whose heads grew again as fast as they were cut off.

wen: a lump or protuberance on the body.

and communicative, and he seemed to enter even with an eager readiness on the circumstances of his past life, while his "soul seemed heightened

"Dennis Hampson, or the man with two heads, is a native of Craigmore, near Garvagh, county Derry; his father, Bryan Darrogher (blackish complexion) Hampson, held the whole town-land of Tyrcrevan; his mother's relations were in possession of the wood-town (both considerable farms in Magilligan). He lost his sight at the age of three years by the small-pox; at twelve years he began to learn the harp under Bridget O'Cahan: 'For,' as he said, 'in those old times, *women* as well as men were taught the Irish harp in the best families; and every old Irish family had harps in plenty.' His next master was John C. Garragher, a blind travelling harper, whom he followed to Buncranagh, where his master used to play for Colonel Vaughan: he had afterwards Laughlin Hanning and Pat Connor in succession as masters.

"All these were from Connaught, which was, as he added, 'the best part of the kingdom for Irish music and for harpers.' At eighteen years of age he began to play for himself, and was taken into the house of counsellor Canning, at Garvagh, for half a year; his host, with Squire Gage and Doctor Bacon, found and bought him an harp. He travelled nine or ten years through Ireland and Scotland, and tells facetious stories of gentlemen in both countries: among others, that in passing near the place of Sir J. Campbell, at Aghanbrack, he learned, that this gentleman had spent a great deal, and was living on so much per week of allowance. Hampson through delicacy would not call, but some of the domestics were sent after him; on coming into the castle, Sir J. asked him why he had not called, adding, 'Sir, there was never a harper but yourself that passed the door of my father's house;' to which Hampson answered that, 'he had heard in the *neighbourhood* that his honour was not often at home;' with which delicate evasion Sir J. was satisfied. He adds, 'that this was the highest bred and stateliest man he ever knew; if he were putting on a new pair of gloves, and one of them dropped on the floor, (though ever so clean), he would order the servant to bring him another pair.' He says that, in that time he never met but one laird that had a harp, and that was a very small one, played on formerly by the laird's father; that when he had tuned it with new strings the laird and his lady both were so pleased with his music that they invited him back in these words: 'Hampson, as soon as you think this child of ours (a boy of three years of age), is fit to learn on his grandfather's harp, come back to teach him, and you shall not repent it;'—but this he never accomplished. [Walker suggested that Owenson incorporate a reference to Hampson in her novel; see Connolly and Copley, lxi. Ed.]

"He told me a story of the laird of Strone with a great deal of comic relish. When he was playing at the house, a message came that a large party of gentlemen were coming to grouse, and would spend some days with *him* (the laird); the lady being in great distress turned to her husband, saying, 'What shall we do, my dear, for so many in the way of beds.' 'Give yourself no vexation,' replied the laird, 'give us enough to eat, and I will supply the rest; and as to beds, believe me *every man shall find one for himself;*' (meaning that his guests would fall under the table). In his second trip to Scotland, in the year 1745, being at Edinburgh, when *Charley* the Pretender was there, he was called into the great hall to play; at first he was alone, afterwards four fiddlers joined: the tune called for was, 'The king shall enjoy his own again:'—he sung here part of the words following—

by the song," with which at intervals he interrupted his narrative. How strongly did those exquisitely beautiful lines of Ossian rush on my

'I hope to see the day
When the Whigs shall run away,
And the king shall enjoy his own again.'
[Traditional refrain associated with
Jacobite song or tune. Ed.]

"I asked him if he heard the Pretender speak; he replied—I only heard him ask, 'Is Sylvan there;' on which some one answered, 'He is not here please your royal highness, but he shall be sent for.' He meant to say *Sullivan,* continued Hampson, but that was the way he called the name. He says that Captain McDonnell, when in Ireland, came to see him, and that he told the captain that Charley's cockade was in his father's house.

"Hampson was brought into the Pretender's presence by Colonel Kelly, of Roscomon, and Sir Thomas Sheridan, and that he (Hampson) was then above fifty years old. He played in many Irish houses; among others, those of Lord de Courcey, Mr. Fortescue, Sir P. Belew, Squire Roche; and in the great towns, Dublin, Cork, &c. &c. Respecting all which he interspersed pleasant anecdotes with surprising gaiety and correctness. As to correctness, he mentioned many anecdotes of my grandfather and grand-aunt, at whose houses he used to be frequently. In fact, in this identical harper, whom you sent me to *survey,* I recognised an acquaintance, who, as soon as he found me out, seemed exhilirated at having an old friend of (what he called) 'the old stock,' in his poor cabin. He even mentioned many anecdotes of my own boyhood, which, though by me long forgotten, were accurately true. These things shew the surprising power of his recollection at the age of an hundred and eight years. Since I saw him last, which was in 1787, the wen on the back of his head is greatly increased; it is now hanging over his neck and shoulders, nearly as large as his head, from which circumstance he derives his appellative, 'the man with two heads.' General Hart, who is an admirer of music, sent a limner lately to take a drawing of him, which cannot fail to be interesting, if it were only for the venerable expression of his meagre blind countenance, and the symmetry of his tall, thin, but not debilitated, person. I found him lying on his back in bed near the fire of his cabin; his family employed in the usual way; his harp under the bed clothes, by which his face was covered also. When he heard my name he started up (being already dressed), and seemed rejoiced to hear the sound of my voice, which, he said, he began to recollect. He asked for my children, whom I brought to see him, and he felt them over and over;—then, with tones of great affection, he blessed *God* that he had *seen* four generations of the name, and ended by giving the children his blessing. He then tuned his old time-beaten harp, his solace and bedfellow, and played with astonishing justness and good taste.

"The tunes which he played were his favourites; and he, with an elegance of manner, said at the same time, I remember you have a fondness for music, and the tunes you used to ask for I have not forgotten, which were Cualin, The Dawning of the Day, Elleen-a-roon, Ceandubhdilis, &c. These, except the third, were the first tunes, which, according to regulation, he played at the famous meeting of harpers at Belfast, under the patronage of some amateurs of Irish music. Mr. Bunton, the celebrated musician of that town, was here the year before, at Hampson's, noting his tunes and his manner of playing, which is in the best old style. He said, with the honest feeling of self love, 'When I played the old tunes, not another of the harpers would play after me.' He came to Magilligan

recollection: "But age is now on my tongue, and my mind has failed me; the sons of song are gone to rest; my voice remains like a blast that roars

many years ago, and at the age of eighty-six, married a woman of Innisowen, whom he found living in the house of a friend. 'I can't tell,' quoth Hampson, 'if it was not the devil buckled us together; she being lame and I blind.' By this wife he has one daughter, married to a cooper, who has several children, and maintains them all, though Hampson (in this alone seeming to doat), says, that his son-in-law is a spendthrift and that he maintains them; the family humour his whim, and the old man is quieted. He is pleased when they tell him, as he thinks is the case, that several people of character, for musical taste, send letters to invite him; and he, though incapable now of leaving the house, is planning expeditions never to be attempted, much less realized; these are the only traces of mental debility; as to his body, he has no inconvenience but that arising from a chronic disorder: his habits have ever been sober; his favourite drink, once beer, now milk and water; his diet chiefly *potatoes.* I asked him to teach my daughter, but he declined; adding, however, that it was too hard for a young girl, but that nothing would give him greater pleasure, if he thought it could be done. [July 11–14, 1792, some ten harpers gathered in Belfast, including Denis Hempson, Arthur O'Neill, and Charles Byrne, to demonstrate their prowess and compete by playing hitherto unknown melodies. The purpose of the event was to help redeem the last surviving fragments of a generally lost tradition. Edward Bunting (1773–1843) was one of three musicians appointed to transcribe the harp melodies, and he went on to publish three landmark collections of Irish music, including *General Collection of the Ancient Irish Music* (1797). Ed.]

"Lord Bristol, when lodging at the bathing house of Mount Salut, near Magilligan, gave three guineas, and ground rent free, to build the house where Hampson now lives. At the house warming his lordship with his lady and family came, and the children danced to his harp; the bishop gave three crowns to the family, and in the *dear* year, his lordship called in his coach and six, stopped at the door, and gave a guinea to buy meal.

"Would it not be well to get a subscription for poor old Hampson? It might be sent to various towns where he is known.

Once more ever yours,

G. V. S."

ADDENDA.

"In the time of Noah I was green,
After his flood I have not been seen,
Until seventeen hundred and two. I was found,
By Cormac Kelly, under ground;
He raised me up to that degree;
Queen of music they call me."

"The above lines are sculptured on the old harp, which is made, the sides and front of white sally, the back of fir, patched with copper and iron plates. His daughter now attending him is only thirty-three years old.

"I have now given you an account of my visit, and even thank you (though my fingers are tired), for the pleasure you procured to me by this interesting commission.

Ever yours,

G. V. Sampson."

loudly on a sea-surrounded rock after the winds are laid, and the distant mariner sees the waving trees."[167]

So great was my veneration for this "bard of other times,"[168] that I felt as though it would have been an indelicacy to have offered him any pecuniary reward for the exertions of his tuneful talent; I therefore made my little offering to his wife, having previously, while he was reciting his "unvarnished tale,"[169] taken a sketch of his most singularly interesting and striking figure, as a present for Glorvina on my return to Inismore. While my heart a thousand times called on hers to participate in the sweet but melancholy pleasure it experienced, as I listened to and gazed on this venerable being.

Whenever there is a revel of the feelings, a joy of the imagination, or a delicate fruition of a refined and touching sentiment, how my soul misses her! I find it impossible to make even the amiable and intelligent priest enter into the nature of my feelings; but how naturally, in the overflowing of my heart, do I turn towards her, yet turn in vain, or find her image only in my enamoured soul, which is full of her. Oh! how much do I owe her. What a vigorous spring has she opened in the wintry waste of a desolated mind. It seems as though a seal had been fixed upon every bliss of the senses and the heart, which her breath alone could dissolve; that all was gloom and chaos until she said, "let there be light."

As we rode back to our auberge by the light of a cloudless but declining moon, after some conversation on the subject of the bard whom we had visited, the priest exclaimed, "Who would suppose that that wretched hut was the residence of one of that order once so revered among the Irish; whose persons and properties were held sacred and inviolable by the common consent of all parties, as well as by the laws of the nation, even in all the vicissitudes of warfare, and all the anarchy of intestine commotion; an order which held the second rank in the state;* and whose members, in

In February 1806 the author, being then but eighteen miles distant from the residence of the Bard, received a message from him, intimating that as he heard she wished to purchase his harp, he would dispose of it on very moderate terms. He was then in good health and spirits, though in his hundredth and ninth year.

* The genuine history and records of Ireland abound with incidents singularly romantic, and of details exquisitely interesting. In the account of the death of the celebrated hero Conrigh, as given by Demetrius O'Connor, the following instance of fidelity and affection of a family bard is given:—When the beautiful, but faithless, Blanaid, whose hand

---

"let there be light": Genesis 1:3.

[167] Macpherson, *The Songs of Selma* (1765), 170.

[168] Macpherson, *Temora* (1763), Book VII, 215.

[169] See *CR* 28, n. 3.

addition to the interesting duties of their profession, were the heralds of peace and the donors of immortality? Clothed in white and flowing robes, the bards marched to battle at the head of the troops, and by the side of the chief; and while by their martial strains they awakened courage even to desperation in the heart of the warrior, borne away by the furor of their own enthusiasm, they not unfrequently rushed into the thick of the fight themselves, and by their maddening inspirations decided the fate of the battle: or when victory descended on the ensanguined plain, hung over the warrior's funeral pile, and chaunted to the strains of the national lyre the deeds of the valiant, and the prowess of the hero; while the brave and listening survivors envied and emulated the glory of the deceased, and believed that this tribute of inspired genius at the funeral rites was necessary to the repose of the departed soul."

"And from what period," said I, "may the decline of these once potent and revered members of the state be dated?"

"I would almost venture to say," returned the priest, "so early as in the latter end of the sixth century; for we read in an Irish record, that about *that* period the *Irish monarch* convened the princes, nobles, and clergy, of the kingdom, to the parliament of *Drumceat;*[170] and the chief motive alleged for summoning this vast assembly was to banish the Fileas or bards."

"Which might be deemed then," interrupted I, "a league of the *Dunces* against *Wit* and *Genius.*"

Conrigh had obtained as the reward of his valour, armed a favoured lover against the life of her husband, and fled with the murderer; Feirchiertne, the poet and bard of Conrigh, in the anguish of his heart for the loss of a generous master, resolved on sacrificing the criminal Blanaid to the manes of her murdered lord. He therefore secretly pursued her from her palace in Kerry to the court of Ulster, whither she had fled with her homicide paramour. On his arrival there, the first object that saluted his eyes was the king of that province, walking on the edge of the steep rocks of Rinchin Beara, surrounded by the principal nobility of his court; and in the splendid train he soon perceived the lovely, but guilty, Blanaid and her treacherous lover. The bard concealed himself until he observed his mistress withdraw from the brilliant crowd, and stand at the edge of a steep cliff; then courteously and flatteringly addressing her, as he approached her presence, he at last threw his arms round her, and clasping her firmly to his breast, threw himself headlong with his prey down the precipice. They were both dashed to pieces. [Possibly Dermod O'Connor (*fl.* 1720), author of a translation of Geoffrey Keating's *Foras Feasa ar Éireann* and reputed to have embezzled £300 from the subscription money. See *WIG* 116, Ed.'s n. Ed.]

"a league . . . *Genius*": common eighteenth-century poetic cliché.

[170] Druim Ceat, near Derry, the site of the Convention of A.D. 575 determining the position of the King of Dál Riata, with possessions in Ulster and Scotland, in relation to the King of Ireland. St. Columba (see *WIG* 245) mediated the settlement and also laid down rules governing the future behavior of the bardic caste.

"Not altogether," returned the priest. "It was in some respects a necessary policy. For strange to say, nearly the third part of Ireland had adopted a profession at once so revered, and so privileged, so honoured and so caressed by all ranks of the state.—Indeed, about this period, such was the influence they had obtained in the kingdom, that the inhabitants without distinction were obliged to receive and maintain them from November till May, if it were the pleasure of the bard to become their guest; nor were there any object on which their daring wishes rested that was not instantly put into their possession. And such was the ambition of one of their order, that he made a demand on the golden broach or clasp that braced the regal robe on the breast of royalty itself, which was unalienable with the crown, and descended with the empire from generation to generation."

"Good God!" said I, "what an idea does this give of the omnipotence of music and poetry among those refined enthusiasts, who have ever borne with such impatience the oppressive chain of power, yet suffer themselves to be soothed into slavery by the melting strains of their national lyre."

"It is certain," replied the priest, "that no nation, not even the Greeks, were ever attached with more passionate enthusiasm to the divine arts of poesy and song, than the ancient Irish, until their fatal and boundless indulgence to their professors became a source of inquietude and oppression to the whole state. The celebrated St. Columbkill, who was himself a poet, became a mediator between the monarch already mentioned and the '*tuneful throng*;' and by his intercession, the king changed his first intention of banishing the whole college of bards, to limiting their numbers; for it was an argument of the liberal saint's, that it became a great monarch to patronise the arts; to retain about his person an eminent bard and antiquary; and to allow to his tributary princes or chieftains, a poet capable of singing their exploits, and of registering the genealogy of their illustrious families. This liberal and necessary plan of reformation, suggested by the saint, was adopted by the monarch; and these salutary regulations became the prominent standard for many succeeding ages: and though the severity of those regulations against the bards, enforced in the tyrannic reign of Henry VIII as proposed by Baron Finglas, considerably lessened their power;* yet

* Item—That noe Irish minstralls, rhymers, thanaghs, ne bards, be messengers to desire any goods of any man dwelling within the English pale, upon pain of forfeiture of all their goods, and their bodies to be imprisoned at the king's will.

Harris' Hibernica, p. 98.

[Baron Finglas was Chief Baron of the Exchequer during Henry VIII's reign, and author of "A Breviat of the Getting of Ireland and the Decaie of the Same," which was included by William Harris in *Hibernica: or Some Antient Pieces Relating to Ireland* (Dublin, 1747–50), 39–52. Walter Harris (1686–1761), Anglo-Irish historian and chiefly important for an expanded edition of the works of Sir James Ware. Ed.]

until the reign of Elizabeth their characters were not stript of that sacred *stole,* which the reverential love of their countrymen had flung over them. The high estimation in which the bard was held in the commencement of the empire of Ireland's arch-enemy is thus attested by Sir Philip Sydney: 'In our neighbour country,' says he, 'where truly learning goes very bare, yet are their poets held in devout reverence.'[171] But Elizabeth, jealous of that influence which the bardic order of Ireland held over the most puissant of her chiefs, not only enacted laws against them, but against such as received or entertained them: for Spenser informs us that, even *then,* 'their verses were taken up with a general applause, and usually sung at all feasts and meetings.'[172] Of the spirited, yet pathetic, manner in which the genius of Irish minstrelsy addressed itself to the soul of the Irish chief, many instances are still preserved in the records of traditional lore. A poem of Fearflatha, family bard to the O'Nials of Clanboy, and beginning thus:— 'O the condition of our dear countrymen, how languid their joys, how acute their sorrows, &c. &c.' the prince of Inismore takes peculiar delight in repeating. But in the lapse of time, and vicissitude of revolution, this order, once so revered, has finally sunk into the casual retention of an harper, piper, or fiddler, which are generally, but not universally, to be found in the houses of the Irish country gentlemen; as you have yourself witnessed in the castle of Inismore and the hospitable mansion of the O'D___s. One circumstance, however, I must mention to you. Although Ulster was never deemed poetic ground, yet when destruction threatened the bardic order in the southern and western provinces, where their insolence, nurtured by false indulgence, often rendered them an object of popular antipathy, hither they fled for protection, and at different periods found it from the northern princes: and Ulster, you perceive, is now the last resort of the most ancient of the surviving of the Irish bards, who, after having imbibed inspiration in the classic regions of Connaught, and effused his national strains through every province of his country, draws forth the last feeble tones of his almost silenced harp amidst the chilling regions of the north; almost unknown and undistinguished, except by the few strangers who are led by chance or curiosity to his hut, and from whose casual bounties he chiefly derives his subsistence."

We had now reached the door of our auberge; and the dog of the house jumping on me as I alighted, our hostess exclaimed, "Ah Sir! our wee

---

[171] Sir Philip Sidney, *The Defense of Poesie* (1583).

[172] Edmund Spenser, *A View of the Present State of Ireland,* 75.

doggie kens you uncoo." Is not this the language of the Isle of Sky? The priest left me early this morning on his evidently unpleasant embassy. On his return we visit the Giants' Causeway, which I understand is but sixteen miles distant. Of this pilgrimage to the shrine of Nature in her grandest aspect, I shall tell you nothing; but when we meet will put into your hands a work written on the subject, from which you will derive equal pleasure and instruction. At this moment the excellent priest appears on his little nag; the rain no longer beats against my casement; the large drops suspended from the foliage of the trees sparkle with the beams of the meridian sun, which, bursting forth in cloudless radiancy, dispels the misty shower, and brilliantly lights up the arch of heaven's promise. Would you know the images now most buoyant in my cheered bosom; they are Ossian and Glorvina: it is for *him* to describe, for *her* to feel, the renovating charms of this interesting moment. Adieu! I shall grant you a reprieve till we once more reach the dear ruins of Inismore.

H. M.

Letter XXVIII

TO J. D. ESQ. M. P.

PLATO compares the soul to a small republic, of which the reasoning and judging powers are stationed in the head as in a citadel, and of which the senses are the guards or servants.[173]

Alas! my dear friend, this republic is with me all anarchy and confusion, and its guards, disordered and overwhelmed, can no longer afford it protection. I would be calm, and give you a succinct account of my return to Inismore; but impetuous feelings rush over the recollection of trivial circumstances, and all concentrate on that fatal point which transfixes every thought, every emotion of my soul.

Suffice it now to say, that our second reception at the mansion of the O'D's had lost nothing of that cordiality which distinguished our first; but neither the cheerful kindness of the parents, nor the blandishments of the charming daughters, could allay that burning impatience, which fired my bosom to return to Glorvina, after the tedious absence of five long days. All night I tossed on my pillow in the restless agitation of expected bliss, and with the dawn of that day on which I hoped once more to taste

Giants' Causeway: a formation of some 40,000 basalt columns along four miles of the Antrim coast in Northern Ireland.

[173] Plato, *Republic,* Book IV.

"*the life of life,*" I arose and flew to the priest's room to chide his tardiness. Early as it was I found he had already left his apartment, and as I turned from the door to seek him, I perceived a written paper lying on the floor. I took it up and, carelessly glancing my eye over it, discovered that it was a receipt from the prince's inexorable creditor, who (as father John informed me) refused to take the farm off his hands: but what was my amazement to find that this receipt was an acknowledgment for those jewels which I had so often seen stealing their lustre from Glorvina's charms; and which were now individually mentioned, and given in lieu of the rent for that very farm, by which the prince was so materially injured. The blood boiled in my veins. I could have annihilated this rascally cold-hearted landlord; I could have wept on the neck of the unfortunate prince; I could have fallen at the feet of Glorvina and worshipped her as the first of the Almighty's works. Never in the midst of all my artificial wants, my boundless and craving extravagance, did I ever feel the want of riches as at this moment, when a small part of what I had so worthlessly flung away, would have saved the pride of a noble, an indignant spirit, from a deep and deadly wound, and spared the heart of filial solicitude and tender sensibility, many a pang of tortured feelings. The rent of the farm was an hundred pounds per annum. The prince, I understood, was three years in arrear; yet, though there were no diamonds, and not many pearls, I should suppose the jewels worth more than the sum for which they were given.*

While I stood burning with indignation, the paper still trembling in my hand, I heard the footstep of the priest; I let fall the paper; he advanced, snatched it up, and put it in his pocket book, with an air of self reprehension that determined me to conceal the knowledge so accidentally acquired. Having left our adieux for our courteous hosts with one of the young men, we at last set out for Inismore. The idea of so soon meeting my soul's precious Glorvina banished every idea less delightful.

"Our meeting," said I, "will be attended with a new and touching interest, the sweet result of that *perfect* intelligence which now for the first time subsisted between us, and which stole its birth from that tender and delicious glance which love first bestowed on me beneath the cypress tree of the rustic cemetery.

Already I beheld the "air-lifted" figure of Glorvina floating towards me. Already I felt her soft hands tremble in mine, and gazed on the deep suffusion of her kindling blushes, the ardent welcome of her bashful eyes, and

*I have been informed that a descendant of the provincial kings of Connaught parted not many years back with the golden crown which, for so many ages, encircled the royal brows of his ancestors.

"*the life of life*": common eighteenth-century poetic cliché.

all that dissolving and impassioned languor, with which she would resign herself to the sweet abandonment of her soul's chastened tenderness, and the fullest confidence in that adoring heart which had now unequivocally assured her of its homage and eternal fealty. In short, I had resolved to confess my name and rank to Glorvina, to offer her my hand, and to trust to the affection of our fond and indulgent fathers for forgiveness.

Thus warmed by the visions of my heated fancy I could no longer stifle my impatience; and when we were within seven miles of the castle, I told the priest, who was ambling slowly on, that I would be his *avant-courier*, and clapping spurs to my horse soon lost sight of my tardy companion.

At the draw bridge I met one of the servants to whom I gave the panting animal, and flew, rather than walked, to the castle. At its portals stood the old nurse, she almost embraced me, and I almost returned the caress; but with a sorrowful countenance she informed me that the prince was dangerously ill, and had not left his bed since our departure; *that things altogether were going on but poorly;* and that she was sure *the sight* of me would do her young lady's heart good, for that she did nothing but weep all day, and sit by her father's bed all night. She then informed me that Glorvina was alone in the boudoir. With a thousand pulses fluttering at my breast, full of the idea of stealing on the melancholy solitude of my pensive love, with a beating heart and noiseless step I approached the sacred asylum of innocence. The door lay partly open; Glorvina was seated at a table, and apparently engaged in writing a letter. I paused a moment for breath ere I advanced. Glorvina at the same instant raised her head from the paper, read over what she had written, and wept bitterly; then wrote again, and again paused; sighed, and drew a letter from her bosom—(yes, her bosom) which she perused, often waving her head, and sighing deeply, and wiping away the tears that dimmed her eyes, while once a cherub smile stole on her lip (*that smile* I once thought *all* my own); then folding up the letter, she pressed it to her lips, and consigning it to her bosom, exclaimed, "First and best of men!" What else she murmured I could not distinguish; but as if the perusal of this prized letter had renovated every drooping spirit, she ceased to weep, and wrote with greater earnestness than before.

Motionless, transfixed, I leaned for support against the frame of the door until Glorvina, having finished her letter and sealed it, arose to depart; then I had the presence of mind to steal away and conceal myself in a dark recess of the corridor. Yet though unseen, I saw her wipe away the traces of her tears from her cheek, and pass me with a composed and almost cheerful air. I softly followed, and looking down the dark abyss of the steep well stairs,

---

avant-courier: French: herald, one who rides before, harbinger.

which she rapidly descended, I perceived her to put her letter in the hands of the little post boy, who hurried away with it. Impelled by the impetuous feelings of the moment I was—yes, I was so far forgetful of myself, my principles and pride, of every sentiment save love and jealousy, that I was on the point of following the boy, snatching the letter, and learning the address of this mysterious correspondent, this "*First and best of men.*" But the natural dignity of a vehement, yet undebased, mind saved me a meanness I should never have forgiven: for what right had I forcibly to possess myself of another's secret? I turned back to a window in the corridor and beheld Glorvina's little herald mounted on his mule riding off, while she, standing at the gate, pursued him with that impatient look so strongly indicative of her ardent character. When he was out of sight she withdrew, and the next minute I heard her stealing towards her father's room. Unable to bear her presence, I flew to mine; that apartment I had lately occupied with an heart so redolent of bliss—an heart that now sunk beneath the unexpected blow which crushed all its new born hopes, and I feared annihilated for ever its sweet but short-lived felicity. "And is this then," I exclaimed, "the fond reunion my fancy painted in such glowing colours?" God of heaven! at the very moment when my thoughts and affections forced for a tedious interval from the object of their idolatry, like a compressed spring set free, bounded with renewed vigour to their native bias. Yet was not the disappointment of my own individual hopes scarcely more agonizing than the destruction of that consciousness which, in giving one perfect being to my view, redeemed the species in my misanthropic opinion.

"Oh, Glorvina!" I passionately added, "if even thou, fair being, reared in thy native wilds and native solitudes, art deceptive, artful, imposing, deep, deep, in all the wiles of hypocrisy; then is the original sin of our nature unredeemed; vice the innate principle of our being—and those who preach the existence of virtue but idle dreamers, who fancy that in others to themselves unknown. And yet sweet innocent, if thou 'art more sinned against than sinning:'[174] if the phantoms of a jealous brain—oh, 'tis impossible! The ardent kiss impressed upon the senseless paper, which thy breast enshrined!!! was the letter of a friend thus treasured! When was the letter of a friend thus answered with tears, with smiles, with blushes, and with sighs? This, this, is love's own language. Besides, Glorvina is not formed for friendship; the moderate feelings of her burning soul are already divided in affection for her father, and grateful esteem for her tutor; and she who, when loved, must be loved to madness, will scarcely feel less passion than she inspires."

While thought after thought thus chased each other down, like the mutinous billows of a stormy ocean, I continued pacing my chamber with

---

[174] Shakespeare, *King Lear*, III. ii. 59–60.

quick and heavy strides; forgetful that the prince's room lay immediately beneath me. Ere that thought occurred, some one softly opened the door. I turned savagely round—it was Glorvina! Impulsively I rushed to meet her; but not impulsively recoiled: while she, with an exclamation of surprize and pleasure, sprung towards me, and by my sudden retreat would have fallen at my feet, but that my willing arms extended involuntarily to receive her. Yet it was no longer the almost sacred person of the once all-innocent, all-ingenuous Glorvina they encircled; but still they twined round the loveliest form, the most charming, the most dangerous, of all human beings. The enchantress!—With what exquisite modesty she faintly endeavoured to extricate herself from my embrace; yet with what willing weakness, which seemed to triumph in its own debility, she panted on my bosom, wearied by the exertion which vainly sought her release. Oh! at that moment the world was forgotten—the whole universe was Glorvina! My soul's eternal welfare was not more precious at that moment than Glorvina! while my passion seemed now to derive its ardour from the overflowing energy of those bitter sentiments which had preceded its revival. Glorvina, with an effort, flung herself from me. Virtue, indignant yet merciful, forgiving while it arraigned, beamed in her eyes. I fell at her feet; I pressed her hand to my throbbing temples and burning lips. "Forgive me," I exclaimed, "for I know not what I do." She threw herself on a seat, and covered her face with her hands, while the tears trickled through her fingers. Oh! there was a time when tears from those eyes—but now they only recalled to my recollection the last I had seen her shed. I started from her feet and walked towards the window, near that couch where her watchful and charitable attention first awakened the germ of gratitude and love which has since blown into such full, such fatal existence. I leaned my head against the window-frame for support, its painful throb was so violent; I felt as though it were lacerating in a thousand places; and the sigh which involuntarily breathed from my lips seemed almost to burst the heart from whence it flowed.

Glorvina arose: with an air tenderly compassionate, yet reproachful, she advanced and took one of my hands. "My dear friend," she exclaimed, "what is the matter? has any thing occurred to disturb you, or to awaken this extraordinary emotion? Father John! where is he? why does he not accompany you? Speak!—does any new misfortune threaten us? does it touch my father? Oh! in mercy say *it does not!* but release me from the torture of suspense."

"No, no," I peevishly replied; "set your heart at rest, it is nothing; nothing at least that concerns you; it is me, me only it concerns."

"And therefore, Mortimer, is it nothing to Glorvina," she softly replied; and with one of those natural motions so incidental to the simplicity of her manners, she threw her hand on my shoulder, and leaning her head on it, raised her eloquent, her tearful eyes to mine. Oh! while the bright drops hung upon her cheek's faded rose, with what difficulty I restrained the impulse that tempted me to gather them with my lips; while she, like a ministering angel, again took my hand, and applying her fingers to my wrist said with a sad smile, "You know I am a skilful little doctress."

The feelings I experienced when those lovely fingers first applied their pressure to my arm rushed on my recollection: her touch had lost nothing of its electric power: my emotions at that moment were indescribable.

"Oh, good God, how ill you are!" she exclaimed. "How wild your pulse; how feverish your looks! You have over-heated yourself; you were unequal to such a journey in such weather; you who have been so lately an invalid. I beseech you to throw yourself on the bed, and endeavour to take some repose; mean time I will send my nurse with some refreshment to you. How could I be so blind as not to see at once how ill you were!"

Glad, for the present, of any pretext to conceal the nature of my real disorder, I confessed I was indeed ill, (and, in fact, I was *physically* as well as morally so; for my last day's journey brought on that nervous head-ache I have suffered so much from;) while she, all tender solicitude and compassion, flew to prepare me a composing-draught. But I was not now to be deceived: this was pity, mere pity. Thus a thousand times have I seen her act by the wretches who were first introduced to her notice through the medium of that reputation which her distinguished humanity had obtained for her among the diseased and the unfortunate.

I had but just sunk upon the bed, overcome by fatigue and the vehemence of my emotions, when the old nurse entered the room. She said she had brought me a composing draught from the lady Glorvina, who had kissed the cup, after the old Irish fashion,* and bade me drink it for her sake.

"Then I pledge her," said I, "with the same truth she did me;" and I eagerly quaffed off the nectar her hand had prepared. Meantime the nurse took her station by my bed side, with some appropriate references to her former attendance there, and the generosity with which that attendance was rewarded; for I had imprudently apportioned my donation rather to my real than apparent rank.

While I was glad that this talkative old woman had fallen in my way; for though I knew I had nothing to hope from that incorruptible fidelity which was grounded on her attachment to her beloved nursling, and her affection

* To this ancient and general custom Goldsmith alludes in his Deserted Village:—

"And kissed the cup to pass it to the rest."
[Goldsmith, *The Deserted Village*, l. 250. Ed.]

for the family she had so long served, yet I had every thing to expect from the garrulous simplicity of her character, and her love of what she calls *Seanachus*, or telling long stories of the Inismore family; and while I was thinking how I should put my jesuitical scheme into execution, and she was talking as usual I know not what, the beautiful "*Breviare du Sentiment*" caught my eye lying on the ground: Glorvina must have dropped it on her first entrance. I desired the nurse to bring it to me; who blessed her stars, and wondered how her child could be so careless: a thing too she valued so much. At that moment it struck me that this *Breviare,* the furniture of the *boudoir,* the vases, and the fragment of the letter, were all connected with this mysterious friend, this "first and best of men." I shuddered as I held it, and forgot the snow-drops it contained; yet assuming a composure as I examined its cover, I asked the nurse if she thought I could procure such another at the next market town.

The old woman held her sides while she laughed at the idea; then folding her arms on her knees with that gossiping air which she always assumed when in a mood peculiarly loquacious, she assured me that such a book could not be got in all Ireland; for that it had come from foreign parts to her young lady.

"And who sent it?" I demanded.

"Why, nobody sent it," she simply replied; "he brought it himself."

"Who?" said I.

She stammered and paused.—"Then, I suppose," she added, "of course you never heard"—

"What?" I eagerly asked with an air of curiosity and amazement. As these are two emotions a common mind is most susceptible of feeling and most anxious to excite, I found little difficulty in artfully leading on the old woman by degrees, till at last I obtained from her, almost unawares to herself, the following particulars:

On a stormy night, in the spring of 17—, during that fatal period when the scarcely cicatrised wounds of this unhappy country bled afresh beneath the uplifted sword of civil contention; when the bonds of human amity were rent asunder, and every man regarded his neighbour with suspicion or considered him with fear; a stranger of noble stature, muffled in a long dark cloke, appeared in the great hall of Inismore, and requested an interview with the prince. The prince having retired to rest, and being then in an ill state of health, deputed his daughter to receive the unknown visitant, as the priest was absent. The stranger was shewn into an apartment adjoining

---

17—: The date likely refers to the United Irishmen rising of 1798.

cicatrised: scarred.

the prince's, where Glorvina received him, and having remained for some time with him retired to her father's room; and again, after a conference of some minutes, returned to the stranger, whom she conducted to the prince's bedside. On the same night, and after the stranger had passed two hours in the prince's chamber, the nurse received orders to prepare the bed and apartment which I now occupy for this mysterious guest, who from that time remained near three months at the castle; leaving it only occasionally for a few days, and always departing and returning under the veil of night.

The following summer he repeated his visit; bringing with him those presents which decorate Glorvina's boudoir, except the carpet and vases, which were brought by a person who disappeared as soon as he had left them. During both these visits he gave up his time chiefly to Glorvina; reading to her, listening to her music, and walking with her early and late, but never without the priest or the nurse, and seldom during the day.

In short, in the furor of the old woman's garrulity (who however discovered that her own information had not been acquired by the most justifiable means, having, she said, by chance overheard a conversation which passed between the stranger and the prince), I found that this mysterious visitant was some unfortunate gentleman who had attached himself to the rebellious faction of the day, and who being pursued nearly to the gates of the castle of Inismore, had thrown himself on the mercy of the prince; who, with that romantic sense of honour which distinguishes his chivalrous character, had not violated the trust thus forced on him, but granted an asylum to the unfortunate refugee; who, by the most prepossessing manners and eminent endowments, had dazzled the fancy and won the hearts of this unsuspecting and credulous family; while over the minds of Glorvina and her father he had obtained a boundless influence.

The nurse hinted that she believed it was still unsafe for the stranger to appear in this country, for that he was more cautious of concealing himself in his last visit than his first; that she believed he lived in England; and that he seemed to have money enough, "*for he threw it about like a prince.*" Not a servant in the castle, she added, but knew well enough how it was; but there was not one but would sooner *die* than betray him. His name she did not know; he was only known by the appellation of the GENTLEMAN. He was not young, but tall, and very handsome. He could not speak Irish, and she had reason to think he had lived chiefly in America. She added, that *I* often reminded her of him, especially when I smiled and looked down. She was not certain whether he was expected that summer or not; but she believed the prince frequently received letters from him.

The old woman was by no means aware how deeply she had been betrayed by her insatiate passion of hearing herself speak; while the curious and expressive idiom of her native tongue gave me more insight into the whole business than the most laboured phrase or minute detail could have done. By the time, however, she had finished her narrative, she began to have some "compunctious visitings of conscience:"[175] she made me pass my honour I would not betray her to her young lady; for, she added, that if it got air it might come to the ears of the Lord M___, who was the prince's bitter enemy; and that it might be the ruin of the prince; with a thousand other wild surmises suggested by her fears. I again repeated my assurances of secresy; and the sound of her young lady's bell summoning to the prince's room, she left me, not forgetting to take with her the "*Breviare du Sentiment.*"

Again abandoned to my wretched self, the succeeding hour was passed in such a state of varied perturbation, that it would be as torturing to retrace my agonizing and successive reflections as it would be impossible to express them. In short, after a thousand vague conjectures, many to the prejudice and a lingering few to the advantage of their object, I was led to believe (fatal conviction!) that the virgin rose of Glorvina's affection had already shed its sweetness on a former, happier lover; that the partiality I had flattered myself in having awakened was either the result of natural intuitive coquetry, or, in the long absence of her heart's first object, a transient beam of that fire which once illumined is so difficult to extinguish, and which was nourished by my resemblance to him who had first fanned it into life.—What! *I* receive to my heart the faded spark, while another has basked in the vital flame? *I* contentedly gather this after-blow of tenderness, when another has inhaled the very essence of the nectarious blossoms? No! like the suffering mother, who wholly resigned her bosom's idol rather than divide it with another, I will, with a single effort, tear this late adored image from my heart, though that heart break with the effort, rather than feed on the remnant of those favours on which another has already feasted. Yet to be thus deceived by a recluse, a child, a novice:—*I* who, turning revoltingly from the hackneyed artifices of female depravity in that world where art for ever reigns, sought in the tenderness of secluded innocence and intelligent simplicity that heaven my soul had so long, so vainly panted to enjoy! Yet, even there—No! I cannot believe it! She! Glorvina, false, deceptive! Oh! were the immaculate spirit of *Truth* embodied in a human form, it could not wear upon its radiant brow a brighter, stronger trace of purity inviolable, and holy innocence, than shines in the seraph countenance of Glorvina! Besides, she never *said* she loved me. *Said!*—God of heavens! were words then necessary for such an

[175] Shakespeare, *Macbeth,* I. v. 45.

avowal? Oh, Glorvina! thy melting glances, thy insidious smiles, thy ardent blushes, thy tender sighs, thy touching softness and delicious tears; these, these are the sweet testimonies to which my heart appeals. These at least will speak for me, and say, it was not the breath of vain presumption that nourished those hopes which now, in all their vigour, perish by the chilling blight of well-founded jealousy and mortal disappointment.

Two hours have elapsed since the nurse left me, supposing me to be asleep; no one has intruded, and I have employed the last hour in retracing to you the vicissitudes of this eventful day. You, who warned me of my fate, should learn the truth of your fatal prophecy. My father's too; but he is avenged! and I have already expiated a deception, which, however innocent, was still *deception.*

In continuation.

I had written thus far, when some one tapped at my door, and the next moment the priest entered: he was not an hour arrived, and with his usual kindness came to enquire after my health, expressing much surprise at its alteration, which he said was visible in my looks. "But it is scarcely to be wondered at," he added: "a man who complains for two days of a nervous disorder, and yet gallops, as if for life, seven miles in a day more natural to the torrid zone than our polar clime, may have some chance of losing his life, but very little of *losing his disorder.*" He then endeavoured to persuade me to go down with him, and take some refreshment, for I had tasted nothing all day, save Glorvina's draught; but finding me averse to the proposal, he sat with me till he was sent for to the prince's room. As soon as he was gone, with that restlessness of body which ever accompanies a wretched mind, I wandered through the deserted rooms of this vast and ruinous edifice, but saw nothing of Glorvina. The sun had set, all was gloomy and still. I took my hat, and in the melancholy maze of twilight wandered I knew not, cared not, whither. I had not, however, strayed far from the ruins, when I perceived the little post-boy galloping his foaming mule over the draw-bridge, and the next moment saw Glorvina gliding beneath the colonade (that leads to the chapel) to meet him. I retreated behind a fragment of the ruins, and observed her take a letter from his hand with an eager and impatient air: when she had looked at the seal, she pressed it to her lips; then by the faint beams of the retreating light, she opened this welcome packet, and putting an inclosed letter in her bosom, endeavoured to read the envelope; but scarcely had her eye glanced over it, than it fell to the earth, while she, covering her face with her hands, seemed to lean against the broken pillar near which she stood for support. Oh! was this an emotion of overwhelming bliss, or chilling disappointment. She again took the paper, and, still holding it open in her hand, with a slow step and thoughtful air, returned to the castle; while I flew to the stables, under pretence of enquiring from the post-boy if there were any letters for me. The lad said there was but one, and that, the post-master had told him, was an English one for the lady Glorvina. This letter then, though it could not have been an answer to that I had seen her writing, was doubtless from the mysterious friend, whose friendship, "*like gold, though not sonorous, was indestructible.*"

My doubts were now all lost in certain conviction; my trembling heart no longer vibrated between a lingering hope and a dreadful fear. I was *deceived,* and another was *beloved.* That sort of sullen firm composure, which fixes man when he knows the worst that can occur, took possession of every feeling, and steadied that wild throb of insupportable suspense, which had agitated and distracted my veering soul; while the only vacillation of mind to which I was sensible, was the uncertainty of whether I should or should not quit the castle that night. Finally resolved to act with the cool determination of a rational being, not the wild impetuosity of a maniac, I put off my departure till the following morning, when I could formally take leave of the prince, the priest, and even Glorvina herself, in the presence of her father. Thus firm and decided, I returned to the castle, and mechanically walked towards that vast apartment where I had first seen her at her harp, soothing the sorrows of parental affliction; but now it was gloomy and unoccupied; a single taper burnt on a black marble slab before a large folio, in which I suppose the priest had been looking; the silent harp of Glorvina stood in its usual place. I fled to the great hall, once the central point of all our social joys, but it was also dark and empty; the whole edifice seemed a desart. I again rushed from its portals, and wandered along the sea-beat shore, till the dews of night, and the spray of the swelling tide, as it broke against the rocks, had penetrated through my clothes. I saw the light trembling in the casement of Glorvina long after midnight. I heard the castle clock fling its peal o'er every passing hour; and not till the faintly awakening beam of the horizon streamed on the eastern wave, did I return through the castle's ever open portals, and steal to that room I was about to occupy (not to sleep in) for the last time: a light and some refreshment had been left there for me in my absence. The taper was nearly burnt out, but by its expiring flame I perceived a billet lying on the table. I opened it tremblingly. It was from Glorvina, and only a simple enquiry after my health, couched in terms of common-place courtesy. I tore it—it was the first she had ever addressed to me, and yet I tore it in a thousand pieces. I threw myself on the bed, and for some time buried my mind in conjecturing whether her father sanctioned, or her preceptor suspected, her attachment to this fortunate rebel. I was almost convinced they did not. The young, the profound deceiver; she whom I had thought

"So green in this old world."[176]

Wearied by incessant cogitation, I at last fell into a deep sleep, and arose about two hours back, harassed by dreams, and quite unrefreshed; since when I have written thus far. My last night's resolution remains unchanged. I have sent my compliments to inquire after the prince's health, and to request an interview with him. The servant has this moment returned, and informs me the prince has just fallen asleep, after having had a very bad night, but that when he awakens he shall be told of my request. I dared not mention Glorvina's name, but the man informed me she was then sitting by her father's bed-side, and had not attended matins. At breakfast I mean to acquaint the excellent father John of my intended departure. Oh! how much of the woman at this moment swells in my heart. There is not a being in this family in whom I have not excited, for whom I do not feel, an interest. Poor souls! they have almost all been at my room door this morning to inquire for my health, owing to the nurse's exaggerated account: she too, kind creature, has already been twice with me before I arose, but I affected sleep. Adieu! I shall dispatch this to you from M. House. I shall then have seen the castle of Inismore for the last time—the last time!!

H. M.

Letter XXIX

TO J. D. ESQ. M. P.

M___ House.

IT is all over—the spell is dissolved, and the vision for ever vanished: yet my mind is not what it was, ere this transient dream of bliss "wrapt it in Elysium." Then I neither suffered or enjoyed: now—!

When I had folded my letter to you, I descended to breakfast, but the priest did not appear, and the things were removed untouched. I ordered

---

Elysium: in Greek mythology, the paradise to which heroes, favored by the gods, were sent to enjoy immortality.

[176] Shakespeare, *King John*, III. iv. 144.

my horse to be got ready, and waited all day in expectation of a message from the prince; loitering, wandering, unsettled, and wretched, the hours dragged on: no message came: I fancied I was impatient to receive it, and to be gone; but the truth is, my dear friend, I was weak enough almost to rejoice at the detention. While I walked from room to room with a book in my hand, I saw no one but the servants, who looked full of mystery; save once, when, as I stood at the top of the corridor, I perceived Glorvina leave her father's room; she held her handkerchief to her eyes, and passed on to her own apartment. Oh! why did I not fly and wipe away those tears, inquire their source, and end at once the torture of suspense; but I had not power to move. The dinner hour arrived: I was summoned to the parlour; the priest met me at table, shook me with unusual cordiality by the hand, and affectionately enquired after my health. He then became silent and thoughtful, and had the air of a man whose heart and office are at variance; who is deputed with a commission his feelings will not suffer him to execute. After a long pause he spoke of the prince's illness, the uneasiness of his mind, the unpleasant state of his affairs, his attachment and partiality to me, and his ardent wish always to have it in his power to retain me with him; then paused again, and sighed, and again endeavoured to speak, but failed in the effort. I now perfectly understood the nature of his incoherent speech; my pride served as an interpreter between his feelings and my own, and I was determined to save his honest heart the pang of saying, "Go, you are no longer a welcome guest."

I told him then in a few words, that it was my intention to have left the castle that morning for Bally____, on my way to England; but that I waited for an opportunity of bidding farewel to the prince: as that however seemed to be denied me, I begged that he (father John) would have the goodness to say for me all—. Had my life depended on it, I could not articulate another word. The priest arose in evident emotion. I too not unagitated left my seat: the good man took my hand, and pressed it affectionately to his heart, then turned aside, I believe, to conceal the moisture of his eyes; nor were mine dry, yet they seemed to burn in their sockets. The priest then put a paper in the hand he held, and again pressing it with ardour, hurried away. I trembled as I opened it: it was a letter from the prince, containing a banknote, a plain gold ring which he constantly wore, and the following lines written with the trembling hand of infirmity or emotion:

"Young and interesting Englishman, farewel! Had I not known thee, I never had lamented that God had not blessed me with a son.

O'Melville,
Prince of Inismore."

I sunk overcome on a chair. When I could sufficiently command myself, I wrote with my pencil on the cover of the prince's letter the following incoherent lines:

"You owe *me* nothing: to you I stand indebted for life itself, and all that could *once* render life desirable. With existence only will the recollection of your kindness be lost; yet though generously it was unworthily bestowed; for it was lavished on an *Impostor*. I am not what I seem: to become an inmate of your family, to awaken an interest in your estimation, I forfeited the dignity of truth, and stooped for the first time to the meanness of deception. Your money therefore I return, but your ring—that ring so often worn by you—worlds would not tempt me to part with.

"I have a father, sir; this father once so dear, so precious to my heart! but since I have been your guest, *he*, the whole world was forgotten. The first tye of nature was dissolved; and from your hands I seemed to have received a new existence. Best and most generous of men, be this recollection present to your heart! should some incident as yet unforeseen discover to you who, and what I am. Remember this—and then forgive him, who, with the profoundest sense of all your goodness, bids you a last farewel!"

When I had finished these lines, written with an emotion that almost rendered them illegible, I rung the bell and inquired (from the servant who answered) for the priest: he said he was shut up in the prince's room.

"Alone, with the prince!" said I.

"No," he returned, "for he had seen the lady Glorvina enter at the same time with Father John." I did not wish to trust the servant with this open billet, I did not wish the prince to get it till I was gone; in a word, though I was resolved to leave the castle that evening, yet I did not wish to go, till, for the last time, I had seen Glorvina.

I therefore wrote the following lines in French to the priest. "Suffer me to see you; in a few minutes I shall leave Inismore for ever." As I was putting the billet into the man's hand, the stable boy passed the window; I threw up the sash and ordered him to lead round my horse. All this was done with the agitation of mind, which a criminal feels who hurries on his execution, to terminate the horrors of suspense.

I continued walking up and down the room in such agony of feeling, that a cold dew, colder than ice, hung upon my aching brow. I heard a footstep approach—I became motionless; the door opened, and the priest appeared leading in Glorvina. God of Heaven! The priest supported her on his arm, her veil was drawn over her eyes; I could not advance to meet them, I stood spell bound,—they both approached; I had not the power even to raise my eyes. "You sent for me," said the priest in a faultering accent. I presented him my letter for the prince; suffocation choaked my utterance; I could not speak. He put the letter in his bosom, and taking my hand, said, "You must not think of leaving us this evening; the prince will not hear of it." While he spoke my horse passed the window; I summoned up those spirits my pride, my wounded pride, retained in its service. "It is necessary I should depart immediately," said I, "and the sultriness of the weather renders the evening preferable." I abruptly paused—I could not finish the sentence, simple as it was.

"Then," said the priest, "*any* evening will do as well as this." But Glorvina spoke not; and I answered with vehemence, that I should have been off long since: and my determination is now fixed.

"If you are thus *positive,*" said the priest, surprised by a manner so unusual, "your friend, your pupil here, who came to second her father's request, must change her solicitations to a *last* farewell."

Glorvina's head reposed on his shoulder; her face was enveloped in her veil; he looked on her with tenderness and compassion, and I repeated a "last farewell!" Glorvina, you will at least then say, "*Farewell.*" The veil fell from her face. God of heaven, what a countenance! In the universe I saw nothing but Glorvina; such as I had once believed her, my own, my loving and beloved Glorvina, my tender friend, and impassioned mistress. I fell at her feet; I seized her hands, and pressed them to my burning lips. I heard her stifled sobs; her tears of soft compassion fell upon my cheek; I thought them tears of love, and drew her to my breast; but the priest held her in one arm, while with the other he endeavoured to raise me, exclaiming in violent emotion, "Oh God, I should have foreseen this! I, I, alone am to blame. Excellent and unfortunate young man, dearly beloved child!" and at the same moment he pressed us both to his paternal bosom. The heart of Glorvina throbbed to mine, our tears flowed together, our sighs mingled. The priest sobbed over us like a child. It was a blissful agony; but it was insupportable. Then to have died would been to have died most blest. The priest, the cruel priest, dispelled the transient dream. He forcibly put me from him. He stifled the voice of nature and of pity in his breast. His air was sternly virtuous—"Go," said he, but he spoke in vain. I still clung to the drapery of Glorvina's robe; he forced me from her, and she sunk on a couch. "I now," he added, "behold the fatal error to which I have been an unconscious accessary. Thank God, it is retrievable; go, amiable, but imprudent young man; it is honour, it is virtue commands your departure."

While he spoke he had almost dragged me to the hall.

"Stay," said I, in a faint voice, "let me but speak to her."

"It is in vain," replied the inexorable priest, "for she can *never* be yours; then spare *her,* spare *yourself.*"

"Never!" I exclaimed.

"Never," he firmly replied.

I burst from his grasp and flew to Glorvina. I snatched her to my breast, and wildly cried "Glorvina, is this then a last farewell?" She answered not; but her silence was eloquent. "Then," said I, pressing her more closely to my heart, "*farewell for ever.*"

In continuation.

I mounted the horse that waited for me at the door, and galloped off; but with the darkness of the night I returned, and all night I wandered about the environs of Inismore; to the last I watched the light of Glorvina's window. When it was extinguished, it seemed as though I parted from her again. A grey dawn was already breaking to the mists of obscurity. Some poor peasants were already going to the labours of the day. It was requisite I should go. Yet when I ascended the mountain of Inismore I involuntarily turned, and beheld those dear ruins which I had first entered under the influence of such powerful, such prophetic emotion. What a train of recollection rushed on my mind! What a climax did they form! I turned away my eyes, sick, *sick* at *heart,*[177] and pursued my solitary journey. Within twelve miles of M. House, as I reached an eminence, I again paused to look back, and caught a last view of the mountain of Inismore. It seemed to float like a vapour on the horizon. I took a last farewell of this almost loved mountain. Once it had risen on my gaze like the pharos to my haven of enjoyment; for never, until this sad moment, had I beheld it but with transport.

On my arrival here I found a letter from my father, simply stating that by the time it reached me he would probably be on his way to Ireland, accompanied by my intended bride, and her father, concluding thus: "In beholding you honourably and happily established, thus secure in a liberal, a noble independence, the throb of incessant solicitude you have hitherto awakened will at last be *stilled,* and your prudent compliance in this instance will bury in eternal oblivion the sufferings, the anxieties which, with all your native virtue and native talent, your imprudence has hitherto caused to the heart of an affectionate and indulgent father."

This letter which even a few days back would have driven me to distraction I now read with the apathy of a stoic. It is to me a matter of indifference how I am disposed of. I have no wish, no will of my own.

To the return of that mortal torpor from which a late fatally cherished sentiment had roused me, is now added the pang of my life's severest disappointment, like the dying wretch who is only roused from total

---

pharos: a lighthouse or beacon.

[177] Shakespeare, *Macbeth,* V. iii. 19.

insensibility, by the quivering pains which, at intervals of fluttering life, shoot through his languid frame.

In continuation.

It is two days since I began this letter, yet I am still here; I have not power to move, though I know not what secret spell detains me. But whither shall I go, and to what purpose? the tye which once bound me to physical and moral good, to virtue, and felicity, is broken, for ever broken. My mind is changed, dreadfully changed within these few days. I am ill too, a burning fever preys upon the very springs of life; all around me is solitary and desolate. Sometimes my brain seems on fire, and hideous phantoms float before my eyes; either my senses are disordered by indisposition, or the hand of heaven presses heavily on me. My blood rolls in torrents through my veins. Sometimes I think it *should*, it *must* have vent. I feel it is in vain to think that I shall ever be fit for the discharge of any duty in this life. I shall hold a place in the creation to which I am a dishonour. I shall become a burthen to the few who are obliged to feel an interest in my welfare.

It is the duty of every one to do that which his situation requires, to act up to the measure of judgment bestowed on him by Providence. Should I continue to drag on this load of life, it would be for its wretched remnant a mere animal existence. A moral death! What! I become again like the plant I tread under my feet; endued with a vegetative existence, but destitute of all sensation, of all feeling. I who have so lately revelled in the purest wildest joys of spiritual felicity. I who have tasted of heaven's own bliss; who have known, oh God! that even the recollection, the simple recollection should diffuse through my chilled heart, through my whole languid frame such vital warmth, such cheering renovating ardour.

I have gone over calmly, deliberately gone over every circumstance connected with the recent dream of my life. It is evident that the object of her heart's first election is that of her father's choice. Her passion for me, for I swear most solemnly she loved me. Oh, in that I could not be deceived; every look, every word betrayed it; her passion for me was a paroxism. Her tender, her impassioned nature required some object to receive the glowing ebullitions of its affectionate feelings; and in the absence of another, in that unrestrained intimacy by which we were so closely associated; in that sympathy of pursuit which existed between us, they were lavished on me. I was the substituted toy of the moment. And shall I then sink beneath a woman's whim, a woman's infidelity, unfaithful to another as to me? I who, from my early days, have suffered by her arts and my own credulity. But what were all my sufferings to this? A drop of water to "the multitudinous ocean."[178] Yet in the moment of a last farewell she wept so bitterly! tears of pity! Pitied and deceived!

I am resolved I will offer myself an expiatory sacrifice on the altar of parental wrongs. The father whom I have deceived and injured shall be retributed. This moment I have received a letter from him, the most affectionate and tender; he is arrived in Dublin, and with him Mr. D. and his daughter! It is well! If he requires it the moment of our meeting shall be that of my immolation. Some act of desperation would be now most consonant to my soul!

Adieu.

H. M.

Letter XXX

TO J. D. ESQ. M. P.

Dublin.

I AM writing to you from the back room of a noisy hotel in the centre of a great and bustling city: my only prospect the gloomy walls of the surrounding houses. The contrast!—Where now are those refreshing scenes on which my rapt gaze so lately dwelt; those wild sublimities of nature—the stupendous mountain, the Alpine cliff, the boundless ocean, and the smiling vale? Where are those original and simple characters; those habits, those manners, to me at least so striking and so new? All vanished like a dream!—

"The baseless fabric of a vision!"[179]

I arrived here late in the evening, and found my father waiting to receive me. Happily the rest of the party were gone to the theatre; for his agitation was scarcely less than my own. You know, that owing to our late misunderstandings it is some months since we met. He fell on my neck and wept. I was quite overcome. He was shocked at my altered appearance, and his tenderest solicitudes were awakened for my health. I was so vanquished by his goodness that more than once I was on the point of confessing all to him. It was my good angel checked the imprudent avowal; for what purpose could it now serve, but to render me more contemptible in his eyes, and to heighten his antipathy against those who have been in some degree

[178] Shakespeare, *Macbeth,* II. ii. 60.

[179] Shakespeare, *The Tempest,* IV. i. 151.

the unconscious accessaries to my egregious folly and incurable imprudence. But *does* he feel an antipathy against the worthy prince? Can it be otherwise? Have not all his conciliatory offers been rejected with scorn? Yet to me he never mentioned the prince's name; this silence surprises me—long may it continue. I dare not trust myself. In your bosom only is the secret safely reposed.

As I had rode day and night since I left M. House, weariness and indisposition obliged me almost on my arrival to go to bed: my father sat by my side till the return of the party from the theatre. What plans for my future aggrandizement and happiness did his parental solicitude canvas and devise! The prospect of my brilliant establishment in life seems to have given him a new sense of being. On our return to England, I am to set up for the borough of___. My talents are calculated for the senate: fame, dignity, and emolument, are to wait upon their successful exertion. I am to become an object of popular favor and royal esteem; and all this time, in the fancied triumph of his parental hopes, he sees not that the heart of their object is breaking.

Were you to hear him! were you to see him! What a father! what a man! Such intelligence—such abilities. A mind so dignified, an heart so tender; and still retaining all the ardour, all the enthusiasm of youth. In what terms he spoke of my elected bride! He indeed dwelt chiefly on her personal charms, and the simplicity of her unmodefied character. Alas! I once found both united to genius and sensibility.

"How delightful," he exclaimed, "to form this young and ductile mind, to mould it to your desires, to breathe inspiration into this lovely image of primeval innocence, to give soul to beauty, and intelligence to simplicity, to watch the ripening progress of your grateful efforts, and finally clasp to your heart that perfection you have yourself created."

And this was spoken with an energy, an enthusiasm, as though he had himself experienced all the pleasure he now painted for me. Happily, however, in the warmth of his own feelings he perceived not the coldness, the torpidity of his son's.

They are fast weaving for me the web of my destiny. I look on and take no part in the work. It is over—I have been presented in form. They say she is beautiful—it may be so;—but the blind man cannot be persuaded of the charms of the rose, when his finger is wounded by its thorns. She met me with some confusion, which was natural, considering she had been "won unsought."[180] Yet I thought it was the bashfulness of a *hoyden,* rather than that soul-born delicate bashfulness, which I have seen accompanied with

---

emolument: profit, reward, remuneration or salary.

hoyden: a rude, boisterous, or ill-bred girl.

[180] See *WIG* 241, n. 129.

every grace. How few there are who do or can distinguish this in woman; yet in nature, there is nothing more distinct than the modesty of sentiment and of constitution.

The father was as usual boisterously good-humoured, and vulgarly pleasant; he talked over our sporting adventures last winter, as if the topic was exhaustless. For my part, I was so silent, that my father looked uneasy, and I then made amends for my former taciturnity by talking incessantly, and on every subject with vehemence and rapidity. A woman of common sense or common delicacy would have been disgusted, but she is a child; they would fain drag me after them into public, but my plea of ill health has been received by my indulgent father. My gay young mistress seems already to consider me as her husband, and treats me accordingly with indifference. In short, she finds that love in the solitude of the country, and amidst the pleasures of a town, is a very different sentiment; yet her vanity I believe is piqued by my neglect: for to-day she said, when I excused myself from accompanying her to a morning concert, Oh! I should much rather have your father with me: he is the younger man of the two! I indeed never saw him in such health and spirits; he seems to tread on air. Oh! that he were my rival! my successful rival! In the present morbid state of my feelings I give in to every thing, but when it comes to a crisis, will this stupid acquiescence still befriend their wishes? Impossible!

In continuation.

I have had a short but extraordinary conversation with my father. Would you believe it? he has for some time back cherished an attachment of the tenderest nature; but to his heart the interests of his children have ever been an object of the first and dearest concern. Having secured their establishment in life, and, as he hopes and believes, effected their happiness, he now feels himself warranted in consulting his own. In short, he has given me to understand that there is a probability of his marriage with a very amiable and deserving person closely following after my brother's and mine. The lady's name he refused to mention, until every thing was finally arranged; and whoever she is, I suspect her rank is inferior to her merits, for he said, "the world will call the union disproportioned—disproportioned in every sense; but I must, in this instance, prefer the approval of my own heart to the world's opinion." He then added (but in an equivocal manner), that had he been able to follow me immediately to Ireland, as he had at first proposed, he would have related to me some circumstances of peculiar interest, but that *I should yet know all!* and seemed, I thought, to lament that disparity of character between my brother and him, which prohibited that flow of confidence his heart seems panting to indulge in. You know Edward takes no pains to conceal that he smiles at those ardent virtues in his father's character, to which the phlegmatic temperament of his own gives the name of *romance.*

The two fathers settle every thing as they please. A property which fell to my father a few weeks back by the death of a rich maiden aunt, with every thing not entailed, he has made over to me even during his life. Expostulation was in vain, he would not hear me: for himself he has retained nothing but his purchased estates in Connaught, which are infinitely more extensive than that he possesses by inheritance. What if he resides at the Lodge, in the very neighbourhood of___. Oh! my good friend, I fear I am deceiving myself: I fear I am preparing for the heart of the best of fathers a mortal disappointment.—When the throes of wounded pride shall have subsided; when the resentments of a doating, a deceived heart shall have gradually abated, and the recollection of former blisses shall have soothed away the pangs of recent suffering; will I then submit to the dictates of an imperious duty, or resign myself unresisting to the influence of morbid apathy?

Sometimes my father fixes his eyes so tenderly on me, yet with a look as if he would search to the most secret folds of my heart. He has never once asked my opinion of my elected bride, who, gay and happy as the first circles of this dissipated city can make her, cheerfully receives the plea which my ill health affords (attributed to a heavy cold), of not attending her in her pursuit of pleasure. The fact is, I am indeed ill; my mind and body seem declining together, and nothing in this life can give me joy but the prospect of its delivery.

By this I suppose the mysterious friend is arrived. It was expedient, therefore, that I should be dismissed. By this I suppose she is · · · · · · · · · · So closely does my former weakness cling round my heart, that I cannot think of it without madness.

After having contemplated for a few minutes the sun's cloudless radiancy, the impression left on the averted gaze is two dark spots, and the dazzled organ becomes darkened by a previous excess of lumination. It is thus with my mind; its present gloom is proportioned to its former light. Oh! it was too, too much! Rescued from that moral death, that sicklied satiety of feeling, that state of chill hopeless existence, in which the torpid faculties were impalpable to every impression, when to breathe, to move, constituted all the powers of being: and then suddenly, as if by an intervention of Providence (and what an agent did it appoint for the execution of its divine will!) raised to the summit of human thought, human feeling, human felicity, only again to be plunged in endless night. It was too much.

*　　*　　*　　*　　*　　*　　*

Good God! would you believe it! My father is gone to M___ House, to prepare for the reception of the bridal party. We are to follow, and he proposes spending the summer there: there too, he says, my marriage with Miss D___ is to be celebrated; he wishes to conciliate the good will, not only of the neighbouring gentry, but of his tenantry in general, and thinks this will be a fair occasion. Well, be it so; but I shall not hold myself answerable for the consequences: my destiny is in their hands—let them look to the result.

Since my father left us, I am of necessity obliged to pay some attention to *his friends*; but I should be a mere automaton by the side of my gay mistress, did I not court an artificial flow of spirits, by means to me the most detestable. In short, I generally contrive to leave my senses behind me at the drinking table; or rather my reason and my spirits, profiting by its absence, are roused to boisterous anarchy: my bride (*my* bride!) is then quite charmed with my gaiety, and fancies she is receiving the homage of a lover, when she is insulted by the extravagance of a maniac; but she is a simple child, and her father is an insensible fool. God knows how little of my thoughts are devoted to either. Yet the girl is much followed for her beauty, and the splendid figure which the fortune of the father enables them to make has procured them universal attention from persons of the first rank.

* * * * * * *

A thousand times the dream of short slumbers gives her to my arms as I last beheld her. A thousand times I am awakened from an heavy unrefreshing sleep by the fancied sound of her harp and voice. There was one old Irish air she used to sing like an angel, and in the idiom of her national music sighed out certain passages with an heart-breaking thrill, that used to rend my very soul! Well, this song I cannot send from my memory; it breathes around me, it dies upon my ear, and in the weakness of emotion I weep—weep like a child. Oh! this cannot be much longer endured. I have this moment received your letter; I feel all the kindness of your intention, but I must insist on your not coming over; it would now answer no purpose. Besides, a new plan of conduct has suggested itself. In a word, my father shall know all: my unfortunate adventure may come to his ears: it is best he should know it from myself. I will then resign my fate into his hands: surely he will not forget I am still his son.

Adieu.

H. M.

Conclusion

A FEW days after the departure of the Earl of M. from Dublin, the intended father-in-law of his son, weary of a town life, to which he had hitherto been unaccustomed, proposed that they should surprise the earl at M__ House, without waiting for that summons which was to have governed their departure for Connaught.

His young and thoughtless daughter, eager only after novelty, was charmed by a plan which promised a change of scene and variety of life. The unfortunate lover of Glorvina fancied he gave a reluctant compliance to the proposal which coincided but too closely with the secret desires of his soul.

This inconsiderate project was put into execution almost as soon as it was formed. Mr. D. and his daughter went in their own carriage; Mr. M. followed on horseback. On their arrival, they found M___ House occupied by workmen of every description, and the Earl of M. absent. Mr. Clendenning, his lordship's agent, had not returned from England; and the steward, who had been but lately appointed to the office, informed the travellers that Lord M. had only been one day at M___ House, and had removed a few miles up the country to a hunting-lodge, until it should be ready for the reception of the family. Mr. D. insisted on going on to the hunting-lodge. Mr. M. strenuously opposed the intention, and with difficulty prevailed on the thoughtless father and volatile daughter to stop at M___ House, while he went in search of its absent lord. It was early in the day when they had arrived; and when Mr. M. had given orders for their accommodation, he set out for the lodge.

From the time the unhappy M. had come within sight of those scenes which recalled all the recent circumstances of his life to memory, his heart had throbbed with a quickened pulse; even the scenery of M___ House had awakened his emotion; his enforced return thither; his brief and restless residence there; and the eager delight with which he flew from the desolate mansion of his father to the endearing circle of Inismore; all rushed to his memory, and awakened that train of tender recollection he had lately endeavoured to stifle. Happy to seize on an occasion of escaping from the restraint the society of his insensible companions imposed, happier still to have an opportunity afforded him of visiting the neighbourhood of Inismore, every step of his little journey to the lodge was marked by the renewed existence of some powerful and latent emotion; and the agitation of his heart and feelings had reached their *acme* by the time he had arrived at the gate of that avenue from which the mountains of Inismore were discernible.

When he reached the lodge, a young lad, who was working in the grounds, replied to his enquiries, that an old woman was its only resident, that the ancient steward was dead, and that Lord M. had only remained there an hour.

This last intelligence overwhelmed Mr. M___ with astonishment. To his further enquiries the boy only said, that, as the report went that M___ house was undergoing some repair, it was probable his lord had gone on a visit to some of the *neighbouring quality.*—He added, that his lordship's own gentleman had accompanied him.

Mr. M___ remained for a considerable time lost in thought; then throwing the bridle over his horse's neck, folded his arms, and suffered it to take its own course: it was the same animal which had so often carried him to Inismore. When he had determined on following his father to the lodge he had ordered a fresh horse; that which the groom led out was the same which Mr. M___ had left behind him, and which, by becoming the companion of his singular adventure, had obtained a peculiar interest in his affections. When he had passed the avenue of the lodge, the animal instinctively took that path he had been accustomed to go: his instinct was too favourable to the secret wishes of the heart of his unhappy master; he smiled sadly, and suffered him to proceed. The evening was far advanced—the sun had sunk in the horizon, as from an eminence he perceived the castle of Inismore. His heart throbbed with violence—a thousand hopes, a thousand wishes, a thousand fears agitated his breast: he dared not for a moment listen to the suggestions of either. Lost in the musings of his heart and imagination, he was already within a mile of Inismore. The world now disappeared—he descended rapidly to a wild and trackless shore, skreened from the high road by a range of inaccessible cliffs. Twilight faintly lingered on the summit of the mountains only: the tide was out; and, crossing the strand, he found himself beneath those stupendous cliffs which shelter the western part of the peninsula of Inismore from the ocean. The violence of the waves had worn several defiles through the rocks, which commanded a near view of the *ruined castle:* it was involved in gloom and silence—all was dark, still, and solemn! No lights issued from the windows—no noise cheered at intervals the silence of desolation.

A secret impulse still impelled the steps of Mr. M___, and the darkness of the night favoured his irresistible desire to satisfy the longings of his enamoured heart, by taking a last look at the shrine of its still worshipped idol. He proceeded cautiously through the rocks, and, alighting, fastened his horse near a patch of herbage; then advanced towards the chapel—its gates were open—the silence of death hung over it. The rising moon, as it shone through the broken casements, flung round a dim religious light, and threw its quivering rays on *that* spot where he had first beheld Glorvina and her father engaged in the interesting ceremonies of their religion. And to think that even at that moment he breathed the air that she respired, and was within a few paces of the spot she inhabited!—Overcome by the conviction, he resigned himself to the delirium which involved his heart and senses; and, governed by the overpowering impulse of the moment, he proceeded along that colonade through which he had distantly followed her and the prince on the night of his first arrival at the castle. It seemed to his heated brain as though he still pursued those fine and striking forms which almost appeared but the phantoms of Fancy's creation.

On every mourning breeze he thought the sound of Glorvina's voice was borne; and starting at the fall of every leaf, he almost expected to meet at each step the form of father John, if not that of his faithless mistress; but the idea of her lover occurred not. The review of scenes so dear awakened only recollection of past enjoyments; and in the fond dream of memory his present sufferings were for an interval suspended.

Scarcely aware of the approximation, he had already reached the lawn which fronted the castle, and which was strewed over with fragments of the mouldering ruins, and leaning behind a broken wall which skreened him from observation, he indulged himself in contemplating that noble but decayed edifice where so many of the happiest and most blameless hours of his life had been enjoyed. His first glance was directed towards the casement of Glorvina's room, but there nor in any other did the least glimmering of light appear. With a faultering step he advanced from his concealment towards the left wing of the castle, and snatched an hasty glance through the window of the banquetting hall. It was the hour in which the family were wont to assemble there. It was now impenetrably dark—he ventured to approach still closer, and fixed his eye to the glass; but nothing met the inquiry of his eager gaze save a piece of armour, on whose polished surface the moon's random beams faintly played. His heart was chilled; yet, encouraged by the silent desolation that surrounded him, he ventured forward. The gates of the castle were partly open: the hall was empty and dark—he paused and listened—all was silent as the grave. His heart sunk within him—he almost wished to behold some human form, to hear some human sound. On either side the doors of two large apartments stood open: he looked into each; all was chill and dark.

Grown desperate by gloomy fears, he proceeded rapidly up the stone stairs which wound through the centre of the building. He paused; and, leaning over the balustrade, listened for a considerable time; but when the echo of his footsteps had died away, all was again still as death. Horror-struck, yet doubting the evidence of his senses, to find himself thus far advanced in the interior of the castle, he remained for some time motionless—a thousand melancholy suggestions struck on his soul. With an impulse almost frantic he rushed to the corridor. The doors of the several rooms on either side lay open, and he thought by the moon's doubtful light they seemed despoiled of their furniture.

While he stood rapt in horror and amazement he heard the sound of Glorvina's harp, borne on the blast which sighed at intervals along the passage. At first he believed it was the illusion of his fancy disordered by the awful singularity of his peculiar situation; to satisfy at once his insupportable doubts he flew to that room where the harp of Glorvina always stood: like the rest it was unoccupied and dimly lit up by the moon beams. The harp of Glorvina, and the couch on which he had first sat by her, were the only articles it contained: the former was still breathing its wild melody when he entered, but he perceived the melancholy vibration was produced by the sea breeze (admitted by the open casement) which swept at intervals along its strings. Wholly overcome, he fell on the couch—his heart seemed scarcely susceptible of pulsation—every nerve of his brain was strained almost to bursting—he gasped for breath. The gale of the ocean continued to sigh on the cords of the harp, and its plaintive tones went to his very soul, and roused those feelings so truly in unison with every sad impression. A few burning tears relieved him from an agony he was no longer able to endure; and he was now competent to draw some inference from the dreadful scene of desolation by which he was surrounded. The good old prince was no more!—or his daughter was married! In either case it was probable the family had deserted the *ruins* of Inismore.

While absorbed in this heart-rending meditation he saw a faint light gleaming on the ceiling of the room, and heard a footstep approaching. Unable to move, he sat breathless with expectation. An ancient female, tottering and feeble, with a lantern in her hand, entered; and having fastened down the window, was creeping slowly along and muttering to herself: when she perceived the pale and ghastly figure of the stranger, she shrieked, let fall the light, and endeavoured to hobble away. Mr. M___ followed, and caught her by the arm: she redoubled her cries—it was with difficulty he could pacify her—while, as his heart fluttered on his lips, he could only say "The lady Glorvina!—the prince!—speak!—where are they?"

The old woman had now recovered her light, and holding it up to the face of Mr. M___, she instantly recognized him; he had been a popular favourite with the poor followers of Inismore: she was among the number; and her joy at having her terrors thus terminated was such as for an interval to preclude all hope of obtaining any answer from her. With some difficulty the distracted and impatient M___ at last learnt, from a detail interrupted by all the audible testimonies of vulgar grief, that an execution had been laid upon the prince's property, and another upon his person; that he had been carried away to jail out of a sick bed, accompanied by his daughter, father John, and the old nurse; and that the whole party had set off in the old family coach, which the creditors had not thought worth taking away, in the middle of the night, lest the country people should rise to rescue the prince, which the officers who accompanied him apprehended.

The old woman was proceeding in her narrative, but her auditor heard no more; he flew from the castle, and, mounting his horse, set out for the town where the prince was imprisoned. He reached it early the next morning, and rode at once to the jail. He alighted and enquired for Mr. O'Melville, commonly called Prince of Inismore.

The jailor, observing his wild and haggard appearance, kindly asked him into his own room, and then informed him that the prince had been released two days back; but that his weak state of health did not permit him to leave the jail till the preceding evening, when he had set off for Inismore. "But," said the jailor, "he will never reach his old castle alive, poor gentleman! which he suspected himself; for he received the last ceremonies of the church before he departed, thinking, I suppose, that he would die on the way."

Overcome by fatigue and a variety of overwhelming emotions, Mr. M___ sunk motionless on a seat; while the humane jailor, shocked by the wretchedness of his looks, and supposing him to be a near relative, offered some words of consolation, and informed him there was then a female domestic of the prince's in the prison, who was to follow the family in the course of the day, and who could probably give him every information he might require. This was welcome tidings to Mr. M___; and he followed the jailor to the room where the prince had been confined, and where the old nurse was engaged in packing up some articles which fell out of her hands, when she perceived her favourite and patient, whom she cordially embraced with the most passionate demonstrations of joy and amazement. The jailor retired; and Mr. M___, shuddering as he contemplated the close and gloomy little apartment, its sorry furniture, and grated windows, where the suffering Glorvina had been imprisoned with her father, briefly related to the nurse that, having learnt the misfortunes of the prince, he had followed him to the prison, in the hope of being able to give him some assistance, if not to effect his liberation.

The old woman was as usual garrulous and communicative; she wept alternately the prince's sufferings and tears of joy for his release; talked sometimes of the generosity of the good friend who had she said "been the saviour of them all," and sometimes of the christian fortitude of the prince; but still dwelt most on the virtues and afflictions of her young lady, whom she frequently termed *a saint out of heaven*, a suffering angel, and a martyr. She then related the circumstances of the prince's imprisonment in terms so affecting, yet so simple, that her own tears dropt not faster than those of her auditor. She said that she believed they had looked for assistance from the concealed friend until the last moment, when the prince, unable to struggle any longer, left his sick bed for the prison of___; that Glorvina had supported her father during their melancholy journey in her arms, without suffering even a tear, much less a complaint to escape her; that she had supported his spirits and her own as though she were more than human, until the physician who attended the prince gave him over; that then her distraction (when out of the presence of her father) knew no bounds; and that once they feared her senses were touched. When, at a moment when they were all reduced to despair, the mysterious friend arrived, paid the debt for which the prince was confined, and had carried them off the evening before, by a more tedious but less rugged road than that she supposed Mr. M___ had taken, by which means he had probably missed them. "For all this," continued the old woman weeping, "my child will never be happy: she is sacrificing herself for her father, and he will not live to enjoy the benefit of it. The gentleman is indeed good and comely to look at; and his being old enough to be her father matters nothing; but then love is not to be commanded though duty may."

Mr. M. struck by these words fell at her feet, conjured her not to conceal from him the state of her lady's affections, confessed his own secret passion, in terms as ardent as it was felt. His recent sufferings and suspicions, and the present distracted state of his mind, his tears, his intreaties, his wildly energetic supplications, his wretched but interesting appearance, and above all the adoration he professed for the object of her own tenderest affection, finally vanquished the small portion of prudence and reserve interwoven in the unguarded character of the simple and affectionate old Irishwoman, and she at last confessed, that the day after his departure from the castle of Inismore Glorvina was seized with a fever in which, after the first day, she became delirious; that during the night, as the nurse sat by her, she awakened from a deep sleep and began to speak much of Mr. Mortimer, whom she frequently called *her friend,* her *preceptor,* and her *lover;* talked wildly of her having been *united to him by God in the vale of Inismore,* and drew from her bosom a sprig of withered myrtle which, she said, had been a bridal gift from her beloved, and that she often pressed it to her lips and smiled, and began to sing an air which, she said, was dear to him; until at last she burst into tears, and wept herself to sleep again. "When she recovered," continued the nurse, "which, owing to her youth and fine constitution, she did in a few days, I mentioned to her some of these sayings, at which she changed colour, and begged that as I valued her happiness I would bury all I had heard in my own breast; and above all bid me not mention your name, as it was now her duty to forget you; and last night I heard her consent to become the wife of the good gentleman; but poor child it is all one, for she will die of a broken heart. I see plainly she will not long survive her father, nor will ever love any but you!" At these words the old woman burst into a passion of tears, while Mr. M. catching her in his arms, exclaimed "I owe you my life, a thousand times more than my life;" and throwing his purse into her lap, flew to the inn, where having obtained an hack horse, given his own in care to the master, and taken a little refreshment which his exhausted frame, long fasting, and extraordinary fatigue required, he again set out for the lodge. His sole object was to obtain an interview with Glorvina, and on the result of that interview to form his future determinations.

To retrace the wild fluctuations of those powerful and poignant feelings which agitated a mind alternately the prey of its wishes and its fears, now governed by the impetuous impulses of unconquerable love, now by the sacred ties of filial affection, now sacrificing every consideration to the dictates of duty, and now forgetting every thing in the fond dreams of passion, would be an endless, an impossible task; when still vibrating between the sweet felicities of new born hope, and the gloomy suggestions of habitual doubt. The weary traveller reached the peninsula of Inismore about the same hour that he had done the preceding day. At the draw bridge he was met by a peasant whom he had known and to whom he gave his horse. The man, with a countenance full of importance, was going to address him, but he sprung eagerly forward and was in a moment immersed in the ruins of the castle; intending to pass through the chapel as the speediest and most private way, and to make his arrival first known to Father John, to declare to the good priest his real name and rank, his passion for Glorvina, and to receive his destiny from her lips only.

He had scarcely entered the chapel when the private door by which it communicated with the castle flew open. He skreened himself behind a pillar, from whence he beheld father John proceeding with a solemn air towards the altar, followed by the prince, carried by three servants in an arm chair, and apparently in the last stage of mortal existence. Glorvina then appeared wrapt in a long veil and supported on the arm of a stranger, whose figure and air was lofty and noble, but whose face was concealed by the recumbent attitude of his head, which drooped towards that of his apparently feeble companion, as if in the act of addressing her. This singular procession advanced to the altar; the chair of the prince reposed at its feet. The priest stood at the sacred table—Glorvina and her companions knelt at its steps. The last red beams of the evening sun shone through a stormy cloud on the votarists: all was awfully silent; a pause solemn and affecting ensued; then the priest began to celebrate the marriage rites; but the first words had not died on his lips when a figure, pale and ghastly, rushed forward, wildly exclaiming, "Stop, I charge you, stop! you know not what you do! it is sacrilege!" and breathless and faint the seeming maniac sunk at the feet of the bride.

A convulsive shriek burst from the lips of Glorvina. She raised her eyes to heaven, then fixed them on her unfortunate lover, and dropped lifeless into his arms—a pause of indescribable emotions succeeded. The prince, aghast, gazed on the hapless pair; thus seemingly entwined in the embrace of death. The priest transfixed with pity and amazement let fall the sacred volume from his hands. Emotions of an indescribable nature mingled in the countenance of the bridegroom. The priest was the first to dissolve the spell, and to recover a comparative presence of mind; he descended from the altar and endeavoured to raise and extricate the lifeless Glorvina from the arms of her unhappy lover, but the effort was vain. Clasping her to his heart closer than ever, the almost frantic M. exclaimed, "She is mine! mine in the eye of heaven! and no human power can part us!"

"Merciful Providence!" exclaimed the bridegroom faintly, and sunk on the shoulder of the priest. The voice pierced to the heart of his rival; he raised his eyes, fell lifeless against the railing of the altar, faintly uttering, "God of Omnipotence! my father!" Glorvina released from the nerveless clasp of her lover, sunk on her knees between the father and the son, alternately fixing her wild regards on both, then suddenly turning them on the now apparently expiring friend, she sprung forward, and throwing her arms round his neck, frantically cried, "It is my father they will destroy;" and sobbing convulsively, sunk overcome on his shoulder.

The prince pressed her to his heart, and looked round with a ghastly and enquiring glance for the explanation of that mystery no one had the power to unravel, and by which all seemed overwhelmed. At last, with an effort of expiring strength, he raised himself in his seat, entwined his arm round his child, and intimated by his eloquent looks, that he wished the mysterious father and his rival son to approach. The priest led the former towards him: the latter sprung to his feet, and hid his head in his mantle: all the native dignity of his character now seemed to irradiate the countenance of the prince of Inismore; his eyes sparkled with a transient beam of their former fire; and the retreating powers of life seemed for a moment to rush through his exhausted veins with all their pristine vigour. With a deep and hollow voice he said: "I find I have been deceived, and my child, I fear, is to become the victim of this deception. Speak, mysterious strangers, who have taught me at once to *love* and to *fear* you—what, and who are you? and to what purpose have you mutually, but apparently unknown to each other, stolen on our seclusion, and thus combined to embitter my last hours, by threatening the destruction of my child?"

A long and solemn pause ensued, which was at last interrupted by the Earl of M. With a firm and collected air he replied: "That youth, who kneels at your feet, is my son; but till this moment I was ignorant that he was known to you: I was equally unaware of those claims which he has now made on the heart of your daughter. If he has deceived you, he also has deceived his father! For myself, if imposition can be extenuated, mine merits forgiveness, for it was founded on honourable and virtuous motives. To restore you to the blessings of independence; to raise your daughter to that rank in life, her birth, her virtues, and her talents merit; and to obtain your assistance in dissipating the ignorance, improving the state, and ameliorating the situation of those of your poor unhappy compatriots, who, living immediately within your own sphere of action, are influenced by your example, and would best be actuated by your counsel. Such were the wishes of my heart; but *prejudice,* the enemy of all human virtue and human felicity, forbad their execution. My first overtures of amity were treated with scorn; my first offers of service rejected with disdain; and my crime was, that in a distant age an ancestor of mine, by the fortune of war, had possessed himself of those domains, which, in a more distant age, a remoter ancestor of your's won by similar means. Thus denied the open declaration of my good intents, I stooped to the assumption of a fictitious character; and he who as an hereditary enemy was forbid your house, as an unknown and unfortunate stranger, under affected circumstances of peculiar danger, was received to your protection, and soon to your heart as its dearest friend. The influence I obtained over your mind, I used to the salutary purpose of awakening it to a train of ideas more liberal than the prejudices of education had hitherto suffered it to cherish; and the little services I had it in my power to render you, the fervour of your gratitude so far over-rated, as to induce you to repay them by the most precious of all donations—your child. But for the wonderful and most unexpected incident which has now crossed your designs, your daughter had been by this the wife of the Earl of M.!"

With a strong convulsion of expiring nature, the prince started from his chair; gazed for a moment on the earl with a fixed and eager look, and again sunk on his seat; it was the last convulsive throe of life roused into existence by the last violent feeling of mortal emotion. With an indefinable expression, he directed his eyes alternately from the father to the son, then sunk back, and closed them: the younger M. clasped his hand, and bathed it with his tears: his daughter, who hung over him, gazed intently on his face, as though she tremblingly watched the extinction of that life in which her own was wrapped up; her air was wild, her eye beamless, her cheek; pale grief and amazement seemed to have bereft her of her senses, but her feelings had lost nothing of their poignancy: the Earl of M. leaned on the back of the prince's chair, his face covered with his hand: the priest held his right hand, and wept like an infant: among the attendants there was not one appeared with a dry eye.

After a long and affecting pause, the prince heaved a deep sigh, and raised his eyes to the crucifix which hung over the altar: the effusions of a departing and pious soul murmured on his lips, but the powers of utterance were gone; every mortal passion was fled, save that which flutters with the last pulse of life in the heart of a doating father, parental solicitude and parental love. Religion claimed his last sense of duty, nature his last impulse of feeling; he fixed his last gaze on the face of his daughter; he raised himself with a dying effort to receive her last kiss: she fell on his bosom, their arms interlaced. In this attitude he expired.

Glorvina, in the arms of the attendants, was conveyed lifeless to the castle. The body of the prince was carried to the great hall, and there laid on a bier. The Earl of M. walked by the side of the body, and his almost lifeless son, supported by the arm of the priest (who himself stood in need of assistance), slowly followed.

The elder M. had loved the venerable prince as a brother and a friend; the younger as a father. In their common regret for the object of their mutual affection, heightened by that sadly affecting scene they had just witnessed, they lost for an interval a sense of that extraordinary and delicate situation in which they now stood related towards each other; they hung on either side in mournful silence over the deceased object of their friendly affliction; while the concourse of poor peasants, whom the return of the prince brought in joyful emotion to the castle, now crowded into the hall, uttering those vehement exclamations of sorrow and amazement so consonant to the impassioned energy of their national character. To still the violence of their emotions, the priest kneeling at the foot of the bier began a prayer for the soul of the deceased. All who were present knelt around him: all was awful, solemn, and still. At that moment Glorvina appeared; she had rushed from the arms of her attendants; her strength was resistless, for it was the energy of madness; her senses were fled.

A dead silence ensued; for the emotion of the priest would not suffer him to proceed. Regardless of the prostrate throng, she glided up the hall to the bier, and gazing earnestly on her father, smiled sadly, and waved her hand; then kissing his cheek, she threw her veil over his face, and putting her finger on her lip, as if to impose silence, softly exclaimed, "Hush! he does not suffer now! he sleeps! it was I who lulled him to repose with the song his heart loves!" and then kneeling beside him, in a voice scarcely human, she breathed out a soul-rending air she had been accustomed to sing to her father from her earliest infancy. The silence of compassion, of horror, which breathed around, was alone interrupted by her song of grief, while no eye save her's was dry. Abruptly breaking off her plaintive strain, she drew the veil from her father's face, and suddenly averting her gaze from his livid features, it wandered from the Earl of M. to his son; while with a piercing shriek she exclaimed,—"Which of you murdered my father?" Then looking tenderly on the younger M. (whose eyes not less wild than her own had followed her every motion), she softly added, "It was not you, my love!" and with a loud convulsive laugh she fell lifeless into the priest's arms, who was the first who had the presence of mind to think of removing the still lovely maniac. The rival father and his unhappy son withdrew at the same moment; and when the priest (having disposed of his unfortunate charge) returned to seek them, he found them both in the same apartment, but at a considerable distance from each other, both buried in silent emotion—both labouring under the violence of their respective feelings. The priest attempted some words expressive of consolation to the younger M. who seemed most the victim of uncontroulable affliction; but with a firm manner the earl interrupted him:—"My good friend," said he, "this is no time for words; nature and feeling claim their prerogative, and are not to be denied. Your venerable friend is no more, but he has ceased to suffer: the afflicted and angelic being, whose affecting sorrows so recently wrung our hearts with agony, has still, I trust, many years of felicity and health in store to compensate for her early trials; from henceforth I shall consider her as the child of my adoption. For myself, the motives by which my apparently extraordinary conduct was governed were pure and disinterested; though the means by which I endeavoured to effect my laudable purpose were perhaps not strictly justifiable in the eye of rigid, undeviating integrity. For this young man!" he paused, and fixed his eyes on his son till they filled with tears, the strongest emotions agitating his frame; then extending his arms towards him, Mr. M. rushed forward, and fell on his father's breast. The earl pressed him to his heart, and putting his hands in those of father John, he said, "To your care and tenderness I commend my child; and from you," he added, addressing his son, "I shall expect the developement of that mystery, which is as yet to me dark and unfathomable. Remain here till we fully understand each other. I depart tonight for M___ House. It is reserved for you to assist this worthy man in the last solemn office of friendship and humanity. It is reserved for you to watch over and cherish that suffering angel, for whose future happiness we both mutually stand accountable." With these words Lord M. again embraced his almost lifeless son, and pressing the hand of the priest withdrew.—Father John followed him; but importunities were fruitless; his horses were ordered, and having put a bank-note of considerable amount into his hands to defray the funeral expences, he departed from Inismore.

In the course of four days, the remains of the prince were consigned to the tomb. Glorvina's health and fine constitution were already prevailing over her disorder and acute sensibility; her senses were gradually returning, and only appeared subject to wander, when a sense of her recent sufferings struck on her heart. The old nurse was the first who ventured to mention to her that her unhappy lover was in the house; but though she appeared struck and deeply affected by the intelligence, she never mentioned his name.

Mean time Mr. M. owing to his recent sufferings of mind and body, was seized with a slow fever and confined for many days to his bed. A physician of eminence in the country had taken up his residence at Inismore, and a courier daily passed between the castle and M. House, with his reports of the health of the two patients to the Earl. In a fortnight they were both so far recovered, as to remove from their respective bed rooms to an adjoining apartment. The benevolent priest who day and night had watched over them, undertook to prepare Glorvina for the reception of Mr. M. whose life seemed to hang upon the restoration of hers. When she heard that he was still in the castle, and had just escaped from the jaws of death, she shuddered and changed colour; and with a faint voice enquired for his father. When she learnt that he had left the castle on the night when she had last seen him, she seemed to feel much satisfaction, and said, "What an extraordinary circumstance! What a mystery!—the father and the son!" She paused, and a faint hectic coloured her pale cheek; then added, "unfortunate and imprudent young man! Will his father forgive and receive him?"

"He is dearer than ever to his father's heart:" said the priest, "the first use he made of his returning health, was to write to his inestimable parent, confessing without the least reservation every incident of his late extraordinary adventure."

"And when does he leave the castle?" inarticulately demanded Glorvina.

"That rests with you;" replied the priest.

She turned aside her head and sighed heavily; then bursting into tears, flung her arms affectionately round her beloved preceptor, and cried, "I have now no father but you—act for me as such!"

The priest pressed her to his heart, and drawing a letter from his bosom, said, "This is from one who pants to become your father in the strictest sense of the word; it is from Lord M. but though addressed to his son, it is equally intended for your perusal. That son, that friend, that lover, whose life and happiness now rests in your hands, in all the powerful emotion of hope, doubt, anxiety, and expectation, now waits to be admitted to your presence."

Glorvina, gasping for breath, caught hold of the priest's arm, then sunk back upon her seat and covered her face with her hands. The priest withdrew, and in a few minutes returned, leading in the agitated invalid: then placing the hands of the almost lifeless Glorvina in his, retired. He felt the mutual delicacy of their situation and forebore to heighten it by his presence.

Two hours had elapsed before the venerable priest again sought the two objects dearest to his heart; he found Glorvina overwhelmed with soft emotion, her cheek covered with blushes, and her hand clasped in that of the interesting invalid, whose flushing colour and animated eyes spoke the return of health and happiness; not indeed confirmed—but fed by sanguine hope; such hope as the heart of a mourning child could give to the object of her heart's first passion, in that era of filial grief, when sorrow is mellowed by reason, and soothed by religion into a tender and not ungracious melancholy. The good priest embraced and blessed them alternately, then seated between them, read aloud the letter of Lord M.

TO THE HON. HORATIO M.

SINCE human happiness, like every other feeling of the human heart, loses its poignancy by reiteration, its fragrance with its bloom; let me not (while the first fallen dew of pleasure hangs fresh upon the flower of your existence) seize on those precious moments which *Hope*, rescued from the fangs of despondency; and bliss, succeeding to affliction, claim as their own. Brief be the detail which intrudes on the hour of new-born joy, and short the narrative which holds captive the attention, while the heart, involved in its own enjoyments, denies its interest.

It is now unnecessary for me fully to explain *all* the motives which led me to appear at the castle of Inismore in a fictitious character. Deeply interested for a people whose national character I had hitherto viewed thro' the false medium of prejudice; anxious to make it my study in a situation and under such circumstances which as an English landholder, as the Earl of M___, was denied me, and to turn the stream of my acquired information to that channel which would tend to the promotion of the happiness and welfare of those whose destiny in some measure was consigned to my guidance; solicitous to triumph over the hereditary prejudices of my hereditary enemy; to seduce him into amity, and force him to *esteem* the man he *hated*, while he unconsciously became his accessary in promoting the welfare of those of his humble compatriots who dwelt within the sphere of our mutual observation: such were the *motives* which principally guided my late apparently romantic adventure; would that the *means* had been equally laudable.

Received into the mansion of the generous but incautious prince as a proscribed and unfortunate wanderer, I owed my reception to his humanity rather than his prudence; and when I told him that I threw my life into his power, his *honour* became bound for its security, though his principles condemned the conduct which he believed had effected its just forfeiture.

For some months, in two succeeding summers, I contrived to perpetuate with plausive details the mystery I had forged; and to confirm the interest I had been so fortunate at first to awaken into an ardent friendship, which became as reciprocal as it was disinterested. Yet it was still my destiny to be loved identically as myself; as myself adventitiously to be *hated*. And the name of the Earl of M___ was forbidden to be mentioned in the presence of the prince, while he frequently confessed that the happiest of his hours were passed in Lord M___'s society.

Thus singularly situated, I dared not hazard a revelation of my real character, lest I should lose by the discovery all those precious immunities with which my fictitious one had endowed me.

But while it was my good fortune thus warmly to ingratiate myself with the father, can I pass over in silence my prouder triumph in that filial interest I awakened in the heart of his daughter. Her tender commiseration for my supposed misfortunes; the persevering goodness with which she endeavoured to rescue me from those erroneous principles she believed the efficient cause of my sufferings, and which I appeared to sacrifice to her better reason. The flattering interest she took in my conversation; the eagerness with which she received those instructions it was my supreme pleasure to bestow on her; and the solicitude she incessantly expressed for my fancied doubtful fate; awakened my heart's tenderest regard and liveliest gratitude. But though I admired her genius and adored her virtues, the sentiment she inspired never for a moment lost its character of parental affection; and even when I formed the determination, the accomplishment of which you so unexpectedly, so providentially frustrated, the gratification of any selfish wish, the compliance with any passionate impulse, held no influence over the determination. No, it was only dictated by motives pure as the object that inspired them; it was the wish of snatching this lovely blossom from the desart where she bloomed unseen; of raising her to that circle in society her birth entitled her to and her graces were calculated to adorn; of confirming my amity with her father by the tenderest unity of interests and affections; of giving her a legally sanctioned claim on that part of her hereditary property which the suspected villany of my steward had robbed her of; and of retributing the parent through the medium of the child.

Had I had a son to offer her, I had not offered her myself; but my eldest was already engaged, and for the worldly welfare of my second an alliance at once brilliant and opulent was necessary; for, dazzled by his real or supposed talents, I viewed his future destiny through the medium of my parental ambition, and thought only of those means by which he might become great, without considering the more important necessity of his becoming happy. Yet well aware of the phlegmatic indifference of the one, and the romantic imprudence of the other, I denied them my confidence, until the final issue of my adventure would render its revelation necessary. Nor did I suspect the possibility of their learning it by any other means; for the one never visited Ireland, and the other, as the son of Lord M___, would find no admittance to the castle of Inismore.

When a fixed determination succeeded to some months of wavering indecision, I wrote to Glorvina, with whom I had been in habits of epistolary correspondence, distantly touching on a subject I yet considered with timidity, and faintly demanding her sanction of my wishes before I unfolded them to her father, which I assured her I would not do until I could claim her openly in my own character.

In the interim, however, I received a letter from her, written previous to her receipt of mine.—It began thus: "In those happy moments of boundless confidence, when the pupil and the child hung upon the instructive accents of the friend and the father, you have often said to me, 'I am not altogether what I seem; I am not only *grateful*, but I possess a power stronger than words of convincing those to whom I owe so much of my gratitude; and should the hour of affliction ever reach *thee*, Glorvina, call on me as the friend who would fly from the remotest corner of the earth to serve, to *save* thee.'

"*The hour of affliction is arrived—I call upon you!*" She then described the disordered state of her father's affairs, and painted his sufferings with all the eloquence of filial tenderness and filial sorrow, requesting my advice and flatteringly lamenting the destiny which placed us at such a distance from each other.

It is needless to add, that I determined to answer this letter in person, and I only waited to embrace my loved and long estranged son on my arrival in Ireland. When I set out for Inismore I found the castle deserted, and learned (with indescribable emotions of pity and indignation), that the prince and his daughter were the inhabitants of a *prison*. I flew to this sad receptacle of suffering virtue, and effected the liberation of the prince. There *was* a time when the haughty spirit of this proud chieftain would have revolted against the idea of owing a pecuniary obligation to any man; but those only who have laboured under a long and continued series of mental and bodily affliction, can tell how the mind's strength is to be subdued, the energies of pride softened, and the delicacy of refined feelings blunted, by the pressure reiterated suffering, of harassing and incessant disappointment. While the surprise of the prince equalled his emotion he exclaimed in the vehemence of his gratitude, "Teach me at least how to thank you, since to repay you is impossible." Glorvina was at that moment weeping on my shoulder, her hands were clasped in mine, and her humid eyes beamed on me all the grateful feelings of her warm and susceptible soul. I gazed on her for a moment,—she cast down her eyes, and I thought pressed my hand; thus encouraged I ventured to say to the prince, "You talk in exaggerated terms of the little service I have done you,—would indeed it had been sufficient to embolden me to make that request which now trembles on my lips."

I paused—the prince eagerly replied, "There is nothing you can ask I am not anxious and ready to comply with."

I looked at Glorvina—she blushed and trembled. I felt I was understood, and I added, "Then give me a legal claim to become the protector of your daughter, and, through her, to restore you to that independence necessary for the repose of a proud and noble spirit. In a few days I shall openly appear to the world with honour and with safety in my own name and character. Take this letter, it is addressed to the Earl of M___, whom I solemnly swear is not more your enemy than mine, and who consequently cannot be biassed by partiality: from him you shall learn who and what I am; and until that period I ask not to receive the hand of your inestimable daughter."

The prince took the letter and tore it in a thousand pieces; exclaiming, "I cannot indeed equal, but I will at least endeavour to imitate your generosity. You chose me as your protector in the hour of danger, when confidence was more hazardous to him who reposed than him who received it! You placed your life in my hands with no other bond for its security than my *honour!* In the season of my distress you flew to save me: you lavished your property for my release, not considering the improbability of its remuneration! Take my child; her esteem, her affections, have long been your's; let me die in peace, by seeing her united to a worthy man!—*that* I *know* you are; what else you may be I will only learn from *the lips of a son-in-law.* Confidence at least shall be repaid by confidence." At these words the always generous, always vehement and inconsiderate prince rose from his pillow and placed the hand of his daughter in mine, confirming the gift with a tear of joy and a tender benediction. Glorvina bowed her head to receive it—her veil fell over her face—the index of her soul was concealed: how then could I know what passed there. She was silent—she was obedient—and I was——deceived.

The prince, on his arrival at the castle of Inismore, felt the hour of dissolution stealing fast on every principle of life. Sensible of his situation, his tenderness, his anxiety for his child survived every other feeling; nor would he suffer himself to be carried to his chamber until he had bestowed her on me from the altar. I knew not then what were the sentiments of Glorvina. Entwined in the arms of her doating, dying father, she seemed insensible to every emotion, to every thought but what his fate excited; but however gratified I might have been at the intentions of the prince, I was decidedly averse to their prompt execution. I endeavoured to remonstrate: a *look* from the prince silenced every objection: and——But here let me drop the veil of oblivion over the past; let me clear from the tablets of memory those records of extraordinary and recent circumstances to which my heart can never revert but with a pang vibrating on its tenderest nerve. It is, however, the true spirit of philosophy to draw from the evil which cannot be remedied all the good of which in its tendency it is susceptible; and since the views of my parental ambition are thus blasted in the bloom, let me at least make him happy whom it was once my only wish to render eminent: know then my imprudent but still dear son, that the bride chosen for you by your father's policy has, by an elopement with a more ardent lover (who followed her hither), left your hand as free as your heart towards her ever was.

Take then to thy bosom *her* whom heaven seems to have chosen as the intimate associate of thy soul, and whom national and hereditary prejudice would in vain withhold from thee.—In this the dearest, most sacred, and most lasting of all human ties, let the names of Inismore and M___ be inseparably blended, and the distinctions of English and Irish, of protestant and catholic, for ever buried. And, while you look forward with hope to this family alliance being prophetically typical of a national unity of interests and affections between those who may be factiously severe, but who are naturally allied, lend your *own individual efforts* towards the consummation of an event so devoutly to be wished by every liberal mind, by every benevolent heart.

During my life, I would have you consider those estates as your's which I possess in this country; and at my death such as are not entailed. But this consideration is to be indulged conditionally, on your spending eight months out of every twelve on that spot from whence the very nutrition of your existence is to be derived; and in the bosom of those from whose labour and exertion your independence and prosperity are to flow. Act not with the vulgar policy of vulgar greatness, by endeavouring to exact respect through the medium of self-wrapt reserve, proudly shut up in its own self-invested grandeur; nor think it can derogate from the dignity of the *English landholder* openly to appear in the midst of his Irish peasantry, with an eye beaming complacency, and a countenance smiling confidence, and inspiring what it expresses. Shew them you do not distrust them, and they will not betray you; give them reason to believe you feel an interest in their welfare, and they will endeavour to promote your's even at the risk of their lives; for the life of an Irishman weighs but light in the scale of consideration with his feelings; it is immolated without a murmur to the affections of his heart; it is sacrificed without a sigh to the suggestions of his honour.

Remember that you are not placed by despotism over a band of slaves, creatures of the soil, and as such to be considered; but by Providence, over a certain portion of men, who, in common with the rest of their nation, are the descendants of a brave, a free, and an enlightened people. Be more anxious to remove *causes,* than to punish *effects;* for trust me that is only to

> "Scotch the snake—not kill it,"[181]

to confine error, and to awaken vengeance.

Be cautious how you condemn; be more cautious how you deride, but be ever watchful to moderate that ardent impetuosity, which flows from the natural tone of the national character, which is the inseparable accompaniment of quick and acute feelings, which is the invariable concomitant of constitutional sensibility; and remember that the same ardour

---

[181] Shakespeare, *Macbeth,* III. ii. 13.

of disposition, the same vehemence of soul, which inflames their errors beyond the line of moderate failing, nurtures their better qualities beyond the growth of moderate excellence.

Within the influence then of your own bounded circle pursue those means of promoting the welfare of the individuals consigned to your care and protection, which lies within the scope of all those in whose hands the destinies of their less fortunate brethren are placed. Cherish by kindness into renovating life those national virtues, which, though so often blighted in the full luxuriance of their vigorous blow by the fatality of circumstances, have still been ever found vital at the root, which only want the nutritive beam of encouragement, the genial glow of confiding affection, and the refreshing dew of tender commiseration, to restore them to their pristine bloom and vigour: place the standard of support within their sphere; and like the tender vine, which has been suffered by neglect to waste its treasures on the sterile earth, you will behold them naturally turning and gratefully twining round the fostering stem, which rescues them from a cheerless and groveling destiny; and when by justly and adequately rewarding the laborious exertions of that life devoted to your service, the source of their poverty shall be dried up, and the miseries that flowed from it shall be forgotten: when the warm hand of benevolence shall have wiped away the cold dew of despondency from their brow; when reiterated acts of tenderness and humanity shall have thawed the ice which chills the native flow of their ardent feelings; and when the light of instruction shall have dispelled the gloom of ignorance and prejudice from their neglected minds, and their lightened hearts shall again throb with the cheery pulse of national exility:—then, *and not till then,* will you behold the day-star of national virtue rising brightly over the horizon of their happy existence; while the felicity, which has awakened to the touch of reason and humanity, shall return back to, and increase the source from which it originally flowed: as the elements, which in gradual progress brighten into flame, terminate in a liquid light, which, reverberating in sympathy to its former kindred, genially warms and gratefully cheers the whole order of universal nature.

FINIS.

Part Two

CONTEXTS: WRITING IRELAND AND UNION

A TOUR IN IRELAND

Arthur Young

Born at Whitehall in London on September 11, 1741 (d. 1820), Arthur Young was a well-established agronomist prior to arriving in Ireland in June 1776. Author of *Farmers' Letters to the People of England* (1776) and *Political Arithmetic* (1774), he served as land agent on the Kingsborough estates in Co. Cork in 1777, was consulted by William Pitt regarding Irish policies in 1785, and from 1784 to 1808 edited the Annals of Agriculture. Young's travels in Ireland were extensive, covering some fifteen hundred miles, although he chose not to venture much west of the River Shannon. His informants were invariably the local resident gentry and nobility to which he added his own observations. In general, he was equally appalled by the landed classes' profligacy and the tenants' laziness, but he did favorably compare the latter with their English counterparts, commenting on their music and dance in particular. As evident in "Of the Tenantry of Ireland," his condemnation of absentee landlords, tithe collectors, and rackrenting middlemen, together with his remarks on the discouraging effect of the Penal Laws and, finally, his indignant portrait of the "unlimited submission" required of the peasantry, made his Tour in Ireland less welcoming to segments of the ascendancy and more pleasing to subsequent nationalist writers. Ultimately, Young was a classic liberal and approved of industry, regularity, and the development of capital. Not surprisingly, given Richard Lovell Edgeworth's utilitarian convictions, Maria Edgeworth considered Young's account of the Irish peasantry the truest. The two sections included here, "Of the Tenantry of Ireland" and "Absentees" provide interesting contextual material for Edgeworth's didacticism regarding the need to reform Irish agricultural practices. Similarly, they suggestively complicate Owenson's characterizations of the tenant, the land agent, and the absentee landlord. [ED.]

From *Arthur Young's Tour in Ireland (1776–1779)*. Edited with an Introduction and Notes by Arthur Wollaston Hutton. 2 vols. London: George Bell & Sons, York Street, Covent Garden and New York, 1892. Section V. "Of the Tenantry of Ireland." V.2, 24–34; Section XIV. "Absentees." V.2, 114–17.

SECTION V

Of the Tenantry of Ireland

IT has been probably owing to the small value of land in Ireland, before, and even through a considerable part of, the present century, that landlords became so careless of the interests of posterity, as readily to grant their tenants leases for ever. It might also be partly owing to the unfortunate civil wars, and other intestine divisions, which for so long a space of time kept that unhappy country in a state rather of devastation than improvement. When a castle, or a fortified house, and a family strong enough for a garrison, were essentially necessary to the security of life and property among Protestants, no man could occupy land unless he had substance for defence as well as cultivation; short, or even determinable tenures were not encouragement enough for settling in such a situation of warfare. To increase the force of an estate, leases for ever were given of lands, which from their waste state were deemed of little value. The practice, once become common, continued long after the motives which originally gave rise to it, and has not yet ceased entirely in any part of the kingdom. Hence, therefore, tenants holding large tracts of land under a lease for ever, and which have been relet to a variety of undertenants, must in this enquiry be considered as landlords.

The obvious distinction to be applied is, that of the occupying and unoccupying tenantry: in other words, the real farmer, and the middle-man. The very idea, as well as the practice, of permitting a tenant to relet at a profit rent, seems confined to the distant and unimproved parts of every empire. In the highly cultivated counties of England the practice has no existence, but there are traces of it in the extremities; in Scotland it has been very common; and I am informed that the same observation is partly applicable to France. In proportion as any country becomes improved the practice necessarily wears out.

It is in Ireland a question greatly agitated, whether the system has or has not advantages, which may yet induce a landlord to continue in it. The friends to this mode of letting lands contend, that the extreme poverty of the lower classes renders them such an insecure tenantry, that no gentleman of fortune can depend on the least punctuality in the payment of rent from such people; and therefore to let a large farm to some intermediate person of substance, at a lower rent, in order that the profit may be his inducement and reward for becoming a collector from the immediate occupiers, and answerable for their punctuality, becomes necessary to any person who will not submit to the drudgery of such a minute attention. Also, that such a man will at least improve a spot around his own residence, whereas the mere cottar can do nothing. If the intermediate tenant is, or from the accumulation of several farms becomes, a man of property, the same argument is applicable to his reletting to another intermediate man, giving up a part of his profit to escape that trouble, which induced the landlord to begin this system; and at the same time accounts for the number of tenants, one under another, who have all a profit out of the rent of the occupying farmer. In the variety of conversations on this point, of which I have partook in Ireland, I never heard any other arguments that had the least foundation in the actual state of the country; for as to ingenious theories, which relate more to what might be, than to what is, little regard should be paid to them.

That a man of substance, whose rent is not only secure, but regularly paid, is in many respects a more eligible tenant than a poor cottar, or little farmer, cannot be disputed; if the landlord looks no farther than those circumstances, the question is at an end, for the argument must be allowed to have its full weight, even to victory. But there are many other considerations: I was particularly attentive to every class of tenants throughout the kingdom, and shall therefore describe these middle-men, from whence their merit may be the more easily decided. Sometimes they are resident on a part of the land, but very often they are not. Dublin, Bath, London, and the country towns of Ireland, contain great numbers of them; the merit of this class is surely ascertained in a moment; there cannot be a shadow of a pretence for the intervention of a man, whose single concern with an estate is to deduct a portion from the rent of it. They are however sometimes resident on a part of the land they hire, where it is natural to suppose they would work some improvements; it is however very rarely the case. I have in different parts of the kingdom seen farms just fallen in after leases of three lives, of the duration of fifty, sixty, and even seventy years, in which the residence of the principal tenant was not to be distinguished from the cottared fields surrounding it. I was at first much surprized at this; but after repeated observation, I found these men very generally were the masters of packs of wretched hounds, with which they wasted their time and money, and it is a notorious fact, that they are the hardest drinkers in Ireland. Indeed, the class of the small country gentlemen, chiefly consisting of these profit renters, seems at present to monopolize that drinking spirit, which was, not many years ago, the disgrace of the kingdom at large: this I conjecture to be the reason why those who might improve are so very far from doing it; but there are still greater objections to them.

---

cottar: See *WIG* 118.

Living upon the spot, surrounded by their little undertenants, they prove the most oppressive species of tyrant that ever lent assistance to the destruction of a country. They relet the land, at short tenures, to the occupiers of small farms; and often give no leases at all. Not satisfied with screwing up the rent to the uttermost farthing, they are rapacious and relentless in the collection of it. Many of them have defended themselves in conversation with me, upon the plea of taking their rents, partly in kind, when their undertenants are much distressed: "What," say they, "would the head landlord, suppose him a great nobleman, do with a miserable cottar, who, disappointed in the sale of a heifer, a few barrels of corn, or firkins of butter, brings his five instead of his ten guineas? But we can favour him by taking his commodities at a fair price, and wait for reimbursement until the market rises. Can my lord do that?" A very common plea, but the most unfortunate that could be used to any one whoever remarked that portion of human nature which takes the garb of an Irish land-jobber! For upon what issue does this remark place the question? Does it not acknowledge that, calling for their rents, when they cannot be paid in cash, they take the substance of the debtor at the very moment when he cannot sell it to another? Can it be necessary to ask what the price is? It is at the option of the creditor; and the miserable culprit meets his oppression, perhaps his ruin, in the very action that is trumpeted as a favour to him. It may seem harsh to attribute a want of feeling to any class of men; but let not the reader misapprehend me; it is the *situation,* not the *man,* that I condemn. An injudicious system places a great number of persons, not of any liberal rank in life, in a state abounding with a variety of opportunities of oppression, every act of which is profitable to themselves. I am afraid it is human nature for men to fail in such posts; and I appeal to the experience of mankind, in other lines of life, whether it is ever found advantageous to a poor debtor to sell his products, or wares, to his richer creditor, at the moment of demand.

But farther; the dependance of the occupier on the resident middle-man goes to other circumstances, personal service of themselves, their cars and horses, is exacted for leading turf, hay, corn, gravel, &c. insomuch that the poor undertenants often lose their own crops and turf, from being obliged to obey these calls of their superiors. Nay, I have even heard these jobbers gravely assert, that without undertenants to furnish cars and teams at half or two thirds the common price of the country, they could carry on no improvements at all; yet taking a merit to themselves for works wrought out of the sweat and ruin of a pack of wretches, assigned to their plunder by the inhumanity of the landholders.

In a word, the case is reducible to a short compass; intermediate tenants work no improvements; if non-resident they *cannot,* and if resident they *do not;* but they oppress the occupiers, and render them as incapable as they are themselves unwilling. The kingdom is an aggregate proof of these facts; for if long leases at low rents, and profit incomes given, would have improved it, Ireland had long ago been a garden. It remains to enquire, whether the landlord's security is a full recompence for so much mischief.

But here it is proper to observe that, though the intermediate man is generally better security than the little occupier; yet it is not from thence to be concluded, as I have often heard it, that the latter is beyond all comparison beneath him in this respect: the contrary is often the case; and I have known the fact, that the landlord, disappointed of his rent, has *drove* (distrained) the undertenants for it at a time when they had actually paid it to the middle-man. If the profit rent is spent, as it very generally is, in claret and hounds, the notion of good security will prove visionary, as many a landlord in Ireland has found it: several very considerable ones have assured me, that the little occupiers were the *best* pay they had on their estates; and the intermediate *gentlemen* tenants by much the *worst.*

By the minutes of the journey it appears, that a very considerable part of the kingdom, and the most enlightened landlords in it, have discarded this injurious system, and let their farms to none but the occupying tenantry; their experience has proved that the apprehension of a want of security was merely idle, finding their rents much better paid than ever. At the last extremity, it is the occupier's stock which is the real security of the landlord. It is that he distrains, and finds abundantly more valuable than the laced hat, hounds and pistols of the gentleman jobber, from whom he is more likely in such a case to receive a *message,* than a remittance.

And here let me observe, that a defence of intermediate tenants has been founded upon the circumstance of lessening the remittance of absentee rents; the profit of the middle-man was spent in Ireland, whereas upon his dismission the whole is remitted to England. I admit this to be an evil, but it appears to be in no degree proportioned to the mischiefs I have dwelt on. It is always to be remembered, that in the arrangement of landed property, the *produce* is the great object; the system of letting, which encourages most the occupying tenant, will always be the most advantageous to the community. I think that I have proved that the middle-man oppresses the cottar incomparably more than the principal landlord; to the one he is usually tenant at will, or at least under short terms, but under the other has the most advantageous tenure. This single point, that the person most favoured is in one instance an idle burthen, and in the other the industrious occupier, sufficiently decides the superiority. To look therefore at the rent, after it is paid, is to put the question on a wrong issue; the payment of that rent, by means of ample products, arising from animated industry, is the only point deserving attention; and I had rather the whole of it should go to the antipodes than exact it in a manner that shall cramp that industry, and lessen those products.

When therefore it is considered, that no advantages to the estate can arise from a non-resident tenant, and that a resident intermediate one improves no more than the poor occupiers who are prevented by his oppressions, that the landlord often gains little or nothing in security from employing them, but that he suffers a prodigious deduction in his rental for mere expectations, which every hour's experience proves to be delusive. When these facts are duly weighed, it is presumed that the gentlemen in those parts of the kingdom, which yet groan under such a system of absurdity, folly and oppression, will follow the example set by such a variety of intelligent landlords, and be deaf to the deceitful asseverations with which their ears are assailed, to treat the anecdotes retailed of the cottar's poverty, with the contempt they deserve, when coming from the mouth of a jobber; when these bloodsuckers of the poor tenantry boast of their own improvements, to open their eyes and view the ruins which are dignified by such a term, and finally determine, as friends to themselves, to their posterity and their country, TO LET THEIR ESTATES TO NONE BUT THE OCCUPYING TENANTRY.

Having thus described the tenants that ought to be rejected, let me next mention the circumstances of the occupiers. The variety of these is very great in Ireland. In the North, where the linen manufacture has spread, the farms are so small, that ten acres in the occupation of one person is a large one, five or six will be found a good farm, and all the agriculture of the country so entirely subservient to the manufacture, that they no more deserve the name of farmers than the occupier of a mere cabbage garden. In Limerick, Tipperary, Clare, Meath and Waterford, there are to be found the greatest graziers and cow-keepers perhaps in the world, some who rent and occupy from £3,000 to £10,000 a year: these of course are men of property, and are the only occupiers in the kingdom who have any considerable substance. The effects are not so beneficial as might be expected. Rich graziers in England, who have a little tillage, usually manage it well, and are in other respects attentive to various improvements, though it must be confessed not in the same proportion with great arable farmers; but in Ireland these men are as arrant slovens as the most beggarly cottars. The rich lands of Limerick are, in respect of fences, drains, buildings, weeds, &c. in as waste a state as the mountains of Kerry; the fertility of nature is so little seconded, that few tracts yield less pleasure to the spectator. From what I observed, I attributed this to the idleness and dissipation so general in Ireland. These graziers are too apt to attend to their claret as much as to their bullocks,

---

asseverations: Solemn or emphatic declaration or assertion.

jobber: A middleman.

slovens: Persons of slothful or indolent habits.

live expensively, and being enabled, from the nature of their business, to pass nine tenths of the year without any exertion of industry, contract such a habit of ease, that works of improvement would be mortifying to their sloth.

In the arable counties of Louth, part of Meath, Kildare, Kilkenny, Carlow, Queen's, and part of King's, and Tipperary, they are much more industrious. It is the nature of tillage, to raise a more regular and animated attention to business; but the farms are too small, and the tenants too poor, to exhibit any appearances that can strike an English traveller. They have a great deal of corn, and many fine wheat crops; but being gained at the expence and loss of a fallow, as in the open fields of England, they do not suggest the ideas of profit to the individual, or advantage to the state, which worse crops in a well appointed rotation would do. Their manuring is trivial, their tackle and implements wretched, their teams weak, their profit small, and their living little better than that of the cottars they employ. These circumstances are the necessary result of the smallness of their capitals, which even in these tillage counties do not usually amount to a third of what an English farmer would have to manage the same extent of land. The leases of these men are usually three lives to Protestants, and thirty-one years to Catholicks.

The tenantry in the more unimproved parts, such as Corke, Wicklow, Longford, and all the mountainous counties, where it is part tillage, and part pasturage, are generally in a very backward state. Their capitals are smaller than the class I just mentioned, and among them is chiefly found the practice of many poor cottars hiring large farms in partnership. They make their rents by a little butter, a little wool, a little corn, and a few young cattle and lambs. Their lands, at extreme low rents, are the most unimproved, (mountain and bog excepted,) in the kingdom. They have, however, more industry than capital; and with a very little management, might be brought greatly to improve their husbandry. I think they hold more generally from intermediate tenants than any other set; one reason why the land they occupy is in so waste a state. In the mountainous tracts, I saw instances of greater industry than in any other part of Ireland. Little occupiers, who can get leases of a mountain side, make exertions in improvement, which, though far enough from being complete, or accurate, yet prove clearly what great effects encouragement would have among them.

In the King's county, and also in some other parts, I saw many tracts of land, not large enough to be relet, which were occupied under leases for ever, very well planted and improved by men of substance and industry.

The poverty, common among the small occupying tenantry, may be pretty well ascertained from their general conduct in hiring a farm. They will manage to take one with a sum surprizingly small; they provide labour, which in England is so considerable an article, by assigning portions of land to cottars for their potatoe gardens, and keeping one or two cows for each of them. To lessen the live stock necessary, they will, whenever the neighbourhood enables them, take in the cattle at so much per month, or season, of any person that is deficient in pasturage at home, or of any labourers that have no land. Next, they will let out some old lay for grass potatoes to such labourers; and if they are in a county where corn-acres are known, they will do the same with some corn land. If there is any meadow on their farm, they will sell a part of it as the hay grows. By all these means the necessity of a full stock is very much lessened; and, by means of living themselves in the very poorest manner, and converting every pig, fowl, and even egg into cash, they will make up their rent, and get by very slow degrees into somewhat better circumstances. Where it is the custom to take in partnership, the difficulties are easier got over; for one man brings a few sheep, another a cow, a third a horse, a fourth a car and some seed potatoes, a fifth a few barrels of corn, and so on, until the farm among them is tolerably stocked, and hands upon it in plenty for the labour.

But it is from the whole evident, that they are uncommon masters of the art of overcoming difficulties by patience and contrivance. Travellers, who take a superficial view of them, are apt to think their poverty and wretchedness, viewed in the light of farmers, greater than they are. Perhaps there is an impropriety in considering a man merely as the occupier of such a quantity of land; and that, instead of the land, his capital should be the object of contemplation. Give the farmer of twenty acres in England no more capital than his brother in Ireland, and I will venture to say he will be much poorer, for he would be utterly unable to go on at all.

I shall conclude what I have to say upon this subject, with stating, in few words, what I think would prove a very advantageous conduct in landlords towards the poor tenantry of the kingdom; and I shall do this with the greater readiness, as I speak, not only as a passing traveller, but from a year's residence among several hundred tenants, whose circumstances and situation I had particular opportunities of observing.

Let me remark, that the power and influence of a resident landlord is so great in Ireland, that, whatever system he adopts, be it well or ill imagined, he is much more able to introduce and accomplish it than Englishmen can well have an idea of; consequently one may suppose him to determine more authoritatively than a person in a similar situation in this kingdom could do. The first object is a settled determination, never to be departed from, to let his farms only to the immediate occupier of the land, and, to avoid deceit, not to allow a cottar, herdsman, or steward, to have more than three or four acres on any of his farms. By no means to reject the little occupier of a few acres from being a tenant to himself, rather than annex his land to a larger spot. Having, by this previous step, eased these inferior tenantry of the burthen of the intermediate man, let him give out, and steadily adhere to it, that he shall insist on the regular and punctual payment of his rent, but shall take no personal service whatever. The meanest occupier to have a lease, and none shorter than twenty-one years, which I am inclined also to believe is long enough for his advantage. There will arise, in spite of his tenderness, a necessity of securing a regular payment of rent: I would advise him to distrain without favour or affection, at a certain period of deficiency. This will appear harsh only upon a superficial consideration. The object is to establish the system; but it will fall before it is on its legs, if founded on a landlord's forgiving arrears, or permitting them to encrease. He need not be apprehensive, since they who can, under disadvantages, pay the *jobber,* can certainly pay the *landlord* himself, when freed from those incumbrances. At all events, let him persist in this firmness, though it be the ruin of a few; for he must remember, that if he ruins five, he assuredly saves ten; he will, it is true, know the fall of a few, but many, with an intermediate tenant, might be destroyed without his knowing it. Such a steady regular conduct would infallibly have its effect, in animating all the tenantry of the estate to exert every nerve to be punctual; whereas favour shewn now and then would make every one, the least inclined to remissness, hope for its exertion towards himself, and every partial good would be attended with a diffusive evil; exceptions, however, to be made for very great and unavoidable misfortunes, clearly and undoubtedly proved. This stern administration on the one hand should be accompanied on the other with every species of encouragement to those who showed the least disposition to improve; premiums should be given, rewards adjudged, difficulties smoothed, and notice taken in the most flattering manner of those whose conduct merited it. I shall in another part of these papers point out in detail the advantageous systems; it is here only requisite to observe, that whatever novelties a landlord wishes to introduce, he should give seed gratis, and be at a part of the expence, promising to be at the whole loss if he is well satisfied it is really incurred. From various observations I am convinced that such a conduct would very rarely prove unsuccessful. The profit to a landlord would be immense; he would in the course of a lease find his tenantry paying a high rent, with greater ease to themselves, than they before yielded a low one.

A few considerable landlords, many years ago, made the experiment of fixing, at great expence, colonies of Palatines on their estates. Some of them I viewed, and made many enquiries. The scheme did not appear to me to answer. They had houses built for them; plots of land assigned to each at a rent of favour, assisted in stock, and all of them with leases for lives from the head landlord. The poor Irish are very rarely treated in this manner; when they are, they work much greater improvements than

---

Palatines: Germans.

common among these Germans; witness Sir William Osborne's mountaineers![1] a few beneficial practices were introduced, but never travelled beyond their own farms; they were viewed with eyes too envious to allow them to be patterns, and it was human nature that it should be so: but encourage a few of your own poor, and if their practices thrive they will spread. I am convinced no country, whatever state it may be in, can be improved by colonies of foreigners; and whatever foreigner, as a superintendent of any great improvement, asks for colonies of his own countrymen to execute his ideas, manifests a mean genius and but little knowledge of the human heart; if he has talents he will find tools wherever he finds men, and make the natives of the country the means of encreasing their own happiness. Whatever he does then will live and take root; but if effected by foreign hands, it will prove a sickly and short-lived exotic; brilliant perhaps, for a time, in the eyes of the ignorant, but of no solid advantage to the country that employs him.

SECTION XIV

Absentees*

THERE are very few countries in the world that do not experience the disadvantage of remitting a part of their rents to landlords who reside elsewhere; and it must ever be so while there is any liberty left to mankind of living where they please. In Ireland the amount proportioned to the territory is greater probably than in most other instances; and, not having a free trade with the kingdom in which such absentees spend their fortunes, it is cut off from that return which Scotland experiences for the loss of her rents.

Some years ago Mr. Morris published a list of the Irish absentees, and their rentals; but, as every day makes considerable alterations, it is of course grown obsolete; this induced me to form a new one, which I got

*Prior's List of the Absentees of Ireland (2nd edition, Dublin, 1729), estimates the total sum remitted yearly out of Ireland at about £627,800. A later list, taken in January, 1769, by including a variety of other out-goings, raises this sum to over a million and a half, the proportion assigned to absentee landlords and pensioners being £645,575. Young's total (£732,200) is thus shown to be not exaggerated, allowing for the increase in the value of the land, which was greater between 1769 and 1779 than during the preceding forty years. Both these lists were reprinted in Vol. II. of "A Collection of Tracts and Treatises illustrative of the Natural History, Antiquities, and the Political and Social State of Ireland," Dublin (Thom), 1861. [Original editor's note.]

[1] See above, vol. i., p. 398 *sq.* [Original editor's note.]

corrected by a variety of persons living in the neighbourhood of many of the respective estates: in such a detail, however, of private property there must necessarily be many mistakes.

Lord Donnegal	£31,000	Mr. Mathew	£6,000
Lord Courtenay	30,000	Lord Irnham	6,000
Duke of Devonshire	18,000	Lord Sandwich	6,000
Earl of Milton	18,000	Lord Vane	6,000
Earl of Shelburne	18,000	Lord Dartry	6,000
Lady Shelburne	15,000	Lord Fane	5,000
Lord Hertford	14,000	Lord Claremont	5,000
Marquiss of Rockingham	14,000	Lord Carbury	5,000
Lord Barrymore	10,000	Lord Clanrickard	5,000
Lord Montrath	10,000	Lord Farnham	5,000
Lord Besborough	10,000	Lord Dillon	5,000
Lord Egremont	10,000	Sir W. Rowley	4,000
Lord Middleton	10,000	Mr. Palmer	4,000
Lord Hisborough	10,000	Lord Clanbrassil	4,000
Mr. Stackpoole	10,000	Lord Massareen	4,000
Lord Darnley	9,000	Lord Corke	4,000
Lord Abercorn	8,000	Lord Portsmouth	4,000
Mr. Dutton	8,000	Lord Ashbrook	4,000
Mr. Barnard	8,000	Lord Villiers	4,000
London Society	8,000	Lord Bellew	4,000
Lord Conyngham	8,000	Sir Laurance Dundass	4,000
Lord Cahir	8,000	Allen family	4,000
Earl of Antrim	8,000	Mr. O'Callagan	4,000
Mr. Bagnall	7,000	General Montagu	4,000
Mr. Longfield	7,000	Mr. Fitzmaurice	4,000
Lord Kenmare	7,000	Mr. Needham	4,000
Lord Nugent	7,000	Mr. Cook	4,000
Lord Kingston	7,000	Mr. Annesley	4,000
Lord Valentia	7,000	Lord Kerry	4,000
Lord Grandisson	7,000	Lord Fitzwilliam	4,000
Lord Clifford	6,000	Viscount Fitzwilliam	4,000
Mr. Sloane	6,000	English Corporation	3,500
Lord Egmont	6,000	Lord Bingly	3,500
Lord Upper Ossory	6,000	Lord Dacre	3,000
Mr. Silver Oliver	6,000	Mr. Murray of Broughton	3,000
Mr. Dunbar	6,000	Lord Ludlow	3,000
Mr. Henry OBrien	6,000	Lord Weymouth	3,000

Lord Digby	£3,000
Lord Fortescue	3,000
Lord Derby	3,000
Lord Fingall	3,000
Blunden heiresses	3,000
Lady Charleville	3,000
Mr. Warren	3,000
Mr. St. George	3,000
Mr. John Barry	3,000
Mr. Edwards	3,000
Mr. Freeman	3,000
Lord Newhaven	3,000
Mr. Welsh (Kerry)	3,000
Lord Palmerstown	2,500
Lord Beaulieu	2,500
Lord Verney	2,500
Mr. Bunbury	2,500
Sir George Saville	2,000
Mrs. Newman	2,000
Col. Shirley	2,000
Mr. Campbell	2,000
Mr. Minchin	2,000
Mr. Burton	2,000
Duke of Dorset	2,000
Lord Powis	2,000
Mr. Whitshead	2,000
Sir Eyre Coote	2,000
Mr. Upton	2,000
Mr. John Baker Holroyd	2,000
Sir N. Bayley	2,000
Duke of Chandois	2,000
Mr. S. Campbell	2,000
Mr. Ashroby	2,000
Mr. Damer	2,000
Mr. Whitehead	2,000
Mr. Welbore Ellis	2,000
Mr. Folliot	2,000
Mr. Donellan	2,000
Mrs. Wilson	2,000
Mr. Forward	2,000
Lord Middlesex	2,000
Mr. Supple	2,000
Mr. Nagles	£2,000
Lady Raneleigh	2,000
Mr. Addair	2,000
Lord Sefton	2,000
Lord Tyrawley	2,000
Mr. Woodcock	2,000
Sir John Millar	2,000
Mr. Baldwyn	2,000
Dr. Moreton	1,800
Dr. Delany	1,800
Sir William Yorke	1,700
Mr. Arthur Barry	1,600
Lord Dysart	1,600
Lord Clive	1,600
Mr. Bridges	1,500
Mr. Cavanagh	1,500
Mr. Cuperden	1,500
Lady Cunnigby	1,500
Mr. Annesley	1,500
Mr. Hauren	1,500
Mr. Long	1,500
Mr. Oliver Tilson	1,500
Mr. Plumtree	1,400
Mr. Pen	1,400
Mr. Rathcormuc	1,200
Mr. Worthington	1,200
Mr. Rice	1,200
Mr. Ponsonby	1,200
General Sandford	1,200
Mr. Basil	1,200
Mr. Dodwell	1,200
Mr. Lock	1,200
Mr. Cramer	1,200
Mr. W. Long	1,200
Mr. Rowley	1,200
Miss Mac Artney	1,200
Mr. Sabine	1,100
Mr. Carr	1,000
Mr. Howard	1,000
Sir F. and Lady Lum	1,000
Lord Albemarle	1,000
Mr. Butler	1,000

Mr. J. Pleydell	£1,000	Mr. Alexander	£800
Mrs. Clayton	1,000	Mr. Hamilton	800
Mr. Obins	1,000	Mr. Hamilton (Longford)	800
Lord M'Cartney	1,000	Mr. William Barnard	800
Mr. Chichester	1,000	Sir P. Leicester	800
Mr. Shepherd	1,000	Mr. Moreland	800
Sir P. Dennis	1,000	Mr. Cam	700
Lady Dean	1,000	Mr. Jonathan Lovett	700
Lord Lisburne	1,000	Mr. Hull	700
Mr. Ralph Smith	1,000	Mr. Staunton	700
Mr. Ormsby	1,000	Mr. Richard Barry	700
Lord Stanhope	1,000	Colonel Barrè	600
Lord Tilney	1,000	Mr. Ashon	600
Lord Vere	1,000	Lady St. Leger	600
Mr. Hoar	1,000	Sir John Hort	500
Mrs. Grevill	1,000	Mr. Edmund Burke	500
Mr. Nappier	1,000	Mr. Ambrose	500
Mr. Echlin	800		
Mr. Taaf	800	Total	£732,200

This total, though not equal to what has been reported, is certainly an amazing drain upon a kingdom cut off from the re-action of a free trade; and such a one as must have a very considerable effect in preventing the natural course of its prosperity. It is not the simple amount of the rental being remitted into another country, but the damp on all sorts of improvements, and the total want of countenance and encouragement which the lower tenantry labour under. The landlord at such a great distance is out of the way of all complaints, or, which is the same thing, of examining into, or remedying evils; miseries of which he can see nothing, and probably hear as little of, can make no impression. All that is required of the agent is to be punctual in his remittances; and, as to the people who pay him, they are too often, welcome to go to the devil, provided their rents could be paid from his territories. This is the general picture. God forbid it should be universally true! there are absentees who expend large sums upon their estates in Ireland; the earl of Shelburne has made great exertions for the introduction of English agriculture. Mr. Fitzmaurice has taken every means to establish a manufacture. The bridge at Lismore is an instance of liberal magnificence in the Duke of Devonshire. The church and other buildings at Belfast do honour to Lord Donnegall. The church and town of Hilsborough, are striking monuments of what that nobleman performs. Lord

Conyngham's expenditure, in his absence, in building and planting, merits the highest praise; nor are many other instances wanting, equally to the advantage of the kingdom, and the honour of the individuals.

It will not be improper here to add that the amount of the pension list of Ireland, the 29th of September 1779, amounted to £84,591 per annum; probably therefore absentees, pensions, offices, and interest of money, amount to above A MILLION.

A FRENCHMAN'S WALK THROUGH IRELAND 1796–7

Chevalier de la Tocnaye (Jacques Louis de Bougrenet)

Born into a French aristocratic family in Brittany (c. 1776), Chevalier de la Tocnaye (Jacques Louis de Bougrenet) became a French Royalist officer and was forced into exile after the Revolution. Tired of London's indulgent lifestyle, he ventured on a walking tour of Scotland and England and subsequently published his memoirs of the experience, *Promenade autour de la Grande Bretagne par un officer François emigré* (Edinburgh, 1795). Moving to Ireland, he also toured the country on foot during 1796 and 1797. He relied exclusively on the hospitality of strangers, as he possessed very little by way of baggage or provisions. Due to the unsettled nature of Irish society leading up to the United Irishmen Rebellion in 1798, de la Tocnaye was forced to curtail his journeying and completed his travelogue quickly. *Promenade d'un François dans l'Irlande* appeared in 1797 (Dublin), and was noted for its unbiased depiction of everyday Irish country life. The section included here, on his visit to Ardfert, presents an outsider's perspective on Irish religious practices, in particular, focusing on popular devotions at holy wells, the segregation of Catholic congregations along gender lines, and the power of the local parish priest. In the process, the excerpt allows for direct comparison with Owenson's treatment of similar cultural phenomena in her novel. The influence of de la Tocnaye on *The Wild Irish Girl* is clearly evident in Owenson's numerous citations from his text. [ED.]

I came to Ardfert,[1] where I presented myself to the Dean, Mr. Grave, and was received as usual with that charming hospitality which always makes me forget, immediately, the fatigues of the road. Ardfert was formerly a bishopric; at present it is united to that of Limerick. In old times there were here many ecclesiastical establishments; the ruins of the old cathedral are

From *A Frenchman's Walk Through Ireland 1796–7*. Translated from the French by John Stevenson, 1917. Introd. by John A. Gamble, 1984. Belfast: Blackstaff Press, 1984. 109–11.

[1] Ardfert is a small village about five miles from Tralee, Co. Kerry. The ruin of a fifteenth-century cathedral sits on the site of a monastery founded there by St. Brendan, "The Navigator," in the sixth century. [ED.]

the most remarkable remains, although nothing very great. The air of the place is said to be extraordinarily healthy. This has induced a celebrated surgeon to choose it for his place of burying; his tomb is constructed, and his epitaph engraved on it while he is still alive.

In ancient times there stood, in the cemetery of this cathedral, a high round tower with not more than the ordinary appearance of wear. It crushed itself, if the expression may be used, some twelve or fifteen years ago. I say crushed because one would expect that such a building would naturally fall to one side or other, but in this case the stones appeared to tumble straight down, forming a large mass on the spot where the tower had stood. I went a little distance to see the venerable ruins of a Franciscan abbey, and, passing through the scattered debris of remains, I found myself in the presence of the two most beautiful and amiable ladies of Ireland, Lady Glandore and Mrs. Woodcock, who had resolved to be cruel enough to society to absent themselves from it for more than a year. I do not know whether it was their good example which affected me so much at the moment. Certain it is that never in my life did I feel such a desire to become a hermit.

At a little distance there is to be found one of those holy wells round which the inhabitants perform their devotions. This well is very famous, and the people come from afar. They pretend or assert that it can cure all evils, and the devotion consists in going round the well, bare-footed, seven times while reciting prayers, kneeling for a moment at each turn before a black stone, which seems to have been a tombstone, and, while kneeling, they rub the hand over three heads which are cut in the stone, and which are much worn by reason of this hand-rubbing and kissing. Afterwards they pass the hand which has touched the stone over the part of the body which is afflicted, drink a large glass of the water, and wash their feet in the current. Children are sometimes plunged seven times into the cold water, and I have seen people, well clad and having the appearance of being in comfortable circumstances, perform these ceremonies just like the others. I have also seen a very pretty young girl kissing these ugly stones, and I could not help thinking that I would have been a much better restorer if she had paid the reverence to me.

This well is widely renowned in the country, and even the Protestants, who are not very numerous here, when they have tried other remedies in vain, will make up their minds to try the well and go through the usual performances like their Catholic friends. The greater part of these peasants, however, come in a rather careless spirit, seemingly more with a desire to meet their friends than to perform penitences. Speaking to one of the visitors I asked him what was the benefit to be derived from this water. His reply was that he could not tell, and when I asked him why he went through the usual performances, all he could say was to do what the others do and to see the women. In effect, it is at these wells that a great number of marriages are arranged. It is in vain that the priest of the parish has often forbidden his people to go to such places; they have followed this custom so long before the establishment of Christianity that they cannot be broken off it.

In reality, there can hardly be anything more innocent than to go round one of these wells a number of times reciting prayers, and afterwards drinking a glass of water. I will go so far to say that it must be very good for the health of the poor women, since it forces them to take some exercise and to clean themselves. The only thing left to the priest is to see that order is observed in these gatherings, and by his exhortations to warn his people against any impropriety or indecency, and in this the priest of this parish has perfectly succeeded. The good folk come here on Saturday morning and finish their devotions by two o'clock. Then the young fellows make up to their girls and see them safe home to their mothers, chatting the while.

Nearly all the people in this part of the country are Catholics, but Catholic and Protestant agree here very well. The priest performs mass, and the minister preaches, and the two flocks seem not to trouble themselves about each other's religion for the rest of the week. I went on Sunday to the Catholic chapel. The women are always separated from the men here. I suppose this to be to avoid distraction. In the middle of the service the priest made a long discourse in Irish, afterwards translating the principal part into English. He consigned to all the devils (although in highly proper terms) all those infamous enough not to pay his dues.

The priests have great power over their people. They are, in fact, the judges of the country and settle everything connected with morals and manners. They excommunicate a peasant and oblige him to leave a parish. Great care, then, must be taken not to displease them, and especially care must be taken that they get their dues. The Government knows perfectly well that the priests have their people in the hollow of their hand, and, nevertheless, they make enemies of them and treat them badly. Can they make the peasants go whatever way they wish? Well, make them your friends and you have gained the people. I am convinced that a dozen benefices in favour of Catholic priests, at the disposition of the Viceroy, would make them all as flexible and courteous and as desirous to please as their dear brethren in God, the ministers and bishops of the Protestant Church.

THREE LETTERS

Maria Edgeworth

The three letters included here shed light on two distinct moments in Maria Edgeworth's life. In addition, each in its own way enriches our understanding of the particular historical context informing the compositional moment of Castle Rackrent's production. Finally, they complicate, in different ways, Edgeworth's position as an Anglo-Irish novelist responding to the emergence of an increasingly nationalist and decolonizing politics. The letters from September 1798, addressed to Edgeworth's aunt and her cousin, detail the proximity of the failed United Irishmen Rebellion to the Edgeworthstown estate at precisely the time Maria was finishing *Castle Rackrent.* On the one hand, the letters' sense of immediacy captures the very real anxiety attending the family's displacement to the garrison town of Longford. On the other hand, they betray—especially in the picturesque description of the battlefield at Ballinamuck—a detachment from the scene of military defeat. The first letter, for instance, documents that French soldiers were taken prisoner; the latter landscape fails to incorporate the native Irish who were refused the right of surrender and fell victim to the "arms all ranged on the grass." The first two letters, then, demonstrate how Maria Edgeworth occludes the United Irishmen Rebellion of 1798 in the novel, and belie her optimism in the "Preface"—based on the belief that the Act of Union would eradicate the problem of Irish identity politics. The third letter stems from a much later stage of Edgeworth's career, but nonetheless retrospectively informs the author's understanding of her role as novelist. In 1834, Edgeworth published her final work of fiction, *Helen*—the first since 1817. The letter to her brother, who was serving the British Empire in India, captures Edgeworth's growing disillusionment with fiction's ability to represent Irish national character. The political strife attending the campaign for Catholic Emancipa-

---

From Augustus J. C. Hare (ed.), *The Life and Letters of Maria Edgeworth.* 2 vols. (Boston and New York: Houghton Mifflin and Company, The Riverside Press, 1895). "Letter from Maria Edgeworth to Mrs. Ruxton, September 5, 1798"; "Letter from Maria Edgeworth to Miss Sophy Ruxton, September 9, 1798 and September 19, 1798," vol. I. 58–64; "Letter from Maria Edgeworth to M. Pakenham Edgeworth, ESQ, February 19, 1834," vol. II. 549–51.

tion and the continued violence of agrarian secret societies ruptured this Anglo-Irish writer's convictions regarding the utility of fiction. Moreover, in noting agrarian agitation and violence in India, Edgeworth's letter suggests that resistance to colonial rule was not specific to Ireland at this time. [ED.]

To Mrs. Ruxton

Mrs. Fallon's Inn, Longford,
September 5, 1798.

We are all safe and well, my dearest aunt, and have had two most fortunate escapes from rebels and from the explosion of an ammunition cart. Yesterday we heard, about ten o'clock in the morning, that a large body of rebels, armed with pikes, were within a few miles of Edgeworthstown. My father's yeomanry were at this moment gone to Longford for their arms, which Government had delayed sending.[1] We were ordered to decamp, each with a small bundle; the two chaises full, and my mother and Aunt Charlotte on horseback. We were all ready to move, when the report was contradicted: only twenty or thirty men were now, it was said, in arms, and my father hoped we might still hold fast to our dear home.

Two officers and six dragoons happened at this moment to be on their way through Edgeworthstown, escorting an ammunition cart from Mullingar to Longford; they promised to take us under their protection, and the officer came up to the door to say he was ready. My father most fortunately detained us; they set out without us. Half an hour afterwards, as we were quietly sitting in the portico, we heard—as we thought close to us—a clap of thunder which shook the house. The officer soon afterwards returned, almost speechless; he could hardly explain what had happened. The ammunition cart, containing nearly three barrels of gunpowder, packed in tin cases, took fire and burst, halfway on the road to Longford. The man who drove the cart was blown to atoms—nothing of him could be found; two of the horses were killed, others were blown to pieces and their limbs scattered to a distance; the head and body of a man were found a hundred and twenty yards from the spot. Mr. Murray was the name of the officer I am speaking of: he had with him a Mr. Rochfort and a Mr. Nugent. Mr. Rochfort was thrown from his horse, one side of his face terribly burnt,

[1] Longford, some seven miles from Edgeworthstown, was an English garrison town at the time. [ED.]

and stuck over with gunpowder. He was carried into a cabin; they thought he would die, but they now say he will recover. The carriage has been sent to take him to Longford. I have not time or room, my dear aunt, to dilate or tell you half I have to say. If we had gone with this ammunition, we must have been killed.

An hour or two afterwards, however, we were obliged to fly from Edgeworthstown. The pikemen, three hundred in number, actually were within a mile of the town. My mother, Aunt Charlotte, and I rode; passed the trunk of the dead man, bloody limbs of horses, and two dead horses, by the help of men who pulled on our steeds: we are all safely lodged now in Mrs. Fallon's inn.

Mrs. Edgeworth narrates:—

Before we had reached the place where the cart had been blown up, Mr. Edgeworth suddenly recollected that he had left on the table in his study a list of the yeomanry corps, which he feared might endanger the poor fellows and their families if it fell into the hands of the rebels. He galloped back for it—it was at the hazard of his life—but the rebels had not yet appeared. He burned the paper, and rejoined us safely.

The landlady of the inn at Longford did all she could to make us comfortable, and we were squeezed into the already crowded house. Mrs. Billamore, our excellent housekeeper, we had left behind for the return of the carriage which had taken Mr. Rochfort to Longford; but it was detained, and she did not reach us till the next morning, when we learned from her that the rebels had not come up to the house. They had halted at the gate, but were prevented from entering by a man whom she did not remember to have ever seen; but he was grateful to her for having lent money to his wife when she was in great distress, and we now, at our utmost need, owed our safety and that of the house to his gratitude. We were surprised to find that this was thought by some to be a suspicious circumstance, and that it showed Mr. Edgeworth to be a favorer of the rebels! An express arrived at night to say the French were close to Longford: Mr. Edgeworth undertook to defend the jail, which commanded the road by which the enemy must pass, where they could be detained till the King's troops came up. He was supplied with men and ammunition, and watched all night; but in the morning news came that the French had turned in a different direction, and gone to Granard, about seven miles off; but this seemed so unlikely, that Mr. Edgeworth rode out to reconnoitre, and Henry went to the top of the Court House to look out with a telescope. We were all at the windows of a room in the inn looking into the street, when we saw people running, throwing up their hats and huzzaing. A dragoon had just arrived with the news that General Lake's army had come up with the French and the rebels, and completely defeated them at a place called Ballinamuck, near Granard.[2] But we soon saw a man in a sergeant's uniform haranguing the mob, not in honor of General Lake's victory, but against Mr. Edgeworth; we distinctly heard the words, "that young Edgeworth ought to be dragged down from the Court House." The landlady was terrified; she said Mr. Edgeworth was accused of having made signals to the French from the jail, and she thought the mob would pull down her house; but they ran on to the end of the town, where they expected to meet Mr. Edgeworth. We sent a messenger in one direction to warn him, while Maria and I drove to meet him on the other road. We heard that he had passed some time before with Major Eustace; the mob seeing an officer in uniform with him went back to the town, and on our return we found them safe at the inn. We saw the French prisoners brought in in the evening, when Mr. Edgeworth went after dinner with Major Eustace to the barrack. Some time after, dreadful yells were heard in the street: the mob had attacked them on their return from the barrack—Major Eustace being now in colored clothes, they did not recognize him as an officer. They had struck Mr. Edgeworth with a brickbat in the neck, and as they were now, just in front of the inn, collaring the major, Mr. Edgeworth cried out in a loud voice, "Major Eustace is in danger." Several officers who were at dinner in the inn, hearing the words through the open window, rushed out sword in hand, dispersed the crowd in a moment, and all the danger was over. The military patrolled the streets, and the sergeant who had made all this disturbance was put under arrest. He was a poor, half-crazed fanatic.

The next day, the 9th of September, we returned home, where everything was exactly as we had left it, all serene and happy, five days before—only five days, which seemed almost a lifetime, from the dangers and anxiety we had gone through.

Maria To Miss Sophy Ruxton

Edgeworthstown,
September 9, 1798.

You will rejoice, I am sure, my dear Sophy, to see by the date of this letter that we are safe back at Edgeworthstown. The scenes we have gone through for some days past have succeeded one another like the pictures in

---

[2]Gerald Lake (1744–1808), general and commander of the British forces in Ulster during 1797, led the campaign in Wexford and at Ballinamuck in 1798 where he ordered subordinate commanders to take no prisoners. [Ed.]

a magic-lantern, and have scarcely left the impression of reality upon the mind. It all seems like a dream, a mixture of the ridiculous and the horrid. "Oh ho!" says my aunt, "things cannot be very bad with my brother, if Maria begins her letters with magic-lantern and reflections on dreams."

When we got into the town this morning we saw the picture of a deserted, or rather a shattered village—many joyful faces greeted us at the doors of the houses—none of the windows of the new houses in Charlotte Row were broken: the mob declared they would not meddle with them because they were built by the two good ladies, meaning my aunts.

Last night my father was alarmed at finding that both Samuel and John,* who had stood by him with the utmost fidelity through the Longford business, were at length panic-struck; they wished now to leave him. Samuel said: "Sir, I would stay with you to the last gasp, if you were not so foolhardy," and here he cried bitterly; "but, sir, indeed you have not heard all I have heard. I have heard about two hundred men in Longford swear they would have your life." All the town were during the whole of last night under a similar panic, they were certain the violent Longford yeomen would come and cut them to pieces. Last night was not pleasant, but this morning was pleasant—and why it was a pleasant morning I will tell you in my next.

September 19.

I forgot to tell you of a remarkable event in the history of our return; all the cats, even those who properly belong to the stable, and who had never been admitted to the honors of the sitting in the kitchen, all crowded round Kitty with congratulatory faces, crawling up her gown, insisting upon caressing and being caressed when she reappeared in the lower regions. Mr. Gilpin's slander against cats as selfish, unfeeling animals is thus refuted by stubborn facts.[1]

When Colonel Handfield told the whole story of the Longford mob to Lord Cornwallis, he said he never saw a man so much astonished.[2] Lord Longford, Mr. Pakenham, and Major Edward Pakenham have shown much warmth of friendship upon this occasion.

Inclosed I send you a little sketch, which I traced from one my mother drew for her father, of the situation of the field of battle at Ballinamuck. It

* John Jenkins, a Welsh lad; both he and Samuel thought better of it and remained in the service. [Original editor's note.]

---

[1] Possibly William Cowper, author of the very popular "The Diverting History of John Gilpin," who also wrote about cats, including "The Retired Cat" (1791).

[2] Charles Cornwallis (1738–1805), appointed lord lieutenant and commander in chief of Ireland in June 1798 in order to effect a military response to insurrection. Led the British forces that surrounded General Humbert's French forces and Irish rebels at Ballinamuck. [ED.]

is about four miles from The Hills. My father, mother, and I rode to look at the camp; perhaps you recollect a pretty turn in the road, where there is a little stream with a three-arched bridge: in the fields which rise in a gentle slope, on the right-hand side of this stream, about sixty bell tents were pitched, the arms all ranged on the grass; before the tents, poles with little streamers flying here and there; groups of men leading their horses to water, others filling kettles and back pots, some cooking under the hedges; the various uniforms looked pretty; Highlanders gathering blackberries. My father took us to the tent of Lord Henry Seymour, who is an old friend of his; he breakfasted here to-day, and his plain English civility, and quiet good sense, was a fine contrast to the mob, etc. Dapple,* your old acquaintance, did not like all the sights at the camp as well as I did.

Maria To M. Pakenham Edgeworth, ESQ

Edgeworthstown, February 19, 1834.

Molly and Hetty, and Crofton and child, are all flourishing; poor old George is declining as gently and comfortably as can be. When we go to see him, his eyes light up and his mouth crinkles into smiles, and he, as well as Molly, never fails to ask for Master Pakenham. Though "Helen" cannot reach you for a year, Fanny has desired Bentley to send you a copy before it is published.[1] I should tell you beforehand that there is no humor in it, and no Irish character. It is impossible to draw Ireland as she now is in a book of fiction—realities are too strong, party passions too violent to bear to see, or care to look at their faces in the looking-glass. The people would only break the glass, and curse the fool who held the mirror up to nature—distorted nature, in a fever. We are in too perilous a case to laugh, humor would be out of season, worse than bad taste. Whenever the danger is past, as the man in the sonnet says,—

> "We may look back on the hardest part and laugh."[2]

Then I shall be ready to join in the laugh. Sir Walter Scott once said to me, "Do explain to the public why Pat, who gets forward so well in other countries, is so miserable in his own." A very difficult question: I fear above my power. But I shall think of it continually, and listen, and look, and read.

Thank you, my dear brother, for your excellent and to me particularly interesting last letter, in which you copied for me the good observations on the state of your part of India, and the collection of the revenue, rents, etc.

* Maria Edgeworth's horse. [Original editor's note.]

---

[1] Maria Edgeworth's final novel, published in 1834. [Ed.]

[2] R. Roderick, "A SONNET. Imitated from the Spanish of Lopez de Vega" (1763), l. 8. [Ed.]

[3] Shakespeare, *Julius Caesar* IV. iii. 74–75. [Ed.]

Many of the observations on India apply to Ireland; similarity of certain general causes operating on human nature even in countries most different and with many other circumstances dissimilar, produce a remarkable resemblance in human character and conduct. I admire your generous indignation against oppression and wringing by "any indirection from the poor peasant his vile trash."[3] Some of the disputes that you have to settle at Cucherry, and some of the viewings that you record of boundaries, etc., about which there are quarrels, put me in mind of what I am called upon to do here continually in a little way.

ANNO TRICESIMO NONO & QUADRAGESIMO

GEORGII III. REGIS.

****

CAP. LXVII

An Act for the Union of *Great Britain* and *Ireland*.
[2d *July* 1800.][1]
Preamble

WHEREAS in pursuance of His Majesty's most gracious Recommendation Preamble to the Two Houses of Parliament in *Great Britain* and *Ireland* respectively, to consider of such Measures as might best tend to strengthen and consolidate the Connection between the Two Kingdoms, the Two Houses of the Parliament of *Great Britain* and the Two Houses of the Parliament of *Ireland* have severally agreed and resolved, that, in order to promote and secure the essential Interests of *Great Britain* and *Ireland*, and to consolidate the Strength, Power, and Resources of the *British* Empire, it will be adviseable to concur in such Measures as may best tend to unite the Two Kingdoms of *Great Britain* and *Ireland* into One Kingdom, in such Manner, and on such Terms and Conditions, as may be established by the Acts of the respective Parliaments of *Great Britain* and *Ireland*:

From Great Britain, Anno Tricesimo Nono & Quadragesimo Georgii III. Regis. CAP. LXVII. An Act for the Union of Great Britain and Ireland—(2d July 1800). London: Printed by George Eyre and Andrew Strahan, printers to the King, [etc.] 1800. 529–60, 529–30.

[1] Although passed on July 2, 1800, the Union came into effect on January 1, 1801. [Ed.]

THE

STRANGER IN IRELAND;

OR,

A TOUR

IN

THE SOUTHERN AND WESTERN

PARTS OF THAT COUNTRY,

IN THE YEAR

1805.

BY JOHN CARR, ESQ.

OF THE HONOURABLE SOCIETY OF THE MIDDLE TEMPLE.

Author of a Northern Summer, or Travels round the Baltic;

the Stranger in France,

&c. &c.

——"Animae, quales neque candidiores

"Terra tulit, neque queis me sit devinctior alter.—Hor. Lib. 1. Sat. 5.

LONDON:

PRINTED FOR RICHARD PHILLIPS, NO 6, BRIDGE-STREET,

BLACKFRIARS.

By T. Gillet, Wild-court, Lincoln's-Inn-Fields.

1806.

THE STRANGER IN IRELAND

Sir John Carr

John Carr (1772–1832), a lawyer and member of the Middle Temple, was a professional travel writer whose opinions on Ireland Edgeworth and Owenson found formulaic and offensive. His work, however, proved a significant purveyor of ideas about Ireland to a British audience, and his rewards included a knighthood conferred by the Duke of Bedford in Dublin (1806). Sydney Owenson's publisher, Richard Phillips, included Carr's *The Stranger in Ireland* (1806) among a list of possible literary models that she might consider when composing *The Wild Irish Girl* (see Connolly, Note on the Text lviii). Owenson, however, would quickly reject Carr's work, and her subsequent travelogue, *Patriotic Sketches,* could be read as her corrective to Carr's more general portrait of life in Ireland under the Union. Similarly, Marie Edgeworth and her father published an anonymous review of Carr's *Stranger in Ireland* in the *Edinburgh Review* (April 10, 1807, 40–60), where they satirically disparage his research, critique his prose, and complain as to the price of his book. That said, Carr's travelogue appeared almost contemporaneous with Owenson's *The Wild Irish Girl,* and in contrast with de la Tocnaye's *Promenade,* Carr depicts post–Act of Union Ireland. The excerpt included here, "Character of Low Irish" suggests, much like Owenson, a positive cast to the Irish national character, but it is rendered in stereotypical terms. [Ed.]

From John Carr, *The Stranger in Ireland; or, a Tour in the Southern and Western Parts of That Country, in the Year 1805*. Introd. by Louis M. Cullen. Shannon, Ireland: Irish University Press, 1970. Excerpt from Chapter XI, "Character of Low Irish," 246–53.

CHAP. XI

Character of Low Irish

I HAVE in the course of this tour mentioned some circumstances to illustrate the character of the low Irish; and a little closer view of it may not be unpleasant.

In this class of society, a stranger will see a perfect picture of nature. Pat stands before him, thanks to those who ought long since to have cherished and instructed him, as it were "in mudder's (mother's) nakedness." His wit and warmth of heart are his own, his errors and their consequences, will not be registered against *him.* I speak of him in a quiescent state, and not when suffering and ignorance led him into scenes of tumult, which inflamed his mind and blood to deeds that are foreign to his nature. We know that the best when corrupted become the worst, and that the vulgar mind when overheated will rush headlong into the most brutal excesses, more especially if in pursuing a summary remedy for a real or supposed wrong, it has the example of occasional cruelty and oppression presented by those against whom it advances.

The lower Irish are remarkable for their ingenuity and docility, and a quick conception; in these properties they are equalled only by the Russians. It is curious to see with what scanty materials they will work; they build their own cabins, and make bridles, stirrups, cruppers, and ropes for every rustic purpose, of hay; and British adjutants allow that an Irish recruit is sooner made a soldier of than an English one.

That the Irish are not naturally lazy, is evident from the quantity of laborious work which they will perform, when they have much to do, which is not frequently the case in their own country, and are adequately paid for it, so as to enable them to get proper food to support severe toil. Upon this principle, in England, an Irish labourer is always preferred. It has been asserted by Dr. Campbell, who wrote in 1777,[1] that the Irish recruits were in general short, owing to the poverty of their food; if this assertion were correct, and few tourists appear to have been more accurate, they are much altered since that gentleman wrote; for most of the Irish militia regiments which I saw exhibited very fine-looking men, frequently exceeding the ordinary stature; and at the same time, I must confess, I do not see how meagre diet is likely to curtail the height of a man. Perhaps the Doctor might have seen some mountaineer recruits, and mountaineers are generally less in all regions, according to the old adage—

"The higher the hill, the shorter the grass."

---

[1] See *WIG* 166 [ED.]

If I was gratified by contemplating the militia of Ireland, I could not fail of deriving the greatest satisfaction from seeing those distinguished heroes, the Volunteers of Ireland: this army of patriots, composed of catholics as well as protestants, amounts to about eighty thousand men; when their country was in danger, they left their families, their homes, and their occupations, and placed themselves in martial array against the invader and the disturber of her repose: they fought, bled, and conquered; and their names will be enrolled in the grateful page of history, as the saviours of their native land.

What they have done, their brethren in arms on this side of the water are prepared and anxious to perform; and whenever the opportunity occurs, will cover themselves with equal glory.

The handsomest peasants in Ireland are the natives of Kilkenny and the neighbourhood, and the most wretched and squalid near Cork and Waterford, and in Munster and Connaught. In the county of Roscommon the male and female peasantry and horses are handsome; the former are fair and tall, and possess great flexibility of muscle: the men are the best leapers in Ireland: the finest hunters and most expert huntsmen are to be found in the fine sporting county of Fermanagh. In the county of Meath the peasants are very heavily limbed. In the county of Kerry, and along the western shore, the peasants very much resemble the Spaniards in expression of countenance, and colour of hair.

The lower orders will occasionally lie, and so will the lower orders of any other country, unless they are instructed better; and so should we all, had we not been corrected in our childhood for doing it. It has been asserted, that the low Irish are addicted to pilfering; I met with no instance of it personally. An intelligent friend of mine, one of the largest linen-manufacturers in the north of Ireland, in whose house there is seldom less than twelve or fifteen hundred pounds *in cash,* surrounded with two or three hundred poor peasants, retires at night to his bed without bolting a door, or fastening a window. During Lady Cathcart's imprisonment[2] in her own house in Ireland, for twenty years, by the orders of her husband, an affair which made a great noise some years since, her Ladyship wished to remove some remarkably fine and valuable diamonds, which she had concealed from her husband, out of the house, but having no friend or servant whom she could trust, she spoke to a miserable beggar-woman who used to come to the house, from the window of the room in which she was confined. The woman promised to take care of the jewels, and Lady Cathcart accordingly threw the parcel containing them to her out of the window; the poor mendicant conveyed them to the person to whom they were addressed;

---

[2]For Lady Cathcart, see *CR* 43, ED.'s n. [ED.]

and when Lady Cathcart recovered her liberty some years afterwards, her diamonds were safely restored to her. I was well informed, that a disposition to inebriation amongst the peasantry had rather subsided, and had principally confined itself to Dublin.

The instruction of the common people is in the lowest state of degradation. In the summer a wretched uncharactered itinerant derives a scanty and precarious existence by wandering from parish to parish, and opening a school in some ditch covered with heath and furze, to which the inhabitants send their children to be instructed by the miserable breadless being, who is nearly as ignorant as themselves; and in the winter these pedagogue pedlars go from door to door offering their services, and pick up just sufficient to prevent themselves from perishing by famine. What proportion of morals and learning can flow from such a source into the mind of the ragged young pupil, can easily be imagined, but cannot be reflected upon without serious concern. A gentleman of undoubted veracity stated, not long since, before the Dublin Association for distributing Bibles and Testaments amongst the poor, that whole parishes were without a Bible.[3]

With an uncommon intellect, more *exercised than cultivated,* the peasantry have been kept in a state of degradation, which is too well known, and which will be touched upon in a future part of this sketch.

Their native urbanity to each other is very pleasing; I have frequently seen two boors take off their hats and salute each other with great civility. The expressions of these fellows upon meeting one another, are full of cordiality. One of them in Dublin met a camrogue, in plain English, a boy after his own heart, who, in the sincerity of his soul, exclaimed, "Paddy! myself's glad to see you, for in troth I wish you well." "By my shoul, I knows it well," said the other, "but you have but the half of it;" that is, the pleasure is divided. If you ask a common fellow in the streets of Dublin which is the way to a place, he will take off his hat, and if he does not know it, he will take care not to tell you so (for nothing is more painful to an Irishman than to be thought ignorant); he will either direct you by an appeal to his imagination, which is ever ready, or he will say, "I shall find it out for your honour immediately;" and away he flies into some shop for information, which he is happy to be the bearer of, without any hope of reward.

Their hospitality when their circumstances are not too wretched to display it, is remarkably great. The neighbour or the stranger finds every man's door open, and to walk in without ceremony at meal-time, and to partake of his bowl of potatoes, is always sure to give pleasure to every one of the house, and the pig is turned out to make room for the gentleman. If the

---

[3] The Hibernian Bible Society was founded on Nov. 10, 1806. [ED.]

visitor can relate a lively tale, or play upon any instrument, all the family is in smiles, and the young will begin a merry dance, whilst the old will smoke after one another out of the same pipe, and entertain each other with stories. A gentleman of an erratic turn was pointed out to me, who with his flute in his hand, a clean pair of stockings and a shirt in his pocket, wandered through the country every summer; wherever he stopped the face of a stranger made him welcome, and the sight of his instrument doubly so; the best seat, if they had any, the best potatoes and new milk, were allotted for his dinner; and clean straw, and sometimes a pair of sheets, formed his bed; which, although frequently not a bed of roses, was always rendered welcome by fatigue, and the peculiar bias of his mind.

PATRIOTIC SKETCHES OF IRELAND

Sydney Owenson

Published just one year after *The Wild Irish Girl,* Owenson's *Patriotic Sketches of Ireland, Written in Connaught* (1807) describes important topographical and geographical features of Ireland and comments incisively on Irish society. Much of the material for the collection was gathered during the time Owenson spent with the Crofton family, relations of her father in Co. Sligo, while she was writing the novel. On the other hand, the collection may owe its existence to a postscript underlining the ready market for commentaries on the state of Ireland that Owenson's publisher, Richard Phillips, forwarded in a letter dated October 1805 (Connolly, Note on the Text lxiv). Sociological in nature, this travel book mirrors her novel's range of historical, intellectual, and political issues. Moreover, it presents a detailed picture of the immediate post-Union decade, and the difference with the excerpt from Carr's *Stranger in Ireland* is readily apparent. There are two sketches included here. "Sketch V" contradicts most contemporary English commentators that look at the Irish as racially and/or religiously inferior, and suggests that the national decline has more to do with poverty and discontent. "Sketch IX" argues that Ireland was ill-prepared for the ravages of empire given its penchant for arts, letters, and music, and Owenson compares the Irish to the Greeks who were defeated by Rome. In addition, Owenson offers a subtle defense for the "threshers"—an agrarian secret society associated with the Sligo region—that distinguishes between their economic motivations and the accepted view of the organization as politically motivated nationalist rebels. [Ed.]

SKETCH V

IT is observed by Zimmerman, that "in the unvaried stillness and stagnation of small remote places, lie buried an acrimony and rancour of the pas-

From Sydney Owenson, *Patriotic Sketches of Ireland Written in Connaught. By Miss Owenson. . . .* Baltimore: Printed for G. Dobbin and Murray [etc.], 1809. 2 v. in 1. "Sketch V." 48–60. "Sketch IX," 79–104. [The copy used belongs to Boston College's John J. Burns Library. Ed.]

sions, rarely found in great cities."[1] That mind indeed must be endued with great native strength, over which a certain peculiarity of situation holds no influence; which can breathe the spirit of liberty beneath the lash of despotism, be true to nature where art only reigns, and in a range of action limited within a narrow circle, disdain to graduate its sentiments and opinions on a scale proportionably contracted.

From the general order of things, the lesser towns of every country must still be as centres, to which the radii of illiberality and cabal point with the greatest force; and Ireland perhaps, beyond any other country in Europe, furnishes the strongest testimony to the truth of the assertion. That destructive spirit of intolerance in religion, and of faction in politics, which has so long and fatally diffused its noxious influence over the whole kingdom and which we hope is now happily fading away in its leading cities, may still be found flourishing in all its pristine vigour, in the hearts of those little towns and great villages, where both are still nurtured by the local intimacy and opinionative distance of those who perhaps agree in fundamentals, and differ only in points merely speculative; where, on one side, opposition is fed by the jealousy of conscious degradation, and on the other, by the pride of conscious prerogative: where each, solely bent on the support of its respective tenets, allows no modification in political principle or religious opinion; where all must be considered as the extreme of orthodox zeal or heterodox error, as the coarse caricature of loyalty or wild outline of rebellion; and where the respective prejudices of each party, tear away in their vortex every unbiassed sentiment of public good, every generous principle of patriotic feeling, and sacrifice at the shrine of religious and political intolerance, the peace, the welfare, and the prosperity, of a nation.*

To minds which slavery has not broken, nor oppression debased, the consciousness of political inferiority and national inconsequence must ever bring with it a sensitive pride, a tenacious reserve, a suspicious timidity, and an irritability of spirit, which are only to be dissipated by the conciliating advances of that superior influence under which a series of certain events has placed them: and when two distinct parties are internally divided by a difference in religious faith, by an inequality of political establishment, and externally coalesced by local circumstances and certain ties of denization common to both; where prerogative rests on one side, and

*"The two factions of protestant and catholic, more intent on thwarting each other, than in maintaining their mutual rights, became an easy prey," &c. *Macaulay's History of England,* vol. ii. p. 177. [Owenson's note.]

---

[1] Johann Georg Zimmerman, *On Solitude: Or the Effects of Occasional Retirement* (originally written in German, translated into French and then English. London, 1791). [Ed.]

submission on the other; the natural suspicions, the cautious vigilant diffidence of the subordinate party, are only to be seduced into amity, or warmed into confidence, by the open, ingenuous, volunteering liberality of the supreme power.*

But in that dominant sect which by adopting a rational scepticism to antiquated error, may be naturally supposed to possess the tolerance towards others which it has claimed for itself, dwells there that mild, that generous, and all-conciliating spirit of charity, which, like the bow of heaven's promise, flings the encircling arch of its mercy round the whole earth, and receives within the great compass of its indulgence every sect and every persuasion? Dwells there among those who vaunt their own abhorrence of fanaticism and bigotry, that pure and sole religion which, in considering the great and only Object of the universal worship of mankind, neither derides nor reviles the medium through which it flows? Does it indiscriminately betray that open smiling confidence which unnerves the hand of vengeance, inspires affection, and turns the gall of hatred to the "milk of human kindness?"[2] Does it feel for the political subjection of a compatriot, but not established sect; endeavour to counteract the effects of an erroneous and fatal policy, by opposing the endeared rites of social conciliation to the chilling

* "Sure I am says Edmund Burke, that there have been thousands in Ireland who have never conversed with a Roman catholic in their whole lives, unless they happened to talk with their gardener's workman, or to ask their way when they had lost it in their sports, or at best who had only associated with ex-footmen or other domestics of the third or fourth order; and so averse were they some time ago to have them near their persons, that they would not employ even those who would never find their way beyond their stable. I well remember a great, and in many respects a good man, who advertised for a blacksmith, but at the same time added, 'he must be a protestant.' It is impossible that such a state of things, though natural goodness in many persons will undoubtedly make exceptions, must not produce alienation on the one side, and pride and insolence on the other."

It is to be hoped, and indeed to be believed, that the fatal spirit of prejudice thus strongly adverted to by Burke, is daily losing its influence; for myself though one among the many in my own country who have been educated in the most rigid adherence to the tenets of the church of England, I should, like the poor Maritornes of Cervantes, think myself endowed with very few "sketches and shadows of christianity," were I to confine virtue to sect; or make the speculative theory of opinion the test of moral excellence, or proof of human perfection. [Owenson's note. The quotation is from Edmund Burke's *A Letter to Sir Hercules Langrishe. . . , 3 January, 1792* (London, 1792); Miguel de Cervantes (1547–1616), Spanish novelist, playwright, and poet, the author of *Don Quixote*. Ed.]

[2] Common eighteenth-century literary cliché. [Ed.]

influence of a penal code; of private intercourse to public distinction; and by endeavouring to produce that compatriot felicity, that national unanimity and brotherly love, over which a fanetical dogma, or an intolerant law, holds no jurisdiction? If these interrogations can be answered by an undeniable affirmative of actual demonstration, what has Ireland to fear? what has Ireland to wish? The unanimity of a nation, and the mutual confidence and confederation of her sons, are the firmest basis of her prosperity, and the strongest bulwark of her freedom.

The odium of bigotry is generally thrown upon the subordinate sect of every country. Bigotry, however, is in fact the cosmopolite of religion, and adheres with more or less influence to every mode of faith. Of the countless sects into which the christian church is divided,* it appears that each, "dark with excessive light,"[3] arrogates to itself an infallible spirit, which shuts the gates of mercy on the rest of mankind, while it condemns or opposes to the utmost stretch† of its ability, all whose faith is not measured by the standard of its own peculiar creed. All perhaps are alike zealots; the

*"Les Chrétiens, says Helvetius, qui donnaient avec justice le nom de barbarie et de crime anx cruautés qu' exerçaient sur eux les payens, ne donnèrent-ils pas le nom de zèle aux cruautés qu'ils exerçaient á leur tour sur ces mêmes payens?"—"Did not the Christians, who justly gave the epithets of *barbarity* and *crime* to the cruelties inflicted on them by the pagans, dignify with the name of *zeal* those cruelties which they retaliated in their turn?" [Owenson's note and translation. The reference is to Claude Adrien Helvétius (1715–71), French philosopher, famous for his work *De l' Esprit* (1758; "On the Mind") that attacked all forms of morality based on religion. Ed.]

†"Ja considerais cette diversité des sectes qui regnent sur la terre, et s'accusent mutuellement de mensonge et d'erreur; je demandais, quelle est la bonne? chacune me repondait, '*c'est la mienne;*' chacune me disait, '*moi seule,* et mes partisans pensent juste; tous les autres sont dans l'erreur.' Et comment savezvous que votre secte est la bonne? 'Parceque Dieu l'a dit. 'Et qui vous dit que Dieu l'a dit? 'Mon pasteur, qui le sait bien; mon pasteur me dit, et ainsi croire, *et ainsi je crois,*'—il m'assure que tous ceux qui disent autrement que lui *mentent,* et je ne les écoute pas."—*Emile,* it. 9 1. 4.—"While I surveyed this diversity of sects prevailing on the face of the earth, and accusing one another of error and falsehood, I inquired, 'Which is the right?' Each replied: 'It is ours: we alone possess the truth, and all others are in mistake.'—'And how do you know this?'—'Because God himself has declared it'—'Who told you so?'—'Our minister, who is well acquainted with the divine will: he has ordered us to believe this, and accordingly we do believe it.—He assures us that all who contradict him speak false, and therefore we do not listen to them." [Owenson's note and translation. The reference is to Jean Jacques Rousseau's *Émile, ou, De l'éducation* (1762; *Emile: or, On Education*). Ed.]

---

[3]The reference is to Edmund Burke, *On the Sublime and Beautiful,* pt. 2, "Light." [Ed.]

difference is, that the zeal of some is their privilege, and of others their crime.* The Irish, nationally considered with respect to their prevailing religion, never were a bigoted people, though the vivacity of their imagination has sometimes devoted them to superstitious illusion. When christianity took the lead of druidism in Ireland, it was preserved and nurtured by the same mild principles of toleration, which suffered its admission; and though the druidical tenets flourished for two centuries after the arrival of the first christian missionary in the island, yet neither historic record, nor oral tradition, advances any detail of religious persecution adopted on either side. The tenets preached by the christian missionary, or the arguments opposed by the heathen controvertists, awakened no further interest in the public consideration, than a desire to embrace that mode of faith, which came home with most force to reason, and to truth. If the arguments held out were not always attended with conviction, the doubtful superiority was never decided at the sword's point; if the cross was sometimes unavailingly raised, the arm† which supported it was not protected from injury by the egis of toleration; nor were tortures invented, persecution enforced, or oppressions exercised, to obtain the abjuration of a long-cherished tenet, to prove the orthodoxy of a doctrinal point, or to establish the infallibility of a speculative theory.‡ As yet free from that fanatic spirit which strews the earth with human victims, and still "opposes man against the murderer man," the Irish would have rejected with horror and incredulity that prophecy, which should have foretold such a series of religious barbarities

* "Hélas! si l'homme est aveugle, ce qui fait son tourment, fera-t-il encore son crime?" *De Volney,* ch. iv. p. 24.—"Alas! if man is blind, shall this blindness, which constitutes his misery, be also imputed to him as a crime?" [Owenson's note and translation. The reference is to Constantin-François de Chasseboeuf, Comte de Volney (1757–1820), French philosopher and author of *Les Ruines, ou meditations sur les revolutions des empire* (1791; *The Ruins: or a Survey of the Revolutions of Empires*). Ed.]

† "Can that church be the church of Christ," says the tolerant bishop of Novogorad, "whose arm is red to the shoulder with human gore?" [Owenson's note. The reference to "Bishop of Novogorad" is likely to Feofan Prokopovich (1681–1736), Archbishop of Novgorad, who reformed the Russian Orthodox church and effected a political integration of church and state. Ed.]

‡ "César et Pompée," says Voltaire in his English Letters, "ne sont pas fait la guerre pour savoir si les *poulets sacrées* daivent *manger* et *boir,* ou bien manger seulement; ni pour savoir si les prêtres devaient sacrifier avec leur chemise sur leur habit, ou leur habit sur leur chemise. Non! ces horreurs étatient réservés pour *la réligion de la charité.*"—"Cesar and Pompey did not fight to determine whether the consecrated fowl ought to eat and drink, or to eat only; nor whether the priests should officiate with their surplice over their gown, or their gown over their surplice. No: these horrors were reserved for the religion of charity." [Owenson's note and translation. The reference is to Voltaire's *Letters Concerning the English Nation* (1733). Ed.]

as attended the expulsion of the Moors from Spain, the *conversion* of the Mexicans in America, the revocation of the edict of Nantz, and the establishment of the popery laws in their own country.

Surely the experience of successive ages should hold out some beacon to those minds, which the pernicious and illusory light of intolerance misleads; and evince the dreadful effects which have been invariably produced, by suffering an abstract opinion to prevail over the social affections of mankind, either in politics or in religion.*

The toleration of the Germans on religious points, is deservedly proverbial. The patron of Luther, and the first protestant potentate, was an elector of Saxony; and notwithstanding the present electoral family has for four generations back been Roman catholics, they continue to live in the most perfect harmony with their Protestant subjects.

Catherine of Russia dispersed among her Mahometan subjects eighty thousand copies of the Koran; while among her Christian subjects she circulated such works as were likely to establish them most firmly in their religion. Yet, during her long and prosperous reign, the voice of revolt or insurrection was never heard to murmur. But in what age, or in what country, has Toleration displayed her radiant banner, and found her standard deserted by peace, by happiness, and unanimity?

SKETCH IX

I AM at present residing in that part of Ireland where the association of thrashers first arose.[1] I am consequently surrounded by those who formed that association: a peasantry poor, laborious, vehement, and enterprising; capable of good or ill; in the extremes of both; left to the devious impulse of either; but oftener impelled by the hardest necessity to the latter, than allured to the former, by kindness, by precept, or reward.—Punished with rigorous severity when acting wrong, but neglected, unnoticed, and unrecompensed when acting right; forming the last link in the chain of human society, and treated with contempt because unable to resist oppression. It was with one of these beings, who in the strictest sense, daily performed

* The catholics of that part of Silesia conquered by Frederic the great, were so sensible of the toleration they enjoyed from the liberal conduct of their conqueror, that they have ever since remained faithful to the Prussians; while those of their compatriots, who had successfully resisted his victorious arms, have since submitted to the French influence. [Owenson's note.]

[1] Agrarian secret society largely associated with the Sligo region in the first decade of the nineteenth century. See Michael Beames, *Peasants and Power*, 59–64. [Ed.]

"the penalty of Adam,"[2] and nightly, perhaps, assumed the daring character of insurgency, that I had some days back the following conversation:

"Are you laying in your winter's fire?" "No young lady, I am cutting this turf for his honour."

"What is your hire by the day?"—"Sixpence one half, and threepence the other half of the year." *

"Have you a family?"—"I have a wife and six children."

"Then of course you must have some ground for their maintenance?"—"Oh! yes, two acres at £5 an acre; but what with the tythe proctor, the priest's dues being raised, and the weaver having doubled his prices, that day goes by well enough, when we can afford a drop of milk to moisten the potatoes for the young ones."[3]

He paused for a moment, cast his eyes to heaven, shook his head expressively, and then abruptly applied himself to his labour with an effort of overstrained exertion, that seemed to derive its energy from feelings that dewed his rough cheek with tears, flowing from the sad heart of the father and the husband.†

"If we do not go to the very origin and first ruling cause of a grievance,"—says Edmund Burke, "we do nothing:"[4] and if we resort to the light of truth and evidence of fact, it will be found that with respect to every national grievance or political disorder in Ireland, for nearly five

* I have been assured, however, that sixpence a day, throughout the year, is in general the averaged hire in most parts of Connaught. Many persons still living remember it so low as fourpence. [Owenson's note.]

† Since the above was written, a young peasant in Westmeath gave me the following account of his family, which I believe is an epitome of the general state of the peasantry in a county not 30 miles from the metropolis.—The boy was the eldest of seven children though scarcely twelve years old, and of course the only one able to labour; in the summer and harvest season he earned fourpence a day, his father worked for sixpence and eightpence a day through the year; they paid six pounds for an acre of oats, forty shillings a year for grass for their cow, and forty shillings for their cabin and a little ground for their potatoes; in winter when the cow was dry, they lived upon oaten bread, and potatoes and salt. Engaged with the care of seven children, the mother could give little assistance except by spinning sometimes: and out of the year's hire of the father, Sundays and holidays were deducted. [Owenson's note.]

---

[2] See *WIG* 111, n. 19. [Ed].

[3] Tithes, a tax levied on Catholics and dissenting Protestants for the support of the minority Anglican Church of Ireland, became increasingly controversial at the turn of the century, leading to the Tithe War during 1830–33. In addition, dues to the Catholic Church and increased agricultural prices resulted in greater demands on laborers' incomes. [Ed.]

[4] Unidentified. [Ed.]

hundred years back, a mode of conduct has been pursued, partial in its effects, unavailing in its influence, and nutritive to public evil by an apparent blindness to the pristine existence of that evil, and by the rigidly coercive measures exerted against its natural but fatal effects. Still careless and perhaps ignorant of the cause, still attentive only to the result, the rest of discontent has only invigorated, by the topping of its branches, and the pruning of its suckers.

The first settlement of the English colonists in the island took place at a moment peculiarly favorable to such an enterprize: the devotional enthusiasm with which the Irish had applied themselves to letters, to the arts of poesy and song, and all their elegant, but frequently enervating concomitants, left them but ill qualified to oppose an hostile and savage enemy; and sharing the inevitable destiny of all polished nations in a certain era of refinement, they sunk beneath the daring inroads of such barbarians as Greece has submitted to, and Rome was unable to oppose. To those who believe their fate has reached its climax of evil, every doubt wears the aspect of a hope, and every change the character of a benefit; and the arrival of a few English barons and their followers on the Irish coast, at a moment when the Irish spirit was harrassed by the ceaseless suffering of civil dissention, awaken a consolatory expectation, and gave to the politic strangers the air of protectors and the epithet of friends.

From that moment the mass of the Irish people became affectionate to the British government; and if the attestations of historians* are to be credited, if the native tone of the minds of the Irish was attentively studied, it will be found that though that affection may be forced, it can never be voluntarily or causelessly withdrawn from its object.

But the government which they, the Irish, loved, was still counteracted in every intention formed in their favour.—The claims which they made in the expecting confidence of their hearts, remained unrealized, because they were unheard:† for it was ever, as it is now, the singular destiny of Ireland to nourish within her own bosom her bitterest enemies, who with a species

* "I am well assured that the Irish desired to be admitted to the benefit of English law, not only in their petitions," &c.—Davis, p. 88.

It was a circumstance, however, not a little flattering to the Irish, that while the benefit of English laws was denied them, the English colonists adopted the ancient Irish system of legislation. [Owenson's note. The reference is to Sir John Davies, *A Discovery of the True Causes Why Ireland Was Never Entirely Subdued*... (1612). Ed.]

† "It is not," says the poet Saadi, "the timid voice of a minister which can breathe to the ears of his king the complaints of the unhappy; it is the cry of the people only that should ascend directly to the throne." [Owenson's note. The reference is likely to the Persian poet, Mosleh al-Din Saadi Shirazi (c. 1210–90), *Gulistan* (1259), "The Rose Garden," Chapter 1, Story 26. Ed.]

of political vampyrism, destroyed that source from whence their own nutriment flowed.—For still did they, who partially ruled over one country under the influence of the other, close every avenue to mutual and conciliating intelligence; and invariably endeavoured to effect a separation, from which *they* alone derived a benefit—a benefit, however, precarious and unstable, as it was selfish and unjust.

It was in vain that the Irish of other times, testified their anxiety to be admitted to the protection of the laws of England; it was in vain, even so early as the reign of Edward III, that they endeavoured to represent the good that would naturally accrue from denization. "For still," says Sir John Davis, "the great lords of Ireland informed the king that the Irish might not be naturalized without damage and prejudice to the crown, or themselves;" * and perhaps it is no unfounded assertion to advance, that the same disposition on the part of the Irish to the English government, and the same obstacle to its accomplishment on the part of their internal enemies, still exist with undiminished force.† Few countries ever suffered more from the ceaseless vicissitudes of civil dissention, than Ireland; and none ever preserved a more general uniformity of character, disposition, and principle, both as to its internal and relative situation, for ages back. The same grievances have furnished the same complaints, and the same causes invariably produced the same effects.—The Irish heart was ever, and is still, warmly alive to the least appearance of confidence and kindness. The Irish spirit has ever been and ever will be, prompt to resist, what it would be dishonour to endure.

It is a corroborating proof of the unvarying system of things in this country, that an assertion of the able minister of Elizabeth[5] relative to the antecedent and then existing state of Ireland, may be in some respects applied to its present circumstances, viz. "That certain great men of Ireland cross and withstand the enfranchisement of the Irish: whereunto he adds, I must acquit the crown of England of ill policy, and lay the fault upon the

* "All the statutes from Henry IV to Henry VII speak of English rebels, and Irish enemies, as if the Irish had never been in the condition of subjects, but always out of the law." [Owenson's note. The reference, both in the text and the note, is to Sir John Davies. Ed.]

† The genius of Palermo, kept in the senatorial palace, is represented as a man with a serpent on his breast, and this motto, *Alienos nutrit, se ipsum devorat;* a figure that might answer equally well for the personification of Ireland. [Owenson's note. The statue in question now resides at the "Palazzo dello Aquile," Palermo's municipal administration building. The full quotation with translation is as follows: *Panormus Conca aurea suos devorat, alios nutrit* ("Palermo the golden shell devours its own and feeds others"). Ed.]

[5] Reference to Sir Arthur Chichester (1563–1625), an English general in the nine-year war, lord deputy of Ireland (1605–16) during the plantation of Ulster. [Ed.]

pride, covetousness, and ill counsel, of the English planted here."*[6] The line of demarcation which distinguished the English-Irish from the native is now indeed smoothed away by the obliviating finger of time; but the sordid spirit and unpatriotic principles, which guided the views, and directed the actions of the naturalized foreigner, still survive in the breasts of some who have no other claim to the title of Irishmen, than that which the accident of nativity bestows; who, unaffectionate to their compatriots, and unendeared to their country, resolve every principle into self; and give to every local disturbance that terrific aspect of public danger, which extends the empire of individual influence, and strengthens the chain of general oppression.† This perhaps was never more strongly evinced than by those efforts made to misrepresent the recent rising of the thrashers; and to call and punish that as a rebellion, which an officer of the crown, even in the act of pleading against the association alluded to, declares "as not partaking of any political complexion, or confined to any particular party or persuasion;" and that "its professed object was to regulate the payments of the church-tythes, of certain dues paid to the clergymen of the catholic church, and the rates of manual and manufacturing labour."‡

It is indeed a fact incontrovertible and asserted by those employed on the part of the crown against the persons termed thrashers, that this association had its rise in that source which at various and distant periods has given birth to such numerous associations among the Irish peasantry: associations unknown perhaps in any other country in the world, and which, animated by the same principle, and sanctioned by the same plea of

*"When," says Burke, "the warfare of chicane succeeded to the war of arms and of hostility, statutes and a regular series of operation was carried on, particularly from Chichester's time, in the ordinary courts of justice; and by special commissions and inquisitions, first under pretence of tenures, and then of titles in the crown, for the purpose of the total extirpation of the interest of the natives in their own soil: until this species of subtle ravage, being carried to the last excess of oppression and insolence under lord Stafford kindled the flames of that rebellion which broke out in 1641." [Owenson's note. The quotation is from Edmund Burke's *A Letter to Sir Hercules Langrishe*..., 3 January, 1792 (London, 1792). Thomas Wentworth (1593–1641), first earl of Strafford, lord deputy of Ireland 1633–41. During the rebellion of 1641, native Irish and "Old English" Catholics joined forces in opposition to more recently settled populations, commonly referred to as the "New English." Ed.]

†It is perhaps necessary to mention, that this sketch was begun and finished at two different and distant periods. [Owenson's note.]

‡While the peasant of Ireland labours from sun-rise to sun-set, for sixpence a day, the working mechanic regulates his prices by his desires, and the extortion of three days enables him to be idle and inebriate the other four. [Owenson's note.]

[6] Sir John Davies, *A Discovery of the True Causes.* [Ed.]

grievance, have taken the various names of *white boys, hearts of steel, hearts of oak, break-of-day boys, right boys, defenders,* and *thrashers.*[7] Yet from the first whisper of insurrection, to its last murmur, the complaint of the people never breathed upon the government,* and their accusations were as local as the grievances which gave birth to them:—but every pecuniary exaction unjustly and exorbitantly levied on those whose hard-earned little "just gives what life requires, and gives no more,"[8] becomes an object of consideration; and while with willing cheerfulness they contribute to the maintenance of the ministers of one church, and from a principle of duty and affection voluntarily support that of another,† it is little to be wondered at, if that extortion which drives them to the very barrier of penury and want should sometimes impel them beyond that of prudence and subordination.‡

In the present instance they endeavour to palliate their conduct, by asserting, that to the usual exorbitant demands of the tythe* farmers, were added the increasing exactions of the middle-man, the impositions of the

*A few days back, I met with two peasants who were making complaints of the oppression they endured. A gentleman asked them if they thought they were worse off since the union. They replied, "they had never heard any thing about the union, and did not know what it meant." After some further questions, they were asked "if they did not know that there was now no Irish parliament. They replied, that all they had heard was, that the parliament-books were sent away, and that the good luck of the country went with them. So full is the heart of an Irish peasant of his own grievance, and so little is his head troubled about public affairs. [Owenson's note.]

†"It is no slight evil for a country sinking under the weight of taxes, to support a double hierarchy; and some share of the expence might perhaps, without injustice, be defrayed from the revenues of the present establishment, in parishes where every inhabitant is a catholic."—*Review of Sir J. Throgmorton on the Catholic Question.* [Owenson's note. The reference is to Sir John Throckmorton (1753–1819), *Considerations arising from the debates in Parliament on the petition of the Irish Catholics,* 8 vols. (London, 1806). Ed.]

‡Lands in Ireland are generally held on free-hold leases, which throws the burthen of tithes upon the tenant chiefly: the collection being also principally in kind, renders it of course more odious, and the alternative is become insupportable from the extortion of the tithe farmers.—*Ibid.* [Owenson's note.]

*The payment of tithes among the Jews formed a part of the foundation of their republic; but on their first introduction into Christendom, Charlemagne, who established them, found them opposed by the people; "who, says Montesquieu, are rarely influenced by example, to sacrifice their interests," and who considered them "as burthens quite independent of the other charges of the establishment." A synod of Frankfort had recourse to their superstition to ensure their obedience, by protesting, that in the last famine the spikes of corn were found to contain no seed, the infernal spirits having devoured it all; and that those spirits had been heard to reproach them with not having paid the tithes." Book xxxi. 339. [Owenson's note. Quotation from Montesquieu unidentified. Ed.]

---

[7] See Beames, *Peasants and Power.* [Ed.]

[8] See *WIG* 125, n. 38.

weaver, and the increased dues of the catholic clergy. These, they asserted, were exactions which sixpence a day was scarcely adequate to answer. These perhaps were the efficient causes which gave to the pitying eye of the traveller, roofless cabins, desponding contenances, squalid figures, and shuddering groups of literally naked children; these were perhaps the latent sources of those emotions in which the lower orders of this country have been so frequently involved, and the main spring of that coalition of imprudent and unfortunate persons called thrashers; who daringly seized in their own hands the power of summary retribution, proportioned and appropriate as they conceived to their real or fancied grievances, and according to the strict letter of their own old Brehon law.[9] That they did thus dare to seize the means of redress in their own hands, was a conduct that no one can justify; but that any other mode was left them, is a fact no one can establish.

The English country-gentleman, full of patriarchal kindness towards his tenantry, will ask, "Why did not these unfortunates apply for counsel and assistance to their land-lord, their paternal adviser and advocate?" But that tie, so firmly bound in days of feudal influence, and which still in a modified sense in most countries unites the extremes of civil society, the lord of the soil to the peasant who cultivates it, in Ireland is broken, or rather wholly dissolved: and the Irish peasant, while he venerates the name of the good old family under whom his forefathers worked, or for whom his forefathers bled, has now but the name only to revere; while his heart turns despondingly from the middle-man, beneath whose influence he lives; and who would scarcely ameliorate his grievances, while conscious that he was himself the cause of many, and the sanction of all.

It ever was, and is still, the conduct of a certain order of persons in Ireland, to shadow the light of government from the mass of the Irish people; to give to causes of local and domestic disturbance, the invidious term of open rebellion; and to drive by pitiless unkindness to acts of fatal desperation, a people who may be soothed into subjection, but who can never be harassed into a tame endurance of oppression; a people whose national character affords the noblest subject to philosophical observance, that human nature ever presented to the eye of reason and philanthropy.*

* "Nations are governed by the same methods, and on the same principles, by which an individual, without authority, is often able to govern those who are his equals or his superiors; by a knowledge of their temper, and by a judicious management of it."—*Thoughts on the Causes of the present Discontents,* &c. &c. *Burke.* [Owenson's note. The reference is to Edmund Burke's *Thoughts on the Causes of the Present Discontents* (1770). Ed.]

[9] See *WIG* 274. [Ed.]

When the thrashers first attracted notice in those counties where they first arose, it was not unusual to hear, even from those whose opinion carried most weight, that there was some ground for complaint among the Connaught peasantry; the nocturnal adventures of the insurgents were then deemed rather whimsical than mischievous; were sometimes listened to with indifference, or laughed at as ludicrous; but the natural consequences of all public commotions, however apparently unimportant in their tendency and trivial in their origin, from their too frequently experienced and fatal result, should have taught those in whose hands the reins of timely suppression were vested, the necessity of crushing the germ, if they had not the power of destroying its root. But if the invariable effects of a long-existing cause were foreseen, no exertion was made towards their early extinction: the thrashers indeed were instantly called a miserable, deluded and misguided people;—degrading epithets, to which, however Irish feelings have become almost callous. But among the many who thus designated their humbler compatriots, and reversing the maxim of Hamlet, taught them "to assume the vice they had not," [10] who was the benevolent the rational being, to step forth, to inquire into the cause of their discontent, to alleviate their sufferings, or dispel their delusion? Did the head landlord, did the middle-man, did the magistrate, collect around them their misguided countrymen, and with an apparent interest in their destiny, investigate the cause of their real, or probe the source of their fancied grievance, promising their best individual efforts to the removal of the one, or simply proving to their untutored understandings the fallacy and danger of the other? Oh, no! a vehement, an impetuous, a brave but misguided peasantry, careless of that life to which so few ties of human happiness attached them, unquestioned, unresisted, were suffered to accumulate in numbers, to strengthen in principle, to pursue that object which their sense of right upheld to them; and neither redressed in one instance, nor opposed in another, to establish the justice of their cause on the basis of their progressive success; and to become inebriate with that flow of fortune which stronger heads seldom resist, and stronger minds seldom contemplate in its probable and approximating reflux.*

As long as the vengeance of the thrashers was confined to the tythe-farmers, the middle-man smiled at a retribution so summarily used; but when its spreading effects threatened the most distant boundary of his own interest, he shrunk back upon himself with the same principle of

*The thrashers were suffered, for a considerable time, to pursue their depredations on the fields of the tythe-farmers, unmolested and almost unnoticed. [Owenson's note.]

[10] Shakespeare, *Hamlet* III. iv. 160: "Assume a virtue, if you have it not." [Ed.]

repercussion which actuates the tarantula when, retiring to the centre of her web, she darts with accumulated venom on the daring insect who flutters within the sphere of her enslaving dominion.

It then became usual, from the well or ill-founded reports of every informer, for a few skirmishing parties to set out in quest of the insurgents; frequently to escape from the hall of social enjoyment, or the banquet of festal revelry, and "hot with the Tuscan grape," to pursue amidst the doubtful shades of night "the idle visions of a heated brain;" or, perhaps less strictly Quixotorial, to fire at random on such fugitives as chance presented to their observation.

That an insurrection which at this period wore so alarming an aspect ought not to have been suppressed in the first era of its existence, or firmly and decisively opposed in its state of maturer being, is there a mind so weak or so inhuman as to assert? To that rational policy which is ever the "flail of faction," which is ever more solicitous to remove the grievance than to punish even the unjustifiable mode of redress imprudently seized on by the aggrieved, be it left to decide on the most efficacious mode to obviate the evil; but that the partial and summary coercion adopted by certain individuals, in the present instance, were neither correct in plan nor effective in execution, the result fully evinced.

It was indeed at last discovered, that though firing at an odd man of an odd night might have been a chivalrous feat, it was far from being either a decisive or a successful one. Every bullet had not the political sagacity to lodge itself in the fervid brain of an insurgent; the innocent had sometimes a chance of suffering with the guilty: and though they might "fill a pit as well as better men,"[11] yet that cause was not weakened, whose professed opposers became obnoxious to the neutral as well as to the active party; while the moan of private sorrow mingled with the murmurs of public discontent, and the pang of individual anguish exasperated the feelings of general disaffection.

But one mode now seemed left to destroy the hydra-monster of a hitherto unavailing vengeance; and unawed by the series of horrid events which, at no distant intervals, for the space of five hundred years have distracted and impoverished their country, a certain order of persons supplicated the governing power of their nation to erect once more the standard of civil discord, and to establish that law which every state reserves as its last resource against the unmasked appearance of open, daring, and avowed rebellion! But what was the result of this *patriotic* application? At the moment when it was eagerly hoped that nothing would be seen "but man

---

[11] Shakespeare, *Henry IV, Part I,* IV. ii. 66–67. [Ed.]

and steel, the soldier and the sword,"[12] the British government rushed between the mass of the people of Ireland and a few of her degenerate sons; and flinging the veil of her mercy over the errors of her imprudent but unalienated subjects, turned aside the poniard that aimed at the lifepulse of their hearts.

For ever honoured be the memory of that administration which gave to the unhappy, the deluded people of Ireland, the full benefit of that sacred justice coeval with truth and with the God of Truth; who, deaf to the interested application of the few, rescued the many from destruction; who mercifully refused to send back the visionary insurgent to his comfortless hut, to brood, in the midst of his helpless family, over that grievance as poignant in idea as in fact, and which neither redressed, nor contradicted, would rankle with added force in his disappointed heart; who saved the hard-earned pittance of the laborious peasant from the ravages of licensed insolence and the oppression of delegated power; who turned aside the musket that would have awed the oppressed master in that home, where (though but the shelter of a banana-tree from the rays of a vertical sun) even the slave feels himself a king; and who gave to the free-born subjects of the freest of all earthly states, the fair occasion to expose the cause by which they believed themselves agrieved, and to prove how far the effects were "to be extenuated," or had been "set down in malice!"* [13]

It was reserved for the representative of the illustrious house of Russel to be the agent of that divine mission, which had for its object the peace and welfare of a nation; and surely in that record where the gratitude of Ireland has traced in imperishable characters the names of her best friends, his will not be registered in an oblivious page.

* How firmly attached the Irish have ever been to the laws of England, and inimical to the slightest appearance of military subjection, is not only proved by Sir John Davis and his contemporaries, but strongly alluded to by Burke in his speech on the conciliation with America. "After," says he, "the vain project of military government attempted in the reign of Elizabeth, it was soon discovered that nothing could make Ireland English in civility and allegiance, but your laws and your form of legislature. It was not English arms, but the English constitution, that conquered Ireland." [Owenson's note. The reference is to Edmund Burke's *Speech on Conciliation with America* (1775, 1778). Ed.]

[12] Oliver Goldsmith, "The Traveler, or A Prospect of Society" (1765), ll. 169–70. [Ed.]

[13] Shakespeare, *Othello,* V. ii. 342–43. [Ed.]

Part Three

RECENT CRITICISM

Another Tale to Tell: Postcolonial Theory and the Case of *Castle Rackrent*

Mary Jean Corbett

Published in the year of the Act of Union, which ended Ireland's nominal independence from England by dissolving the Irish Parliament, *Castle Rackrent* (1800) has been read mainly as a regional tale, a novel of place. Said to inaugurate the Anglo-Irish novelistic tradition, it is likewise understood to be a comic work, an exemplar of the ironic mode in which Maria Edgeworth's narrator, Thady Quirk, is rather less knowing than he realizes about the full implications of the tale he tells. But it is also, in Suvendrini Perera's words, "the first significant English novel to speak in the voice of the colonized,"[1] and the conjunction among these classificatory categories—regional novel, ironic comedy, and colonial tale—is no mere coincidence: its Irish narrator and its Irish setting are what give *Castle Rackrent* an ironic bent. Situating her colonized Irish narrator and his reckless masters in a position of inferiority to the (so-called) mother country, Edgeworth represents the strangeness of the geographical other to her metropolitan reader; in the gap between "us" and "them" lies the ironic humor of the novel.

Given the colonial politics of this comedy, however, to be moved only to laughter by *Castle Rackrent* means to overlook the novel's implication in systems of colonial control, and so to reproduce the very structure of dominance and subordination the novel replays. For *Castle Rackrent*'s irony depends on how it establishes our readerly distance from the narrator: Thady Quirk and his masters are laughable only to the extent that we persist in seeing them as beneath or below us. And this ironic distance is not only a

Criticism, Summer 1994, Vol. XXXVI, No. 3, pp. 383–400.

[1] Suvendrini Perera, *Reaches of Empire: The English Novel from Edgeworth to Dickens* (New York: Columbia University Press, 1991), 15.

literary device, but also a political one, which works to construct and secure the superiority of the domestic English reader over the Irish subject.

If Edgeworth's irony is complicit with a colonial strategy, so, too, does the novel's generic status as a regional tale occlude a colonialist mentality within the very categories of literary history. As Perera points out in her study of imperialism and colonialism in the nineteenth-century English tradition, "the diverse fictional genres" of the period "are preeminently interested in *place*"; specific sites within the emerging British empire "become the locus of particular moral and cultural values" (35), usually represented as opposed to and inferior to English ones. As Edward Said and Patrick Brantlinger have also effectively demonstrated, British imperialist projects in non-European places—Asia, Africa, the Caribbean—became sites for imaginative conquest as well as economic exploitation, so much so that the two often worked hand in hand, all the while working to consolidate a native English identity.[2] Critics have not generally recognized, however, that the English performed similar operations in arenas even closer to home, within the very geographical borders of Great Britain: the Irish locale of *Castle Rackrent*, like the wild, romantic Scotland of Scott's novels, is every bit as available as the more far-flung outposts of empire for imaginative and imperial appropriation in the nineteenth century. As a regional tale, then, *Castle Rackrent* produces a vision of Irish comic disorder for properly English readers, while its generic status both incorporates it within and makes it peripheral to the English novelistic tradition.

Postcolonial theory here figures as a means of re-viewing the colonial relations within this novel and its contexts; in briefly showing, for example, how a seemingly neutral generic category such as "the regional tale" confirms the "Englishness" of a particular literary tradition, I aim to indicate how postcolonial thinking challenges the critical categories that have seemed so natural to many of us.[3] My intention is not to displace the

---

[2]Edward W. Said, *Orientalism* (New York: Vintage Books, 1979); Patrick Brantlinger, *Rule of Darkness: British Literature and Imperialism 1830–1914* (Ithaca: Cornell University Press, 1988).

[3]The theoretical and critical sources for my thinking are various, but include Bill Ashcroft, Gareth Griffiths, and Helen Tiffin, *The Empire Writes Back: Theory and Practice in Post-Colonial Literatures* (London: Routledge, 1989); Homi K. Bhabha, "Of Mimicry and Man: The Ambivalence of Colonial Discourse," *October* 28 (Spring 1984): 125–33, and "Signs Taken for Wonders: Questions of Ambivalence and Authority under a Tree Outside Delhi, May 1817," *Critical Inquiry* 12 (Autumn 1985): 144–65; Abdul R. JanMohamed, "The Economy of Manichean Allegory: The Function of Racial Difference in Colonialist Literature," *Critical Inquiry* 12 (Autumn 1985): 59–87; Ania Loomba, "Overworlding the 'Third World,'" *Oxford Literary Review* 13:1–2 (1991): 164–91; and Benita Parry, "Problems in Current Theories of Colonial Discourse," *Oxford Literary Review* 9 (1987): 27–58.

recent focus on non-European literatures and so to reinscribe the hegemonic force of the British literary tradition; rather, I hope to decenter that tradition from within by appropriating postcolonial tools to recover the heterogeneity that has been suppressed within British studies itself. The central concerns of postcolonial theorists—the creation of otherness as a material tool of domination, the place of language as a means of both oppression and opposition, the deployment of racial stereotyping in securing the subordinate status of the colonized, to mention but a few—have clear applications to analyses of literary and cultural production in Ireland past and present, and as such are the primary concerns of this essay.

The "particular moral and cultural values" associated with Ireland most often appear as negative ones, but they are certainly productive in the English context; it is the comic distance between English and Irish, relatively unmediated by their geographical closeness, that Edgeworth exploits in *Castle Rackrent.* Investigating the construction of that distance within the novel, and in Edgeworth's biography, I focus here on linguistic, cultural, and gender differences and their relation to extant structures of colonial power and authority. Not a reading of the novel as such, this essay aims to demonstrate how a postcolonial perspective might defamiliarize the familiar, and so to explore the relations between a colonizing literature and its colonized subjects.

1

The Preface to *Castle Rackrent,* undertaken by Edgeworth's editorial persona in the familiar eighteenth-century way, begins by articulating some differences between historical and biographical writing, incidentally revealing what Elizabeth Kowaleski-Wallace has called "a voice of a particular class in the making."[4] Defending "the prevailing taste of the public for anecdote" (27)[5] against the censure and ridicule of the critical establishment, the Preface argues for the value of biography by pointing out the shortcomings of historical writing. One problem with such discourse is its devotion to a particular style: "the heroes of history," the editor claims, "are so decked out by the fine fancy of the professed historian; they talk in such measured prose, and act from such sublime or such diabolical motives, that few have sufficient taste, wickedness or heroism, to sympathize in their fate" (27). "The heroes of history," as created by historians, are

---

[4]Elizabeth Kowaleski-Wallace, *Their Fathers' Daughters: Hannah More, Maria Edgeworth, and Patriarchal Complicity* (New York: Oxford University Press, 1991), 140.

[5]All parenthetical references to *Castle Rackent* are to this New Riverside Edition.

either so far above or so far below us in moral terms as to be beyond ordinary sympathies; "decked out" as they are, dressed in the language of high life and having life only in that very public sphere, their social and linguistic differences from the readers the editor addresses, presumably middling sort of folk, make them inaccessible and unreal to such readers. Like the sphere in which those heroes move, the language by which historians represent them obscures their "true" characters.

The editor prefers "a plain unvarnished tale" of the kind Thady Quirk will offer over "the most highly ornamented narrative" (28), and this preference has a particular class valence to it, for like her contemporaries, Wollstonecraft and Wordsworth, Edgeworth's editorial persona distrusts linguistic sophistication. Here she associates aristocratic vices, linguistic and moral, with a rhetorical power unjustly employed to advance the claims of a literary elite. "Those who are used to literary manufacture know," the editor tells us, "how much is often sacrificed to the rounding of a period or the pointing of an antithesis" (28); in this view, elegance of style masks an underlying incompleteness or emptiness. Those who in writing about high life take on its worst aspects should not be trusted, because "the appearance of candour, which men of great abilities best know how to assume . . . endangers our judgment sometimes, and sometimes our morals" (28). Linguistic sophistication—the writing of those who make it difficult to read them—duplicitously conceals where it promises to reveal, obscures where it should enlighten. Edgeworth's linguistic project can be understood, then, as an attempt to create an alternative to this hegemonic discourse, undertaken in, as Marilyn Butler puts it, "the name of metropolitan knowledge and linguistic correctness."[6] In presenting herself as an acute reader and demystifier of aristocratic language, the editor attempts to win our assent to her own way, which she defines not only against linguistic sophistication, but also against the "illiteracy" of Thady Quirk.[7] For Thady's "plain unvarnished" language is, by the editor's own account, as problematic as the ornamental language of the highbrow historian, and for reasons that have much to do with class and national origin.

Then as now, language use marked—and was marked by—cultural and class differences. Olivia Smith argues that in the 1790s, "language was

---

[6]Marilyn Butler, Introduction to *"Castle Rackrent" and "Ennui"* (London: Penguin, 1992), 16.

[7]In the Preface, the editor uses the word "illiterate" to describe Thady, yet he can most certainly read (28, 61), if not write. My feeling is that Edgeworth uses this word, somewhat ironically, in the eighteenth-century sense as defined by Chesterfield in 1748: "The word *illiterate,* in its common acceptation, means a man who is ignorant of [Greek and Latin]" (*OED*).

generally understood to be a transparent manifestation of value": "a vulgar language was said to exist, a refined language was said to exist, and others were not recognized"; in particular, "the baser forms of language were said to reveal the inability of the speaker to transcend the concerns of the present, an interest in material objects, and the dominance of the passions."[8] Edgeworth's editor, however, seeks to create a third term, situating her own discourse between the "refined" and the "vulgar": historical style aims too high, but Thady's non-style is too low and also needs correction, which the editor supplies through the Preface itself, explanatory notes, and a glossary. Edgeworth's editorial apparatus thus enacts, in Kowaleski-Wallace's phrase, a "process of class and racial positioning" (154) whereby the editor represents her own position, albeit obliquely, as a middle ground between two extremes, a position we might term "Anglo-Irish." This strategic mediation, in its attempt to establish a new norm, also figures Edgeworth's own colonial situation: she seeks to produce the colonized for the colonizer and to establish her own authority for doing so, yet also to reform or reconstitute the relations between those two entities.

To do so, she must impugn Thady's authority just as she did the historians', but on slightly different terms. Whereas the elegance of elevated discourse might disarm middle-class English readers, the advantages of reading the works of "the ignorant" are all on "our" side. "That the ignorant may have their prejudices as well as the learned" she willingly allows, but the balance of power between "the ignorant" and the better-informed lies, of course, in favor of the latter: "we see and despise vulgar errors; we never bow to the authority of him who has no great name to sanction his absurdities" (28). The Irish Thady Quirk—a fictitious, poor, aged retainer who provides the intimate biography of "the family"—clearly has no name at all until his English author endows him with one; whatever authority he may possess he receives at her hands, or so it seems here. And through the editor, Edgeworth ingeniously and deliberately undercuts Thady's authority as teller of the tale in hope of securing her own.

As a carrier of the "vulgar language" Smith delineates, Thady is implicitly represented as one of "those, who without sagacity to discriminate character, without elegance of style to relieve the tediousness of narrative, without enlargement of mind to draw any conclusions from the facts they relate, simply pour forth anecdotes and retail conversations, with all the minute prolixity of a gossip in a country town" (28). While "careless conversations" and "half-finished sentences" were previously cited in the

---

[8] Olivia Smith, *The Politics of Language, 1791–1819* (Oxford: Clarendon Press, 1984), 21, x, 3. But see Marilyn Butler's Introduction to *Castle Rackrent* for another view of late eighteenth-century language politics.

Preface as the linguistic stuff that makes up "the characters of men" (27), in Thady's mouth they have no such value; what his discourse lacks, as the editor represents it, are the literary qualities that weave mere yarn into fabric. Thady's storytelling, indebted to an oral tradition, thereby functions as the other pole to historical discourse; against the shortcomings of the two extremes, Edgeworth's editor defines a literate "middling" style and a literate middle-class reader. Through her own editorial devices, Edgeworth transforms the raw matter of Thady into a text fit for literary consumption, *Castle Rackrent* itself.

As the events of the tale to follow illustrate, Thady is Edgeworth's most fully realized example of one kind of erring reader. He fails to discern the patently ridiculous habits and manners of many of his masters, resorting instead to a blind obedience to his quasi-aristocratic betters; he lacks the acuteness to see through the deficiencies of those whom he serves, effectively placing himself outside the middle-class English community Edgeworth's preface constructs, whose readers observe both the faults of the Rackrents and the blindnesses of their historian. In his role as "native informant," to borrow a term from anthropology, Thady Quirk is thus positioned as the source of our knowledge, yet at the same time subtly discredited; his account requires the correction of the enlightened colonialist perspective.[9]

But even though the editor clearly links the native Thady's reading practices to error, she also worries that "Thady's idiom," "incapable of translation" (29), will be, by its difference, beyond the grasp of her English readers, who will fail to perceive this native's errors. This anxiety motivates a series of pointed editorial moves, designed to insure that members of her intended audience meet the literate standard, which is explicitly linked to the possession of accurate colonial knowledge. For while those who "know" the Ireland of the mid-eighteenth century "will want no evidence of the truth of honest Thady's narrative," to "those who are totally unacquainted with Ireland, the following Memoirs will perhaps be scarcely intelligible, or probably they may appear perfectly incredible" (29). The presumed otherness of "Thady's idiom," represented by the editor as the authentic language of the Irish peasant, compels her to provide "*ignorant* English" readers with interpretive aids—not only notes and a preface, but also a glossary. While the class superiority of middle-class English readers might well enable them

[9]See Edward W. Said, "Representing the Colonized: Anthropology's Interlocutors," *Critical Inquiry* 15 (Winter 1989): 205–25, and Trinh T. Minh-ha, *Woman, Native, Other: Writing Postcoloniality and Feminism* (Bloomington: Indiana University Press, 1989), 47–76, for recent critiques from outside anthropology of this concept as an anchor for neocolonial knowledge production.

to form a proper reading of their own indigenous inferiors, Edgeworth assumes that the linguistic difference of the Irish—the difference her own novel helps to constitute as inferiority—necessarily complicates the interpretive process undertaken by English readers. Thus "the narrative voices of *Castle Rackrent*," in Perera's words, "counterpoise an editorial presence, established as rational, professional, and English against that of the oral, premodern, and 'racially' different Thady" (16).

As John Cronin comments in his study of the Anglo-Irish novel, anxiety about the linguistic otherness of the Irish (many or most of whom still spoke Gaelic at the turn of the nineteenth century) was common to Anglo-Irish writers of the period, who produced their work primarily for an English market: "the Irish novel of the early part of the century," he states, "nearly always comes to us with its footnotes or afternotes packed with details of regional explication."[10] Such reading supplements help to produce the Irish as deficient for their colonial masters while simultaneously enabling this other to be read; the editorial apparatus thus confirms both the address of the text to an English audience and the Englishness of its creator. Introducing the cultural other to the English reader brings Thady near—domesticates him, so to speak—while also distancing him and his eccentric language. But while the apparatus Edgeworth creates works in part to contain and control the unruly Thady, I want to suggest that her relationship to her creation is yet uneasy and unstable; her ostensible mastery of his idiom belies a certain dependence on it, a dependence which operates as well in other registers throught the novel and in the larger context of English-Irish relations.

2

Edgeworth's literal appropriation of another's discourse in *Castle Rackrent* is very much a function of her family's anomalous position as liberal Anglo-Irish landlords in late eighteenth-century Ireland. Unlike the scurrilous

---

[10] John Cronin, *The Anglo-Irish Novel,* vol. 1 (Belfast: Appletree Press, 1980, 11. In Edgeworth's case, notes and glossary were belatedly added to the text of the novel rather than being integral to its conception and production; as Marilyn Butler points out in her definitive biography, the novel was already in press when the Edgeworth family—Maria's immediate reading audience—"decided that some further explanation for the public was needed" (Marilyn Butler, *Maria Edgeworth: A Literary Biography* [Oxford: Clarendon Press, 1972], 354). Butler further notes "the self-conscious . . . *Englishness* of the Glossary," reading it as the Edgeworth's effort "not merely [to interpret] Thady to an audience unfamiliar with his type," but especially "to dissociate themselves from his primitive attitudes" (354).

absentees whose indifference to their Irish tenants Edgeworth was strongly to criticize in such later works as *Ennui* (1809) and *The Absentee* (1812), her father, Richard Lovell Edgeworth, had returned to Ireland from England in 1782 "with a firm determination," in his words, "to dedicate the remainder of my life to the improvement of my estate, and to the education of my children; and farther, with the sincere hope of contributing to the melioration of the inhabitants of the country, from which I drew my subsistence" (quoted in Butler 77). Via the naive Thady, whose loyalty to "the family" transcends all other possible considerations, *Castle Rackrent* reveals some of the abuses that historically had been perpetrated against the agrarian Irish working class by the agents and middlemen whom English and Anglo-Irish landlords had employed to work in their interests.

Because the Edgeworths understood themselves to be a breed apart from their improvident and uncaring ancestors, Richard Edgeworth took it upon himself to correct the wrongs that had been done to his estate and his tenants; yet his benevolent paternalism also sought, in Kowaleski-Wallace's words, "to contain and regulate impulses that might otherwise become inimical and hostile to his purposes" (150). In this endeavor, as in many literary ones, Maria Edgeworth served as her father's assistant, and ultimately as his successor, carrying on his program until she was well into her seventies; in Michael Hurst's words, she became "something between a colonial civil servant and a missionary rescuing the masses from inferior material and spiritual practices."[11] While such a characterization underlines the colonialist assumption of English superiority, it is important to recognize, as Richard Edgeworth did, that Ireland was not only a resource to be exploited, but the very source of the Edgeworths' "subsistence." In other words, they were indebted to and dependent on those "inhabitants of the country" whom, through the cultivation of paternalism, they sought to constitute ideologically as wholly indebted to and dependent on them.

Maria Edgeworth committed herself to her father's project in several ways. She educated herself through a course of reading about her new home, studying English "constitutional authorities" as well as "Spenser and Sir John Davies, Arthur Young and Adam Smith" (Butler 91) and thus steeping herself in the colonialist understanding of Ireland. At the same time, her duties on the estate brought her into contact with a number of her father's tenants and employees, and one especially important family retainer—the estate steward, John Langan—became the original inspiration for Thady Quirk: as Butler reports, Edgeworth "liked to entertain the

---

[11] Michael Hurst, *Maria Edgeworth and the Public Scene* (Coral Gables, FL: University of Miami Press, 1969), 23.

family circle by mimicking [his] brogue and strange opinions" (174). Like Thady himself, who is described in the Preface as roused from "his habitual laziness" and "persuaded to have [the story of the Rackrents] committed to writing" (29), Edgeworth transferred her invention to paper only at the urging of her favorite aunt, a trusted literary advisor, who convinced her that her powers of linguistic impersonation were too great a gift to waste (Butler 174). Edgeworth's text, then, has at its core her ability to appropriate the tone, accent, and idiom of another, and to put them to a variety of literary, political, and economic uses. And that appropriation of a dependent's persona makes her, to some extent, dependent on him, as a copy is to the original.

Along these lines, we can read Edgeworth's ploy as an authoritative act by which she assumes—and so subsumes—the identity of another; just as Butler would have it when she asserts that "down to incidental gestures Thady was a faithful copy" (241) cunningly drawn. Catherine Gallagher makes the point yet more forcefully, arguing that Edgeworth's appropriation of Thady's idiom, her possession of the language of the dispossessed, makes a commodity of him: the goal of the text "is to possess the non-identity of the other and then put it into circulation," with all profits accruing to the family estate.[12] "Thady's language is . . . constantly put to use against 'the family' to which his only sense of self"—his only sense of identity—"is so indebted" (17), and within the tale told this is undeniably so. Even though Thady speaks as a loyal family retainer who draws his identity from theirs, his tale ironically exposes the excesses of a debased aristocracy; moreover, it is Thady's unhesitating divulgence of family affairs to a stranger that puts his well-beloved master, Sir Condy, in the hands of a cunning entrepreneur and ultimately puts Sir Condy's estate into the hands of Thady's own less-beloved son. In Gallagher's words, Thady "circulates the stories that lead to the dispossession . . . and then tells the stories we read, the story of the dispossession" (16). By capitalizing on the personality and idiom of the family steward and commodifying him for an English reading public, Edgeworth makes him her literary property.

Edgeworth's act of linguistic appropriation repeats and reproduces other acts of colonization; she represents the world of the Irish other, making it readable to those safely ensconced in their English homes. In this light, the only really "Irish" thing about *Castle Rackrent* is its subject matter: as Butler puts it, "the viewpoint [Edgeworth] wanted to adopt was

---

[12] Catherine Gallagher, "Fictional Women and Real Estate in Maria Edgeworth's *Castle Rackrent*," *Nineteenth-Century Contexts* 12:1 (Spring 1988): 14. Gallagher's comment is apropos of two other works by Edgeworth, *Letters for Literary Ladies* (1795) and the *Essay on Irish Bulls* (1802), but applies equally well, I think, to *Castle Rackrent*.

English and forward-looking" (306). The prevailing Edgeworthian prescriptions for Ireland—that the Irish needed to be reformed, disciplined, and reimagined on English models, and so subjected in new ways to a more just English authority—all depend on substituting this properly intelligible, properly English viewpoint for a despised and inferior colonial Irish identity. We should not, however, assume that all the power at this cultural crossing is held by a single agent: Edgeworth's appropriation of Thady's "non-identity" (to use Gallagher's term) may enable her to establish her own literary identity, but the logic of the literary marketplace is not the only crucial factor here. As Homi K. Bhabha asserts, those who subject are also subjected, for the ambivalence of colonial discourse necessarily cuts both ways: "it is difficult to conceive of the process of subjectification as a placing *within* orientalist or colonial discourse for the dominated subject without the dominant being strategically placed within it too."[13] Bhabha thus reminds us that even the colonizing Edgeworth is also a participant in "the process of subjectification," which takes place in terms of gender and class as well as race, and as such her position in relation to her colonized creation may well be less stable than Gallagher assumes. While Edgeworth is the bearer of hegemonic English values and powers, her own authority is crosscut by at least two kinds of dependency—one having primarily to do with cultural and linguistic difference, the other regarding issues of gender.

Edgeworth's own admittedly fanciful description of her writing process gives Thady agency as a motivating force in the production of the text: "When, for mere amusement, without any ideas of publishing," she wrote to a friend, "I began to *write* a family history as Thady would *tell* it, he seemed to stand beside me and dictate and I wrote as fast as my pen could go" (quoted in Butler 240–41; emphasis mine). Here Edgeworth figures her own writing as dependent on Thady's oral presentation: while she denies him authority in her public preface, in the private letter she assigns Thady a power that both enables and rivals her powers of literacy. The efficacy of John Langan's oral idiom as against Edgeworth's literate standard, the priority of the so-called "primitive" culture over the "civilized" one is, ironically, mobilized by Edgeworth as a means of distancing herself from her own act of appropriation, suggesting an ambivalence at the heart of the relationship between copy and original. Even as her written text transforms orality into literacy, making Thady's "non-identity" a condition of her newly emergent literary identity, she simultaneously undercuts her literary authority by granting primacy to Thady's powers of speech.

[13] Homi K. Bhabha, "The Other Question: The Stereotype and Colonial Discourse," *Screen* 24:6 (1983): 25.

Edgeworth's image of dependency, which figures her relationship to another's discourse as mere recording from dictation, partially undercuts what the Preface works so hard to establish: the effort to represent an English style as the superior medium for all literate readers and writers breaks down in the face of another style, another idiom, an Irish tongue that Edgeworth may be able perfectly to imitate but which also in some sense masters her. The very act of introducing Thady's idiom into her text generates the anxiety which the editorial apparatus attempts to control; thus "English" and "Irish" lock into a relation in which each constitutes the other in a relation of mutual dependence. Without the presence of the one—another language or culture, as native to some as English is to others—there would be no call for the continual reassertion of the other's superiority. The very ground of *Castle Rackrent,* then, is its indebtedness, its dependence on the idiom it seeks to construe as wholly dependent on English for its articulation.

The ironies of this structure of mutual dependence come into sharper focus when we consider the role that gender plays in the production of the text. *Castle Rackrent* marked Edgeworth's first "independent" literary effort; unlike her earlier works, and most of what she produced before Richard Edgeworth's death in 1817, it was written without her father's guidance and only after its completion submitted for his approval. But her figuring of her subordination to Thady rehearses, perhaps unintentionally, what Edgeworth presented as her quintessential scene of writing: she accorded her father most of the credit for her works, styling herself a mere mediator of his ideas and so minimizing her own participation in deference to the patriarchal authority she feared to offend. As Thady stands by her side dictating, he does not stand alone, for her father's literal absence does not efface his symbolic omnipresence. Edgeworth thus demonstrates, as I have argued elsewhere with reference to other women writers, the uneasiness many nineteenth-century literary women felt about literary production and literary authority; for her as for others, the norms of gender make any act of writing potentially threatening to the culturally constructed "feminine" self.[14]

Like class and culture, gender effects a certain difference in Edgeworth's position, revealing one among other instabilities within the ostensibly dominant term of the opposition between colonizer and colonized. But subjected as Edgeworth may be to patriarchal authority, or even to the linguistic power of Thady's idiom, her position as a colonial mediator simultaneously assigns her the power that accrues to one who represents those

---

[14] See Mary Jean Corbett, *Representing Femininity: Middle-Class Subjectivity in Victorian and Edwardian Women's Autobiographies* (New York: Oxford University Press, 1992), especially chaps. 2 and 3.

who cannot represent themselves, at least not in print. *Castle Rackrent* may thus be read as an articulation of the shifting relations of power between colonizing and colonized women and men in which no one group—not even the ostensibly dominant one—can be said entirely to lack agency, given that all, including its author, are located within "the process of subjectification" of which Bhabha writes. Within the text of the novel, asymmetries of power between women and men—master and mistress, mistress and servant—primarily surface in regard to matters of inheritance, cultural difference, and language, complicated by analogous (though not precisely equivalent) asymmetries of power between colonizer and colonized; by exploring those relations, we can, I think, better estimate Edgeworth's position. Attending to gender and race as interlocking yet sometimes internally contradictory structures of oppression within *Castle Rackrent,* as I hope to suggest below, provides another means of seeing how the figure of the colonial woman writer instantiates the doubleness of power relations in this cross-cultural encounter.

3

As most critics of *Castle Rackrent* have recognized, the disorderly transmission of family property in the novel signals what Edgeworth thinks of as a serious disturbance in social order among the Anglo-Irish. In its linking of familial stability to social reproduction of the established relations of property and authority, Edmund Burke's celebrated discussion of inheritance in *Reflections on the Revolution in France* can serve as the exemplary statement on the matter:

> The power of perpetuating our property in our families is one of the most valuable and interesting circumstances belonging to it, and that which tends the most to the perpetuation of society itself. It makes our weakness subservient to our virtue, it grafts benevolence even upon avarice. The possessors of family wealth, and of the distinction which attends hereditary possession (as most concerned in it), are the natural *securities* for this transmission.[15]

In Burke's thinking, familial inheritance, proceeding from father to son, secures "the perpetuation of society." In *Castle Rackrent,* however, "weakness" and "avarice" rule, as the estate rarely passes on in orderly patriarchal fashion.

---

[15] Edmund Burke, *Reflections on the Revolution in France,* ed. J. G. A. Pocock (Indianapolis: Hackett Publishing Company, 1987), 45.

Such abuses are sanctioned in part by institutionalized English prejudice against Irish Catholicism: "by Act of Parliament," Sir Patrick O'Shaughlin must "take and bear the sirname and arms of Rackrent" (31) in order to inherit due to the Penal Laws (of which Burke himself disapproved), which prohibit Catholic ownership of property. Yet patriarchal deficiencies play an equally central role. The drunken Sir Patrick gives up his religion and his family name so as to secure his estate and pass it along to his son, Sir Murtagh, who exploits his tenants and produces no heir; upon his death, Murtagh's younger brother, Sir Kit, an inveterate gambler and absentee, inherits and squanders it. Finally, the estate passes to Sir Condy, the "heir-at-law," who belongs to "a remote branch of the family" (48); raised among the common Irish Catholic children of the town, he has a character consequently formed far below what his adult station requires.[16] The breaks in the transmission of the estate and the concomitant degeneracy of the family itself, Edgeworth implies, contribute to the social instability of the world she portrays: as Gene W. Ruoff puts it, "the generations of Rackrent do not need generation to propagate themselves," as several Rackrents inherit only by "claims traced along precarious routes of male protestant descent."[17] What Ruoff's statement, like Burke's patriarchal logic, tends to occlude, however, is the participation of the female body in the generation of heirs: the degeneracy of the Rackrent men, foregrounded by Edgeworth herself, also entails a less visible but no less vital absence of "generation" on the part of women.

Rackrent marriages, seemingly without exception, are made for money, not for love, yet the women who make these marriages are no mere victims; as Ann Owens Weekes points out, "each wife escapes upon her husband's death, her fortune intact and indeed in two cases increased" (42). Sir Murtagh chooses his wife, for example, on the basis of the fortune she may bring: he "looked to the great Skinflint estate" (33–34) as a means of enhancing his own purse. But his wife is every bit as grasping as he, and runs a so-called charity school only so her duty-yarn may be spun *gratis* by its pupils. As Edgeworth herself did in fictionalizing John Langan for the market, the novel's women make material profit from the colonial project and so are directly implicated in it. Like their husbands, Rackrent women display a

---

[16] For a thorough reading of the Rackrent men as husbands and masters, see Ann Owens Weekes, *Irish Women Writers: An Uncharted Tradition* (Lexington: University Press of Kentucky, 1990), 41–59.

[17] Gene W. Ruoff, "1800 and the Future of the Novel: William Wordsworth, Maria Edgeworth, and the Vagaries of Literary History," in *The Age of William Wordsworth: Critical Essays on the Romantic Tradition*, ed. Kenneth R. Johnston and Gene W. Ruoff (New Brunswick: Rutgers University Press, 1987), 309.

decided preference for property and no interest in securing the means of its transmission; they have no commitment to the estate, leaving it behind when their husbands die or when things go bad. That they do not reproduce biologically may be taken as emblematic of the disorder Edgeworth locates in familial and social relations: themselves treated as the site and medium for property exchange between men, the ladies Rackrent fetishize what they accumulate, seeing self-interest as the limit of their interests.

Within the family economy, these women thus exercise several different kinds of economic power. Despite the fact that they are largely used by their husbands as means of access to property, they resist their husbands' efforts to control them. Their ostensible dependency on men masks the fact that the patriarchal system of property transmission, properly ordered, depends in great part on them, just as the Edgeworths depended for continued subsistence on their tenants. Within the constraints of patriarchal limitations on feminine agency, the Rackrent women thus refuse their subordination by spurning their "natural" reproductive role and remaining childless. The lack of female subordination in this important arena of patriarchal control is another sign of how far short Irish affairs fall from the Burkean model Edgeworth implicitly supports.

The "unnaturalness" of the feminine figures in the novel is best exemplified by one character who experiences the utmost in patriarchal abuse of power. Sir Kit, characteristically short of money and long on debts, marries "the grandest heiress in England" (40) to revive the family fortunes. When the lady balks at giving him her valuable diamond cross, he locks her in her bedroom for seven years, and she is freed only at his death. Kit's wife is thus subject to patriarchal power in one of its crudest forms, yet she continues to resist and, like the other Rackrent women, her resistance concerns her right to her own property. What makes her most unnatural, however, at least in Thady's eyes, is not her refusal to indulge Kit's avarice, or her failure to produce an heir, but her racial difference, for this resister is "a *Jewish*" (41), a "heretic Blackamore" (41) of "dark complexion" (41).[18] Through this figure's relationship to the narrator, Edgeworth's text reveals how each positions the other as subordinate in terms of gender, class, or race, raising important questions about the distribution of power within the text.

Prepared to welcome his new lady with open arms, Thady is "greatly shocked" to discover that "she was little better than a blackamoor" (40) in appearance. Not only her looks but her habits—her refusal to eat pork, for example—draw Thady's uncomprehending wonder, even condescension.

[18]See Sander L. Gilman, *Difference and Pathology: Stereotypes of Sexuality, Race, and Madness* (Ithaca: Cornell University Press, 1985), 31–35, for analysis of the nineteenth-century racist links forged between blacks and Jews.

The lady also turns out to be wholly indisposed to talk, and invariably responds to Thady's solicitous inquiries with a silence he reads as a lack of comprehension: "never a word she answered, so I concluded she could not speak a word of English, and was from foreign parts" (40). And once she does speak, to inquire of her husband about an Irish term Thady uses, Thady interprets her lack of information as "ignorance." She fails properly to identify the (to her) unfamiliar features of the Irish landscape, calling a bog "a very ugly prospect" and seeing Irish "trees" as equivalent to English "shrubs" (41–42). "To hear her talk, one might have taken her for an innocent" (41), Thady says, applying a linguistic and cultural standard to her similar to the one that Edgeworth has applied to him in the Preface. Licensed perhaps by his master's subsequent ill-treatment of her, Thady regards "the Jewish" as his inferior, and thereby takes up a position of power ordinarily denied him by representing her as truly other.

Throughout this episode, we are meant to see, I think, yet another example of Thady's "prejudices"; "in the process of exposing the wife's ignorance about indigenous Irish practices," Kowaleski-Wallace comments, "Thady often exposes his own" (151). The anti-semitic tone of his remarks ostensibly belongs to him, not to Edgeworth.[19] Yet "the Jewish" displays her own form of prejudice, which also concerns the language of the other: she treats Thady's discourse—and especially a particularly rambling anecdote on "the bog of Allyballycarricko'shaughlin" (42)—with utter contempt, just as any native English aristocrat might.[20] On hearing the tale of the bog, "the Jewish," Thady reports, "fell to laughing like one out of their right mind, and made me say the name of the bog over for her to get it by heart a dozen times—then she must ask me how to spell it, and what was the meaning of it in English" (42) Here gender and class position firmly link "the Jewish" to the English establishment in ways that Thady fails to recognize. For all the new lady's perceived foreignness to Thady, and despite the logic that makes

[19]Other works by Edgeworth that include stereotyped representations of Jews include *Belinda* (1801) and *The Absentee* (1812). *Harrington* (1817) was written in part to expunge the anti-Semitism of these earlier works, yet its fortuitous ending—the hero discovers that no religious impediment to his marriage exists, since his beloved is revealed not to be a Jew after all—seems to confirm that Jewishness, like Irishness, signified for Edgeworth as a kind of alien otherness.

[20]As P. F. Sheeran points out in "Colonists and Colonized: Some Aspects of Anglo-Irish Literature from Swift to Joyce," *The Yearbook of English Studies* 13 (1983): 97–115, the differences of view among Sir Kit, Thady, and "the Jewish" in this scene are "a function of their cultural and social differences," and he goes on to reveal that the very name of the bog "testifies to a history of conquest and enclosure" (105): the name contains Sir Patrick's original family name, O'Shaughlin, within it; moroever, the true Gaelic name for it, which even Thady does not use, is "portach."

all non-English others subordinate to an English standard, she is, in linguistic and cultural terms, more of an insider than he is; her "Englishness" is clearly a function of a linguistic sophistication that takes the other's language as a mere joke.[21] Despite her subjection to her husband, and Thady's willingness further to marginalize her as a "blackamoor," "the Jewish" is thus not wholly without power, derived from her association with the very structures Thady uses to indict her. Her race marks her as not-English, but her command of the English language and her contempt for the Irish align her, if only precariously, with the colonizer.

Thady and "the Jewish" thus have similarly doubled positions: each could function as a mirror for the other, but neither registers any likeness between their situations. The linguistically deficient native other sees no similarity between himself and "the Jewish," whose subordination to his master is even more pronounced in some respects than his own; "the Jewish" derives her sense of superiority to Thady from her class position and her place as his mistress, but her racial otherness, from English and Irish alike, makes her, in a way Thady's other masters and mistresses are not, as subject to his condescension as he is to hers. Edgeworth, however, covertly links the two by assigning them to structurally equivalent places. Each of them is positioned as unequal: as Perera remarks of similarly marginal characters in Edgeworth's *Belinda* (1801), Thady and "the Jewish" "are linked within a scale that structures them . . . as outsiders yet pits them simultaneously against one another" (26). Caught as they are in a hierarchy of structural gendered and racial inequalities, Thady and "the Jewish," like Edgeworth herself, understand the other's otherness as inferiority, failing to perceive their own subordination to English patriarchal rule while still accruing certain benefits from it.

Within *Castle Rackrent*, then, the Rackrent women, like Thady, are both agents of and subject to patriarchal colonial rule, just as Edgeworth herself was, yet one of the central recurring ironies of the text—that those who are doubly positioned as powerful and powerless fail to recognize their implication in the systems that subject them—works at their expense, not hers. Edgeworth takes as her explicit function the ideological task of mediating the otherness of others, such as Thady or "the Jewish," representing and revealing it, conveying and correcting it, making the specification of linguistic differences her primary tool for imposing the hegemonic English standard with which she identifies. Yet in crucial ways, Thady and "the Jewish" figure Edgeworth's own unspoken, unrecognized position as a colonial

[21] See Gallagher on the *Essay on Irish Bulls*, especially 11–13, for further analysis of this point.

woman writer, subject to as well as of the patriarchal colonial discourse she produces. Her identification with the dominant power, however tenuous, effectively militates against her developing both a more nuanced perception of her own otherness in patriarchal thought and a more thoroughgoing critique of the structures of colonial domination.

In the last analysis, however, the point is not to criticize Edgeworth for her ideological blindnesses, but rather to reflect on our own. Postcolonial theory, as represented particularly by the work of Homi Bhabha and Gayatri Spivak, has offered a serious challenge to normative modes of figuring relations among the powerful and the disempowered, while the critical work of numerous scholars in African, Caribbean, and Indian postcolonial literatures, Anglophone or not, demands that those of us trained in "English literature" rethink that category in both our research and teaching as a way of exposing the muted dynamics of inclusion and exclusion. If decentering the hegemony of Englishness by emphasizing the Welsh, Scots, and Irish components of the great tradition is not the only way to continue the process of decolonization, it is nonetheless a necessary step. And recognizing the otherness even of such putative insiders as Edgeworth provides a further means of coming to terms with the colonial experience.

Miami University

Narrating Cultural Encounter: Lady Morgan and the Irish National Tale

Ina Ferris

The ear is receptive to conflicts only if the body loses its footing.
—*Julia Kristeva,* Strangers to Ourselves

Writing early in this century Niilo Idman noted the persistence in Anglo-Irish literature of a certain plot: "A person of eminence arrives in Ireland; he (or she) possesses every qualification for a rich and interesting life, yet nothing noteworthy has ever happened to him, and he is full of spleen until, once there, he is dragged into a whirl of undreamt-of-adventures; his former habits, prejudices and ways of thinking suddenly give way to an all-absorbing passion, which irresistibly hurries him towards bliss or destruction, as the case may be."[1] The plot he outlines derives from the first national tale, the highly successful romantic fiction *The Wild Irish Girl: A National Tale* (1806) by Sydney Owenson (better known as Lady Morgan), which focuses on the initiation of a young Englishman into Gaelic Ireland through romance with the not-so-wild Irish Girl of the title. Idman's plot summary, concentrating as it does on the transporting of a "person of eminence" out of familiar categories, usefully points to the way in which the narrative genre founded by Morgan effects a certain unhinging of the metropolitan figure, subjecting this figure to a *bouleversement* whose outcome is uncertain. In contrast to most recent commentators, who focus on the imperial complicities of this generic plot, Idman sees in it an aggressive energy located in the peripheries: he understands it as "the revenge of a subdued and oppressed country upon her masters" (p. 70).[2] Idman's sense of

Nineteenth-Century Literature 51 (December 1996): 287–303.

[1] *Charles Robert Maturin: His Life and Works* (Helsingfors: Helsingfors Centraltryckeri, 1923), p. 70.

[2] The national tale has only recently begun to move into critical purview as a distinct genre founded in the British peripheries in the early nineteenth century, and when it is

the particular *relation* of this narrative to imperial power seems to me to be worth taking seriously, for he draws attention to the fact that the significance of the national tale may lie not so much in what it means as sociopolitical discourse (its reproduction of or resistance to imperial discourse) as in what it *does* as narrative in exploiting the romance trope of encounter. What it does, I want to suggest, is deploy the pragmatics of narrative to effect a breach in metropolitan reason so as to gain Ireland a particular kind of hearing. Building out of romance modes and the proto-ethnographic discourse of travel, the national tale relocates the scene of cultural encounter, confounding the distinction between "over here" and "over there" in order to move the modern metropolitan subject/reader into a potentially transformative relation of proximity.

As a worldly and impure genre that sets out to do something with words, the national tale makes central to its whole project the often obscured, performative notion of representation itself. The concept of representation, as Wolfgang Iser has pointed out, is so closely identified in our critical thinking with mimesis (understood as duplication or imitation of a given) that its performative sense has been largely overlooked.[3] Iser himself emphasizes the Aristotelian notion of representation as the performance of a potential, and if we adopt Benedict Anderson's well-known definition of the nation as an "imagined community," then to represent a nation is to perform a potential in this sense.[4] But of more direct concern to the work of the early Irish national tale, it seems to me, is another performative sense of representation: the presentation of something to someone so as to create a certain effect.[5] The first reviewers of *The Wild Irish Girl* understood the

---

discussed, it is mostly read as a colonial genre that harnessed nationalist energies in the Celtic territories on behalf of an imperial "British" identity. See, for example, Gary Kelly, *Women, Writing, and Revolution, 1790–1827* (Oxford: Clarendon Press, 1993), pp. 178, 184–86; and Nicola J. Watson, *Revolution and the Form of the British Novel, 1790–1825: Intercepted Letters, Interrupted Seductions* (Oxford: Clarendon Press, 1994), chap. 3. The most extensive and complex discussion of the genre to date is by Katie Trumpener, "National Character, Nationalist Plots: National Tale and Historical Novel in the Age of *Waverley*, 1806–1830," *ELH*, 60 (1993), 685–731.

[3] See "Representation: A Performative Act," in *The Aims of Representation: Subject/Text/History*, ed. Murray Krieger (New York: Columbia Univ. Press, 1987), pp. 217–32. For a theorizing of narrative itself as interactive and performative, see Marie Maclean, *Narrative as Performance: The Baudelairean Experiment* (London: Routledge, 1988).

[4] See *Imagined Communities: Reflections on the Origin and Spread of Nationalism*, rev. ed. (London: Verso, 1991).

[5] In a related point, Trumpener notes that the national tale sought "not only to reflect but to direct national sentiment" (p. 689).

novel very much in this way, reading it in terms of the pragmatic pole of advocacy and frequently complaining that Morgan's disquisitions on Irish culture and history (both within the narrative and in the elaborate paratext accompanying it) disrupted the pleasure of immersion in the fiction. So the *Monthly Review* protested that the narrative was "much interrupted by many intrusive subjects, which are forced on us, no doubt, because the tale *is* a *national tale*. . . . Milesian pride in so many forms must make us smile."[6] The reviewer's remark draws attention to two points: first, the degree to which the performative notion of representation was received as distinctive of the national tale ("no doubt, because the tale *is* a *national tale*"); and second, the way in which Ireland emerged in the national tale as not simply the scene of representation (an object of discourse) but the scene of enunciation, the site from which a claim is made ("Milesian pride"). As an enunciation it was motivated by the desire to make a case for the stigmatized nation, to provide what we might call (drawing on the title of Alexander Welsh's recent book) a "strong representation" before the court of middle-class English public opinion.[7] Morgan in fact typically invokes the legal metaphor and adversarial model, describing her writing in phrases like "national defence" and defining her national tale as a "fictitious narrative, founded on national grievances, and borne out by historic fact."[8]

The context of law that Morgan generally invokes is less the abstract, discursive framework of written laws and rights (although this does enter into the tales, as in their campaign on behalf of Catholic Emancipation) than the concrete, agonistic scene of advocacy, a scene of public speaking necessarily attached to a particular voice and body. Thus when she responds to the charge of being "political" in the 1835 preface to the revised edition of *O'Donnel* (1814), for instance, Morgan declares: "Born and dwelling in Ireland, amidst my countrymen and their sufferings, I saw and I described, I felt and I pleaded; and if a political bias was ultimately taken, it originated in the natural condition of things."[9] Re-charging the categories of discourse with categories of presence, Morgan here foregrounds not so much the truth of her representation as the truthfulness of her act of representing. The suffering body of Ireland makes "natural" her political intervention, while this intervention, itself rooted in feeling, takes the form of a "pleading," a term conflating both the agonistic public speaking

---

[6]Rev. of *The Wild Irish Girl*, *Monthly Review*, n.s. 57 (1808), 379.

[7]See *Strong Representations: Narrative and Circumstantial Evidence in England* (Baltimore: Johns Hopkins Univ. Press, 1992).

[8]Morgan, Prefatory Address, *The Wild Irish Girl*, rev. ed. (London: Henry Colburn, 1846), p. xxvi.

[9]Preface to *O'Donnel*, rev. ed. (London: Henry Colburn, 1835), p. ix.

of the law court and the personal appeal of a woman's voice. In the kind of pragmatism that will mark her entire career, Morgan draws on her femininity to sanction a move out of the strictly feminine and into public argument. "I am not the one," she once remarked, "to give up any of the *privileges* of my sex, *en attendant, their rights*!"[10]

The pleading that Morgan sets in motion in her first national tale explicitly engages rival representations and is fueled by a combative textuality that will become characteristic of the genre. *The Wild Irish Girl* not only offers a history of Ireland countering the official London-based narrative, but it also sets up an elaborate subtext of footnotes in which a personal, authorial voice criticizes, revises, commends, and otherwise engages a plethora of texts on Ireland written from different points of view (and sometimes in different languages). The acute awareness of a metropolitan addressee informing the text recalls Terry Eagleton's observation that "Irish fiction constantly overhears itself in the ears of its British interlocutors . . . holding the prejudices of its implicit addressee steadily in mind."[11] But where Eagleton's formulation (overhearing oneself in the ears of another) suggests the potential of a debilitating self-alienation and self-inhibition in a writing so acutely aware of itself as being read, Morgan overrides the inhibiting possibility by making the context of response the explicit condition of her narrative rather than its paralyzing shadow. Throughout, she directly and energetically engages texts and readers.

In activating the discourse of representation *of* the peripheries in order to make a clearing for representation *from* the peripheries, Morgan performs an act of autoethnography (to use Mary Louise Pratt's useful term).[12] The important point about an autoethnography is that, as a speaking from the peripheries that engages the language of the metropolis, it derives its authority from the impurity or hybridity of its site of enunciation. And Seamus Deane helps to locate the significance of this site in the "hyphenated culture" of Anglo-Irish in the early nineteenth century, when he remarks that in this period it is difficult to separate Irish novels from both travel literature "written by foreigners" and "folk or folksy reminiscences

---

[10] Prefatory Address, *The Wild Irish Girl*, p. x.

[11] *Heathcliff and the Great Hunger: Studies in Irish Culture* (London: Verso, 1995), p. 201. Bakhtin's comment in "The Problem of Speech Genres" on the determining role of the addressee in speech genres seems to me of special pertinence to literary genres like the national tale: "Each speech genre in each area of speech communication has its own typical conception of the addressee, and this defines it as a genre" (*Speech Genres and Other Late Essays*, ed. Caryl Emerson and Michael Holquist, trans. Vern W. McGee [Austin: Univ. of Texas Press, 1986], p. 95).

[12] See *Imperial Eyes: Travel Writing and Transculturation* (New York: Routledge, 1992).

and reports, written by natives."[13] Deane's observation underscores the way in which the Irish national tale operates in between standard binaries, seeking to effect their crossing. Moving *around* rather than within or against colonial and metropolitan categories, it produces itself as the writing of one who, to invoke Anne Grant's memorable phrase describing her own writing on the Scottish Highlands, "is not absolutely a native, nor entirely a stranger."[14] In an important sense the national tale is a tale that can be written neither by a foreigner nor by a native. It may gesture toward the presentness and interiority of a "native" writing, and it may move within the textuality and exteriority of a "foreign" narrative, but its specificity derives from its eluding both categories: standing neither inside nor outside, the national tale occupies the space of their encounter. And through the dynamism and mobility of encounter that it activates, the subjected nation becomes not so much a "picture" gratifying curiosity (although the picturesque always remains in play) as a participant in an event through which metropolitan perceptions themselves undergo a certain estrangement.

Central to this estrangement is the transposition of the targeted reader. The national tale addresses the external chronotype of reception not simply through the authorial move of representing the case of Ireland but also through the relocation of narrative ground—that is, through the apparently obvious move of dislodging the reader from English space. Travel writing of course had long been removing the reader from English space, but it typically retained an English enunciation: someone from "here" traveled "over there" and reported back. The national tale altered the site of enunciation even as it retained the same (or similar) language, and the implications of this move were nicely registered by T. H. Lister in an article on Irish novels for the *Edinburgh Review* in 1831. Until the turn of the century, Lister comments, the Irish were generally known to English readers only as "solitary foreigners, brought over to amuse us with their peculiarities."[15] Because they were never represented "on Irish ground," Lister explains, "we never

---

[13] Deane, "Irish National Character 1790–1900," in *The Writer as Witness: Literature as Historical Evidence*, ed. Tom Dunne (Cork: Cork Univ. Press, 1987), p. 103. The term "hyphenated culture" I take from Julian Moynihan's *Anglo-Irish: The Literary Imagination in a Hyphenated Culture* (Princeton: Princeton Univ. Press, 1995). See also Benedict Anderson's analysis of creole nationalism in chap. 4 of *Imagined Communities*, which is pertinent to the emergence of Anglo-Irish nationalism in the nineteenth century.

[14] *Essays on the Superstitions of the Highlanders of Scotland: To which Are Added, Translations From the Gaelic; and Letters Connected with those Formerly Published*, 2 vols. (London: Longman, Hurst, Rees, Orme, and Brown, 1811), I, 10.

[15] "Novels Descriptive of Irish Life," *Edinburgh Review*, 52 (1831), 411–12. Comments like this bring to mind Jerome Christensen's recent charge that the Edgeworths "depeculiarized" the Irish. It is certainly the case that they sought to discipline and regularize the

viewed them as natives of a kindred soil, surrounded by the atmosphere of home, and all those powerful accessaries [*sic*] which made *them* natural, and *us* comparatively strange and foreign" (p. 411). Lister's memorable phrasing ("*them* natural, and *us* comparatively strange and foreign") draws attention to the reversal of trajectory in the national tale. Displacing its English readers, the genre compelled them to consider Ireland as a habitat (a native and independent place) and not simply as the primitive, ridiculous, or dangerous colony of English imaginings.[16] As a corollary, they themselves became the strangers. A small moment early in *The Wild Irish Girl* is emblematic. As the English hero, Horatio M___, walks through the Irish countryside, he is attracted to a ruined barn by the sound of "a full chorus of females." There he finds a spinning circle of young women led by an old woman, and he listens to their song until it abruptly stops when the women perceive his presence. He reports that "the old woman addressed me *sans ceremonie*, and in a language I now heard for the first time." Horatio responds in English, and his words are greeted by repressed laughter on the part of the younger women and by what seems a gesture of contempt on the part of the old woman. Never, he declares, did he feel himself "less invested with the dignity of [a man] than while I stood twirling my stick, and 'biding the encounter of the eyes' and smiles of these 'spinners in the sun.'"(114–16)[17] Having gone for a look, Horatio is now himself subjected to a certain looking, suddenly made aware of the existence of another world in which his usual (English, masculine) identity no longer quite sustains itself.

Thus transported to Irish ground, the metropolitan protagonist, and the reader, of the national tale are asked to operate neither as tourists (passing through for a "look") nor as foreigners (bringing along familiar norms) but as strangers, moving into a new zone. "A stranger," William Hazlitt notes, "takes his hue and character from the time and place."[18] To be a stranger is

---

native Irish in conformity with their liberal ideology, but it is also the case that the glamour of remaining "peculiar" is generally more apparent to those already safely inside dominant discourses (see Christensen, "The Romantic Movement at the End of History," *Critical Inquiry*, 20 [1994]. 473).

[16] Claire Connolly is one of the few commentators on *The Wild Irish Girl* to draw attention to its displacement of English sensibilities (see "Gender, Nation and Ireland: The Early Novels of Maria Edgeworth and Lady Morgan," diss., Univ. of Wales, 1995). Deidre Lynch has argued that tactics of displacement are characteristic of female-authored narratives of the nation in the romantic period (see "Nationalizing Women and Domesticating Fiction: Edmund Burke and the Genres of Englishness," *Wordsworth Circle*, 25 [1994], 45–49).

[17] All paranthetical references to *The Wild Irish Girl* are to this New Riverside Edition.

[18] "On Going on a Journey," in *Table-Talk*, ed. P. P. Howe, vol. 8 of *The Complete Works of William Hazlitt* (London: Dent, 1931), p. 185.

thus to suspend one's own identity and to enter what we might call the rim of another's space. Strangers do not belong within the space, but nor do they invade that space, as foreigners do. A stranger may certainly decide to become a foreigner—the two roles do not rule one another out—but the key point is that the stranger denotes the point of hesitation in cultural encounter: neither side has yet made up its mind. Each behaves according to a certain decorum, and it is significant that this decorum is set by the culture one enters. "Stay, Sir, you are I apprehend a stranger in this country?" asks a judge in Morgan's *Florence Macarthy* (1818) when the unknown hero of the novel finds himself arrested on false charges:

> "I am, my lord, an utter stranger."
> "You have then, Sir, a prescriptive right to courtesy and protection, in a land where the name of stranger is still held sacred."[19]

The motif of Irish hospitality to strangers may have rapidly become a sentimental cliché, producing stock scenes like the peasants' sharing of meager food stocks, but it served to establish the point of home ground. Once the stranger moves onto this ground and into the neutral space of hesitation, the stranger can choose to transform it (into the positive pole of receptivity, for instance, or the negative pole of hostility), but the definitive narrative move of the national tale is to effect the initial unhinging that offers the possibility of a rearrangement of relations and positions.

On that deliberate dislocation depends the power of the genre to gain a hearing for the stigmatized nation. "The ear is receptive to conflicts," Julia Kristeva has recently written, "only if the body loses its footing. A certain imbalance is necessary . . . for a conflict to be heard."[20] Over and over again the protagonist of the national tale registers the shock of cultural encounter (which opens out onto a submerged history) through a loss of balance, and the genre as a whole is informed by figures and effects of dislocation. Of special interest is the way in which the initial loss of balance is brought about by an alien sound. From Horatio M___ in *The Wild Irish Girl* to Glenthorn in Maria Edgeworth's *Ennui* (1809) to Armida in Charles Robert Maturin's *The Milesian Chief* (1812), the metropolitan stranger in the national tale undergoes a stumbling of the body on hearing an unknown voice. *The Wild Irish Girl* offers the classic instance. Horatio M___, banished to his father's remote estates in the west of Ireland, one evening enters the Gaelic enclave of Inismore, where lives the remnant of the clan dispossessed by his own ancestors during the Cromwellian wars. Himself unseen,

---

[19] *Florence Macarthy: An Irish Tale*, 4 vols. (London: Henry Colburn, 1818), III, 44.

[20] *Strangers to Ourselves*, trans. Leon S. Roudiez (New York: Columbia Univ. Press, 1991), p. 17.

Horatio watches ("spell-bound") the celebration of a mass in a ruined chapel by the sea, and he exhibits the familiar aesthetic posture of the tourist.[21] "What a captivating, what a *picturesque*, faith!" he exclaims, identifying the nature of his scopic pleasure and reinforcing it by drifting into narcissistic fantasy: "I . . . almost wished I had been born the lord of these beautiful ruins . . . the adored chieftain of these affectionate and natural people" (145, 146). He turns to leave, but just as he does so he hears "the low, wild, tremulous voice" of a woman playing a harp (146), and this moment alters his entire history, jolting him out of the controlling spectatorship of the gaze into the proximity and implication of response.[22] Like Wordsworth's speaker coming upon the solitary Highland reaper, Horatio is stopped by an unknown sound; unlike the Wordsworthian speaker, however, he does not stay to wonder what it means. Instead, Horatio's body responds to the voice as to a calling; forgetting caution, he moves toward it and loses his bearings. Following "the witching strain," he climbs a ruined wall, and as he clings to the parapet "to prolong this rich feast of the senses and the soul," the loose stones give way, and Horatio falls, losing consciousness. Upon awakening he finds himself inside the castle and experiences an "irresistible desire" to prolong his status as guest and patient at Inismore (146–149).[23]

I read this scene as an instance of what Michel de Certeau, in his account of "ethnological eroticism," calls "ravishment."[24] Ravishment is a moment of excess in cultural encounter, a moment implicating the body and suspending (for the moment) linear and cognitive structures of temporality, language, and thought. So for Morgan's Horatio the voice of the unknown

---

[21] For an analysis of the nineteenth-century trope of the tourist, see James Buzard, *The Beaten Track: European Tourism, Literature, and the Ways to Culture, 1800–1918* (Oxford: Clarendon Press, 1993).

[22] Although in general the eye seems to me too negatively coded in current criticism (not all looking signifies detachment and control), the play of seeing and hearing in this scene of Morgan's novel recalls the distinction Susan Stewart makes in her discussion of travel writing between the separating function of the gaze (aestheticism) and the implicating function of the dialogic (ethics) (see *Crimes of Writing: Problems in the Containment of Representation* [New York: Oxford Univ. Press, 1991], chap. 6).

[23] For two recent readings of this scene, see Vivien Jones, "'The Coquetry of Nature': Politics and the Picturesque in Women's Fiction," in *The Politics of the Picturesque: Literature, Landscape, and Aesthetics since 1770*, ed. Stephen Copley and Peter Garside (Cambridge: Cambridge Univ. Press, 1994), pp. 120–44; and Joseph W. Lew, "Sidney Owenson and the Fate of Empire," *Keats-Shelley Journal*, 39 (1990), 39–65.

[24] See Certeau's chapter on "Ethno-Graphy: Speech, or the Space of the Other: Jean de Léry," in his *The Writing of History*, trans. Tom Conley (New York: Columbia Univ. Press, 1988), pp. 209–43. See also Robert J. C. Young on "colonial desire" in *Colonial Desire: Hybridity in Theory, Culture, and Race* (New York: Routledge, 1995).

woman (who turns out to be Glorvina, the Princess of Inismore) produces a response that bypasses the circuits of rationality. Where the earlier scene of the eye was governed by terms like "interest" and "curiosity," the scene on the parapet features "nerves" that thrill at what the ear hears: "I listened—I trembled"(146). The importance of such moments of ravishment, as Certeau underlines, is that they *do* something (rather than mean something), and what they do is prompt the "gesture of coming nearer." This gesture, reducing but not eliminating distance, seems to me to embody the desire of the national tale: its bid to turn the foreigner into the stranger-who-comes-nearer.

If such gestures inevitably "return" to the terms of standard discourse, as they do, a residue of the initial ravishment remains and serves to mark a limit within the enclosing discourse. In the case of Horatio, the ravishment of Glorvina's voice unsettles the English idiom he has hitherto taken for granted and ushers him into an idyllic chronotope that turns Ireland into an erotic, pastoral body and renders time (as Bakhtin evocatively puts it) "a dense and fragrant time, like honey."[25] Deploying the erotic plot in order to signal engagement with, rather than simply observation of, the hidden nation, Morgan rewrites Ireland as the locus of desire, unsettling colonial readings in the process. But the locus of desire is at the same time the locus of guilt. In Inismore, Horatio confronts the scene of violent usurpation that underpins his own family history. The image of Glorvina thus mingles fearful guilt with ardent longing, as evidenced by an evocative dream directly after his arrival. The injured Horatio falls asleep, suggestively in the midst of alien sounds: "while the sound of the Irish harp arose from the hall below, and the nurse muttered her prayers in Irish over her beads by my side, I fell into a gentle slumber." The dream follows: "I dreamed that the Princess of Inismore approached my bed . . . and raising her veil, discovered a face I had hitherto rather guessed at, than seen. . . . it was the face, the head, of a *Gorgon*!" (154). The eye, it seems, has its terrors as well as its complacencies. Horatio sheds his guilty name. He adopts the mask of an itinerant artist and calls himself Henry Mortimer, recognizing that entry into the nation hidden from the English colonizer is possible only on condition of a feignng and a splitting. Strangely enough, the identity prudently assumed proves oddly compelling, bringing about a disconcerting reversal. "It is absurd," Horatio says at one point, "but I *cannot* divest myself of a feeling of inferiority in [Glorvina's] presence, as though I were actually that

[25] "Forms of Time and of the Chronotope in the Novel," in his *The Dialogic Imagination: Four Essays*, ed. Michael Holquist, trans. Caryl Emerson and Michael Holquist (Austin: Univ. of Texas Press, 1981), p. 103.

poor, wandering, unconnected being I have feigned myself" while she, the impoverished Glorvina O'Malley, was "a *real Princess*" (162).

The disruption of his familiar identity deepens as Horatio learns (quite literally) another language in Inismore. Glorvina, at once erotic goddess of nature and ardent nationalist heroine, teaches him Irish and instructs him in the lore of "ancient Ireland."[26] Taught and learned "*con amore,*" the Irish language becomes entangled with the nonverbal language of the body: sighs, tears, glances, and the gaze of mutual absorption. "Delicious" is the word Horatio invokes most readily to describe this language, and such metaphoric crossings underline the pastoral harmony in which Glorvina lives. As she sings, dances, teaches, and moves around the valley, nature and art pass smoothly into one another. But, at the same time, she is framed by a self-conscious artfulness, thematized most clearly when Horatio draws her as she sings. The moment draws attention both to his technique and to the way in which Glorvina is immobilized as cultural icon: "That peculiarly pensive expression which touches the countenance of Glorvina, when breathing her native strains, I have most happily caught; and her costume, attitude, and harp, form as happy a combination of traits, as a single portrait can present" (194). Thus turned into artifact, Glorvina and her Gaelic trappings threaten the transformation of history into decor and point to the "staging" of folklore that Susan Stewart finds characteristic of literary ballads of the period.[27] For even as Morgan's novel helped to shape the cultural-political categories underwriting nationalist movements like Young Ireland, her first national tale also produced, as Ian Dennis has observed, a rage for the Wild Irish Look.[28]

As a narrative act rooted in pragmatic notions of performance and effect, the national tale founded by Morgan constantly risked producing simply a picturesque thrill for jaded urban palates or material for a fashion statement. If the figure of Glorvina dislodged some English preconceptions and shed a glamour for the Irish themselves over their degraded national

---

[26] On Morgan's doubling of the erotic and the political, see J. Th. Leerssen, "How *The Wild Irish Girl* Made Ireland Romantic," *Dutch Quarterly Review of Anglo-American Letters,* 18 (1988), 209–27.

[27] See *Crimes of Writing,* p. 122.

[28] "'What a Land is This, Where All the Women are Fair, and the Men Brave!': The Historical Novel, Nationalism, and Desire," diss., Univ. of Toronto, 1995, chap. 2. Morgan herself of course was a highly theatrical figure, playing the role of Glorvina in real life with some relish. For differing interpretations of her theatricality, see Seamus Deane, *A Short History of Irish Literature* (Notre Dame: Univ. of Notre Dame Press, 1986), pp. 97–98; Tom Dunne, "Haunted by History: Irish Romantic Writing 1800–50," in *Romanticism in National Context,* ed. Roy Porter and Mikulás Teich (Cambridge: Cambridge Univ. Press, 1988), p. 73; and Eagleton, pp. 184–85.

identity, it was also readily recuperated into the metropolitan narrative—as into Horatio's drawing. And it is noteworthy that starting with her second national tale, *O'Donnel,* Morgan rewrote her "ravishing" performative heroine and the trope of seduction and reimagined her nation. Increasingly she began to detach Ireland from exclusive identification with the unifying figure of place (the nostalgic Gaelic chronotope) and to reconstruct it as an internally stratified and dispersed agency. The heroine herself underwent a similar scattering, as Glorvina's *thereness* (her fullness of being, her rootedness in place) gave way to an oddly elusive and deterritorialized figure who belongs nowhere, exactly, and who typically operates in the interstices of culture, keeping herself hidden and in reserve.[29] But what remains constant is the effect of encounter with this heroine: she disconcerts and confounds the assumptions and identities of the strangers who come across her in the hinterland.

The key to the Irish national tale inaugurated by Morgan is thus her rewriting of the romance trope of transformative encounter. Recasting encounter as a breaching of the universals of metropolitan reason by the specificities of body and voice, she allows for an unsettling of imperial identity in colonial space through the attainment of a problematic proximity.[30] The national tales that followed in the wake of *The Wild Irish Girl*—even when dismissive of Morgan or opposed to her politics—found themselves turning to this suggestive and mobile narrative trope as they worked through their own sense of colonial relations. In Maria Edgeworth's first and quirkiest national tale, *Ennui* (1809), for example, it is the voice of a native Irish-woman that effects the initial displacement of the young English hero. The more rational Edgeworth de-eroticizes Morgan's trope, replacing the enchanting young Glorvina with a stubborn old nurse, but English-Irish encounter in the novel functions in a remarkably similar way. As the bored Lord Glenthorn of *Ennui* rides out on his birthday to kill himself, he comes across an old woman he does not know, who greets him "in a strong Irish tone" and identifies herself as his early nurse. She spooks his horse, and Glenthorn tumbles to the ground: "I was stunned by my fall, and senseless."[31] Curious to test the feelings of those around him, he feigns

---

[29] For Morgan's later heroines, see Ina Ferris, "Writing on the Border: The National Tale, Female Writing, and the Public Sphere," in *Reforming Genre in British Romanticism,* ed. Tillotama Rajan and Julia Wright (Cambridge: Cambridge Univ. Press, forthcoming).

[30] For a compatible reading of colonial encounter, see Sara Suleri, *The Rhetoric of English India* (Chicago: Univ. of Chicago Press, 1992).

[31] Maria Edgeworth, *Ennui,* in *Castle Rackrent and Ennui,* ed. Marilyn Butler (Harmondsworth: Penguin, 1992), p. 155. In her excellent introduction to this volume Butler draws special attention to the fact that women writers produced the first national

death, and discovers himself abandoned by those he trusted. As he lies there he also hears the voice of the old nurse: "I did not understand one word she uttered, as she spoke in her native language, but her lamentations went to my heart, for they came from hers" (p. 156). This moment, which will prompt his crucial decision to go to Ireland, underlines the doubleness of voice (hence of cultural encounter): as sound, an emanation of the body, the voice of lamentation pulls the two figures into proximity (my heart to hers); as language, however, voice is also the bearer of estrangement ("I did not understand one word").

In such moments, which typically involve confrontation with a female Irish body, the male English hero faces an opacity that blocks sense. As here, or in Horatio's encounter with Glorvina in *The Wild Irish Girl,* such blocking may release another (or perhaps *the* other of) meaning, but it may also simply defy and shut out the metropolitan subject. So when Glenthorn later arrives at Ellinor's surreal cabin in the Irish countryside, he is blocked by sheer sound: "the dog barked, the geese cackled, the turkeys gobbled, and the beggars begged, with one accord, so loudly, that there was no chance of my being heard" (*Ennui,* p. 186). It is not surprising that this experience decides him on building Ellinor a cottage "in the most elegant style of English cottages" (p. 189). But this too, when completed, resists his will and reason, uncannily turning itself into the Irish cabin he had attempted to erase, and in his frustration Glenthorn summons up the demeaning categories of the metropolis: "I reproached Ellinor with being a savage, an Irishwoman, and an ungrateful fool" (p. 200). Encounter can thus threaten as well as liberate, open up the muddiness of origins (Ellinor turns out to be Glenthorn's mother) as well as the sensuous pleasures of erotic transcendence.[32] Whichever the case, it unfixes identity—sets it adrift—as witnessed by the shifting names, the disguises, and the other forms of self-estrangement that typically mark the protagonists of national tales, including Glenthorn himself, whose family name changes several times in the course of the novel.

In *The Milesian Chief* names may not drift in the same way, but identities certainly do. Maturin's little-known national tale pushes the dynamic of dislocation characteristic of the genre to the limit, stripping the ground completely away from the protagonist and producing death and destruction for all of the major participants. Based on Morgan's plot of love between a

---

tales, and she highlights the distinctive national-symbolic resonance of Irishwomen in Edgeworth's fiction (see pp. 50–53).

[32] Elizabeth Kowaleski-Wallace reads *Ennui* as articulating an anxiety about the grotesque mother's body in *Their Fathers' Daughters: Hannah More, Maria Edgeworth and Patriarchal Complicity* (New York: Oxford Univ. Press, 1991), pp. 159–66.

dispossessed native and a dispossessing stranger (but reversing the genders), *The Milesian Chief* darkly rewrites her trope of encounter.[33] The novel focuses on the pampered and adored Italian-English Armida—a performative heroine in the mode of Madame de Staël's Corinne—who travels to her father's Connaught estate, where she meets and falls in love with Connal O'Morven, grandson of the Milesian chief of the title whose lands now belong to Armida's father. The meeting of native and stranger here leads not into the idyllic erotic pastoral space of *The Wild Irish Girl* but into a bewildering historic-Gothic realm that shatters Armida's very being. To set the stage for this more radical fall and crossing, Maturin writes an arrival scene that takes place on a literal edge and turns the stumble of the newcomer into a potentially deadly plunge. As the carriage bearing Armida enters the castle of the O'Morvens, situated on a precipice, there rises a sound of anguish from the remnant of the displaced clan watching from the rocks below: "a cry, the most bitter that ever pierced the human ear, burst from the crowd below."[34] At this sound the horses bolt, and Armida's carriage hangs precariously over the edge. When a figure suddenly appears Armida assumes its murderous intent, and she loses consciousness. But the figure rescues her, as the horses and carriage plunge to the rocks below. Armida thus experiences encounter as terror but also as rescue, and that double coding will characterize her experience throughout the novel as she moves deeper and deeper into romance with her rescuer, Connal. In the limit-world that Ireland becomes in this novel, Armida is stripped of her cosmopolitan categories and confidence, and all former coherence gives way. When late in the novel she finds herself on the run with the weary rebel band following Connal, watching children die of hunger and confronting violence and murderous rage, Armida experiences even herself as a fall into incoherence, repeatedly enduring fits of madness. And from this incoherence there is no rescue. The novel ends in a Gothic *liebestod,* a bizarre scene of mad and sacrifical lovers tangled up in a state execution, as Maturin concludes his un-writing of the hopeful trope first articulated by Morgan.

Through its narratives of encounter the Irish national tale sought to place certain forms of metropolitan reason under pressure and loosen their configuration. This does not mean, it should be stressed, that the genre

---

[33] Despite its title, Maturin's earlier novel *The Wild Irish Boy* (1808) bears little relation to Morgan's national tale. In one of the few critical discussions of *The Milesian Chief,* Fiona Robertson draws attention to Maturin's reversal of gender and argues that this change allows Ireland to emerge as more tragic and less assimilable than in Morgan because it is now linked to serious, male power (see *Legitimate Histories: Scott, Gothic, and the Authorities of Fiction* [Oxford: Clarendon Press, 1994], p. 219).

[34] *The Milesian Chief: A Romance,* 4 vols. (London: H. Colburn, 1812), I, 57.

repudiates the rational. Neither of its main practitioners, Morgan and Edgeworth, valorized a resistance to modern reason all the way down. Acutely aware in their very different ways of the disadvantages of remaining outside modern power, they were not content to leave Ireland in the speechless realm of Unreason, even as they challenged the forms of reason that denied it national existence. For them the gesture of unfixing had to be accompanied by the complementary gesture of seizing: a seizing for oneself of the discursive ground on which that reason operated. And it was such a seizing that the young Sydney Owenson attempted in Dublin when, from a peripheral and hybrid site of Anglo-Irish enunciation, she published in London the heavily footnoted romance *The Wild Irish Girl.* Attempting at once to seduce and to challenge English opinion, this novel—and the genre it founded—may usefully be thought of as the kind of "skirmish" advocated by Jean-François Lyotard in his defence of storytelling in "Lessons in Paganism": "The only way that networks of uncertain and ephemeral stories can gnaw away at the great institutionalized narrative apparatuses is by increasing the number of skirmishes that take place on the sidelines."[35]

As a short-lived genre from the European sidelines, the national tale lived out its uncertain and ephemeral life in such skirmishing. It operated as a timely utterance rather than a permanent writing, understanding itself in the political-pragmatic context of particular words directed at other words in anticipation of a response. What it offered was the "pagan" lesson that Lyotard calls "replying" rather than "reacting." To react, he explains, is to repeat (to insult someone who insults you), but to reply is to displace (to turn the tables, to rearrange the narrative positions) (p. 137). In its tactics of displacement the national tale founded by Morgan in *The Wild Irish Girl* effected less an overturning than a troubling of the imperial narrative, and to return it to the field of early-nineteenth-century literary genres is to recognize in this field more destabilizing energies than are often acknowledged by the disciplinary narratives of our own time.

University of Ottawa

[35] "Lessons in Paganism," in his *The Lyotard Reader,* ed. Andrew Benjamin (Oxford: Blackwell, 1989), p. 132.

Maria Edgeworth and Lady Morgan: Legality versus Legitimacy

Robert Tracy

Maria Edgeworth's first Irish novel, *Castle Rackrent* (1800), ends with a funeral. Her three other Irish novels, *Ennui* (1809), *The Absentee* (1812), and *Ormond* (1817), end with weddings, but there is a puzzling ambivalence about her treatment of these weddings. Each one resolves a plot and represents a conventional happy ending, but the novelist herself seems uneasy about the rewards she confers. As the end of each novel approaches, she deliberately foils the plot she has been developing—the marriage which seems inevitable and desirable—and creates an alternative marital outcome. At the same time, she contrives to suggest that somehow the earlier plot and marriage have not been foiled after all and have indeed been validated and brought to a successful conclusion.

There is a strongly didactic element in all four Irish novels, though at times didacticism is threatened by Maria Edgeworth's eagerness to exploit the more bizarre aspects of her material. This conflict is presumably due to her own awareness of having not one audience but two. Her didactic material is aimed at readers of her own class, at other Anglo-Irish landlords. She explains to them how to succeed—in *Castle Rackrent,* how to fail—as landlords. But she is also conscious of English readers, and for them she emphasizes the strange and flamboyant—that is, the un-English—nature of Irish life, those very habits and traits which work against the prudent husbandry she is endorsing.

In all four novels the basic issue is how the relationship between Anglo-Irish landlords and Irish tenants can be improved. Maria Edgeworth's father, Richard Lovell Edgeworth, settled on his estates at Edgeworthstown (now Mostrim) in County Longford in 1782, determined to be a successful and enlightened landlord. Writing as her father's disciple, Maria urged her

Nineteenth-Century Literature 40 (June 1985): 1–22.

Irish readers to practice fair dealing and careful husbandry. Landlords, she suggests, will prosper if their tenants prosper; tenants will prosper if their landlords treat them fairly and introduce them to efficient farming methods. Landlords and tenants must recognize mutual interests and will in time develop mutual loyalty. The Irish will lose their foreign "identity" and become more like their English fellow subjects (29).[1]

It is a decent, rational aspiration, but Maria Edgeworth was too shrewd an observer of the Irish scene to believe that things could be settled so sensibly. She knew how irresponsible many landlords were, how lazy or how greedy. And she knew well what barriers of religion, race, tradition, and sometimes even language prevented landlords and tenants from recognizing a mutual loyalty. These barriers were higher and stronger than ever in the aftermath of the 1798 Rising and its brutal repression, which had revealed an implacable hatred between the two classes. Anglo-Irish landlords were well aware that they were a minority surrounded by a disaffected majority and that their legal right was not backed by any freely accepted social contract which would lead Irish peasants to concede that their Anglo-Irish landlord's claim to his place was in harmony with the legitimate and natural order of things. "Confiscation is their common title," announced the Earl of Clare, describing the Anglo-Irish landowners in his speech advocating the Act of Union in 1800, "and from their first settlement they have been hemmed in on every side by the old inhabitants of the island, brooding over their discontents in sullen indignation." Clare's intention was to frighten the Anglo-Irish into voting for the Union by persuading them that they "never had been, and . . . never could be, blended or reconciled with the native race."[2] He succeeded in his purpose, but he was not wholly wrong in his evocation of Irish resentment, and the structure and plots of Maria Edgeworth's Irish novels suggest that she was well aware that Irish tenants were not going to forget their wrongs easily, nor accept the legitimacy of the Ascendancy order of things.

Her four Irish novels are simple in structure. *Castle Rackrent* is a chronological account of four successive owners of the Rackrent estates, whose follies and extravagances become an object lesson in how *not* to be an Irish landlord. In *Ennui* the owner of an Irish estate is taken on a tour of Ireland, during which he learns something of Irish life and Irish resources, and observes examples of proper and improper estate management. Maria Edgeworth found this tour structure so useful for her didactic purposes

---

[1] All parenthetical references to *Castle Rackrent* are to this New Riverside Edition.

[2] Quoted by W. E. H. Lecky, *A History of Ireland in the Eighteenth Century*, abridged by L. P. Curtis, Jr. (Chicago: Univ. of Chicago Press, 1972), p. 463.

that she employed it again in *The Absentee* and in *Ormond.* After *Ormond* she wrote no more Irish novels, though she continued to gather material for one during the eighteen-twenties, until O'Connell's successful appeal to Catholic-Irish identity led her to believe that her themes of reconciliation would be unacceptable. "It is impossible to draw Ireland as she now is in a book of fiction," she wrote in 1834; "realities are too strong, party passions too violent to bear to see, or care to look at their faces in the looking-glass. The people would only break the glass, and curse the fool who held the mirror up to nature—distorted nature, in a fever."[3]

In both *Castle Rackrent* and *Ennui* the Anglo-Irish landlords are depicted as Lord Clare depicted their class, "hemmed in on every side by the old inhabitants of the island." The decline of the Rackrents, from Sir Patrick through Sir Murtagh and Sir Kit to Sir Condy, the last of the line, is narrated by Thady Quirk, who tells us that "I and mine have lived rent free time out of mind" upon the Rackrent estate (30). Thady controls the story by choosing what he will tell us and how he will tell it. He has conventionally been taken as a naive narrator whose awe at the Rackrents' wasteful and reckless behavior is a comic device used to heighten our sense of the Rackrents' self-induced tragedy. But Thady is not naive. He is well aware that the more foolishly the Rackrents behave, the more he and his family will prosper. He is resentful of Lady Murtagh because she keeps track of supplies and expenses, and he delights at any carelessness with money or land. Thady's praise of extravagance and scorn of prudence hints at his own prosperity as that of the Rackrents declines, and he deliberately shapes the behavior of the last Rackrent, Sir Condy, by instilling in him the desire to live up to the family tradition of waste: "I told him stories of the family and the blood from which he was sprung, and how he might look forward, if the *then* present man should die without childer, to being at the head of the Castle Rackrent estate. . . . The old people always told him he was a great likeness of Sir Patrick, which made him first have an ambition to take after him" (48–49).

Sir Condy proves an apt pupil and manages to emulate the different fooleries of all his predecessors until he loses the estate to his attorney Jason Quirk, Thady's son. Jason had become manager of the estate, partly at Thady's suggestion and partly as a result of his own calculated toadying to Sir Condy. Though Thady disapproves when Jason takes over the estate, their dispute seems to be about tactics: Thady would rather live off the estate and its owners; Jason would rather be owner. In any case, the Rackrents are surrounded by the predatory Quirks, eager to rob them in one way or

[3]Quoted by Marilyn Butler in *Maria Edgeworth: A Literary Biography* (Oxford: Clarendon Press, 1972), p. 452.

another. Along with Thady and Jason, there is Judy M'Quirk, "daughter to a sister's son of mine," Thady tells us (51), who is Sir Condy's mistress and who almost becomes Lady Rackrent. One way or another, the Irish peasants will take back the land from its Anglo-Irish owners—the nightmare of Anglo-Ireland.

In *Ennui* Maria Edgeworth combines her instructive series of good and bad examples of estate management with a bizarre plot that simultaneously allows and refuses to allow the estate to fall into the hands of the Irish peasantry. Lord Glenthorn is bored and unhappy; his marriage has ended in divorce. He resolves to visit his Irish estates and thereafter undergoes a course of instruction in Irish mores and estate management. The novelist emphasizes the strangeness of Irish life and its dangers to landlords: rebellion—presumably the '98—breaks out, and Glenthorn is threatened by the rebels and then scorned by his fellow landlords when he does not seek bloody vengeance. Literally surrounded by the peasantry, Glenthorn describes himself as "kept a state prisoner in my own castle, by the crowds who came to do me homage, and to claim my favour and protection. In vain every morning was my horse led about saddled and bridled; I never was permitted to mount."[4] These comic sieges prepare us for the rebels in the countryside and the hostility of the Anglo-Irish.

Glenthorn is also in search of a wife, and eventually he proposes to the witty and very Irish Lady Geraldine. Marriage with her seems to offer him a chance to assume an Irish identity and to manage his estates justly, but also with due regard for Irish tradition and Irish sensibility. Her name suggests an identification with the great family of Fitzgerald (the Earl of Surrey's love poems to "the fair Geraldine" addressed one of the Fitzgeralds). From the revolt of "Silken Thomas" Fitzgerald in 1534 to that of Lord Edward Fitzgerald in 1798, that family often supplied leaders for Irish rebellions against the English. Marriage with Lady Geraldine will give some direction to Glenthorn's life and presumably will make him a better landlord and a true Irishman.

But Lady Geraldine rejects Lord Glenthorn and eventually marries someone else. And then Glenthorn discovers that he is not Lord Glenthorn at all. He is Christy O'Donoghoe, an Irish peasant, and the true Earl has been brought up in a peasant cottage as Christy O'Donoghoe; the infant Earl's nurse substituted her own child for her noble charge. The false Earl insists on relinquishing title and estates to their rightful owner, and sets off for London, where he works hard, passes the bar, and then returns to

---

[4] *Ennui* (London: J. M. Dent, 1893), p. 55; hereafter page references appear parenthetically in my text, indicated by *E.*

Ireland to practice law. His honesty and industry attract favorable notice, and he marries the rather vapid Cecilia Delamere, a character introduced into the novel in its antepenultimate chapter for this purpose. He recognizes as legitimate her mother's objections to the name O'Donoghoe and agrees to accept the name and arms of Delamere. Meanwhile, the true Earl is unable to overcome his peasant upbringing and live up to his position. His son and heir becomes a drunkard, sets fire to the Castle, and perishes in the flames. The Earl relinquishes his position to return to his smithy, begging the pseudo-Earl to "come to reign over us again" (*E*, pp. 243–47). As it happens, Cecilia Delamere is heir-at-law to the Glenthorn estates; the Delameres rebuild the Castle and resolve to settle there.

This resolution ends the novel, but it raises a number of questions. Why is Lady Geraldine shunted away, especially when the hero remarks at the end of the book that she and the man she married "first awakened my dormant intellects, made me know that I had a heart, and that I was capable of forming a character for myself"? and why does he consider their presence the only "wish of my heart that remains ungratified"? (*E*, p. 244). If Lady Geraldine is Maria Edgeworth's self-portrait, perhaps she cannot be shown as happily married to the hero. But I suspect a political motive for her banishment.

The plot calls into question certain assumptions about the role of the Anglo-Irish and their mandate to rule. The true Earl's birth is not enough to make him a gentleman. His failure undermines the whole notion of hereditary rank, hereditary right, and of the natural capacity for leadership, which the Anglo-Irish allegedly possessed and the Irish allegedly lacked. The pseudo-Earl's instinctive nobility and honesty is equally subversive. Properly educated, the Irish can rule.

When the novel ends, the Irish peasant has changed his name, has learned how to rule, and has the legal right to do so through his wife. It is not the *national* right that marriage with Lady Geraldine would have conferred—there is nothing personally or characteristically Irish about Cecilia Delamere. But the peasants know the hero and respect him as a gentleman and as one of their own. He is triply legitimized by his education, his legal right, and his Irish identity. Once again an Anglo-Irish estate has fallen into Irish hands; the process is more honorable than in *Castle Rackrent*, but the result is similar—the Anglo-Irish have failed to hold on to what they had. In its tortuous way the plot undercuts all the sensible advice about fair dealing and prudence which the didactic portion of the book offers so freely. Good husbandry is not enough, it seems. The plot suggests that some other vaguely defined legitimacy is needed: the commitment to Irish tradition, which Lady Geraldine seems to represent and from which Maria Edgeworth draws back; or an unhyphenated Irish identity, which the hero half embodies, half evades.

There is some uncertainty as to precisely when Maria Edgeworth finished *Ennui.* She describes herself as "finishing *Ennui*" in a letter written in April 1805, but a striking description of an Irish hackney chaise and driver in chapter 6 is apparently based on a conversation with Humphry Davy in July 1806; and later Richard Lovell Edgeworth assured a correspondent that the novel had undergone "patient changes" and had been "totally rewritten."[5] We can probably assume that she worked on *Ennui* between 1804 and 1807 or 1808, though not continuously. It was during that period that Sydney Owenson—not to become Lady Morgan until her marriage in 1812—published her successful *The Wild Irish Girl* (1806). We do not know precisely when Maria Edgeworth read that novel, nor her initial opinion of it; later, in *Patronage* (1814), she was to caricature Lady Morgan as a governess turned author, and later still to deplore "a shameful mixture" in Lady Morgan's *Florence Macarthy* (1818) of "the highest talent and the lowest malevolence and the most despicable disgusting affectation and *impropriety.* . . . Oh that I could prevent people from ever naming me along with her—either for praise or blame . . . God forbid as my dear father said I should ever be such a thing as that—."[6] But it is probable that the character of Lady Geraldine in *Ennui* represents both a response to and a rejection of a theme Lady Morgan develops in *The Wild Irish Girl,* a theme Maria Edgeworth again develops but then again rejects in *The Absentee.*

The Wild Irish Girl is an epistolary novel in which Horatio, second son of the Earl of M____, describes his banishment to his father's Connaught estates. Horatio has wasted time and money, played the libertine, is heavily in debt, and is addicted to "polite literature and belles lettres" to the detriment of his legal studies (100).[7] In a half-ruined castle by the sea, Horatio discovers the aged Prince of Inismore, last of a line of ancient Irish chieftains, and his lovely daughter, the Princess Glorvina. The estates of Lord M____ were once the estates of the Prince's ancestors, confiscated in Cromwell's time when the ancestor of the M____s, a Cromwellian soldier, killed the then Prince in his own castle.

Horatio conceals his identity and gains admission to the castle, first as an invalid—he hurts his leg trying to spy on Glorvina—and later as the Princess' drawing master. There he hears and duly reports a series of lectures on the Irish language, Irish history, antiquities, grievances, and customs from the Prince, Glorvina, and Father John, the Prince's chaplain. He also falls in love with Glorvina, only to find that he has a rival, his own father. The Earl has long felt guilty about his own prosperity and the Prince's

---

[5] Butler, *Maria Edgeworth,* pp. 237, 247, 366–67, 291.

[6] Quoted by Butler in *Maria Edgeworth,* p. 448; see also p. 258.

[7] All parenthetical references to *The Wild Irish Girl* are to this New Riverside Edition.

poverty, but the Prince has refused any communication or help from his hereditary enemy. The Earl has also managed to enter the castle by concealing his name and pretending to be an Irish rebel fleeing after the 1798 Rising. He has persuaded the aged Prince and Glorvina to agree to a marriage, so that Glorvina can live in a way appropriate to her rank, and so that the ancient wrong of murder and confiscation can be righted. But the Earl gladly relinquishes Glorvina to Horatio and gives the young couple those estates which were once her ancestors' domain. She and Horatio will rule them together with a double right: to his legal right she adds her own traditional right, and from her he will learn respect for Irish history, Irish ways, and Irish tradition. Their children will be both Anglo-Irish and Irish, heirs to both rights and both traditions; the peasantry will accept them as legitimate masters in a way they have never accepted the M____ family alone, for peasant loyalty has always been with the "old" Catholic-Irish family.

In her subsequent Irish novels Lady Morgan introduces other descendants of ancient Irish families and emphasizes the strength of their traditional claims on their confiscated lands and on the loyalty of their peasantry. These are far stronger than the merely legal rights of the Anglo-Irish, and the very nature of those legal rights—based as they are on confiscation and usurpation—is a barrier to their acceptance as legitimate and binding by the peasantry. Only the restoration of the old Irish heir or an intermarriage that will merge Irish and Anglo-Irish claims, Catholic and Protestant, modern knowledge and traditional attitudes, can evoke that loyalty which guarantees that a landlord will be eagerly obeyed and even loved and thus assuage that "sullen discontent" which Lord Clare describes.

This happy coalescence of apparently mutual and irreconcilable enmities makes an attractive literary and political solution, and it became almost a cliché in the novels of Walter Scott, as when Catholic Stuart-supporting Diana Vernon marries Protestant Hanoverian Frank Osbaldistone in *Rob Roy* (1817) or when Saxon and Norman are reconciled in *Ivanhoe* (1819). Scott acknowledges a debt to Maria Edgeworth in his "postscript, which should have been a preface" to *Waverley* (1814), and in the "General Preface" to his novels (1829). His chief debt is to *The Absentee*,[8] but I suspect an unacknowledged debt to Lady Morgan—unacknowledged because Scott was a Tory, Lady Morgan a notorious Whig, and even, according to her sister, "an elegant artist, / A radical slut, and a great Bonapartist."[9]

---

[8] Butler, *Maria Edgeworth*, pp. 394–95.

[9] Lionel Stevenson, *The Wild Irish Girl: The Life of Sydney Owenson, Lady Morgan* (London: Chapman and Hall, 1936), p. 250. Stevenson's book is the standard modern biography of Lady Morgan.

Maria Edgeworth seems to be grooming Lady Geraldine to be a less flamboyant version of Glorvina before she exiles her from *Ennui.* If this is so, Edgeworth is not just toying with Lady Morgan's plot device of intermarriage. She is close to admitting that legal title and fair dealing are not enough to justify an Anglo-Irish landlord's possession of his estates. He must also make some emotional appeal to the deeper traditional loyalties of his peasants, must become in some way a part of the older tradition. An irrational element must be added to Richard Lovell Edgeworth's rational recipe. But to the Edgeworths, as Marilyn Butler points out, "Irish traditions meant . . . the survival of irrational and inefficient habits: they thought that extensive education among all classes was the best remedy for tradition." [10] To endorse Lady Geraldine's Irishness by marrying her to the hero would be to accept and endorse Irish tradition and Irish identity. Clearly Maria Edgeworth's instinct as a novelist, as well as her own awareness of the Ascendancy's failure to put down roots in Ireland and failure to evoke loyalty from the Irish, impels her toward such an endorsement of Irish tradition and Irish identity. But at the same time, her acceptance of Richard Lovell Edgeworth's principles makes her draw back from such an endorsement and, ultimately, deny it. As a novelist, Maria Edgeworth values Irish tradition and Irish strangeness; as an economist, she deplores these things and justifies her hero's success by his hard work, seriousness, and his marriage to the legal heir to the Glenthorn estates. But there is a perfunctory air about this resolution.

The uncertainty about what we may call the Glorvina solution—the intermarriage/assimilation of Irish and Anglo-Irish, of modern efficiency and ancient tradition, of legal right and traditional loyalty—is even more marked in Maria Edgeworth's third Irish novel, *The Absentee,* in which she first develops, then denies, and finally suggests such a solution. The structure of *The Absentee* is once again that of the exemplary tour. Lord Colambre, son and heir of the absentee Lord Clonbrony, visits Ireland and sees both well-managed and badly managed estates, including some of the properties he is to inherit, which he visits incognito. His tour also provides Maria Edgeworth with an opportunity to portray Dublin society, considerably lowered in tone since the Union, and the consequent departure of lords and commons to Westminster. Colambre learns the evils of absenteeism and the necessity for economy and prudent husbandry.

But there is also a plot. Lord Colambre is looking for a wife as well as a definition of his duty. He has two imperative conditions about his marriage: he will not marry for money, as his mother wishes him to do—"if

---

[10] *Maria Edgeworth,* p. 364.

you don't marry Miss Broadhurst"—an heiress—"we can't live in Lon'on another winter," she declares;[11] and he will on no account marry a woman who is not of legitimate birth. He has, we learn, "the greatest dread of marrying any woman whose mother had conducted herself ill. His reason, his prejudices, his pride, his delicacy, and even his limited experience, were all against it"(*A*, p. 193). Though even some contemporary readers described this attitude as "prudery,"[12] this attitude is for Colambre a basic principle and one that Maria Edgeworth endorses both here and, more elaborately, in *Patronage* (1814): a child brought up by an unchaste mother will be subtly corrupted, and so rendered unfit to raise her own children properly, an attitude in keeping with the Edgeworths' educational theories about the effect of environment and early training on character.

Colambre has allowed himself to fall in love with his mother's ward, Grace Nugent. Grace is beautiful, intelligent, and "not a partisan, but a friend" to Ireland (*A*, p. 155). She is the last heir of the old Irish family that once owned the Colambre estates. But there is a question about her legitimacy. In a plot whose complexity hints at Maria Edgeworth's uneasiness with some of its implications, Grace Nugent's parentage is explored and her legitimacy established in such a way as to suggest her relationship to the old Catholic owners of the estates and to deny that relationship. Grace is initially introduced as Colambre's cousin, the daughter of his "uncle Nugent," whose place in the family tree is never explained; we never learn if he is a paternal or a maternal uncle. We do, however, hear that the Nugents were an ancient Irish family who once owned the Colambre estates; the squalid local village is still called "Nugent's town" (*A*, p. 266).

During his travels Lord Colambre meets an Irish gentleman, Count O'Halloran, who is a Catholic aristocrat. He received his title after a distinguished career in the Austrian army. (Irish gentlemen traditionally served in the army of one of the Catholic powers, since they were not allowed to be British officers.) Now retired to Ireland, he spends his time advising the government about defense against Napoleon and studying Irish antiquities. O'Halloran, who is named for Sylvester O'Halloran of Limerick, one of the earliest Irish antiquarians,[13] represents Colambre's first encounter with

---

[11] *The Absentee*, in *Castle Rackrent; The Absentee*, Everyman's Library (London: J. M. Dent, 1910), p. 101; subsequent references in my text, indicated by *A*, are to this edition.

[12] Butler, *Maria Edgeworth*, p. 333, n. 1.

[13] Sylvester O'Halloran (1728–1807) was angered by what he considered Macpherson's theft of Irish material in the Ossian poems, and so became an antiquarian. He published *Insula Sacra* (1770); *An Introduction to the Study of the History and Antiquities of Ireland* (1772); *Ierne Defended* (1774); and *A General History of Ireland* (1778). A chance encounter with this last work made Standish O'Grady determined to study ancient

Irish tradition. Learned in Irish history, culture, and even fauna, O'Halloran has reassembled the skeletons of an Irish elk and a moose-deer, and his pets are "an eagle, a goat, a dog, an otter, several gold and silver fish in a glass globe, and a white mouse in a cage"; the dog is "a tall Irish greyhound—one of the few of that fine race, which is now almost extinct" (*A*, p. 195).

When a British officer who accompanies Colambre stumbles over the goat, the eagle attacks him until O'Halloran summons the bird; then "his first care was to keep the peace between his loving subjects and his foreign visitors. It was difficult to dislodge the old settlers, to make room for the new comers: but he adjusted these things with admirable facility; and with a master's hand and master's eye, compelled each favourite to retreat into the back settlements" (*A*, p. 197).[14] This episode suggests the same reconciliation with the older Catholic and Celtic Ireland that was Lady Morgan's theme. Count O'Halloran is a slightly more plausible version of the Prince of Inismore, endowed, like the Prince, with ancient lineage, antiquarian lore, aristocratic but not English manners, and loyalty to an older tradition. He too is of a "fine race . . . now almost extinct." He saves the British officer from the eagle, a hint at his role in assisting Britain against Napoleon; and he mediates between native and foreign, "old settlers" and "new comers." Colambre and the Count become friends, and he offers Colambre another model for success as an Irish landlord. Fair dealing is important, but so is a knowledge of and a respect for Irish tradition.

The Count has noticed Colambre's interest in a black letter book open on the table to a chapter entitled "Burial-place of the Nugents" (*A*, p. 197), and he presents him with an urn "enclosing ashes . . . lately found in an old abbey ground" where the Nugents are buried (*A*, p. 201). It is a symbolic gift representing Colambre's initiation into the Irish tradition and foreshadowing that restoration of legitimacy which his marriage with Grace Nugent, like Horatio's to Glorvina, will bring about. And the scene implicitly endorses that irrational Irish obsession with tradition which made Maria Edgeworth and her father uneasy.

Ireland; see Phillip L. Marcus, *Standish O'Grady* (Lewisburg, Pa.: Bucknell Univ. Press, 1970), p. 14. Thomas Flanagan emphasizes Count O'Halloran's Catholicism and continental service in his discussion of *The Absentee* in *The Irish Novelists, 1800–1850* (New York: Columbia Univ. Press, 1959), pp. 88–90.

[14] Count O'Halloran remarks that "a mouse, a bird, and a fish, are . . . tribute from earth, air, and water, to a conqueror" (*A*, p. 197), a pointed though inexact allusion to *Herodotus* IV, 130, in which the Scythians send a bird, a mouse, a frog, and five arrows to the invading Darius. Darius interprets these objects as signs of submission, but a wiser counselor sees them as warnings to depart. Colambre alone catches the Count's hint that the "foreign visitors" are unwelcome invaders.

But then Colambre discovers that Grace Nugent is not Grace Nugent at all. She was born before her mother's marriage to "uncle Nugent," who "adopted the child, gave her his name, and, after some years, the whole story" of her mother's premarital affair "was forgotten" (*A*, p. 204). Grace seems to be the illegitimate daughter of one Captain Reynolds and a Miss St. Omar. The St. Omars are described to Colambre by Lady Dashfort, who has her own reasons for preventing his marriage to Grace, as "*that* family, where, you know, all the men were not *sans peur,* and none of the women *sans reproche*" (*A*, p. 191).

But Count O'Halloran saves the day. He has already shown Colambre the way to a kind of national legitimacy by his example and by his gift of the burial urn. Now he is able to establish that Grace *is* legitimate. Her father, Captain Reynolds, was a young Englishman in the Austrian service and O'Halloran's friend. Her mother, also English, was educated in a Viennese convent. The couple were properly and provably married. When O'Halloran and Colambre call upon Grace's English grandfather and show him the certificate of marriage, he immediately agrees to recognize Grace as his granddaughter and heiress. There are no further obstacles to her marriage with Colambre, and even her poverty has been magically removed.

But she is no longer Irish, and her English legitimacy removes her apparent ability to reconcile two traditions and to bring the legitimacy of the old Irish owners of the land to Lord Colambre's legal rights to his estates. Maria Edgeworth has worked toward Lady Morgan's resolution, then foiled that solution. She has drawn back from the implications of her own plot; Count O'Halloran, despite appearances, is only the guarantor of formal legality, not of traditional rights. A legal title and prudent habits are, after all, sufficient to justify Colambre's rule of his estates and his choice of Grace as a wife.

But even as she changes the story's direction and implication in this way, Maria Edgeworth simultaneously continues to hint that Grace is, after all, somehow Catholic, Irish, and the heir to ancient traditions. Her father, we are told, has been in the Austrian service with Count O'Halloran—why? We know that Irish Catholics often entered the Austrian army and why they did so. The Irish-Catholic aristocrat who has served in the army of one of the Catholic powers is almost a cliché in Lady Morgan's novels. But why would a Protestant Englishman do so? or even a Catholic Englishman? There is an unmistakable hint of the Irish-Catholic aristocrat about Reynolds despite his English identity. And what of Miss St. Omar? Sometimes English Protestant girls were educated in Catholic convents abroad, but in context she too has a vaguely Catholic aura. Her name confirms this suspicion. St. Omer, in Belgium, was the location of a famous Catholic seminary, where priests were trained to serve in England and Ireland during the Penal Times—Father John, the chaplain in *The Wild Irish Girl,* has studied there.[15] Finally, why did Maria Edgeworth, in establishing Grace's parentage, decide to call her Grace *Reynolds?* The name had had some recent unpleasant notoriety in Irish history: Thomas Reynolds was the informer who caused the arrest of the United Irish leaders, his friends and companions, in March 1798. At their trial John Philpot Curran denounced him as "a vile informer, the perjurer of a hundred oaths, a wretch whom pride, honour and religion cannot bind."[16] He was particularly hated for his role in the betrayal of Lord Edward Fitzgerald. Does the name suggest Maria Edgeworth's uneasy awareness that she had in some way betrayed her Irish theme? or is it one more example of her ambivalence? Her juxtaposition of the names Nugent and Reynolds seems to point, not to the traitor Thomas Reynolds, but to the Irish nationalist poet George Nugent Reynolds (1770?–1802), the descendant of an ancient family of Catholic landowners in County Leitrim. Reynolds' once popular poem, "The Catholic's Lamentation," also known as "Green were the Fields where my Forefathers dwelt O," addresses that very dispossession of the old Irish families that is a partially submerged theme in *The Absentee.*[17]

By advancing and then denying Grace Nugent's Irish identity, Maria Edgeworth seems at cross purposes with her own intentions, but she implicitly continues to assert that Irish identity by hinting at a Catholic and implicitly Irish identity for Grace's parents. In the last few pages Grace seems inescapably Irish despite all we have previously heard. The novel ends with a letter from Larry Brady, a positilion at Clonbrony Castle, to his brother Pat in London, describing the triumphant homecoming of Colambre and Grace. The letter, which gave Maria Edgeworth a chance to return to a narrative voice like that of Thady Quirk, was a last-minute solution to the problem of how to end the novel, and was approved, perhaps even suggested, by Richard Lovell Edgeworth.[18] It has the effect of giving an

---

[15]Lady Morgan, *The Wild Irish Girl,* I, 250. Cf. the Glossary to *Castle Rackrent,* prepared by Maria Edgeworth and her father: "It was customary amongst those of Thady's rank, in Ireland, whenever they could get a little money, to send their sons abroad to St. Omer's, or to Spain, to be educated as priests. Now they are educated at Maynooth"(89).

[16]Thomas Pakenham, *The Year of Liberty: The Story of the Great Irish Rebellion of 1798* (1969; rpt. London: Panther Books, 1972), pp. 328, 50–52, 87–88. W. J. Fitz-Patrick quotes another scathing passage from Curran's speech in *"The Sham Squire" and the Informers of 1798,* New ed. (Dublin: M. H. Gill, 1895), pp. 149, 123.

[17]"Reynolds, George Nugent," *DNB,* and authorities there cited; also see Donal O'Sullivan, *Carolan: The Life, Times, and Music of an Irish Harper,* 2 vols. (London: Routledge and Kegan Paul, 1958), I, 39; II, 66. Reynolds was one of Carolan's patrons and is the subject of one of his songs, No. 157 (I, 247).

[18]Butler, *Maria Edgeworth,* p. 285; see also p. 375.

Irish voice the final word and of letting one of the tenants express the satisfaction that he and his fellows feel at the coming reign of Grace and Colambre. The evil bailiff is gone. The tenants have been offered fair leases. An enthusiastic welcoming crowd takes the horses out of the traces and pulls Colambre, his parents, and Grace up the avenue, and then "the blind harper, O'Neil, with his harp, . . . struck up 'Gracey Nugent'" (*A*, p. 344), a song by the famous Carolan, described by Goldsmith in an essay as "The Last of the Irish Bards." "Gracey Nugent," like many of Carolan's songs, celebrates the daughter of one of the old Irish families who were his patrons; Maria Edgeworth would have known it from its inclusion in the first collection of poems translated from Irish, Charlotte Brooke's *Reliques of Irish Poetry* (1789), which prints the original Irish as well as a verse translation, and which quotes from the brief life of Carolan in Joseph Cooper Walker's *Historical Memoirs of the Irish Bards* (1786). The song is also included in Miss Owenson's [Lady Morgan's] *Twelve Original Hibernian Melodies; with English Words, Imitated and Translated from the Works of the Ancient Irish Bards* (1805). Charlotte Brooke cites one of Walker's notes that identifies the subject of the song as "sister to the late John Nugent, Esq; of Castle-Nugent, Culambre"[19]—presumably the source of Lord Colambre's title. Culambre or Colambre is Coolamber in County Westmeath, near the Longford border. Harper and song are a traditional celebration strongly suggesting an old Irish restoration, as does the general air of enthusiasm and good will among the people. And everyone continues to refer to Grace Reynolds as Grace Nugent despite the change in her identity.

The Absentee represents Maria Edgeworth's most elaborate development of the Lady Morgan plot, with its potential endorsement of the

---

[19] Miss [Charlotte] Brooke, *Reliques of Irish Poetry* (Dublin: George Bonham, 1789; rpt. Gainesville, Fla.: Scholars' Facsimiles and Reprints, 1970), p. 246. Charlotte Brooke acknowledges Sylvester O'Halloran's help. For the tune to "Grace Nugent," see O'Sullivan, *Carolan* (Song No. 110), 1, 221. The woman of the song married about 1708; three of her brothers were "killed in the Emperor's service" as Irish-Catholic officers in the Austrian army. She seems not to have been related to George Nugent Reynolds. See *Carolan*, II, 66, 68–69. Maria Edgeworth would presumably have been aware of the career of Earl Nugent (1702–1788), an Irish poet and politician of an old Catholic family, described by Richard Glover in his *Memoirs* (1813; new ed., London: John Murray, 1814) as a "jovial and voluptuous Irishman, who had left Popery for the Protestant religion, money and widows" (p. 64); and perhaps of Lavall, Count Nugent (1777–1862), an Irish soldier in the Austrian service who distinguished himself at the battles of Monte Croce (1800) and Caldiero (1805). Sir Murtagh Rackrent has a lawsuit with "the Nugents of Carrickashaughlin" (35). This is an interesting conjunction when we remember that the Rackrents changed their name, and presumably their religion, to inherit the Rackrent estates; their original name was "O'Shaughlin, related to the Kings of Ireland" (31). For the presumed changes of religion, see Flanagan, *The Irish Novelists*, pp. 70–71.

legitimate rights of the old Irish to their lands despite the legal ownership of the Anglo-Irish; and it also represents her most tortuous refusal to let that plot and its implications fully work themselves out. She simultaneously hints that the Anglo-Irish order must connect itself with the older tradition if it is to evoke that loyalty which is essential to its survival. After nervously contemplating the displacement of the Anglo-Irish Rackrents by the Irish Quirks in *Castle Rackrent,* and the ambiguous identities of lord and peasant, Anglo-Irish owner and Irish tenant, in *Ennui,* and after creating, then destroying, then obscuring an heiress to the old Irish tradition for the hero of *The Absentee* to marry, she is equally if less tortuously evasive in *Ormond,* her last Irish novel.

As young Harry Ormond, her hero, enters adult life, he is offered three models for possible emulation: Sir Herbert Annaly of Anglo-Irish stock, an enlightened landlord who strongly resembles Richard Lovell Edgeworth; Sir Ulick O'Shane, an Anglicized Irishman, Scottish on his mother's side, who is a government lackey and an unscrupulous speculator with his own and other people's money; and Cornelius O'Shane, known as King Corny of the Black Islands, an old Irish chieftain, Catholic, who lives among his people in the traditional manner and is a less sentimental version of Lady Morgan's Prince of Inismore. Choosing to combine elements of Sir Herbert and King Corny, Ormond will be a prudent agriculturalist but will practice his Edgeworthian virtues on the Black Islands, which he purchases after King Corny's death; Corny had earlier proclaimed him Prince of the Islands. Ormond refuses to buy Sir Ulick's more prosperous estate, which is also available. His choice indicates at least a partial allegiance to the traditions King Corny represents.

Maria Edgeworth's treatment of Ormond's marriage once again approaches and then retreats from the Lady Morgan solution of intermarriage and the consequent achievement of legitimacy by uniting a legal owner of land with the heiress of older and more sentimental rights. Ormond falls in love with King Corny's daughter, Dora O'Shane. But Corny has promised her to White Connal, a son of Connal of Glynn. Corny prefers Ormond as his son-in-law and heir, but his word is sacred to him, even after White Connal breaks his neck on an unmanageable horse; Dora is then offered to Black Connal, White Connal's twin brother.

Dora is sardonic about some of the ancient customs maintained at King Corny's castle, and she is a coquette. When Ormond pities her during her first engagement, she responds with a believable mixture of pride, annoyance, and tears. She is perhaps Maria Edgeworth's most interesting Irish woman, and the interest she arouses seems to bar her from the role of heroine. Ormond is most attracted to her when she is safely unavailable and he can pity her as a sacrifice. When she is unexpectedly free because of White

Connal's death—in his excitement Corny has temporarily forgotten Black Connal—Harry becomes as ambiguous about Dora as Maria Edgeworth seems to be, and as uncomfortable:

> What were his feelings at this moment? They were in such confusion, such contradiction, he could scarcely tell. Before he heard of White Connal's death . . . he desired nothing so much as to be able to save Dora from being sacrificed to that odious marriage; he thought, that if he were not bound in honour to his benefactor, he should instantly make that offer of his hand and heart to Dora, which would at once restore her to health and happiness, and fulfil the wishes of her kind, generous father. But now, when all obstacles seemed to vanish, when his rival was no more, when his benefactor declared his joy at being freed from his promise, when he was embraced as O'Shane's son, he did not feel joy: he was surprised to find it; but he could not. Now that he could marry Dora, now that her father expected that he should, he was not clear that he wished it himself.
>
> Quick as obstacles vanished, objections recurred; faults which he had formerly seen so strongly, which of late compassion had veiled from his view, reappeared: the softness of manner, the improvement of temper, caused by love, might be transient as passion. Then her coquetry, her frivolity. She was not that superior kind of woman, which his imagination had painted, or which his judgment could approve, in a wife.[20]

One might well ask, who is being coquettish here? And Maria Edgeworth has already made, in her authorial voice, the same sardonic comments about the arrangements at King Corny's castle that Dora offends Ormond by making.

Once again Maria Edgeworth thwarts the marriage she seems to have been preparing us for, though, as with Lady Geraldine in *Ennui,* she has also hinted at some reservations about the lady's vivacity and equated that with a subtly unsuitable Irish quality. Lady Geraldine, we are told, "was not ill-natured, yet careless to whom she gave offence, provided she produced amusement; and in this she seldom failed; for, in her conversation, there was much of the raciness of Irish wit, and the oddity of Irish humour" (*E,* p. 87). Lady Geraldine is sent off to India to a presumably happy marriage; Dora rejects Ormond and willingly goes to Paris, briefly infatuated with Black Connal and his Parisian elegance—he is an Irish officer in the French service—but her marriage is unhappy. Ormond will rule the Black Islands, but without the legitimacy that marriage with King Corny's daughter would have conferred.

---

[20] *Ormond: A Tale,* Irish Novels Series (1900; facsimile rpt. Shannon, Ireland: Irish Univ. Press, 1972), p. 142.

Instead he marries the colorless Florence Annaly, Sir Herbert's sister. But there is an intriguing, almost subversive detail that complicates this resolution of the marriage issue. Florence is without personality and therefore without markedly Irish characteristics. She has been educated in England. But though her name sounds English, it is the name that County Longford bore—Annaly or Analé—until the old Irish families were driven out early in the seventeenth century, to be replaced by "Britons and Protestants": "The chiefly names and all survivals of Irish law and custom were to be abolished. . . . the intention was to establish English landlordism and its dependent tenures."[21] As Maria Edgeworth well knew, those "Britons and Protestants" included her ancestor, Francis Edgeworth, who received the six-hundred-acre Edgeworthstown estate (involving a change from the old Irish place name, Mostrim or Mastrim) in 1619: "This grant was in accordance with James I's policy of settling Protestants of English descent on lands confiscated from Irish Catholics."[22] Florence's surname seems almost a desperate though concealed attempt to reintroduce that theme of legitimacy through marriage into the older Irish tradition, which the plot of the book has explicitly rejected.

Maria Edgeworth's flirtations with the theme of intermarriage indicate her awareness of Lady Morgan's themes. They seem to have attracted her strongly, yet she could not bring herself to yield to that attraction, deterred perhaps by the implicit reservations about the position of the Anglo-Irish. Her gingerly handling of the theme suggests how uneasy she must have been about the estrangement between Anglo-Irish and Irish, Protestant and Catholic, legality and ancient traditionary right, landlord and tenant. It suggests too her bleak sense that this estrangement could not be made to vanish by an appeal to mutual interest and mutual fair dealing, longer leases and improved agricultural methods. Perhaps she feared that the Anglo-Irish were incapable of creating among their tenants those emotional ties of

---

[21] Edmund Curtis, *A History of Ireland,* 6th ed. (1936; rpt. London: Methuen, 1950), p. 233. The new name, Longford, sounds English but is in fact the Irish *Longfort* or *Longphort,* a fortified place or camp—an appropriate metaphor for the newly planted settlers who often fortified their houses. Annaly, the old Irish name for the county, presumably derives from the Irish *eanach,* a watery place, a swamp, but one can also speculate that it derives from the goddess Ana or Dana, the tutelary goddess of the Tuatha Dé Danann, the ancient rulers of Ireland. It is unlikely that Maria Edgeworth knew of this derivation. See Brendan O Hehir, *A Gaelic Lexicon for Finnegans Wake* (Berkeley: Univ. of California Press, 1967), pp. 355–59, 380. Cormac's Glossary (c. 900) calls Ana "mater deorum hibernensium," *Cormac's Glossary,* trans. and ed. John O'Donovan (Calcutta: Irish Archaeological and Celtic Society, 1868), p. 4.

[22] Butler, *Maria Edgeworth,* p. 13.

loyalty and even love that would make their position secure by connecting them with Irish tradition.

There is one final element in the theme of legitimate rule through marriage with the heiress of ancient rights that Lady Morgan and even Maria Edgeworth may have partially sensed. We can only guess how much each novelist knew about ancient Ireland and its ideas about legitimate chieftainship. Maria Edgeworth, as we have seen, professed little interest in tradition; Lady Morgan sentimentalized it. But both would certainly have been aware of certain echoes of these ancient ideas that can be heard in popular Irish songs of the seventeenth, eighteenth, and early nineteenth centuries. Maria Edgeworth's knowledge of the Irish language was probably very slight. Lady Morgan did know Irish, though we cannot be sure how much or how well: her *Twelve Original Hibernian Melodies* (1805) is described on its title page as "Imitated and Translated from the Works of the Ancient Irish Bards." But by 1800 the themes of older nationalist songs in Irish were being reworked in English and were being sung and printed all over Ireland in that language.

A favorite form for these songs, in both languages, concealed a patriotic theme under the guise of a love poem or a poem describing a vision—*aisling*—of a beautiful maiden. The maiden is Ireland, alone, defenseless, robbed of her rightful inheritance, and the poem promises her a strong husband—successively James II, James III, Bonnie Prince Charlie, Napoleon, even L'Aiglon—who will rescue her, restore her lands, marry her, and father strong children upon her.[23] She is variously named—Banba, Cathleen ni Houlihan, Rosaleen, Granuaile or Granu Waile—but fairly consistently depicted: the frontispiece to *Paddy's Resource,* later subtitled *The Harp of Erin,* a booklet of patriotic songs published in Belfast in 1795, is "Ireland as a woman standing under the Tree of Liberty, holding a harp and a pike topped with a Phyrgian cap, some broken chains at her feet: a fairly complete epitome of the contents."[24]

Cathleen ni Houlihan and the other popular female personifications of Ireland are not merely a convention of eighteenth-century poets. They are

---

[23] Georges-Denis Zimmermann, *Songs of Irish Rebellion: Political Street Ballads and Rebel Songs, 1780–1900* (Dublin: Allen Figgis, 1967), pp. 31–33, 54.

[24] Zimmermann, *Songs of Irish Rebellion,* p. 38. Zimmermann cites James Porter's satire *Billy Bluff and Squire Firebrand* (Belfast, 1796) in which the Squire announces his hatred of ballad-singers and especially "Grawny Wail, and all things that have a double meaning" (p. 55). In *Irish Melodies* Thomas Moore footnotes "The Irish Peasant to his Mistress" to explain that the mistress is "allegorically, the ancient Church of Ireland," and uses the female personification of Ireland in "As vanquish'd Erin"; see Zimmermann, *Songs of Irish Rebellion,* p. 77, n. 13.

also a recollection, faded and altered over the centuries, of the ritual which legitimized an ancient Irish king or chieftain, the source of his right to rule over his lands and people. "The inauguration of the [ancient Irish] king," writes Myles Dillon, "was a symbolic marriage with Sovereignty, a fertility rite for which the technical term was *banais rígi*, 'royal wedding.' Sovereignty was imagined as a goddess whom the king must wed, presumably to ensure the welfare of his kingdom. . . . There are many Irish tales in which this idea is expressed, and it persisted into modern times. . . . In the seventeenth century Ó Bruadair refers to a king as 'the spouse of Cashel.' Even in the eighteenth century the poets called Ireland the spouse of her lawful kings."[25] Ancient Irish literature has many references to such symbolic matings between a king and "the sovereignty of Ireland" or the sovereignty of a local area.

Lady Morgan's Glorvina, with her harp, embodies the iconography of Ireland as it was known at the end of the eighteenth century in song and emblem; she is a twin for the figure in a song written to mourn the death of Robert Emmet (1803):

> Despair in her wild eye, a daughter of Erin
> Appeared on the cliff of a bleak rocky shore,
> Loose in the winds flowed her dark streaming ringlets
> And heedless she gazed on the dread surge's roar,
> Loud rang her harp in wild tones of despairing,
> The time past away with the present comparing,
> And in soul-thrilling strains deeper sorrow declaring,
> She sang Erin's woes and her Emmet's no more.[26]

And Glorvina—elusive, mysterious, hardly a real woman—clearly represents a memory of that old tradition by which marriage with the local tribal goddess gave a chieftain legitimacy. In *The Wild Irish Girl* she can legitimize even an Anglo-Irish "chieftain" and evoke for him a traditional loyalty that Grace Nugent and Dora O'Shane can only remotely hint at. But Maria Edgeworth refuses to let Grace and Dora fulfill the roles they seem destined for, though she is also reluctant to relinquish those roles entirely for them.

---

[25] Myles Dillon and Nora K. Chadwick, *The Celtic Realms* (London: Weidenfeld and Nicolson, 1967), p. 93. See Brendan O Hehir, "The Christian Revision of *Eachtra Airt Meic Cuind ocus Tochmarc Delbchaime Ingine Morgain*" in *Cellu Folklore and Christianity: Studies in Memory of William W. Heist*, ed. Patrick K. Ford (Santa Barbara: McNally and Loftin, 1983), p. 165; O Hehir summarizes the scholarship about ritual marriage in the Irish tradition and lists the most important studies.

[26] The complete song, "My Emmet's No More," is in Zimmermann, *Songs of Irish Rebellion*, pp. 175–76.

Both writers seem to grasp intuitively the broader importance of the theme. For the Anglo-Irish to rule, it is not enough to have legal right or British protection. It is necessary to connect in some way with Irish tradition, to recognize and respect that tradition and the attitudes it embodies, to become a part of it. "History," exclaims a character in William Trevor's story "Beyond the Pale" (1981), "is unfinished in this island." That uneasy awareness was to become the subject of most of the Anglo-Irish writers as they examined their role and their rule as a privileged but endangered minority.

University of California, Berkeley

WORKS CITED

Beames, Michael. *Peasants and Power: The Whiteboy Movements and Their Control in Pre-Famine Ireland.* New York: St. Martin's Press, 1983.

Burke, Edmund. *A Philosophical Enquiry into the Origin of Our Ideas of the Sublime and the Beautiful.* London: Routledge & Kegan Paul, 1958.

_____. *Reflections on the Revolution in France.* Harmondsworth: Penguin, 1986.

Butler, Marilyn. "Edgeworth's Ireland: History, Popular Culture, and Secret Codes." *Novel* 34 (Spring 2001): 267–92.

_____. Introduction. *Castle Rackrent and Ennui.* By Maria Edgeworth. 1–54.

_____. *Maria Edgeworth: A Literary Biography.* Oxford: Clarendon Press, 1972.

Butler, Marilyn, and Tim McLoughlin. Introductory Note. *Castle Rackrent, Irish Bulls, Ennui.* By Maria Edgeworth. vii–lxi.

Carr, John. *The Stranger in Ireland or a Tour in the Southern and Western Parts of that Country in 1805.* Introd. by Louis M. Cullen. Shannon, Ireland: Irish UP, 1970.

Connolly, Claire. "'Completing the Union?' The Irish Novel and the Moment of the Union." *The Irish Act of Union, 1800: Bicentennial Essays.* Ed. Michael Brown, Patrick Geoghegan, and James Kelly. Dublin: Irish Academic Press, 2003. 157–75.

_____. "'*I accuse Miss Owenson*': *The Wild Irish Girl* as Media Event." *Colby Quarterly* 36 (June 2000): 98–115.

_____. "Introduction: The Politics of Love in The Wild Irish Girl." *The Wild Irish Girl: A National Tale.* By Sydney Owenson, Lady Morgan. xxxv–lvi.

———. Note on the Text. *The Wild Irish Girl: A National Tale.* By Sydney Owenson, Lady Morgan. lvii–lxvi.

Connolly, S. J., ed. *The Oxford Companion to Irish History.* Oxford: Oxford UP, 1998.

Corbett, Mary Jean. *Allegories of Union in Irish and English Writing, 1790–1870: Politics, History, and the Family from Edgeworth to Arnold.* Cambridge: Cambridge UP, 2000.

_____. "Another Tale to Tell: Postcolonial Theory and the Case of *Castle Rackrent.*" *Criticism* 36 (1994): 383–400.

Deane, Seamus. "Irish National Character, 1790–1900." *The Writer as Witness: Literature as Historical Evidence.* Ed. Tom Dunne. Cork: Cork UP, 1987. 90–113.

_____, gen. ed. *The Field Day Anthology of Irish Writing.* 3 vols. Derry: Field Day, 1991.

de la Tocnaye, Chevalier [Jacques Louis de Bougrenet]. *A Frenchman's Walk Through Ireland 1796–7.* Trans. John Stevenson, 1917. Introd. by John A. Gamble. Belfast: Blackstaff Press, 1984.

Dunne, Tom. "A Polemical Introduction: Literature, Literary Theory and the Historian." *The Writer as Witness: Literature as Historical Evidence.* Ed. Tom Dunne. Cork: Cork UP, 1987. 1–9.

_____. *Maria Edgeworth and the Colonial Mind.* O'Donnell Lectures, 26. Dublin: National University of Ireland, 1984.

Edgeworth, Maria. *Castle Rackrent, Irish Bulls, Ennui.* Ed. Jane Desmarais, Tim McLoughlin, and Marilyn Butler. London: Pickering & Chatto, 1999. Vol. 1. of *The Novels and Selected Works of Maria Edgeworth.* Marilyn Butler and Mitzi Myers, gen. eds. 8 vols. to date. 1999–.

Edgeworth, Maria, and Frances Anne Beaufort Edgeworth. *A Memoir of Maria Edgeworth, with a Selection from her Letters by the late Mrs. Edgeworth.* 3 vols. London: Joseph Masters and Son, 1867.

Edwards, Ruth Dudley. *An Atlas of Irish History.* London: Methuen, 1973.

Ferris, Ina. "Narrating Cultural Encounter: Lady Morgan and the Irish National Tale." *Nineteenth-Century Literature* 51 (1996): 287–303.

_____. "Writing on the Border: The National Tale, Female Writing, and the Public Sphere." *Romanticism, History, and the Possibilities of Genre: Reforming Literature, 1789–1837.* Ed. Tilottama Rahan and Julia M. Wright. Cambridge: Cambridge UP, 1998. 86–106.

Foster, R. F. *Modern Ireland: 1600–1972.* New York: Viking Penguin, 1988.

Hare, Augustus J. C., ed. *The Life and Letters of Maria Edgeworth.* 2 vols. Boston and New York: Houghton, Mifflin, Riverside Press, 1895.

Hutton, Arthur Wollaston, ed. *Arthur Young's Tour in Ireland (1776–1779).* 2 vols. London and New York: George Bell & Sons, 1892.

Kirkpatrick, Kathryn, ed. *The Wild Irish Girl, A National Tale.* By Sydney Owenson, Lady Morgan. Oxford: Oxford UP, 1999.

Lecky, W. E. H. *A History of Ireland in the Eighteenth Century.* Abr. ed. and introd. L. P. Curtis. Chicago: U of Chicago P, 1972.

Leerssen, Joep. *Mere Irish and Fíor-Ghael: Studies in the Idea of Irish Nationality, its Development and Literary Expression Prior to the Nineteenth Century.* Cork: Cork UP in association with Field Day, 1996.

_____. *Remembrance and Imagination: Patterns in the Historical and Literary Representation of Ireland in the Nineteenth Century.* Cork: Cork UP in association with Field Day, 1996.

Maguire, W. A. "Castle Nugent and Castle Rackrent; fact and fiction in Maria Edgeworth." *Eighteenth-Century Ireland* 11 (1996): 146–59.

Moody, T. W., F. X. Martin, and F. J. Byrne, eds. *A Chronology of Irish History to 1976: A Companion to Irish History, Part I.* Oxford: Clarendon Press, 1982. Vol. 8 of A New History of Ireland. 7 vols. to date. 1976–.

Neill, Michael. "Mantles, Quirks, and Irish Bulls: Ironic Guise and Colonial Subjectivity in Maria Edgeworth's *Castle Rackrent.*" *The Review of English Studies* 52 (2001): 76–90.

Newcomer, James. "The Disingenuous Thady Quirk." *Family Chronicles: Maria Edgeworth's Castle Rackrent.* Ed. Cóilín Owens. Dublin: Wolfhound Press, 1987. 79–86.

O'Halloran, Claire. "Irish Re-Creations of the Gaelic Past: The Challenge of Macpherson's Ossian." *Past and Present* 124 (1989): 69–95.

Owenson, Sydney, Lady Morgan. *Patriotic Sketches of Ireland, written in Connaught, By Miss Owenson. . . .* Baltimore: Printed for G. Dobbin & Murphy, 1809.

_____. Preface. O'Donnel: A national tale. Introd. by Robert Lee Wolff. New York: Garland, 1979. vii–xii.

_____. "Prefatory Address to the 1846 Edition." Appendix. *The Wild Irish Girl: A National Tale.* By Sydney Owenson. 245–63.

_____. *The Wild Irish Girl: A National Tale.* Ed. Claire Connolly and Stephen Copley. Fwd. Kevin Whelan. London: Pickering & Chatto, 2000.

Sommer, Doris. *Foundational Fictions: The National Romances of Latin America.* Berkeley: U of California P, 1991.

Spenser, Edmund. *A View of the Present State of Ireland.* Ed. Andrew Hadfield and Willy Maley. Malden, MA: Blackwell, 1997.

Stevenson, Lionel. *The Wild Irish Girl: The Life of Sydney Owenson, Lady Morgan (1776–1859).* London: Chapman & Hall, 1936.

Tracy, Robert. "Maria Edgeworth and Lady Morgan: Legality versus Legitimacy." *Nineteenth-Century Literature* 40 (1985): 1–22.

Trumpener, Katie. *Bardic Nationalism: The Romantic Novel and the British Empire.* Princeton: Princeton UP, 1997.

Waingrow, Marshall. *James Boswell's Life of Johnson.* 4 vols. New Haven: Yale UP, 1994.

Watson, George, ed. and introd. *Castle Rackrent.* By Maria Edgeworth. Oxford: Oxford UP, 1964. Rpt. with introd. by Kathryn Kirkpatrick, 1995.

Weekes, Ann Owens. *Irish Women Writers: An Uncharted Tradition.* Lexington: UP of Kentucky, 1990.

Welsh, Robert, ed. *The Oxford Companion to Irish Literature.* Oxford: Clarendon Press, 1996.

Whelan, Kevin. *The Tree of Liberty: Radicalism, Catholicism and the Construction of Irish Identity, 1760–1830.* Cork: Cork UP in association with Field Day, 1996.

FOR FURTHER READING

Bartlett, Thomas. *The Fall and Rise of the Irish Nation: The Catholic Question 1690–1830.* Dublin: Gill and Macmillan, 1992.

Campbell, Mary. *Lady Morgan: The Life and Times of Sydney Owenson.* London: Pandor Press, 1988.

Connolly, Claire. "Reading Responsibility in *Castle Rackrent.*" *Ireland and Cultural Theory: The Mechanics of Authenticity.* Ed. Colin Graham and Richard Kirkland. London: Macmillan Press, 1999. 136–61.

Deane, Seamus. *Strange Country: Modernity and Nationhood in Irish Writing Since 1790.* Oxford: Oxford UP, 1997.

Dunne, Tom. "'A gentleman's estate should be a moral school': Edgeworthstown in Fact and Fiction, 1760–1840." *Longford: Essays in County History.* Ed. Raymond Gillespie and Gerard Moran. Dublin: Lilliput Press, 1991. 95–121.

Eagleton, Terry. *Heathcliff and the Great Hunger: Studies in Irish Culture.* London: Verso, 1995.

Ferris, Ina. *The Romantic National Tale and the Question of Ireland.* Cambridge: Cambridge UP, 2002.

Keogh, Dáire and Kevin Whelan, eds. *Acts of Union: The Causes, Contexts and Consequences of the Act of Union.* Dublin: Four Courts Press, 2001.

Kreilkamp, Vera. *The Anglo-Irish Novel and the Big House.* Syracuse: Syracuse UP, 1998.

Lloyd, David. *Anomalous States: Irish Writing and the Post-Colonial Moment.* Durham, NC: Duke UP, 1993.

Newcomer, James. *Lady Morgan the Novelist.* Lewisburg, PA: Bucknell UP, 1990.

_____. *Maria Edgeworth.* Lewisburg, PA: Bucknell UP, 1973.

Owens, Cóilín, ed. *Family Chronicles: Maria Edgeworth's Castle Rackrent.* Dublin: Wolfhound Press, 1987.

Smyth, Jim. *The Making of the United Kingdom, 1660–1800: State, Religion and Identity in Britain and Ireland.* New York: Longman, 2001.

CREDITS

Reprinted material from Corbett, Mary Jane, "Another Tale to Tell," *Criticism* Vol. 36:3 (Summer 1994), with the permission of Wayne State University Press. Copyright 1994, Wayne State University Press.

Ina Ferris, "Narrating Cultural Encounter: Lady Morgan and the Irish National Tale." © 1996 by The Regents of the University of California. Reprinted from *Nineteenth Century Literature*, Vol. 51, No. 3 Issue: December 1996, pp. 287–303, by permission. www.ucpress.edu.

Robert Tracy, "Maria Edgeworth and Lady Morgan: Legality versus Legitimacy." © 1985 by The Regents of the University of California. Reprinted from *Nineteenth Century Literature* Vol. 40, No. 1 Issue: June 1985, pp. 1–22. www.ucpress.edu.